Wild Magic

Book Two of Fool's Gold

Jude Fisher

POCKET
BOOKS

LONDON · SYDNEY · NEW YORK · TORONTO

First published in Great Britain by Earthlight, 2003
This edition first published by Pocket, 2004
An imprint of Simon & Schuster UK Ltd
A Viacom Company

1 3 5 7 9 10 8 6 4 2

Simon & Schuster UK Ltd
Africa House
64–78 Kingsway
London WC2B 6AH

www.simonsays.co.uk

Simon & Schuster Australia
Sydney

F120,873

€10

A CIP catalogue record for this book is available from the British Library

ISBN: 0 7434 4041 2

Typeset by Palimpsest Book Production Limited,
Polmont, Stirlingshire
Printed and bound in Great Britain by
Cox & Wyman Ltd, Reading, Berkshire

Jude Fisher is a pseudonym for Jane Johnson, publishing director of HarperCollins' SF imprint, Voyager. She holds two literature degrees, specialising in Anglo Saxon and Old Icelandic texts, and is also a qualified lecturer. For the last seventeen years, Jane has been the publisher of the works of J.R.R. Tolkien. She is the author of the official Visual Companions to Peter Jackson's movie trilogy of *The Lord of the Rings*, and with M. John Harrison has had four novels published under the pseudonym of Gabriel King.

Praise for SORCERY RISING, Book One of Fool's Gold:

'This tale of magic, mystery, intrigue and feud works well, and the characters are so convincing (including a strong and appealing female lead) that I can't wait to read the next instalment.' *The Times*

'My, but *Sorcery Rising* has a plethora of characters. There's Katla, the rock-climbing swordmaker; Saro, the unwanted younger son; the lusty, vengeful Tycho; and dozens of others. The amazing thing is that author Fisher manages to make each of them integral to the plot. Fisher ultimately pulls it all together to form a compelling and intriguing whole that will have readers eagerly awaiting the next volume.' *Starlog*

'A marvellous tapestry, deftly woven, with a masterfully colourful complexity. *Sorcery Rising* left me breathless and shouting for more' *Janny Wurts*

'I enjoyed Jude Fisher's debut very much ... a well-written work, leading the reader deftly on to fascinating scenes and unusual characters' Anne McCaffrey

'An impressive debut' Roz Kaveney, AMAZON.CO.UK

Also by Jude Fisher

Sorcery Rising
Book One of Fool's Gold

Thanks are due to Emma and Fiona for their constant encouragement, to Darren, Jess and Neal for their unwavering support; to the wilds of New Zealand and the Mojave Desert and to the limestone cliffs of southern Spain for inspiration and escape. To Ian and the cats and Freddie the Parrot who made it so hard to concentrate; to Ariel, for the website; and to all those enthusiastic and impatient people who read *Sorcery Rising* and sent emails and letters urging me to get on with the sequel: here it is!

What Has Gone Before . . .

From the ashy wastes of the Moonfell Plain, where the trading event known as the Allfair is held every year, there rises a great rock. The Istrians know it as Falla's Rock and claim it as sacred ground, while the northerners call it Sur's Castle in honour of their god. Katla Aransen, daughter of the Rockfall clan, has come to the Allfair for the first time. At home in the barren Westman Isles of Eyra she spends her time climbing the granite cliffs, running across the moors, forging weaponry in the steading's smithy – her long red hair wild and tangled, her clothes torn and stained. Pigheaded and rebellious, she would probably have climbed it even if forbidden; but no one told her not to; and in the dawn light it looks magical and inviting. So she scales the sacred Rock and is spotted by two old Istrian men, whom she easily escapes, but the Allfair Guards may be a harder prospect. Sacrilege is a capital offence: in order to obscure her identity at the Fair, and thus save her life, her father hacks off her hair.

The peoples of the north and south of the world of Elda have long been in conflict. In ancient days, the southerners drove their enemies steadily north out of the abundant farmlands of Istria until there was nowhere left for them but the rocky Eyran islands battered by the icy Northern Ocean. Since then, their customs and practices have become sharply delineated; the Istrians worshipping the cruel fire-goddess, Falla, and keeping their women shrouded; the northerners giving obeisance to the god Sur. The divergences between the two cultures have caused ever-increasing friction, resulting in raids and incursions, battles and full-blown wars: even in peace-time hostilities are close to the surface. Little does she know it, but by setting foot on the Rock, Katla is about to become the spark for a mighty conflagration – in a young man's heart, and in a wider context, which may claim the lives of thousands.

Meanwhile, from Sanctuary, an icy fastness at the top of the world, there has come to the Fair a strange, tall, pale man called Virelai, a mage's apprentice who has stolen away from his master two of the three most powerful beings in Elda: the Rose of the World, a woman of perfect beauty whose merest glance fires men with desperate lust, and a cat called Bëte. By use of a powerful spell, Virelai has left the Master wrapped in sorcerous sleep; but if the mage awakes, his vengeance will surely be terrible. Already constrained by a geas which prevents him from dealing death to the mage in any direct manner, Virelai devises a cunning plot: at the Allfair he distributes a number of forged maps, each imbued with a little magic, to tempt adventurers to Sanctuary, where they are promised treasures beyond imagination. All they have to do in return is to promise to take the life of one old, sleeping man. Among the many so duped is Katla's father, Aran Aranson, head of the Rockfall clan, a man in sore need of some excitement in his life. Now all he needs is to raise sufficient funds to have a hardy ice-breaker built which can brave the mighty arctic seas around Sanctuary.

Elda was once a world filled with magic and wonders, a world in the guardianship of three benign deities: the Woman, the Man and the Beast. There remain legends of that lost age, and of the people of the Far West, with their vast jewelled ships and golden artefacts. For centuries now Elda has been a world bereft of magic; but with the arrival of the bizarre trio of Virelai, the Rosa Eldi and the cat, sorcery seems to have returned. It begins in small ways, as the charms and potions of the wandering folk known as the Footloose suddenly begin to take greater effect than they were ever designed to do, as Erno Hamson is about to find out. He buys a love-charm from the ancient nomad healer, Fezack Starsinger, and wears it under his tunic. The object of his desire? Katla Aransen, who has never shown any interest in him before. Love charms and potions may seem harmless enough; but sorcery is destined to erupt in a far more unsettling manner.

The Vingo clan, a once-illustrious southern family now fallen on harder times, are at the Fair to trade horses, and their elder son – the arrogant, vicious Tanto – in marriage to the daughter of an equally arrogant and vicious nobleman: Tycho Issian, Lord of Cantara, a man well known for his religious fervour and fierce oratory. Their younger son Saro, already entranced on the very first day of the Fair by the vision of a bare-legged girl with long red hair shining in the dawn sun atop the forbidden Rock, is already finding his first visit to the Moonfell Plain an extraordinary experience; the more so as he makes his way through the wonders of the nomads' quarter. But while he is buying a gift from the moodstone-seller for his absent mother, a fight breaks out nearby between some Istrian and Eyran youths. Violence escalates and before long the moodstone-seller, old Hiron Sea-Haar, lies dying in Saro's arms, stabbed by Tanto. As the old man passes into the beyond he bestows upon Saro a gift: a moodstone with strange and perilous powers, and the ability to know another's mind by the merest touch. Such empathy is soon to prove more of a burden than a blessing. By way of recompense for the murder, Tanto agrees, falsely and under duress, to donate half the winnings he takes from the Games to the old man's family, but when his marriage settlement to Lord Tycho Issian's daughter Selen falls short of the agreed sum, he reneges on the deal and it is left to

Saro to take the money without his family's leave and pay it over to Hiron's family.

Lord Tycho Issian, meanwhile, has struck his own deal. Afflicted by the need to 'worship the Goddess' with a willing woman, he seeks for a whore, but glimpses instead the Rose of the World, and is lost utterly. Stricken with lust, he agrees to pay Virelai a fortune if he can take the Rosa Eldi as his own: if he can extend his debt to the Ruling Council of Istria and swiftly settle the marriage arrangement with the Vingos, he will have just enough to pay the sorcerer. But all goes awry.

The Vingos do not have the sum agreed on the night of the Gathering – the event at which Ravn Asharson, King of the Northern Isles, will choose himself a wife. In the midst of the festivities, Tanto decides he will take his bride whether the marriage settlement is made or not and makes his way to her pavilion, where he kills her maid and takes Selen by force. Selen Issian fights back, stabbing Tanto in the groin. Covered with blood, she runs naked into the night.

Meanwhile, Aran Aranson, consumed by the dream of Sanctuary's gold, 'sells' his daughter to the shipwright who will build his ice-breaker. Trussed up in a red dress at the Gathering, Katla Aransen is due to be betrothed to the fat old shipmaker; until she persuades Erno Hamson to help her escape. Erno does not need much persuading: he has loved Katla since he was a child; but when he kisses her, the love charm he wears smoulders to the ground, and with it go his dreams. Katla is furious, but she still needs his help. The plan is to steal a boat and row away down the coast; but as they run across the plain, they encounter Selen Issian, and then a troop of guards. Katla insists that Erno rescues the terrified young Istrian woman, while she doubles back to confuse the soldiers; but this plan too, will go awry.

At the Gathering, King Ravn is bored – bored with shrouded southern women whose beauty he cannot assess, bored with the machinations of the northern lords, all manoeuvring for their advancement – until he too is captured by the power of the Rosa Eldi. Forsaking all others, he claims her as his bride.

The Gathering is already in turmoil as the Allfair Guards burst in with a captive: Katla Aransen – mistaken for a man with her hair cut all rough and short – is accused of murdering Selen Issian's slavegirl and stabbing Tanto Vingo. Even when the error of her gender is resolved, there remains the matter of her climbing the Rock. The northerners claim it to be Sur's Castle, but the Istrians insist it is sacred ground to the Goddess. There are calls for a burning: the traditional Istrian punishment for sacrilege. The Moonfell Plain is neutral ground; but Lord Rui Finco, a southern lord bearing more than passing resemblance to the northern king, quietly points out that the Rock was ceded to Istria in an agreement made by Ravn's father, the Shadow Wolf himself, Ashar Stenson. Katla will be burned, according to Istrian law.

Fights break out across the fairground. The nomads, who have seen omens of bloodshed and a return of their own persecution, flee the plain. Amidst the chaos, the northern king is abducted, revealing a plot by a number of Istrian lords to gain control of the northern fleet and thus the ocean ways, which will render them great power and wealth. But the plot is foiled and Ravn Asharson flees with his bride, leaving Katla Aransen to burn and his countrymen in fierce and furious conflict with the Istrians.

Tied to a pyre, flames all around her, it seems nothing can save Katla. But young Saro Vingo, following a mystical encounter with the Rosa Eldi, wades into the fire to set her free, the moodstone he carries killing all in his path. Katla's kin take her to safety; but even when the crisis has passed, cries for war fill the air.

Meanwhile, Erno Hamson has done as Katla told him – rowed away with Selen Issian: his heart is broken, and she is now a refugee who can never return to her home. Tanto Vingo, his wound poisoned, is saved only by drastic surgery. Tycho Issian, obsessed by the loss of the woman who has enslaved his soul, devotes all his efforts to fanning the flames of war: under the pretence of rescuing his daughter from her barbarian abductors and liberating all the women of Eyra from the sacrilegious lives their menfolk have forced them to lead, he calls for the south to carry fire and sword to the Northern Isles until they have laid it waste (and he can claim the Rosa Eldi for himself). He has the sorcerer, Virelai, and his magical cat to aid his cause; as well as Lord Rui Finco and his conspirators, for whom war with Eyra would suit many of their purposes.

Katla Aransen, carried unconscious from the Moonfell Plain, recovers slowly at home in Rockfall; disfigured and damaged by the fire, her precious right hand fused into a clublike lump of scar tissue. She fears she will never climb another cliff, never forge another blade. Disconsolate, she wanders the island, trying to avoid doing household tasks. At Winterfest the mummers, under the charismatic leadership of Tam Fox, arrive; and with them comes a *seither*, one of the mysterious ancient folk who have but a single eye, which sees more than mortals' two. The *seither* sees in Katla an adept, a channeller of earth-magic. To Katla, despite her great skill with rock and metal, this comes as a shock. The healer lays hands upon her and together they begin to work on Katla's burned arm; but this act is tragically misinterpreted by Katla's twin brother Fent, who attacks the *seither*, running her through with the Red Sword, Katla's finest blade. Appalled, Katla attempts to turn her newfound abilities to the aid of the *seither*, but strength fails her and she feels herself ebbing away into the darkness, a darkness in which a distant and infinitely powerful voice calls to her . . .

Prologue

The Rose of the World hovered over her sleeping husband and the ends of her pale hair grazed his cheek. Wrapped in the strangest of dreams after his night's exertions, King Ravn Asharson – known, confidingly, by the women of Eyra and, enviously, by the men, as 'the Stallion of the North' – stirred briefly as those silky fibres brushed him, his eyelashes fluttering like the lift of a crow's wings.

The Rosa Eldi smiled. It was an expression she had been practising each day in the privacy of these chambers, with the aid of one of her husband's many gifts to her – a mirror of polished silver, glass and mercury, bought from traders from the Galian Isles: a miraculous thing in itself; but all the more so to the Rose of the World, who had never seen her own face, except as a reflection in the eyes of enraptured men.

They told her she was beautiful and rare, the most perfect of women: but she had no means to judge if they meant what they said: she had spent all of the life that she could recall cloistered away in Sanctuary, that remote icy stronghold, whose only inhabitants had been a black cat, Bëte, the mage, Rahe; and Virelai, the Master's apprentice. Rahe had told her she was beautiful over and again: but since he had also given her to believe that he had created her in an image most pleasing to his own eyes, it seemed a subjective judgement.

Then, when Virelai had stolen her away and they had travelled out into the world she had had the opportunity to assess for herself the concepts of beauty and perfection; but in the beginning the assault on her starved senses had been so overwhelming that she had found everything – from the commonest dungfly to the mightiest tree – beautiful and perfect as and of itself. And yet, at the same time, everything she saw had seemed oddly familiar to her, as if the images that had populated her dreams had suddenly slipped from her head to swarm around her in all their myriad forms and colours.

But people were the most disconcerting. She had no idea of how to react to them; and so usually she said nothing and just drank in their images to recall later in the darkness of the wagon in which she, the cat and the apprentice lived while they travelled; but what struck her repeatedly was how women recoiled from her, smiling with their mouths, but rarely with their eyes, as if they mistook her silent gaze for insolence, or a threat. Men, on the other hand, appeared to fall in love with her in an instant and become so helplessly enraptured that they wanted to have congress with her there and then, no matter how inappropriate the time, place or circumstances. The women did not like that, either. It seemed that in the making of her, the Master had invested her with sufficient magic to seduce every man on Elda (though that had clearly not been his intention, which was surely to keep her to himself alone) and from what she now understood about such matters, it seemed that Virelai had understood her power early in their journey and had made himself a considerable sum of money from these men and their use of her as they travelled across the world.

She felt her smile fade at these memories: felt it by the release of the muscles in her face. Turning, she reached over and retrieved the mirror from its place on the tapestried settle beside the bed, and tilted the pretty artefact until the first rays of the dawn's light were caught between its sheeny plate and her pale, pale skin. The silver gave back to her an oval face as white as milk, except where her husband's beard had during the night rasped her chin and cheek and brought a faint pink flush to the surface, and a pair of green eyes, more sea-green than leaf-green. Ravn called them 'mermaid's eyes' and laughingly insisted on checking her feet each morning for signs of her secret nightly excursions: for fronds of seaweed, he said; for seahorses, flippers or scales! She had no idea what he meant by this, and had solemnly told him so, which surprised him much, for surely everyone knew the tales of the selkies of the Northern Isles, who borrowed human form to seduce unwary sailors and fishermen, and then slipped into their fishy skins at night and returned to their ocean homeland, leaving their lovers mazed and heartbroken? She smiled again into the mirror and watched her lips curve up into a pale pink bow, saw how her cheeks rounded and the skin around her eyes creased. She relaxed the expression and stared mercilessly at her changed image in the reflective surface. In this strong morning light she was able to spy out the vaguest of lines running from the sides of her nose to the corners of her mouth, fanning outward from her eyes. She had not thought she knew how to smile, or make any other such expression; but these faint marks told another story.

The Master had always treated her as a thing rather than any sort of person, a solace and pastime for his pleasure alone in the chilly, empty world of Sanctuary, and until this time she had never questioned her place in that world: but now a new thought came to her.

In some lost past, she must have smiled and frowned and pursed her lips enough times to have etched these small lines into her skin.

In some lost past, therefore, she must have had another life.

Feelings that she could put no name to welled up in her. She dropped the mirror to her lap, barely registering its cold touch on her naked skin. Beside her, her husband stirred briefly, eyelids flickering, then he stilled and slipped back into deep sleep. She reached out and brushed a frond of his black hair away from his brow, and felt herself calmed by the sheer simplicity of the act. *Such a man of many parts*, she thought, taking in the conjunction of the weatherbeaten skin of his face and neck with the vulnerable whiteness of his chest and belly; at the dark hands and forearms flung wide upon the linen sheet which contrasted with legs so pale they were like limbs belonging to another man. Only the curling black hair that grew everywhere upon him knit the whole together, blurred the seams, confused the edges.

Leaning towards him, she laid the mirror now on its side before his sleeping face and watched as his breath bloomed on the cold metal. The bloom faded and died, then was restored with each new passage of warm air. Then she wiped the mirror on the sheet and breathed on it herself.

Nothing.

The metal remained pristine, unblemished.

'For all your reputation, there is no heat in you,' she remembered the Master saying to her. Then, under the binding of his magic, it had been as much as she could do to concentrate on the sound his words made; it was only now, away from his influence, that she began to see what he might have meant by this, yet no matter how many times she tried the test, the result was still the same and she still had no better understanding of who she was or where she had come from. It was a mystery that was coming to obsess her, to drive her mind ceaselessly through every hour of the day and night.

All she knew was that she had owned no knowledge, no identity or volition while she lived with the Master. It was as if his sorcery had smothered them as a wet cloak might smother flames before a fire could catch hold. All she had known in her years in Sanctuary was how to arouse Rahe's ardour and slake his lusts: other than this, she had drifted as in a dream. It was only after she had left the island that she had felt any sense of herself return. But even after several months of travelling amongst the fantastic people and places of Elda, she had still been quiescent, content to drift in Virelai's wake; content to do what he asked of her with the men he brought to the wagon. Content, that is, until he had tried to sell her to a southern lord – a man whose touch had made her skin creep, made her shudder with a revulsion she could neither name nor comprehend except to know with a deep, primal instinct that he was full of death and she wanted no part of him.

The fact that she was here, now, in the royal chambers of Halbo Castle was all her own doing, and she felt some satisfaction in that. When she had escaped Virelai on the night of the Gathering, she had not known her own intention. To remove herself from the grasp of the deathly southern lord meant putting an ocean between them; and a ship bound for the north required the protection of an Eyran captain; but when she laid eyes upon Ravn Asharson the future came into clear focus. Assessing him at a glance as a powerful man, a man who could defend her against all comers, she knew at once that his soul cried out for the exotic; and so she had stepped into his orbit and drawn his eyes to her.

In her short experience of the world beyond Sanctuary she had learned that women used whatever wiles they possessed to attract men to them, and that the conquest of a king would be regarded by most as a triumph, not an undertaking to be entered into lightly or by a woman of no breeding or heritage. But for the Rosa Eldi, this was no game of statesmanship, no play for status: it was a gambit made simply for survival, and so she had exerted the full force of her seductive magic upon him; he was utterly, inextricably bewitched.

What she had not bargained for were the odd sensations he drew forth from her. These sensations, which she learned to term 'feelings', started with a vague tenderness toward a man so vulnerable her mere glance could bring him to his knees; then had grown into something altogether more demanding of their connection in the weeks of the voyage back to the northern capital and his careful introduction of her into the great castle he called his home. Now it had become something she could only think of as a slow fire burning deep inside her, so that instead of abandoning him as soon as the ship docked in Eyra as she had planned, she now experienced an almost physical pain every time he left her side.

This pain was made all the worse by the fact that she knew she had wrought a powerful enchantment upon Ravn: she could not be sure that, without it, he would feel anything for her at all. And since she had thrown this veil of bewitchment over him, it was impossible to know his true character. It was like viewing an island through fogs: she sensed, beneath the miasma of the magic, something adamantine in him, something uncompromising and elemental; something that might challenge and thrill her into a greater understanding of love, of life, of the world and her place in it. But he moved and talked as if in a daze when he was with her; and when he was away, she knew nothing of him.

It would, she pondered, leaning closer to trace the chiselled line of his mouth with the tip of her finger, be curious to withdraw the glamour and see just who this man she had chosen to ally herself to might truly be. But she did not yet dare to do it.

And so, she moved further down the bed until her face was level with her husband's chest. Then she laid her head down upon him and listened to the steady draw of his breath, to the powerful slow beat of his heart – like a tide, like a tide – and wondered whether she would ever learn what it was to be human in this world of Elda.

One

Intrigues

Aran Aranson, Master of Rockfall, stood in the doorway of his smithy with the moon leering over his shoulder like the eye of some vengeful giant, and watched with disbelief as the dead woman came to her feet.

In front of him, his second son Fent was on his knees, gazing up at the apparition he had killed only moments earlier, while his only daughter, Katla Aransen, lay as still as stone on the cold floor with blood all over her face and hands. The dead woman took a step towards him and the moonlight shone from her single eye so that she looked like an afterwalker, recently returned from the quiet of the burial howe to haunt those who had done it wrong in life, to straddle the rooftree of the houses till the timbers broke, to hag-ride the livestock till they ran mad; to terrorise all and sundry until the whole settlement was cursed and abandoned.

His hand tightened on the pommel of the dagger he wore at his waist-belt. *Severing the head, that's the only thing that works with ghosts*, old Gramma Garsen had told them, her face lit ghoulishly by the embers of the firepit, as he sat with all the other little boys of the steading, held rapt and terrified breathless by her words, *You have to cut off the head and bury it as far from the body as you can.* But would such simple advice work on a seither, one of the legendary magic-channellers of the Northern Isles? Aran drew the dagger and held it out before him, knowing it an inadequate weapon for the task at hand. Katla's Red Sword, the prize weapon she had forged last year, with a carnelian set into the hilt, lay out of his reach; but if he could disable the seither with the dagger, then spring past her to retrieve it—

'Put away that pin, Aran Aranson.'

The seither's voice was deep and resonant: too powerful for a woman heart-pierced only moments earlier. He found his hand faltering, as if there were more power in her words than just their meaning.

'Would you bring down the same curse on yourself as I placed on your murderous son?'.

May all your ventures meet with disaster.

Aran had never thought himself as a particularly superstitious man but now he felt an icy dread upon him as if the dead woman had reached out and placed a chilly finger on his heart.

'I do not understand what has happened here,' he managed at last.

The seither, Festrin One-Eye, smiled grimly. There was blood on her teeth and gums, blood which looked black in that garish light. *They do not bleed as we do*, Gramma Garsen had said; *they swell to twice their normal size and their veins fill with black fluid, one drop of which would sear a hillside for eternity.*

'Do you really think me *aptagangur*, Aran Aranson?' Festrin said with remarkable sweetness, and began to unlace the ties of her tunic.

Aran's eyes dropped unwillingly from the seither's face to where her clever fingers pulled apart the bows and knots. Beneath her hands the torn and bloodstained fabric parted easily; but although he had seen the Red Sword rammed home to the hilt by a panicked Fent there was no sign of any hurt there – no ragged hole, gouting the blood that had spurted over Katla as she tended to the dying woman; not even the closed purple of a stab-wound newly healed.

Nothing but smooth white skin, and the swell of her breasts. Aran felt his mouth drop open like any fool's.

Fent spun to regard his father, his face waxy with shock. 'I killed her,' he whispered. 'I saw her die.'

Festrin stepped around the boy as if he were of no more consequence than a stray dog, keeping her eyes all the while on the Master of Rockfall. 'Your daughter is a rare creature, Aran Aranson. She tried to give her life for mine, but do not fear – she is still alive. She will recover herself. Mark well what I say. Do not waste her. Do not bargain her away like a prize ewe; nor wrap her in silks and mothballs. Earth-magic flows through her, and something else as well—' She leaned towards him and poked him hard in the shoulder with one long, lean finger. 'Look well to your daughter, Master of Rockfall; because if you do not, I shall return for her and you will wish I had never set foot on this island.'

And having delivered this pronouncement, she was past him, her form silhouetted for a moment, tall and straight as a monolith, in the frame of the smithy door; and then she was gone.

No one saw the seither leave. No boat was missing from its moorings the next day, nor was any horse gone from the stables. All Tam Fox, the leader of the group of mummers with whom Festrin One-Eye had come to Rockfall, could offer by way of explanation was to tap the side of his nose and declare: 'Best not to enquire how seithers travel the world.'

Katla spent two days in the bed to which Aran carried her, sleeping as deeply as a sick child, waking briefly, then sleeping again. But on the third day when he came to sit by her he found the bedclothes thrown off onto the floor in a heap and her boots missing from their place beside the door.

Aran walked the enclosures and checked the outhouses, but to no avail. At last he took the path down to the harbour where, reduced to simple methods by the club-hand she had earned from the burning, she would sometimes sit and dangle a crabline from the seawall, but the only folk down there were the fishermen taking their boats out on the early tide.

He went out to the end of the mole anyway and turned back to stare inland. The steading at Rockfall was no grand affair like some of the other great halls of Eyra's clan chiefs, but it was a fine and sturdy longhouse constructed from timbers shipped out from the mainland in the time of Aran's great-grandfather, from stone dug out of the surrounding hillsides, and roofed in the traditional fashion with peat and turf. Even on this fine summer morning a curl of smoke rose from the central fire that maintained all day and night throughout the year. *My home*, Aran thought with pride, taking in the bustle of activity in the enclosures, the shimmering field of barley, the white specks of sheep up on the mountain pastures. When he had taken over responsibility for Rockfall after the last war, the hall had been in a state of disrepair, the crop-fields fallow, the outhouses tumbled down. Aran Stenson had paid little mind to his land, preferring a life on the sea, 'trading' as he liked to call it, though others might consider it simple piracy. The Istrians, for example. Aran Aranson smiled. He had done his duty by his family; he had made Rockfall a steading to be proud of. It had taken years of hard and selfless work; he had rebuilt much of the hall with his own hands, in the days when they could barely afford to feed themselves, let alone their retainers. He and Bera had raised a family, and lost five children to stillbirth and disease along the way. He had won support from his neighbours and from lords and clan chiefs across Eyra for his steady voice and fair dealings in a hundred lawsuits, and his strong arm in enforcing them. He had made himself a man to be reckoned with by walking the line of sense and responsibility all these long years; and now he considered he had earned the right to follow his own dreams and enjoy the adventures he had missed out on as a young man, and had been promising himself ever since. That promise had propelled him through the difficulties of his marriage and the dullness of the farming. It had kept him steady all these years, and now he would have his reward.

He patted the pouch he wore about his neck. In it there nestled a scrap of parchment, an ancient map he had come by from a nomad trader at the Allfair. That map would bring riches his forebears could never have imagined. His pursuit of the treasure it guaranteed was hardly, therefore, a selfish thing: it would provide for his family far better than his staying on Rockfall and managing the farm, or by mining and trading the rare sardonyx out of the heart of the island, which was both costly and time-consuming. No, in one fell swoop, with some luck, some audacity and the right vessel, he would make their fortunes. Bera could live like the rich woman she had always dreamed she would be. His sons could buy a veritable fleet of longships, sail the Ravenway, or, in Fent's case, go raiding the Istrian coast, before they settled for some good land and a wife to plough. And as for Katla, wherever she might be . . .

He scanned the landscape absent-mindedly for his daughter, his thoughts already drifting out onto the high seas, to the north, with their drifting floes and towering bergs and secret islands wreathed in mist . . .

Drawn back to the ocean by the seductive images in his head, he watched the last of the fishing boats sail out of the bay, passing the dramatic spike of the Hound's Tooth, the rocky headland which provided the island with its look-out position to all points south and west. On its very apex, a detached rock stood out, balanced precariously on its seaward lip. He narrowed his eyes, and as he did so, the sun crested the mountains of the island's interior and cast their light across the cliffs so that he was suddenly able to make out – instead of a rock – a tiny figure, its red hair haloed by the sun.

Katla!

★   ★   ★

Katla Aransen sat on the top of the Hound's Tooth, her face thrust out towards the sea, her feet dangling over three hundred feet of clear space to the water breaking over the rocks below. She had risen at dawn filled with an energy she could put no name to and had fled the house before any of her family were awake. In these last few days, she had seen and heard so much that it had all become a great jumble in her head: Festrin's talk of earth-magic, her father's plans to steal the King's shipmaker for his mad expedition into the frozen north; the voice in her head that had rumbled like thunder when she had channelled whatever force it was that had brought the seither back from the brink of death . . .

The implications of this last act in particular were so mystifying that she could not bear to talk to another soul until she had made some sense of it for herself. And so she had run down to the water's edge and climbed to the top of the cliff by her favourite route.

Climbing always cleared her head of troubles, especially a dizzying ascent like the dauntingly sheer seaward face of the Hound's Tooth, which required every bit of her concentration. Being unable to climb all these months because of her injuries, and believing that she never would again, on account of the awkwardness of the clubbed hand, had been the worst punishment of all.

She held the afflicted arm up in the air now, twisted it this way and that. Still she could not believe the marvel of it. Where before there had been a great welted mass of red-and-white scar tissue, now she had four fingers and a thumb again, albeit pale and thin in comparison with her other tanned and muscular hand. It was hard to believe she was healed; harder still to comprehend that she had brought about that healing herself. It was perplexing and strange, and she half-expected at any moment to look down and find the old monstrosity there again. So she tried not to think about it at all, in case doing so might tempt the

Fates and remind them of her unworthiness as a recipient of this miracle.

But as she laid a hand on the first hold of the cold granite a fine trembling had started up in her fingers, followed by a hot buzz which had suffused her whole arm, then her shoulders, neck and head, and at last her entire body, as if the rock were speaking to her in a language her blood alone could understand, a language like thunder; and that had been the most confusing thing of all.

For Katla, climbing was her ultimate escape – away from the chores of the steading and her mother's doomed attempts to make her more ladylike – out into the most inaccessible places on the island where no one could follow her, even if they knew where she was. To be able to look down onto the backs of flying gulls, to share a sun-drenched ledge with fulmars and jackdaws, to watch the folk of Rockfall from way up high, and them not even aware of their audience, was a special pleasure to her: at once a discipline of controlled movement and the ultimate expression of the wildest part of herself. Whenever her life became frustrating or alarming she would climb. The necessities of the activity brought a great simplicity to life, she found: move carefully, hold tight; do not fall. When she climbed she was forced to make these her only concerns, so that all other anxieties receded into insignificance; but to be assailed by this tangible flow of earth-magic, with all the complexities and consequences it brought into her life turned simple escape into a perplexing discussion of the nature of the world.

The sea, she thought now, looking out over that wide blue expanse. *The sea's the answer. I may feel the magic running out of the reefs and skerries; but surely over the deepest ocean it will leave me be? I'll put my case to Da, make him take me on his expedition . . .*

Aran's lungs and legs were complaining long before he crested the final ridge, even though the landward path was far more kindly than his daughter's route to the top. It had been a long time since the Master of Rockfall had even walked to the summit of the Hound's Tooth; indeed, it was with some chagrin that he realised that 'some time' meant in truth almost twenty years – before the island had become his domain, after his father's death in the war with Istria. In all that time it had been a succession of lads he'd sent up here on look-out duty: immediately after the war, looking for enemy ships, which could be hard to spot: since native Istrian vessels were not designed for ocean crossings, the Southern Empire used captured Eyran ships against the north; then, when the uneasy truce had been established, looking for independent raiders intent on pillage, and more lately, with rather less urgency, looking for merchant ships and those bearing men and news from the King's court at Halbo. In his father's day, the look-outs commanded respect in the island community, but since the perils of war had ebbed away the task had fallen to green lads – second, third and fourth sons of Rockfall retainers with no land of their own to work and few other prospects. Young Vigli and Jarn Forson were the current pair of look-outs, and Sur knew how feckless those two could be: with war looming again, he should set about the matter of finding reliable replacements . . .

'Hello, Da.'

Katla waved her hand at him. Her right hand, the one that had been maimed. The bandages with which Bera had thought to conceal the sudden improvement from the superstitious eyes of the world had gone, he noticed. But of course, no one had yet had the chance to tell Katla to keep them on.

With some trepidation – for Aran did not share his daughter's nonchalance around precipitous cliffs – he sat down on the rocky outcrop, rather further from the edge than Katla, and took the proffered hand in his own. In his meaty grasp it was tiny, almost fragile. He turned it over, palm up, then palm down, and gazed at it in amazement. He had pulled her out of the pyre the Istrians had made for her at the Allfair, for her sacrilege (as they saw it) of climbing their sacred Rock, and for the part they claimed she had played in the abduction of Lord Tycho Issian's daughter Selen, before she could be swallowed by it, but her right hand had been burned raw and red, her fingers fused into a clublike mass. He had thought she would never forge another sword, never decorate another dagger, never climb another cliff; but now here was she was with a full complement of pristine fingers and a separate thumb once more, sitting cheerfully on top of her favourite route. Aran had never been much of a believer in magic, but what he had experienced of late had given him considerable pause for thought.

'So,' Katla grinned at him, the sun adding mischievous sparks to her tawny eyes, 'now that I'm whole again, can I go with Fent and Halli to Halbo to capture the King's new shipmaker?'

Aran dropped her hand as if it had burned him. It was impossible that anyone else had crept up the Hound's Tooth to overhear them; but even so, he could not help but glance around anxiously.

'What? How could you know?'

Never an accomplished liar – partly through laziness, for it was simpler to tell the truth – Katla opted for the easy explanation: 'I overheard you and the lads plotting in the barn after the feast. To bring Morten Danson back here, whether he will or no, and all the timber and tools and men too, so that he can make an ice-breaking ship for your expedition north, through the floes.'

Aran's eyes hooded themselves briefly, as if he cloaked his thoughts from her. When he looked up again his face was dark with some hidden passion. 'You cannot tell anyone.

F120,873

You know that, don't you? The future of our family is at stake here.'

'So you'll let me go with them?'

'It's strong men that are needed, not girls,' he said roughly.

Katla's nostrils flared. 'I can fight as well as my brothers: I can wrestle better than Halli and wield a sword better than Fent—'

'You are not going. Your mother needs you here.'

'My mother! All I do is get under her feet and remind her what a hard job it's going to be to marry me off—'

Aran gripped her so hard that she almost yelped. 'When I make this expedition you will be running Rockfall with Bera: you'd better start learning the way of things now.'

'But Da!' Treacherously, Katla's eyes had filled with sudden, scorching tears. If she could not sail to Halbo, she'd been consoling herself that at least she'd be sailing with the expedition force, to find the legendary island of Sanctuary and the treasure that was hidden there. She blinked furiously. 'You *need* to take me with you – who else can shin up the mastpole when the lines get tangled? Who else can feel the draw of the land when there's none to be seen?'

'I've nearly lost you twice, girl: I'd not forgive myself if I lost you again.'

Katla wrenched herself free of his grasp so violently that Aran fell backwards, his head striking an outcrop of granite splotched with rosettes of gold lichen. She leapt to her feet, her shadow falling across him for a moment, then she took off down the cliff path without looking back.

With a groan, Aran levered himself upright, an expression of pain tightening the lines on his handsome face, though it could not be said whether this expression were brought about by the knock he had taken from the granite or from some other, more interior, sensation.

Overhead, a black-backed gull slipped sideways on a current of warm air, its shadow long in the low sun.

'She said I must look well to you, Katla,' the Master of Rockfall said softly, watching his daughter running wildly down the cliff, oblivious to the gorse and brambles which choked the path. 'Or she would be back for you.' He knew he would never tell her of the exchange he had had with the seither, not just because Katla would toss her head like a wayward pony and have her way out of sheer, cross-grained will, but out of some obscure shame in him that there might be other influences on their lives that he could not control, that some other force might already be pulling on the lines of his fate, and those of his family, too.

Even downhill and at the breakneck speed that drove her it took Katla more than twenty minutes to reach the harbour. The first person she encountered there was Min Codface, Tam Fox's right-hand woman, whose specialism within the mummers' troupe was the throwing of knives with such accuracy that Tam liked to joke she could trim your beard and your nails and then kill you dead before you knew it. Min was a big woman, but even she was staggering under the weight of a huge wicker chest, around which she could see nothing at all: two more steps and she'd be in the sea. Katla caught hold of the chest and turned Min sideways with a foot's length to spare.

'Close one!' grinned the knife-thrower, revealing the huge gap in her teeth that had caused some obscene merriment between Fent and Tam, before Min had threatened to punch their lights out, and even Fent had recognised someone potentially more violent than himself and had mumbled what amounted, almost, to an apology. 'Thanks, chubb.'

Min had developed a habit of referring to everyone as some type of fish or another. 'He's a right strange mullet,' she'd said of one unfortunate lad who'd lost his balance on top of the human tower they'd been practising before the feast or, referring to one of the village girls, 'Pretty as a speckled trout'; and 'Your brother Halli seems like quite a fair carp,' which was apparently a compliment. Katla had wondered whether Min had chosen her own name, or whether its imposition had coloured her view of the world.

Min dumped the chest unceremoniously on the seawall and wiped her brow. Behind her, a cavalcade of mummers was winding down the steep hill from the steading, their arms full of costumes and props and provisions for the voyage ahead.

'You're sailing today?' Katla asked, appalled at how time had overtaken her.

The knife-thrower nodded quickly. 'Aye, we'll catch the late tide, Tam says. He couldn't be arsed to make an early start, lazy great halibut. Got us all running around while he sweet-talks your ma out of her best yellowbread.'

At the very mention of this delicacy, Katla's stomach rumbled loudly. Her mother's yellowbread was known across all the islands, though she baked it rarely now that the cost of the flowers that gave up their stamens to the spice that gave it its distinctive taste and colour had become so expensive. The crocuses grew only in the foothills of the Golden Mountains on the southern continent, and this was one reason Gramma Rolfsen cited as clear evidence that the Eyrans had been driven out of their rightful homeland: for how otherwise would yellowbread have become a staple of the Northern Isles when all the southerners did with the flowers was to crush them for dyeing or use them in their rituals?

Katla gave the knife-thrower a distracted smile, then started up the hill towards the hall. Breakfast first, she thought; then some serious plans to be made. She passed the tumblers, dressed not in their bright motley but in ordinary brown homespun, with casks of water and stallion's-blood wine balanced precariously on their heads, then some more of Tam's women stumbling down the path with a freshly dead cow which seemed to be refusing to cooperate with them. It would, Katla thought, watching them wrestle awkwardly with the stiff-legged carcass, have been far simpler to joint and carve the creature up at the hall and haul down a portion apiece, or to have butchered it down on the strand, close to the ship. The mummers were not always the most practical of folk, for all their skill and tricks. Towards the end of the procession she saw her twin brother Fent carrying a long, finely made box of polished oak. Katla's eyes narrowed suspiciously.

'What've you got there, fox-boy?' she said, stepping in front of him so that he was forced to halt. She knew the casket well enough: Uncle Margan had made it as a gift to her father by his brother-by-law, for keeping his sword in, 'now that we are no longer at war and you will be providing for my sister by becoming a great landsman'. Bera liked to tell the story of how Aran's face had fallen, thinking Margan had brought him a new sword, and how long it had taken for him to recover his manners sufficiently to thank him for the box alone.

Fent looked surprised at first to see his twin up and about; then he turned shifty. He had not shaved in several days, Katla noticed with some surprise, for her brother was vain of his looks and never let a beard grow to cover them up. Now, however, a fine orange fluff had coated his chin and upper lip like some sort of exotic mould. 'It's for Tam,' he mumbled, and tried to press past her.

Katla stood her ground. 'There's only one sword in Rockfall good enough to find Tam's favour,' she said grimly, 'and that's my carnelian, which I have my own plans for.' She nipped forward and neatly tipped the lid of the casket. Inside, on a bed of white linen, lay the Red Sword. Katla swore. 'Who said you might take the finest blade I ever forged and give it away to a mummer?'

Fent coloured, but his chin came up pugnaciously. He

snapped the lid shut, barely missing her hastily withdrawn fingers. 'Father said Tam Fox should have it as part payment for the voyage. It's tainted now, anyway.'

It was said that the blood of a seither would make the blade that had drawn it chancy and untrue, liable to turn on its owner.

'Even so, no one asked me.'

'You were dead to the world.'

'You're damn lucky you aren't,' Katla fumed, her grey eyes sparking dangerously.

They stood eye to eye in this way, as like as a pair of birth-hounds, neither prepared to back down, until Halli, appearing suddenly with a couple of wheels of muslin-wrapped cheese in his arms, intervened.

'It's good to see that you're well enough to argue with Fent, but let him take the sword, sister,' he said quietly. He gave Fent a cold look that made his younger sibling quail in a new and unusual manner.

He knows, Katla thought, remembering with sudden clarity the conversation she had overheard after the feast. He knows that Fent is a murderer, that he killed Finn Larson in hot blood at the Allfair. And how much, she wondered, did he know of the episode with the seither, Festrin One-Eye? As if in answer to this, she watched his gaze fall to her miraculously mended right hand, saw how his brows drew together into a single straight line just as their father's did when he was confounded. Taking advantage of this moment of inattention, Fent shouldered past them both with the box and trotted smartly down the path, his red head bobbing with suppressed energy.

'Let him go,' Halli said, placing a restraining hand on Katla's shoulder. 'The sword is cursed and so is he. Why do you think he hasn't shaved these last few days?'

Katla shrugged. 'Laziness?'

Halli gave out a brief, harsh shout of laughter. 'After the

seither told him all his ventures would meet with disaster, he
hasn't dared take a knife to his face for fear it will slip and cut
his throat!'

Katla grimaced, feeling almost sorry for her twin.

'And you—' He stared down again at her arm, lost for
words.

Feeling uncomfortable, Katla tugged her sleeve down over
her hand. 'Oh, that,' she said inadequately. 'It's better.'

'Rather too quickly for nature.'

One of their farmhands came into view carrying a roll of
sailcloth and, catching the end of their conversation, gave
Katla a curious glance. Halli took her by the arm and drew
her out of the way until the man was out of earshot.

'Was it the seither did this to you, made it whole?'

Katla warded him off and started walking up the path again.
She didn't want to think about this now. 'I don't know.' Past
Feya's Cross, where the path forked, she took the way up
towards the mountain pastures. 'I don't care, either,' she
added, firmly. 'All I know is that it's whole again and that's
all that matters to me.' She flexed her fingers, revelling once
more in the healthy sensation of separate fingers and strong
muscles.

'It may be all that matters to you, but there are those who'll
talk of witchcraft if you don't keep it hidden. They'll shun
you for it, and the rest of our clan, too.' He frowned. 'And
with Da set on this mad plan, we're likely to be outcast soon
enough as it is.'

'Not if the stories about Sanctuary are true. Not if he brings
back the gold.' Katla's eyes shone at the thought.

'It's all nonsense.'

'Da doesn't think so.'

'Da's head's been turned inside out by that nomad mapseller
and his fairytale maps.'

'If Da hears you say that he'll pound your head. Anyway,
who's to say the map's not real – it's most accurately drawn.'

'Aye, well there's something odd going on,' Halli glowered. 'For his is not the only map I've seen.'

Now it was Katla's turn to frown. 'Showing the oceanway to Sanctuary?'

'Keep your voice down. Aye. I caught a glimpse of a map that Hopli Garson was showing to Fenil Soronson at the Allfair.'

Katla considered this in silence for a moment. 'Then they'll be planning an expedition too?'

Halli nodded. 'No doubt. Fenil is just as mad as Da for tales of treasure and lost islands and the like.'

'But we must get there first!' she cried, her face lit with fervour. 'Can we not just take the *Fulmar's Gift* and set out straight away? It'll be *months* if we have to wait for a new ship to be built, and that's even if Morten Danson agrees to it, which he's hardly likely to do, even if you abduct him — *especially* if you abduct him!'

'Even Fenil is not such a fool. The sea freezes as far south as Whale Holm from Spirits' Day to gone Firstsun: and beyond that they say the ice goes on to the top of the world. He'll need an ice-breaker just as we do.'

'But he'll already have gone to Morten Danson . . .'

'Tam says the shipyard's taken in six months' production of iron ore from the Eastern Isles.'

'That's more than's needed for a single ice-breaker. If he binds that much iron to his ship the only course it'll be taking is straight down to the Great Howe!'

'I think the King's shipmaker has plenty of orders on his hands. I suspect he may have turned down Da's commission because of the rumours as to how the last King's shipmaker perished.'

He stated it as flatly as if it had been a goat Fent had skewered at the Allfair, rather than a man, and his sweetheart's father to boot, Katla noted with surprise. Older and harder his face looked, too; more than ever like Aran's. Halli was a man to be reckoned with, she realised with surprise; not a boy any more at all. Between the actions of their father and brother he'd lost every dream he'd ever cherished for himself – his own ship, the wherewithal to make a match with the girl he loved and the price of the farm on which they'd raise their stock and their family.

'Jenna will come round in the end,' she said softly. 'She's really very fond of you.'

Halli's head jerked as if she had hit him. 'You know?' he asked incredulously.

'Fent told me. On the voyage back.'

'But instead of telling me you thought you'd let me find out for myself,' he said bitterly. 'Why would she ever ally herself to the clan who killed her father?'

'She doesn't know for sure. No one does.'

'And that makes it right, does it? I say Fent should be a man and declare the killing and offer blood-price to the Fairwater clan and take the years of exile for the manslaughter that he's due.'

'But Da won't let him?' Even as she said it Katla knew this to be so: Aran was so fixed on his dream of gold that he'd not let a small thing like law or principle stand in his way. Paying blood-price for the King's shipmaker would ensure that the Rockfall clan would never afford another ship, even if anyone was willing to trade with them again.

Halli shook his head wordlessly, his jaw rigid.

Katla shrugged. 'Easier to move mountains than to shift our father a knuckle-length when he's set on something.'

'I hate him.' Dark blood suffused his face.

'Da?' Katla was taken aback.

'Fent.'

'He's a hot-tempered—' she started.

'He's a monster.' Halli said it with a vehemence Katla had never heard from her mild-mannered sibling. 'He's as dangerous as a mad dog. At best he should be muzzled

and tied to a post where his poisonous bite can do no
one harm.'

A curious expression – part avidity, part calculation – passed
over Katla Aransen's face like a high cloud above clear sea.

'I have an idea,' she said.

By the height of second tide, the mummers' ships were fully
laden and the Rockfallers had come away from their various
tasks and had trailed down to the harbour to wave them off
on their voyage back to Halbo. Only three of those gathered
on the quay knew that there was anything more to the venture
than a simple return to the mainland, and one of those knew
more than the other two. In a tight knot on the end of
the seawall a little distance from the crowd, Aran Aranson,
Halli Aranson and Tam Fox stood with their heads together,
talking quietly.

'Only his best oak will do for the keel,' Aran said urgently
to his son. 'Don't let him palm you off with anything but
the finest single timber he's got in his store – I'll have no
botched-together vessel for this voyage. I've heard he has
oaks from the Plantation, and trees from that sacred grove
can reach a hundred feet tall. For the ship I have in mind,
nothing else will do: that keel will need to be as whippy as
a cat's spine to weather the big seas of the far north.'

Halli nodded impatiently. He had the air of one who
had heard these instructions a dozen times or more. 'And
heartwood for the planking, yes I know.'

'Come back with strakes of sapwood and I'll send you back
to Halbo in a rowing boat—'

'Heartwood, not sapwood.' Halli rolled his eyes, but his
father had turned his attention to Tam Fox.

The chief mummer matched Aran for height, but seemed
taller for the mass of sandy hair he wore in a bizarre combination of topknots and braids and fierce-looking crests, some
of which had been turned by years of air heavy with seasalt to

a bright, streaky yellow. Plaits wove in and out of his long red beard like snakes; look closer and it became clear that some of the decorations *were* snakes, cured and withered, or stripped to their skeletal forms, their heads poised to strike.

'Be careful with the shipmaker,' Aran was saying. 'If you have to knock him unconscious just make sure you have all the information you need from him first – men, timber, tools: I want nothing left to chance. And don't hit him too hard, for he'll be no use to me if he's addled—'

'Aran.' Tam Fox gripped his old friend by the shoulder. 'Do you think I have the memory of a chicken that you tell me this again and again? We will bring you Morten Danson, bruised if necessary, but in full possession of his wits; we will bring you the oak and the tools and the men to wield them, and we will be back here by Harvest Moon.' He paused, his eyes scanning the crowd over the Master of Rockfall's broad shoulder. 'I had hoped to bid farewell to your daughter,' he added casually.

'I haven't seen her since this morning when we had an altercation,' Aran said stiffly.

'I saw her,' Halli offered helpfully. 'She came storming past me into the longhouse, grabbed up some bread and wine, then ran out to the stables, leapt on one of the ponies and galloped off into the hills.'

Aran grimaced. 'She'll be back when her temper's cooled.'

'She's a tricksy little minx, your Katla,' Tam Fox said with a grin, 'but I like her fiery temperament well enough. Why not make her part of our bargain, Aran Aranson, and save yourself the trouble of civilising her for another? I'll wager you'll not have her wed by next Winterfest otherwise!'

'The last time I included Katla in such a deal was ill-fated,' Aran growled. 'I'll not be tempting the gods again.'

'I mean to have her, Aran.'

The older man held the mummer's gaze. 'Did I not know you to be more than you seem, this discussion would be ended for good and all. Besides, persuading Katla to be wed at all is likely to be the harder part of the bargain.'

Tam Fox gave the Rockfaller his lupine smile. 'Despite all appearances to the contrary, I am a patient man. Time weighs differently for me than it does for you, my friend.'

The ship's boat came bumping against the seawall below them and Halli threw his leather sack down to the men at the oars, then lowered himself nimbly into the stern. 'Fare well, Father,' he said tightly. He turned his gaze to the *Snowland Wolf*, its prow rising and falling on the tide, as sleek and elegant as a swan's neck, scouring the decks for one slight figure.

Katla Aransen watched the group of men on the mole with curiosity; but when they stopped talking and looked out towards the ship, she swiftly ducked her head and made herself busy about the lines. None of Tam Fox's crew had noticed anything amiss when Aran Aranson's younger 'son' had boarded the *Snowland Wolf*; but that might have had more to do with the skins of stallion's blood she had brought with her than the efficacy of her disguise. Even so, she thought, fingering the unfamiliar fuzz on her chin, the honey had done a remarkable job of keeping in place the snippets of fox-fur she had stolen from the edge of one of her mother's best capes, even if the hound, Ferg, had tried to lick it off. One good gale was likely to whip it away; but the weather looked set fair to see her safely beyond the point of no return. She stretched her arm up to reach for another of the lines off the yard and was assailed by a rich, rank stench.

Whoo! She wrinkled her nose in distaste. Wearing Fent's clothing for the duration of the voyage was going to be punishment in itself. A picture of her twin, securely gagged and bound to the central pillar of the main barn, eyes sparking blue murder as she and Halli bade him farewell at the door, flickered briefly and satisfyingly through her mind.

Then Katla turned her face to the ocean and grinned with the utmost glee.

Two

Tanto

'Take this vile stuff away! Are you trying to poison me now, not content with having rendered me a gross and stinking cripple?'

Saro watched the silver plate spin through the air and hit the wall on the other side of the bedchamber, emptying its contents down the pale terracotta like vomit. It was curious, he thought, that his brother could have the strength required to hurl a plate so hard that it left a dent in the plaster, but be apparently too weak to feed himself.

It had been three months since Tanto Vingo had regained consciousness after succumbing to the trauma of the wounds he had received at the Allfair, and the equally dangerous ministrations of the doctors which had followed. Their parents, Favio and Illustria, had been tearful with relief and gratitude at the return of their favourite son – albeit in his new form; but on hearing that familiar voice rend the air of the darkened room on the night when the merchants had passed through, with their rancorous gossip and the fateful moodstones which had played their part in resurrecting the patient, Saro's heart had contracted in misery.

He had much preferred his brother when he lay like a dead thing, suppurating silently.

'Clean it up, you toad! Lick it off the wall, like the revolting spew it is – it's all you're fit for, anyway.' Fat tears welled in Tanto's eyes and burst out onto his pale, fleshy cheeks. He balled his chubby fists and started to batter the counterpane with them. Then he began to roar in the way he did when there was no one else but Saro to hear him. 'Why *me*? Why has the Goddess visited this mischance on me – why not you? You're such a shit-filled, cowardly little worm – what good are *you* in the world? No one loves *you*, no one expected anything of *you*: to have seen you reduced to this would have been no loss. But *me—*'

The wailing grew to tidal proportions until Tanto's face went a putrid purple and he was forced to stop to gasp for breath.

Saro studiously ignored this outburst, as he had learned to do (nothing infuriated Tanto more) and applied himself to scraping the remains of the roasted chicken, peppers, onions and zucchini off the wall. They had been pureed, like infant food, since Tanto refused even to make the effort to chew; but they had been prepared by their mother's own hand, mixed with the most expensive herbs and spices and slow-cooked for hours to bring out the delicate flavourings. To see such love and effort treated with such childish scorn was painful to Saro. Though it was hardly surprising that Tanto was in such a permanent foul temper: he was somewhat changed from the young man who had set out from Altea bound for the Allfair those short months ago. Then he had been handsome, athletic and adored – the favourite son, of whom great things were expected. A fine marriage was talked of, an alliance which would bring status, land, influence and, it was hoped, not a little wealth. Through Tanto, the Vingo clan would claw back the economic and political standing it had enjoyed several generations back, before fortunes were squandered by delinquent sons and the war with the North had claimed the rest.

And so Tanto had been raised as the golden hope of the family, every favour and luxury showered upon him: the best tutors (or rather, when the best were dismissed for gainsaying him, those clever, weak men who had learned not to complain at his laziness and lack of application, nor to suggest that the handwriting in which his exercises were delivered might not be his own); the best fencing masters and weaponry, the best tailors and the fabrics (though Tanto had never acquired good taste: his preference ran to ostentation and obvious expense); and later, the most costly courtesans and body-slaves. But none of this indulgence had done anything to improve what was already showing itself to be a dangerous personality, and in encouraging Tanto's dreams of power and glory their father had succeeded only in fuelling an arrogant and overweening nature. Tanto did not simply walk: he swaggered. He did not laugh: he brayed, and usually at his own remarks, for he rarely listened to anyone else's. He did not merely win: he triumphed, at everything he assayed; or there would be tantrums and blood shed, usually a servant's.

In short, Tanto had been well on his way to becoming the monster that the Goddess had, in her own inimitable way, now shown him to be, as if his ugly interior had been turned inside-out to show his true face to the world, so that his erstwhile tanned, healthful and darkly handsome exterior was displaced by a bloated, foul-smelling, evil-humoured slug. The beauty of it was that Tanto had brought his fate down upon himself by his own cruel hands (and other parts of his anatomy that were now sadly missing), no matter how vehemently he tried to heap the blame for it upon Saro. *So it seemed that there was*, Saro thought, scrubbing the last of the dinner off the tiled floor, where it had slid down the wall and congealed, *some poetic justice in the world after all*.

'Perhaps some dessert, brother?' he offered now, turning back to survey the ravaged creature in the bed. 'There's an apricot frangipan, or some fig jelly . . .'

'Go fuck yourself, *brother*,' Tanto returned viciously, his black eyes blazing baleful as coals in the soft blubber of his new face.

Ever since the parts of his gangrenous manhood had been cut away by the chirurgeon's knife and sealed with Falla's fire, Tanto had swelled in size, lost all his muscle-tone and most of his hair. The fat was likely due to the fact that Favio and Illustria, while Tanto had been so blessedly unconscious, had equated parental love with the stuffing of liquid food into their son's throat by day and night, by long spoon and then by ingenious tubes made from sheep's intestines while a slave sat by the bedside and stroked his throat to make him swallow. Being bed-bound had converted all that food into these great swells and bloats of flesh: the hair, and the smell of putrefaction which seemed to boil up out of every orifice Tanto owned, well, that seemed a just punishment from the Goddess.

No matter how hard Tanto railed against the barbarian Eyran raiders who had, he swore, burst into Selen Issian's pavilion, intent on rape and destruction and wounded him in his brave defence of the girl, Saro knew his brother too well. Tanto had elaborated on the tale so much now, embroidering ever more unlikely details into it, that Saro suspected a far simpler explanation for the events and their consequences, and one that was far more in keeping with what he knew of his elder sibling. Tanto was not used to being denied anything: so when the marriage settlement with Selen had fallen through for lack of funds, there was surely only one reason why Tanto would have gone to the girl's tent: to take (by force if necessary) what he thought should rightfully be his. And succumbing to a stab wound to the genitals spoke of a woman's desperate defence rather than a brawl with a band of northerners, especially since the only other marks Tanto bore looked suspiciously like the tiny crescent-shaped cuts which might be made by a woman's fingernails. They said the Goddess looked after her own . . .

No one else had remarked on those small wounds, dis- tracted, no doubt, by the horrifying nature of his other wounds, but Saro had been forced to spend a lot of time tending to his brother after the attack. It had been Favio Vingo's way of punishing him for giving half his winnings from the horse race at the Allfair to the nomad child whose grandfather Tanto had butchered, rather than donating it to the marriage settlement, as a more dutiful (and hard-hearted) son should have done.

He collected the plate and spoon, and felt for a moment as he did so a disconcerting buzz of energy tingle through his fingertips, as if some ghost of Tanto's temper haunted the objects and was finding a way to discharge itself through him. As he left the room, he could feel his brother's eyes boring into his back all the way. In the corridor outside, he shook his head: being alone with Tanto was an unpleasant experience: it could do strange things to his head.

It was a blessed relief just to breathe clean air as he crossed the courtyard to run the plate, spoon and cloth under the tap from the water-butt there. Tanto would doubtless lie to Mother that Saro had not fed him, that he had taken the food away without waking him for his meal, or most likely had eaten it himself. And Saro would probably end up reviled and punished in like manner: by being refused any supper. But as he felt the sun beat down on his face and was assailed by the hot, spicy scents of the honeysuckle and marigolds which had been planted against the whitewashed wall there, Saro did not care. He was used to his brother's spitefulness, and to his parents taking Tanto's word against his own. *So much for the loving bonds of family*, he thought. There were times when he felt he had made a deeper connection with the nomad folk he had met at the Allfair than with those with whom he had spent his entire life.

He crossed the courtyard and leaned against the wall, looking out across the landscape. Their villa stood on a hill below which tiers of cultivated land stretched away in myriad steps, bearing their hard-won crops of limes and lemons, pomegranates and figs down into the orange groves, planted in serried ranks along the valley floor so that the land below appeared like a cloth boldly striped in alternating bands of dusty red and glossy green, shot through with a single sweep of glinting blue where the river ran through. Beyond, maybe sixty miles away or more, the land rose white and rocky to form the foothills of the Farem Heights; beyond that again rose the sawtoothed mountain range known as the Dragon's Backbone, standing as clear and affirmative against the blue horizon as a voice calling his name.

All I want, he thought, wringing the cloth out over the wall, *is to be away from here. To call my life my own.*

But only the nomads could exist in the wild places beyond the bounds of the Empire. Travelling with their placid pack-beasts, the shaggy-looking yeka, they traversed Elda, never putting down roots, never founding settlements, nor claiming ground, never doing damage to the world. And because they trod so lightly on the land, the land appeared to allow them sustenance and passage through even its most inhospitable areas. The only nomads he had encountered had been at the Allfair, where both northerners and Empire folk travelled to do business, to trade their goods and services, to make alliances, marriages and gain political favour. Had this been the extent of the Fair's attractions, Saro would have found it dull indeed: but the nomad people – known by the southerners as 'the Footloose', though they pre-ferred to call themselves 'the Wandering Folk' – had also come to the annual fair, and their presence had provided wonders aplenty. He remembered watching them arrive in their garishly painted wagons and their outlandish costumes, bearing the fantastic array of goods they brought with them to trade and to sell: lanterns and candles, jewellery made from dragonclaws and bear teeth; ornaments, pottery and weavings; potions and charms. His fingers strayed unconsciously to the small leather pouch he wore around his neck. Inside, there lay the most dangerous object in the world, though when he had first come upon it at a nomad peddler's stall he had thought it merely a pretty trinket, a moodstone which changed colour according to the emotional state of the person who handled it. Since that innocent time, however, he had seen it absorb an old man's death and pass to him the wearer's gift – a deep, and entirely unwanted, empathy with anyone with whom he made physical contact. He had seen it flush red in anger and poisonous green with jealousy; he had seen it flare to a white that hurt the eyes; he had seen it steal men's souls out of their bodies and leave them stone dead upon the ground. Until three months ago, he had thought he had seen the utmost the moodstone could show him. Then, accessing some nexus of power he could not comprehend, it had brought his brother back to the world; and for that alone he felt like pounding it to dust and scattering its magic to the winds.

Magic, he thought sourly. Surely it was only magic that was likely to spirit him out of this place. If he could just take his courage in his hands and ride out of here in the dead of night he might chance upon a band of Wanderers who would take him in. And then perhaps he might find Guaya again, the little nomad girl whose grandfather Tanto had so needlessly killed and who, up to that horrible moment, had been his friend. Or he might travel north and try to discover what had happened to Katla Aransen. The red of the soil here was a daily reminder of her, for it was the exact dark, sandstone red of her hair; just as the pale blue of the sky on the northern horizon was the colour of her eyes. He found reminders of her all around him: in the curve of a piece of fruit, in a well-turned blade or a shout of laughter; in any mention of Eyra or talk of the imminent war with the North. She was everywhere, and nowhere. He did not even know if she was still alive. She had escaped the burning, Fabel told him, by sorcerous means; but Saro had touched her soul when she had laid hands on him at her knife-stall, and he knew there was no witchery in her; just a pure, natural energy. But night after night she continued to visit him in his dreams, her presence there as vibrant and physical as it had been in life, and his heart still yearned for her. That energy could not be gone from the world: he would surely know in his heart if she were dead . . .

'Saro!'

His reverie shattered, he turned to find Favio Vingo striding across the courtyard toward him, his face dark with anger. *By the Lady*, Saro thought unhappily, *now what?*

His unspoken question was answered in no uncertain manner by a roundhouse slap from the man he had until recently believed to be his father, up to the moment some months back when he had been visited by that unwelcome, disturbing vision of his uncle lying with his mother . . .

Fury rushed through him; but whether it was his own reaction to the painful assault upon his now-pounding ear, or a less tangible legacy of Favio's temper, he could not ascertain.

'How dare you treat your brother so!'

Ah, thought Saro heart sinking. *So that's the way of it.*

'To strike a bed-ridden invalid is the worst and most cowardly act – and to strike him so hard as to leave such a mark—'

Saro could hardly believe his ears. While his calumnies against Saro had so far been many and varied, Tanto had never yet accused him of physical violence, so this new allegation represented an escalation in Tanto's lies. Although Saro knew it to be an exercise in futility, he felt that he should make some attempt to defend himself. 'I did not hit Tanto,' he said steadily. 'If he has a mark on him it must be one of his own making.'

This just antagonised Favio further. 'Come with me!' he roared. His fingers closed around Saro's biceps with brutal force and he began to drag him bodily back towards the house.

Saro was overcome by a flood of righteous anger which approached hatred, followed by a wave of scalding sorrow: for the wrong son was lying like a great white maggot in the sickbed while this mendacious, useless boy strode about glowing with health. Saro went bonelessly with Favio Vingo, his limbs and his mind no longer his own while the physical contact remained in place. On the threshold of Tanto's chamber, however, Favio shoved Saro away from him so hard that the boy sprawled upon the tiles, and the maelstrom of emotions ebbed slowly away.

When Saro gathered himself and looked up, he found his mother, swathed in her customary blue sabatka, weeping silently on a chair beside the bed and his brother propped up by a multitude of white pillows (*no doubt*, Saro found himself thinking incongruously, *stuffed with the feathers of the most expensive Jetran geese and costing a good cantari apiece, while I sleep on a pallet stuffed with straw and a bag filled with chicken feathers from our own coops*) staring at him with outraged eyes. Tanto's bedshirt was torn open to reveal a dark bruise over the collarbone, or where the collarbone must be, hidden somewhere under all that soft white flesh. The wound was a livid red, already purpling. It must have required considerable force and determination to have done such damage to himself, Saro thought, once more taken aback at the extent of Tanto's loathing for him.

'I was not eating fast enough,' Tanto complained in a miserable whine, his black eyes glinting with self-induced tears, all the while clasping Illustria's thin hand in his own flabby great paw. 'He kept hitting me again and again with the spoon—'

Saro turned to their father. 'This has nothing to do with me,' he said through gritted teeth. 'How can you believe I would do such a thing?'

But Favio's expression was one of purest disgust; and not for the puling creature in the bed, either.

Tanto savoured his triumph. 'And when I cried out for him to stop, he took out his belt–dagger and thumped me so hard with the pommel that I thought he had stabbed me!'

In victorious evidence of this he reached beneath the bed-clothes and flourished what was in truth Saro's own dagger.

Saro stared at it, dumbfounded. His hand went to his waist, but he knew before he felt there that he was not wearing the belt on which he habitually carried the dagger. He could picture it now, slung over the back of the little cane chair in his own chamber on the next floor of the house. And the dagger had been in its tooled leather scabbard beside it when he left the room that morning. So how had Tanto managed to lay hands upon it?

Tanto saw the doubt on his brother's face and smiled evilly. 'But of course I forgive you, Saro,' he said softly, his eyes like gimlets. 'I know I am a trial to nurse and that such care is not your natural calling. Which is why I have suggested to Father that since the Council is bound to be calling soon on all good men and true to take up arms for the Empire, we should be training you up as a soldier.'

Saro stared at him in disbelief. Tanto knew well that he had no warrior skills. His swordsmanship was clumsy, his lancework worse: he had neither the taste nor the ability for combat. Nor could he rely on archery – he was a poor shot with a bow, too, not least because he could never stand to harm a living thing. He was fleet of foot and had an affinity with horses which enabled him to ride better than most; but as far as he could see all this qualified him to do was to leave the field of battle rather more swiftly than most, which would certainly be his inclination, since he had neither the aggression nor the blind patriotism required to split another man's skull for no good reason other than to save his own skin.

He opened his mouth to protest in horror, then closed it again as a new thought occurred to him. If he were to train as a soldier well enough to bring no dishonour to the Vingo name, then he might be allowed to leave Altea and make his much-wished-for escape. He turned his face to the man he called his father, who stood blocking the doorway, hands on his hips in a most uncompromising manner.

'It is most magnanimous of my brother,' he said through gritted teeth, 'to make this suggestion. If it would please you, sir, to allow me to redeem myself thus, then I will do my best to take on this task and acquire the skills necessary to a good soldier.'

Favio Vingo looked taken aback. He had been surprised when Tanto had advocated the idea, but had put it down to the fact that since Tanto would never be able to don the Vingo armour and go into battle at the head of the Altean troop as the hero he would surely be, then the next best thing was that his brother should carry the family's honour. But he was even more surprised at Saro's response. He had been expecting a storm of protest from the boy who had, he knew well, little liking for such activities. That, or downright, surly refusal. This gracious acceptance spoke of filial responsibility, of humility and, at long last, a bit of manly pride. But while the boy's attitude might have taken some of the sting out of his fury, there was still the matter of attacking Tanto to be attended to.

'Since it is not in your nature to take good care of your brother, then you shall learn that care the hard way. I do not know why Tanto should feel warmly towards you when you have shown him such violence and malice, but he has made a special request of me, arguing that the bond between the two of you needs to be strengthened. So, for the weeks to come, before, between and after you begin your training with Captain Bastido, you shall take over the duties of washing your brother's person, clearing away his waste and applying the ointments prescribed by the chirurgeon. You will start these duties at dawn tomorrow. Tonight, though, you shall retire to your own chamber without food or light, and reflect upon the qualities that make for proper fraternal relations. Now, go to your room.'

Saro was appalled. To have to train for soldiering, and give himself up to the untender mercies of Captain Galo 'the Bastard' Bastido was bad enough, for the man was a brute, and a sadistic one at that; but to have to touch his brother with his bare hands now Tanto's thoughts were no longer cloaked by a miasma of his unconsciousness was truly the most horrible torment Saro could imagine.

It was with leaden steps that he made his way upstairs.

Three

Halbo

Lit from landward by the crimson rays of the fallen sun and from the sea by the ghostly light of the newly risen moon, the King's capital of Halbo appeared between the silhouettes of the Pillars of Sur like a mirage. Amid the swells and folds of land which rose steeply from the narrow inlet, tiny amber lights twinkled in strings and clusters, and a large fire appeared to be burning down near the shore, illuminating the dark water and several dozen ships bobbing at anchor in the inner harbour.

Then the Pillars themselves hove into full view, stretching three hundred feet into the black air and Katla gasped in amazement. Contrary to first impressions it seemed that these two great sentinel towers were no mere natural feature of the landscape, for as they closed upon them a myriad of tiny lights were revealed inside the rock, one upon another, to the height of maybe ten longhouses. Tiny figures moved past the lights at various junctures so that from a distance the lights seemed to jump and skitter; then a web of stairways and arches came into focus, running from the waterline to the summits, winding around and about the towers and into the cliff-face on either side of the inlet.

It was a miracle of architecture: Katla stood there, hands on the gunwale, staring up into the night sky until her neck cricked, until she felt the touch of a finger drawn lightly down the line of her chin, which made her leap away with a shout. 'Sur's nuts! Keep your hands off me!'

'Much better without the beard, my dear, if I may say so.' Tam Fox was at her shoulder, his keen eyes boring into her, his white teeth gleaming in the silvery light. 'And you really should be much more grateful that I did not cast you off in the faering and send you back to your Da.' He took another step towards her, but Katla dodged away.

'You're a randy old goat,' she said with a grin. 'Go find yourself a nanny to tup.' She stared back up at the pillar.

'Extraordinary, isn't it? A work of genius, or madness, if you believe the tales.'

'I've never seen anything like it,' she said, and it was true: the houses of the Westman Isles were sturdy and constructed low to withstand the fierce winds off the Northern Ocean, and all she had seen on her visit to the Allfair had been pavilions and tents and simple booths; nothing made to last or serve any function beyond that of temporary accommodation. She had heard, though, that the great cities of Istria – Jetra and Cera and Forent – were built around magnificent castles which mazed the eye and took the breath right out of your lungs.

'The Pillars were hollowed out in the time of King Raik Horsehair, when the Eyrans were first driven north to these islands. He fortified the city in many cunning ways, and when he fell in the battle of the Sharking Straits, his wife carried on his work. They say it's impregnable, you know. Much like you—'

Katla rolled her eyes at him. 'I know,' she said crossly, ignoring his inference. 'It's what the city's name signifies – Hal-bau – "safe house" in the old form, and no enemy has ever sneaked past its defences.'

From the watchtower, a man shouted something that she could make neither head nor tail of, though the sound carried clearly in the night air; and after a moment Tam shouted back, 'White Rose!'

Katla looked at him.

'The password,' he said with a shrug. 'It changes every few weeks; but since the King returned with the nomad woman they've all had to do with her: Rosa Eldi; the Rose of the North; Heart's Desire; the King's Rose.'

'And what would happen if you didn't know the password?' Katla asked, puzzledly.

Tam grinned. 'Look there,' he said, pointing to the rocks on which the tower was founded. A rim of white surf marked its seaward edge. 'And there.' He indicated the opposite pillar at the same level.

Katla strained her eyes in the darkness. 'I can see nothing.'

'Just beneath the surface of the water there lies a chain forged of iron and blood and *seithers'* charms,' the mummers' chief explained. 'It's attached at either side to two great winches in the towers. Our ships are shallow-draughted enough to skim the chain but any southern vessel that by some miracle made it across the Northern Ocean would ground upon it – one word from the watchmen and up it goes, tipping them over into the Sound. And then—'

'What?'

Tam shook his head. 'Won't speak of that,' he said, making a superstitious gesture. He looked past her into the channel ahead. Behind them, the oars dipped and rose quietly and the steerboard man made delicate adjustments to their approach, so that the *Snowland Wolf* slipped into the lee of the eastern pillar and was swallowed by the cold shadow cast by the rising moon.

There was a low grating noise, then the soft sound of water parting cleanly, and a moment later they were inside the inner harbour. Here, they changed course so that the ship angled to hug the land ever more closely – though as far as Katla could see, the middle way into the docks was wide and clear – so closely that Katla could see the gleam of green weed, swathes of limpets and barnacles, splashes of white guano on the rocks. They rounded a small headland, and suddenly Halbo spread itself before them. The hills rose sharply from the water, so that street after street of little low-built stone houses seemed to have been piled one on top of the other. Candles glowed in windows. Curls of cooking smoke spun up into the night air. In the midst of all this domesticity and order rose the pale walls of Halbo's fortress, the High Castle, home of the Eyran kings since they first made the mainland their home. Squat and bleak, it was not beautiful, to Katla's eye at least: but there was no denying that it was imposing. Thick turrets rose at the corners of the building, and the walls were pierced through with eyelets so that archers might lay waste an approaching enemy from the safety of the interior. The battlements were crenellated, and a steep bank rose up to the foot of the castle walls: it looked a difficult stronghold to overcome. Rows of barracks led away from the castle down to the harbour where they met a jumble of wharves and jetties and a harbour full of vessels. On the far western strand a great bonfire had been constructed to light the work of a hundred men, all of whom were stripped to the waist and covered from head to toe in the sheeny red of something that must surely be blood. Before them on the beach lay a huge shape from which protruded great white staves amid dark and glistening slabs of meat. Even from here, the stench was appalling.

'By Sur,' Katla whispered, 'they look like the goblins that brought down the Giant Halvi to end the Battle of the Sun.'

Tam laughed. 'Haven't you seen men butcher a whale before, Katla Aransen?'

'A whale? But it's vast! No whale that I have seen has been a quarter the size of that monster!'

'Ah, the Westman Isles, where even the whales are as minnows! Sur was not smiling on your ancestors when he blew their settlement ship in to Rockfall, my dear.'

Katla shot him a furious look.

'Towering cliffs, windy uplands and women bred between wildcats and trolls; Rockfall's speciality. Just the way I like them.'

Tam Fox grabbed her by the waist and crushed her against his chest. Katla promptly spat in his eye and at the same moment brought her knee up hard into his groin, but the mummers' chief had been manhandling women all his life and knew himself an expert in such matters. Swivelling his hips, he evaded the main threat and took the wad of saliva on the cheek where it hung for a moment like cuckoo-spit, then bubbled off down his chin. Then he grinned from ear to ear.

'They say that a bit of resistance gets the blood up,' Tam said cheerfully. 'But I'd rather you came to me of your own free will.' When she started to struggle he said, 'Hear me out!' and imprisoned her arms in a time-honoured wrestling manoeuvre executed so neatly that Katla could not help but experience a brief moment of admiration. 'I have a place close to the docks where we can go and get better acquainted,' he added, nuzzling her neck. Katla's teeth came close to catching his ear; but the mummer craned his head away with a laugh. 'It's not luxurious, but you'll not notice once we're started. I've been waiting all week for this, little troll. Did you not think I'd see through your disguise in seconds? I could spot you in a crowd of a thousand other women, all naked and with bags over their heads!'

Katla stopped wriggling and stared at him. 'You have a most bizarre imagination, Tam Fox,' was all she could say.

The mummers' chief laughed. 'Aye, it is quite creative. You should make the effort to discover its horizons for yourself . . .'

'Take your hands off her!'

The speaker's voice was pitched low and soft, but his tone

was menacing. 'If you don't take your hands off her at once I'll prick out your kidney and feed it to the gulls.'

Katla spun around and saw that her brother, Halli – who had killed two men in all his life and was still suffering nightmares as a result – had appeared as silently as a stoat and had a belt-knife pressed into the small of the mummer's back.

She laughed and extricated herself without too much difficulty from Tam Fox's grasp. 'It's all right, Halli. No harm done.'

Tam shrugged and stepped away. 'Your loss, little wildcat.' He winked. 'We'll see what your Da says when we get back to Rockfall, eh?' And with that he moved smartly past the pair of them and made his way between the curious rowers to where the tillerman stood shouting out his instructions. A few moments later the crew shipped their oars as the *Snowland Wolf* entered the inner harbour and then everything else was subsumed by the bustle of landing and unloading.

It was close to midnight before Katla and Halli were able to step into the last of the faerings, as if Tam Fox's punishment for the insult to his pride was to delay their discovery of the city as long as he possibly could.

Fretting with impatience, Katla craned her neck over the others in the boat, avid for every detail. There were ships everywhere – merchant ships, wide-bellied and short-ribbed; knarrs and longships and fishing vessels. They rowed so close to the *Sur's Raven*, the King of Eyra's own ship, that she was able, by leaning out as far as she could and with Halli holding her legs and the rest of the crew egging her on, to brush the very tips of her fingers against its elegant strakes. 'It's so beautiful!' she cried, looking back at the swell of its bow, the clean lines of the stempost, the roaring dragon's head.

A moment later they passed a ship of oak so dark and weathered it was almost black. Its stempost boasted an ugly figurehead, roughly carved and of grim aspect, a great round head of no recognisable creature on Elda, mouth wide open as if to devour the world. Katla stared at it, fascinated. As they skimmed past it, the moonlight struck the single lump of glass that had been set as its eye, and a memory clicked into place. A moment later, she cried out, 'It's the *Troll of Narth!*'

Everyone laughed good-naturedly at her wild enthusiasm: many of them were Halbo-born and bred, and none but Katla first-time visitors. They had seen the *Troll* a hundred times and more: it was a way-station, a landmark, a dull piece of ancient history.

Katla, however, was transported back to winter firesides and her father's tales of the old war, the war before the one he had fought in, the one in which his grandfather had been killed. Those times and their artefacts had taken on almost legendary status for Katla. While the other females in the steading had put their hands over their ears and groaned at the bloodthirsty tales that Aran Aranson told, Katla had been enraptured. She stared back at the great black hulk. So this was the ship in which Ravn's grandfather, King Sten, had escaped from the Battle of Horn Bay by sheer brio and superior seamanship, outrunning a dozen Eyran vessels which had been captured by the enemy and were now crewed by mercenaries and slaves under Istrian command. The *Troll* was already an ancient ship then, but Sten had worked on it all his life and he knew every vibration of its rudder, every gradation in the tension of its lines and sheet and so, confident in his knowledge of his ship and on home territory, he had steered a dangerous course right through the middle of the Bitches, that treacherous range of reefs that lie like sharks' teeth off the eastern coast. Eight of the pursuing ships, sure of their prize, had come straight after him; six had foundered on the invisible rocks. The remaining ships, surrounded by chaos, had altered course and lost the wind, and by the time they had found it again, the *Troll* was gone, vanished into the labyrinth of islands up the coast. Sten had rejoined his fleet off Wolf's

Ness and together they had turned back and fallen upon the Istrians in their borrowed ships. It was a short battle, for the enemy were outnumbered and at a loss in these tricky waters. Forced to choose between the Bitches and the mercy of the northern king, many Istrians made the fatal error of choosing the latter; for although Sten ordered that the survivors be saved and taken back to Halbo, it was only the slaves he freed, and they had wept with gratitude. Many had stayed in Eyra, for there was nothing awaiting them in the south, and worked on farms and in nobles' houses until they could afford their own piece of land. Many took ship to the Eastern Isles where land was cheap, which accounted for the preponderance of dark-haired folk, and for a slightly disdainful attitude towards the easterners from the wealthier Eyrans. The mercenaries Sten had brought back into his own service, for he appreciated good fighting men and had no illusions about loyalty and patriotism; but the Istrians he hanged and quartered on the very docks which they had planned to sack; and then catapulted their bodyparts across the lower half of the city. 'As a message to the others,' he had famously informed the single Istrian he had spared – a gangling, black-haired boy from Forent, who had wisely not revealed himself as the heir to the lord of that city. And now, as the tale played itself to an end in her head, another thought struck Katla: she had encountered that man's son at the Allfair. Rui Finco, Lord of Forent, had presided over her trial, pronounced her guilt, sentenced her to burn. She made the sign of Sur's anchor to ward off evil, and focused her eyes on the town ahead.

At last, the faering grounded on the shingle below the quay. The crew splashed up onto the beach, the ground oddly stable and unmoving beneath their feet, and dragged the boat up above the tideline. By the time they had got their bearings, Katla and Halli found themselves alone, the rest of the crew having dispersed like mist into the night of their home town.

'We should find lodging,' Halli said, sensible as ever.

But Katla's eyes were shining. 'How can you *think* of sleep? There's a whole city to be explored!'

She raced up the narrow stone steps onto the docks and stared around with delight, even though there was little to see here beyond the usual paraphernalia of such an area – tarpaulins stretched over sacks of grain, casks and chests piled higgledy-piggledy, drying racks and nets, carts and sleds and livestock pens; and behind these a shantytown of marine industry – ropemakers, sailmakers, netters and caulkers. Beyond, another Halbo beckoned: Katla could sense its seamy presence in the air – a miasma of smoke and ale and sex.

'Come on!' she grabbed her brother by the arm and dragged him around the corner into a place marked by a bedraggled twist of string upon a pole with the name knotted into it in the traditional Eyran fashion: Fish-eye Lane. The first tavern they passed offered the gorgeous sight of two men puking in its doorway. Katla regarded them with interest but Halli guided her quickly past. He had been to Halbo before. The Bosun's Cur was not the sort of establishment to take your sister into, even one as unladylike as Katla; but then again, it was hard to think of anywhere he could.

Farther up the lane they passed a group of women in split-fronted breeches and bizarrely stiffened corseting which spilled their pale breasts up and over the whalebone like an offering to eager hands. Katla grinned widely at their regalia.

'Come up the steps with me, little lad,' the oldest of the group called in the broad, coarse accent of the east mainland. She parted the fabric of her pantaloons for a better sight of her wares. 'I'll teach you a couple of new tricks. Have you tried "the Rose of Elda"? It's what they all want at the moment. Guaranteed to make you shoot before your friend here has had time to count his coin.' She leered at Halli. 'I might even do you for free, since you're such a handsome fellow, if your mate here pays for the Rose—'

Katla, puzzled as to why anyone should want to pay a greater price for a briefer encounter, and curious to know exactly what 'the Rose' entailed, opened her mouth to ask, but Halli pushed her roughly in the back.

'We've just arrived, ladies,' he called over his shoulder, 'and we'll need considerable sustenance before we have the strength to do your skills true justice.'

Katla quirked an eyebrow. How strange to hear her diffident brother so confident and self-possessed.

'I'll take the Rose!'

The cry came from behind them. Katla turned to see a motley bunch coming up Fish-eye Lane led by a small round figure in a boiled leather jerkin. Behind him was a tall, gaunt, one-handed man in full wargear, an ugly fellow wearing a skullcap and a lugubrious expression and, some steps in arrears, a fearsome-looking woman with a cropped head and a mouthful of pointed teeth. Walking beside her was a giant of a man with a long sword banging against his leg.

'Sell-swords,' said Halli in a low voice.

'Aye, I know,' Katla returned cheerfully. 'Joz! Hey – Joz Bearhand!' She waved and whistled.

The big man stopped in his tracks. He squinted ahead, then turned to the woman beside him. 'Well, now, Mam: look what the tide threw up: it's Katla Aransen, by Sur!'

The woman strode forward until the light cast by the sconce in the brothel's doorway fell squarely upon her. The whores took one look at this new arrival and without further discussion took their business further up the street.

'We thought you were dead,' Mam grunted, looking Katla up and down suspiciously.

'You looked dead the last time we saw you,' the small fat man said, grinning up at her. 'Laid out on the shoreline like a half-burned trout, you was, and yer hair all frizzled off.'

'Fish don't have hair,' the skullcapped man pointed out with deadpan logic.

'She didn't neither, Doc—'

'Shut up, Dogo.' Joz Bearhand pushed the little man aside and gave her a hug to suit his name. 'I'm glad you're alive, girlie.' He stepped back and patted the sword at his side. 'Best blade I've ever had, this. I've a hankering for a dagger to match.'

Katla smiled delightedly. 'Ah, the Dragon of Wen.' It was indeed the best sword she had forged, other than the carnelian blade which Tam Fox now had in his possession. *And much luck may it bring him*, she thought. 'It'd be a pleasure, Joz.'

Mam glanced at the sword and curled her lip. 'Lost me a fortune, that thing. I'd say it carried bad luck.'

It was hard to believe the Dragon of Wen could have lost the mercenary woman a fortune, Katla thought. At the worst she could sell it for a good sum. 'Bad luck?' she asked.

Mam laughed and the light from the sconce gave her filed gnashers a grim and bloody aspect. 'Your sweet brother,' she said, 'borrowed this little beauty and proceeded to use it to make a kabob of the shipwright.'

Katla frowned. Quite how Fent had come by the Dragon with which to carry out the deed she had no idea; nor why the death of Finn Larson should be such a loss to a mercenary troop.

'The King promised us one of Larson's ships,' Joz said helpfully, as if reading her mind. 'Thought we'd take to the high seas in our own right, instead of in the service of some other rich bastard, make our own fortunes. Bit of a problem now he's a goner.'

'But you still got the price of one—' the small man called Dogo started, then stopped with a yelp as the tall man in wargear kicked his shin. 'No need for that, Knobber, I was just thinking of that coffer of coin we fished out of his ten—'

'Aye, well Danson's prices have gone through the roof since old Larson's demise,' Mam said dourly.

Katla went uncharacteristically quiet. She found herself wondering about the coffer of coin, and whether it might have contained the money her father had stolen from his sons and taken to Finn Larson in order to commission the ice-breaker which obsessed him to the point at which he had even agreed to throw her into the bargain – *Knots within knots*, she thought, frowning. 'This coin—' she started, but Halli, aware of the reputation of these apparently mild-mannered folk, and witness to their considerable violence at the Allfair, stepped in front of her and changed the subject rapidly. 'Since it seems my brother lost you a fortune,' he said, 'the least I can do is to offer you an ale as some reparation for your trouble.'

Mam grinned horribly. 'It'll take more ale than you've ever seen, little bear, to win my favour; but I suppose it's a start.'

The Enemy's Leg boasted a crudely painted sign and a tally-board outside on which a number of frayed old strings had been knotted in various complex arrangements. Halli, Katla and the mercenaries perused the board, complete with inventive mis-knottings and unintentional errors with interest. 'Shepherd's Eye' sounded like a dish worth avoiding, but: 'Kipper's Ale,' Doc said, smacking his lips appreciatively. 'Two bits a flagon. That'll do me.'

'Don't know how you can drink that stuff,' the one-handed man observed. 'Tastes as bad as it sounds. Fish's piss.'

'It's a bit salty,' Doc conceded. 'But you know, Knobber, it reminds me of home. Tastes – well, I'd say "authentic", but then I'd have to explain the meaning of the word to you. So I'll stick with right good.'

The ugly man took a cheerful swing at Doc, who sidestepped neatly so that Knobber's fist connected dully with the top of Dogo's skull. In the ensuing confusion, Katla slipped into the inn ahead of the rest of the group. Inside, the taproom was low-ceilinged, dark and wreathed with a smoke so pungent it made her eyes burn. The place was still crammed with customers even at this late hour. Unable to look down for the press of the crowd, Katla could feel wood shavings crunch under her feet with each step she took. *A proper seagoing, shipmaking town*, she thought approvingly. Everywhere she looked there was evidence of it – tables and seats made from old seachests, a nook constructed out of an upended, broken faering in which four men were noisily playing knucklebones, antique figureheads caked in the greasy black oil from the lamps and the cooking adorned the walls; ales entitled Deep Anchorage and Double Fisherman's, Marlinspike and Old Bilgewater. Katla hoped the latter was someone's idea of a joke and not an accurate description, and ordered a flagon to find out, despite Halli trying to purchase her a small glass of light wine which he evidently regarded as a more suitable beverage for his little sister.

Old Bilgewater proved to be a dark and supple ale with the sort of bitter aftertaste that could pickle walnuts and probably your tongue if you drank the stuff for too long; but Katla gulped it down and left most of the talking to Halli.

'You came in with Tam Fox, then, did you?' Mam asked straight out.

Halli nodded. There was no point in denying it, since no other vessel had followed them in. 'Da sent us for supplies,' he said truthfully, if economically. 'Since the *Snowland Wolf* was sailing.'

'How'll you get back then, I wonder?' Mam canted her head enquiringly. 'Last I knew it, Aran had a perfectly good knarr of his own for fetching his necessaries in.'

'It's being repaired,' Katla supplied quickly, knowing that her stolid brother was not quick with a good lie. 'The *Fulmar's Gift*.'

Knobber cackled. 'Good name that!'

Joz Bearhand grinned.

Dogo stared at Knobber, then at Katla and finally at Mam, his brow wrinkled with puzzlement. 'Eh?'

Knobber made a great play of retching deep in his throat, then gobbed copiously onto the tabletop. 'Fulmar's gift,' he said delightedly, pointing at the gleaming spittle. 'That's what they do, see, them fulmar-gulls.'

Dogo looked pained. 'Don't see what's so funny,' he mumbled. 'Nor why you'd name your boat so.'

'They're like that, the Westlanders,' Joz said, winking at Katla. 'Strange sense of humour they have.'

'Aye, run you through as soon as look at you, too,' Mam said darkly. She turned to Katla. 'You look a lot like your fox-haired brother,' she remarked.

'People often say that.'

'He's not with you, then?'

'No. He stayed behind.' An image of Fent straining at his bindings in the barn, his eyes bulging with outrage, rose irresistibly to the surface of her mind. She dropped her head to hide the smile she was unable to suppress, but Mam saw it anyway and narrowed her eyes.

'I heard Tam Fox's troupe is giving an entertainment for the King's wedding at Halfmoon, night after next, and that the *Wolf* would be sailing in this evening,' Knobber interjected into the moment of silence that fell. 'Some folk were talking about it down on Rats' Wharf this afternoon.'

'But we didn't know ourselves how fair the winds would be or when exactly we'd put in,' said Halli, bemused. 'How could they have known?'

'A message-bird came from the ship – one of Tam's pretty pigeons.'

Katla frowned. She'd seen no pigeons on board the *Snowland Wolf*; but just before dusk fell she had been surprised to see a raven settle on the top yard, just to the left of the mast-head. It had seemed odd, for ravens were not sea-going birds, but she had been so distracted by the draw of the land that she had thought little more about it at the time.

'Not that there'll be a welcome for the likes of us,' the skullcapped man the others called Doc said, glaring at Dogo. 'Not after we tried to recoup our loss.'

'It was dark, wunn it?' the small man pleaded. 'How'd I know it was Ravn's own ship?'

Katla stared disbelievingly from one member of the group to another. 'You tried to steal *Sur's Raven* from under the King's nose?'

Dogo shrugged. 'They all look the same to me, and Knobber wasn't much help.'

The tall man laughed. 'Got the anchor up and a few of them strong Farem lads on the oars; but with Dogo on one side and me on the other with only the one hand, all we managed was to bang into some other great hulk and go around in a circle!'

'Lucky the King's preoccupied, shall we say?' Mam declared dourly. 'Thought it a fine joke, they say; but Stormway's no fool. Told the guard to keep an eye on us, and that on no account were we to enter the castle or be allowed near the ship. Still,' she brightened. 'Plenty of entertainment to be had away from the rich folks. Why don't you and your brother come spend Moonday night with us so's we can show you the sights, eh?' She grinned evilly.

Katla saw Halli's dark eyes gleaming with momentary panic. 'Relatives to visit,' she supplied smoothly. She rolled her eyes at the tedium of such a duty. 'Greetings to bear to our mother's sister and a dull night hearing of her aching hands and swollen knees, no doubt.'

Mam grimaced. 'Life's easier as a sell-sword. These lads here are my family. I pay their wages and they watch my back. There's more trust and honour between us than from any family I've ever known.'

After that, the talk turned to old campaigns and jobs undertaken, and Katla was surprised to find herself a little shocked that Mam, Dogo and Joz had all fought at the Battle for Hedera Port, in which her own father had nearly lost his life, but on the enemy side.

'Why fight for nothing?' Joz said. 'Especially with the Istrians offering good money.'

'Do you feel no loyalty to your own country?' Katla pressed, feeling a little naive even as she did so.

Mam laughed. 'All I ever got from Eyra was the pox and the need to forge my own weaponry at a tender age.' She clicked her sharpened teeth together in an alarming fashion. 'I've no love for any king, be he the Old Grey Fox or the silly young raven. They all think they can charm or coerce you into doing their bidding, even when it's clearly against your own interests. The Istrians are oily bastards, but at least they're realistic enough to know a job worth doing's a job worth paying for. I'll take Istrian coin over Eyran promises any day.'

Put like that, Katla thought, with no family to defend and nowhere to call your home, the mercenary woman's argument seemed hard to gainsay.

'Sides,' said Joz, 'the coin the Istrians pays us comes back to folks like you as the price of our swords.' He patted the Dragon of Wen.

'Aye,' said Halli in an undertone. 'And often enough the blood on the blade, too.'

Four

Curse

Saro was already awake when the sun came up the next day. He had been awake for hours. In fact, he was fairly sure he had not slept at all, for thoughts of what awaited him seemed to have spun endlessly around his head, leaving him dizzy with dread. He dressed as if in a trance, registering for a brief, irritated moment, the absence of his belt-knife from the chair beside his bed – he must have left it in the kitchen, though he did not remember doing so – and dragged on his boots.

Downstairs, Tanto lay in his bed like a grub in its cocoon. His eyes gleamed. He, too, had been awake for some time, anticipating the exquisite nature of the revenge he would exact from his beloved brother. Everything that had happened was Saro's fault: if he had not taken the winnings from the race to the little nomad whore, Tanto would have been a lord in his own right by now; a lord with his own castle and a beautiful, devoted wife. He would be whole and admired, looked up to by all those fools who thought themselves better than him – Fortran Dystra and Ordono Qaran, for example – with their money and their lands and their fine, uncomplicated, privileged futures stretching out before them as smooth and shining and endless as the surface of Lake Jetra. He hated them all. But he hated Saro more than any of them. He summoned a great effort and shifted slightly in the bed until he felt his bowels spasm.

*　　*　　*

The smell was suffocating. Saro stood over his brother for a few moments, clenching and unclenching his hands, fighting down the nausea that threatened to assail him. Tanto's eyes were firmly closed, his breathing regular and steady. The ghost of a smile played around the corners of his mouth. He looked as if he slept wreathed in innocence, dreaming of better times; except for the pulse that throbbed insistently in the vein at the side of his temple and the flush of exertion on his cheeks. Saro stood over him suspiciously for a minute or more, waiting to see whether or not he would stir or betray himself in some way. Then, jaw tight, he went down the corridor, heated some water on the stove in the little utility room there, and fetched some washcloths and a lidded tin pot for the waste.

When he returned to the chamber Favio Vingo was inside standing at the bedside, staring down at the sleeping form of his eldest son. Favio's chin was dark with stubble and he wore a stained red dressing robe furled about him, tied with a frayed blue sash. His bald head gleamed in the light admitted by the room's only window. It was rare that he allowed anyone to see him like this, for usually he was most fastidious: shaving close each morning and hiding his lack of hair beneath a winding of cloth. It just showed, Saro thought, how little care he had for anything any more now that the pride of the Vingo clan lay bedridden and seeping like an incontinent dotard.

When Saro entered, Favio took his hand hastily away from his nose and straightened up. His eyes were damp. *Smarting from the stench*, Saro wondered uncharitably, *or from the grief of it all?*

His eyes travelled over the objects Saro carried, lingering bemusedly for several seconds over the tin pot, then his head came up and he fixed his second son with a scoriating look. 'I blame you for this,' he said, his voice clogged with emotion. 'No matter what you do; no matter how hard you try, you'll never be a tenth as good as Tanto: do not think you will ever replace him in my heart or in this home.'

And with that he shouldered past Saro, leaving him to his unenviable tasks.

Saro swayed, caught in the backwash of his father's contempt. He had thought himself used to such pain; but it seemed that even though such tirades occurred at regular intervals, he had never developed the ability to steel his heart against them. Squaring his shoulders, he set about the task at hand and pulled back the bedclothes, recoiling as the smell hit him anew. Quite suddenly, the invalid sat bolt upright, leering horribly, his gaze bright with malice.

'Nasty, isn't it?' Tanto was gleeful. 'Since you can walk at your leisure to the earth-closet, take a bath or swim in the lake with all the other pretty, naked boys, I thought you should spend as much time as possible elbow-deep in the disgusting state you've reduced me to: all that shit and piss and filth. If I could spew on you, I would, just to give you the full picture.'

Saro reared back, appalled. 'You know I did not do this to you, Tanto,' he said in a low voice, proffering the tin pot and ducking away from that glittering black stare. 'I don't understand why you are trying to punish me for the misadventure that overcame you.'

'Misadventure!' Tanto howled with bitter laughter. He pushed the tin pot away so viciously that it slid from Saro's grip and clattered on the tiles. 'A mischance, an unfortunate mishap, brought me to this, did it? A little jest on the part of our beloved Lady Falla the Merciful, eh? The Fates crossing their threads in error? I think not, brother—'

Fingers like claws, he reached out and caught Saro by the arm. Skin to skin, gripped by his brother's powerful malevolence, the impact on Saro was merciless. He found himself standing paralysed as if on a night shore as wave after wave – midnight-black, boiling with effluents and tentacled monsters, sawtoothed sharks and poisonous serpents – piled up on the horizon, poised to sweep him away, catch him in their undertow and pin him helplessly to the seabed to be pummelled and beset by horrors. Then the first wave engulfed him, and he experienced:

The sight of a note, written in his own hand, propped against a depleted pile of coin; a blur of movement, then the ransacking of his chamber, details rendered with hallucinatory precision: he saw how an inkpot spilled its contents with infinite exactitude across a neat pile of smallclothes and his favourite doeskin slippers, how the fabrics soaked up the dark liquid, absorbing it with lazy hunger; something silver, protruding from beneath a snowy pillow. A violet-clad arm snaked out, a hand – dark, tanned, muscular: Tanto's – grabbed up the weapon, the fingers closing around the hilt. A combination of hatred and fury overcame him then, followed by murderous triumph. *I will kill him. I will take this dagger and—*

A plunging knife. Feathers. Feathers everywhere.

Had someone killed a bird? He did not understand. The fingers dug into his arm, unrelenting, bruising.

The scene changed, became unfamiliar, disorientating. A ridiculous pair of purple shoes with curling toes in Ceran style crunching into black, ashy ground: the Allfair on its volcanic plain, then. Moonshadow and firelight. An altar to the Goddess, kicked over with vicious glee. The skitter of broken terracotta, then the sudden scent of safflower, aromatic and heady.

And then he was outside a tent lit from within by sconces, could see the outline of two female figures therein, one veiled, the other's profile clearly delineated: Selen Issian. A hot flush of lust washed over him, followed by a voice echoing in his head, quotations from the *Lay of Alesto*, candlelight playing on the pattern-welded blade of a dagger . . .

Then all he could see was blood. Blood everywhere, in the air, floating in tiny globules as if time had slowed almost to death; blood on the blade of the knife, gleaming slickly on his hands. Blood flowing in a great, dark stream out onto a golden shawl . . .

Something in Saro convulsed then. He staggered back, clutching his head, and Tanto's grip slipped from his arm. But even with the contact broken, afterimages still chased one another through his skull. He concentrated, trying to make sense of them. The note and the fury it must have engendered he understood well enough: his own note to his brother warning him that he had taken the half-share of the winnings to Guaya, as they had agreed; or as he thought they had agreed, though he should have known never to trust to Tanto having any sense of honour, especially where a blood price to one of the nomad folk was concerned. The feathers, the altar, the scent of safflower; all these images were too random for him to fit into any coherent pattern. His mind kept returning to the knife. He turned it over and over in his imagination, took in its distinctive silver knotwork and elegant pattern-welding. An Eyran blade, he was sure of it. It was surely the one *she* had given him: *Katla*, Katla Aransen . . .

The very memory of her – her competence, her good cheer, her hawklike beauty – gave him the clarity he sought for. *Yes*, it was the very dagger he had stowed under his pillow, and which had then disappeared. But Tanto had claimed to have been stabbed with it while he tried to defend Lord Issian's daughter from Eyran raiders, so he must have stolen it from Saro's chamber; which explained the feathers, the pillow stabbed in fury . . . then the walk – for those shoes were indubitably Tanto's own, no one else would have such a vulgar taste in footwear – to the tent with the two women inside; which must surely have been Selen Issian's pavilion, but there had been no sign of Istrian raiders: no disturbance at all until . . .

His eyes came open, fired by a sudden horrible gush of knowledge.

'By the Goddess, Tanto: what have you done?'

His brother stared at him curiously.

'By the Goddess, Saro, what are you talking about?'

'It was you! When you touched me I *saw*—' He cut the sentence off abruptly, but it was already too late. He watched Tanto's mien change; but not, as he had expected to one of guilt or remorse, or even fear of discovery: but to an expression of utter calculating avidity.

'I knew it!' Tanto's tone was triumphant. 'You can see my mind! When I touch you, you read my thoughts! You always were so *sensitive*, so *sweet*, such a lily-livered, little milksop, always so considerate to the slaves, so gentle with the animals, mollycoddling even the most vicious of the beasts; and they never bit *you* did they? Oh, no: they bit *me*: because you knew their minds and *you made them bite me*!' His hand shot out again and caught Saro by the wrist. He watched, delighted, as his brother writhed away from him, grimacing as if gripped by some deep inner pain. Hatred flashed in the black holes of his eyes. 'For years I thought you could not possibly be my true brother – *you* – such a miserable, timid, spineless child, a brother to *me*: ridiculous thought! Mother must have lain with a travelling charm-peddler to make you while Father was away at war, and you've been left tainted by that forbidden union, shot through with some disgusting magic of the mind . . . So let's see if my theory bears fruit, shall we? Let's see if your holier-than-thou, unsullied little soul can read these thoughts, shall we?' His face contorted with depraved glee. Then he closed his eyes as if summoning his very finest memories.

A torrent of images began to thrust themselves into Saro's mind, though he tried all he could to block them, to pull away from his brother's grip – too strong, too hard for such an invalid, surely?

A pretty slavegirl, her veiling sabatka ripped in two and tangling around her ankles as she tried to ward off his advances, her hands batting at him ineffectively as pigeon's wings until he caught her roughly, almost breaking her arm, and bent her double over the table – the table in their dining chamber, the slavegirl poor little Sani, who had died last year of the blood-cough, Saro noted with helpless misery – then kicked her legs apart and pushed his hand into her until she cried out in pain . . . Down in the orange grove, a slaveboy on his knees, crying out incoherently in some guttural hill-language as, thrilled by the boy's terror and disgust, he gripped him by the hair and forced his head back while with his other hand he freed his cock . . . A pair of brown, long-lashed eyes flashing defiance and despair. A pair of swollen white breasts marbled with pale blue veins that filled his hands to overflowing. A woman's face, all wet with tears, pleading, pleading in such an appealing fashion that it made him want to hit her yet more. A round, white belly, distended by a six-month child . . . his own . . . his first bastard! The dulled resignation on the bruised face of the whore he came back to again and again, for he paid the brothelkeeper well for his unusual practices . . . The slavegirl expiring at his feet in a crimson sea, Selen Issian staring up at him with that mouth, pink and full-lipped, open in a perfect 'O' of surprise. His wife – his *wife*! Or she would be soon after; for how could Lord Tycho or his father gainsay the marriage once the goods had been spoiled so, whether the marriage-price were paid in full or no? That little shift: so provocative, so flimsy: surely designed to draw him on? He could see the pale moons of her breasts, the aureoles dark as eyes returning his gaze through the sheer fabric. It had been a moment's work to rip it away from them; and then there was the rest of her, soft and yielding: the breasts exactly as he liked them, ripe and round and just a little heavy, her slim belly ready to do service as the receptacle for his seed; and that place below, untouched by any other man: his to claim, now, now! The first dark, boiling plunge into her was a glorious combination of pain and divine pleasure: he felt the resistance of her maidenhead, slick with his own juices, felt it tear beneath the power and the pressure of his thick erection and admit him, willingly, willingly he was sure . . . Then there followed the thrilling build towards his climax as he ploughed and ploughed this virgin field and her strong fingers gripped his back, her nails digging into his skin with the intensity of her own desire for him; then the gorgeous release . . .

Tanto's hands came off his brother just before that next fateful moment. He didn't want to think about *that* again, let alone share it with Saro. In any case, he could hardly believe it had happened at all, that she, his beloved, his wife to be— No, surely, it was others, taking his own dagger, plunging it into him: he had almost convinced himself of that now, could almost form their faces in his mind.

'You monster!'

Freed from his brother's touch, Saro had backed himself against the wall, out of reach of grasping hands. His chest heaved. His face was flushed. He felt contaminated by what he had just been witness to: he felt filthy. He had been aware of enough of Tanto's less-than-praiseworthy characteristics prior to this point: had seen with his own eyes the slyness, the cheating, the lying, the random cruelty to the villa's cats and dogs, his deliberate roughness with the horses; the way he hit the servants, once to the point of rendering poor little Deno blind in one eye. And he had heard Tanto brag about his escapades with women, but had closed his ears to such claims, dismissing them as at best unlikely and empty boasting and at worst as his brother's fantasies as to what he would like to do to them, had he the opportunity. To know the full extent of Tanto's depravity was nauseating.

In response, Tanto just grinned. He pointed below Saro's waist.

'Not such a milksop, after all, I see. Perhaps I may call you "brother" after all.'

Saro stared down and was horrified to find that his body, possessed by Tanto's wicked thoughts, had betrayed him, for his tunic was tented out by the stiffness of his own erection.

With a cry of despair, he hurled himself from the room and out into the harsh light of the courtyard.

Tanto listened with malicious satisfaction as his brother threw up noisily into the marigolds outside the window. *That will teach him*, he thought. *If he thinks he's so perfect and I'm so unnatural.*

The sound of retching continued unabated. Tanto Vingo threw back the counterpane and swung his great, soft legs over the side of the bed. He put his weight on them gingerly, then levered himself upright. The tiling was cold beneath the soles of his feet. Taking up the washcloths that Saro had discarded, he scraped the worst of the waste he had made off his own skin and onto the sheet and wiped himself down as best he could, grimacing at the smell and the stickiness of it all. Then, sweating and trembling with the effort, he staggered over to the window and peered out. There was Saro on the other side of the courtyard, leaning against the wall. Every line of his body spoke of defeat and despair: his shoulders were slumped, his head hung down, his hands were splayed against the sun-warmed stone as if they were the only things keeping him upright.

Tanto smiled to himself. It had been a most satisfying morning so far: the best he could remember in months. To have engineered the situation of having his father order that Saro attend him through all the worst aspects of his sick state had been delicious in itself, but this new development was finer than he could ever have dreamed of: for now he would be able to drive Saro insane through a bond of fear and torture, rather than simply through the daily horrors of cleaning up after him and tending to his every need and whim. Of course, he could require Saro to carry out all those pleasant small tasks as well. With very little trouble on his own part (which was how he liked it) he could ensure that his brother's life became an utter misery; and by the time he went away to be a soldier – a soldier! the very idea of Saro attempting to lead a troop to battle, to wield a weapon in anger at all was wonderfully absurd – he would be as mad and loagy as a late-summer wasp, all its sting drawn and its understanding of the world a bleary miasma. He'd die in the first engagement: probably fall on his own sword, and thank the Goddess for it!

Making sure that his brother was not yet coming towards the house, Tanto slipped back to the bed and withdrew from beneath the pile of cushions there the belt-knife he had the previous day stolen – with his own hands – from Saro's room. It would not do to have Illustria find it when she came to look in on him: it served his purposes well to have everyone continue to regard him as the bed-confined weakling they believed him to be. The knife weighed heavily in his hand. Making the bruise on his chest with its pommel had hurt considerably at the time, but the investment had paid off far more handsomely than he'd expected.

Being able to wound Saro's mind was so very satisfying that it outweighed by far the discomfort sustained in hurting his own body.

He edged over to door and stuck his head outside. No one was in sight. Father and Uncle Fabel would most likely be engaged in the morning's observances, kneeling on their prayer mats like the superstitious fools they were; the women – well, they would hardly dare report his movements even if they spied him: they had learned to their cost what was likely to happen to them if they crossed his will. Using the wall to keep himself upright, he made his way down the corridor with remarkable speed for an invalid; and took the stairs on his hands and knees like a gigantic cockroach.

* * *

It had been, Saro thought, as the sun dipped in the west, the worst day of his life, and that was truly saying something. After returning to his brother's room to clear away the filth from the bed, he had changed the sheets and been forced to wash them by hand; and while the servants brought Tanto fresh linen and a breakfast fit for a lord, *he* was sent out to the practice field with one of yesterday's loaves and whatever fruit he could find on the way, and was there beaten black and blue on every part of his anatomy, ostensibly for his slowness and clumsiness by Captain Galo Bastido. 'The Bastard', as the captain was colloquially known by the young men he had flogged and beaten into some semblance of swordsmanship, was during time of war the leading officer of Altea's standing army; but currently, during what still purported to be peacetime, even with the threat of conflict hanging heavy overhead like those anvil-shaped clouds which concealed the makings of storms within them, he held merely the position of overseer for the Vingo estates, and was responsible for managing the family's work-force of hillmen and slaves in their lowly tasks around the fields and groves. Another man (Santio Casta) held the more highly regarded position of estate manager, and it was to Casta that he was forced to report (which he saw as a great slight, since Casta had been one of his subordinates in the last conflict with the North). None of this had made Bastido a pleasant man, and that without his natural tendency towards physical and mental brutality, his arrogance and boar-thick skin, all of which had served him well in his soldiering career. The demeaning task of working the land with slaves and riff-raff who barely spoke any Istrian but grunted away in their own incomprehensible languages had further engendered in him a complete disregard for the sensibility of others; except when they were clearly in pain. A sharp yelp, a low groan, watering eyes and an agonised grimace – these were the sort of responses he understood, and causing them in the course of teaching a skill seemed to produce quick and effective results.

Being asked to turn his rough attentions to his master's second and least favoured son appeared to have cheered him considerably, for whenever Saro fell face down in exhaustion or at the brunt of the Bastard's huge training sword, he would bellow with laughter.

'"Treat him hard" your father said to me,' Bastido had informed Saro cheerfully, standing over him after flooring him for the third time that morning. Despite being half a head shorter than Saro, he was a good twice his width and sinewy as dried mutton. '"He's lazy and unwilling and shows little aptitude with a blade. Make a man of him" he said, "a soldier the Vingos can be proud of" – and that's exactly what I'm being paid to do.'

So now, with every inch of his skin, as it seemed, raw with grazes and cuts, every fibre of every muscle throbbing with bruises, Saro dragged his feet back up the stairs to his chamber, aware that once he fell upon his bed he would likely fall into a sleep so welcome and so deep that he would probably never make it back down again to the kitchens in time for any hot food, and that if he did not, he stood less chance than ever of withstanding the Bastard's tender mercies the next day. But at the moment he could not find an iota of energy or will in himself to do anything more than collapse in the privacy of his own chamber. He was no more heedful than a beaten cur, no more intelligent than a mauled wolf, returning to its den. Tomorrow was tomorrow. With luck he might not live that long.

He shouldered open the heavy wooden door, fell inwards with it and staggered in. He managed to kick off his boots and begin to struggle out of his dusty tunic. Arms and head still wrapped in its neck and sleeves, he fell backwards onto the bed. His exhausted brain registered the existence of something cold and hard beneath the aching muscles of his back. Rolling over, he stripped the swaddling tunic away and cast it onto the bedside chair. His right hand closed over a familiar object. He retrieved it from beneath himself and held it up. In the dying light of the day, he found he held his own belt-knife, which he had been unable to find that very morning. Its hilt was shit-smeared and foul.

With a shudder of repulsion he dropped it on the floor, where it lay, shining dully, its blade as red with the sunset as if it had been freshly dipped in blood.

And he knew, with a sudden fierce, instinctive knowledge, just where it had been in the time it had been absent from him, and how it had returned here.

He slept no more that night.

Five

The King's Shipmaker

They slept that first night in the King's city in the loft above a fletcher's with whom the mercenaries had business. When Katla asked what this business might entail, Dogo had pulled an idiot face and girned at her horribly and Halli had shaken his head. So Katla had desisted from asking more until she and Halli had parted from the sell-swords the next morning and they were on their way to Morten Danson's shipyard to carry to him Tam's 'royal' invitation to the mumming – no common knotted string this, but a fine parchment of goatskin inscribed with fish-ink in Tam's careful hand. For authenticity, Katla had donned a quartered tunic in green and red borrowed for this very purpose before they had left the ship from Silva Lighthand, one of the tumblers; and Halli was looking most uncomfortable crammed into a ridiculous suit of gold and green, its garishness partly mitigated by an all-encompassing cloak in sober grey on which the Snowland Wolf and its serpent enemy were picked out in neatly stitched red silk. Surprised though she had been by his skill in writing, Katla had been rather more amazed to discover that Tam Fox had sewn this piece himself. It was hard to think of those great, hairy hands engaged in anything much beyond wielding knives, hauling sail or squeezing women, let alone something so delicate, or so traditionally feminine, as embroidery, but the leader of the mummers had been unconcerned when she had laughed at him. 'Mumming's not all fun and games,' he had said. 'You're on the road all the time. It can get very boring, especially when some pretty lordling's decided to keep you waiting for a day or three while he hunts some mythical dragon or swives his latest piece to death. Besides, we can't afford to keep a seamstress, a cook or a laundress, so we all have to muck in. We make and maintain all our own costumes, men and women alike: my troupe need to be as proficient with a needle as they are with batons, balls and knives.' And Katla had to admit the workmanship on the clothes they had borrowed far exceeded her own. If she had to produce her own costumes, the audience would be entertained by rather more than they had bargained for, she thought wryly.

The first half hour of the walk through Halbo city had been an entertainment in itself for Katla. She could not help but exclaim at every turn – *Look, brother, windows with glass! – See that woman, her hair is purple! Oh, 'tis a headdress! – What sort of person lives in such a house? – Why are there bars on the door and spikes on the wall? – What are those marks there like burned tar? Oh, they are burned tar. From the war? – But why would an Eyran lord fight his king? A woman? Surely not* – and so on, until Halli had threatened to knock her cold and leave her in a ditch for the next beggar to find. Then, nearing the outskirts of the city, they had witnessed a veritable cavalcade trotting smartly towards them: mounted men in fine cloaks and shining helms, their long hair braided and their beards knotted with brightly coloured fabric, pennants fluttering from spears that gleamed as if they had never been put to any other use; women peering out of covered wagons pulled by the sturdy ponies of the Northern Isles whose manes and plaited tails had been all threaded through with ribbons. One of the wagons, bearing a group of giggling girls combing out each other's long hair, passed so close to Katla and Halli that they were forced to leap out of the way; but when Katla leapt back, shouting furiously and waving her fists, Halli grabbed her by the arm.

'Don't!'

She stared at him incredulously. 'They could have killed us—' She stopped. Halli's face was pale and strained, his eyes dark with some unreadable emotion. 'What is it? What's the matter?'

But he just shook his head and started walking again, head down, wrapped in grim thought and Tam's fine cloak, and said not a word more all the way to the shipyard.

Morten Danson's yard lay encircled by the arms of a wide lagoon, beyond which the hills of the firth rose into the wide blue sky. Once, this vista must have been one of the most beautiful in the Northern Isles, for the land would have been forested as far as the eye could see with native oak, ash and pine, and the waters of the firth would have mirrored in its clear surface a dozen shades of green, the dark, serrated mountain peaks, the high white clouds scudding across bright northern skies. Now not even tree-stumps were visible in this place, for the forests had been replaced in the shorn uplands by a dense tangle of bracken and bramble and bilberry or by blackened mats of burned roots, producing a forlorn-looking landscape that was of little use to man or beast. Down on the river plain, ramshackle buildings had colonised the open areas – sheds of weathered planking with rusting tin roofs, structures of stone and turf, log cabins and warehouses, temporary shelters made from hide and poles – a miserable-looking shanty town. The hulls of a hundred vessels in various stages of completion lay amid all this chaos, their staves and stems poking up into the air like the skeletons of butchered whales. It looked, Katla thought, as if a great sea battle had been fought here millennia since and the waters had retreated, leaving in their wake the carcasses of the slain as a warning to others.

In the lagoon a great litter of vessels lay scattered, most of them stationary, some slowly weaving a line in and out of the dozens of moored pontoons, barges and rafts of timber. Clearly the local area had been stripped of every suitable tree for miles around, and demand for new ships ensured that Morten Danson had to source his materials from rather further away. The largest of the logs must surely have come from the sacred Barrow Plantation, since the trees which had been cut and stripped of their branches to provide this timber must once have towered to over a hundred foot in height, ancient giants now laid low.

A tributary stream of the river that flowed into the southern end of the lagoon had been diverted from its original course, which now lay abandoned, marked only by a line of darker grasses and a bed of dry pebbles through which tall weeds protruded, so that it now ran between culverts of stone right into the heart of the yard. Men ran from the stream to the steaming sheds with great leather buckets brimming with this diverted water, and so much vapour billowed up from these sheds into the air of the valley that from a distance it seemed that the manufacture that went on in this valley was not that of ships but of clouds: a weather-factory such as only Sur himself could possibly command.

Katla and Halli made their way down the road leading into this well of industry and stared in amazement. Even Halli, who had travelled more than his sister, to Ness and Fairwater, and once, after an Allfair, as far as Ixta in the north of Istria, had never seen such evidence of man's will exerted over the natural world.

'It's extraordinary,' he breathed, taking in the great swathe of activity below them.

'It's awful,' said Katla. 'I think I'll never take sail again.'

'This place provides the lifeblood of Eyra, sister. How else can we master the oceans? Did you think the *Fulmar's Gift* was whittled by our grandfather on an idle day from a couple spare branches from his favourite oaks?'

Katla looked unhappy at his jibe. 'I don't know. It's just—'

She spread her hands to take in the view. 'There's nothing . . . given back.' She frowned. 'I can't explain what I mean. It's all so grim.' She stopped, at a loss. When she worked her metals in the forge she could feel the power of Elda flowing up out of the heat, through her and back into the ground. It was a kind of blessing, a bargain with the world. But this—

'Can I help you?'

The man who addressed them was small of stature and richly dressed. He was beardless in the southern fashion, but had a thin moustache neatly cut to reveal thin, chiselled lips and his sideburns had been trimmed to a sharp line accentuating the shape of his jaw and cheekbone. His collar was knife-sharp and edged with expensive brocade quite out of place in these surroundings; his under-tunic such an improbably perfect white that it must have been donned new today. Katla thought she had never seen a man who presented himself with such conscious effort at precision and contrived elegance. His voice, though, gave away his origins: an accent from the poor far east of the islands, flat and harsh, had yet to be turned out to quite the same level of perfection as the rest of him.

'We have come to see Morten Danson, the owner of this yard,' Halli said.

The man looked him up and down, then turned his attention to Katla. She felt his eyes travel across her, taking in the ravaged hair, the outlandish costume, the smallness of her breasts. 'More beggars and ne'er-do-wells no doubt come to seek employment,' the man sighed. 'We have enough pig-ignorant labourers here without casting about for the likes of you. Take your motley and thievery elsewhere and good day.' He turned on his heel.

Halli opened his mouth to reply, but Katla was quicker.

'Never mind, brother,' she said loudly enough that her words would reach the retreating figure. 'If this gentleman wishes to prevent us from delivering an invitation to Morten

Danson on behalf of the King then that's up to him. I'm sure a mere shipmaker will hardly be missed among such an august crowd of nobles and men of influence.'

The small man turned in a flurry of silks. 'An invitation? To me? From the King, you say?'

So this strutting cockerel was Morten Danson himself. Katla felt a keen stab of dismay. How could such an over-weening and snobbish fool be the finest shipmaker in Eyra? His hands, pale and smooth as a lady's, looked as though they had held no tool – at least not one used in the pursuit of carpentry – in decades. It made no sense at all.

Halli reached into his bag and removed the roll of goat-parchment, tied with a silken band. He held it out to the shipwright, who took it avidly, his long fingers play-ing up and down the shaft of the roll as if in a par-oxysm of excitement. Then he unfurled it with shaking fingers. Katla watched how his eyeballs flickered up and down the unfamiliar markings and his brow knit in conster-nation. He cannot read, she thought delightedly. It means nothing to him at all; so much for pig-ignorance. She coughed delicately and took the parchment away from the shipmaker deftly.

'You know we were instructed to declaim the invitation properly, brother,' she said to Halli, extending the paper to him. ''Tis hardly polite to expect a gentleman to do his own reading—'

Halli's face became carefully bland, although behind his smooth expression she could sense his mind working furi-ously. 'Ah yes,' he said after a bare moment's hesitation. He held the parchment out at arm's length. 'The King – Lord Ravn, son of Ashar, son of Sten of the Northern Isles – requests the presence of his most loyal and esteemed shipmaker, Morten Danson, to an evening of entertainment on Halfmoon Night by the world-famous mummers under the chieftancy of the great Tam Fox at Halbo Castle to celebrate his marriage to the beauteous Rose, Queen of his heart.'

'An entertainment? Tomorrow night? At Halbo Castle? By Tam Fox's mummer troupe? Invited by King Ravn himself?' The shipmaker's eyes gleamed.

'You are invited to attend the feast, and to enjoy the King's hospitality overnight in the guest chambers.' Halli finished loudly. He furled the parchment back into its roll and proffered it to Danson who took it from him greedily.

'My, my, what delight. What a charming prospect. And what should I wear for such an occasion?' Danson's eyes flicked to Halli, then shot away again. 'Whatever am I thinking, to ask the messenger such a question? Let alone a messenger clothed as if he has dressed in the dark out of someone else's wardrobe—'

Katla grimaced at her brother. 'He's got you there,' she mouthed silently.

'We have been asked, also,' Halli said, ignoring her, 'to make an inspection of the yard and bear word back to our master of the marvels you carry out here.' He was careful to avoid being too specific about who their 'master' might be. Let the shipmaker believe they answered to the King rather than to the chief of the mummers if he was so arrogant that he thought Ravn would have sent them personally with such a request.

The deception worked. Katla could almost see the man preening. 'Of course, of course. Follow me.'

The tour was perfunctory, and delivered amid such a torrent of self-serving verbiage that by the end of it Katla felt ready to knock the shipmaker over the head there and then and save everyone the bother the following night. They had, however, gathered all the information they had come for. Morten Danson had commissions for three ice-breakers, was in the process of smelting the iron for a fourth, had felled every big oak in the eastern isles, including the sacred grove above Ness – 'for they say war is coming, you know,' the shipmaker had said, bobbing his head like a robin sighting a worm, 'and then it'll be he who has the wood who makes good' – had cut a swathe through the Barrow Plantation, too, and had in his employ not only his own yard foreman, Orm Flatnose – a master craftsman of the finest order – but Finn Larson's man, Gar Fintson, too. Any Eyran who wanted an oceanworthy ship built would be forced to beat a path to Morten Danson's door and take their place in a growing queue. They would also have to pay his extortionate prices – 'so little competition any more,' the unpleasant little man had leered. 'With Larson dead and what's left of the Fairwater clan chopping rowing boats and rough knarrs out of the last of their seasoned timber. No wonder they're reduced to selling off their prize cow.' At which point Katla had seen Halli's face cloud over as thunderously as their father's could in the worst of his tempers.

They had had the foremen pointed out to them; also the master steamer, who steamed the planking to shape by eye alone; and the riveter and the rabbetter too, and had ascertained that, given the number of urgent orders to be fulfilled, all lived on or near the yard site. Sailmakers and ropemakers they had aplenty in the western isles; there would be no need to bribe or kidnap any with these skills. They had marked the whereabouts of the finest heartwood and the best oak for the stempost. It would be hazardous sailing two barges through all the obstacles on the lagoon and out into the firth, but the barges were huge, the other vessels were tiny in comparison and the problem would be lack of speed rather than manoeuvrability. Katla did not envy her brother that task at all. She was, on the other hand, looking forward to rendering the shipmaker unconscious and carting him off to the *Snowland Wolf* as ungently as she could.

The next day dawned with ill omen. The sun's red light

edged piling clouds with a fiery glow; then minutes later the whole sky turned as dark as dusk and a fork of silver stabbed down through the gloom. With a dull groan the heavens opened and rain came sheeting down. Katla stared out into all the greyness and took in the rain-slick stones, muddy streets and filth-choked gutters with a sinking heart. For the first time since she had slipped aboard the mummers' ship, she wished she were at home in Rockfall, where storms over the sea seemed more like the theatre of the gods and the rain served merely to clear the skies, green the fields and clean the birdshit off her favourite climbs.

Beside her, wrapped in a pair of old flour sacks, Halli mumbled something inaudible, rolled onto his side and began to snore again. He had slept badly, and as a result so had Katla, since she had been forced to elbow him forcibly on several occasions to quiet him. The word 'Jenna' recurred eight times in the course of his nocturnal ramblings. Katla knew: she had counted.

Now, she inserted a chilly bare foot beneath the sacks and placed it firmly on the hot skin of her brother's belly. Halli sat up, snorting wildly.

'Wha—'

'Time to leave your happy dreams behind,' she said sternly. 'You've a raid to lead and I've some tumbling to learn.'

'She'll be there. Tonight. I won't even see her.'

Katla stared at him. 'What on Elda are you talking about?'

'Jenna.' Halli's face looked grey, though perhaps it was just the light.

'How do you know she'll be there?'

'I saw her, yesterday, riding in with the rest of them.'

Katla remembered the cavalcade of wagons that had rumbled past them on the road from the east the previous day – the group of giggling girls, the long blonde hair; Halli's stormy mood thereafter – and felt a fool. 'Oh, Halli – the wagon that nearly ran us off the road . . .'

He nodded. She could tell how his jaw was tensed by the cords of tendon that stood out on his neck.

'That stuff the shipmaker said about the Fairwater clan—'

'—selling off their prize milch cow,' he finished bitterly. 'She's up for marriage to some ancient, crippled retainer, no doubt. Or some fat lordling jostling for position and favour, thinking he'd do well to take the runner-up to the nomad whore.'

Katla made a face. 'You had best not say such things in the King's city if you care to keep your head.'

'My sister, the diplomat.' Halli laughed shortly, then moved to the window of translucent membrane made from the stretched stomach lining of a seal, or suchlike, and peered out. 'Is that a shadow I see up there, or a flying pig?'

Katla stared up into the clouds, her eyes narrowed in mock concentration. 'A pig, definitely.'

They stood there in silence for a few minutes, just gazing out into the racing sky. Then: 'What can I do, Katla?' Halli asked in an anguished tone. 'I have Father pushing me one way and my heart and conscience another . . .' He passed a hand across his face. 'If I carry out Da's plan, I'll be miles off down the coast, stealing ships and timber, while Jenna is parcelled off without a friend in the world to save her, and I'll have lost her forever.'

Katla didn't know what to say. She squeezed his arm. 'Do you really love her?'

Halli nodded. 'But I fear she doesn't love me.'

Katla grinned. 'Jenna knows how to love no one but herself, and that not as well as she could. I will find her tonight and talk to her. Trust me, brother.' She pushed herself off the wall into an awkward back-flip and landed in a tangled heap on the floor. There was straw in her hair and dust streaked across her cheek. She looked about four years old. Halli could not help but smile. 'A fine and limber serpent you will make tonight. Best run along. You need as much practice as you can get.'

By the time Katla got to the stables where the mummers had arranged to meet to rehearse, it was clear she was late, which was not entirely surprising since she had got lost and had then compounded the error by deciding to explore the town beneath the castle, finding a pie-shop and a knife-maker in the winding lane below the walls and had eaten her fill in the first and got into an interesting conversation about quenching metal in the second.

The performers in Tam's troupe, their first exercises completed, stood around in knots, sweating profusely. The men had stripped down to linen clouts or soft leather breeches, while the women had bound their breasts flat and their hair into long tails. They all stared at her as she ran in. Tam Fox, resplendent in his shaggiest cloak, gave her a cool, assessing glance that took in every detail of her attire, and every inch of flesh beneath it, and beckoned Urse One-Ear, his huge deputy, to him. 'Tie the second and third fingers of her left hand together,' he bade the hulking creature. 'It may serve as a reminder to her to be punctual later.' He turned back to Katla. 'Four fingers, fourth hour after noon. The Great Hall. If you're late then, I'll have Urse cut both fingers off.' He walked away without a backwards glance.

'You can't treat me so!' Katla shouted furiously after his retreating figure. 'Not with my father paying—'

She regretted this as soon as she'd uttered it. Not just because it sounded peevish and spoiled, but because it was stupidly indiscreet and now everyone had stopped their chatter to listen. Tam Fox turned back slowly. His eyes were steely. 'Your father, my dear,' he said softly, 'is a fool and a madman, and penniless to boot. I do this for my own reasons, and you had best remember that and knot up your loose tongue.'

Urse turned his ruined face to Katla. It was hard to read an expression, she thought, that was half-missing. Some accident with an axe, she'd heard from one of the women; a run-in with a white bear, said one of the men. But had she been pressed, she'd have said he was smiling, and not pleasantly. 'Hand out, girlie.'

Turning cartwheels came naturally to Katla. She'd been tumbling her way around the islands since taking her earliest steps; but with the leather binding on her fingers it required a lot more concentration, and Tam Fox's punishment took on a rather more subtle significance. Urse had tied the thong with a series of bowlines and hitches so that the whole arrangement remained tight and unmovable even under the strain of her whole body. She became aware of the pressure of the ground beneath her palm in a way she would never previously have noted had she been springing freely in her usual way, could feel the buzz of energy released in an ever-replicating, increasingly focused arc between her body and the stone of the floor. By the end of the rehearsal, she was exhausted, but glowing with pleasure from the intense satisfaction of her body's coordination and control. It was a simple routine, to be truthful: all she had to do was to cartwheel across the floor, then, in a series of handsprings and leaps, threaten the actor playing the god, and fall over when he hit her with a gigantic straw-stuffed anchor, as they played out the tale of Sur and his encounter with the Serpent whose desire it was to swallow the world; then Bella, another of the tumblers, would come running out of the shadows with her striped costume and mad whiskers and play the Fire Cat; at which point 'Sur' would whistle up the Snowland Wolf, who would toss the Fire Cat into the audience, before turning to do battle with the Dragon of Wen. It was childish stuff, but apparently the King's favourite tale; and at least she had no lines to deliver.

She accepted gratefully the flask of spiced water Bella

handed her, swigged from it greedily and then started trying
to untie the thong. It was a finicky business, with one hand.
She had just started to loose the first knot when she suddenly
realised there was more to the arrangement than functionality:
Urse had tied a message into the binding. She angled her hand
away from the other mummers and stared at it in disbelief.

Meet – a goat-hitch twisted back on itself.

End – a single granny knot.

Practice – an elaborate knot, the name of which eluded her.

I have – two simple hitches, crossed.

Plan – a bowline and half of an eight.

3 Tree – three twists and an oak-hitch.

Gate – a double bowline to finish the binding.

She looked around. The way she had come in had been
oblique: through the postern and a snaking path between
the outbuildings. No gate that warranted the name there.
Still fingering the knots, she got to her feet and began to
wander away from the group. She passed a group of men
in long cloaks, then a gaggle of women bearing baskets of
bread heading up the hill towards the castle's kitchens. No
one paid her any attention. She skirted a pond on which ducks
and geese clacked and honked, climbed the hill beyond it and
found herself looking down on a line of oak trees leading to
a tall wooden gate.

Grinning, she ran down the avenue, stopping at the third
oak from the gate. There was no one there. *Sur's nuts*, she
cursed silently. She circled the tree. Nothing. He must have
despaired of her intelligence and given up the tryst. She could
hardly blame him. Annoyed with herself, she walked slowly
back up the line of oaks.

'Hoooo—'

It was odd to hear an owl in daylight. She looked back.
High up in the boughs of the third oak from the gate there
indeed was Tam Fox, now making himself visible to her, his
long legs dangling.

He cocked his head at her. 'Get up here, and make sure no one sees you.'

Katla looked around. There was no one in sight. The oak was broad, and the first branches were out of reach. She wasn't used to tree climbing: in the Westman Isles the only trees that could survive the hard winters and horizontal north-west winds that came howling straight off the ice floes were low-growing birches and goat-willow and a few oaks and ashes that never reached their full potential. But she hadn't been climbing rock her whole life for nothing. At waist-height there was a small depression in the bole of the trunk, and above it a protuberance where a branch had lived and died and fallen away. Standing up on the tallest of the spreading roots, she inserted a toe into the depression, grasped the protuberance with her right hand and nimbly levered herself upright. Now she could reach the lowest branch; and after that it was easy. A moment later she was seated astride a huge gnarled branch facing the mummers' chief.

'Very ladylike,' he observed, grinning to see how her kirtle had ridden up to her waist.

Katla, who never had much thought for such proprieties, firmly tugged the fabric down. 'It cannot be a very crucial plan if you have time to waste on staring up my tunic.'

'How could I consider that wasted time?' His teeth were white amid his beard. And when Katla's eyes sparked at him, he said swiftly, 'I have a role for you tonight I believe you'll enjoy.'

Katla lay on the floor, gasping. Flint Erson was standing over her, triumphant in his tattered robes of sea-grey and storm-grey and his huge black beard of dyed sheepswool. His vast, straw-stuffed anchor came down again.

'Damn it,' she hissed, dodging the direct blow. 'Not so hard!'

But the crowd were roaring with laughter, whistling and

stamping their feet, clearly enjoying the show. Though not
nearly so much as Flint Erson seemed to be. Then there were
oohs and ahs, and here was Bella as the Fire Cat, sewn into a
supple costume of painted horseskin in such a way as to best
show off all her lush assets. Flames licked their way from the
soles of her feet to the crown of her head, played suggestively
over her thighs and chest. The Fire Cat dropped to her hands
and knees and began to purr. She twisted herself around the
god's legs in ways no mere woman should be able to. Bella
was double-jointed.

Katla smiled. With the crowd suitably distracted, she
slithered quickly out of view and took off the Serpent's
head, stitched neatly from cured salmon skins. It had held up
remarkably well to the tumbling, she thought, turning it this
way and that; but it smelled awful. Her first task was done; but
it was not yet time to carry out her next piece of play-acting.
For the first time this evening, she was able to relax sufficiently
to gaze around the Great Hall, taking in the monumental
architecture of its carved pillars, stretching fifty feet or more
to meet the great fans of wooden beams that spanned the high
roof, the fabulously-coloured tapestries adorning the thick
stone walls depicting scenes from myth and history – King
Fent and the Trolls of the Black Mountains; The Battle of
the Sharking Straits; Sur standing waist-deep in the Northern
Sea, skimming his stones into the ocean to make the islands of
Eyra. Then she turned her attention to the assembled guests.
It was like the Gathering all over again, she thought: the
Eyran nobility all turned out in their gaudiest, least tasteful
costumes, all vying with one another to be noticed by the
King. Ravn Asharson – who had let the Istrians take her to
be burned without lifting a finger or his voice to prevent it –
had eyes for no one apart from the woman he had now taken
officially as his wife, and therefore Queen of the North. He
sat with his handsome head turned from the entertainment
(so much for all that rehearsal, Katla thought crossly) speaking

softly with his companion, his hand in her lap, her long white fingers fluttering along the underside of his wrist in the sort of sensual, hypnotic rhythm of one stroking a favourite cat. Behind the pair sat an austere-looking woman dressed all in black with the hawkish nose and bearing of Eyran royalty. She was not watching the entertainment, either: rather, she had her eyes fixed with undisguised loathing on the new Queen of Eyra. The Lady Auda, Katla realised: the King's mother, widow of the Night Wolf, the Shadow Lord himself, Ashar Stenson, now displaced as the first lady of the realm by the nomad woman who sat before her, her only son bound tightly under her spell. *No wonder she looks so sour*, Katla thought, *to be forced to give way to a Footloose woman with no name and no heritage, and to lose not only your status, but your son as well.*

Her eyes strayed back to the nomad woman again. It was the first time Katla had had the chance to examine the Rosa Eldi at her leisure: being manhandled by a troop of Allfair guards on her way to the stake had hardly been conducive to giving the nomad woman her undivided attention. She was, thought Katla, used to the robust females of Eyra, an odd-looking creature, being so thin and pale and delicate that she might have been raised in a snow-cave without sun or sustenance all her life: but there was something more to her than met the eye. Others had called the Rosa Eldi 'blonde' and 'fair' and 'fragile', but Katla had seen the pelts of the white-bears from the coldest regions of the Northern Isles and been intrigued by the hairs on them that on closer inspection when held up to the light revealed themselves not to be the pale, yellowish-white colour you might expect from seeing the beasts at a distance (always the safest way to view them, for despite the deceptive way they ambled along, they were renowned for their speed and ferocity, as Urse could probably attest to), but as translucent as an icicle trapping frozen fire. And that was how this woman appeared to Katla: pale and cold and beautiful, with her finely drawn features and her willowy limbs, yet filled with some dangerous, invisible energy that at any moment might break its deceptively fragile bonds, flare out into the hall and kill everyone there in an instant.

She looked away, discomfited by this bizarre thought, and as she did so her eye was snagged by another fall of blonde hair: truly gold this time, rather than the green of an unripe wheatfield, as it had been the last time Katla had properly seen her friend: for there, seated a few places down from the King, between a scrawny young man in a purple tunic and a greybeard in an overstuffed doublet, was Jenna Finnsen. And next but two from Jenna was the shipmaker, Morten Danson.

Perfect, thought Katla. *Two birds with one shot.*

There came a great burst of raucous applause. Katla turned to see that in the middle of the players' circle, Sur had just polished off the Dragon of Wen with a great flourish of his oversized sword, and Tam Fox had taken the floor. He clapped his hands and called for quiet.

'And now,' he declared. 'It is time for a miracle of mutability, a magical, mirth-making mystery of tantalising trickery, a phenomenal phantasmagoria, a triumph of transformation, a veritable spectacle of shape-shifting!'

The crowd applauded. They enjoyed the troupe-chief's wordy introductions. Four of the players carried on a striped tent made of flexible poles and densely woven cloth and set it down behind Tam Fox, shuffling around to situate it exactly where it was required. It stood maybe a head taller than Tam himself, and a tall man's length in diameter, looking remarkably sturdy for all its lightweight components.

'I need two volunteers,' Tam Fox proclaimed. 'A gentleman, and one of the fairer sex. They will enter the magical booth and – well, what they get up to together in there is their own affair of course—' This encouraged a number of crude comments and whistling. 'All I can promise is that what you are about to perceive is the rare and ancient art of shape-shifting!'

'Any volunteers?'

Only one person – Silva Lighthand, seated between the shipmaker and the old, fat man next to Jenna Finnsen, and primed to play her part – answered his call.

Tam Fox smiled. 'Is there no gentleman brave enough to take my challenge?'

This was Katla's cue. With the Serpent's head jammed hastily down over her face, she came cartwheeling out of the shadows, a lithe figure all in sheeny silver, all the way to the royal bench, where she stopped, panting slightly, before Ravn Asharson and his new wife. There she executed a flamboyant bow, then turned enquiringly to Tam, as she had been told.

'Shall my lord take the challenge?' Tam Fox cried out.

The crowd fell hushed and shocked at his effrontery, but almost immediately Katla was on the move again, with a grin and a back-flip which brought her directly in front of Morten Danson. The shipmaker stared at her, aghast, as she leapt up onto the table and took him by the arm. Then, hauling him to his feet, she ignored Silva's outstretched hand and moved beyond her.

'What are you doing?' Silva hissed; but 'Shhh,' Katla replied and reached across for the daughter of the Fairwater clan.

Jenna opened her mouth to protest; but the Serpent dipped its head and – she was quite sure of this – winked at her out of the eye-slit that had been cut between the salmon-skins. In the moment of hesitation that followed, Katla grabbed her friend and pushed her and the shipmaker out onto the floor.

'Why,' Tam declared with a slightly bemused frown, 'it seems the Serpent has found two brave souls to take with him on his journey into the underworld.'

The crowd cheered wildly.

It was too late to escape. Morten Danson decided to try to make the best of the situation and began to grin and to wave with his free hand, but the hand that Katla held imprisoned was damp with sweat. *He isn't enjoying this at all*, she thought gleefully. *And how much less is he going to enjoy what comes next . . .*

Tam Fox gave the pair a loud lecture on their proper behaviour when they were together in the tent (since the presence of the Serpent could lead only to greater temptation). He made to look under Jenna's skirts to ensure she was wearing stout undergarments, which caused her to slap his hands away and to blush furiously. The crowd cheerfully roared its encouragement to the shipmaker, who looked equally embarrassed by the proceedings. Then Katla led them inside the canvas, gripping their hands with all her might. In the seconds before chaos ensued, she heard the musicians strike up, and the sound of dancing feet encircling the tent; then the floor gave way beneath them and they were falling.

The hooting of the pipes and thumping of the drums camouflaged most effectively Morten Danson's shriek of outrage and the grating of the trapdoor, before Urse had the shipmaker secured under his massive arm and gagged with impressive speed and dexterity.

Katla extricated herself from the hay-bales that had been placed there to break their fall and hauled Jenna out of the way so that the two mummers who were taking the place of the shipmaker and what should have been Silva Lighthand could climb back up through the hole. The replacement for Danson was a little, wiry, bald man called Lem, who wore nothing but a pair of oversized boots and a breechclout into which had been inserted a vast sausage.

'Ready, my fine pike?'

Min Codface, dressed in a flimsy, low-cut shift and a ludicrous wig, hefted Lem through the hole, then levered herself up with athletic ease. As she exited the trapdoor,

Katla could see that she had tied strips of linen around her calves and thighs to accommodate an armoury of throwing knives. Just in case of trouble.

'By Feya's tits, Katla, what are you playing at?' Jenna was red in the face. It looked as though she might at any moment burst into tears.

'Right,' said Katla grimly, removing the Serpent head with a flourish. 'Is it the skinny runt or the fat old goat they've got you down to marry?'

Jenna blinked. 'I knew it,' she said at last. 'I knew it when you winked at me, though it seemed such a mad notion that you should be travelling with a troupe of mummers.' She thought about this. 'Or maybe not, actually.'

'So? Which one?'

'The goat,' Jenna said humourlessly.

'And do you want to take him?'

'I have no choice. They tell me there's no money coming in and he's a rich man.'

'Halli still loves you.'

Jenna stared at her. Then she started to cry. 'Oh, Katla, I've been so unhappy . . .'

Above them, the music stopped. Then there was a scuffling sound as the tent was removed, and after a moment's stunned silence the crowd started to shout with laughter and clap enthusiastically.

Katla grabbed her friend. 'No time to talk. Are you coming with us or staying to marry the goat?'

For a moment the blonde girl hesitated. Then she nodded vigorously. 'Coming with you.'

There was a commotion behind them as Morten Danson was stuffed into a roll of theatrical backcloths and thrown into a covered wagon. Jenna looked alarmed. 'Is he all right?'

'Bit of a jape,' Katla grinned. 'He'll be fine.' *If just a little incandescent with rage*, she thought cheerfully, *when he finds out where he's going. And why.*

Six

Exiles

Erno Hamson sat quietly in the corner of the inn and listened. He had been there, listening, for close on two hours now. It was a great deal warmer and more comfortable inside the Leopard and Lady (known by the sailors and dock-workers of Hedera Port rather more colloquially as the Cat and Quim) than it was outside, especially in the rather basic shelter he had managed to rig up from the overturned faering in which he and the woman had made their escape from the Moonfell Plain, branches and driftwood and a large sheet of sailcloth he'd managed to steal from a shipyard as darkness fell the previous day. They had been travelling for several weeks now, drifting from place to place, living off the land and the sea, without any sort of plan. The woman complained about this a lot; but Erno did not care. Since Katla Aransen had died his world felt cold and empty: so wandering and living rough was the same to him as living in a palace.

But being in the Cat and Quim was certainly preferable to being down on the small shingle beach. It meant, apart from anything else, that he did not have to listen to the woman's soft, sibilant southern voice as she sang those peculiar little nonsense rhymes she was so fond of. To begin with, he'd thought it was his poor ear for Istrian that was at fault, as he caught a word and a phrase in strange conjunction – something about a frog and a spoon; or a cat in a well, a spider and some curds and whey – then he'd realised she was crooning nursery songs to herself, songs which had their equivalent in the Northern Isles of his own homeland. For a time, that had made him sad for her, displaced as she was from her own people; but lately he had begun to find it irritating, as if it was her way of shielding herself from him and their situation. By now, after three moon-cycles and more in Selen Issian's company, he could converse well enough in the southern language, though when he ventured into public places like Hedera Port, he'd had to claim his ancestry and bizarre accent hailed from the mountains in the far south in order not to draw unwelcome attention.

And the amount she ate! It was hardly credible that one so small could eat so much without doubling in size. It was becoming a trial travelling with her: when he was lucky enough to come by more bread than they could eat in a day and stockpiled it for later, he would wake the next morning to find it gone, along with all the dried fish and the round of cheese he'd been saving for harder times. Given the desperate nature of her situation – as a fugitive from the vaunted 'justice' of Istria for killing the man who had attacked her at the Allfair – he felt duty-bound to stick with her, even though it was because of her that they had consigned his beloved Katla to the fires. There were days when he could hardly bear to look at the Istrian woman: and this was one of them, which was why he was here now, with his hood up, and his eyes cast down, sipping from the flagon of weak beer he'd been nursing for the past hour. He'd spent his last coin on his first flagon, which had gone down rather too quickly for prudence or savouring, but when he'd left the inn to visit the outhouse at the back he'd found a single cantari trodden into the mud there – dropped by some customer too sozzled to mind his coin-purse, he'd bet – and that had bought him this current flagon and would either buy another two; or some food, if sense prevailed. Either way, he reckoned, Sur must be smiling on him.

The Leopard and Lady was the first Istrian tavern he'd been able to pluck up the courage to go into; but it was the similarities between the inns back home and those in the Southern Empire that were most striking to him, even so. It was cramped and dark and smoky, you had to shout your order over the noise, and the beer was weak and cost more than it should. Despite the great differences between the cultures of the two countries, inns were still, it seemed, places where men came to get away from women, from the dullness of their work and the responsibilities of their home lives. They came to drink; they came to be in the comfortable company of other men; and they came to talk. It was amazing what you could hear in a place like this if you sat quietly enough that no one paid you any mind. So far he had discovered many small and interesting facts.

He had learned that one Pico Lansing was offering special rates at the brothel he ran – the Maiden's Arms, down at the end of the docks – where you could now get two girls for ten cantari, and probably eight if you bargained hard enough, since business was so poor as a result of the greatly increased workload at the local metalworks; he had learned that the tall fellow with the shining bald head and hooked nose standing morosely at the bar over a tall glass of rose araque, that vile, smoky-flavoured spirit the Istrians favoured so highly, was having a hard time having his parents' house repaired up on Sestria Hill, since it seemed impossible to lay hands on a carpenter at the moment for love or money, even with the rain pouring through and ruining furnishings that his wife had had her eye on these last seven years; and that the price of tin and brass had unaccountably gone sky-high, while silver values had fallen, the money market was so glutted with coin. He learned that a band of Footloose travellers had passed through the environs of the port town the previous week and been chased off the land on which they had traditionally camped these past twenty years and more, and that in their

wake the wife of the merchant Paulo Foring had prematurely
given birth to a monster – a child with a huge head and wings
instead of arms, that had torn her apart as it breached, and that
she would probably not survive. Much muttering followed
this pronouncement, and others had their own stories to
contribute: how a pregnant brood-mare had produced a pair
of full-grown lions and then expired, since they had eaten
her from within; how a fish had been pulled up in the nets
last week that had tiny fingers on its fins and toes on its tail
– it was hanging on a post down at Calabria Dock if anyone
wanted to go and see it; how a girl from a good family –
the Layons, from that estate in the valley – had escaped the
Sisters of Fire, where her father had sent her in punishment
for refusing to marry the man he had chosen for her, and had
fled to the nomads, pleading with them to take her in; but
they in their turn had stoned her away, but only after she
had been raped by a dozen of their number, and now lay
close to death. She could not, it was whispered, even pray
to the Goddess for forgiveness, since the evil men had taken
her tongue as well as her chastity. Many around the inn had
made the fire-sign at this terrible news. *The Footloose should
be burned once and for all*, one man had cried and others had
nodded in agreement. Magic was wicked and dangerous: all
the years of potions that had little effect and charms that never
worked, were surely to lull folk into a false sense of their own
safety, while the nomads gathered their strength and prepared
to take the Empire apart in vengeance and spite.

Erno listened to these latter rantings with a grimace.
He gave little credence to the superstitious nonsense the
southerners attached to the nomad folk whom, Sur knew,
he had little reason to love, but who had seemed, on the small
acquaintance he'd had with them, pleasant, gentle people
with no interest in the acquisition of wealth or power: and
that was more than he could say for the larger part of Eyrans
or Istrians he'd encountered, most of whom devoted their

lives to the pursuit of one or the other, and frequently both. The girl had most likely been assaulted by men of her own kind and lost her tongue to prevent her speaking out. Nothing would surprise him: the Istrians behaved strangely around women – setting them up as worshipful beings, then treating them like possessions, using them as lust dictated, as if they were merely chattels without any sentience, let alone a will and a soul of their own. But something about the arrangement must work, for no one protested against it or fled the country: there were, as far as he knew, no southern women in Eyra, where women were known for speaking their minds and having the run of the household.

From the first two snippets, however, he learned that plans for war with the North were well advanced: if the shipyards and the craftsmen were kept so busy, then the Istrian Council had clearly given orders for the preparations of a fleet. And if that was the case, then if discovered he would be even more unwelcome here than he already felt. His left hand went unconsciously to his hair. He had persuaded the Istrian woman to cut it for him, when it became clear that the southerners rarely wore their hair long, let alone in braids with shells and rags bound into it. Every object carried its own freight of significance. One had been a braid in memory of his mother, dead of a fever, bearing little strips of her clothing and a shell she had given him. One he had made for Katla, which included a small plait of red–gold hair wound around the silver-white of his own in a complex, formal knot, and a pebble she had once taken a liking to, and he had spent hours boring a tiny hole in it with the awl he used for repairing his leather. The silver wire with which he had tied it into the braid had come, unbeknownst to Katla, from her smithy. She used it for laying delicate knotwork patterns into the engraved head of a fine axe or the blade of a dagger, and it was expensive stuff, but at the time he'd tucked it into his money-pouch all those months ago he had not thought she'd miss a finger's length. And now, of course, she'd have no use for it wherever she was, weaving cloth with Feya in the women's hall, while Sur feasted in the Great Howe. He'd kept the braids (they were wrapped in a corner of sailcloth and packed into the storage compartment in the faering: he'd thought it best not to carry them with him on these forays) shaved off his beard with a well-sharpened knife, and kept it shaved every other day which was an almost unbearable nuisance, and dyed his hair black with octopus ink purchased at a small harbour further down the coast; but his light eyes were impossible to disguise, and so he wore the hood.

He was just about to allow prudence to triumph over pleasure by removing himself from the tavern and buying some food in the market, when he heard the name 'Vingo' dropped into a conversation somewhere to his right, and his head shot up like a wolf scenting prey.

'Howled like a dog, he did, and claimed he was blind, that's what Foro said: but it 'twas the darkness of the room fooled him. There was never a happier man than Favio Vingo then, to have Falla return his son to him.'

'Aye, well maybe she didn't want to keep the lad for herself. Tales I've heard . . .'

'Tanto Vingo? He's a national treasure, that boy. Came second in the swordplay at the Allfair, you know; and then ran himself onto an Eyran blade trying to save some northern ruffians from stealing his wife—'

'Wife-to-be,' another corrected. 'They were not even handfasted by the night of the Gathering. Lord Tycho went off the deal and refused to complete the bargain.'

'I'd heard it was the Vingos pulled back,' said the first man. 'He's a strange one, right enough, is Tycho Issian.'

'He's a pious man: a most righteous lord, out preaching every day on the iniquities of the Eyran oppression of women. I heard him speak in Forent last week, and he was most convincing. Truly, I felt like taking ship there and then for the Northern Isles and bringing back every woman I could find to do the Goddess's service—'

'To do your own service, most like!'

There was a great chuckle at this piece of wit, and then the conversation moved on to the more specific uses of women and how best to worship the Goddess with their aid. Erno frowned, trying to make sense of the nuggets of information he had gleaned. Then he drained the dregs from the flagon and swiftly and silently threaded his way through the revellers and out into the chilly street beyond.

He went first to the market, before he was tempted to spend his remaining coin on anything other than food, and bought two cheap loaves of heavy rye bread, a bag of rice and a piece of smoked ham. He'd passed a field of trees still bearing their crop of apples on the path from the coast; and he'd check the crab-pot he set that morning on his return: and that should last the two of them a few days, if they eked out the meat with the rice. At the last minute, he counted his coin and realised he had just enough to buy a second piece of ham, which would keep for a week or more – but then he passed a stall where a man was crying his wares and found that he had exactly the price of a single hen, which seemed remarkably fortuitous; but when he opened his mouth to say so, the stallholder took the money straight off his palm, grabbed up a chicken from the coop and throttled it so quickly and expertly that Erno did not have a chance to ask him to leave it alive and merely tie its feet together for him and he found he had drunk just a little too much to be able to argue coherently in Istrian with him. Now they'd have to cook it that night, whether the crab-pot contained a catch or not.

Erno took a path westwards along the cliffs, and once he was out of sight of the town shook his cowl loose and walked with his head high and the cold onshore breeze in his hair. The path cut through fields that prior to the harvest would have contained a great sea of barley and rye, but now were filled with muddy stubble. Great sheaves and stacks marked the cornfields further inland: he could see for miles, for the countryside here was rolling and open. And everywhere he looked, the soil was fertile and the crops plentiful. All this, Erno thought, his jaw tight, had once been Eyran land, all the way to the Golden Mountains, or so the old folk said. He had felt a powerful, instinctive hatred against the Istrians when he'd learned what had happened to Katla; but now that he saw this fine lost land stretching away on all sides and compared its lush contours with his memories of the storm-lashed, barren, rocky wastes of the Northern Isles, he could feel that anger refining itself, burning deeper, burning brighter. He began to understand the angry things Tor and Fent said about the southerners being their ancient enemy, words that at the time had seemed cruel and stupid. And yet here he was, on Istrian soil, in Istrian disguise, walking back to feed and care for an Istrian woman, when all around him the Southern Empire prepared itself for war against his own people.

He shook his head. Tor would have something to say about this. If he ever saw him again.

In the next valley down a plume of smoke marked the position of a farm. He skirted a small wood until he was close enough to see washing flapping on a line outside; chickens running hither and thither across the yard. Something stirred in his head.

A few moments later he was loping quickly towards the coast, his sack bulging with its new addition. The bark of an outraged dog echoed in the smoky air.

By the time he had checked the crab-pot, found it empty and made his way back to the beach, the sun had dipped below the horizon and night was setting in. The woman was sitting on a log of driftwood in front of a little fire and poking with a stick at the two mackerel he had caught and cleaned that morning and left in a rockpool to keep fresh for dinner. The fish lay in the embers, their patterned skin bubbling and crisping. The light of the flames illuminated her face in the darkening air. Had she been any other woman he would have said she looked beautiful, but he hardened his heart against her and dug in his sack.

'Put this on!'

He flung the dark fabric at her and watched as her face changed.

'Why have you given me this?' Selen Issian shook out the plain black robe with its integral veil, slit to reveal only the mouth: the traditional dress of an Istrian woman, and this a particularly poor quality example. She stared at the Eyran in bewilderment. 'I thought we had agreed after the last time that it was best I was not seen with you.'

'I'm not taking you into the town: I'm taking you to your father. He is in Forent with Lord Rui Finco at the moment. It is not far: three or four days at most, less if we can avail ourselves of a ride.'

Even in the rosy light, the woman's face blanched. 'You can't – you promised you would take care of me. You promised I would not have to go back to him—'

'The man you thought you had killed is not dead, so circumstances have changed.'

'Tanto – Tanto Vingo lives?' How could any man survive the loss of so much blood? When she had stabbed him – three, four times? she had lost count in the terror of the moment – it had gushed out everywhere: over her hands, the knife, the floor. She could not believe it.

'There was a man at the inn who was visiting the family house when Tanto Vingo revived from his long sleep.' He did not add that the Vingo boy had 'howled like a dog' on his return to consciousness. 'And that he is now rallying. So it seems that at the worst your father need only pay the family the price of a wounding, rather than confer you to the flames. You can go back in safety and in honour.'

Selen searched his face for any sign of untruth, and failed to find it there. He watched, expecting an outburst; but she set her jaw and stared into the cook-fire with such intensity that it appeared as if she had rather cast herself upon it than do as he suggested. Then, quite matter-of-factly, she retrieved the fish carefully from the embers and stoked the fire with the discarded sabatka, and when he gave a shout of protest and bent as if to grab it up, she waved the stick she had been using to tend to the mackerel and flourished it at him in warning.

'I tell you now,' she said and her voice was low and determined, 'and I swear to all that is holy in the world that I shall never wear one of these monstrous robes again. Why should I cover my face as if I am ashamed for the world to see me? Why should I allow myself to be hidden away as if I am less than a man, less than human? We are confined in these things as surely as if we were behind bars, disallowed any identity except our husband's or our father's. Well, I have had enough of being treated so, by my father, by you or by anyone else on Elda.'

The flames billowed and roared as they consumed the sabatka, lighting the beach with a hellish effulgence.

'I refuse to be bought and sold to satisfy any other's desires than my own. I will no longer be regarded as a chattel, or bartered away as part of a marriage settlement that serves no more purpose than to swell my father's coffers and extend his estates. I utterly refuse to go back to my father: I renounce him, my family, my country and—' she drew a deep breath '—and the Goddess!'

Erno dropped to his haunches beside her and his face was grim. 'For your own good, Selen, go back to your family. What good is this ranting? The world is the way it is, and you and I cannot change it. Whatever we do, it all comes to ashes in the end.' He took the stick from her and prodded at the charred rag at the heart of the fire. Little flakes of burned fabric eddied upwards in the hot draughts of air, winking with red light like tiny fireflies, then drifted away all dead and dark.

The woman started to cry.

'I cannot go back, Erno. I have no place in Istria now.'

'Your father will care for you.'

Selen gave a bitter little laugh. 'My father cares for no one but himself. I am of no use to him now, for I am spoiled goods. Even if I would countenance it, no man will want me for his wife. My father will have no choice but to give me over to the Sisters and they will find me out, for I have no belief in their Goddess or her goodness any longer. So it will be the fires for me one way or another, you see.'

Erno rubbed a hand across his face. He had rehearsed the scene over and over in his head on the long walk back to the beach and it had all seemed perfectly simple then: the boy was not dead; there was no crime to answer to: she could go home and he—

—well, he had not got that far.

'Are both those fish yours?' he said quietly.

Sensing that something had gone out of him, Selen wiped her tears away with the back of her hand. Her wet cheeks gleamed in the firelight. She risked a glance at the northerner, but his eyes had gone hooded and dark and she could not guess his thoughts. Instead, she took a breath and met his enquiry direct. 'I— No. Take one if you wish to. I thought you would have eaten something in the town.'

Erno removed one of the loaves from the sack and hacked a large piece off it with his belt-knife. 'Here.' He handed it over, his eyes averted.

It was a peace offering, of a sort. He could not think of anything else to say in the face of her distress. Why did everything always turn out to be so much harder and more complicated than you'd imagined it would be?

Selen took the bread from Erno and felt him blench when the tips of her fingers brushed his palm. Even so, he still would not look at her; indeed, was making a very great effort to stare fixedly at the ground, the fire, the fish: anything that did not involve making eye-contact. *I have to save myself*, she thought. *But I do not know how with a man like this.* She gazed at him wordlessly, taking in the anxious lines furrowed deep into his brow, the bunch of hard muscle at the jawline. Conflicting emotions warred inside him: that much she could tell. He did not want to be responsible for her, but innate decency was making it hard for him to carry through an abandonment. *He cannot even look at me*, she thought. *Does he hate me so much? Perhaps I should tell him—* She felt her self-pity rise up again, the tears pricking at her eyes, and her mind flew wide. Now was not the time: in his volatile state he might panic and simply leave her anyway, knowing she would have no choice other than to go home and throw herself on the mercy of her father. To distract herself as much as him from this line of thought, she blinked hard and then, gesturing at the provisions sack, said in as steady a voice as she could muster: 'Is that a chicken I can see?'

Erno forced a laugh. 'It is, but it will stay fresh enough till tomorrow if I leave it in the tideline.'

'Leave it in the tideline and the crabs will have it.'

'That would be a waste.'

'Give it to me and I will roast it now.'

'If I give it to you, you will simply fling it on the fire, gizzards and all and we shall have a hen that's black on the outside, red on the inside and painful bellies for a week!'

She shrugged. 'They do not teach us the way of these things in my country.'

'You have seen me prepare a bird a dozen times and more,

and have learned nothing. It's as if you would have me be your slave!'

He spoke more angrily than he had meant to, but he saw her draw herself up to meet his attack.

'It is not my fault that I was born into the nobility and have not acquired these skills. I am doing my best to learn, but it is hard when you are always so impatient.'

Clenching his jaw in case he said something more he would regret, Erno took the chicken from the sack and went down to the water's edge to clean it. When he came back, he found that she had eaten both fish and the rest of the loaf and was looking up at him with huge round eyes.

'If you want a mackerel, I can go back and cast the line again,' she said guiltily.

Erno looked skyward and mastered his temper with difficulty.

'Why don't you boil some rice?' he suggested at last, and when she looked helpless he sighed and retraced his steps to the sea with the cook-pot in his hand. He would speak to her again in the morning. Things would seem less hopeless after food and a good sleep. In the light of day, she would surely see the impossibility of the situation she placed him in, now that there was no need for his protection any more, no need for all this dangerous, mad subterfuge.

Tomorrow would be better.

Later, bedded down inside the shelter with his back to her and the sound of her soft breathing filling the dark space around him, he found he could not sleep a wink.

Seven

Illusions

There was definitely something wrong with it. Virelai had thought it was the case the night before, but candlelight was fitful at the best of times and it had been difficult to be sure. Now, in the unforgiving light of a chilly Istrian dawn, there really could be no mistake. The skin between the thumb and forefinger of his left hand was starting to dry and flake off just as it had on his right hand a week or two ago, revealing an unpleasantly dull, chalky texture underneath. Unguents and emollient creams had ameliorated the damage on the other hand for a while, but eventually he had had to resort to an obscure renewing spell, dragged forcibly out of the cat, which had seemed to be rather too much enjoying his plight and had played very hard to get. Now the skin to which he had applied the spellcraft was just a half-shade too pink, too 'alive' where the rest of him was so pale; though it was unlikely anyone else would notice while the affected areas remained small. But if this kept happening, he would look like a patchwork quilt before long.

Was it his diet that was causing this curious effect, he wondered; or perhaps the stress of using too much magic? It might just be that such a long exposure to Istrian life was proving too rich for his palate, for the Master had never bothered to teach him the use of spices or those combinations of herbs with which the southerners flavoured their food when he had taught him the basics of the culinary arts. His fare on Sanctuary had been dull indeed: he could make unleavened bread, boil roots and turnips and those rather scrawny chickens that Rahe had conjured out of the air and tasted barely more substantial. The Master had never been very interested in food: indeed, he had seemed rather uninterested in most things by the time Virelai had left the island, letting things go to wrack and ruin, or even smashing them quite deliberately to pieces. Most things: but not the Rosa Eldi, a creature Virelai had come to hate in these past few months. They had enjoyed a complex and difficult relationship whilst they travelled together, though if he had been unable to profit directly from her charms, he had certainly ensured that others had paid over the odds for them. But now she was free and he was labouring under the yoke of a cruel new master, driven to produce ever more demanding sorceries in the name of the man's unswerving obsession . . .

He sighed, and turned to look for the cat. He would need to speak a few words over his flaking hand if he were to stop the progression of this new disorder.

But of Bëte, the beast in which Rahe had stored a large number of his most important spells, there was no sign.

'By Falla's fiery quim!'

It was the worst curse he knew. If Tycho Issian heard him utter it, he would be punished most severely. But the Lord of Cantara was still closeted with the girl Virelai had provided for him the previous night: he would not be abroad for an hour or more yet. Life here in the castle at Forent under Rui Finco's regime was one of discreet debauchery, for the lords, at least. Even the cat seemed to get up to no good; for although it was not allowed to stray beyond the tower, still it managed to discover and murder a remarkable number and variety of smaller beasts. So far, Virelai had been gifted with – or perhaps tormented with was a more accurate term – several families of mice, laid out in neat rows; a pair of lark's feet, complete with hooked spurs (but no lark: that had obviously proved too tempting a morsel); three fat rats; a pigeon bearing a message coiled around one grey-pink leg; and once, rather alarmingly, a half-dead rabbit, which had sprung disconcertingly to life when Virelai had reached a hand to it. Where the cat had come by these new acquaintances, he had no idea. Mice and rats infested every keep; and the pigeon must foolishly have landed on the sill of the window. But a lark? A rabbit? These were creatures of open farmland, of which there was precious little in the vicinity of Forent Castle.

The message had been interesting, though.

Consisting of an unhelpful length of thin twine tied into a combination of knots and twists and strange little curlicues, it had taken him several days to decipher and appeared to have something to do with the fact that a plan had gone awry and that a shipman named Dan, or something approximate, had disappeared.

Virelai had no idea why this Dan was so important that his absence had to be reported by messenger-pigeon, but perhaps he should try to find out. One thing he had learned in these long months out in the world of Elda was that information could be as valuable as silver, women, ships; or any other tradable object.

He went to the window and leaned out over the dizzying precipice beneath. They liked to build high in Istria, it seemed: the tower-room he had occupied in the great castle at Cera had also been lofty. But where the view from the window at Cera had been one most pleasing to the eye – parklands, woods and formal gardens all dappled with sunlight and caressed by gentle breezes; milling streets and markets ablaze with colour and buzzing with the noise of all the folk running around below him just like little ants ferrying their supplies to and fro – the prospect here at Forent was quite another matter. All he could see from this north-facing window was rock and sea. And a lot of sky. And all of these were grey. A thick mist had, as was quite common in this goddess-forsaken place – rolled in off the Northern Ocean, melding all three elements – solid, watery and ethereal – into a single monotonous blur. He hated this view; had hated it from the first day he had been incarcerated here. It reminded him too much of Sanctuary, with its grim ice cliffs and frozen gardens, a landscape rendered in a thousand shades of grey. A more poetic man – or one who had travelled more widely and had a greater ability to make comparisons – might have discerned an extraordinarily subtle palette of blues and greens and purples in that scene: but until he had fled the place, Virelai had never seen anything beyond the Master's icy hell and loathed that too heartily to be bothered to find any poetry in it.

Down below, a larger than average wave crashed onto the jagged rocks at the base of the keep with a roar, sending up a great geyser of white water. Flecks of spume eddied up into the damp air. The sea retreated, leaving behind it a sucking vacuum.

Virelai shuddered – an instinctive reaction to bad memories and the chilly air; but when he felt the hairs on the back of his neck start to rise, he knew the cause was more tangible. Bëte had returned.

Ever since the bizarre vision he had been afforded back in Cera, he had been wary of her. He turned now quickly, unhappy at the thought of the beast's eyes on his unguarded back.

She sat in the doorway as neat as a statue of Bast, Falla's feline companion: head up, paws together, tail tucked seamlessly around her feet and regarded the sorcerer with a merciless green gaze. There was no love lost between the two of them: Virelai had the strange feeling the cat blamed him for its separation from the Rosa Eldi. A whole continent away from the hypnotic hands of the woman who had been able to reduce it to a dribbling, purring pet and now forced to eject spells at another's whim, the cat was developing a nasty temper. Not that it had ever been of a particularly pleasant disposition (and his hands and forearms carried enough thin white scars to testify to *that* fact). Watching it carefully out of the corner of his eye, Virelai crossed the room and sat down upon his bed to allow the animal to pass unchallenged. He had given up trying to stare it down. Ever since he had thought he saw it grown vast and demonlike in that room in Cera, he was trying to avoid the sort of confrontation that might suddenly bring on the same manifestation. He had almost managed to persuade himself that his vision of it in that monstrous state, and the echoing voice that accompanied that vision, had been brought about by his fevered mind, a mind subjected to unbearable stress by the Lord of Cantara.

Almost, but not quite. There had been the small matter of the dead hound he had found at the threshold of the room the next morning, its throat agape, its wiry grey coat all matted with gore. The hound was one of the Lord of Cera's hunting pack and was a huge beast in itself: how much larger and more savage, therefore, must be the predator which had taken its life and dragged it to the topmost tower-room?

'Well now, my Lord of Cantara, I can well see why you are late to table this morning.' Rui Finco, Lord of Forent, leaned casually against the door-jamb surveying the contents of the bedchamber with some amusement. Tycho Issian, that hard-faced hypocrite, pushed the woman who sat astraddle him roughly aside, drew the covers up to his chest and glared at his host.

'Is nowhere private to you?'

'Nowhere in this castle.' Rui watched regretfully as the woman gathered her sabatka more decorously around her and glided away into the dressing-chamber. She had a good shape, if a little slender for his tastes: he could tell that much quite easily even though she was swaddled in the all-encompassing robe: you developed an eye for such things if you had bedded as many women as had the Lord of Forent. It was his right and his privilege, after all, as lord of the domain, and he'd spent much of his time, income and effort on acquiring the finest seraglio in the Empire. Was it Raqla? he wondered. The height and the size of her hips and breasts looked slighter than he remembered them under that rich blue sheeting, but then she might have suffered from the wasting sickness which had taken hold earlier in the year. Raqla had been a favourite of his: a tireless girl, given the right encouragement, who had been happy enough to climb aboard and ride him so that he could watch her breasts sway and jounce with her efforts. None of this sabatka nonsense for him behind his closed doors: he liked the way a woman's body was made, could not understand how it could possibly be more holy to worship the Goddess's image through some holes in a robe rather than to appreciate the whole glorious creation in full sight. But he could have sworn he had glimpsed a strand of pale blonde hair caught for a moment in the mouth-slit of the sabatka; and Raqla was so dark to be almost ebony-haired . . .

Curious. He could not place the woman amongst the hundred or so he kept in the castle seraglio; had the Lord of Cantara possibly have had the temerity to spurn his host's more than generous hospitality and had a girl from the town smuggled in to service him? It seemed unlikely, especially given the network of informers he paid well to keep their eyes on Tycho's comings and goings; but the southern lord was strange indeed, and obsessed enough to try anything.

'If your lordship is sufficiently rested, perhaps we might continue our discussion?'

Tycho waved an impatient hand. Beneath the walnut-brown tan his face appeared sallow and unhealthy. It looked as if he had not slept in a week, rather than spent a pleasurable night locked in some lusty courtesan's embrace. 'Give me a few minutes and I'll attend you presently, Rui. Is there no door that locks in this damned place?'

Rui Finco did not bother to answer this naive question. Of course no door but that to his own chamber – and the stronghold below – bore a lock. How effective a politician would he be if he did not know the comings and goings of every visitor to Forent Castle? With a humourless smile and a nod of barest politeness, Rui left the room, swinging the oak door closed behind him.

Tycho pushed himself out of bed and stormed across the room to the mirror that hung over the stone basin and ewer there. Framed by the exquisite mosaic of the frame, his eyes were bloodshot, his cheeks haggard and his chin was dark with stubble. The lines that ran across his brow and beside his nose were more deeply incised than ever, and a whole forest of wrinkles had appeared around his eye-sockets. Rather than the forty-three years he owned to, today he looked closer to sixty. He was not, in truth, getting much sleep; and not just as a result of his exertions with the whores he required Virelai to bring to him night after night, for they were mere distractions, an attempt to exorcise the demon that had his soul in its thorny grip. He had not been sleeping properly now for— He made a mental calculation: he had come from Cantara, via Cera, to Forent around Harvest Moon and the Allfair had taken place at Quarteryear – so it was now over four moon-circles since he had been thus afflicted. It was enough to turn any man's wits, and his health, too. Before his fateful encounter with the woman they called the Rose of the World he would have called himself a rational man: one given rather more to consideration of the outcome of his actions, one who could always be counted on to choose the best course to progress his own fortunes and status. More than that, in many areas of the Empire his name was a watchword for piety and patriotism: he was known as an orator and upholder of Falla's laws. A man of shining reputation. True, his heritage was obscure – and he intended to keep it that way – and he had owed the Council a large sum of money (now repaid, with interest); but in all other ways he had worked hard through his life to show to the world a man of great character, a man who lived well but purely; a man who was known to be hard on sinners and the causes of sin, but had himself an unblemished record. And now? All he could think about, at every hour of the day and night was the Rosa Eldi – her milk-white skin, the long golden hair that would tangle silkily around him, the slender waist he could encircle with his hands, the full breasts that would surely spill over his palms, the heat of her softly hairless—

He caught himself up, appalled for the thousandth time at the potency of the image, at the profoundly physical effect it had on him. He had never, he reminded himself now, seen even a glimpse of the nomad woman's naked flesh; but somehow that one kiss he had shared with her in the map-seller's wagon at the Fair had been all it had required for her to enspell him, body, thought and soul: she had, he was sure, gifted him with a full understanding of how it would be to *know* every crevice of her in that single encounter, and he had been haunted by this insatiable hunger for her ever since.

Not only was he constantly exhausted, but his wretched cock was eternally hard. It was – apart from being a potentially desperate embarrassment – a practical horror, and no matter what he tried, nothing seemed to reduce the size or insistence of his erection. Cold baths, cold compresses, hours of prayer: nothing worked. So instead he had turned to the professional efforts of the castle's seraglio: for surely women such as these must have come across problems worse than his in their lustful careers. The whores wore him out and made him sore with their exertions, but still he could not ejaculate. Even this latest experiment did not seem to be doing the trick.

He took a new length of linen bandage and bound himself

tightly, wincing at the discomfort. *It is my punishment*, he thought savagely, *for allowing the Rosa Eldi to be taken into heathendom. I must bear it until I can liberate her from that foul barbarian and his wicked, heretical followers. I must take her and purge her thoroughly; rinse her through with my own sacred libations. Together we shall worship the Goddess from whence we all came; I shall cover her flesh from the view of the lustful; I shall show her the true and steady Way of Fire: I shall lead her back to the paths of the righteous . . .*

He was beginning to believe the words he cried out in town squares, the words that brought people crowding around him, calling for a holy war against Eyra: a war to end all wars.

Rui Finco tarried in the hallway outside until he heard the water running in the ewer and the lord bidding the whore leave by the secret way; then he ran swiftly down the stairs and entered the elaborate Galian Room below. Behind the vast freestanding bed, with its plush hangings and massively carved posts, he located the panelled door and slipped into the narrow staircase beyond. His great-grandfather, the notorious Taghi Finco, had constructed this neat little maze of secret passageways in the castle walls. In the last century social mores had been strict and congress with a woman not one's Goddess-given wife a crime punishable by castration. Taghi was a man of enormous appetites, his wife a sickly creature who refused to bed him after the birth of their only son, or to have the Goddess-given good grace to fade away and die. Via the passages, Taghi had smuggled women into the Galian Room and had there pleasured himself and them through many a torrid night. He had, it was rumoured (though never in polite company) fathered half a hundred bastards. Rui blessed his forebear daily: it was not just the castle he had inherited from Lord Taghi Finco.

He heard a click above him and then the sound of feet

on the wooden steps, and a moment later a lithe figure in a dark robe emerged, barefoot and in a hurry, from the room above.

'Aha, my lovely!'

Stepping out of the shadows, Rui caught the girl in his arms and propelled her with him through the doorway into the Galian Room. Even before he unveiled her, he knew by the touch of her alone that it was Raqla. With a practised hand he flipped the sabatka over her head until it fell to the floor in a shimmer of silk.

'Bast's teats!'

If he were blind, and working solely on the shape and feel of her, he would still have sworn it was Raqla. But the evidence of his eyes told him otherwise. The woman standing before him with one hand over her breasts and the other modestly concealing her hairless crotch, was pale and blonde – a rare colouring in the southern lands, where men and women tended to dark skin and darker hair. He stared and blinked, suddenly lost for words.

Then something occurred to him.

'Turn around!' he ordered the woman suddenly.

She looked alarmed but turned a shapely shoulder to him and presented him with her elegant back and rounded buttocks, on the right of which a large brown mole was displayed in sharp contrast to the milky skin. He traced it with a finger and felt the woman tense. He knew that marking: he had caressed it often enough after the throes of their lovemaking. Rui felt a ripple of superstition tremble down his spine. He made the sign of the Goddess, bent to retrieve the fallen robe and threw it to the woman.

'Clothe yourself.'

The girl caught the fabric, shook the robe out into its proper form with swift efficiency and shrugged her way in it. She was about to adjust the veil that covered the face when the Lord of Forent took a step towards her.

'No, wait.'

Inserting his hands into the mouth-slit, he tore the head-piece in two with a single, violent gesture and stood there, assessing her face. Then he caught her chin, angling her head this way and that. The girl's eyes were as big and as black as coals: and he knew them well. Was the hair a wig? He wound its silky length around his finger and gave a sharp tug. The woman exclaimed in pain. Not a wig, then.

'Why have you dyed your hair?'

The woman stared at the ground, unable to meet his gaze. She had performed acts with this man that would bear favourable comparison to those of the famous lovers in the forbidden erotic book, *Cestia's Journey*; she had seen every part of him in the most intimate detail, had watched him at his most vulnerable while he slept or when he lost himself in ecstasy; but still she could not look him in the face. It was truly a shameful thing she had done, shameful and punishable by death . . .

Rui's tone was softer than she had expected as he asked, 'Who has done this to you, Raqla?' but when she answered, her voice barely above a whisper, she saw his jaw clench and his eyes go hard.

'Stay still. No, don't stand like that: I need the light on your face—'

This one was difficult. Her jawline was too pronounced, and she had an overbite. He had managed the hair with much less effort this time, but it seemed there was always some aspect of the remaking that would compensate for the easier bits. And the eyes – he could never quite get the eyes to change. He had read in one of the tomes in the Master's icy library how one of the poets so favoured by the Southern Empire had referred to the eyes as 'the windows to the soul' and had then had no idea what nonsense the man had meant by this; but finding they were immutable, immune to the most powerful magic he could extract from the cat, he was beginning to wonder whether there might not be some truth in poetry after all.

He was, on the other hand, quite proud of what he had achieved with the form of the woman. The hips were almost right – lean and slight as a boy's, with just a swell of flesh at the haunch; and the breasts were perfectly shaped. It had been a pleasure to cup them himself, even though he risked dire punishment if discovered.

He brought the cat up level with the girl's face and watched as her eyes widened at the struggling beast's snarl of protest. Tightening his grip on the thick skin at the back of its neck, he closed his eyes, focused his mind carefully on the clean, taut line of the face he recalled so perfectly from memory, and repeated the refining spell.

'Stop this travesty now or you will shortly be making a sharp downward exit from this window.' The voice was dangerous and cool. 'The sharks have had a thin summer this year: a paucity of storms has meant that there have not been the usual number of shipwrecked sailors for them to feast on; and they do so enjoy the taste of human flesh—'

Virelai's eyes shot open. He had not heard the footsteps, nor the door come open; and so to see Lord Rui Finco standing on the threshold, his keen face taut with controlled anger, and the girl he had worked on so successfully yesterday on her knees before him with the veil of her sabatka ripped away was a surprise indeed. Even so, he could not prevent his gaze from wandering between the faces of the two women and noting with some satisfaction that Balia's jaw was closer to the template than his earlier attempt on Raqla had been. His skills were improving all the time.

'Whatever in the fiery pits do you think you are doing?'

Virelai came back to his predicament with a guilty start. He had not seen the Lord of Forent angry before and he suspected of those who had faced his fury, not many had survived.

'My lord— I—'

Rui shut the door behind him silently. Virelai did not like that. When Tycho was angry he had a tendency to scream his displeasure and lay about him with his fists. He'd received a myriad of bruises as a result of the Lord of Cantara's temper; and once a whipping, but no worse. The Lord of Forent, on the other hand, looked as if he might well be quietly true to his word about feeding him to the fishes, and probably the two girls as well. And no one would hear – and even if they did, it was the lord's own castle they were in: who would dare to question him over the loss of one poor nomad?

'Sorcery. I can smell it.' Rui Finco's face twisted in disgust. 'I knew there was some perversity in the air, some filthy practice between you and your master.' He looked down at the black cat, currently gone uncharacteristically limp and quiet in Virelai's hand. 'And let that poor creature go, for Falla's sake!'

Virelai released his hold on Bëte. She fell on her feet, gave him an unforgiving look which promised that she would add this latest degradation to her ongoing tally, and with the teeth-setting sound of claws on wood, leapt up the tall chest of drawers on the opposite side of the room and took up position there where she might view proceedings in safety.

'We burn magic-makers in this realm,' Rui said softly, his eyes never leaving Virelai's face.

'I know, my lord.' Virelai could feel a quaking begin in his knees, as if the bones there were liquefying.

'Do you know when the nomads started to be persecuted in earnest in this country?'

'No, my lord.'

'In my late father's time. He had cause to believe a nomad sorcerer had betrayed him by casting a glamour over his enemy. I shall not burden you with the entire sordid tale, but suffice it to say that I have a brother in this world who is not truly my brother, and my father was less than happy that those who trod Istrian soil should dare to bring disgrace on his house in so foul a manner. He took against the Footloose peoples from that day forward. He must have burned—' Rui cast his eyes ceilingward and began to count '—let's see, there were two, three, four hundred – no, no, what am I saying? – a thousand of them. There were several dozen in that first caravan of travellers – men, women and children: that made a considerable bonfire, I can tell you, Master Virelai. As a child of eight, I was brought out onto the viewing platform and forced to watch. I think my father considered it some form of punishment for me, that I had been at home and not protected his hearth and his wife as a true Istrian warrior should; but truth to tell, I was most morbidly fascinated to hear their wails and to watch the way their skin crisped and blackened, and boiled off their bones like tallow candles. Do you know that when you burn a human creature the smoke that billows up from them can coat the buildings for the distance of half a league or more with a very unpleasant sticky black fat?'

Virelai's knees began to buckle.

The Lord of Forent caught him by the elbows. 'How now, my sorcerous friend: is your stomach too weak for such details? Do you perhaps see yourself entering a similar fire? Would you shriek, think you, or go with quiet dignity? It must be said, that's hard to achieve when the flames begin to make your eyeballs sizzle.'

At this, Virelai crumpled. He sat there on the floor of the tower-room, shaking with terror. It was as he thought: where the Master was harsh and the Lord of Cantara both brutal and cruel, this man was more dangerous by far: he would see them all in the fires and laugh as they burned.

'I am sorry, my lord,' he managed to say. The words bubbled up and out of him in a torrent now as the floodgates of caution gave way. 'It's my master, my lord: Tycho Issian, Lord of Cantara, for whom I work this glamour. He has become ill with his need for – for a certain lady, and I am trying to help him ease his distress. It's very difficult work, my lord, and my efforts have not always been met with appreciation. Many times he has beaten me when the spell fades before its time. It is very hard to make a glamour which will hold for any while, my lord, much less so one that depends for its effect on counterfeiting another so perfectly.'

But Rui Finco was barely listening to him now. Rather, he was staring first at Balia, then at Raqla. He pulled the latter from where she had subsided onto the floor and stood her alongside the first girl. He spent some time looking from one to the other; then he came back to Virelai.

'You will not continue this practice, do you hear me?'

Virelai nodded mutely. Tycho would doubtless beat him black and purple; but he would prefer such treatment than to incur the Lord of Forent's displeasure any further.

'He is not to spend himself on these creatures. I cannot afford to have his obsession lessened in any degree.'

This last the lord uttered in a voice so low and so bland that it was clearly not meant to be any part of their conversation, but Virelai nodded anyway.

'Can you bring them back to themselves?'

Understanding that he was not to burn, at least for the time being, Virelai scrabbled upright. 'There is no need, my lord. Very shortly Raqla will be herself again, her hair black and her body wider. And if Balia sleeps for an hour or so the glamour will fade of its own accord: it requires some effort of concentration on the part of the subjects themselves to maintain the illusion you see, my lord—'

'Yes, yes.' The Lord of Forent waved his hands. Then his eyes narrowed as if something else had occurred to him. 'The silver that the Lord of Cantara has so fortuitously come by in recent months; was it sorcerously made?'

Virelai's terrified expression told him the answer to that question.

'Even the silver he has given me to aid our venture?'

Virelai shook his head vigorously. 'No, my lord. Lord Tycho thought it best to ensure that we traded the silver I made for true silver for your own coffers, my lord. Although I am finding that my skill in changing other metals to silver is improving all the time: I have some in my possession that has retained its new form for almost two moons now.'

The Lord of Forent became contemplative. 'I see. How interesting. However, while I may not share my father's penchant for the aroma of the roasted flesh of the Footloose, do not think I shall hesitate to skewer you personally if I find you carrying on your perverse practices—'

'My lord, I—'

'Do not interrupt me. I will personally skewer you if I find you making magic for anyone other than *me*. Do you understand me, nomad? You will remain here as my guest, as will your erstwhile master, the Lord of Cantara, and your damned pet cat, and from now on you will all three of you do my bidding, or face the fires for sorcery.' He turned to the women. 'It's been some time since I took a golden-haired girl to bed. Shall we see if your changed appearance has taught you any new tricks?'

The two women followed their lord to the door with remarkable alacrity, Virelai thought; as if they were not simply being obedient to his command, but were eager to remind themselves of his abilities.

A moment later he was left alone in the chamber. Alone, that was, apart from the cat, whose eyes he could feel boring into him with the utmost contempt and loathing.

Every time he thought his life could get no worse, it seemed Fate had another unlucky card to deal him. He sighed, remembering the Master's words to him: *You should thank me for bringing you here to Sanctuary and saving you from all that greed and horror.*

Yet again he felt the old doubts assail him.

Eight

Messages

'Sur's nuts, how I hate the blasted sea!'

She leaned over the gunwale again, catching her bleached and knotted braids in one hand and retching so horribly that anyone not privy to the situation might be forgiven for believing that a sheep was being slowly and grotesquely strangled.

The tall, gaunt man next to her watched this performance dispassionately, and when she straightened up, her face now almost as haggard as his own, he raised an eyebrow. 'Picked the wrong profession for such a delicacy of stomach in that case, Mam.'

The weatherbeaten brown of the woman's skin had taken on the faintest tinge of spring-green. Privately, Knobber thought it suited her: made her look a little more vulnerable, a touch more womanly. He hadn't seen her look vulnerable since a distant evening in Jetra and that strange matter of the hillman whose disappearance had caused the mercenary leader such excess of emotion that he'd actually caught her shedding a tear. Only the one, mind, and that dashed away angrily with the back of a hand: but that one tear in itself had seemed a very abomination against nature. Generally, Mam looked barely female: it was hard to think of her as a woman at all, even if you scrubbed and combed out her hair and dressed her in one of the sheer gauze shifts the new queen was reported to wear, that were currently causing such a stir in court circles in Halbo. He shuddered. Actually, that image was not a pleasant one on which to dwell, and if Mam caught him entertaining it – and she did have an uncanny way with such matters – she'd not be amused. And Mam not amused was something to be avoided, and that was the truth.

'Have you reckoned on what to tell him yet?' he asked, changing the subject, though judging by the mercenary leader's expression, probably not for the better.

Mam snarled. 'You think I should concoct some fiction that sounds less bizarre than the truth?'

Knobber shrugged. Certainly their employer, Rui Finco, the Lord of Forent, was not going to be a happy man; for while they had managed to successfully stow the shipload of good Eyran weaponry they'd been paid to fetch south, they had signally failed to bring aboard their main cargo, the man without whom all the rest would prove pointless, for unless the range of a bowshot arrow had improved dramatically since he'd last heard about it, there was still no weapon that could fly across the wide Northern Ocean from Istria to Eyra without a boat to carry it within striking distance.

When he and Joz had arrived at the shipyard, not only was Morten Danson missing, but most of his workers and the best timber had gone, too. No one they spoke to seemed to know where he was: some lame excuse about the mumming in Halbo had been offered; but that hardly explained the missing men and wood, and it seemed more likely to Knobber that one of the King's rivals had decided to make a little investment of his own. When they had got back to Halbo and reported their failure, Mam had seemed already distracted, full of unfocused fury, and rather than stick around to find out exactly what had caused her famously volatile temper, they had blurted out their own disappointing findings and headed swiftly for the safety of an anonymous tavern.

It was not, Knobber thought, a situation he'd want to explain to the Lord of Forent. No ships meant no war.

Correction: no *Eyran* ships; no war, for those coast-hugging little Istrian vessels were worse than useless in a heavy sea. So, no Eyran shipmaker, no Eyran ships. No war: no more lucrative work for them. *Perhaps*, he thought speculatively, *we'd be better off fermenting a civil war in the Southern Empire. Or . . .*

'We could get the captain to turn around, take this lot north through the Sharking Straits and flog it to the Earl of Ness—'

'This captain couldn't find the Sharking Straits if it bit him in the arse. Besides, Ness has no money,' Mam returned flatly, indicating that she had already considered and dismissed this possibility.

'Erol Bardson?'

'That man works by stealth, not open conflict. When he makes his move, it won't be by force of arms, but by clever words and a knife in the back. War with Istria might suit his purpose well; but buying a shipment of arrows from us would be too obvious by far. No, Bardson has other plans, I'll wager, though I'm not sure I'd take his coin even if he called me in.'

Knobber scratched his chin thoughtfully. 'That sounds choosy, Mam. You developed a soft spot for young Ravn?'

Mam snorted. 'Our stallion? Poor lad hardly knows which end's up at the moment. They'll be needing a new king in Halbo soon, and not through any treachery Bardson might devise: that woman must have worn Ravn's cock to the size of a worm by now, so she can't be getting much satisfaction from him.'

Knobber regarded his leader askance. He'd heard some women did receive pleasure from the act of love, but he'd yet to encounter one who'd admit to it. Though that might have something to do with— He pushed the thought aside.

'You think Bardson will try to take the throne?'

'There's enough would take his side. Ravn did himself no

favours when he took to wife an unknown nomad woman over the flower of the Eyran nobility. And he pays no heed to his counsellors, even when he sits with them, which I hear is rare in itself. Spends most of his waking and sleeping hours in the arms of his new queen and lets the rest go hang. They say Stormway and Shepsey are doing what they can, but they're old men now, and their hearts aren't in it any more. They've got ambitious lords and greedy farmers yapping round their feet like feists.'

'Southeye was the one could have held it together.'

'Aye. Well, we did what we had to do, and got well paid for it – one way or another.'

After the debacle at the Gathering and King Ravn's subsequent escape, it had proved quite difficult to persuade the Lord of Forent to hand over to them the rest of the money, even though, as Mam had pointed out in no uncertain terms, they had kept their side of the bargain by delivering the King, and it was his and Varyx's stupid fault that Ravn had got away from them. Rui had been less than impressed at the ease with which Mam had switched sides when the odds had shifted but when it looked as if a rumpus might ensue he'd paid up, albeit with ill grace. It had come as something of a surprise to be offered a new commission from the Lord of Forent: but work was work, and not so plentiful that they could afford to turn a job away.

The two sell-swords stared morosely over the side at the endless procession of grey rollers and contemplated their ill-fortune. But while Mam inwardly cursed her tardiness and lack of foresight in the matter of abducting the shipmaker, Knobber found himself wishing he was back on the little island a day's sail east of the Galian Isles on which he had once fortuitously been washed up – the result of no shipwreck this, but an unfortunate altercation with some Circesian pirates – where the sun had shone day in and day out, and the light striking down through the gentle inshore waves was the identical cloudy, opalescent green of a stone pendant he had once scavenged from a mortally wounded southern warrior in a small skirmish in the foothills of the Golden Mountains when they'd found themselves caught on the losing side and had quickly switched allegiance. He'd put the thing around his neck and given its owner a quicker death than he deserved and thus regarded the stone as a good-luck charm, a symbol of his personal survival, though sometimes when he took it off and studied it he could swear that it appeared to change colour. He had lain on that painful, glorious, shining beach of crushed white seashells, with the sun beating down on his back, drying his shirt into stiff, salty folds, and stared into that softly polished stone as it shifted from grey to aqua-green in front of his eyes just like the flow of a sea, or the tide of his life— He was blasted out of this gentle memory as a particularly large wave struck the ship such a hard broadside blow that the timbers creaked and a bone-shaking rattle shuddered through the vessel's frame and transferred itself deep down into his poor mortal bones.

'Sur! Give an Istrian captain an honest, Eyran-made craft and he'll still do his damnedest to sink it. Don't they have the least understanding of seamanship? It's a miracle we've not capsized a dozen times already. If we were closer to land, I'd drown the blasted man myself and take the helm!'

Another wave hit them hard. Mam groaned. Then she grabbed the gunwale and heaved desperately over it once again.

'Whoo, that was a big one! Rough, isn't it?'

A small, round man had appeared at Knobber's elbow, grinning from ear to ear. His cropped piebald hair stood up in stiff little peaks – partly from an accumulation of airborne brine, partly because it had not seen clean water for – well, Knobber couldn't remember the last time he'd seen Dogbreath bathe any part of his anatomy, let alone anything so frivolous as his hair. Dogo claimed that washing took off

a much-needed layer of skin: and since there was so little of
him in the first place he could hardly risk losing any more.

'What's the matter, Mam? Something you ate? Was it the
hogfish last night – that smelled a bit off to me – or that
rather ripe crab soup this morning?'

The sound of retching reached a crescendo, became more
productive, then ceased abruptly. Mam shot upright, grabbed
the little man by the throat in a single fluid movement and
hoisted him until his feet dangled.

'Why don't you go and play in the rigging, Dogbreath?'
A shake accompanied each word. 'Keep out of my way and
don't mention food in my presence, or you'll find yourself
making close acquaintance with the keel!'

When she put him down again, Dogo dodged swiftly
behind Knobber. 'Joz sent me to get you,' he rasped, rubbing
his sore neck. 'Bird's arrived from Forent.'

'Damn me.' Knobber made a superstitious sign. 'How in
seven hells do those pigeons find a single boat in the middle
of a bloody ocean?'

'I get paid to fight and steal; not fill my head with
arcane knowledge. That's Doc's province. Why don't you
go ask him? Myself, I think we'd better go and find out the
worst. I knew we should have throttled that sneaky bastard
pigeon Lazlo claimed was his pet bird before he got the
chance to send word of our little disaster to Rui Finco.
Pet bird, I ask you. Whoever had a pet bird on board a
ship? Get roasted the second day, it would, on any boat of
mine—'

'Sur did,' Dogo interrupted.

'What?'

'Sur had his raven, came everywhere with him.'

Mam fixed the little man with a grim stare. 'Shut up,'
she said.

'And?'

'Get ready to threaten that little weasel of a captain if it sounds bad. He's got the balls of a mouse, that one: he'll tell tales on us as soon as blink.'

'I could spit him for you, Mam,' Dogbreath added cheerfully, from the safe shelter afforded by Knobber's broad back. 'I could run him right through the gizzard and be away so fast he'd think a fly had bit him!'

'Likely that'll be the way your women feel when you've bedded them, little man.' The troop leader adopted a bewildered, mimsy air and a gratingly high-pitched voice: 'Ooh my, was that a tiny wee gnat gnawing on my privy parts, or have I just been visited by the mighty Dogo?' Mam leered at the little man. 'Don't spit Lazlo, you numskull: he's steering the ship: I just want him threatened, and that only if we have to. Let's cross the bridge before we cut the ropes, eh?'

The pigeon had now made itself comfortable on the rakki above the wide sweep of the sail and was refusing to come down.

Two of the mercenaries – Joz and Doc – and a motley group of sailors from half a dozen Istrian provinces had gathered in a little knot at the foot of the mast and were gazing upwards. In their midst, a short, worried-looking man in expensively tooled leather was directing a thin, dark child from the Empire's southern mountains, a boy they referred to as 'the Monkey', for his climbing skills, and for the legendary creature of the Far West, to shin up the mast to fetch the pigeon down and the boy was protesting, sensibly enough, to Mam's mind, that as soon as he got within a body-length of the bird, the thing would take fright and fly off elsewhere, maybe to another ship entirely. And then where would they be? For this, Monkey received a sharp clip around the ear and a stream of abuse from the captain.

Joz Bearhand sighed and shook his head. These people had a tendency towards histrionics and impracticality that he found extremely irritating. He took a couple of steps backwards, reached around behind him, took aim. A moment later, the bird fell to the deck, twitching. In the middle of the stunned silence that followed, Joz retrieved the pebble (one of his favourites – a seawashed round of white quartz he'd taken from a beach in the Fair Isles), put it back in his pouch along with the catapult, pick up the limp form of the pigeon, untied the message scrip from its leg and handed it to Mam.

She unwound it carefully and started to read its odd combination of dots and dashes.

'That message is for me!'

The Istrian captain came at her furiously with his hand extended, palm up, fingers flicking imperiously.

Mam gave him her ghastliest smile, making sure every single one of her pointed teeth were visible to him. *Imagine what it would be like if I were to bite you,* that look said. *Imagine what it would feel like if I bit you, down there* . . . Then she handed the scrip to him with a nonchalance that spoke volumes. Joz caught Doc's eye and was rewarded with a wink. Dogo looked disappointed: he'd been looking forward to showing his little blade to the man.

The mercenaries melted away, to regroup up by the stempost. 'So?' Knobber asked impatiently. 'What did it say?'

'Sadly it seems the captain's last bird didn't make it through,' Mam grinned. 'The Lord of Forent is most displeased with the lack of information he's received thus far and is demanding news of the whereabouts of the shipmaker by return.'

Joz grinned. 'That's a shame,' he said laconically. 'He won't be making old Lazlo very happy when we get back and he's still received no word of Danson.'

Lazlo, the captain, appeared to be rather unhappy already.

Mam looked suddenly and unaccountably delighted. 'We may not get our pay for this one, but for my part I'm really quite looking forward to seeing his lordship's face when I tell him his precious shipmaker's been kidnapped by the Rockfall clan!'

Joz and Knobber exchanged glances. Here was an unexpected snippet of news. There were times when they suspected that the way Mam managed them so efficiently was by withholding crucial information from them. After all, as she kept pointing out, knowledge was power, and somehow she always seemed to have more knowledge than the rest of them.

Erno rose before the dawn, every muscle stiff with the anticipation of what he must do that day. He ducked out into the grey light of a world balanced precariously between night and day and as quietly as he could, given the crunching of the pebbles under his boots, made his way across the little shingle beach and down to the water's edge. It was a chilly morning. In it he could sense the leading edge of winter: something he had never previously experienced in the southern continent. It would be a lot milder here than it was at home, he mused, watching his breath ghosting out into the air. They probably had no snow at all in this area; even sleet would melt away as soon as it touched ground that had been charmed by the sun all summer long. Whereas in the Westman Islands the snow came down in flurries, tumbling out of the sky in a great swirling chaos as if Sur himself had upended a gigantic sack of eider feathers all over the world, and settled itself determinedly across the land for a whole season at a time. As a child, fostered by Aran Aranson at Rockfall, Erno would be the first to rise in the mornings before any of the rest of the household were stirring, always knowing with some inexplicable primal instinct when snow was in the air. He loved to stand out in the enclosure with his face turned up to meet those first spiralling flakes, to feel them brush the warm skin of his cheeks and gather like moths on his hair and cloak. Winter was when Rockfall was at its most beautiful, when snow covered the fields and the uplands in a perfect, clean, enveloping swathe of white that shimmered and sparkled in the early light and ice bound both land and water, turning lakes and ponds and even the fringes of the coastal sea into a churned, wrinkled, translucent solid that would bear the weight of gulls and geese and seals and even, if you were lucky, the weight of a boy moving quickly on long wooden shoes bound with hide and greased with walrus-oil. The purity of a Rockfall winter had never ceased to amaze him, even living with it as he did every day, surrounded by others who complained about the bitter cold and the smoky hall and the dried meat and salted fish that became their sole diet in those hard months and spun yearning tales around the fire at night of lands where the sun shone constantly, things called pomegranates grew on trees and the wheat came as high as your shoulder. But for Erno, nothing could match the sight of the sky above the Blue Peak as the sun set on a Last-Moon afternoon: how it gave way from a luminous pale blue that mirrored back the white of the snow at the crest of the mountain to the delicate purple of budding heather and thence to a rose-pink so fragile that the bowl of the sky looked as though it might shatter like an ice skin if even the smallest bird flew across it. Once, feeling foolhardy, but driven by some inner compulsion he could not name, he had climbed up onto the slopes of the Blue Peak just as the sun was finally dipping out of sight, even though he had known he would have to make the long, dangerous descent in the dark. Seated on a granite boulder, as close to the top of the world as he had ever been in his life, he had taken out one of the skeins of twine he carried with him for such purposes and tied into it the knots that would forever remind him how smoky trails of scarlet streaked the blue sky; how the low bank of cloud that hung over the western end of the island was limned with a deep, firecrest gold; how plumes of vapour from the hot springs below him had streamed out across the frozen peat-hags and ancient, laval outcrops like the spirits of the island, released into the darkening air.

He fingered that twine now, braided as it was around his left wrist, where he had tied it on that long-ago night, and remembered the scene so clearly that he could almost feel the hairs in his nostrils prickling with ice.

It was time to go home to Eyra.

'He's *where*?'

Rui Finco's voice, normally so well modulated, so controlled and refined, rose to a howl of outrage.

Mam leaned back in her chair, tilted it so that the two supporting legs screeched on the polished wooden floor and rudely swung her feet up onto the Lord of Forent's priceless Gilan oak desk. Her boots – vast, unstructured and covered in seven kinds of unnameable filth – made a striking counterpoint against the neat piles of books, the carefully tied rolls of parchment, the map set square with the lower righthand corner; the single ink dish and pot of cut quills.

'Rockfall, my lord, in the far Westman Isles, home to Aran Aranson and his clan.'

The Lord of Forent frowned. 'Aranson?' A vague memory stirred – a dark man in a temper, with piercing eyes, a close-cropped beard, long dark hair shot through with grey and an arrogant manner. 'Aranson . . . whose daughter we burned? The little witch who climbed Falla's Rock?'

Mam nodded grimly. She saw no advantage to be gained in telling him Katla Aransen had survived that ordeal; was informing him of the likely whereabouts of the shipmaker precisely because there was nothing he could do about it, Rockfall being so very remote across the expanse of the Northern Ocean and so out of his reach.

Rui paced the room, digesting this new piece of information. Then he turned back, his face dark with fury. 'And get your damned feet off my desk!'

Mam cocked her head sideways, gave him a slow, indolent smile, then very carefully and deliberately removed her feet. Little scuffs of mud and who knew what else marked the pristine surface of the desk. The lord was hardly likely to stoop to clean up after her himself, but it gave her a small, childish pleasure to think of him having to call a slave in to do it, and for that slave to intuit the circumstances whereby a significant smear of dogshit had made its way onto the prized furniture of this Istrian noble.

Rui crossed to the desk and studied the map intently, trying to keep his temper at bay. It was an old map he had helped himself to out of the great library at Cera; where it had lain so dusty he doubted anyone would notice it was missing. It was a beautiful piece of work, and so antique that it referred to Jetra as Ieldra, the ancient name for the Eternal City before the Istrians had crossed the Tilsen River during the Long War and driven their enemy out of that rich agricultural land, ever northwards until there was nowhere left for them to go other than to take ship and head out into the unknown. No islands were marked, of course. Beyond the northernmost tip of Istria, at Hedera Port, there was nothing but a pale parchment wasteland marked, unhelpfully, 'uncharted waters'. He looked up to find Mam watching him, one eyebrow raised quizzically.

He glared at her. It was insupportable to be made to feel a fool by a common mercenary; and worse, so much worse, to be made to feel so by a woman. He rolled the map away hastily and took a deep breath.

'So why did you not pursue them to this . . . Rockfall . . . and take the man by force?'

'My orders were to return here with the shipment before Bast's Day, which is, by my reckoning, three days hence. To have pursued the Rockfallers to the Westman Isles and thence back to Forent would have added at least another ten days to the voyage; besides, it was only rumour that Morten

Danson was taken there: it could have been pure coincidence that the Rockfall contingent and the shipmaker disappeared at the same time.'

The southern lord's expression told her exactly what he thought of that line of reasoning. 'And did you not stop to think for a moment that it was hardly worth the expense or the trouble of bringing the damned armaments back here without the man to build us the ships so that we might *use* them?'

Mam's eyes gleamed. 'As a mere sell-sword, my lord, I am paid to fight, not to think; and since your lordship did not honour me with any explanation as to the link between the two cargoes I was sent to fetch, I carried out the commission as best I was able under the circumstances.'

The Lord of Forent gritted his teeth. 'I should have known better than to trust such a task to an ignorant barbarian.'

'So your lordship thinks he might have achieved his goal had he sent a team of loyal Istrians in to the northern capital, does he? Who would, of course, have been as unobtrusive as whores at a temple—'

'Get out!' Rui roared.

'Not without our pay.'

'Your pay?'

'I will not ask you for the entire sum, but given that we have brought half the shipment back as contracted, I am sure your lordship will concede that he owes us half the monies due—'

'You shall have not a single cantari from me for this fiasco. You'll be lucky if I do not have you flayed alive and your remains dangled over the harbour for the gulls to pick at.'

Mam took a step forward and thrust her face at him. 'If I'm not out of here and back to my men unscathed by the hour of the Second Observance, Joz Bearhand will be seeking audience with the Duke of Cera to offer him information in the matter of your relationship to the northern king . . . My lord. I am not so sure the members of the Ruling Council will welcome you so warmly if they feel your ambitions and loyalties do not tally closely with their own.' She had been nurturing this suspicion ever since the night of the Gathering, when she had unceremoniously dumped Ravn Asharson in the Lord of Forent's pavilion, made her own keen observations and overheard a conversation between the two men that she could never have been intended to understand. She had stored that conversation away, and like a magpie sifting through the shiny things it had collected for its nest, had brought it out again and again into the light until she thought she had made sense of it all. It was a calculated risk, to name her suspicions now so baldly, and to trust that the Duke of Cera was not one of the Lord of Forent's inner circle; but all she had heard of the leader of Istria's Ruling Council led her to believe the old man was too straight a traditionalist to be involved with an ambitious chancer like Rui Finco. She had had dealings with men like the Lord of Forent all her life: she knew the sort of cronies they made. It was a high card to play for what might seem an insignificant trifle: but the eight thousand cantari the man owed them was no small matter. Nor was that where it ended.

With intense effort, Rui maintained the coolest demeanour he could manage. He cursed himself for underestimating the woman's intelligence, and her nerve. He would have to play this one very carefully indeed. His mind spun through the possibilities. Call her bluff and order the castle guards to run her through here and now? He'd had the good sense to have her disarmed before she entered his chambers; but he suspected she could still take down his personal guards with her bare hands, and likely him as well, even if she did not have other weapons concealed about her person (and no Istrian was likely to want to soil their hands searching a barbarian woman too closely: Falla knew what dubious crevices such a woman might hide a small blade in). And if she meant what she said about dispatching her man to the Duke of Cera . . . Haro would surely never take a sell-sword's word against his own, unless . . . Perhaps he should pay her what she demanded, then send an assassin to do away with her and her small troop in the night. Yes, that would be best. That lanky hillman from Farem, the one with the ritual tattoos on his face. Persoa: that was his name. Varyx had used him to remove that entire family in Sestria when they had defamed him . . . He would not come cheap, but he could recoup the money from what he was to give the woman now. Eight thousand? He was tempted to give her the lot to make her go away, but if he did not bargain hard enough she would surely suspect him.

He mustered a rueful smile. 'Well, maybe you have some of the right of it. You can't possibly expect me to hand over a full half for such a miscarried job, though—'

'Eight thousand,' Mam said firmly.

'I'll give you six.' He could not be bothered to play out this scene again.

'Eight.'

Rui took a huge key out of the desk drawer, strode across the room and unlocked a brass-bound chest in the alcove beneath the shrine to the Goddess. He came back to her bearing three bulging bags of coin.

'For Falla's sake, woman, take the six and think yourself lucky.'

Mam gave him her best grin, the one that exposed the silver-capped molars with the double points. 'Done.'

The Lord of Forent watched her saunter from the room, braids swinging. The coins chinked with every step she took.

'You will be,' he promised grimly. 'You will be.'

Nine

Quietus

Selen Issian pushed the hair out of her eyes and struggled to wake. Lately she had been finding it hard to rouse herself; harder still to forsake the comfort of the thick cloak that enveloped her and face the prospect of dragging herself out into the cold dawn air and down to the cove's edge to check the fishlines Erno set every night. What little light that seeped through the small cracks in the shelter the northerner had rigged for them from the upturned boat, the close-packed wall of stones and the handfuls of moss and fern that filled the gaps was this morning grey and thin and particularly uninviting.

Selen turned over, pulling the cloak more snugly around her shoulders, closed her eyes and tried to catch the trailing fringes of the dream that had wrapped her. In that other place she had been sitting on the top of a steep hill with a tall stone cold against her back and the wind whipping her hair back and forth, which made her aware that she wore no veil. She was watching a black dog trying to herd a flock of straying sheep which veered crazily first to the right, then sharply to the left as if they owned but a single mind between them, and every time they dodged like this, the dog howled its irritation and bounded at them, snapping its jaws furiously. She had been drowsily watching the animals zigzagging across the cropped turf – tiny white running stitches in a great, undulating cloth of green – before surfacing from her sleep, and had noted how when the dog ran too fast or barked too loudly it sent its charges into such panic that she had wanted to go down the hill to the dog and calm it, speak to it in a soothing voice, persuade it to slow its pace and break the mad pattern of chase and flight it had set up. Now, the dream beckoned her back, pulling softly at her consciousness and she let it take her. A moment later, the air felt thinner, less easy to breathe: it made the blood rush to her cheeks. It was very clear, very sharp: superreal. Details lurched up at her: moss and stone and twig; the virid green of the pasture, the unnatural size of the dog. She got to her feet and felt how the world felt tilted and skewed, as if it had suddenly become a less welcoming place. Standing up, the wind howled around her and she realised that she was wearing nothing but a thin white shift which plastered itself to her body, revealing every jut and contour. The dog stopped dead in its tracks and watched her and the flock milled around, not sure what to do with themselves now that they were no longer being chased. The black dog's scrutiny was avid: disturbing. Selen felt concern; but her feet carried her down the path towards it even though her mind urged her to turn back, to wake up. Only a body's length away now, she saw how the dog panted and rolled its eyes: strange eyes for a dog – too expressive, too . . . human . . . The whites that presented themselves on either side of the irises, which were a deep, rich brown flecked with gold, were bloodshot and yellowing, like the eyes of a man deep in his cups and fighting mad. Flecks of white foam showed at the corners of its mouth. Despite her terror, she found herself reaching out to touch the beast's head and it snarled at her, elastic black lips curling back to expose jagged teeth; and it was then that she noticed the collar of sardonyx it wore, all rust and brown. Something jagged in her memory. As it sank its teeth into her, she remembered where she had seen that banded chalcedony before. She opened her mouth to scream and then the black dog had her by the arm. She felt the points of its fangs jar the bones in her forearm, felt its jaws bear down . . .

A moment later, she was cast to the ground, and there was another dog standing over her: a white dog, larger than the first, and she cowered away in terror.

This time Selen came properly awake.

In her mind, she could still feel the dog's hot breath on her and hear the snarl in its throat; but here, in the sheltering faering, the only hot breath was her own, and the only sounds she could hear were the distant cries of gulls as they wheeled across the bay and the gentle susurrus of the waves. Even so, the anxiety remained with her as a small, tight feeling in the pit of her stomach. Something was different. Something was wrong.

She crawled outside the shelter, convinced that some disaster had befallen Erno; but when she stood up and scanned the cove, there he was, at the far end of the beach, gazing out to sea as still as a stone carving of himself. She saw him glance at her and then away, which did not make her feel any happier. Sighing, she made her way down to the water's edge. Behind the rocks there, she squatted out of his sight and relieved herself. Then, hoicking up the red dress, now streaked with dirt and ragged around the hem, she walked into the lapping waves and washed herself as thoroughly as she could manage. The salt would dry and streak, but they did not have enough fresh water to spare for such luxuries as washing, as Erno so frequently reminded her. She washed her face and tasted the brine. She ran wet fingers through her sticky, wind-roughened hair. Then she scooped up a handful of water and washed carefully between her legs. As they had these past two months and more, her fingers came away unsullied by the blood she would usually have expected to see on the day before the moon was full.

It was no longer a surprise.

She pushed the realisation of what this might mean away

as hard as she could and, setting her jaw, picked a path
gingerly across the reef to check the fishlines Erno had set
the night before. Three mackerel had attached themselves to
the northerner's well-made hooks. They lay quiescent in the
dark water below the rocks, their cat-striped skins flickering
as the waves passed over them. Selen felt a moment's pang of
misery for their doomed condition; then she hauled the cold,
wet lines in hand over hand and carried their catch back to
the beach.

By the time she returned, Erno had moved away from
his stance on the far rocks. She scanned the cove, and was
surprised to find him dismantling the shelter. He had pushed
the faering off the stones and onto its keel so that it now lay
the right way up on the shingle, a boat again rather than a
roof. She had been so immersed in hauling in the fish, so
determined not to think her own thoughts, that she had not
heard the noise this must have made. Now he was engaged
in kicking the stone wall down, giving to the task rather
more energy than it required. Rocks skittered and bounced
off one another. The dry, thick sound of them echoed off
the cliff walls. Moss and furze scattered in the wake of his
flying feet.

Their belongings – few as they were – had been piled up
separately.

Dropping the lines and the mackerel, Selen covered the
ground towards the northerner in an awkward, lurching
run.

Behind her, the mackerel flopped helplessly, drowning
in the air.

'What are you doing?'

Her tone came out more imperious than she had intended.
Erno spun around. The effort and the chill wind had brought
a hectic flush of red to his cheeks. His blue eyes looked wild
and hazed. There was a determined set to his jaw she did
not like.

'I'm leaving,' was all he said.

Then he turned his back to her and picked up his sack, his knife and his fishing kit and stowed them under the crossbench at the stern of the faering.

Selen felt the blood drain from her face. Hastily, she gathered her own pathetically small pile of acquired possessions – the cloak, purloined from another washing line; the underwear she had fashioned of strips torn from a stolen shirt; the belt-knife Erno had given her for gutting fish with; the long spoon he had carved for her after she had complained at having to eat with her hands – and bundled them into the other end of the boat. Erno stared at them, then at her. Then he bent and fished the things out, and tossed them down onto the beach.

'Alone. I'm leaving alone.'

This pronouncement flew past her like a bird, barely regarded. He couldn't possibly mean what she thought he had said. She frowned, tried to form a question: failed; then watched as he shoved the wooden boat with tremendous force down the shingle and into the shallow water. For a moment, the faering grounded itself on a raised bank then, as he splashed after it and pushed at it again, the muscles in his arms and back ridging under his thin shirt with the effort, it sailed off into clear water.

Erno waded after it until he was up to his waist in the waves. Then he grasped the far side of the boat, threw a leg over the gunwale and began to lever himself aboard. The faering rocked in protest and threatened to capsize, but Erno waited until the little vessel found its equilibrium, then completed his manoeuvre.

Without a look back at the shore, he settled himself on the rowing bench and unshipped the oars.

He was abandoning her. Leaving her here, miles from anywhere, without conscience, without a thought.

'No!'

The outrage she felt was astonishing. Adrenalin flooded her system, lending her determination, speed, aggression. Grabbing up the bits and pieces he had cast down on the shingle, she stuffed them under her arm and began furiously to wade after him. The water cleared her shins, her knees, her thighs. She felt its resistance as a momentary irritation and ploughed on, still shouting.

'Come back! How dare you leave me, Erno Hamson! You are a coward, a cur, a barbarian!'

In the faering, Erno braced himself against her words and began to scull away. Selen forged on. The waves lapped at her waist, her breasts, tugged at her robe, made her suddenly buoyant. A moment later, she felt her feet lose contact with the seabed. She kicked in panic, struck out with her arms, lost the bundle of belongings. The fabric of the cloak tangled her thrashing arms. White water sprayed up around her, soaked her hair, filled her mouth. She spat out the water and yelled again:

'Will you let me drown? Will you row out to sea and never once look back?'

She saw the figure in the boat ahead stiffen and she thought he would turn around, but then a wave came over her head and for a moment she could see nothing of the sky but a terrible watery light. Then it was gone, taking the cloak with it, and she was out of her depth, the red robe floating up around her like a pool of blood. She struggled to stay afloat, kicking hard and splashing out with her arms.

'I am pregnant, Erno! If you leave me now you will not just be responsible for the death of the woman you blame for causing Katla's death, but that of a blameless infant, too!'

Down she went again, the water cold and heavy around her. She felt it close over her head, seal her off from all contact with the air, claim her as its own. She sank. Her arms flapped uselessly; her feet scrabbled. The pressure of the sea against her chest felt like someone forcibly pressing the air out of her. Water rushed into her mouth. She felt its cold passage, a horrible invasion, felt herself losing the warmth that made her human and alive. As she began to drown she felt a sudden pang of empathy for the poor mackerel she had left to perish on the beach, drowning in a hostile, unnatural element.

Then the light faded and she felt nothing at all.

Instead of the usual fleapits they stayed in, this night the mercenary troop had been treated by Mam to rather splendid accommodation, which boasted a common room as well as sleeping quarters above the stable belonging to a good inn, close to the smartest whorehouses Forent had to offer; which was saying something. This being Rui Finco's town, the brothels were plentiful indeed, their women famed the length and breadth of Istria for their beauty and their clever tricks. Forent was where the women came to avoid Falla's vengeful fires – for adultery, for impiety, for saying the wrong thing at the wrong time to their fathers, their brothers or their husbands. Rui Finco was known to have a somewhat laxer attitude to such misdemeanours than the other Empire lords and that, in addition to his prowess behind closed curtains, made him popular with the women of Forent, as Doc had learned to his cost.

'All I said to her was that I bet his nose was bigger than his cock, and she kicked me out of bed there and then and refused to take a cantari from me.'

'And had you done the deed with her?'

Doc smiled reminiscently. 'Several.'

Dogo looked contemplative. 'What did you say her name was?'

'Sestrina.'

'And which whorehouse was this?'

'The Tower of Earthly Delights, second left past the market square: has a pair of pink pillars either side of the door. Knobber introduced me to it.'

Dogo patted his pocket and took out his money-pouch. Fat with the coins Mam had earlier doled out among them, it swung smugly back and forth on its leather thong. 'Shan't be needing this, then,' he grinned. Then he tossed it up, snatched it out of the air with his other hand and stuffed it back into his tunic again. 'Still, who's to say I might not wear her out and need to take myself off to another establishment later?'

Joz Bearhand, seated on a bench off to the side where he was engaged with a complicated system of whetstones and assorted cloths in sharpening his many weapons, snorted contemptuously. It was rare that he accompanied his companions on these nocturnal excursions, and when he did, rather than going in to avail himself of the services on offer, he would stand outside the premises, leaning on his sword and eyeing visitors as they went in, 'in case of trouble'. Although the only trouble that came their way tended to be when brothel-owners took exception to Joz's presence giving their customers such pause for thought that many turned away and decided to visit an alternative establishment where they were less likely to be scrutinised by a man who looked like some vengeful giant out of legend, ready to lop their heads off for their lewd intentions. And then Doc and Knobber and Dogo would have to bundle Joz away before he got stuck into his customary lecture on the evils of paying women for sexual congress. It was curious really, that a man who was happily prepared to murder for money would draw the line at the idea of spending a little of his hard-earned coin on having a pretty girl make him forget the troubles of the world for a while, but there it was.

'You be careful with that money,' Mam warned. 'You don't want to be flashing it around too obviously in a place like this.'

She said this wherever they went. Sometimes it was like having your mother along, which felt very bizarre when you were about to go off and visit a whore. Dogo rolled his eyes at Doc, who shrugged. They got used to it.

Dogbreath tapped his left thigh. 'Got me knife,' he said. He tapped his right calf. 'And me other knife.' Then, with a flourish, he produced the two he had secreted down his boots. 'Oops, nearly forgot these.'

'For pity's sake just go!'

'I'm coming with you.' Knobber appeared in the doorway, gleaming and pink from his annual bath. His hair, which he normally wore tied and knotted in a dozen braidlets around his head, to keep it out of the way in a fight, was unbound and still damp and beginning to frizz around his shoulders. He wore his best shirt, the one he had bought off a nomad stall at the Allfair, a pale blue affair with gaudy green and silver piping at the collar. It looked as if he had even passed a hot stone over it to take out the worst of the creases. His pendant lay nestled in the opening of the tunic amongst his copious chest hair. He looked about nineteen, rather than the thirty-odd years he owned to, and about to visit his sweetheart.

'You've taken your cap off,' Doc observed with surprise, glancing down at the truncated stub that was all that remained of Knobber's left hand. Without the stained leather wrapping which the sell-sword usually wore to cover the wound, the appendage looked as vulnerable as a newborn pup: all hairless and puckered and pink. The conjunction with the dark, weathered skin of his forearm was almost shocking. Looking at the soft, pale flesh of the stub, you could almost believe that Knobber might once have owned a childhood away from all the violence and harshness of a mercenary's world.

'It's been itching me,' the tall man said uncomfortably. 'Gia soothes it with her hands.'

'Is that the same girlie you've been seeing all week?'

Knobber blushed to the roots of his beard. 'Aye.'

Dogbreath guffawed. 'I've got a little stump she could soothe—'

'Shut up, Dogo.' Doc cuffed the little man around the head, made him yelp. 'We'll be moving on soon,' he reminded Knobber. 'It doesn't pay to get too tender-hearted about any one of these whorehouse girls. Better to spread your money around, I always think.'

'Sample the full range,' Dogo grinned, unabashed.

Knobber looked offended. 'Some of us know when we've found a good thing. Just because I don't feel the need to find out what's under every skirt in Forent doesn't make me soft in the head. Besides, she's a nice girl: only working where she does out of the worst sort of adversity and ill chance. We've spent a fair while talking, she and I. It's amazing how much we have in common.'

Dogbreath guffawed. 'Aye. Like lying down and humping like rats in a sack—'

This time it was Mam who caught him a whack. 'Shut your hole, Dogo. There's nothing wrong with treating a girl like a human being rather than just a convenient place to stick your tool. Now get out of here and leave me and Joz in peace so's we can make some decisions. Someone's got to do some planning that involves something a little more constructive than deciding which whorehouse to visit next.'

The chill outside took them by surprise and Dogbreath and Doc had an entertaining time teasing Knobber for his refusal to spoil his appearance by wearing his manky old cloak over his fine shirt, or even wanting to crease the thing by the addition of his swordbelt.

'Fine sell-sword you are!' Doc admonished.

'It's only a couple of streets away, and Gia doesn't like to see me wear a weapon. Besides, what's to fear with a couple of bodyguards like you two with me?'

None of them noticed the pair of shadows that detached themselves from the alley behind Cutter's Lane as they passed, nor the movement of another pair in the opposite direction.

*   *   *

Erno gazed down at the body of the woman lying in the bottom of the boat and felt hot tears prick his eyes. It had not come easily to him to abandon Selen Issian, nor to hear the understandable fury in her voice as he had rowed away, but it was all he could think to do at the time. Reasoning with her had achieved nothing and every time he began to think about the sort of life that awaited her return to her family, despite the survival of Tanto Vingo, he felt his mind shy away. It was hardly fair that women in the southern continent should be bought and sold and passed from the hands of one man to another in the way they were, to endure lives of misery and servitude without an iota of choice in the matter, but it was the way life was in Istria; likely the way it had always been and always would be, and therefore not, as he kept reminding himself, something he could change. The situation was not his fault: all he'd done was lend a helping hand.

But if it was not his fault, then why did he feel such guilt? For it was guilt that had driven him to leave with barely a word that morning, guilt that had pushed the faering out into the water; guilt that had made him row away without looking back, without realising that she had waded after him so far that the sea had taken her.

The truth of the matter was, he admitted to himself now (now that it was too late) he had known she was with child for several weeks. He had known it in the way any lad brought up in a large family on a farm would know such things, and without giving the matter a second's conscious thought. Something in him had recognised changes that were taking place in Selen that even she had probably not recognised in herself: in the way she seemed to luxuriate, seeking ever more food and warmth and comfort, as if the tiny life that grew inside her were making a nest of her body. Something in him had noted how her breasts ripened without a lascivious eye, seen how her curves took on ever lusher proportions, and yet had intuited that her gradual expansion was not simply due to the food that kept disappearing, had understood, somehow, that those provisions had not been taken out of simple greed. For he had never once chastised her for stealing from their store, nor for singing her strange little nursery songs, nor for sleeping late and taking over all the cloak in the night. He had certainly been wary of her sudden changes of mood – her temper with him and with her situation – but that he had put down to the way of all women, and particularly to being noble-bred. But when she had cried out to him as the waters closed over her that she was pregnant and that if she drowned he would responsible for two deaths, not one, he had known it to be no more than the simple truth.

Even then, he had hesitated. It was remarkable how much could pass through your mind at such a crucial moment. He had seen himself a year hence, a stranger in a strange land, forced to dye his hair and shave his beard and speak the language of his enemy so that he might be hired to carry out menial jobs in order to provide for a woman and child not his own. And then he thought how things might have been in a different world a year from now, a world in which Katla had not perished and it had been because of no Footloose charm that he had won her love. In his mind's eye, he had seen the sun shining on a smallholding on North Isle, a group of turf-roofed houses at the head of a cove in which fishing boats bobbed at anchor and a fine longship lay in its winter cradle on the strand. On the hills around the hall, sheep and goats cropped grass and grew fat. And in the doorway of the biggest house stood a slim woman with long red hair braided about her head, a baby nursing at her breast. He saw all this with such hallucinatory clarity that for a moment it seemed it might be a true vision of the future and not some impossible dream, but then reality rushed in at him and he realised firstly that even if Katla had not burned, she would never want such a life; and that just thirty feet away from him, a woman was drowning.

He had covered the space between them in three powerful oarstrokes, determining the location by the dim red shadow of the gown that sank with Selen into the depths. And then he had hurled himself overboard and, grabbing that fateful robe, had hauled it up until he was able to catch the Istrian woman by the arms, and though she had hung there, limp and unresponsive, he had somehow fought them both up through the water till his lungs were burning and ready to burst.

It had been a desperate struggle to get her into the faering without overturning it, but terror had lent him immense strength. Then she had lain in the bilges like a great, wet, dead seal, while he remembered how Thoro Twistarm had nearly drowned off Sand Isle the winter before last, and Gar Otterson had roughly pressed the water out of him on the beach there till he had choked and coughed and had the strength to curse the lot of them. A lot of water had come out of her, in big gushes and spurts to begin with, then in weak trickles. And still she did not stir, nor seem to breathe. But when he had touched her neck and her wrist in a terrible panic (all the time a tiny voice chanting in his guilty mind, *you did this, you did this, you did this*) there had been a small flutter of life there, and so he had taken off all his clothes, saving one rag for his modesty, had wrapped her in them as close as he could and had chafed her hands, her face, her feet. Even in these dire circumstances, even knowing that the core of a body's heat resided in the chest and belly, he could not bring himself to put his hands on the more intimate parts of her. And so he sat there, shivering in the chilly wind, watching over her as if the power of his will might bring her back to the world, and fearing all the while that she might be allowing her spirit to simply drift away rather than face the dreadful alternative that coming back to life offered.

*   *   *

'We could try our luck in Cera.'

'We could.' Joz ran the whetstone down the edge of the Dragon of Wen, then rubbed the blade with his oiled cloth and sat back and admired Katla Aransen's artistry for the thousandth time.

'I heard the Duke was assembling troops.'

'He won't take Eyran mercenaries since Cob Merson turned tail on him and took the Duke of Gila's coin at Calastrina.'

Mam considered this. 'Further south, then, maybe? Where there's less competition?'

'Less money, too. Though Jetra might be worth a visit.'

'I wouldn't mind visiting the Eternal City again.'

To Joz's sensitive ear, Mam sounded almost wistful. He glanced up and saw that her eyes had become unfocused, as if they gazed on something far beyond the inn room in which they sat. 'It's a curious place, Jetra,' he said carefully. 'Full of odd folk passing through.'

Mam sighed. 'I suppose they do pass through and rarely stay,' she said at last. She smiled brightly at him, without showing the dreadful teeth. 'Long way to go on a chance, though we'd best move on from Forent, I'd say. I would not trust the lord here as far as I can throw him.'

Joz grinned. 'Still, we got paid, and that's more than I'd expected, given the circumstances. You're a wonder, Mam, for truth.'

Mam tapped the side of her nose. 'I know more than he would like me to know,' she said cryptically, 'and that's what keeps us safe.' She got up, crossed the room and looked out of the window onto the streets below. Outside, revellers wandered unsteadily up and down with flagons in their hands and coin in their purses. 'Should be a good night for the whores,' she said tightly. 'Looks as if most of their customers'll be too addled to get their wicks stiff enough to use 'em.'

Joz grimaced. 'I could sink a few jugs of ale myself. Why don't we take ourselves downstairs and carry on our discussions in the snug?'

Mam folded her arms. 'And who guards the money if we get legless?'

'We could take it with us.'

'We might as well hang a banner out of the window inviting every thief in Forent to help himself as clank through the bar with this lot.'

The mounds of cantari they had accumulated in the past few months – by fair means or foul – lay in a large, Eyran-made wooden coffer. It now contained almost two dozen bags of coin: far more than the two of them could carry without drawing considerable attention to themselves, even if they used all the moneybelts and the cloaks with the hidden pockets.

'Tell you what,' Mam said after a while. 'Why don't you break into the funds and go down and buy us a few jugs of that good red wine they make round here and bring it back up? A meat pie wouldn't go amiss, either.'

Joz got to his feet with alacrity. He opened the coffer, helped himself to a handful of coin and was out of the door before she could change her mind. The Dragon of Wen lay on the bench where he had left it, gleaming in the candlelight.

As the door swung closed, Mam turned and surveyed the town of Forent again. It was not a bad place, she thought. The food was good, and its ambience was a little less stuffy than some Istrian cities, though she did not like its lord, and keeping track of the lads in a town that contained quite so many distractions could prove to be something of a problem. But they'd be out of here tomorrow, and maybe it was time to head south and confront the demon she had encountered in Jetra: if indeed he was still there.

Her reverie was broken by the creak of a floorboard in the room behind her. It was far too soon for Joz to be returning.

She whirled around, knife in hand, but the assassin's blade took her in the side of the neck all the same.

Knobber, Doc and Dogo crossed the market square, and took the second turning on the left past a pair of drunken brawlers. It seemed the lighterman had not yet made it to Tiger Alley to ignite the dozen sconces there, for the street was dark and gloomy, although the Tower of Earthly Delights was apparent about halfway down on the right-hand side where pale porticoes marked its entrance. Knobber ran a hand nervously through his hair.

'Dark,' he noted laconically.

Doc laughed. 'Bet you can find your way blindfold – you've been here every night since we arrived, haven't you?'

'D'you think Mam would let me bring her with us?'

'Gia? You're joking! What can she do, other than f—'

'She's not a whore by choice,' Knobber interrupted grimly. 'She had a decent life before her bastard husband got fed up with her and paid one of his slaves to say she took him as a lover and cast her off by law. If she hadn't got to Forent, she'd have been burned.'

'They've all got some sob-story. There's always some web of lies they've concocted to appeal to your better nature and get a bit more money out of you, and this Gia sounds like she's spun you up as cosy as a she-spider. Just nod and smile and get back to work on her, that's what I say,' Dogo grinned. 'But don't believe it for a second, or you're a bigger fool than you look.'

Knobber stopped dead. When he turned around, moonlight fell full upon the broad bones of his face. 'Say another word about her and you'll be skipping with your guts.'

Dogo shrugged. Then his eyes flickered away from his companion and his face became a mask of ferocity. Snarling with fury, he drew one of the blades strapped to his leg and leapt away from Knobber, who stared at him in bemusement.

It was the last thing he did. A moment later, his face met the cobbled street with a sickening thud and he died wondering what had caused the sudden burning pain in his back and whether Gia would think him disrespectful for turning up with mud on his shirt.

The moodstone on the pendant around his neck changed in swift succession from green to cloudy grey to unsullied white, as if its colour had drained out of it to meet the dark pool that spread out from Knobber's body. Neither of his comrades remarked upon it, for they were fighting for their lives.

When Joz shoved open the door to their common room, his hands wrapped around a trayful of bread and meat and broth, and with two capped flasks of the innkeeper's best wine balanced precariously under each arm, it took him several seconds to make sense of what he saw. Mam was on her knees in the middle of the chamber in front of a wiry, dark man who had her hair caught in his fist, forcing her head back. For an insane moment, Joz wondered whether his troop leader was engaged in an unthinkable sexual act; then he saw the bright gore leaking from her neck and the sheen of a silver blade in the man's right hand. With a roar, he hurled the victuals at the intruder. The tray skimmed Mam's head, raining bread and broth down on her. One of the wine flasks flew wide, but the other caught the man a glancing blow, shattered against the wall behind him and spewed its deep red liquid down the plaster like blood.

Staggering away from her attacker, Mam rounded on Joz, hand clamped to her neck. Blood leaked through her fingers. Broth leaked from her hair. 'What the fuck do you think you're doing?' she croaked. 'Don't try to drown the bastard – stick him with your sword!'

The Dragon of Wen lay glittering on the bench beside

the door where Joz had left it. He could feel the tug
of the metal like the breathing presence of a live thing
behind him. And he could see how the black eyes of
the assassin slid for an instant towards the blade. In that
instant, Joz moved: not for Katla Aransen's finest work, but
straight at the hillman, taking him fast and low in the gut
with his head in a time-honoured and hardly subtle Eyran
wrestling manoeuvre. His left hand clamped itself around
the man's wrist, twisted mercilessly. Bones crunched; the
assassin screamed. The curved southern blade clattered to the
floor and spun harmlessly away. Carried backwards by Joz
Bearhand's powerful momentum, the hillman lost his balance
and fell heavily beneath the mercenary. Joz clamped his knees
down on the man's shoulders and prepared to squeeze the
life out of him; then a moment later found himself falling
sideways, propelled by an insistent kick. By the time he had
come to his feet, the man was dead. Breathing raggedly, Mam
stood over the fallen assassin, propped up by the greatsword
which she had driven so hard through the hillman's chest that
it was buried to the depth of half a hand in the wooden boards.
Fingers caressing the dying wolf that lay strangling in the coils
of the intricately carved dragon etched into the hilt, she stared
down at the foe who had so nearly taken her life, a strange
little half-smile on her broth-and-blood-smeared face. In the
preternatural silence that followed the death, Joz could hear
the steady drip from Mam's wound onto the floor.

'You'd better bind that—' he started, but she put her finger
to her lips.

Footsteps sounded on the stairs below, heavy and
awkward.

With terrifying determination, Mam set her foot on the
dead assassin's chest and dragged at the Dragon of Wen with
what little strength remained to her, working the blade back
and forth so that metal grated repulsively on bone, but it
remained stuck fast. Joz extended his short sword towards

her, hilt first. Mam gave him a mulish look. Then with a shrug she took the weapon from him and stepped away. Joz wrenched the Dragon free in a moment and took up his stance facing the door.

A moment later, Dogo appeared, prodding a tall, cloaked man with a tattooed face before him with his dagger. He was followed by Doc, a body slung over his shoulder.

Mam's legs suddenly gave way beneath her and she crumpled to the floor. Joz was at her side at once; but it appeared it was not solely the loss of blood that had caused her collapse.

'Persoa,' she breathed. 'I thought you were dead.'

The cloaked assassin smiled thinly.

'Several times,' he said in heavily accented Eyran. 'Just like the proverbial Bast, I seem to have nine lives.'

'Must have reached your ninth, then,' Doc growled, dropping Knobber's corpse onto the floor. The dead sell-sword fell with a thud to lie between them like an accusation. The pendant on its leather thong swung clear of the body to rattle on the wooden boards, and its stone as empty as his gaze. 'I thought you might care to question this bastard yourself, since he claims to know you,' he said, turning to Mam. His eyes became round at the sight of her blood-soaked tunic and gaping neck. 'By the seven hells what happened here?' He had never seen his leader wounded before: it shook his faith in the rightness of the world.

Mam gave him her ghastly smile, made all the more ghoulish by the blood on her teeth. Then she wound a kerchief tightly around her neck and crawled over to Knobber. Head on one side, she scrutinised his corpse. 'No swordbelt?' she asked at last.

'He said Gia was scared of his weapon.'

Dogo stifled a tasteless chuckle.

Mam glanced at him sharply, then ran her fingers gently over the dead mercenary's face. When she withdrew her hand, Knobber's eyelids were closed. 'Why'd you bring him back here?'

'I thought you'd want to question him,' Doc repeated. 'Find out who paid him.'

Mam rolled her eyes. 'Not *him*, you fool: *Knobber*.'

Doc exchanged appalled glances with Joz. 'Couldn't just leave him out in the street . . . it wasn't right.'

The mercenary leader levered herself upright and thrust her face at him. 'Right? Since when have we been interested in what's right? We're sell-swords – and Knobber died because he forgot that small fact. No sword – he dies. Simple as that. You die as a sell-sword, you get left where you fall. We don't do funerals: we kill people.' She leaned down and unhooked the pendant from around Knobber's neck, weighed it in her palm, then pocketed it. 'Waste not, want not.'

The hillman made a superstitious gesture. 'Unlucky,' he said.

Mam eyed him with hostility. 'I don't ever remember you having such scruples in your previous life. In fact, I'd go so far as to say you're the least principled man I ever met. Which is saying something. You and Rui Finco make a good team.'

Persoa grinned. Except for the ritual tattoos of his tribe, which ran in complicated whorls and flourishes from chin to brow, he had the face of a young man – smooth skin stretching over strong cheekbones, a disingenuous expression. Laughter lines ran from his engaging smile to the corners of his wide-set brown eyes. The tattoos tended to frighten people, so he had learned early in life how to make people trust him: as a weapon it was more useful than even the best Forent steel. But his eyes were a hundred years old: those eyes had witnessed and stored away sights that would set weaker souls to gibbering. 'I never could fool you.'

'You did pretty well in Jetra.'

'Who was fooling whom? I was enchanted, enraptured; bewitched.'

Mam coloured.

Dogbreath grimaced at Joz Bearhand, who winked. Doc gawped from the prisoner to the mercenary leader, hardly believing his eyes or his ears. Mam and this . . . southerner? Mam . . . bewitching?

'So enraptured that you went out one morning to fetch us bread and kaffee and never came back,' she croaked.

Persoa's eyes went solemn. 'I had no choice.'

'And did you have a choice about taking on this little commission from our Lord of Forent?'

'Had I known—'

'Oh, you knew,' Mam stated grimly. 'You always know.'

Persoa acknowledged the fact with a tilt of the head and a barely perceptible shrug.

'I hope Rui paid you damn well,' Mam snarled.

'He did.' Doc held up a heavy belt lined with bags of coin. He hefted it consideringly. 'I made him take us to this. Haven't had a chance to count the contents, but I'd say there's at least four thousand cantari in here.'

The hillman made a face. 'I would not have accepted less for such a . . . challenge.'

Mam laughed, then winced. 'Didn't have the nerve to take me on yourself, then.'

'Perhaps I did not wish to see you die.'

'I'm so touched.'

'Hami never was as accomplished as he liked to think.'

The fallen assassin's blood had crept across the floor in an ever-expanding puddle. Under the dark tan of his skin, Hami's face had already begun to take on its death-pallor, the cheeks shrinking in on themselves, the eyes staring hollowly up into the rafters. All five sell-swords regarded the corpse dispassionately.

'He nearly took me out,' Mam said softly. 'I must be getting slow and deaf in my old age.' She removed the dagger she wore strapped to her left thigh and tested the blade on her thumb. A thin red line appeared in the skin. She sucked the beads of blood away, looking thoughtful.

'To me, you look as young and as beautiful as you always did,' Persoa said gallantly.

Dogbreath guffawed, then tried to disguise his lapse in social etiquette as a cough.

'Well that's an accurate enough statement, even if it was phrased as slimily as by a southern lord, since I never did look young or beautiful.'

'To me you did.'

'Are you really so desperate to save your neck?' Mam asked curiously, placing the point of the blade under the hillman's chin and pressing hard enough that he was forced to raise his head to expose the entire length of his throat. The tail end of the left tattoo that marked him as one of the Catro clan from the south-east quarter of the Farem Heights curled lazily past his ear and disappeared from view amid the folds of his cloak. Mam ran the blade lightly down his neck, tracing the line of the pattern. The dagger tickled the skin, then reached the fabric of the cloak and slipped abruptly sideways and down. Sheared from its fastening, the cloak slid to the floor around Persoa's feet. Little beads of perspiration popped out onto his brow. Mam grinned. The blade wavered, then continued its journey along the inked design where it ran down the throat and came to rest at the collarbone in a curlicue that completed itself with a delicate bifurcation and three elongated dots. 'I always did like your tattoos,' she said nostalgically.

'I remember,' Persoa said, looking distinctly nervous.

'Do you still have the others?'

It was a pointless question. Once marked by the tribe leader, nothing less than flaying was going to remove a Farem tattoo. The assassin nodded. Mam raised an eyebrow, then slit his shirt fastenings till the fabric gaped open to the waist. Joz whistled. Where above the markings had appeared abstract and stylised, those covered by the man's clothing were figurative and extraordinarily detailed. They depicted a scene from mountain legend: the imprisonment of the god Sirio beneath the Red Peak and the flight of his sibling, the goddess Falla. The tail and hindquarters of her magical cat, Bast, could just be seen disappearing into the waistband of Persoa's leggings. Mam knew the markings well: she had spent many hours tracing them across the hillman's smooth, dark skin. She knew exactly what lay between the cat's forepaws. Ah yes, she remembered that all too well . . .

'Why, Persoa, you remain a work of art,' she smiled. 'It would be a shame to lay such craft to waste.'

The assassin breathed a sigh of relief.

'Though of course I could simply carve the skin from you as a keepsake, to remind me of . . . interesting times.' She looked away from his alarmed face, took in the curious expressions of her troop. 'Shall I spare him, lads, now that we're one down?'

Doc stared hard at the corpse he'd carried back from Tiger Alley. 'I'd sooner run him through and have done with this sorry place,' he said shortly.

Dogbreath polished his knife on his leg. 'I'd be happy to oblige.'

Joz's face remained stony. 'Knobber's dead and there's nothing that'll bring him back. But I guess Persoa was doing the job he was paid to do, same as us: we've all taken the Lord of Forent's money and done worse.'

Mam nodded. 'If we're to steal a ship and get ourselves out of here by morning, we'll need all the help we can get.'

'Steal a ship?' Doc echoed disbelievingly.

The mercenary leader grinned. 'Ah yes, hadn't had time to expound my newly devised plan to you,' she croaked. 'We're going down to the docks with – well, I was going to invest some of our own hard-won earnings in the venture, but since Sur has seen fit to provide us with an alternative source of cantari—' she indicated the money-belt Doc held '—and a remarkably able navigator—' she indicated the hillman '—it would be churlish not to make the most of our good luck.'

'A navigator?' Now it was Joz's turn to be sceptical. 'The man's from the mountains: what on Elda does he know about crossing oceans?'

Persoa bowed his head. 'I have . . .' He paused. The admission he was about to make would get him stoned or burned in regular company in Istria. But Finna Fallsen's mercenary troop hardly counted as regular company. He took a deep breath. 'I have a certain affinity with rock and mineral.'

'And what's that when it's at home? An *affinity*?' Dogo waved a limp wrist at the hillman.

'Among the hill-tribes of the Farem Heights there are those who are born with the magical ability to divine the land: folk who can "see" every aspect of it even when it's hidden from the eye. They call them *eldianni* – "landseers", and Persoa is one of the best. It means he can sense rock – below the water, across the sea, in the middle of a desert. He can follow a mineral vein a hundred miles with his mind; he can feel islands, continents, reefs,' Mam declared with a certain proprietorial pride. 'In Eyra, he'd be prized beyond worth; in Istria, he landed himself in trouble digging crystals and precious stones out of the Golden Mountains as a boy; got most of his tribe murdered or enslaved as a result.'

Doc gave the hillman a fierce look. 'You stabbed Knobber in the back when he was weaponless. But if you can do what Mam just said and not give us any trouble, I'll stomach you.'

Dogo grinned at the assassin. 'Efficient, though, taking him out like that. I'll be watching you.'

'Knobber was a friend of mine,' Joz Bearhand said quietly. 'And there aren't many who've earned that distinction. A man who kills my friend might by definition be regarded as my enemy: and my enemies rarely live long. You'd better prove yourself to be invaluable to our diminished team, or I shall personally rip your throat out.'

Persoa eyed the big man warily. Then he extended his hand. Joz nodded briefly, then engulfed the hillman's wiry hand in his own great paw. 'Welcome to our world.'

The world was red and full of pain, but when she opened her eyes, everything became a desperate, blinding white. She blinked and coughed, blinked again. Red; white; red; white; red. Her chest felt as raw as if it had been laid open to the winds and she was cold to the bone. When she tried to move, she found herself constricted and began to panic. She rolled and wailed and the world rolled with her.

'Selen! Selen!'

Strong hands gripped her shoulders. A face came into view. It was a good face, strong-boned and healthy-looking: a man, with long hair and wind-darkened skin. His blue-grey eyes were anxious. She tried to speak but the words wouldn't come out right. When she struggled again, the man bent and eased her bindings, put an arm under her and helped her to sit up. His shadow afforded her eyes respite. She looked around and realised she was in a small boat, which explained the rolling. It seemed very familiar, while at the same time bizarre in the extreme.

'Thank Sur you're alive! I thought you'd died for sure. I've never prayed for anything and meant it before. Perhaps there is a god, after all.'

She frowned. Sur? Who was Sur? Died? What was he talking about?

'Who are you?' The words came out as an indistinguishable croak. She watched his brow furrow as he tried to understand her. With an immense effort, she concentrated on what she could remember and came up only with the image of a dark man with a hooked nose coming at her with a leather strap and malice in his black eyes. He was not the man she saw before her now; but beyond that piece of information, nothing in the world seemed certain. She tried again. 'Who am I?' This time the words managed to separate themselves into distinct sounds, though why she had asked this particular question, she had no idea, since it was not the one she had originally framed; was not even sure whether she wished to know the answer.

'Selen. Selen Issian,' the man said. 'Don't you remember?'

She shook her head, coughed again. Her throat felt like hot ashes.

Almost as if he read her thoughts, the man offered her a skin of liquid. She took a mouthful and found it was fresh water. She had never tasted anything so marvellous in her life, whatever that life might have been. She laughed. The man looked surprised.

'Selen Issian,' she repeated. 'What a ridiculous name!'

It really wasn't the best day to be trying to make a swift escape from Forent City with a longship stolen from the dangerous lord of that province and a depleted crew of thugs and ne'er-do-wells, though the sun beat down and the sky was a perfect, cloudless blue. But there wasn't a breath of wind to be had and therefore they had had to row the whole damn way until they were out of sight of any likely pursuers. They had, judging by the height that merciless bright gold disc had now attained, been rowing without pause for over three hours, and still the outline of Forent Castle could be seen in the distance behind them as a vague and geometric extension to the tall black cliffs. Mam's arms – as brown and gnarled as old oak – burned with the effort. Her back ached. Her palms felt raw. On the back of her neck – above the bandage – she could feel the hot breath of a man whose presence had once made her knees go weak with desire, though she would never, ever admit to it, to him, or to anyone else. A man, moreover, she reminded herself, who had just caused the death of one of her troop and sent one of his own to dispatch her and Joz. 'Couldn't do it, myself,' he'd said to her softly, head slightly cocked in that confiding way of his that she remembered so well. 'Too many pleasant memories.'

She had nearly killed him on the spot for that insolence alone.

'Over there! See, over there to steerboard—'

Mam jumped, nearly lost her grip on the oar.

The man who had called out was a swarthy sailor who hailed originally from the foothills of the Golden Mountains and had been pressed into service some twenty years before by a predatory Istrian merchant in need of new crewmembers following a disastrous voyage through the infamous storm zone of the Gilan Sea. He had a sore head from the skinful of wine he had drunk at the mercenaries' expense in the Skarn Inn the night before; it made his thickly accented Old Tongue even more impenetrable.

'What?'

The man made an impatient gesture. He was less than pleased to have woken aboard this purloined northern vessel, pressganged onto an oar yet again, but there was coin chinking in his purse and more promised once they reached Eyra and while his new employers were a ramshackle team – a group of Eyran mercenaries and an *eldianna* from the Farem Heights – at least they owned no whip-man like that bastard Oranio. He said something unintelligible in his native language and pointed out across the sparkling water.

Mam shaded her eyes and peered where he pointed. 'A small boat,' she said after a while. 'I think it's a small boat.'

'It's a faering,' Doc said, from the crossbench to her right. 'An Eyran faering.'

'Long way from any shore for a faering,' Joz noted. 'Let alone from Eyra.'

'Take her alongside,' Mam instructed the rowers. 'Quickly now.' Quite what she was expecting to see in the tiny vessel that pitched awkwardly up and down on the gentle swell she did not know; but it certainly was not what they found.

Inside the faering was a big man whose blond hair had at some point been inexpertly dyed black: for in contrast to the parti-coloured locks on his head, the new beard that was sprouting on his chin was so pale as to be white-gold. And beside him sat a black-haired girl in a tattered red dress with huge eyes and a proud neck.

'I know you,' Mam breathed, staring at the man. 'I do: I know you.'

The big man bowed his head, then looked her in the eye. 'Erno Hamson,' he said at last. 'Of the Rockfall clan.'

Joz Bearhand laughed. 'By Sur, life has a habit of making strange knots sometimes!'

'And you?' Mam asked his companion.

'My name matters not,' the dark-haired girl said in a rather stilted form of the Old Tongue. 'I am a free woman, and I shall make my future for myself.'

Mam grinned. 'Good girl. Still,' her eyes dropped to the soft curve of the girl's belly where the red fabric had dried plastered tight against her skin, 'it looks as if someone else had other ideas about allowing you a free hand with your own life.'

Selen blushed. 'You have sharp eyes.' She placed a hand on her belly and sat there for a moment, considering. 'This child shall also choose its future,' she said at last.

'Is it yours?' The mercenary leader asked Erno curiously. 'The baby?'

He looked horrified. 'No . . . no, of course not.'

Mam laughed. 'I like a mystery. And at least you look strong enough to manage an oar. If we don't get some wind soon, we'll be rowing all the way to Halbo. If you'll row with us while the wind fails, we'll offer you passage.'

It was a tough bargain. Erno's heart thumped. This was the chance he needed to return to his homeland, but if it rested on Selen Issian's uncertain temper, they might both be lost, abandoned to the sea once more. He waited for her usual outburst of indignation at the idea of having to carry out any task she might regard as beneath the standing of the daughter of an Istrian noble. If skinning a rabbit was something she would barely deign to do, even to feed herself, how she was likely to react to the idea of being taught to man an oar on a merchant vessel, of being treated like a common crewmember, and in her delicate condition, he didn't dare to imagine. He felt the breath stand still in his chest, heard the mournful wail of a loon as it slid past overhead in search of better fishing grounds, caught a sudden sharp odour of brine and sweat off the clinkered boat that rose above them, and waited.

Selen said nothing. Instead, she got gingerly to her feet, steadied herself with a hand on Erno's shoulder and waited for the faering to stop rocking. Then she stepped to the gunwale, took Mam's extended hand and clambered up onto the merchant ship. For a moment she surveyed her new surroundings blank-faced. Then she grinned. The expression felt unfamiliar to her; but it was as if everything in the world was unfamiliar to her now. She turned back to the mercenary leader.

'I've no idea how to work an oar, but I'm sure you will teach me. My name is Selen Issian, and I can see that this will be the start of my new life.

'I hope you have something more practical that I can wear.'

Ten

The Three

They had had to take a long detour to avoid Gibeon, and now their provisions were running low. Alisha Skylark passed a weary hand across her face, tucked a frond of curly hair behind her ear, took hold of the stone again and tried to concentrate. The crystal was being more than usually uncommunicative this day, the interior it offered to her sore eyes being as streaked and dark and blurry as a rainwashed sky.

'What do you see, amma?'

She almost jumped, Falo had crept in so quietly. What sort of seer was she, that she could not even intuit the comings and goings of her own child?

She held an arm out to the boy, caught him to her and buried her nose in the fragrant black fuzz of his hair. 'Nothing, my honeybee. Nothing at all.'

And that was the truth, and the curse of it. Ever since the old woman, her mother, Fezack Starsinger, had passed on during their journey over the Golden Mountains, howling out something unintelligible about the Three even as she toppled from the wagon, it had been as if the crystal had swallowed her essence and made of it a cloud between Alisha's vision and the far-sights of Elda. As the caravan's scryer, she was proving to be of remarkably little use. The insights the stone afforded her were fragmentary and unsatisfactory: partial glimpses so fleeting that sometimes she could not even determine the town or even the region she was being shown.

Not that any of the company had criticised her for this failure: but Alisha found herself burdened with doubts and fears and a growing lack of faith in the world's providence. She suspected that this mistrust might in some part stem from her parentage; for misgivings were uncharacteristic in one of the true Wandering Folk, who knew with the utmost certainty that their place in the world was unique and ordained, that they each fitted into Elda's fabric like a single perfect stitch in a vast tapestry. But the Istrian soldier who had taken her poor mother by force on the fateful day after her grandparents had unearthed the great crystal was likely a man racked by guilt and unworthiness, qualities his seed had carried into Fezack's womb and thence into the soul of her only child. Or perhaps it was not her fault that the stone was recalcitrant; perhaps it was true what they said: that the really great seeing-stones yielded themselves fully only to those with whom they bonded in life, and that with the death of the principle seer, the gift of the crystal dwindled and dimmed.

But she sensed there was more to it than that. She had begun to find herself uncomfortable in the presence of the great stone, as if it were indeed haunted by Fezack's spirit, or by something worse ... Ever since the incident in the mountains, Alisha had been plagued by the sense that they were being pursued, that somehow Fezack's death into the crystal had opened a doorway somewhere and had allowed something both powerful and possibly malevolent access into the world. But since Falo never showed any fear of the great stone, she was learning to take comfort from that.

'Let me see, amma.'

Falo clambered up onto her lap. He was getting too big to be doing this, she thought, as his hard little feet dug painfully into her thighs, and when she made a small noise of protest, the boy turned his shining face to her and smiled. It was a smile of extraordinary, sunny charm, and at once she was cast back into painful memories of his handsome, charismatic father. Long gone now, of course. Their liaison had been shortlived, and she regretted that. You were not supposed to regret such things, as a nomad, she knew, and took it as further evidence of her mixed heritage.

She watched the boy grasp the crystal with a confidence born of long hours watching his mother and grandmother at their scrying, saw how odd gleams and shadows chased across the planes of his skin like a glamour. Sometimes he looked younger than his six years, eager and wide-eyed and opened out to life. She hoped it would last. She hoped he would have a chance to experience the best that being one of the Wanderers had to offer before he experienced the worst.

'Can you see anything, Falo?'

The lad's expression was one of intent concentration. The tip of his tongue protruded from his mouth; his eyes were round. He shook his head impatiently and shifted his grip on the stone, raising one shoulder slightly against her, as if to exclude her.

Alisha settled back against the wall of the wagon and let the rhythm of the passage lull her. After a moment she closed her eyes. She must try to decide what they should do next, where they might safely go to trade for food. Gibeon had been their best chance; but there had been red streaks in the sky in the morning and Elida had dreamed of buzzards alighting on a corpse. When she had interrogated the crystal, it had offered up a brief glimpse of flames and a woman running, her mouth stretched in a soundless scream; then had gone dark and uncooperative, showing nothing more than a shower of red sparks shooting through its interior like a swarm of fireflies. Three bad omens, she had decided; and they had taken the cattle road to the south of the slave-town and passed into the hills that would take them through to the Tilsen Plain and the villages where their magic samples were less likely to be regarded with superstitious horror. They were likely to go hungry before they reached them, though: all the

supplies they had bartered for at the Allfair were long gone.
The only member of the caravan they had recently lost to this
lack was the ancient yeka, One Eye Brown One Eye Green,
who had released her spirit as they threaded their way back
down through the steep Skarn Mountains, and there they had
buried her; for the Wandering Folk did not eat their own, nor
any flesh.

Their caravan had been constantly on the move for nearly
four moon-cycles now, rarely staying more than one night in
the same place, skirting the towns and villages, trading warily
and selling no charms. They had stopped in Cantara for a
while, since its notorious lord was away in the north, and
the people of the town seemed more relaxed about trading
with nomads in his absence. Some of the dancing women
did good business there, for the town had no whorehouse
and the sight of a naked female face was a great novelty
to those younger men who had not yet made the annual
journey to the Allfair, and many of them had stayed, reducing
the caravan further. They ate well in Cantara, and received
generous gifts from the lady at the castle, too, from the
lord's elderly mother, Constanta Issian. This benefactress
had sent out spiced wines and savoury rice dishes to them,
a great basket of freshly baked sweet-cakes and pastries full
of dried fruits. It was interesting, Alisha thought now, that
she had selected the food so thoughtfully. She had sent out
no killed meat, no fish or game. It was possible that the
Lady of Cantara spent her time in the library, reading of
their customs in one of the ancient books that told of such
things, but Alisha had seen her briefly, in the crystal, and
she suspected the lady's knowledge came from other origins
entirely.

'Oh!'

The child's exclamation brought her sharply from her
reverie.

'What is it, Falo? What can you see?'

'Look, amma: look there.' Falo marked the spot with a careful finger.

Alisha craned her neck. All she could make out was a swirl of movement in the globe, and a flash of light, as if she were glimpsing a bright fish swimming in the depths of a murky pond. She frowned and placed her hands one on either side of her son's. The great stone felt warm to the touch, and at first she thought this was due to the transferred heat of Falo's hands; but then the crystal began to buzz, so that the bones of her forearms juddered and throbbed. She narrowed her eyes, forced her mind open to the stone. And then she was falling into its centre . . .

A great, green-gold eye held her gaze. Its pupil was vertical, a shining black slit amid all that luminous colour. Under its rapt inspection, Alisha felt herself go hot, then cold. The eye blinked, once, then withdrew as if to allow her to gain perspective and she found that she was staring into the face of a cat. It was no small domestic creature this, though: no family pet that had wandered into the vicinity of another far-seeing stone and pressed its curious muzzle at the crystal as it might on seeing its reflection in a puddle. No, this was another order of cat entirely. It towered over the crystal globe on the carved wooden table before it as an eagle might loom over a mouse, and its eyes were ancient and intelligent. Its fur was as black as night and when it opened its mouth to roar, the interior of its maw appeared as hot and fiery as the heart of a fire.

No sound emanated from the crystal, but deep in her head, like the ghost of an itch, Alisha heard a voice.

Alisha, it said.

It knew her name. Alisha found that she was trembling.

Alisha, hear me. We are all Three in the world, it said. *The Power is here, but divided. The Lady is taken north; the Lord lies in his prison of stone. And I, who am full of the Power, find myself drained for petty trifles and cruel play. She does not know herself; he cannot free himself, and I am in the hands of incompetents, fools and those who walk upon the surface of Elda when they should have passed beyond—*

The voice ceased abruptly and the perspective in the globe flickered and slid sideways.

When the cat appeared again it was tiny, and it seemed agitated. Behind it, a large shape moved in shadow.

Jetra, the voice came again in her mind, and its timbre was the same as when the cat had been vast. *They are taking me to the Eternal City—*

The crystal in the chamber moved, rose into the air. A hand appeared around it, then a face. Alisha cried out and took her hands off the stone.

'Amma? Amma?'

Falo was staring up at her, his eyes huge and round.

'It's all right, my sparrow,' she said shakily. 'It's all right.'

She sat there with her arms around him and waited for her pulse to stop racing. The crystal sat glowering on the table before them, its surfaces gone opaque and unreflective once more.

'Did you see the cat, amma?' Falo asked excitedly. 'Did you hear it talk? I did not know that cats could talk. Can I have a talking cat?'

Alisha jerked upright. 'You heard it speak?' she asked unnecessarily.

Falo nodded. 'It wants us to go to Jetra,' he said cheerfully. He thought for a moment. 'Perhaps we can get a talking cat in Jetra.'

His mother smiled, though anxiety gnawed at her.

'Perhaps,' she said. It seemed the easiest thing to say.

Eleven

From the Depths

Katla turned her face into the wind and felt the airborne brine thrown up by the charging waves sting her skin. Her chin-length hair – too short to tie back out of her eyes – whipped her cheeks painfully, but her eyes were sparkling and her hands gripped the good wood of the *Snowland Wolf*'s prow more for thrill than for safety. She had begun to notice that she could feel the connection between the land and the ancient oak planking *through the motion of the sea*. It was not something she could ever have explained to anyone else without having them think her mad, but it was oddly exhilarating. She had never felt so alive. A good easterly filled the sail so that the wolf depicted there seemed swelled with pride at the capture of his prey: a great writhing red dragon, its tail looped extravagantly in and out of the wolf's legs and all around the border of the oiled cloth. They would be home in four days – less, if this big wind persisted – but she wished they could just keep sailing until they fell off the edge of the world.

It was not that she dreaded the return to Rockfall – as another disobedient daughter might have done; but then, Katla had never really regarded obedience as a major priority – but that the prospect of a winter on the land, with no excitements to look forward to at least until the spring and the launch of the new ship, was becoming a grim thought. In the last half year her life had been a dramatic round of triumphs and disasters. It had been a life in which nothing could be taken for granted. It was, she reflected now, rather like the business of cliff-climbing: there was always some unexpected obstacle, some lurking peril, some lucky hold to be found, while beneath you the sea roared and paced back and forth like a hungry wolf waiting for you to make an error and fall into its maw. She suspected she was becoming rather addicted to the edginess of this sort of existence; the delicious scariness of not knowing what would come next was so much more fun than the endless round of winter chores and cooped-up company that awaited her at home.

But at least work on the expedition ship could be started, the ship that would carry her out of home waters and into the icebound seas of the far north. Now that would be an adventure. She would have to be patient and carry out her dull duties well enough that her father would have no excuse for leaving her behind. He would surely, she thought, be delighted with the ease and success of their mission. Every time she thought about their wonderfully skilful abduction of the shipmaker, the swift departure, the amazing lack of pursuit, she laughed aloud and hugged herself with glee. She could just envisage the excitement that reports of their return from the lookouts posted on the Hound's Tooth would elicit, could picture her father's delight when he saw the *Snowland Wolf* round the ness and sail triumphantly into the harbour, followed by the two great barges from the shipyard stacked high with the finest oak to be had in all of Eyra. The barges made heavier weather of the passage than Tam Fox's vessel; even shading her eyes now, she could barely make them out in the distant haze behind them; but they were seaworthy and strong and sailed by two competent captains Tam had with his usual foresight taken on in Halbo, men who knew their way through the treacherous channels that led into Rockfall and could be depended on to set a fair course even in a fog.

She turned around to survey their captive. Morten Danson

huddled uncomfortably amidships, his knees drawn up to his chin, his eyes closed against the world, his arms gripping the massive mastfish against which he pressed his cheek as if it were the only solid place that he could imagine in all this churning, rolling, inconstant universe. Since they had left Halbo, he had refused to take a single bite of food from anyone. Katla presumed that Danson meant his gesture to be taken as a noble protest at the ignominy of his abduction; but she suspected that it had rather more to do with the fact that he had neither sea-legs nor a sea-stomach, since even the water he drank so sparingly seemed to come back up again with regular monotony as a thin, pale trickle of vomit. Ironic really, she mused, that a shipmaker could be so profoundly unsuited to life on the ocean.

Morten Danson was not the only one suffering. Beside her, there came another muffled groan followed by a disturbing gulping sound. Katla found herself grinning uncharitably.

'Oh Jenna, poor Jenna – I thought it was only your hair turned green!'

The *Snowland Wolf* hit another swell and her friend grimaced horribly. Jenna Finnsen had been holding back the contents of *her* stomach these past few days: Katla had never seen anyone so determined not to spoil their clothing; but it was a wasted effort, since Jenna's fine blue robe – the only thing of her own she now possessed since being spirited away from the feast at Halbo with only the clothes she wore on her back, despite her complaints – was already spotted with salt-stains from the inevitable spray caused by the passage of the ship. What Jenna did not yet know, since there were no mirrors on board the vessel, and since no one had mentioned it, was that a very fine dollop of gullshit had streaked its way down the back of the garment, adhering itself to the weft of the velvet all the way from the shoulder to the hip. Sur knew what the bird had eaten that had disagreed with it so: it was a truly prodigious amount. Still, Katla reasoned, it was Jenna's own fault, since she had refused the loan of any of the suitable gear that Katla and others among Tam Fox's crew had offered her when she set foot on the ship, exclaiming in horror at the unflattering cut of the breeches, the salt- and sweat-stiffened shirts, the serviceable leather jerkins. 'I can't wear that!' she had cried when Katla shook out a crumpled, but relatively clean, tunic of pale green linen. 'It'd make me look so washed out!' It would, Katla reflected, have gone rather well with her complexion at the moment.

Katla knew why Jenna behaved so. It was out of vanity, yes; but not a vanity that was born of an overweening sense of her own beauty, but rather more out of anxiety, an anxiety that seemed always to revolve around some man or another; at the Allfair, when she had foolishly taken the nomad woman's hair-charm that had turned her golden tresses into the unfeasible likeness of a cornfield, mice and all, it had been born of her obsession with Ravn Asharson; now, Katla had more than an inkling that her brother lay at the vortex of Jenna's thoughts. Their reunion had not been quite the happy event she had hoped for.

'Feeling poorly, missy?'

It was Urse again, Tam Fox's lumbering great deputy. He seemed to have taken quite a shine to Jenna, and although on the first day she had squealed at the sight of his ravaged face, she seemed to have got used to its bizarre contours and was not doing a great deal to discourage him. Katla watched her now as she simpered and protested that no, she was fine – just a little tired and chilled – and the big man offered her his cloak, saying that it was a shame to hide such a pretty form, but that he couldn't stand to see her shiver.

She rolled her eyes. Jenna could be a flirtatious little minx.

Halli Aranson scooped up the knucklebones in his huge fist, closed his fingers over them and shook them together so that they rattled hollowly. He was trying to concentrate on the game, but his mind kept wandering away from it like an errant lamb. He had already lost eight cantari to Tam Fox and he knew he should stop, since the mummers' leader was a proficient cheat who owned not a shred of conscience in his dealings with friends or foes; but to stop meant getting up off the sack of grain he was sitting on and moving past Jenna Finnsen, who was standing just a few feet away at the gunwale, smiling up at some huge bear of a man; and he just did not know what to say or do.

He had been shocked rigid to find his erstwhile sweetheart on board the *Snowland Wolf*: it was, quite literally, the last place on Elda he would have expected to find her, and not just because of the rumours of her forthcoming wedding in the capital. Jenna, for all she was the daughter of the King's dead shipwright, hated the sea and would never voluntarily set foot on a vessel unless it were under the most exceptional circumstances. As he had steered the first barge up along the coast from Halbo, on his way to the rendezvous with Tam Fox's ship, he had been in a sombre mood. Here he was, he thought, stealing timber and men and tools – the theft of any of which might land him in an unpleasant lawsuit – so that his father could take him on some damnfool expedition which was likely either to kill him or make him a man rich beyond his most extravagant imaginings. And if the latter were the case, it would all be for naught, since his heart's desire would be wed to another.

So when he had seen that unmistakable flag of golden hair blowing in the wind beside his fox-maned sister, he had thought he was suffering from a sea-dream, one of those strange miasmas that steals over a sailor's soul when he has been on the ocean for too long without sleep or sustenance. Except that he had both eaten and slept perfectly well and against all the odds.

On board, Katla had run to meet him, bubbling and

fizzing like Old Ma Hallasen's mad cat, dragging her friend reluctantly behind her. 'Do you see who I have here, Halli? Pretty Jenna – do you see? I saved her! I rescued her from being married to that stinky old goat!' She had capered around them until Halli's head spun. 'She's all yours, brother, to have and to hold, stolen right out from under the nose of the King (not that he'd notice if you stole his throne from under him, the way he looks at that pale nomad queen of his) and some thin, rich old buzzard of a suitor! I *improvised* – I think that's the word Tam Fox used, after he used a whole load of ruder ones – dropped her down a hole in the floor of the Great Hall down into the cellars, and then we were away, and here she is! Don't say I never give you anything!'

Halli had stared from Katla's shining eyes to Jenna Finnsen's sweet, upturned face and felt his heart expand and thump painfully. He had opened his mouth to say something, then been unable to utter a single word. And Jenna, mistaking his confusion and silence for something worse, had dropped her eager glance from him and stepped away as if scalded, blushing to the roots of her hair. In the end, he'd managed to greet her gruffly, then had made his escape, mumbling something about having to find Tam Fox and report in. And ever since, though all the fine words he knew he should have said to her had he not been caught so horribly unawares tumbled through his mind over and over again, he had not been able to bring himself to address her at all.

He had seen how other men had no such inhibitions. He had watched Tam Fox make her giggle, had listened grimly while Tam's huge, ruin-faced lieutenant clumsily paid her compliments about her hair and her hands and her pretty shape; and had clenched his jaw and cursed himself for being a fool for saying nothing. But it was as if some old witch-woman had laid a curse on him: gone was the confident, cheerful young man who had courted Jenna at the Allfair and teased her for kissing the image of Ravn

Asharson in the mirror he had given her; and in his place was
the tongue-tied lump she had once accused him of being.

He threw the bones and watched them both land,
unsurprisingly, on their lame side.

Tam Fox laughed. 'Ten cantari!' He reached down and
picked up the bones, tossed them into the air and caught them
neatly. As he jiggled them around his palm, his big square
fingertips caressed the polished brown curves and jags as if he
were imbuing them with magic. Perhaps, Halli thought, he
was. He had never seen the mummers' leader lose at knucklebones, and though it might just be that he had a knack for
throwing them so that they always landed nose-up, somehow
Halli doubted it. There was more than met the eye with Tam
Fox. He was as crafty and as elusive as his namesake and his
luck was supernaturally good, whether it was in the matter
of games, stratagems, or women. Katla was probably the only
one who had ever knocked him back, Halli thought.

'Ten cantari, my man!' Tam grinned, his teeth sharp and
white amidst the complex braids of his beard. 'What's the
matter with you today? It seems a gull's got your luck, a cat's
got your tongue and a bear's got your girl!'

Halli smiled ruefully and made to reach into his money-
pouch to settle the debt.

'No, wait!' The mummers' leader gripped him by the arm.
'I have a better idea. Let's make it double or quits.'

Halli shook his head. 'I've no skill for this game, nor any
wish to lose more to you.'

Tam Fox laughed. 'I have something different in mind.'
His eyes gleamed. 'It's more a bargain than a game of chance.'
He leaned close to Halli and said something in a low voice.

Halli blinked in surprise and his brows became a single
black line of furious concentration. For a moment it looked
as if he might hit the mummer; then his face brightened. 'All
right,' he said. 'You're on.'

*　　*　　*

Katla left her friend to Urse's tender mercies. Despite his size, he wasn't harmful: besides, what could anyone get up to under open skies on the *Snowland Wolf*? The only shelter was the ablutions tent, and that was hardly conducive to romance. Behind her, she heard Jenna's laugh tinkle like a ewe's bell and watched her brother's head come up sharply out of his conversation with the mummers' leader and his dark gaze fix itself hungrily upon his sweetheart.

Poor Halli.

Match-making was not Katla's forte; but it was just plain irritating to see two people who clearly cared for one another behaving so stupidly. She resolved to do whatever she could during the voyage to bring them together. The idea of spending the winter in close quarters in the steading at Rockfall with the pair of them trying to avoid one another was too ridiculous to imagine; although it had to be admitted that spending the winter with the two of them making eyes at each other and whispering secretly in corners might be even worse.

She stepped over a coil of rope lying on the deck like a sleeping serpent, grabbed up an empty bucket, tipped it upside-down and sat on it, grinning like an imp.

'Lost again, have you, brother?'

Halli glared at her.

'It's only a game.'

'Ah, it wasn't the knucklebones I meant.'

'How's my favourite sharp-tongued troll today?'

Tam Fox leant back against the side-planking, stretched his long legs out luxuriously and surveyed her coolly. He was dressed in layers of cream wool and linen, with a fine brooch of silver and some shining blue stone holding his huge fur-lined cloak closed at his throat. Beads of brine glinted in his abundant sandy hair and on the shells and bones he wore in it. His eyes – the silvery-green of a forest pool – appraised her minutely. Katla became abruptly aware of the tightness of her tunic (she had borrowed it from Bella, who was smaller than she was, while her own recovered from the latest dunking she had given it to get rid of the last of Fent's smell) and it was stretched uncomfortably across her breasts; and the gaping hole in her breeches where an expanse of tanned flesh showed through.

She watched his gaze drop to the torn leather as if he had read her thoughts. When she spread her fingers to cover the hole, he looked up and scanned her face guilelessly, his expression as bland and benign as a child's. Then one side of his mouth curved upward into a wicked grin that bared a single sharp incisor. Tilting his head, he gave her a slow, provocative, assessing look which made her feel naked to his gaze.

To cover her confusion she said, 'Which island is that up ahead?'

A dark shape showed on the horizon, as dark and as round as the hump of a whale.

'That will be Kjaley,' Tam Fox said, his light eyes flicking away from her. 'Keel Island. Site of many a wreck.' He gathered his legs beneath him and stood up as lithely as a cat. 'Take her in!' he hailed his crew. He glanced down at Katla again. 'Tonight we shall feast and sleep in comfort!'

Keel Island lived up to its name. On the approach, Katla had spied the carcasses of a dozen or more stricken vessels – some whose wooden planking had taken on a dark and peaty texture, others in which it had weathered to a dull, flaking silver. Still more littered the black strand, strewn like the ribs of so many whales across the volcanic shore. Driftwood lay tangled in fantastic contortions, its original form smoothed and rounded by the sea as if polished by a giant's hand. Here and there, bones gleamed against the black sand. It seemed a strange, forlorn spot to put in for the night, but Tam Fox appeared to be very at home on the island, knowing exactly where to anchor the ship to save it from being dashed on the cutting reefs, sending one party to gather driftwood for fires and another to fill the leather buckets with fresh water from a stream that coursed down from the sheer black cliffs, more to raise tents and bring the ale ashore. By the time sunset fell and crimson light flooded the island, a festive air had overtaken the crew. A huge fire roared, sending spirals of sparks up into the darkening sky; fishskin bubbled and crackled on spits; one barrel of ale was already upturned and empty. Bella and Silva Lighthand were performing handsprings and somersaults; Flint Erson threw himself in cartwheel after cartwheel, until he cannoned into Min Codface and she bellowed at him and chased him into the shallows, where he tripped and fell headlong; and one of the jugglers was trying to teach Jenna how to throw and catch three coloured balls stuffed with dried beans in a fluid rhythm, without much success.

Morten Danson sat apart from the mummers, glowering at everyone who crossed his path. It seemed, though, that his appetite had returned now that they were on dry land: the skeletons of at least three mackerel lay scattered on the ground before him, their stripy heads staring sightlessly out to sea.

By full dark, Katla had downed her fifth mug of ale and was beginning to feel pleasantly fuzzy around the edges. Someone was tapping out a dance measure on a set of hand-drums and a band of musicians had retrieved their pipes and horns from the ship and joined in. A knot of folk were dancing around the fire. The costumes were out too, Katla saw, rather to her surprise. Tam Fox ran a tight crew most of the time and the costumes had been carefully stowed, wrapped first in unbleached linen and then in greased canvas to keep out the sea and the weather, and folded away into the big brassbound seachest in which he also kept Katla's carnelian sword, which seemed to have been a significant part of Aran's payment to the mummers' chief for his part in the abduction. Someone was wearing the gigantic red head belonging to the Dragon of Wen costume and was chasing one of the singers in and out of the tents, and someone else swathed in the enveloping blue and green robe and headpiece of Mother Ocean was in the process of forming an unnatural and unholy union with the Lady of Fire. Katla helped herself to another mugful of the spiced ale and paid rapt attention as it warmed its way down her gullet.

'Easy there!'

She turned around, too quickly. The world spun and she fell over her elder brother. 'Whoops,' she said from the ground, grinning lopsidedly. ''Lo, Halli.'

Halli sat down beside her. 'You're drunk,' he accused.

'No. Not really.' Katla shook her head. It felt unpleasant, so she stopped and gazed at him owlishly instead. 'Only a bit giddy. Still got my sea-legs,' she explained solemnly after a bit.

Halli laughed. 'Sea-legs! Well, have it your own way. I came to bring you Tam Fox's greetings and invite you to dine with him.'

'I ate. I think.' Katla was nonplussed. Had she eaten? She remembered seeing mackerel roasting, and white bones scattered around the fire, and she remembered thinking about helping herself to one of them, then getting distracted by the arrival of the ale. She frowned, then sniffed her hands. They smelled salty: but that would be from days of handling wave-wet ropes; there were no scales on them, no fish-oil. She shrugged, narrowed her eyes and scanned the crowd, trying to spot the mummers' leader. There was no sign of him by the fire with the rest of the crew, though the light of the flames gave everyone's hair such a wild red halo that it was hard to know whether she had seen him or not. A cool onshore breeze carried the sudden, unmistakable scent of roasting lamb to her and her stomach rumbled its approval noisily. Lamb! Now that was a proper treat after days of dogfish and eel. 'All right: take me to him.'

She tried to get up, managed to get her feet under her and swayed awkwardly. Halli – always more temperate in his habits than his sister – leapt up and caught her under the arms before she fell again. 'I do think it would be a good idea to get some food in you,' Halli said again. 'Before you get completely sozzled.'

Katla cocked her head on one side and regarded him knowingly. He slid out of focus: became two grim-faced, dark young men, their four eyes boring into her earnestly. This scrutiny was acutely uncomfortable: she felt like a small child caught peeing where she shouldn't. By concentrating hard she managed to make the two figures coalesce into Halli again. 'You can be very . . . dull sometimes,' she enunciated carefully, hardly slurring at all. 'Very . . . grown-up.'

'Someone has to be,' Halli said crossly, thinking of his wayward father, his mad brother; this irresponsible sister. Tam was right: it was about time she was married and settled.

Tam Fox had his own fire burning at a little distance away from the main group, and it was from this blaze that the scent of roasting lamb had originated: a crisping carcass hissed fat into the flames. The mummers' leader turned the spit once more with his foot, then sat back. He had constructed a roomy shelter from a large piece of sailcloth draped over branches and oars and a comfortable-looking seating area out of several bags of soft goods covered with furs and cloaks and there he reclined with a flask of wine in the crook of his arm and a plateful of steaming meat at his side. It looked quite rare still: blood leaked out onto the tin plate all red and glistening, though it might just have been the radiance of the flames reflecting in the cooked juices. Firelight played across Tam Fox's face, illuminating his broad cheekbones, his wide brow, and the myriad braids and decorations in his copious beard and hair; it caught the band of silver he wore at his throat, rendering it a flawless gold, and fiery sparks lit the wells of his deep green eyes. He looked as magnificent as a great cat guarding its fresh-caught prey: all tawny grace and indolent power. Katla caught her breath.

His companion was as richly arrayed as any queen. An abundant white dress swathed her, its hem and sleeves adorned with intricate silver brocade. The neckline plunged dramatically, revealing a fine pair of white breasts. Katla squinted. She recognised that dress: it was the one worn, along with a ludicrous wig of yellow straw, by Flint Erson at the Rockfall mumming in his role as the Rosa Eldi. But Tam Fox's companion was clearly not the hirsute Flint: there was far too much soft female skin on show for anyone to make *that* mistake; nor yet was she the nomad queen. Clearing the dancing, deceptive light of the fire, Katla got a clear view of the richly attired woman sitting beside Tam Fox. With a shock, she realised it was Jenna Finnsen.

Jenna's cheeks were flushed and she wound a long coil of her golden hair round and round her finger as she giggled throatily at something the mummers' chief had just said. When she saw Katla and Halli, she went very still and her eyes became round and wide.

'Why, Jenna,' Katla said thickly, 'you've changed your dress I see.'

Jenna blushed a shade deeper. 'You could have told me there was birdshit all over it!' she replied defensively. 'Tam kindly pointed it out and had Silva take it away for a wash.' She smiled up at the tawny man under her eyelashes. 'He's been looking after me: he told me I looked pale and wan and needed good red meat and red wine to bring my colour back.'

'I also said she needs a man who'll appreciate her beauty and fill her full of seed, give her a score of fine, fat babies.'

Jenna choked so hard with laughter so that a bubble of wine burst from her mouth and dribbled down her chin.

Her hands flew up to her face. 'You're outrageous!' she cried, peering at him between splayed fingers. Katla could tell she was delighted by his teasing. 'I think you're the rudest man I ever met!'

The mummers' leader gave Halli a heavy-lidded look that seemed almost a gesture of encouragement, or assent.

'I am not a man fit for civilised company, it's true,' he conceded. 'I've spent far too long on the high seas with the lowest of the low. And I am clearly too scurvy and rough-tongued a rascal to claim the attentions of such a well-bred and beauteous maiden. What you want, my dear, as I have been telling you this past hour, is a fine young man who's unspoilt by the world, a man who's upstanding and honourable, a man who'll wed you and make you a proper home. Why, a man just like handsome Halli Aranson here—' Tam Fox pushed himself upright and odged sideways to make space for the Rockfaller, then when Halli hesitated, caught him by the arm and hauled him down so hard that he almost fell into Jenna's capacious lap. Katla giggled: so this was their game, and it was hardly subtle: get Jenna drunk on strong wine and Tam Fox's lavish compliments then let Halli take over the seduction. And with luck, it seemed that Tam's more direct attempt at match-making might be more successful than her own, for although Jenna looked a little put out at the ease with which the mummers' chief had abandoned her, she did not seem entirely sorry to find herself in close proximity to Katla's brother; indeed, was simpering away like a fourteen-year-old virgin. She was about to say as much, jokingly, when powerful hands grabbed her and swung her around until she tripped and almost fell upon the cushions. A moment later, the world stopped spinning and she found herself jammed up against the solid bulk of Tam Fox.

Tam reached around behind them and miraculously produced two more flasks of wine and handed them to the Rockfallers.

'Stallion's blood?' Halli asked, sniffing at it warily. He had not had much exposure to any wine other than the thin, bitter stuff that owned the name in the Northern Isles.

Tam Fox snorted. 'I may be a brigand and a thief, a jester and a fool; but I am neither mean of purse nor eager to rot my guts! Stallion's blood is fit only for sousing herring and fixing dyes: but this – this, my friends, is Jetra's finest vintage, dating from the reign of Raik Horsehair who liberated it himself from the cellars of the Lord of the Eternal City. It has come to me by a long, circuitous and not entirely legal, route, so do not waste a drop of it and do not guzzle it back like ale. Take time to savour the fine abundance of the rich blackberry aroma; treat your palate to its glorious buttery finish!'

He demonstrated the latter with such overstated theatricality that Halli and Katla exchanged a look and burst out laughing.

'I quite like stallion's blood actually,' Katla declared cheerfully, not believing a word of the mummer's nonsense. 'I find it rather . . . bracing.' She took a huge swig from the wine flask, swilled it around and then gargled with it in a thoroughly unladylike fashion. Two seconds later it all went down the wrong way and she found herself coughing like a cat trying to dislodge a particularly recalcitrant hairball. Jenna began thumping her on the back, rather too hard, Katla thought, for mere aid.

Tam Fox began to cut dripping slices of the lamb from the roasting carcass. He proffered the laden plate and his belt-knife to the now-silent Katla, who regarded him askance.

'Are you sure you trust me with your little knife?' she asked slyly. 'Especially in the state I'm in?'

'I have heard you have such magic in your fingers, that you can take the most inoffensive blade and turn it to a deadly weapon.' The mummers' leader returned her glance without

a smile, though there was a glimmer in his eye. 'I would love
to discover your mettle with my . . . metal.'

Katla frowned. What was he talking about? 'I forge swords,'
she said. 'It's true.'

'Ah, but do you quench them?'

Was she imagining it, or had he just winked at her? She
examined his face, bemused by the alcohol and annoyed
to be unable to read the situation, and was caught by the
intensity of his gaze. *He has the most remarkable eyes*, she found
herself thinking, *as intense and as wild as a feral cat's*. Almost,
she expected his pupils to be vertical slits, for the moonlight
to shine off them in flat silver discs.

'Eat before it goes cold,' Tam said, and thrust the plate
at her and she took it from him, wondering what had just
passed between them; but before she could consider the
matter further she heard Halli say something in a low voice
to Jenna, then he stood up and pulled her to her feet. She
was a little unsteady, and the white dress was unwieldy, but
Halli put a supportive arm around her waist and she curled
herself into his embrace, and it seemed to Katla then that
the two of them looked very fine together: all contrast and
complement – Halli so tall and dark, his black hair lifted by
the light breeze; Jenna all gold and white, the pair of them
limned with moonlight, and the black strand stretching away
behind them and the white surf rolling onto the shore. Then
Halli bent and kissed her, and Katla felt her heart contract in
something like regret.

'They make a handsome couple,' Tam Fox said as if reading
her thoughts, and his voice was soft and melodious. They
sat there together for a while in companionable silence
punctuated only by the crackling of the fire and the muted
sounds of revelry. Then he turned to Katla and asked, 'Will
you be Jenna's witness?'

She gawped at him. 'For what?'

'Tomorrow I shall handfast her to your brother.'

Katla laughed. 'Halli will have to wait till he returns to Rockfall for any handfasting, and that's only if my father and Jenna agree.'

'As the captain of the *Snowland Wolf*, which sails Sur's moon path and on which Halli serves as crew and Jenna travels as my guest, I have the god's authority to handfast the two of them if they so wish it,' Tam said mildly.

Katla raised an eyebrow. 'And what if she doesn't wish it?'

Tam Fox shrugged. 'More fool her. I think she will, though. She's a woman much in need of a man's regard, and anyone with half an eye can see that your brother loves her well.'

'Are you such an expert on love?' Katla chewed a piece of lamb, took another swig from the flask to wash it down with. The meat felt hot and greasy on her tongue: she swallowed the mouthful quickly before she gagged.

'Some might consider me such.'

'But you never wed.'

'In another lifetime, I did.'

Katla was surprised. She looked up from her plate of food to find that the mummer's eyes had gone distant and unfocused. Something in his face had softened, making him look at once younger and yet older than his years.

'What happened? Where is she now, your wife?'

Tam Fox shook his head. 'It's not a subject for a pleasant evening like this. I'd rather talk about you, Katla Aransen.'

'Me?'

The mummers' chief took the platter away from her and set it on the ground. Then he took both her hands in his own. They were very large, his hands, and very warm, with big, square, capable-looking fingers decorated with several intricately worked silver rings. It felt quite comforting to be held so; but if it was so comforting, why was her heart starting to pound?

'Katla, you're a very beautiful young woman.'

Katla almost choked on her wine. Beautiful was not a word she would think of applying to herself; nor was it a term anyone else was likely to confer upon her. Possibly Erno had thought her so, but that had all been trickery. The young Istrian – Saro Vingo – had looked at her in such a way and made her feel as if she might be beautiful: but that had been before the burning, before he had come at her through the fire with his sword drawn. She pushed away the haunting memory of the Istrian's intense, black-eyed gaze. Tam Fox was another matter entirely. She had always known his attraction to her, but had dismissed it as being a part of what she had thought of as his indiscriminate womanising. But having spent a month in his company she had not in all that time seen him with another woman, nor heard others gossip of his affairs, and realised that she might have to reassess her judgement of him. Not that a month was long enough to make such a judgement; but curiously she found she didn't much care.

'My advances towards you as we sailed into Halbo were boorish and ill-timed,' the mummers' chief went on, his voice barely more than a murmur. 'But being in close quarters with you on the ship made me rash.' His hand brushed her cheek and she felt the blood race through her abdomen and chest; felt it travel up her throat and make her face and ears burn. Tam Fox's face was suddenly very close to hers: she could feel his warm breath on her neck, smell the wine fumes as he spoke, but whatever he was saying now washed over her unnoticed, a jumble of meaningless sound. All she could focus on was his mouth, for the rest of him was a delicious blur: and so she found herself staring at his sharply chiselled top lip, its deep runnel partially masked by the red-gold beard; the long, full lower lip, a pale, dry, fleshy pink. Then, without taking her eyes from that mesmeric mouth, she placed the wine-flask carefully on the sand, cupped his strong jaw in both her hands and kissed it. The mouth was as she had imagined it might be: hot and muscular, tasting of spices and smoke. And then she abandoned herself to Tam's insistent tongue and roving hands, caught up fistfuls of his wild hair — beads and shells and snakeskins and all — and pressed herself against him till she thought the heat of her body might just burn all their clothes away. It was only a little while later when she felt the onshore breeze brush her skin that she realised he had managed to remove her tunic and leggings without her having had any conscious knowledge of the fact at all.

When she awoke the next morning, it was to the sound of a horde of small trolls painfully excavating the inside of her skull with their vicious little picks and hammers. Each thump made her wince, and that was before she opened her eyes. Sunlight lanced her pupils like hot needles; she shut them again immediately, only to be assailed by a horrible, flaring red that scoriated her eyeballs. Her mouth felt as furry as the thing she was lying on, and she felt an overwhelming need to pee, throw up or merely die.

Feeling something hard pressing uncomfortably into her naked buttock, she shifted her weight and reached down. Her fingers closed over a number of small, unidentifiable objects. Very slowly, she opened her eyes again, shielding herself from the worst of the light with her other hand, and held her discoveries aloft. In her grasp were a pair of pale pink cowrie shells, and a twist of silver wire with several long red hairs still attached to it. More shells were scattered across the blanket; the shrivelled husk of a snakeskin lay beside her on the pillow. Mystified, she looked around. It took a while to register her surroundings or, indeed, her companion. Inside a makeshift tent of sailcloth and lashed-together oars, the chief of the mummers' troupe lay propped on one elbow, regarding her with a hugely satisfied smile. Some of his braids had come undone and his hair was in disarray.

Events from the previous night started to come back to her in hallucinatory little flashes, and suddenly she became aware that the only item of clothing she was still wearing appeared to consist of a single felt sock, and that was half off her left foot.

Katla groaned. Now death definitely seemed the most welcome option.

'Well, that's a most charming greeting, Katla Aransen. Good morning to you, too. And so far I've found it to be a very beautiful morning: the sun is shining, the wind is true and there appears to be a naked girl in my bed. Not a bad way to start the day.'

'Did we—?'

It was a pointless question. The bearskin beneath her hip was still slick and damp. Katla was no virgin: she knew what that must mean. This time her groan was louder.

'By Sur, I must have been drunk.'

Tam Fox regarded her curiously. 'You could not imagine engaging with me unless you were rats'-arsed?'

It was a quaint term used predominantly by Fair Islanders. Inconsequentially, amidst all the other confusions, Katla wondered whether that was where he had originated. Her short, bitter laugh was her only reply: his question had surely been hypothetical. When Tam leaned closer and put a hand out to her face she jerked away like a skittish mare.

'Ah,' he said. 'I see. Even so, perhaps I will ask your father again for the right to wed you, when we return.'

'Again?'

Tam nodded.

Katla was aghast. 'Why, what did he say the first time?'

The mummer tapped the side of his nose. 'That's my secret.'

'I will never wed,' she said vehemently.

'Never?'

'Never.'

Tam raised his eyebrows. 'If that is your choice, then so be it. 'Twould be a terrible waste, though, if such a lovely body were not to grace a good man's bed on a regular basis, most preferably mine . . .'

Then he pushed back the covers and ducked out of the tent to stand stark naked in the sun. The light fell on his long, lean muscles, his narrow waist and neat buttocks. He was a well-made man, that much was undeniable, but what really caught her eye was the mass of scar tissue across his back and shoulders.

She called his name to catch his attention, meaning to ask him what had caused such despoliation to his flesh, but when he turned to face her full on, the question went right out of her head, and when he smiled and came back into the tent she made only the most cursory protest when he slid under the furs beside her once more and started to run his big hands gently down her flanks.

Later, it was her turn to prop herself up on an elbow and survey his drowsy face. 'Do not get the idea that this means more than it does. I still will not wed you, or any man.'

'It means enough; and enough, as my mother always said, is as much as a feast.' He smiled like the cheesemaker's cat. 'Besides, I only said that perhaps I would ask your father. I may have changed my mind now that I have sampled the goods.'

Katla thumped him furiously and got dressed in such haste that it was only when she stomped off across the beach with the mummer's laughter ringing in her ears that she realised she had put her leggings on back to front and that the rip in them must have revealed to anyone she passed (and there were quite a few, most of whom seemed to be well aware, from the knowing smiles they conferred upon her, where and how she had spent the night) a very considerable expanse of her bare arse.

* * *

They cast off from Kjaley around noon and sailed west-south-west until the sun began its slow dip towards the horizon. They had made good time: a strong wind filled the sail all the way so that they sped along at such a clip Katla could have sworn the prow of the *Snowland Wolf* barely skimmed the surface of the sea. This time tomorrow they would be home. She could feel the draw of the islands in her bones, like an aroma scented on the air, acknowledged but not yet identified.

Halli must have had the same thought; though prompted more by his understanding of dead reckoning and navigation than by some uncanny intuition. She watched him take Tam Fox aside, watched the two of them in deep conversation; saw Tam take a handful of Halli's hair in his fist and shear it off with his belt-knife. Katla frowned, remembering a similar occurrence of her own. A little while later, Tam crossed the ship and took a bundle of old, faded twine from the bottom of the costumes chest and passed it to Urse, who made his way steadily up the length of the *Snowland Wolf*, tied one end of the twine carefully to the sternpost and then let the other down over the stern to trail in their wake. Then nobody did anything for the best part of an hour; except Jenna, who had donned her best blue dress again and was now fussing with her hair.

Katla marched boldly up to Tam Fox, who was now sitting on the chest, plaiting together a black and yellow braid.

'What's going on?' she demanded, hands on hips.

The mummers' chief did not even look up from his task. 'You'll see.'

'I'll see what?' Katla persisted.

Tam said nothing. His fingers flicked the strands of hair expertly in and out of one another until he reached the end of the braid. There he wound the remaining strands into a complicated knot and finished off the binding neatly. He waved it in front of Katla's nose, then whisked it out of her reach and stowed it in his belt-pouch.

'Wait and see.'

And with that, he leapt to his feet and padded his way down to the stern, where he drew the soaking twine aboard, unhooked its dry end from the post and brought it dripping back up to the centre of the ship. There, he squeezed the seawater out of it until there was a small pool at his feet; then he called Jenna and Halli to him. Katla watched curiously as Tam Fox made the pair face one another, then wound the wet twine about their wrists in a complicated series of figure-of-eights so that their palms were inextricably pressed together. Then he crouched, dabbled his fingers in the puddle of brine and anointed each of them on the forehead and tongue.

By now, a group of the mummers had gathered around their captain and the lovers: Katla had to move nimbly to get herself to the fore of the crowd in time to hear Tam Fox intone: 'This salt you taste is for remembrance, that the Lord Sur has witnessed your promises.' Then he raised his voice. 'The Lord of the Waters, Lord of the Storm, Lord of the Isles watches the vows which you, Halli Aranson and you, Jenna Finnsen, make this day in your handfasting. This twine that I have bound about you symbolises the endless circle of life, which is the Lord's gift. In exchange, I offer this braid as a token of their vow to take one another as man and wife within a year from this day, and to honour Sur's name with their lives and the lives of the children they will bring into your world.'

He took the braid of black and gold hair from the pouch at his belt and held it aloft so that all might see. Then he cast it over the side. Jenna followed its arc, her upturned face lit golden by the setting sun. The saltwater gleamed on her lips, which were curved into the most blissful smile. Halli's face was blithe: he looked, Katla thought, like the child he had

once been. Apart from the beard, and that big strong jaw . . .
The braid lay bobbing on the sparkling waves for a second,
then it filled with water and sank slowly from view.

Everyone started to talk at once, congratulating the couple,
exclaiming at the tightness of the binding Tam had made, and
at the unusual configuration of knots.

'Look,' Min Codface was saying, 'he's woven in a blessing
for five children. Five! Imagine that!'

'Are you sure it's not five sheep?' someone else said. 'The
knots are very similar for "babes" and "ewes" . . .'

They all laughed.

Katla laughed with them, though she was more than a little
annoyed that no one had thought to include her in their plans
before the fact. She was about to swallow her irritation and
offer her own good wishes to her brother and her friend when
she felt a vague tremor beneath her feet. The vibration she
felt from it travelled through her soles and into the bones of
her shins, setting up a faint aching sensation. The ship rocked
slightly, then it was gone.

She frowned, shifted her feet. When she looked up, she
found that Tam was watching her curiously and she looked
away quickly, just in time to catch sight of an oddly forked
tail emerging out of the foam of the steerboard wash, and
then disappear again.

She ran to the gunwale, looked overboard. Nothing.
Nothing except a serried rank of greying waves tinged
with the last of the sun's red light and the bright white
of the scudding surf. But the wood under her palms told
another story. The planking was filled with weird energy:
her hands tingled and buzzed, but not in the familiar way
that denoted the approach to land, the passage of the ship
over reefs or veins of crystal, lodes of metal; deep-buried
ores. The charge was more frenetic, as if it were tangled and
knotted, caught in cross-currents; confused, warped, even. So
when the surface of the sea began to behave in a strange way

— swelling out in slow, broad circles, heaving upward like a welling geyser — she held her breath and waited, beguiled, hypnotised, unable to move. Gradually, the waves swamped away from whatever they had been hiding, to reveal the thing that had been following them, that had brushed the keel of the ship a few moments ago, the thing that owned the forked tail she had glimpsed, and she was barely more than a little surprised.

It was vast: at first she thought it some sort of whale, though of a far larger species than any normally caught off Rockfall's waters, or even the great grey whale that had washed up on the northern coast of the island some years back, that had kept them all in meat and oil the whole winter and more. But when it raised its head out of the sea, she knew it was no whale, nor any other natural thing.

Its vast, bulky body was variegated in every shade of grey and green so that it looked as though it were patched with lichens and moss; indeed, as it drew down upon the *Snowland Wolf*, great swags of vegetation — kelp or weed — were revealed, clinging to portions of its anatomy as if growing on sea-washed rocks, trailing out behind it in long clusters like the ragged hem of a vast robe. An array of fins alternated down its knobbly spine with what seemed to be the tentacles of some enormous squid that it had somehow absorbed into itself, digested and then partially expressed. The forked tail which Katla had spied flicking through the waves served only to deceive the eye as to the true size of the thing: for it was only one of many small appendages attached to the creature, and each completed itself in a different manner: soft fronds, an ugly knot; what looked almost like a hand. Its true tail, if it had one, remained below the water; but clearly some huge device was at work down there beneath the visible monster, for a great vortex of sea churned and sucked behind it, producing an alarming whirlpool in its wake. As the creature rose out of the waves, its maw opened to reveal a black cavern of a mouth fringed with lethal-looking teeth surrounding a leprous purple tongue liberally furred with grey. Katla, suddenly and inconsequentially gifted with a moment of utmost clarity, saw how some parts of its skin were as sheeny and smooth as the skin of a seal, repelling the water in great sheets and beads; whilst other patches – all mottled and boggy with retained moisture – appeared to be porous, as if the thing were only partly adapted to life in its ocean home.

Up it came – fully twenty feet into the air, its silhouette red-lined by the failing light – to reveal a livid green and white belly studded with further mouths. Behind her, Katla was vaguely aware of cries of horror and despair from her crewmates, then Tam Fox was at her side, a reversed oar in his hands, his hair wild in the sunset. Someone cast a fishing spear into the monster. It buried itself neatly in the creature's back, in one of the porous patches of skin, and water and other foul liquids gushed out around the puncture. Something silver flashed past Katla's head; followed by another and another. Katla turned to see that Min Codface had shimmied halfway up the mast and, with one arm and one leg crooked around the pole, was delivering her throwing knives with murderous accuracy at the brute, all the while yelling with great snarls of defiance: 'Get back, you vile squid, you hagfish, you overgrown guppy; you abomination of a megrim! Back to the depths, to the ocean-cracks where you belong!'

In a trice, a dozen separate gouts of blood had erupted from the monster's hide and it roared its distress with a bellow like thunder. For a moment, it seemed that the crisis might be over, for the great fish now turned tail and dived beneath the ship, a red tide bubbling in its wake. Katla had time to turn and scan the faces of her fellow sailors – aghast, excited, terrified, or in Min's case, utterly elated.

'That taught the foul morwong its business!' The knife-thrower slid down the mast, her eyes shining. 'That great garfish won't be back in a hurry!'

She was wrong. A moment later there came a hideous grinding sound and every timber in the ship groaned in protest. Water sprang up between the boards at Katla's feet. Someone tumbled past her, cursing. The ship tilted danger-ously, then righted itself with a booming crash. Displaced water shot skywards like a fountain, then rained down on them so that they were splattered with a glistening mixture of brine and fishblood, and the sunset reflected on them, turned them all into red things.

Katla felt instinctively that, against all the odds and despite all she knew of the great fish of the oceans, the beast had deliberately tried to overturn them instead of fleeing for its life. This was, clearly, no ordinary creature. She remembered suddenly the rash of superstitious tales that had recently been told around the cookfires: tales of bizarre sightings, peculiar corpses washed up on deserted beaches; strange objects netted in the midst of a catch of herring. The creature was not going to leave them alone: something must be done.

People were running this way and that, trying to save oars and belongings, chests of clothing and tradegoods that had been dislodged and strewn around the deck. In the midst of it all, the handfasted couple clung together with Jenna's head buried against her lover's shoulder as if by this means she might shut out the horrible reality beyond. Others were strapping on swords and sharpening oars and staves under Tam Fox's command. He strode around the deck, issuing orders like a man born to lead, the short stabbing sword he carried habitually – a brutal enough weapon at close quarters – beating against his thigh as he went.

A subconscious hum took up residence in Katla's skull; a zinging: a call. The Red Sword. She could *feel* its blade singing to her like a grasshopper in a thicket. Instinctively she knew its whereabouts: in the casket Fent had loaded onto the ship in the harbour at Rockfall, that she had thought would make a gift to King Ravn; but the mummers' leader had clearly had other ideas. Dodging skittering pots and pans, snaking lengths of rope and stumbling companions, she found herself in the stern; and there was the casket, still securely lashed down. With strong fingers and raw determination, Katla undid the sea-wet knots, dragged the lid open and liberated the great blade. In the light of the setting sun, it gleamed a bloody red, as if already anticipating the damage it would do. The sword fitted her hand as she had always remembered, the polished beauty of the carnelian pommel contoured snugly against her palm, the crosspiece hard against her fist. Exhilaration filled her, an inebriating song which filled her veins, running from her right hand through her arm and shoulder, suffusing her neck and head; coursing down through her torso, heating her abdomen, running like molten iron through her legs. The Red Sword! With the weapon buzzing in her hand she felt invincible.

She shook her head, trying to clear the thrill of the metal's spell. Wielding the carnelian blade was all very well, but she was hardly going to get close enough to the monster to simply run it through . . .

Grabbing up the cord that had lashed the casket down, she ran back towards the stempost, where even now the beast was looming up again, wrapped about by foaming pink surf, its spines and tentacles shaking in wrath, its great, blank forehead bearing down upon the prow of the *Snowland Wolf*, eclipsing its carved dragonhead entirely, like a snowy owl mantling over a sparrow. A discarded oar nearly felled her, and when she leapt it, caught her a numbing blow to the shin. Swearing hideously, Katla cast herself down beside the oar and set about it with her belt-knife. In mere seconds she had hacked out a sizeable chunk of the good oak. The violated inner wood gleamed palely amidst the deeper gold of the handpolished exterior, but Katla was in no mood to appreciate such aesthetics. While Tam Fox and his men fired arrows from the ship's few shortbows into the monster, Katla fitted the hilt of the Red Sword into the gouge she had made in the oar-handle and lashed the two together using the cord she had taken from the casket and every swift knot she knew.

There came another huge thud, followed by cries of terror. The monster had rammed the vessel. Timbers shrieked in protest; then, with an ear-splitting crack, the prow of the ship sheared away. Katla looked up just in time to see Flint Erson fly over the side and into the weltering sea, where he disappeared soundlessly beneath the boiling, creamy surf. Enraged at the loss of one of his crewmen, and his best tumbler to boot, Tam Fox roared imprecations at the monster, and hurled his shortsword with such aggressive finesse that it sank without trace into the creature's gill-striped cheek; but still the sea-beast came at them.

Katla leapt to her feet, makeshift harpoon in hand, and made for the mutilated prow. There, for an instant, she found herself staring into one of the creature's eyes. At first all she saw was her own reflection, a horrible red parody waving a pathetic length of wood with a pin stuck to the tip; then her heart lurched horribly. She was looking, unmistakably, into a human eye.

The eye regarded her. It was the deepest velvet brown, the brown of a cow's eye; but around the iris, white cornea showed, tapering at either end. The eye was fringed with lashes. It blinked as if startled at the intimate contact, and then Katla heard a strangely familiar voice in her head. It spoke her name, haltingly, pleadingly, so low as to be a subterranean rumble, coming not from the bizarre creature before her, but from a thousand and more miles away, deep below Elda's surface. Then water filled the eye and it blinked again. What looked horribly like the largest tear in the world rolled slowly down the vast fish's face. Katla found herself caught neatly between empathy and revulsion; but the Red Sword knew its task. Of its own volition, or so it seemed to a stunned Katla, her arm drew back the spear she had fashioned and released it with brutal power. Hard and true the carnelian blade flew, burying itself to the hilt in the monster's eye-socket. For a moment, all was still. The *Snowland Wolf* settled itself; everyone took a breath. Then the creature reared up and its wail of agony rent the air. Up it went, propelled almost to the vertical by the frantic beatings of its many tails and fins, all of its mouths opening and closing in hellish concert, each uttering a different cry of hurt.

Katla stood teetering on the gunwale where her cast had brought her, engulfed by the monster's shadow. Even with the thing hanging in the air above her, she found she could not move.

'Katla!'

She heard the voice, but it sounded far away, swallowed as it was by the cacophony of the wounded beast.

And then it pitched down.

Halli's free hand wrapped itself firmly around Katla's ankle, dragging her backwards, just as the sea-creature plunged. Flying backwards, barely registering the pain of her landing on her elbows, her back, her left shoulder, Katla watched as the monster crashed down upon the *Snowland Wolf*, watched as the splintered stempost pressed delicately for a second against the mottled skin of the beast's belly, puckering the area between two gaping mouths. Then the pale skin gave up its futile resistance and swallowed the spar, impaling it down the full length of the shattered prow. With a final mournful bellow and a gush of vile-smelling fluids, the monster died.

But the worst was still to come.

Under the weight of its new burden, the ship tilted violently. There was a moment of uncanny calm, then the

sail came free of its rigging and, flapping wildly, swept Bella
and two other tumblers over the gunwale. Barrels and boxes
tumbled headlong; the iron cauldron and its tripod rolled the
length of the ship, gathering speed, and caved in the other
half of Urse's smashed head. Down the creature went and
the *Snowland Wolf* went with it, inexorably bound for the
vile maelstrom of the beast's death-throes.

With a groan, the mastfish – fashioned two centuries ago by
the Master of Hedebu from the heartwood of the greatest oak
in his ship-grove – split asunder. No longer firmly anchored,
the mast wavered desperately, then plummeted to the deck,
carpeting the ship with the great sail, which writhed as those
trapped beneath it tried to fight free, so that the wolf and the
serpent appeared to do battle for the fate of the world once
more. Then the ship tilted crazily again and the mast, sail and
all, slid sideways and crashed through the larboard gunwale,
taking another half dozen shrieking figures with it. In its wake,
two men lay screaming amidst a wreckage of tortured wood
and rope; Katla could see the white of their legbones shining
through a mess of cloth and blood.

The last thing she saw as water flooded into the fine old
ship that had been the *Snowland Wolf* was her brother, with
Jenna plastered against him like a drowned kitten, sawing
desperately at the well-knotted bonds which tied the pair
of them together. Then the sea rushed in and carried them
all away.

Twelve

The Master

Abandoned by the thing he had made, the thing he had stolen and the beast in which he had stored much of his magic, the Master paces his chambers in the icy fastness of Sanctuary like a madman. For lack of any other society, he has over the passage of the last few months attempted to create new companions for himself – with spit and earth and a little, just a little, of his own blood to give them life – but without the presence of the cat, they have proved to be hopeless experiments, shambling, misshapen creatures who bumble into walls and knock off pieces of their new anatomies, who drown in the lake, or stumble away into the snowy wastes, never to be seen again; or simply grind to a halt, staring into space as though they have discovered some new existence in an entirely other world. He makes no effort to patch them up or reanimate them; indeed, he makes no effort even to tidy their remains away, so that the tunnels and grounds of the stronghold have become littered with these failed creatures in varying states of decay. The long sleep seems to have sapped all energy and will from him, and now he has given up his experiments; since even the best of his creations have barely been able to string two words together. It is discourse that he craves, he lies to himself; the lively interplay of minds, and not mere company – he has the wailing seabirds and the visitations of corpse-whales and seals to serve the purpose of mere fellowship. But at night, in his fitful rest, it is the Rosa Eldi's body he sees, pale and gleaming, lithe and inviting, always ready for him, never questioning, her lost will bolstering his own. And each morning he awakes more enervated than he had been before pitching into the night's sleep.

Most of the time it is as much as he can do to forage through the neglected gardens that Virelai used to tend and there procure himself sufficient ingredients from which to make a meal. There is not much left, after the unadulterated arctic winds and the feral things he made and then forgot to dispose of have had their way. More often than not he eats what he finds raw, gnawing upon it like a rat, and when he is able to summon the vigour to boil turnips or roast onions, it is always without artifice or condiment. Everything tastes of ashes to him: what point can there be in disguising the taste of the truth? – that he has failed in all he has attempted. For he held a whole world, and what should have been the recipe for eternal happiness, in his grasp and yet allowed it all to fall away from him. Lost, lost, forever lost.

He spends many lonely days in the tower room, surveying the world he once regarded as his own through his complicated device of crystals and levers and clever reflecting glass, and is by turns perturbed and exhausted by what he sees. He turns the levers to show him the barren Northern Isles, but other than the appearance of the odd sea-monster (only to be expected, given the sudden unnatural influx of magic back into the world) finds nothing particularly surprising – people fishing; people fighting; people birthing and dying in much the same way as they have always done in their pathetic little existences.

In the Southern Empire, he searches for the Rosa Eldi, in vain. Instead, after much random casting about, he finds his hapless apprentice engaged in some bungled attempt at sorcery for a man who looks as if he might very soon lose his temper. Here he stays for some time, watching.

At least he has located the damned cat.

But even the sight of Virelai attempting to use the magic he has stolen fails to keep his interest for long. Listlessly, he seeks again for the woman, the perfect one, but although he trails the length and breadth of the Southern Empire, which is surely the only place a woman of such perverse refinements is likely truly to be appreciated, he can find no sign of her: except for the little incidents of magic that appear to have seeped out into the fabric of the world in a variety of warped and bizarre manifestations. By swinging the crystals to and fro without any deliberate pattern he comes upon wells and watercourses in the deep south of the world that once were pure and potable and have now become poisoned by the ingress of heavy metals ejected from veins in the earth far, far below; he finds streams in which fish have developed legs; birds which have suddenly grown teeth and turned upon their own; feral chickens which have escaped the barnyard and have scurried out into the woodlands and meadows. He comes upon other oddities and phenomena which pique his curiosity for a little while, then he resumes his search for the Rose of the World, trawling once more through the towns and cities of Istria.

Yet again, it seems, the people of the south are in preparation for another war, its people angry and unfocused, preferring to turn their attentions outside their own lives to rail against their northern neighbours for yet another imagined slight. Something to do – if his mouth-reading is accurate – with a barbarian king's rejection of a swan. A piffling matter, clearly; as is usually the way with the seed of such disturbances. He remembers the immolation of two entire clans in the Northern Isles after a bloodfeud caused by one drunken man pissing on some piece of ground designated as 'sacred' by some other idiot. As if the fools had the least idea of what the word 'sacred' really meant: for if they did, it would hardly be small squares of hallowed turf that concerned them, oh no!

Bored with the southerners' narrow rages and inhumanity, he shifts his view to the nomads – those wandering souls he had so easily displaced from their own lands and set about their random excursions – and finds little ant-lines of them trekking across the great wastelands, carefully skirting the cities wherein might lie renewed persecution and cruelty. It appears that the fervour which has the southerners in its grip once more has prompted a hatred of strangers and a fear of even the smallest magics, or indeed anything not immediately comprehensible to the dullest mind. He sighs. It was ever thus. Magicians and their kind were always distrusted: he had had to be rather more forceful with his own people when he had dwelled in the world than he might otherwise have chosen. A taste of pain, a terrible glimpse of what might be, was always one way to bring them back into line; the focused hatred of a third party another, even more effective, method.

He deploys the pulley system and brings one small caravan of yeka into closer focus. A young woman sits the leading yeka, her hair and skin an indeterminate reddish colour which suggests some miscegenation. She has light-coloured eyes, too, unlike most of her people. But the lad who sits beside her is one of the travelling folk through and through: dark-haired, black-eyed, lean-featured. He scans the rest of the troupe and notices that there looks to be no flesh to spare between them: they are a skinny bunch, all bones and sharp lines, stringy muscles and sagging breasts. Times have been hard for these folk. They have no unharnessed beasts left to them: an unlikely scenario, given inevitable lameness and the need for the rotation of mounts. They must surely have lost a number of the beasts along the way; had them stolen, he'd wager. (If such a thing were feasible – even when he lived in Elda, there had been few so stupid as to take a bet with a magician. Although one or two had been arrogant enough to try . . .)

Following this line of thought, he swings the crystals far to the south, deep into the mountains, to the foot of the Red Peak. There, he finds more evidence of disturbance, and this time a chill runs through him, making his skin creep into gooseflesh. Little chasms and vents have appeared in the flanks of the great mountain itself, revealing the blood of the world within, all red and boiling. Directly over its cap the most profound aperture of them all is gusting out clouds of fouled yellow vapour, vapour which, even as he watches, kills a bird stone dead as it foolishly takes a course through the mist, so that one moment it is gliding effortlessly through the evening air on wide, powerful wings and the next is tumbling senseless end over end to disappear silently into the mountain's maw.

He sits back now, his hands shaking. Is there anything he can do to avert the likely disaster to come? he wonders. Perhaps a hundred years ago, when he felt stronger and more confident of his powers, more in love with the possibilities of his future than he does now, he might have gathered his energies and his remaining magic and set sail for the south; exacted revenge upon his erring servant and taken back the cat by force, then made swift passage into that wilderness, there to reinforce the ancient spells and bindings he had put in place. From the perspective of great age and weariness, it seems a monumental task, too great a venture to undertake. But if he does not . . .

He puts his head in his hands. For the first time in two hundred years the greatest mage the world has ever seen, Rahe the Magnificent, as he liked to term himself in the days of his prime, puts his head in his hands and weeps.

Thirteen

Ghosts

'Ha!'

The Lord of Forent's hawkish face was alive with triumph. He flourished a roll of parchment at Tycho Issian. The unmistakable green-and-red knotted ribbon denoting that the missive had come direct from the Duke of Cera himself fluttered discarded to the floor of the tiled bathchamber. In the midst of the room, chest-deep in a tub filled with a foaming mess of chopped brome and ramsons, sat the Lord of Cantara. The old woman who was tending to Tycho – a bent crone by the look of her, even swaddled as she was in the most traditional of slave sabatkas in the coarsest black hessian – took one look at Rui Finco and scuttled from the room as if her life depended on it.

'Phew!' Rui wafted a hand in front of his nose. 'What in Falla's name has the old bag been adding to your treatment now?'

'Wild garlic,' Tycho answered plaintively, reaching for a length of bleached linen that was hanging just out of his reach. The tub rocked dangerously. Little rivulets of pale green water spilled over the side, followed by a watery salad of crushed leaves.

The Lord of Forent stepped carefully over this noxious puddle, caught up the fabric and handed it to Tycho. The agreement he had made with the crone was that if all else failed to cool the southern lord's insatiable ardour, she was in some other way to ensure that Tycho was rendered entirely undesirable to even the lowest whore, let alone the fastidious women of Rui's seraglio. Steeped as he was in the vile liquid, he was likely to stink of the ramsons she had added to his bath for many days to come.

The Lord of Cantara stepped out of the tub and wrapped himself carefully in the cloth, but no matter how he tried to conceal the fact it was eminently clear to Rui that none of the crone's other remedies had had any ameliorating effect on the man's condition: his erection remained as recalcitrant as ever. Rui could not help but grin: if they did not launch their war effort on the north and recover the nomad whore soon, the man was likely to explode.

'Still no surcease, my lord?' he asked courteously.

Tycho regarded him with slitted eyes and wound the linen tighter. 'No,' he said shortly. He surveyed the scroll the Lord of Forent still grasped. 'What's in the letter?'

'My lord Lodono, Duke of Cera and the Lords Dystra, by divine edict joint heads of the Ruling Council, do summon together all the nobles of Istria for a Council gathering, to be held on the day after full moon next in the Grand Hall of the Dawn Castle in the Eternal City of Jetra,' Rui intoned with great pomp and ceremony, without unrolling the parchment. 'Or some such nonsense. It's particularly interesting, I think, that they should be holding this so-called "gathering" in Jetra though, don't you think?'

Tycho frowned. 'To honour the Swan?'

'It must surely be a council of war.' The Lord of Forent scanned the contents of the scroll once more. 'Though it does not actually say so. Why else hold it in the home city of the Dystras and their beauteous sacrifice, so despicably scorned by the barbarian king?' He looked up again and his eyes glinted. 'And you, my lord, are singled out for special mention.'

'I am?' He was surprised. The Duke of Cera had hardly deigned to speak to him before; for while Lodono could trace his ancestry back to the glorious days of the Hundred Day War, in which his family had routed and massacred every clan dwelling in the rich foothills of the Skarn Mountains down to the smallest child, he, Tycho Issian, could not even tell civilised company the true name and nature of his own father. He snatched the parchment from the Lord of Forent's hand and read aloud:

'"To Lord Tycho Issian, who husbands so well the city of Cantara, we extend a particular welcome in this time of his grievous loss."'

He paled.

'What grievous loss?' He looked wildly about him, suddenly terrified that his shameful lust for the Rosa Eldi had been spied out. Then he realised what was meant. 'Ah – no – Selen . . . Have they word of my daughter? Is it worse than I feared? Have they perhaps found her broken body washed up on some desolate shore?'

Rui shook his head. 'Do not panic, my friend. I smell politics at work here, rather than disaster. Make the sorcerer scry for you if it puts your mind at rest. It seems to me that the Council may think to use you as a rallying point for the people, to work on their sympathy with a touching tale of abduction and horror . . .' He paused, musing. 'Or maybe, just maybe, our tactics have worked rather better than we had thought and public opinion is forcing their hand, for I cannot believe the old guard would welcome war anew. There must surely be considerable unrest to cause them to call us all away from our duties at such short notice. "The day after full moon next" – that's barely a week away. We shall have to make swift provision for the journey.' He clapped the Lord of Cantara hard on the back, leaving a sharply defined handprint on the other man's bare shoulder. 'Fine news, eh Tycho? Get ready to preach and rant in every market square on the way south to fan the flames. Better ask the crone to prepare you a new tincture that won't drive the crowds away!'

*   *   *

'Harder, boy, harder. Put some muscle into it!'

'Oh, for the Lady's sake!'

Saro Vingo hit the ground of the practice field with a thud, sending a little cloud of red dust spiralling into the air. Captain Galo Bastido stood over him, grinning maniacally out of his lopsided, broken-nosed face, his vast fists wrapped around the gigantic wooden sword with which Saro had just been thwacked. His arms ached; his shoulders ached; his head ached. And now his shins had added their own protests to his body's general groan of complaint: they had been out on the field for well over an hour and a half without halt, and in all that time Saro had done little more than land a few glancing blows on his opponent. Quite the opposite was the case with the captain. The Bastard sweeping his legs from under him in this last ignominious fashion had been the latest degradation in a long sequence of humiliations that seemed designed to prove to the men watching – his father, his uncle and a visiting group of horse-traders – that the younger Vingo son would never have the strength, skill or guts to make up for the tragic lost promise of the elder; and that instead of passing the title of captain of the Altean militia to this pathetic specimen, Galo Bastido should reclaim the prestigious (and remunerative) role he regarded as his by right.

Saro reached for the sword he had dropped and used it to lever himself wearily to his feet.

'Again!' the Bastard called, and took up his stance.

Saro looked to his father for respite, but Favio stared at him stonily; indeed, appeared to be looking right through him to the enclosure beyond where the finest of the Vingo bloodstock cropped contentedly at the only green grass for miles in any direction. Saro knew this to be the case: he had last year helped to dig the irrigation system which kept it watered while the rest of the land parched in the late autumn sun. Tanto, of course, had not been expected to engage in such menial labour: he had spent the baking afternoons while Saro hacked at the rocky ground with pickaxe and spade riding one of the geldings over to the neighbouring estate and seducing their newest acquisition, a slavegirl purported to have spent time in the seraglio at Forent, and therefore a most accomplished and imaginative courtesan; or at least, that was how Tanto had reported the use of his time. Saro had had his doubts even then as to the veracity of his brother's lurid tales of conquest. Now, after weeks of being subjected to the filthiest corners of Tanto's memory and imagination, which entities appeared to be almost indistinguishable, Saro was becoming convinced that the tales his brother had told of those sultry afternoons had been very edited indeed.

Tanto was seated now in the contraption that Favio and Fabel had commissioned for his use: a long, wickerwork chair with two small cartwheels attached in which the invalid would be able to propel himself along the flatter pathways surrounding the villa. That had been the idea, anyway; but Tanto had made no great effort to be self-sufficient, but had instead insisted on having two servants follow the chair at all times to lift it down steps or over thresholds, or even to push the vehicle along if he could no longer be bothered to do it for himself. A lever at either side brought the chair to rest and anchored it firmly; and if Tanto was overcome with exhaustion from all this exertion, another lever allowed the back of the chair to tilt until the thing had become a perfectly comfortable bed-on-wheels. Favio had worked on the design for long hours, sketching on parchment with goose quills and expensive inks, before handing over his plans to a man in Altea town who specialised in the construction of horse-drawn racing carts. It had cost the family a small fortune they simply did not have: Saro had heard his father and uncle arguing into the small hours about the grievous nature of the family's finances. The deal for Night's Harbinger, their finest horse, had fallen through, and no one seemed to be buying much at the moment anyway. There was too much uncertainty in the air, too much talk of war for anyone to be committing their capital to breeding programmes or such frivolities as racing; but Favio had been insistent about the need to provide his beloved son with his own means of transport around the grounds. 'It will do him a power of good to regain a little independence, you'll see.'

But as far as Saro could see, it just afforded his brother more excuses to follow him around the estate to ensure his torments never became stale.

Wincing, he pushed himself to his feet now and brought his sword up to signal his readiness to continue the bout. He was so exhausted that when the Bastard came at him again, instinct took over and had him moving out of the man's way without his conscious mind intervening in his response at all. Suddenly, he found the captain's wide back offered to him and his wooden blade descending in a stinging blow as he passed. His arms tingled with the momentary contact, then he was back in himself again, bemused by the shouts of surprise from the stockade.

'A hit!'

'By the Goddess, boy, you got him!'

He looked up to see Fabel there, grinning widely.

'Go on, lad!' he called. 'You've got the measure of him now.'

This seemed palpably unlikely to Saro, but he could not help but experience a brief moment of amazed self-congratulation. A moment later, he found himself unable to breathe. Under the guise of a complicated spinning attack, the Bastard had caught him with a vicious fist to the gut. Out of the onlookers' view, it was designed to seem that Saro had been caught napping in his moment of triumph. The audience at the fence groaned in resigned acceptance. The strike on the captain had clearly been an aberration; a lucky blow.

Finding his knees giving way, Saro clutched for balance at his opponent's arm. He knew it was a mistake even as his fingers closed on Bastido's hard muscle. Ravening ambition spiked through him, as bitter as bile; hurt pride, overweening arrogance – for here he was, Captain Galo Bastido – the finest warrior in the province – forced to play-fight this piteous creature grovelling in the dirt before him when by rights he should be training the troop he was born to lead, parading through the streets of Altea town in a red-plumed helmet and silk-lined cloak, with the ladies remarking favourably on the fine figure he cut, and the men in proper awe of his discipline. It was insupportable. It was unfair. He _could_ not allow the plume to pass to this _worm_ of a boy—

Saro _saw_ the disabling stroke – a neat, twisting downward cut designed to detach the plate over the knee—

He rolled away just in time. The Bastard's heavy practice blade came whistling down, grazed his shin and buried itself in the red soil with a thud. The look in the man's eyes as he backed away was quite enough to confirm his suspicions: Galo Bastido would cheerfully have crippled him in that moment.

'Enough!'

Favio Vingo strolled wearily into the enclosure, every line of his body speaking his disenchantment, and his resignation. The boy was hopeless, but it would be shame indeed to have the Altean militia led by any other than a Vingo, as Tanto kept reminding him . . .

The messenger had arrived from Jetra that afternoon. The Vingos were summoned to join a Council gathering in the Eternal City. 'They must be scraping the barrel, brother,' Fabel said, looking up from Cera's missive, 'to require our presence.'

They were not members of the Ruling Council, but only of the extended governance of the provincial states: Altea provided scant revenues to the Council's coffers even in a good year.

'It must surely mean war,' Favio returned gloomily, taking the scroll from his brother and casting a suspicious eye over the curt invitation as if seeking some further message written in an ink only he might perceive. 'But if it does, why don't they come right out and say it? I don't want to haul myself all the way to bloody Jetra for no good reason.'

Tanto thumped the table. 'I hope it does!' He grinned at Saro, who was balanced precariously on the bench on one buttock, trying desperately to avoid even the slightest touch from his brother. For his part, Tanto had been edging his way minutely along the bench they shared during the course of the meal and was thoroughly enjoying Saro's obvious discomfort.

'Why so, my son?' Favio turned a puzzled face to his favourite.

'Then Saro may avenge my injuries on the barbarians who brought me to this lamentable plight.'

Fabel nodded sagely. 'Indeed, I am sure your brother is eager to do just that. Has he not been training hard these past weeks for just such an opportunity?'

I certainly had no such thing in mind, Saro thought. *Quite the opposite: were it not for the torment I've suffered as a result, I'd bless the one who brought my beloved brother to this pass.* Rather than say such, he smiled dutifully and inclined his head. 'Of course, Uncle, although it seems to me that I have little talent for war.'

In normal circumstances, Tanto would have delighted in taking up this chance to humiliate his sibling further; but instead of agreeing with Saro's unchallengeable statement, he said: 'Excellent, brother. I knew you would not fail me. You will make us all proud.' And the look he gave him then was opaque and hard to read. But Saro knew him well enough to sense some other game at hand. And so he watched through narrowed eyes as Tanto leaned across the table to their father and said something in a low tone that he could not quite catch. Then, with cumbersome care, the invalid swung his apparently lifeless legs over the settle and snapped his fingers at the two body-servants currently lolling beside the hearth, who sprang into action with an alacrity born of long experience of Tanto's impatient rages and swift fists, installing him in the rolling chair before he had had time even to utter the command.

Favio rose; but as Saro got to his feet, too, he waved his hands. 'No, no – stay here and entertain our guests, my dear son. We'll be back shortly.'

Saro could not remember the last time Favio had addressed him thus. Something was surely afoot. He sat back down and watched his brother and father disappear through the chamber's door with cold dread seeping into the pit of his stomach.

Their guests for the evening were a pair of bloodstock traders from the north-east. Some sort of deal had been struck for three of the mares to augment their stud; but they had no need of more stallions, so the Vingos were left with Night's Harbinger and precious little money to show for the day's discussions. The cost of the meal alone – a lavish affair – would probably undo what little profit the family had taken; but at least the men were good company. They were a lively pair: one portly and wicked-humoured, the other as thin as a fence-post with a laugh like the rattle of a pied crow. They had been in business together since the last war and seemed closer than man and wife, for when one started a sentence the other was likely to finish it for him, and they seemed to delight in setting up each other's jests and punchlines. It hardly seemed necessary to entertain them, but as ever Fabel played the good host.

'So,' he said now, rubbing his hands together as if in anticipation of a treat, 'what's been your best deal of recent weeks?'

The squat man – Dano – winked at his partner. 'Better not mention the widow, eh Gabrio?'

The thin man's rattle echoed off the walls. 'Or her silly daughter – ah, no; but the bay—'

'—with the star; thought its spine would surely snap!'

'Thirty cantari—'

'Thirty-one – don't forget the one!'

'Thirty-one: you are correct as ever, my friend.'

'She was a big woman—'

'Quite huge. I'm sure Figuero's back looked bowed when she finally clambered off him.'

'No more than her legs even before she got aboard—'

'She might fit you, then, Dano!'

And they were off and chortling again. Saro exchanged a look with his uncle, who rolled his eyes and tried a different tack. 'So you say you came down through Jetra then, gentlemen?'

The thin man – Gabrio – swallowed his clattering laughter and regarded Fabel solemnly. 'Ah yes, the Eternal City, flower of the Empire. Strange to see a town so renowned for its tranquillity in such a ferment.'

'Ferment?'

'I've never seen so many lords gathered in one place: Cera, Prionan, Gila, the Bear – even one of the Circesian lords; and the Dystras, of course – all preparing for this Council meeting, I suppose.'

Fabel frowned. 'What about Rui Finco, Lord of Forent?'

Dano leaned across the table. 'Taken up with a madman, they say.'

'Oh?'

'The Lord of Cantara – who never used to be one of the Ruling Council, unless my memory's poorer than I remember?' Gabrio scratched his head. 'Anyway, they were both travelling south when we left, preaching and railing all the way.'

'Preaching? Rui Finco? Surely not? The man's a libertine – about as different to Tycho Issian as can be.'

Dano quirked an eyebrow. 'The Lord of Cantara a friend of yours?' he asked carefully.

Fabel snorted. 'Hardly.'

An expression of relief crossed the trader's face. 'That's all right then. Nutter. Crazy as they come. Whipping them into a frenzy all the way around Forent, calling for a holy war against the North.'

'Holy?' Saro asked. The last he had heard of the southern lord, he had been urging raids upon Eyra in response to the abduction of his daughter Selen. Understandable vengeance; but hardly a sacred cause.

'Takes a tall, pale man with him—'

'—wherever he goes. He just stands there—'

'—behind him. With a cat.'

'With a cat in his arms, all trussed up like a roasting bird—'

'—poor thing.'

'Poor thing.'

'And what do they do, the pale man and the cat, I mean?' Saro asked.

'Why, nothing,' Dano said. 'It's like . . .'

'. . . theatre,' finished Gabrio, and the two men grinned at one another. 'A bit of stage-dressing. Catches the eye and draws a crowd. Keeps 'em riveted, too: spellbound.'

Saro and his uncle exchanged glances. 'A strange alliance,' Fabel said at last. 'And there's really talk of war?'

'The people seem to want it,' Dano said simply. 'Not the Council, not really: they're more cautious.'

'Older lords have been there before,' Gabrio added. 'They've seen what war can do, the atrocity and the disruption. They're less keen. Plus, they know the state of the country's treasury. Not good.'

'Not good,' Dano echoed. 'War's expensive.'

'Affords opportunities, though,' Gabrio said brightly. 'Money to be made—'

'—power to be mongered.'

Saro shivered. If there were a war then he'd have to fight in earnest. He imagined having to fend off some huge veteran northerner with a bloodstained axe, a big man with murder in his eyes and death in his hands. He'd better start learning how to run faster.

There was a commotion at the doorway and an exchange of voices heralded the return of his brother and father. Then Tanto's wheeled chair came into view, heaped high with unfamiliar objects which glittered in the flickering gold light of the candles like a treasure-horde.

The traders whistled.

'For you, brother,' Tanto said softly, positioning himself in such a way as to block any escape. 'All for you.'

It was the armour of Platino Vingo, legendary hero of their house, Lord of Altea, Pex and Talsea and head of the Ruling Council in those days before the Vingo fortunes had plummeted and drought had gripped their land like a rabid dog. On top of a faded linen surplice in the family colours of blue and silver lay a breastplate of bronze all chased with silver in the form of a rising hawk, its talons encircling a coiling snake. Tooled leather vambraces and greaves lay jumbled in Tanto's lap; gauntlets and mailed boots. On top of the whole pile sat the helm: a mighty lump of bronze and iron as forbidding as a severed head, its eye-slit a vacant gash, its horsehair plume the faded red of sun-bleached plush.

Saro felt the breath ooze out of him.

'Since I will never have the honour of bearing these arms, it is only fitting that they pass to you, brother,' Tanto said, smiling. For all his pallor and sunken cheeks, he looked as sunny and innocent as a child offering meadow flowers to its mother.

Unable to meet this unnerving regard, Saro stared down at

the helmet instead, taking in the little dents and scrapes that marred its polished surface; at the gouges in the crest and cheek-guards where the weapons of enemies had glanced off; at the jagged widening at the right of the eye-slit.

When he looked up again, he found Tanto's gaze upon him; and now the pupils were black with some powerful emotion.

'Here,' Tanto said. He picked up the helmet and held it out. 'Take it. It's yours now, brother.'

Saro glanced past Tanto to where Favio stood in the doorway. His father gave him a chilly look, then nodded almost imperceptibly.

'Go on, lad,' Fabel said cheerfully from behind him. 'It may be an antique, but you'll never see better. It was forged by Culo, you know: they say it was his apprentice piece before he became Constantin's smith.'

It had been a hundred and sixty years since Istria had deposed its last emperor; which made the armour over a hundred and eighty years old, Saro calculated rapidly. He stared at the thing, unwilling to take it into his hands, which had begun to shake.

'A little bit of history, that helmet,' Fabel went on, apparently unaware of Saro's discomfort. 'Been through the Battle of Six Hills, the Fords of Alta, the War of the Ravens. Lady knows how many other conflicts.'

There was no escape: Saro could feel the room closing in, could sense the weight of four pairs of curious eyes upon him. Gritting his teeth, he reached for the artefact, but Tanto was faster. With a feint, he brought the helmet up past Saro's extended hands and, with a remarkably swift and deft manoeuvre for an invalid, jammed it down over his brother's head.

Death flowed around Saro, a freezing tide. Somewhere, horses screamed, swords rang, men roared. In a dozen different times, in a dozen different places, he heard the same

cacophony: a mad jumble of sound denoting agony, desperation and rage. The sweet, iron tang of blood filled his nostrils,
the acrid sweat of men and animals, dung and hacked earth.
In one time he felt the bones in his forearm jar as his sword
locked with another man's; in another, a weapon pierced his
back. The rings of a mailshirt were crushed into his chest by
the savage fall of an axe; he saw the swordpoint that ended
his life angling through the eye-slit of the helmet, grating
through the bronze. Bright sparks against a dark sea. Despair
washed through him; despair and disbelief and a stream of
unanswered, unanswerable questions:

*Is this truly the end, does it happen so simply? Stupid: a stupid
error — I never saw his second blade.*

*Why were we fighting this battle, anyway? Was not the rumour
that we had won the war yesterday at Talsea?*

*Should have blocked that last thrust and gone left. If I fall, I
will be trampled. Hold the cantle, hold tight. Why cannot I feel
my fingers?*

*Is that a crow up there, circling; or a gull? My eyes are getting
so bad. Who will oversee the harvest? Can Pali be trusted to run
the estate?*

Ah, Falla, now I know what pain means.

*Will I never see my Corazon again . . . my sons . . . my
beloved hounds?*

Is this all there is?

A thin, keening cry reverberated from one wall of the
helm to the other, growing ever louder, like the clang of
the Crier's bell.

He felt darkness and blessed silence reach out for him.
Something in him then rushed to embrace that quiet place
which beckoned; but hands fell upon him and the images
changed from those of war and death to concern and distress.
Apart from one, light touch, a mere brush of fingers on
the skin of his neck. A voice sounded quite clearly in
his head.

'You see, brother, what I can do? I will have you yet.'

Then there came a babble of noise, followed by a brief sensation of tugging and a moment of acute discomfort; and at last the helmet was off and all the images fell away.

Fourteen

The Eternal City

Virelai had dreamed of entering the Eternal City ever since he had come across a tiny black etching tucked away between the pages of a treatise on the anatomy of dogs which he had purloined late one night from the Master's study. Neither concept – 'dog' nor 'city' – held much meaning for him at that time, since he had not yet been introduced to the miraculous viewing contraption in Rahe's secret chamber and therefore had seen neither any place beyond the icy wastes of Sanctuary nor any creature other than Bëte: but he had been fascinated by the detailed pictures of flayed skin and lurid organs and the very idea that such peculiar component parts might be comprised in a single living thing; and then the sketch of the city had fluttered out of the book and landed on the floor at his feet.

At first, he had not been sure what he was looking at: a great array of blocks and curves, spikes and arches shimmered in one half of the picture and were repeated in sharper, inverted form below. He had picked up the parchment to examine it more closely and only eventually, after turning it around and around and around, had he realised that he had been looking at the image upside-down and that rather than offering him an abstract pattern, the picture was of some sort of citadel, carved from the living rock on which it stood, a citadel which stood on the edge of a lake so that its spires and crenellations, its arches and roofs were reflected in the water below in a perfect echo of the structures above.

Something about the picture pleased him immensely: something about its balance and symmetry seemed at once transcendent and reassuring, though he had no words for these concepts, either. The image had haunted his nights ever since, so that time and again in a dream in which he scurried about the corridors of Sanctuary, he would find himself standing suddenly at the towering carved gate in the etching, gazing up at its vast door, drawn by the mysteries he sensed within.

Now, here he was, barely a mile from that very place, negotiating a steep defile through a tangle of boulders and thorn bushes, with his thighs and backside aching fiercely from the unrelenting jolt of the little nag his new masters had put him on; and rather than being filled with anticipation, he had never felt so uncomfortable in all his existence. Even after five days of riding he had still not mastered the beast. He had never sat astride any animal before: when driving the yekas, it had always been from the safety of the wagon; but Tycho had been characteristically unsympathetic. To take in every possible rallying point on the way between Forent and Jetra and still arrive in time for the Council meeting, it was necessary to take the fastest route, which involved such rocky terrain and dense forests, narrow tracks and steep tors that any sort of wheeled vehicle was out of the question; so Virelai had been forced to strap Bëte's wicker box onto one side of the pannier they had slung over his animal – a bad-tempered pony with a dirty white coat and virulent yellow teeth, which it liked to show a lot – and his grimoires on the other, and then clambered into the saddle, where he had sat for the past few days, feeling as precarious as a perched block ready to tumble off down the hillside at any moment. There were times when he thought he would be able neither to walk nor sit properly ever again.

The cat, however, and with its usual perversity, had made no complaint. If anything, the rocking of the horse seemed to lull it into a hypnotised doze: he had not heard a peep out of it during the journey (though getting it out, and then back in, to the box when they made their scheduled stops along the way was a different matter). Virelai almost envied it its comfortable captivity, its capacious rug-lined box. He was just thinking this when the nag stumbled on a loose stone and attempted to catapult him from the saddle. He lost the reins immediately and grabbed wildly at the beast's mane. The girth slipped. When, a moment later, he opened his eyes, he found himself hanging upside-down beneath the nag's sweating belly, gazing down across the plain at the very image of the Eternal City he had first seen on the Master's parchment etching.

The Vingo clan had travelled to the Eternal City across the Altan Plain, skirting the rocky defiles of the White Peak and crossing the Golden Mountains at Gibeon, where Fabel had settled a small debt (which meant putting off another creditor for a little while), and stayed overnight at the Three Ladies Inn, reputed to have been a notorious brothel in the time of Lord Faro – as Tanto reminded everyone with glee – but was now known far and wide for the excellence of its food and wine. 'We deserve one night of luxury,' Favio had declared after his brother had protested the expense, 'after three days on the road.'

Even after downing several glasses of the rich red vintage for which the region was renowned, Saro found it impossible to sleep. Being forced to share a room with Tanto did not help, although his brother, exhausted by the jolting of the wagon and by the effort it had required to sink three bottles of the most costly wine in the establishment, was snoring loudly. The episode with Platino's helmet seemed to have sensitised Saro even more to the echoes around him: he

could sense the thousand lives that had previously touched
the bed on which he lay. Many had done far more than
merely sleep there, of course. The imprints they left behind,
as if ingrained in the wood of the furniture itself, were blurred
and manifold, but sufficient to prevent his rest. Instead, he
sought the quiet of the stables and spent that night with the
horses: their memories were short and their lives simple; and
even Night's Harbinger, high-strung as he was, caused him
no disturbance.

The next morning, as they took the old trade road
that wove through the foothills where the Golden Range
debouched onto the Tilsen Plain, they spied a nomad caravan,
moving with slow grace across the infinite grasslands. Some
ponies grazed nearby, untroubled by the passage of the
Wandering Folk and overhead a flock of the region's geese
streamed effortlessly past, their long necks outstretched, their
long wings beating the air. The rest of their entourage paid
far more attention to the latter than to the distant nomads:
Jetran geese were fine sport, and produced the feathers
which the great fletchers used to flight their most expensive
arrows – Tanto was loudly holding forth on the subject. Saro
shaded his eyes against the heat haze and concentrated on the
Wanderers. He counted only five wagons and less than a dozen
yekas, which must surely represent only the vanguard of the
travellers. He scanned the horizon for the rest, having read
that the nomads travelled in great caravans often consisting
of half a hundred wagons and thrice as many of the shaggy
great beasts that pulled them. Certainly, the troupe he had
witnessed arriving at the Allfair conformed to this description;
but he had heard in recent months that these huge caravans
were splintering into smaller groups in an attempt to be less
conspicuous, to be able to melt away into the landscape in
times of trouble. Persecution was rife; but to travel in so small
a group surely offered no protection at all. If the five wagons
were outriders, there was no sign of their companions in any

direction that he looked. Had they started out with more? And if so what had become of them? With a shudder, he remembered the rotting, mutilated bodies they had passed on the riverbank south of Pex on their journey back from the Allfair and found himself praying again that little Guaya was not amongst the dead.

Above the startling blue of the water soared red and ochre walls; red and ochre reflections shimmered back out of the lake. *Jetran blue*, Virelai (now upright and with the girth tightened and the reins gripped firmly in his fists) thought with a sudden shock of recognition as he remembered the exotic names on the pots of ink stacked on Rahe's study shelves. Shadows of umber and violet constrasted sharply with the sun-washed stone, exaggerated the details of the carvings, the arrowslits and the caryatids. Turreted towers punctuated the walls; ornamented spires pierced the skyline. His mouth fell open. Ahead of him, Lords Tycho Issian and Rui Finco rode on unconcerned, untouched by the magnificence of the view. They had seen Jetra too many times to be captivated by its spell: its presence held little mystery for them now.

As they passed beneath the arch of the Dawn Gate, Virelai nearly fell off his nag again; this time for leaning back too far while trying to concentrate on the complex carvings adorning the gateway. From a distance they had appeared to be little more than a series of interlocking patterns that offered little to him in the way of interpretation, but now that they were closer, Virelai could make out the shapes of figures and creatures; a man grasping the talons of a vast raptor, a woman twined with a cat-headed snake, or possibly a snake-bodied cat; great winged beasts too large for any eagle, if the scale of the horses and yeka that danced around the arch was to be believed – a dragon, then, or some other mythological monster? Virelai wished he had paid more attention to the Master's books. Some of the carvings remained indistinguishable no matter how hard he stared at them, their details erased as if by a giant's hand, but most likely sand-blasted by centuries of desert winds.

They had come south via the Blue Peak, over the White Downs, and then had followed the steep valley carved out by the Tilsen River, their passage broken by rest-stops in those towns deemed useful by the lords for stirring up religious zeal. Virelai had gathered audience after audience for Tycho, drawing them out of their own houses by the sudden mysterious need to purchase bread, eggs or goose feathers they did not actually require, while stroking Bëte's throat to coax yet another Spell of Attraction out of her gullet. When a sufficient number had materialised in the market square there seemed to be no further need for magical intervention, since the sight of so many folk gathered in a public place seemed always to draw others merely out of curiosity and Virelai soon discovered he could fill a decent-sized forum within a third of an hour or less. Then Tycho would begin his rousing orations, alternately working upon the audience's sympathies (the terrible abduction and likely violation of his only daughter by the barbarians) and stoking their xenophobic tendencies in the name of Falla (liberating the women of the North from the heretical treatment of their men, who kept them scandalously unclothed in the sight of the Lady, to whom they made no obeisance). There was little need for Virelai to add to this volatile mix a Charm of Coercion, but he found himself doing it anyway: Tycho was not a pleasant man to work for, and it was better to be safe than savaged. As areas of settlement became more dense on the approach to the Eternal City, Tycho took to performing three times a day, urging the horses to a gallop between towns, which was why Virelai ached as badly as he did. Everywhere they went they left behind a fermenting stew of bigotry, fanaticism and murderous intent.

*   *   *

Inside the Star Chamber, many of Istria's ruling lords and their retinues had already arrived and were either milling about, helping themselves to araque and almond biscuits, or were locked in deep discussion. More would arrive as the day lengthened; the Council meeting would begin after First Observance the next day.

Saro stared about him in amazement. It was his first visit to the Eternal City, though he had read about it in a dozen stories and knew well the work of the poet Fano Cirio, who served the Swan at the Jetran court.

> Teach me, my Lady Falla
> In all things thee to see
> In the pillars of thy city
> In its great antiquity
>
> A man who looks on Jetran glass
> On it may stay his eye
> Or if he pleases, through it pass
> And your heaven there espy
>
> This is the famous city
> That turneth all to gold
> For that which the Lady does possess
> Cannot for less be told.

Which was, Saro thought, struck for the first time by the final sentiments of the poem, a clever way to coerce payment from the nobles for whom he had created and performed such verse. He gazed around now at those gilded pillars, the fabulous tapestries clothing the walls, the massively carved furniture with its distinctive clawed feet – a trademark of the craftsmen of the White Woods – and the intricate fan-vaulted ceiling fully fifty feet overhead, pinpointed with the constellations of glittering silver which gave the hall its name. It was not surprising that Cirio had been so

inspired. Saro himself felt both dwarfed and enchanted.
He could feel the age of the place, its 'great antiquity' in
every detail. The carvings that twined around the pillars and
crawled across the walls, slipping under the tapestries and
re-emerging around the high windows, were too simple in
form to be truly Istrian. Animals and people wove in and
out of one another in patterns that on first glimpse appeared
abstract, then resolved themselves suddenly, revealing dogs
and horses, yeka and winged creatures, hunters and warriors.
One particular carved panel caught his eye. On the opposite
side of the chamber, a group of men in long tunics, bearing
spears carried in elegant parallel, were pursuing a figure which
had vanished mysteriously behind one of the tapestries. Just
one perfect foot could be seen of the fleeing figure: a slim
ankle and the first few inches of calf. The carving intrigued
him. He looked around. Behind him, his father and uncle
were engaged in conversation with Lord Sestran, and Tanto
was taking his ease in their chambers. Saro knew from the
brief touch his brother had conferred upon him that Tanto
had spied there a particularly attractive bodyslave, and while
there appeared to be little he could do in practical terms to
avail himself of her charms, he still intended to make some
attempt to molest her, so Saro had approached the girl himself
before they had come down to the Star Chamber with the
intent of warning her clear of his brother, but she spoke
no Istrian and only a word or two of the Old Tongue
and just whistled and clacked at him in a bizarre fashion
that reminded him of nothing so much as the old nomad
woman who was Guaya's grandmother. They had parted
in mutual misunderstanding, leaving Saro with the horrible
suspicion that she thought he meant to have her for himself.
The shadow of that anxiety was with him still as he detached
himself from the group of men and crossed the chamber to
the tapestried wall. The hanging which covered the running
man was especially fine: its field largely of deep crimson, its

detail picked out in jewel-like greens and golds. Safflower
and desert rose entwined around the feet of Bast and the
Lady; great trees blossomed overhead, dropping their creamy
petals in their path; birds arrayed the branches, flew between
the trees, alighted on the ground; but it was not the tapestry
that drew Saro's attention, but the disembodied owner of the
foot. Slipping behind Lord Varyx and a tall thin man with a
gleaming bald head, Saro lifted the tapestry a little away from
the wall and peered behind it.

The fleeing figure, naked and laughing delightedly over its
shoulder, luring the eager soldiers onward through a tumble
of hair, was a naked man with a vast erection. And in front
of him was another and another and another, all equally
endowed. Saro gasped and dropped the fabric back into
place. His cheeks flamed. The figures were imprinted in
his vision as surely as if they had been tattooed onto the
inside of his eyelids.

The congress of men with men was forbidden in Istria:
had been so for a hundred years and more, though there
were many hero-tales of bygone days in which men partnered
closely with a comrade, to defend or avenge the other. And
then the general – less threatening and unpalatable – was
replaced very suddenly by the very particular, as yet again the
fleeting memory of Tanto forcing himself upon the slaveboy
in the orange grove assailed him. He retched at this memory,
the bile rising suddenly in his throat, and turned quickly away
in need of a discreet place – a plant-pot, maybe, or an open
window – where he might vomit.

'You must be the surviving Vingo boy.'

The voice was as polished as a river-washed stone. Saro
spun around, to find the Lord of Forent regarding him
curiously.

He swallowed. 'My brother lives still,' he said stiffly.

Rui Finco quirked an eyebrow at him. 'Not many survive
the attentions of Chirurgeon Brigo. He's a lucky man.'

Saro thought of his brother's mutilated form, his suppurating wound and increasingly poisonous temper and gave a bitter laugh. 'Hardly.'

At that moment, another figure arrived at the Lord of Forent's shoulder and his great height blocked the light from the sconce behind him. Saro felt the shadow he cast even before it fell across him.

The man who had appeared so silently was tall and wan, as white and stooped as a Farem ice-flower, his hair was the same yellow-white as a snowbear's pelt, and his eyes were as pale as a squid's. When he smiled, Saro felt as though his guts might turn to water. Under his arm, the man carried a small black cat wearing an elaborate red harness and muzzle. Unable to look the ashen man directly in those unnerving eyes, Saro found himself focusing on the cat instead. Everything about its demeanour spoke its discomfort: the bristling of the fur along its spine, the twitching of its sleek black tail; the way it pulled its head away from the long white fingers of the man's right hand, which flickered rhythmically up and down its neck. He saw how its claws – pearly pink and needle-sharp – flexed and bit into the man's forearm at each stroke; he saw how its vivid eyes flared and sparked at the indignity of its imprisonment; and he remembered what the horse-traders had said about a tall, pale man with a cat 'all trussed up like a roasting bird' who stood behind Tycho Issian while he ranted for war against the North.

When Saro looked up again, he found that the man's eyes were fixed upon him: not upon his face, however, but upon the exact point above his heart where, beneath his tunic, the pendant nestled in its leather pouch, as if that bleached and ashen stare could divine the presence and nature of the object which was hidden there. And for its part the moodstone seemed alert to the proximity of the newcomer, for it seared a sudden chill into the skin of Saro's chest and began to pulse there, a steady, drumming beat that made him feel dizzy and a little faint. Once more, Saro felt an urgent need to be elsewhere. He turned to leave, but his path was blocked by the arrival of Lord Tycho Issian.

The Lord of Cantara barely threw Saro a glance, but instead gripped Rui Finco excitedly by the arm and drew him a little aside. He looked as if he had drunk a gallon of araque, or inhaled an entire stack of sweetsmoke, for his eyes were bulging and bright with passion, and the usually tight, reserved planes of his face were flushed and mobile.

'Our stratagem is working better than we could ever have hoped!' was all Saro managed to catch of their conversation for, at almost the same moment at which Tycho Issian started to speak, the pale man leaned towards him and laid a hand on his shoulder. A terrible cold filled Saro's bones. It felt as though ice had been poured into him, buckets of it, filling up his limbs, his belly, the cavity of his chest. He could not move, could barely breathe. He waited for a torrent of images to engulf him – the typical deluge of memories and desires, random thoughts and uncontrolled urges – but instead there was nothing but a terrible, empty, paralysing chill, and images so faint as to be phantasms in his own mind. Then, as swiftly as it had come upon him, the cold retreated, and Saro realised that the pale man had taken his hand off him as if he had been burned and was even now stumbling backwards in an uncoordinated trot, so that the cat, sensing its captor's distraction, writhed cleverly out of his arms and ran beneath the table trailing its red leash. The pale man, however, did not even appear to notice its escape, for his eyes were fixed upon Saro and the look in them was one of sheer terror. Saro had seen such a look in the eyes of the slaves that Tanto tormented, in the eyes of a rabbit struck but not quite killed by a quarrel. But the last time he had seen it so clearly had been in the eyes of the old nomad woman whom Favio had brought aboard the barge at Pex to cure his unconscious brother. The death-stone, she had termed his pendant, and fled, leaving his dreams haunted by the men he had killed so unknowingly at the Allfair.

His hand came up now reflexively to cup the hidden stone, and the pale man began to gibber, as if he thought Saro might remove the talisman from its pouch and strike him dead with it on the very spot.

'For the Lady's sake, Virelai,' the Lord of Forent said sharply, staring at the magician around Tycho Issian's shoulder. 'Try not to make a complete fool of yourself and the rest of us in this august company.' Then his eyes narrowed and his gaze dropped to the floor, where a black tail could be seen protruding beneath a damask table cover, flicking angrily up and down against the fabulous mosaics. 'And may I suggest you rescue your animal and confine it safely upstairs in your chamber?'

The pale man – Virelai – hesitated. It was imperative that he recapture the cat, but he had no wish to brush past the young southerner who bore the most terrible weapon in the world around his neck as nonchalantly as if it were a mere trinket.

Saro watched the man's discomfort with curiosity. Then: 'Excuse me,' he said, and took his chance. He bobbed his head to the Lord of Forent, who was watching him suspiciously, and to the Lord of Cantara, who was not, and walked swiftly away.

'I came through Monvia Town, and there were people on the streets howling for war like a pack of wolves.'

'They burned an effigy of the northern king in the market square at Ina, in the Blue Woods.'

'And at Yeta, too.'

'I came from Gibeon, and even there where folk care little about such things, they were cursing the barbarians.'

'The Lord of Cantara is well known in Gibeon: they will take the abduction of his daughter personally.'

*   *   *

'The Duke will not sanction hostilities, surely?'

'Cera is vulnerable to Eyran attack.'

'Aye, but who says they'll attack? Ravn has his hands full with his new acquisition, from all I'd heard.'

'A fact that has incensed the people. To choose a nomad woman over the Swan of Jetra is an abomination.'

'That face, though . . .'

'Viro, you should watch your mouth or you'll find yourself heading for a pyre.'

'The treasury will not stand for the cost of another war.'

'There may not be much choice: the people want it, and as we have always known, our people are most determined when they set their hearts on something. Woe betide the leader of a province who stands out against the wishes of his people.'

'Hearts, though: therein lies the problem. All this talk of war is fuelled by dangerous passions, rather than sound economics. What do we gain by sacking the North? They have nothing left for us to covet. We've driven them onto a pile of rocks in the middle of a ferocious sea.'

'They could navigate the Ravenway for us—'

'Not Forent's ludicrous scheme again! I do not even believe in the existence of this "Far West"; and everyone knows that such treasure is a myth. Besides, if we carry war to the north, they'll hardly give up their secrets willingly, and who would trust information extracted by duress? No: this is bigotry run mad. I for one will vote against the very notion of a war – it's taken us twenty years to recover from the last one.'

'That poor woman: stolen away by those dogs for their perverted pleasures. I can hardly bear to think of what may have become of her. See her father over there, a man racked by the horror of it all. He has been preaching the good cause, they say, persuading the people to pray with him to Falla for the Lady Selen's safe return.'

'That or sending ships north to take her back by force.'

'And saving as many of the women of the Isles, too.'

'The brothels of Sestria would profit from some new blood.'

'Varyx, that's a disgraceful thing to say!'

'Well, what else will happen to them if we "liberate" them from the barbarous yoke of their menfolk?'

'Why, we shall offer them honourable protection, give them over to the Sisters for instruction in Falla's ways.'

'Ha! I doubt the Sisters will welcome the sudden intrusion of a thousand Goddessless Eyran bints to clutter up their precious Contemplation Grounds.'

'Varyx: you are a profane scoundrel.'

'Pragmatic, Palto; I prefer pragmatic.'

'It would take six months – more – to build a fleet. And such an expense we cannot afford.'

'The Lords Issian and Finco seem well in funds and much in favour of a conflict.'

'That is, I must say, a curious reversal of fortunes. Has anyone any idea whence all this newfound wealth has sprung? Last I knew of it, Prionan and Cera were demanding the late repayment of Cantara's debt to the Council. Balto Miron was rubbing his hands in glee at the thought of acquiring himself a new castle.'

'You are behind the times! The Lord of Cantara has, I have heard, discovered a silver mine in his lands. Certainly, all his debts are repaid in full and he has been most generous to a number of charitable causes of late.'

'Doesn't their alliance strike anyone other than me as rather odd? After all, Rui Finco has had the reputation as the most licentious man in Istria for many years. He must surely have fathered an entire dynasty of bastards by now.'

'May I suggest you keep your voice down, Gabran: they're just behind us! Come, let us move away into the gardens. Now then, what I had heard was that the Lord of Forent has changed his ways, is making daily sacrifice and spending much time exhorting the people to holy thoughts and deeds.'

'Preaching war, you mean?'

'Well, certainly carrying the Word of the Lady to the pagan Isles.'

'Carrying fire and sword, you mean.'

'If that is what it takes to civilise our northern neighbours, then they have all my support.'

'I took this scar from the last war with Eyra.'

'My father lost his life.'

'My estates have never recovered from the destruction the northerners visited upon them.'

'Do you not wish a chance for revenge? I am vowed to seek the men who killed my father. If war is declared, I shall volunteer to crew the first ship north!'

'What do you know of seamanship, Festran? You would perish from wave-sickness before you even passed the harbour wall at Hedera Port.'

The assembly was convened as soon as First Observance had been made. The echoes of the Crier were still reverberating from the rose-red walls of the city's towers as the lords of Istria, and their sons and nephews and cousins, all took their seats in the Council Chamber, until the room was packed tight and humming with conversation. Over a hundred of Istria's most powerful men were gathered there: hereditary peers and nobles whose bloodlines could be traced back to the days of the First Dynasty; clan heads representing every major town and city in every province of the Empire. At the head of the table set in the centre of the chamber – a vast affair carved, it was said, from the trunk of a single

great oak from the forest around Sestria before the call for
a new fleet in the Third War had decimated the area's trees
– sat Lord Prionan, the Duke of Cera and the Lords of Jetra,
Greving and Hesto Dystra. The latter appeared to have aged
by years in the space of mere months: already elderly men,
they now appeared stooped and frail, their grey hair thin
streaks across the identical shiny pink domes of their heads.
They had taken the insult to their granddaughter hard, it was
said by some; though others argued that she had surely had
a most lucky and narrow escape, and that if she had been
carried off to Eyra, they would surely have borne her loss
more grievously. Prionan, on the other hand, appeared to
have been living rather too well. Florid of complexion and
rotund of frame, he looked as if he might burst out of his
elaborate robes of state at any moment. By contrast, the
Duke of Cera was elegance personified; slim and understated
in his midnight blue and discreet silver, he occupied his chair
with all the poised grace of one of his snow leopards, his
black eyes darting glances around the chamber as if assessing
every nuance of atmosphere, every detail offered in the faces
present, every thought lurking in men's minds. He did not
welcome a war: like Hedera, Cera had much to lose in any
war with the North, as had proved to be the case time and
time again down the centuries. The walls of his city – held
by his family for two hundred and fifty years, ever since they
had ousted the resident barbarians from their homes – had
been scaled and smashed down on four separate occasions,
and rebuilt higher after each attack; the castle walls bore the
scars of fire and siege; new wells had had to be dug after water
supplies were poisoned. And for the first time in years, there
were sufficient funds to construct the fine aviary he had been
planning: he had far rather spend his waning years with his
creatures than waging an unwinnable war.

Saro was assigned a seat at the end of a bench just one
row back from the table, while his brother was reverently

manoeuvred in the wheeled chair they had had to convey
all the way from Altea to a position at his side. It was,
Saro thought, an unlikely honour to be seated so close to
the centre of power; and probably a mistake on the part of
some bored official.

However, the Lord of Cantara, if he had been expecting
to be offered a seat at the high table, was about to be sorely
disappointed; for when he entered the chamber confidently
at the side of Rui Finco, who strode up to his rightful seat at
the left hand of the Duke, Lord Issian was discreetly shown to
the row where the Vingo clan were seated so that Favio and
Fabel were forced to stand to allow him to pass. Saro saw his
father's face darken with loathing as the southern lord pushed
by and knew his thoughts at once.

Saro got to his feet to allow Tycho to sit beside his brother;
but the Lord of Cantara took one appalled look at the white,
hairless, sluglike creature in the wheeled chair and sat down
abruptly and without a word between Saro and his uncle.

Tanto's eyes flashed his fury and a moment later he dug a
spiteful finger into Saro's thigh. It was a momentary touch,
but even so, a welter of bile burned through him.

'Sit back so I may address the Lord of Cantara.'

Saro would have given much to be seated elsewhere
entirely, but he leaned back as far as he could.

'My lord,' Tanto began in his new, high, wheedling
voice.

Tycho pretended not to realise that he was being addressed
thus.

Tanto coughed and spoke louder. 'My lord of Cantara.'

It was impossible to ignore him: others were shifting in
their seats, craning to listen to the exchange. This was, after all,
the hero of the Allfair, the man who had almost died in trying
to save Tycho Issian's daughter from dishonour at the hands
of Eyran brigands; a man, moreover, who had once been
the flower of Istrian manhood and would, it was rumoured,

never walk again and never father children of his own. It was a scandal, a disgrace: a tragedy of the first order.

Tycho inclined his head as graciously as he could manage. 'Tanto Vingo: an honour to see you again.'

'What news of your daughter, my lord?'

Tanto's voice rang out across the Council Chamber so that people stopped in the middle of earnest discussions and looked around to see who had called out so loudly. Tycho forced down all signs of the delight he felt at this so very public question: he could hardly have engineered the situation more neatly if he had been seated at the head of the table.

Pitching his voice to carry much farther than was necessary to cross the space between him and Tanto, he replied: 'There is no news, my boy. No news at all. I fear she is dead, or worse enslaved by those filthy miscreants who stole her away and murdered her companion. I have slept not one full night since she was taken from me. I sacrifice to the Goddess every day for a sign of her survival, but I have yet to be rewarded.'

'They are monsters!' Tanto cried. 'Surely we cannot sit quietly by and see such an act unavenged. Were I fit and able, I would carry the Lady's flame to their shores myself; but as you can see, their venomous blades have reduced me to this miserable state. My brother, however, has avowed time and again that he wishes nothing more than to take up sword and shield and cross the seas to the Northern Isles in order to requite the harm done to your family and to mine.'

Saro did not have the time or the opportunity to protest this horrible untruth, for the Lord of Cantara turned to him with blazing eyes and embraced him with a sob.

At once, his whole being was invaded so that he knew every vile thought and desire of this man whose outward appearance was one of such gentility and piety. There was no care for his daughter there; no wish for justice, dignity nor fairness at all. The beacon that burned so brightly inside the southern lord was neither devout nor honourable: it was an inferno of lustful desire that would threaten the very balance of the world, would see every man on Elda dead and trampled underfoot, if he would gain his prize. And at the heart of that ravening appetite was the image of the woman who had in the middle of the carnage at Katla Aransen's pyre, on the ashy black shores of the Moonfell Plain, reached out and touched the stone that hung around his neck, and had by that touch and by the means of some weird power she held rendered its simple magic lethally destructive. But the woman he had seen then – as pale and beautiful as a frosty day, with her fine silver-gold hair and sad green gaze – was carried in the soul of the Lord of Cantara as a barely unrecognisable harlot, a lewd and shameless voluptuary who paraded her nakedness before his eyes, proffering first her rose-tipped breasts to him and then spreading her long white legs to afford him a shockingly sacrilegious, heart-stoppingly unholy view. Then there came a bright hallucinatory flash of King Ravn Asharson as he had appeared at the Gathering, handsome and impressive in his Eyran robes, with his long dark hair, his lean muscles and sharp eyes, and the woman shining in the candlelight beside him with her hand resting possessively upon his arm; and then that pretty picture was replaced by an image of the same man ripped and eyeless and covered in running gore, hung upside-down from a pole while Tycho, with his fingers knotted in them up to the knuckle, pulled his entrails from his still-living flesh.

With a gasp, Saro broke contact with the southern lord, but the images surrounded him like a miasma through the course of the next hour, revisiting him in greater detail, both violent and profane.

So it was that he barely registered the Lords of Jetra babbling on about the indignities that had been visited upon the South, by the desecration of the garden they had made for the Swan, by the insult to the Goddess implied thereby. While the Duke of Gila complained of his failing revenues and lack of resources to fund the well-being of his people, let alone an army, he saw again cities burning and men screaming, and the green-eyed gaze of the woman superimposed upon them. When Cera spoke in his light, clear voice of the necessity to consider their position carefully and not rush into any foolish decisions, he saw her open her legs to him. As Rui Finco rose to his feet and demanded justice on behalf of his friend, and by extension to every man, woman and child in Istria; as he carried the chamber to a veritable frenzy by the most passionate and eloquent speech in the annals of the Council; as the vote was taken and carried by a vast margin; as the Lords of Forent and of Cantara were assigned joint command of the fleet that would bear arms, holy fire and the word of the Goddess to the Isles of Eyra, and as his own name was announced as the Lord Issian's personal lieutenant, Saro sat blind and deaf to the proceedings, wrapped around by a disorientating haze of abominations. The last vision that presented itself, before a hail of well-meaning compliments, pats on the back and shaking of hands assailed him and dislodged it in a welter of relative normality, was of the Lord of Cantara beside the tall, pale man called Virelai, in whose arms lay the nomad woman, standing atop a mountain overlooking a plain on which a mighty battle was taking place. Hundreds of feet below a great horde of Eyrans and Istrians fought and fell, charges were made and repulsed. Flights of arrows flew like crows. Swords rang and spears flashed. Blood flowed and horses screamed. And then there fell a moment of supernatural silence as Lord Tycho Issian held aloft the very moodstone which Saro Vingo bore now about his neck and, summoning all the power he could channel from the magician, his cat and the unconscious woman, blasted its white rays out across that dark landscape and laid waste every other living being in sight.

Fifteen

Bindings

'What is it, my love? You look so sad.'

Ravn crossed the chamber in two strides and wrapped his arms around his wife. Instead of leaning back into his embrace in her usual passive fashion, the Rosa Eldi turned to face him and her wide green eyes were troubled. But just as she was about to speak her mind, the white ermine robe which he had commissioned for her at immense expense slipped seductively down off one smooth, pale shoulder, exposing the top of her breast. She caught at it in consternation, but the moment had already imprinted itself on her husband. She watched Ravn's gaze drop, saw how it was drawn automatically to the falling edge of the fur: how his pupils flared wide and black and his hand rose to cup the exposed flesh.

Seeing him thus, desire rendering his handsome face bland and generic – a man, any man; Ravn Asharson, King of the Northern Isles no longer – its tide coursing through him to erase all marks of his true personality as thoroughly as the waves might carry away the driftwood, footprints and crabshells that had laid their character on a strand, to leave behind no more than a featureless expanse of sea-washed sand, she felt an enormous sorrow. As his hands pulled down the other side of her robe so that the velvet pooled about her feet; as his hot mouth fell again and again on her neck and she felt him grow hard and urgent against her, she felt that instead of possessing his spirit, as she had believed to be the case when she had first ensnared him; rather than sealing their connection, tying their bodies and souls into a single inextricable knot, she was losing him – the essence of him – once again.

And that was not all.

The truly bizarre matter in all this, though, was that even as they fell upon the bed and his mouth met hers, she felt she was losing herself, too. In all the lessons of love the Master had taught her in his icy fastness at the top of the world, not one had concerned the sensations she might experience during the acts that might be performed upon her. And so she had expected none, and had passed through each successive encounter – with Rahe, and then with the men to whom Virelai sold her on their travels – untouched by the experience. Until now.

On the ship which had carried her safely away from the Moonfell Plain, she had found that Ravn's touch awakened something in her. At first, she had thought this some effect of the rhythm of the waves beneath the hull of the vessel; or some proximity of the ocean's great swell. But then, when they had made dry land and were ensconced in Halbo's well-walled castle, whatever it was had announced itself in a myriad of different signs. She had become aware of a curious sense of her own displacement whenever her husband was not at her side for, despite all the ease of the northern court, where people largely spoke their mind and did not ring around their words and actions with hieratic posturings or meaningless ceremony, she knew in some deep place in herself that this was not and could never be her true home; though whether she owned such a place it was impossible to say. But when he was with her somehow she felt more at her ease, more complete in herself. Then she began to notice that if she observed Ravn speaking with another woman, let alone laying a hand upon her arm or shoulder, even in the least suggestive manner, she would feel a twinge in her chest or gut – a chill like a cold wind whistling among her bones. And when he lay with her – each night, or early in the morning, at snatched moments in the afternoon, or before they dressed for dinner – the touch of him made her skin burn, as if her blood were rising up to meet his, as if it would sear away any physical barrier between them so they could mingle as one entity. Moreover, with increasing frequency, she would often find herself swept away in the tide of passion. The most extraordinary sensations would ripple through her, possessing her, overriding any consciousness she had to match her exertions to her husband's so that her breath came in the same great heaves, her incomparably pale skin flushed pink from top to toe, and her cries – those of a distant seabird skimming lonely seas – echoed his own. At times, it seemed, she lost herself entirely and became that bird, at the mercy of strange new elements, swept here and there by salt and stormy winds. And sometimes she exulted to feel herself so lost and powerless. But the temptation to slip beneath those dark waters and never return was hard to resist.

When she came back to herself after these bouts of desire she was frightened. She had been lost all her life, and through no fault of her own; what would become of her now if she allowed herself to slip beneath those waves forever?

And so this time, as his mouth closed upon her and the two of them fell naked and urgent onto the fur-covered bed, she fought her own will. For her own sake – as well as his own – she would have to lift some measure of the enchantment she had thrown over her lord and bring him back to himself. Then, she would learn more of the actual nature of the man to whom she was bound. Then, and only then, she would learn the extent of her powers, and his response to her as a woman, rather than the sorceress she believed – and feared – she might truly be.

The banquet that night had been thrown in honour of the

marriage of the Earl of Black Isle, a pitiful rocky outcrop in
the eastern channels between the mainland and the Fair Isles,
and the daughter of Ravn's oldest and most trusted adviser,
the Earl of Stormway.

They had done their best with Breta Bransen, but they
had not had the best material to work with in the first place.
Stormway's daughter might have been a prepossessing girl,
being wide of shoulder and hip and as tall as any of Ravn's
warriors. But she carried herself with such contrition for her
size that she appeared almost hunch-backed, she stooped so
badly. Her hair – a pale, sandy colour much like her father's,
and with the same wiry unconcern for any confining style –
had been plaited into a series of braids that had then been tied
with silver ribbons about her head and threaded through with
little sprigs of pale blue flowers. On another woman it might
have looked both girlish and charming; but on Breta it looked
more as if she had been pulled backwards through someone's
kitchen-garden and taken half its contents with her. The wiry
hair escaped its bounds in little strands and clumps, marring
the elegance of the braiding, and the flowers were becoming
limp in the dry heat of the hall-fires. They had swathed her in
a dress of pale blue linen, the colour of Sur's calm sea, for luck;
but the linen had crumpled and stretched hideously. Above
it, Breta's large, lumpy face was a perfect picture of misery.

She had not wanted to marry at all, let alone Brin Fallson,
the Earl of Black Isle, a man with a sweating head and a
laugh like a distressed donkey. It was not that he was cruel
or unpleasant – she did not actively dislike him in any way
– but he represented for her the final affirmation, if such
were needed, that all the love and wit and gentleness you
could possess would never make up for a lack of looks in
this world. Not to mince words, she was plain; and that
one unfair accident of birth – whereby she had inherited
the sturdy looks of her beloved father, instead of the fey
beauty of her mother – weighed heavy in the balance against

all her other fine attributes in the eyes of the man whom she truly craved. She had been in love with Ravn Asharson since the age of seven, though to him she had never been more than a slower, weaker, more foolish playmate with whom he played his castle-games of hiding and ambush, stag-and-hounds, wrestling and duelling. She had borne his teasing, his thoughtlessness and his bullying with resignation, but time had neither erased nor eased the pain of knowing that her adoration was not one whit returned. She had conceded to herself some time ago that Ravn would likely never look upon her as an object of desire, but she had hoped in time that friendship and generosity of spirit would win him over. In fact, she thought now, he had probably never even looked upon her as a woman, let alone as a potential lover, until her father had presented her at the Moonfell Gathering. For Ravn, he had been kind then: even praising the cut of her dress, rather than laughing in her face, but it had been a humiliating experience all the same.

Her betrothed, on the other hand, had apparently watched her make her progress to the dais with trepidation, and such had been his relief at the northern king's choice of another woman for his bride that he had straightway sought out the Earl of Stormway and asked if he might call on his daughter on their return to the isles. To have any man smitten with her was a novelty to Breta, but rather than console her, it prompted in her an even greater despair in the impenetrable minds of men. However, for all that he was twelve years her senior and going thin on top of his big pink head, there was little she could really object to in him as a suitor. Ever since that heart-striking moment when she had seen Ravn look into the pale woman's eyes at the bride-taking and watched there and then as he fell in love – like a diver plunging from a cliff – she had lost all her hope in the world. And so when her father had come to her with Brin Fallson's proposition she had merely shrugged and acceded. If she could not have the one man she wanted, then she would give herself up to the first man who asked for her and damn the consequences.

But even though she tried hard not to think about it, the imminent prospect of the bedding was atrocious.

Once the feast was over, the bride and her betrothed would be led from the hall amid immense ribaldry and merriment, and be bound together in the best guest chamber, tied hand to hand and foot to foot (with a certain amount of room to manoeuvre) with the blue and green cords that symbolised the marriage of sea and land, woman and man, in Sur's eyes. They would not be untied until the sun was at its highest point the next day.

Breta shuddered and moved to take her unwanted seat of honour beside her love's new queen, whose task it was by tradition to pass the evening giving the wed-maid her best womanly advice. To have the wife of your heart's desire giggling in your ear as to the best way to please a man – how to touch him *here* and *there*, and lay your lips just *so* – would have been quite unbearable; the one consolation of the evening, Breta thought, was that the pale woman had no conversation, barely said more than a couple of words at the best of times, and was hardly likely to confide secrets to her. She nodded politely to the Rose of the World, and sat down.

The Rosa Eldi smiled briefly, then her eyes dropped to the blue wedding cords tied loosely about Breta's waist and suddenly, with a great flash of memory unlike any she had ever experienced, remembered her own wedding night – the crowds, the noise, the raucous laughter, the bawdy songs – and the look in Ravn's mother's eyes as she had tied the traditional first knot. She had known a kind of fear then, which had nothing to do with the wedding itself, but all to do with the unpredictability of being amongst too many people over whom she had little or no influence: for it seemed her charms had but small effect on women.

And remembering this moment, the Rosa Eldi felt uncomfortable again. There were too many people here, and she had the disturbing impression that they were all watching her and speaking about her just out of earshot. She kept catching little snatches of their conversation; but even when she concentrated, could not capture them whole. 'Night and day,' she heard; 'Four months now'; 'should have taken the Fairwater girl' and then, most clearly of all, 'if she will not breed, he'll have to have to take another'. But the gaze of the forbidding Lady Auda was the most unnerving thing of all.

The King's widowed mother had tonight been seated – by some horrible error, or by her own contrivance – directly opposite the new queen, and her eyes seemed always fixed on the Rose of the World, who felt those chill, violet eyes on her every minute they were in each other's company, and instinctively knew this regard for what it was: the possessive dislike of one woman for another who had usurped her position. Auda sat there gaunt-faced and shrivelled, a queen-spider fallen on hard times, her dark, white-streaked hair bound severely back into an elaborately knotted coif, her lips pursed so tight it seemed her face might sink suddenly inwards on itself. She radiated a regally compelling disapprobation; and the new Queen of the Northern Isles knew she was at all times the focus of her enmity.

In all the time that the Rosa Eldi had been in Halbo, Auda had uttered barely three sentences to her.

The first, on the evening she had set foot inside the Great Hall after landing on Eyran soil but moments earlier, had been: 'If you think your whorish nomad tricks will hold my son, you are sadly mistaken.' The second had been the traditional words with which a man's mother passed her son into the care of another woman, and hissed between bared teeth. After which Auda had taken to her chambers and refused to share a table, a room or even a breath of the same air with her son's new wife. And the third, a few weeks later, had been only after Ravn had ordered that the Lady Auda's chambers be refreshed with new Circesian hangings and rugs, which necessitated the removal of all her furniture and the lady herself, and under this ploy, had persuaded her down to his solar, where, with Ravn's big hands cupping his mother's as she grasped the Rosa Eldi's crushed fingers, had been muttered under duress: 'Welcome to Halbo, my son's wife.'

The last part of the greeting, 'and my queen', had gone unspoken and the Rose of the World had watched as her husband lost both the heart and the courage to press the point.

Since that time, Ravn had insisted on his mother's presence at all public occasions, and she had complied with pressed lips and a haughty demeanour, watching and watching the Rose of the World, and had never addressed her directly again.

Tonight she looked especially sour, though there was a gleam in her eye. A little while after the repast had been served, she leaned forward suddenly past her son and, without any polite acknowledgement of her daughter-by-law's presence, spoke across her to address the Earl of Shepsey, who was seated at the Queen's right hand.

'Back still playing you up, Egg?'

Egg admitted that this was the case, but that he ascribed his condition to his age and a draughty chamber. He started to include the new queen in this conversation by asking whether she found the castle chill, when Auda spoke over him.

'Well, it will take no less than sorcery to amend your age.' She gave the Rosa Eldi a pointed stare, and when this failed to provoke a response, launched into a lengthy treatise on just which herbs he might add to his bath for ameliorative effect. 'And make sure you test the temperature of the water before you get in: too cold and the muscles will seize; too hot and you'll just make it worse.'

Egg thanked her.

'No magic, that,' the former queen said loudly. 'No nomad

fakery required at all: good old-fashioned Eyran methods will do the trick every time.'

The Earl of Shepsey looked uncomfortable, but Ravn was intent on a conversation across the table, and if he heard his mother's barb, he gave no sign of it.

Auda made further remarks on the subject to a lady on the opposite side of the table, and then called her maid, an equally poisonous creature called, for no apparent reason, Lilja (for she resembled no lily, but rather a burdock, being both wide and dark) and made requests that she 'pass the wine by that woman's platter'. Lilja did so, awkwardly jostling the Rosa Eldi's shoulder as she retrieved the flask. The Rose of the World looked around, startled, but the moment had passed. A few minutes later, Auda raised her voice. 'Bring me a spoon that is untouched by that woman's hand!'

Quiet fell across the top end of the hall. Even Ravn heard this.

'Mother,' he said, his voice edged with warning.

Breta Bransen, seated on the old queen's right, silently passed her own spoon to Auda with a frown. She had no love for the woman who occupied Ravn's bed and all his thoughts, but such rudeness was a blight on an evening which was already sorrowful enough.

Auda took the spoon from her without a word. A little later, she beckoned Lilja to her and whispered something in her ear which caused the serving woman a sly smile and to hasten off.

'You'll be wanting babies straight away,' the old queen now addressed herself to Breta, who coloured. 'Not getting any younger, are you, girl? Left it a bit late getting wed, though. What are you now — twenty-three, twenty-four?'

Breta nodded grimly.

'The same age as my boy. I always suspected you might have had a bit of a soft spot for him,' Auda went on mercilessly. 'And why on Elda he wouldn't take you or another like you, Sur only knows. Good stock, I told him you were, just what the kingdom needs: a fine Eyran bloodline and a sturdy set of hips: you'd give him all the babies he could want to save his throne; but he's always been a fool for a pretty face, and now he's got himself a wife looks more like a skinny white serpent than a proper woman. Still, I'm sure he'll learn his lesson the hard way: men always do.'

Breta stared helplessly along the table, her cheeks flaming, but the subject of this tirade was currently feeding his new wife with a morsel of chicken from his own plate and was oblivious to his mother's remarks. She tried to think of something to say to the old woman, but was reprieved by the return of Lilja Mersen bearing a new pitcher of the bitter dark wine they pressed from the grapes grown in the chalky valleys around Fairwater. At Auda's gesture, goblets were filled around the table; but when Lilja came to the new queen's shoulder, she stumbled and cried out a great curse. Wine splashed all over the Rose of the World – over her hair, which still lay smooth and unbound like any maid's, spilling over her shoulders – over her pale robe, and over the ermine stole, which soaked up the liquid greedily, turning it an ugly, sodden red. Little runnels of the wine ran unchecked down the Rosa Eldi's white flesh, to disappear in dark runnels beneath the embroidered bodice into the milky space between her breasts.

Conversation ceased.

Auda gasped; and looked stricken. Her eyes went wide, as if shocked at the clumsiness of her maid. Then she leaned across the table and grasped the Rosa Eldi by the wrists so tightly that the pale woman cried out. But rather than uttering any word of apology, instead she declared: 'Blood will come from the South, and mar the snows of Eyra; white skin will gape and run red. Sorcery has risen: wild magic all around. Fire will fall on Halbo. Hearts will wither; many will die.'

Then her eyes rolled up in her head and she fell sideways in her chair.

If it had been staged, Breta Bransen thought, having watched the interplay between Auda and her hand-servant, it was beautifully done. Even so, it was surely incumbent on her as the one closest to the old queen to enquire as to her health. 'Are you well, my lady? Can I help you in some way?'

But the old woman neither stirred nor spoke. Curious, Breta took up her hand in her own large grasp. It felt limp and frail, the pulse beneath her fingers beating as light and as fast as the wings of a moth trapped under the skin there. And still Auda did not move. She looked across the table in some distress, but the King was intent first on the damage done to his wife's costume, and then to that done to her composure; for when the old woman had uttered her pronouncement, the Rose of the World had gone still as stone, her green eyes had become huge and she had begun to tremble from head to toe. It was Brin Fallson who came quickly to the old queen's side, who lifted her head and peered beneath her quivering eyelids and declared that she had fainted and must be removed to a place of comfort and quiet.

Breta watched as the man to whom she would be bound – tonight and beyond – took considerate charge of the situation, sent a boy to fetch the King's own healer, dispatched servants to stoke the fire in Auda's own hearth, and to lay out for her there food and wine of which she might partake when she recovered sufficiently, and carried the old woman from the room as carefully and lightly as if she had been a child; and thought for the first time that after all she might not have made such a bad bargain for the rest of her life.

The feast had been brought swiftly to a close; drinks supped up, food left for the dogs. The married pair were seen off to their room with rather less ceremony and high spirits than would usually have been expected. Lacking a living mother, Breta had been forced to ask the Rosa Eldi to tie the first knot – a figure-of-eight for eternity – and through it thread the ends of the blue cord that would bind her right hand to her partner's left; but the new Queen of the Northern Isles had never knowingly tied a knot in all her life, and Breta was forced to make the initial working for her, then explain the path the cord must follow thereafter. It had felt less than auspicious.

Her father tied the green cord to Brin's wrist and then turned to his daughter. He squeezed her hand as he made the intricate knot, and dropped his normally booming voice to a whisper: 'He's a good man, my dear. He won't hurt you.'

Breta felt tears prick her eyes, but she nodded quickly and kept smiling as the King stepped up and blessed her with a kiss on the forehead and the final knot – usually a complicated affair involving a double-sailmaker's and Sur's anchor, for good wind and safe ground – but in this case a simple sheepshank finished with a hitch, which he completed in barely two seconds, before running after his own swiftly departing wife.

The Rosa Eldi felt an unaccustomed pain gnawing at her temples. The blood beat there, hot and angry – if blood was what flowed inside her. She had begun to wonder. Since Virelai had stolen her away from Rahe, since they had left Sanctuary in that tiny boat, with her locked in the oak casket in which the Master used to keep her hidden, she had drifted as if in a dream, taking little notice of the world or the people around her: it was all too confusing, too strange. She took little notice of time passing, either. Life had been better when they had travelled with the nomads, for at least then Virelai had been unable to sell her body to any man who wished it: no money passed hands amongst the Wandering Folk themselves, though several of the men had asked whether she might wish to spend some time with them. But Virelai had seen them off angrily when he had seen there was no profit to be made from their interest, and she had been left to herself. Just before they arrived at the Allfair the daughter of the old seer – Fezack Starsinger's girl, Alisha, who had sometimes shared her body with Virelai – had come to her one morning and asked if she had need of a charm against conception. And when the Rose of the World had asked what she meant by this, Alisha had laughed and shown her the little pouch of dried herbs she wore about her neck. 'Like this: toadflax and chervil and Creeping Gilly. Wear one of these and you'll not need to worry about babies.'

Even then, the Rosa Eldi had been puzzled. Did the herbs repulse children, as the scent of an orange seemed to repel a cat? Alisha had clapped her hands together and laughed. But when she had seen that the pale woman meant the question seriously, she had questioned her further. Did she have her normal courses? And when this, too, was met with incomprehension, Alisha had done a bit of explaining, about the tides and the moon and the movement of blood around a woman's body, and how the womb prepared itself anew each month ready for a man's seed to take root there. The Rose of the World had frowned and replied, 'I have no blood,' before turning and leaving Alisha standing open-mouthed outside the door of the wagon.

Now she wondered if that statement were no more than the simple truth. She had learned rather more about the world in the intervening months. It had been four moon-cycles since Ravn Asharson had taken ship with her from the Moonfell Plain, four moon-cycles during which he had spilled his seed in her nightly, and often several times in a day. And yet her belly remained as flat as a plate, her waist as neat as ever. Girls at the court who had wedded and bedded their men since she had arrived in Halbo already bragged of their fertility and gone around showing off the growing curves of their bodies. She had learned to prevaricate with the women who discreetly asked to take her linen for washing by telling them she liked to see to her own things. But from the snippets of conversation she had overheard even tonight, tongues were beginning to wag. And the Lady Auda would only become more insistent as time went on.

'Babies to save his throne,' she crooned to herself, though she did not fully understand the old woman's import.

'What did you say, my dove?'

Ravn had entered the chamber silently behind her: she whirled around, her hand flying up to her mouth.

'Who am I?' she asked then.

It was a question she had not needed to ask him in some weeks. Ravn crossed the chamber, caught her gently by the shoulders and held her at arm's length where he could see her face clearly by the light from the wall sconces.

'You are the Rosa Eldi, the Rose of the World, the Queen of the Northern Isles and of my heart.'

Usually this quieted her; but not tonight.

'And am I not enough for you?'

Ravn frowned. 'What do you mean? You are all I have ever wished for, the most beautiful woman, the most perfect wife any man – any king – could want.'

'But you need babies to save your throne.' She said it without intonation, let the words make their own sense to him.

'Babies to save my throne? Ha! Children from you: babies to seal my succession; babies to stop the wolves circling.' He grinned at her, his teeth white amid the close black beard. 'What are you telling me, my love?'

She could not help but mirror his expression: it was an automatic response.

His whole face lit up. It was as if someone had started a fire inside him: his eyes blazed with expectation, with sharp, uncontrolled joy. Golden candleflame reflected in his dark irises, softened the hard planes made by his cheekbones and long jaw. He flung his head back and released a great laugh into the vault of the ceiling.

The Rose of the World watched this sudden outpouring of delight with a sinking heart. Whatever it was she had asked he had misunderstood: but now she had the gist of it, and it was too late. When he enfolded her in his arms and carried her tenderly to the bed, she could think of nothing to say to him. When he undressed her with undue care and ran his hands wonderingly down her concave flanks, she merely smiled and smiled. But when he laid his head on her belly and slept there without touching her further, water began to leak from her eyes. She blinked them furiously, jolted from this sudden access of emotion by the sheer unfamiliarity of the sensation. The tears ran down her face and into her mouth. They were hot and salty, unexpected.

Then she remembered something.

It was nebulous and impossible to place; but it was a memory, nevertheless. She stood staring down at a great rock-choked chasm. Dust was still settling, and there was a dull, distant booming sound beneath the noise of the falling rocks. She remembered a physical pain in her chest, a sensation in her throat as if she had swallowed one of the falling stones herself, a painful prickling at the eyes, and then the same hot, salty water gathering and spilling. Dust had covered her feet. It was red and fine. It clung to the hem of her white robe. Her feet were bare. A drop of water fell, as slowly as a feather, splashed down onto her foot, leaving a white mark amongst the red. And then a rough hand had pulled her away, and she had stumbled blindly, her eyes hazed by the first tears she had ever wept.

Sixteen

Survivors

Only about half the crew of the *Snowland Wolf*, the finest ship Morten Danson ever built, made it back to Rockfall.

Tam Fox was lost; and so were Silva Lighthand and Min Codface and half a dozen of Elda's finest tumblers and acrobats, whose skills counted for nothing in the depths of that swallowing sea. Bella, the Firecat, and two of the other women survived, along with the tumbler, Jad; and the shipmaker on account of whom the entire expedition had been formed. One of the ship's boats remained intact; the rest of the survivors clung to the broken mast and bits of floating timber until they were hauled aboard it by Urse, a new gash marring his already-spoiled face. Katla Aransen had sat in the bow for hours, even after Urse and one of the male acrobats whose name she had never known took an oar apiece and rowed away, shivering and scanning the choppy waves for any sign of the mummers' leader, her brother and new sister-by-law, Jenna Finnsen. Despite the evidence of her own eyes — for the last time she had last seen Halli and Jenna they had been inextricably bound together by their handfasting cords and were being swept over the side of the vessel — it still seemed impossible to believe they had drowned. And Tam Fox had such life force, such a power of personality and physique that he could surely not have perished. She saw, for a second, his face above her in the darkness, his braids swinging wildly and his eyes shining in the moonlight, and then shut her eyes and pushed the image away.

They rowed for three days without sustenance. On the second day it rained and they turned their faces up to the sky and drank whatever they could catch.

The rowers changed places every few hours. Saltwater blistered their palms. Some of the women cried, but the sound of their weeping left Katla feeling hollowed out, empty. She gripped her oar and stared at the grey waves and felt nothing. Was she so unnatural? In the space of a few minutes she had lost her beloved brother, her friend and – she had no idea how to think of Tam Fox. So she tried not to think about him at all.

For Jenna, she felt curiously little: seeing her brother grieving over her silly inconstancy seemed to have diminished whatever friendship they had once had. Memories of Halli, however, washed around her: the sea reminded her of him – it was his element. A hundred times, more, they had rowed out of the harbour at Rockfall in the little wooden faering Aran had made for Halli when he was six. They had fished around the skerries and further out, where they were not supposed to venture. They had brought back mackerel and pollack, and occasionally, after something of a struggle, some big seabass. He had once caught a garfish and, as the strangely beaked creature flapped madly around in the bilges, had leapt into the water in sheer panic just to get away from it, leaving Katla to grab the thing, remove the hook from its mouth and be rid of it. Except, of course, that instead of simply casting the fish back in, Katla had waited for Halli to surface once more and had thrown it right at him. It had caught him neatly on the head. She could still remember the wet slap of it, Halli's anguished howl, the great splash he had made as he dived away from the snapping creature. He was such a strong swimmer, he'd got halfway back to Rockfall before she'd been able to turn the boat around and overtake him.

She grinned at the memory of it, at Halli's furious face, at how he'd pulled her overboard and made her swim home; how they'd dripped into the hall like a pair of drowned cats, only to be scolded by their mother for ruining the new rushes she'd laid that afternoon.

'That's more like it, girlie.' Urse leaned across and patted her knee. 'See the bright side. They're with Sur now, and we're still living and breathing his air.'

She smiled bleakly, unsure as to which was the preferable state. Some while later they encountered a fishing vessel netting in the seas around Cullin Sey and were taken aboard and carried under full sail back to Rockfall.

Of the rest: sailing into the home bay, where the two shipyard barges were already moored; the faces of the folk gathered at the quay, curious as to why two great timberloads should have arrived ahead of the faster vessel; staggering into the hall on Urse's arm; her mother's wailing, Aran's silent, black-browed misery, Fent's pale-faced shock, the unnatural quiet of the steading as everyone tiptoed around, not knowing what to say, she remembered blessedly little, but drank a pitcher of milk, promptly threw up, and slept like a dead woman for the best part of two days.

'It should have been me,' Fent said for the ninetieth time. 'The seither's curse was meant for me, not Halli.'

Katla was bored with hearing him, tired of talking about it; she felt frayed and exhausted. Fent had made her describe the creature's attack, their defence, the capsize and the aftermath so many times now that the sequence of events was beginning to take on a false shape in her mind, as if somehow in the retelling he were stealing the truth of it away from her, jealous of her crucial role. It was almost as if her twin craved some part of the drama he'd been absent from, was trying to claim some part of it for himself. 'You can't really believe that. It's just superstition.'

'Katla!' He looked appalled. 'Don't say that: if you say such things you'll bring disaster on our heads for sure.'

'What greater disaster could there be? Truly, Fent, it was just a great narwhal or something like, and much bad luck. There was nothing anyone could have done differently.' She picked up a piece of wood and hurled it across the pasture for Ferg, but the old hound merely watched the arc of the stick with mild interest and then sat down heavily to lick his parts. He had not left her side since her return, and his mute presence had been of greater comfort to her than any amount of words or human contact.

'But what about the barges?' he persisted. 'Surely they would have witnessed the attack.'

'The *Snowland Wolf* made a stop on the journey back,' Katla told him, tight-lipped. She wasn't going to be drawn into describing the passage of *that* night, not to Fent. Misgiving fretted at her, a sharp little pebble rolling around and around her skull. Irritated and impatient, she pushed it away. 'The barges sailed on before we left: they wouldn't have seen a thing.'

It had been curious how everyone else's memory of the sea-creature had varied, as if they had been attacked by a dozen different beasts. Even on the ship's boat, within hours of the incident, their memories of what had occurred had begun to veer away from what Katla herself recalled. And from there, the entire episode had taken on its own life; as the survivors added their own details, and these were embellished by the listeners and passed on in a subtly (or not-so-subtly) different version to folk from other settlements and visiting traders, to women at the market or travellers passing through. She had overheard Fotur Kerilson telling the eldest of the Erlingsons that the *Snowland Wolf* had been overturned by a freak wave, and knew that Urse – whose version up until recently had been circumspect in the extreme – must have struck up acquaintance with the old man; but Stein Garson would have it that the ship had been attacked by a shoal of merwomen wreathed in weed and skulls, come to add to their dwindling collection of sailors and fishermen. After all, there had been many months of fine weather now, and no ships lost from the isles since the *Eider* went down off Fail Point.

For her part, she could see little point in fuelling speculation by adding her own bizarre observations of the thing to the fireside tales; and no one but her appeared to have noticed its eyes. As the days wore on she had begun to think this particular detail had been her own misapprehension, some trick of the light, or of her own devising. But then she remembered the weird energy she had sensed in the wood of the ship and the waters beneath its keel, the absolute certainty she had had on first sight of the thing that it was no natural creature, and she was overcome once more by a terrible sense of doom. She found herself increasingly unable to shake the feeling that there was something wrong in the world, something warped and out of true, and that some aspect of that wrongness had chosen to manifest itself to her, and in the process had taken her brother, his betrothed and Tam Fox, as well as half his troupe. It was this very sense that made her so abrupt with Fent now: he had pressed on a wound too close to the bone.

She watched as her twin walked moodily away, kicking stones out of the turf as he went. He always hated it when she refused to join in with his games; and becoming a man had not improved his temperament. Halli had acted both as shield and arbitrator between the two of them, doing all he could to prevent their disputes turning too hot or violent. She wondered what it would be like at home without him, and found she could not dwell on that thought at all.

Instead, she found her mind nagging at another matter, one that was beginning to torment her a little more with each day that passed. She had tried ignoring it, but as soon as her day became quiet, on waking or just before she fell asleep, it

would be back with renewed force. Turning her back on
the dwindling figure of her brother, she headed back towards
the hall. Nearing the enclosure, she saw a familiar figure sitting
outside. It seemed her grandmother had had enough of the
company of the other women and had dragged her big carved
chair outside to make the most of the warm weather. She sat
there with her face turned up to the sun, and the golden wash
of light smoothed out her accumulation of lines and wrinkles
so that she looked more like her daughter than a woman of her
own advanced years. A yellowed bone comb lay in her lap, her
hands curled idly to either side of it. At her feet was heaped a
mound of the oily, brown wool which grew so profusely on
the Rockfall sheep.

Katla smiled. She looked so peaceful. But at the approach
of her granddaughter's footsteps, Hesta Rolfsen's eyes flew
open and fixed her with a gimlet stare.

'Can't I shut my eyes for a second around here without
interruption?'

'Sorry, Gramma. I'll leave you.'

The old woman's clawed hand shot out and wrapped itself
with the speed of a striking snake around Katla's arm. 'Might
as well stay with me now you've disturbed my rest.' And
as Katla hesitated: 'Well, sit down, child. You're blocking
the sun.'

Katla sat crosslegged at her grandmother's feet. 'Why are
you out here, Gramma, and not inside with the others? Did
they have enough of your sharp tongue and cart you out here,
chair and all?'

'Impudent creature! As it happens, I couldn't bear another
minute in that dingy hall with a great stickful of wool stuck
under one arm and my distaff spinning away with Magla
Ferinsen's whiny little voice going on and on about how
salting the fish is beginning to ruin her fine skin. Bloody
woman. As if she was anything to look at in the first place,
with her big nose and her cow-eyes.'

'Gramma!'

Hesta Rolfsen grimaced. 'Actually, my dear, I can't spend too much time around your mother at the moment. We all have our own way of grieving, and I'd rather do mine out here in the air than watch Bera trying so hard to hold herself together. I keep waiting for her to burst apart at the seams like one of Morten Danson's god-cursed boats.'

It wasn't the most comfortable of analogies. But once Gramma Rolfsen hit her stride, there was no stopping her.

'And that bloody man keeps coming in and helping himself to a dish of stew or a loaf of bread without a word of asking or thanks – just glares at us all and stamps off again; and Aran won't say or do anything to stop him for fear he'll stop his work on the damned ship, and that's just making your mother worse. Which is no surprise: if any husband of mine persisted in such an idiot scheme having lost his own son to the sea because of it, I'd throw him off my farm and renounce our marriage vows without a moment's regret.'

For once, Katla couldn't think of anything to say. Her parents were barely speaking; her mother went about her daily chores all pinched and silent, her red-rimmed eyes the only clue to her misery, while her father stalked the steading like an afterwalker, and spent his nights sleeping alone in the barn. The silence stretched out uncomfortably. In the face of all her grandmother had said, she felt shallow and foolish to have any concerns of her own. She was just about to make an excuse and head back down to the harbour to fish for crabs, when Hesta said crossly, 'Well, if you're going to sit there, you may as well be of some use.' She held out the comb to Katla, who took it uncertainly, and then sat back in the chair again and closed her eyes against the sun.

So Katla picked up a vast hunk of the wool, wrinkling her nose against the smell, and set about it with the comb. Within minutes, however, the entire thing had transformed itself at first into a complicated series of knots, and then into an impenetrable type of felting which defied all her efforts to separate out the strands. Cursing under her breath, Katla cast the mess down and picked out a far less ambitious handful of the wool and had another try. No matter how much care she devoted to it, the stuff seemed to have an independent will; now it tangled around the teeth of the implement, and then around her fingers.

'Sur's nuts!'

Gramma Rolfsen started to cackle. 'What are you doing, chook, trying deliberately to get me into trouble with your mother?'

Katla grinned ruefully. 'I don't seem to have inherited many of her abilities, and that's the truth.'

'You're a lot more like her than you think.'

'Really?' This seemed unlikely to Katla. 'I thought it was just her hair I'd got.' Even under the sort of stress that would render another woman insensible, Bera ran a fearsomely orderly household, juggling tasks as disparate as descaling a fish with one hand while manning a heddle with the other with all the ease of Silva Lighthand at her best. Damn. She closed her eyes with a groan as she was visited by an image of the acrobat describing a final graceful arc into the dark waters.

'And her temper. And her terrible impatience. You could never teach Bera a thing: always thought she knew how to do it without a word of instruction. And run around like a little hoyden? I thought she'd never settle down, never take a husband. No one was good enough for her it seemed: not Gor Larson, nor Joz Ketilson, nor even Lars Hoplison, though his father had left him the biggest farm this side of Halbo. Ran them all ragged. Till your da came along.'

Katla hugged her knees. The idea of her mother – so prim, so organised and stern – as a hoyden was beyond belief. 'And did she run him ragged, too?'

Hesta Rolfsen chuckled. 'He didn't know which way was

up. Poor Aran. Once he has his heart on something, it's all he can think about until he's got his hands on it. Trekked over here day after day on that tiny pony of his, his feet dangling on either side so close to the ground he might as well have been walking, and sometimes she'd be out the back door and up into the hills like a sprite, and wait till sundown and he gave up before she appeared again. Other times, she'd be making him daisy-chains and threading them through his hair. Poor lad didn't stand a chance: loved her to distraction and she just kept saying no to his offer. He's a handsome man, I said to her: think how beautiful your children will be; and so strong and practical, too. But all she could say was that she wanted no children and was quite strong and practical enough in herself, and would she listen to me? I might as well have been talking Istrian for all the notice she took of my advice.'

'To take him and be glad of it?'

'He's a good man, your father, for all his dangerous obsessions.'

'I know.'

They fell quiet for a little while. A cloud passed across the sun, and a moment later a flock of starlings burst out of the trees bordering the enclosure with a great clatter of wings.

Katla girded up her courage. 'Gramma?'

The old woman took note of the change of tone in her granddaughter's voice. She opened her eyes and settled her direct grey gaze on Katla's upturned face. 'A man?'

Katla coloured. She nodded.

Hesta Rolfsen tilted her head to one side and her eyes glittered just like a hawk's spying its prey. 'At first I thought it was mourning for your brother that was making you so lacklustre. But I've been thinking there was more to it than that.'

'I loved Halli with all my heart.'

'I know that, my dear. We all did: he was so like his father.'

Two fat tears started to roll down Katla's cheeks, and suddenly she could not stop the flood that had been swelling up inside her ever since the disaster, so many tears that it was as if all the water displaced by the sinking of the *Snowland Wolf* were suddenly gushing up out of her eyes. After some time during which her grandmother held her tight and they rocked back and forward, and Ferg came bounding up the field and ran around and around them with his tail down and his great bark reduced to a puzzled, questioning yelp, Katla managed to gasp out: 'It's Tam, too. Tam Fox.'

Gramma Rolfsen held her at arm's length and scrutinised her so closely that Katla found her gaze hard to bear and had to look away. 'Ah,' she said. 'Ah. So that's the way of it. It doesn't surprise me: he is a very remarkable man – full of energy, full of life. Compelling eyes. Good hands, too. Ah, my dear, it's hard to lose them. Very hard. The sea takes the best of them.'

Katla's only memory of her maternal grandfather was of a tall, stern man with hair like beaten bronze shot through with silver, and a beard that stuck out this way and that, but still failed to disguise his long jaw and dimpled chin; a man whose face could transform itself in an instant when he laughed. She had seen him only a few times between his voyages, and then the sea had claimed him, as it traditionally claimed the men of Rockfall: sailors and fishermen all. And remembering her grandmother's loss, and Jenna's death, as well as Halli's and Tam's and those members of the troupe who had perished, Katla felt suddenly unworthy and deeply selfish. She knew why she had sought out Hesta Rolfsen: for she could surely not talk to her mother or, Sur forbid, her father, about what troubled her beyond their loss.

Firming her jaw, she managed to blurt out:

'It's worse than that, Gramma. I think I may be pregnant.'

For a moment it was as if all of the island was holding

its breath, then Gramma Rolfsen smiled. It was a smile of beneficence, a smile of the utmost calm, and suddenly the weight that had borne down on Katla these many days fell away from her, flowed out into the grass, into the rock beneath it; into the wind. 'It's just more life, child, if you are.' She took Katla's right hand – the one that had been maimed until the seither worked her magic on it – in her own thin grasp and squeezed it gently. 'When was your last course?'

Katla grimaced. 'I'm not sure. I don't seem to be very good at keeping track of these things. I'm not entirely certain Sur meant to make me a girl at all.'

Hesta Rolfsen sucked her teeth, clicked her tongue chidingly. 'We'll go visit Old Ma Hallasen, see what she has to say. She's a wonder with sheep and goats, that one; never wrong.'

Katla was about to protest that she was neither sheep nor goat, but the sudden arrival of her father put an end to the conversation.

Aran Aranson looked as if he had not slept in weeks. Black shadows hung beneath eyes that seemed unnaturally bright; his skin appeared thin and waxy, and his beard had grown unkempt. His long dark hair was tangled and knotted, but in no orderly fashion. He had made no remembrance braid for his first son, Katla noticed now for the first time, recalling with a sharp pang the one Erno Hamson had made for his dead mother. She sometimes wondered what had become of Erno, but it was yet another subject on which she did not dare to dwell too long.

'I need you to forge some more rivets for me, Katla, and braces for the bow.'

Katla spread her hands. 'The rivets I can make; but the braces?'

'Danson will show you,' was all her father said; and with that he turned on his heel and headed back down the hill.

Katla watched him go in consternation. She looked to her

grandmother, but all Hesta could do was to shrug. 'Better do as he says, child. He'll not stop till the damned thing's built and he's taken every fool in the islands aboard it for his insane expedition.'

Morten Danson was already waiting for her at the smithy – indeed, looked as if he might have been waiting for quite some time; for his arms were folded across his chest, his feet had scuffed all the pebbles away from the path up to the forge, and his face was set in a thunderous scowl. He carried nothing in his hands – no measuring cord, no length of notched wood. Katla wondered whether his obvious impatience was for her late arrival, or for that of his foreman, Orm Flatnose, bringing the necessary calculations with him.

All he said was: 'Aran Aranson tells me you're the finest ironworker in the Northern Isles; and I replied to him that such vaunting statements would serve him for naught if it were not the truth.' And then he sneered at her; a queasy half-smile that made her skin crawl. 'I offered him my own smith's services, but he waved the suggestion away with contempt. Your father must be keen to make an early acquaintance with the god's seabed home if he thinks to entrust such a crucial task to a stripling girl, and one who surely knows better how to use what's between her legs to win her way in the world than to wield a hammer on an anvil.'

Katla surprised herself by not punching the man hard in the eye, as would be her usual response to an insult. Such a slur deserved at least that the giver be summoned to the duelling ground by herself or by one of her kin; but she could tell by the way he grimaced at her, his teeth showing through the ostentatiously decorative trim of his beard, that he knew himself entirely safe in his role as the Master of Rockfall's shipmaker; at least until the vessel was finally constructed and launched. *Then*, thought Katla; *then we shall see how brave you are*. Instead, she gave him a hard stare and shouldered past him into the smithy. Inside, it was dark and stuffy, and the air was heavy with smoke. Ulf Fostason had been reassigned by Aran to his new task of keeping the fire going; so currently he was failing in both of his appointed roles, for his goats were no doubt wandering the fells; or worse, eating every new shoot in the arable fields; while the fire had dwindled to a feeble glow. He stood now, looking thoroughly bored, leaning against the bellows, his face all red-lit from beneath by the hot charcoal, but as soon as Katla came in, he drew himself smartly upright and gave the bellows a quick pump. Little coils of disturbed ash spiralled up into the air and the coals flared hungrily.

Katla nodded at him, then looked around at the state of her forge, newly revealed by the burst of light. Little bits of pig iron were strewn around the stone floor, and someone had upset half a bucketful of new rivets and roves amongst the detritus and not bothered to gather them up. All her tools lay scattered here and there; and some clumsy workman had missed his stroke with the heavy sheet-hammer at some point and taken a corner off her best granite anvil. Katla had her own suspicions as to who was the likely culprit: her father seemed beset by a demon where this ship was concerned.

Cursing under her breath, she set about the pig iron, rivets and roves with a broom, got it all into a heap and squatted to sort the nuts and nails from the scraps, and then through the latter to find the better quality pieces that might be smelted again. Then she picked up each tool and replaced it in its accustomed place on the rack, turned the big anvil, with a great deal of heaving and puffing, so that the chipped corner was closest to her and less likely to be problematic. Then she stood up and wiped her hands on her breeches.

'So,' she said to Morten Danson with the barest civility she could muster. 'What about the measurements for these braces then?'

The shipmaker tapped his brow.

Katla frowned. It was hard to know quite what he meant

by the gesture: was he indicating she was mad – 'touched', as Gramma Rolfsen would say, with the same indication – or that he was? 'What?' she asked, rudely.

'Everything I need to know about the crafting of any part of a ship lies in my head,' Danson said, smirking with insufferable complacency.

'Well, that's not how I work,' Katla said furiously. 'Unless it's in *my* head, how can I gauge the amount of iron I must smelt, or the shape and thickness I must hammer out?'

The shipmaker shrugged. 'I will tell you.'

Taking orders from anyone was not Katla's way. She bristled. 'I don't think that will work.'

'Then what do you suggest?' Danson asked sharply.

'I need to see how the brace will fit the wood, how it will be fixed, the strain it will be subjected to by the movement of the ship.'

The shipmaker looked at her in surprise. This was not at all what he had been expecting: he was used to most of the men he employed doing exactly what he told them as if they had no greater brains than sheep, and as for a woman thinking to take such an active hand in the making . . . Well! He would show her the working in its current state and let her make the fool of herself that seemed inevitable by this show of arrogance.

'Come with me,' he said briskly, and turned on his heel.

'Keep that fire hot, Ulf,' Katla grinned at the goatboy, and trotted after the shipmaker.

She had not been down to the home ground, close by Whale Strand, to see how the ship was progressing for a week and more. Her other concerns had obscured all else around her. When she had last visited the site, there had been little of any great interest to see. Four of the great logs they had towed and barged from Danson's shipyard had been hauled up out of the water, and one of the largest oaks – a monster of eighty feet or more, and as straight as a taut rope – had been neatly split to reveal the heartwood, all golden and fragrant and close-grained. Workmen had skimmed the bark from the second great oak, a tree that had also grown perfectly upright and true; the other two logs curved gently through their entire length, which had surprised Katla: these latter pair did not look as if they would produce good strakes, for which the graceful arc of the planking would be achieved through careful steaming. There were a dozen men busy at the site with axes and adzes and the air was full of the lovely smell of fresh-cut wood; but Katla, unable to concentrate on anything for long in her current predicament, had soon found her mind wandering, and had then allowed her feet to follow its inclination away from all the noise and bustle.

Now, though, there was a great deal more to see. Two dozen men or more were hard at work on the flat, grassy lawn above the shore's seaweed-strewn tideline. A handful had come on the barges from Morten Danson's shipyard, lured by the promise of good pay for their expert work; but most were Rockfallers through and through: wiry, dark men with deft hands and strong faces. They had worked with boats all their lives, even if they were not master craftsmen; and the chance to work on Aran Aranson's ambitious ship seemed as fine a way as any to pay tribute to the loss of his well-liked son. Many of them hoped, in their hearts, to be selected for the expedition, too: they had heard stories of the Island of Gold, and of those a good number were young men, youngest sons with little hope of land of their own unless – Sur forbid – disaster carried off a fair number of their siblings. And so all worked with care and pride to make the Master of Rockfall's great ship. They hewed fine planks out of vast tree trunks with sure and steady axe-strokes; those proficient with hatchet and chisel cut cleats and oarholes; while the less skilled soaked withies in seawater and oil to make them flexible enough to use as lashings, while others were engaged in heating new-cut pine, so that now the pungent smell of the resin thus rendered mixed headily with the clean scent of hewn wood. Katla recognised most of the men there: men she had grown up with and seen every day of her life: there was Bran Mattson and Stein and Kotil Garson; Lars Hoplison; Finn Erlingson and his brother Rolf; the handsome Stensons from the north of the island, Felin Grey Ship and his sons Gar and Bran; even Kar Treefoot and her Uncle Margan were there, although they had their own land to work and should hardly be labouring on Aran's mad project. She grinned: her aunt – Bera's sister, Gwenna – was a formidable woman; he'd be in trouble when he returned to the shieling, if return he dared.

Her pulse quickened as she scanned the scene. The excitement was palpable: an adventure was being crafted before her very eyes. This expedition belonged to every man present and would be theirs to cherish: everyone here was a participant in her father's dream. Something about this romantic notion appealed to her, made her grin from ear to ear. And there, visible in momentary glimpses through the knot of men who laboured around it, was the heart of the enterprise: the most elegant thing she had ever laid eyes on; and that included the most costly jewellery worn by any lady at the Halbo court, the finest bred pony in the isles or the best sword she had ever made. Set upon a frame of hewn pine and supported by crossed spars at top and toe was the spine, head and tail of a great ship. Threading her way through busy men and stacks of timber, stepping over cut angles of scrapwood, propped tools and sacks of wool and horsehair as if in a dream, Katla came to a halt at last beneath the skeletal prow and there craned her neck upwards. Carved out of a single treetrunk, the stempost curved outwards from the base and then back on itself with the graceful sweep of a swan's neck. She followed its line groundwards. The deep and massive keel must surely have been coaxed from the huge oak she had last seen split upon the strand by a master craftsman, for it had been fashioned as a single piece, despite extending to almost seventy feet in length. Nowhere did such mighty trees grow in the Northern Isles any more: it must have originated in the sacred grove above Ness. Reflexively, she made a warding sign, hoping that all the attendant spirits of that ancient grove had been suitably propitiated when this awesome tree had been felled. She could not help but reach out and touch it. At once, a jolt of energy coursed down her arm. She gasped, finding herself caught up in the ecstatic rush of life she encountered there; yet at the same time was able to retain enough detachment to allow her to appreciate the artistry of the workmanship which had taken a fine tree and made from it this elegant form. Where the prow met the keel, a clean joint had been made, the wooden edges smoothed flush and the rivets bedded so neatly that when Katla knelt and ran her hand over it, there was hardly any change to the sensation beneath her fingertips. The entire frame seemed to vibrate against her skin like a purring cat. It was suddenly a great temptation to sit there for the rest of the day just stroking the thing; with considerable resolve, she took her hand off the prow and stared up at the shipmaker in wonder.

'It's extraordinary.'

In response, Danson merely inclined his head.

Katla's head felt dizzy, displaced. She rose slowly, for fear of losing her balance and sprawling on the ground in front of him. 'So: show me where it is that the braces will go,' she said at last, mustering herself.

The shipmaker indicated the hollow inside the ship where keel met stempost and where the first of the overlapping garboards had been nailed in place. 'Here, and here, running down past the keel scarph to strengthen the bow for the ice-breaker. It should extend from here—' he indicated a point above the second board '—to here—' a foot past the scarph. 'It needs crosspieces here and here for strength, and that would best be made of a piece than welded, if you can manage such a thing.' He knew perfectly well that she could not: it was more than he'd ask of his own smith, but he would enjoy seeing her fail. 'Then we'll rivet the exterior piece through the wood to the interior brace. It'll make the prow rather less flexible than I'd prefer, but your father is adamant on the need for it.'

Katla walked to the other side of the vessel and peered over the top strake, marvelling at the way all the different pieces of handcut wood melded together with an almost supernatural perfection and something in her view of the loathed shipwright began to make a shift towards a rather grudging admiration. Grabbing up an empty wooden pail that gave off a strong reek of fish, she turned it over and stood on it so that she could reach over to the place where the ironwork was to be riveted. Then she closed her eyes and let her hands move up and down the joinery.

Danson watched her, one brow raised in disbelief. The girl was either mad or brilliant, and he most definitely erred towards the former judgement. Let her do her worst: when she had wasted a goodly amount of rare iron and produced some useless monstrosity that clearly would not fit, then he would make sure that her strangely blinkered father would see the truth of it. Shaking his head, he walked off to check his foreman's progress with the plank-steaming.

Katla made her way back to the smithy as if she were sleepwalking and when Ulf Fostason addressed her she barely even acknowledged his presence. All afternoon the forge rang with the sound of hammer on anvil and smoke and embers billowed from the windows. As the sun dipped behind the Hound's Tooth and the men trailed in from their labours to eat in the hall, the goatboy stumbled out into the twilight, his limbs shaking with fatigue. Lit by torchlight, her face and arms sheeny with sweat and her hair hanging in rats' tails, Katla quenched the ironwork in pine tar and linseed oil and regarded her handiwork with satisfaction.

While Aran Aranson conferred with Morten Danson and Orm Flatnose over the dinner board as to the best ratio of sail and mast to keel to bear the strong winds of the arctic north, his daughter staggered down to Whale Strand bearing a most bizarre-looking contraption in her arms. The thing she had made bore little relation to the simple iron brace the shipmaker had specified.

It was far lighter than she had expected when she had started to beat it out of the smelted metal, for she had heated it until the iron was blue, beaten and quenched it, and cut away the excess; then beaten it thinner and quenched it again, and then again; but it was strong, far stronger than the sturdy but coarse frame that had originally been envisaged. And although it was beaten so fine, she had smelted out the impurities so thoroughly that she knew the metal would withstand first the indignity of the riveting, and then the strain of the moving wood and the counter-pressure of the ice-breaker that was to be added below the waterline. That was the dangerous part of the design: even the most finely made ship might be thrown entirely out of true by such an addition, especially if the ice-breaker were made by lumpen hands; but then she recalled the fine joinery and the clean lines of the vessel and knew that Danson was too prideful a man to allow poor workmanship to mar his creation.

Isolated on its clumsy pine cradle upon the empty strand, with the moonlight limning every line of its structure, the bones of Aran Aranson's emerging vessel appeared more austere than ever. Katla breathed deeply and approached it in some trepidation. Something had prompted her to place the armature she had made inside the ship when there were no witnesses to the act: but whether this was out of fear that the thing would not fit and that her efforts would be ridiculed; or out of some more obscure, almost religious urge to commune with wood and iron, both of which had come up out of Elda's roots, she had no clear idea: both concepts were terrifying.

And so, teetering on the upturned bucket that was still where she had left it, she lifted the armature over the riveted boards – noticing with some small part of her mind that was not entirely frozen with fear, that another two planks had been added since she had left the scene that afternoon – and placed it inside the bow. The shock that travelled up her hands as wood and metal made contact nearly threw her off her perch. It was as if the oak – even in its mutilated, man-worked form – reached out for the iron, embraced it, took it into itself. The brace fitted like a second skin, even to the ridges in the overlap of the strakes. She stood there, on the bucket, with the palms of her hands glowing against the metal, feeling the life in the wood beneath it, and the life of the world below that, where the keel met the pine frame, and the frame met the ground, and the rock veins beneath the beach ran out into the sea and down, far down, into the heart of Elda itself; and then the voice came.

'Do not take sail in this ship, Katla Aransen, for I have need of you.'

Her head came up with a start, and involuntarily she searched the strand for the speaker, although she knew full well there was no one but herself there in that dark place.

That night she slept fitfully, her dreams haunted by crashing seas, by the sound of breaking wood and the cries of dying men. She awoke in the grey light of dawn with painful cramps in her belly, and when she went outside to piss before the rest of the household were about, found that her monthly bleeding had come upon her with a vengeance.

Seventeen

Seers

Frost had etched feathery patterns on the flagstones of the herb garden and crazed the puddles on the ground made by the melt of last night's hailstones. The Rose of the World steadied herself against a tall clay planter filled with dead and twiggy herbs and watched her breath blossom in the air. She knew by these signs that it must be very cold but she felt the change in temperature not at all. Part of this might be due to the way in which she was swathed: over an underdress of soft white linen and a tunic of red velvet she wore a heavy cloak lined with the furs of ermines and minks; the black and white of the pelts gaudily chequered. Around her shoulders as she was leaving the castle gate, her husband had then insisted on wrapping a sealskin cape with a wide snood trimmed with snowbear fur which he had drawn up over her pale golden hair. Then he had kissed her on the forehead and walked quickly away before desire overtook him. Ever since the night on which he had stumbled on the mistaken belief that she was carrying the heir to the Northern Isles, Ravn Asharson had been extravagantly solicitous, and rather than reveal the truth and break his heart, the Rosa Eldi had taken to layering her clothing in accordance with his wishes. He had also been exercising the most remarkable self-control. Since that night they had lain together but once, and that in the pitch-dark so he would not see the pristine flatness of her belly. She was beginning to doubt her own powers, such as they were; and the fact that she had been unable to conceive, no matter with what diligence she had tried, had done nothing to improve her peace of mind.

It was not just to maintain the illusion that she wished herself with child; nor yet to please her lord's heart, though she yearned to do so more desperately with each day that went by, for there could be no doubt in her mind, or whatever passed for her own heart, that she loved him utterly; but also out of a growing fear for her own safety in the northern kingdom. The announcement of the pregnancy would provide her with some protection; but she had sworn her husband to secrecy until, as she put it to him, 'she could be sure'; but it would be hard to postpone the declaration for much longer without incurring his suspicion. She had good reason to be concerned. Now that Ravn had unbound himself somewhat from her enspellment, she found herself rather more free to wander the halls and mazelike corridors of the great castle, and had thus overheard many a conversation never designed for her ears. It was true that her hearing was preternatural, and her footfall soft; but she seemed to come upon new conspiracies and whisperings every time she ventured from her chambers.

The manoeuvrings of Erol Bardson came of little surprise, even to one so poorly versed in the complexities of court intrigue; she had heard Ravn's lords many a time warn him of his cousin's plottings and urge their King to send the man away on some pretext or another before he could rally enough supporters to make his bid for the throne. What had surprised her had been just how many other nobles and commoners whispered against the King when they thought themselves safely out of earshot. Ravn was not popular, even in the hub of his own capital, even within the thick walls of Halbo Keep. And it was her they blamed most: that much was abundantly clear. 'The sorceress', they called her; and 'the white seither': this latter was a term she had not heard before and it puzzled

her. Like so much else, she stored it away for future reference
and listened on. Some of the women were vicious in their
comments. 'A heathen witch, that's what she is,' one bony
creature in an ill-fitting yellow dress had declared to her
companion, a vast woman all hips and bosom and nothing
to differentiate the shape between. 'Trapped him between
her legs and squeezed all the life out of him. I remember
when he ran up and down these passages of a night, slipping
into one bedchamber after another and swiving everything
in sight!'

Her companion had nodded her agreement vigorously,
though even to the Rosa Eldi's untrained eye, it seemed
highly unlikely the Stallion of the North had ever been so
starved of his oats that he would have snuffed at these poor
nosebags.

'Of course,' the dandelion-robed one continued, 'if she
doesn't bear him a son within the first year of their marriage,
he will surely have to cast her off and take a more fertile
woman to his bed.'

'If the Lady Auda has anything to do with it, she'll not even
last that long,' the vast woman had concurred cheerfully. She
lowered her voice so that the Rose of the World had to calm
her breathing to hear the rest of her remarks. 'I heard our
esteemed ex-queen has sent for a seither.'

'Indeed?' The thin woman was intrigued. 'A seither to treat
a seither? That's a thing I never heard of.'

A shiver ran through the Rosa Eldi's frame that had nothing
to do with the winter's chill. It was the second time she had
heard the word, and the context boded ill.

'Treat? To help the Queen conceive? No, you fool!' The
fat woman chuckled in disbelief. 'To seek herbal intervention.
To do away with her in such a way as it will appear she's
expired from natural causes, before the King's seed takes
root, which Auda would hate to see: she could hardly dare
to lay a finger on her then. "That nomad whore", that's how

the Lady Auda refers to her, you know. Abhors her, and all her like.'

'Whores?'

'No, nomads, Sera: nomads and all their witching ways.'

'But why? I've never seen a nomad in my life till this one turned up; and as far as I know, Auda's never left the Isles.' The skinny one sounded perplexed. 'Besides, if she has such a loathing for magic, why call on the skills of a seither?'

'Good northern magic is quite different to the vile practices of those Footloose folk,' her companion declared matter-of-factly. 'It's well known that seithers merely draw on the natural energies of the world; while the nomads . . . Well, they draw no line, even at the use of blood and men's seed in their spells. It's said old King Ashar fell in love with one when he went a-raiding in Istria. From what I'd heard, he never sought his wife's bed again once he'd returned, all aflame with desire for his witch-lover a thousand miles away.'

'No!'

'Yes! And that's why the Lady Auda hates nomads,' the big woman concluded triumphantly. 'She can't bear to see her own son follow his father's heart.'

'Heart? Cock, more like!'

'Sera!'

And the two of them had collapsed into mirth and begun a different sort of conversation entirely.

The Rosa Eldi had never known anxiety; but she was beginning to learn its potency now. Added to this, she had been visited by strange thoughts of late – it was hard to think of them as dreams, since she did not truly sleep. Images came to her in flashes, more and more frequently since the haunting vision of the rock-choked cavern. She had no idea what to make of them, for they tallied with nothing she had experienced in this world since leaving Sanctuary. She saw a city of gold, its turrets gleaming in the sunlight. She saw gigantic trees towering into a summer sky. She saw cliffs so white they seemed carved from ice: but they were warm and vibrant, pocked with coloured flowers and with trailing ivies, nothing like the ice-cliffs of the Master's sorcerous island. More than once, she saw the image of a woman in a red dress, her long, pale hair all decked with blossoms, mirrored in the clear surface of a lake. The woman's head was thrown back and she was laughing, so the Rose of the World could not clearly see her face; but something about her was terribly familiar, made her pulse race. Beside her, a step behind, stood a tall man dressed all in blue, his long flaxen hair blowing in the breeze. His hand was on her waist, the gesture both proprietorial and affectionate. At his feet sat a huge beast, black-furred and sleek. It stretched and yawned and she saw the deep, dark-red interior of its mouth, its sharp fangs, its long tongue. Something about this vision kept returning to her in slightly different forms through the days and nights; but never could she make out the man's visage, or fully recognise the female figure, though some part of her knew it was herself she saw there, knew it as well as if she looked into a mirror now. Had she truly once been so happy? The woman in her flash of memory had appeared powerful, ecstatic, free. She could not equate such a figure with the woman she was now; had no idea of the identity of the man who was with her. That he might be her husband, in another time, another life, seemed like some cruel trick.

Cruellest of all, however, had been the unmistakable swell of her belly. In this other time, this other place, with this other husband, she had conceived a child.

And if that were the case, why could she not now?

She sighed and pressed her hand against the defiantly flat muscles of her abdomen. 'Grow,' she whispered fiercely. 'Grow.'

But what good was such an instruction if there was no seed planted within? It had been almost two weeks since Ravn had made love to her, and that one time he had withdrawn before ejaculating: some old wives' tale about a man's seed deforming the growing babe in the womb. And when she had stared at him in disbelief and dismay he had merely stroked her face and reassured her that once the child was born they would take even greater pleasure from one another than they had ever before, since no one would be able to begrudge them such, with one healthy heir already the consequence of their enjoyment.

She was called back to herself by something stirring beneath her hand, the hand which rested amid the herbs in the clay planter against which she leant. She blinked and looked down. A sturdy green shoot had forced its way between her first and second fingers, its continuing upward progress bizarrely visible. She drew back, at once afraid and fascinated. And still the shoot grew; unfurled its green head, put forth a pair of tiny leaves on its stem, then a second pair. A moment later the new herb had produced nascent shoots and tiny buds; and then – in the middle of a bitter Eyran winter, surrounded by plants which lay blackened and frost-withered – it burst into a dozen pale pink flowers.

The Rose of the World stared at this miracle, then at her hand. She bent to touch the plant, and the aromatic scent of its flowers engulfed her. No illusion, then. Her fingers tingled. She touched them experimentally to a patch of creeping thyme, its twiggy runners bare and leafless. 'Grow,' she whispered again.

And it did.

The Rosa Eldi gazed at the herb, wide-eyed. Then, as a thought occurred to her, she smiled. If she could bring such magic out of herself for the sake of a tiny plant, should she not be able to channel the same power, and more, inwards? She returned to her chambers, her cheeks flushed by something more than the nip in the air, and finding her husband just returned from the hunt and in the midst of changing his mud-spattered clothes, she dropped her furs and her robes to her knees and embraced him in such a manner that no amount of self-control could possibly withstand.

King Ravn Asharson, Lord of the Northern Isles, announced his wife's pregnancy that very evening; sent ravens and runners out across the mainland and to every Eyran island with the joyous news that his queen, the Rose of the World, had conceived him an heir. A great feast of celebration was planned. Across the realm, many would breathe great sighs of relief. But there were others yet who wished the royal pair ill, whose plans would be thwarted by these tidings. The King's mother took to her chambers under the pretence of an ague and awaited the visitor she had summoned ever more impatiently.

The magic kept flowing. She grew apples in the frosty garden; then buried them for the worms. She healed one of the castle dogs when it was gored by a wild pig and the wound turned septic. None knew she had done this, for the dog had been left in the stables to survive or expire; there was much rejoicing from the houndsman the next morning when he found his favourite bitch up and about, if limping heavily: it had not seemed wise, the Rosa Eldi thought, to make the healing seem too miraculous. Ice bound the earth so hard that the castle's well ran dry. Unseen, the Rose of the World laid her hands on the rock floor of the well chamber and sent her thoughts down into the land. Ranging out through the rock-veins, she at last located a small stream which ran down from the mountains above the city, then veered away through the forests to pour itself dramatically in a great waterfall into a mossy chasm above the sea. Making a subsidiary branch of this stream, she guided it deep beneath the frostbound earth, through the ancient volcanic rocks on which Halbo stood; and then, unnaturally, upwards so that it carved a strange new course into the well.

This last exhausted her; but it also exhilarated her. She felt the thrill of a deep connection with the world which bore her name, had the sense that something at its heart had heard her call and answered it. And surely, surely if she could move rock and water, manipulate the core of the world to her will, she could bring life into herself?

But for all her efforts, the Queen felt not one tiny change in her own body. Her belly remained as empty and as flat as ever it had; and now she began to learn the true sharpness of despair.

And the voice that had called to her as she had laid her hands on the rock and called forth the water, and now quested after her – joyful, sharp with unanticipated hope and desperate yearning – went unheard.

Some days later a small vessel drew into the harbour of the capital at dead of night, its sail filled with a non-existent wind. It came sweetly into the lee of the seawall, bumped gently against the stonework as its occupant disembarked onto the weed-covered jetty, and then drifted out into the night again as if it had a mind of its own. Which, perhaps, it did.

A tall, thin moon-cast shadow preceded the sailor who had thus arrived as he – or she – made their way through the sleeping streets. More than one cat stopped its midnight prowling in mid-stride and stared, one paw raised, tail a-quiver, the silver light reflecting from its eyes, as the figure passed; and then slunk quickly into a safe dark place, and did not stir till morning. The castle hounds, usually more than a nuisance with their incessant bayings and howlings at the moon, fell uncharacteristically silent as the eastern lych gate creaked open and then closed; though as the shadow passed by one or two of the older bitches lifted their heads, sniffed the air, and gave the merest whimper of recognition.

The guards on duty at the entrance to the castle saw nothing out of the ordinary that night, though an observer might have noted how their conversation ceased for the space of a few seconds and their eyes flickered closed; only for the argument as to the merits of the beer to be found in the Stag's Head as compared with that served in the Enemy's Leg to ensue again in the middle of a sentence as if there had been neither pause nor lacuna.

The Rosa Eldi, however, felt an itching inside her skull; a little vibration through her bones; an unwonted shimmer of heat. She sat bolt upright in the bed she shared with the King of Eyra and, like a cat, her green eyes went wide and reflective. Like a cat, she trembled: if she had had whiskers, she would have twitched them, felt the movement of air currents through the castle walls; but as a woman, she listened and looked and every pore of her body opened itself wide to sense whatever was out there – and now *in here*, in Ravn's castle. The palms of her hands began to grow hot; the base of her spine tingled: she could *feel* the approach of magic, like a change in atmospheric pressure, like the coming of a storm.

Slowly, she rose up out of the bed, pulled on the gown she had learned was seemly to wear if she went abroad, and slipped out into the corridor. There was no guard outside the royal chamber: Ravn preferred to avoid such formalities in his home, though Stormway and Shepsey would no doubt soon win their argument over this omission now that the Queen was with child. So no one saw the Rose of the World as she passed soundlessly through the passages of Halbo Keep, her bare feet white and fragile against the massive granite flags. The sound of voices – conspiratorially low – came floating to her through the night's thin air: one was sharp with spite, the other as mellow as a sun-ripened fruit. The itching in her head and hands grew stronger: heat pulsed through her extremities, conducted by the length of her spine. Something she remembered, something she *knew* . . .

Turning a corner, she could see that the end of the passageway was aglow with flickering light: a candleflame guttering in the draught from an open door. A large and lumpy knapsack sat propped up against the wall: a poor-looking item, all frayed hessian and patching. She walked toward it, intent and alert, frustrated recognition clawing at her scalp. At the door, she paused. This was Auda's chamber: she had never set foot here before, but she knew as much at once from the heavy scent of lilies permeating the air. That much was no surprise to her; what made her catch her breath was the candle-cast shadow that leapt and danced on the wall opposite the door: it was tall and lean, impossibly so; but unmistakably that of a woman. Words came to her then: *seer, scryer, seither . . .*

As if called, the shadow's head turned. The Rosa Eldi could see its profile clearly: a sharp nose, flat brow, well-defined jaw; long hair in a tail. More words now, as if spoken, though there was no sound to be heard: *You! It cannot be . . . Yet I knew: I felt you all the way here, beneath my feet, in the air . . .*

And then the figure came swiftly through the door and stared at her with its single eye.

The Rose of the World dropped like a stone.

'Rajeesh, mina kuenna. Segthu mer. Mina dea, mina dea: rajeesh . . .'

The pale lids fluttered, revealing a flash of emerald green. The exquisite lips parted, framed a question, whispered into the air.

'Hverju? Hvi segthu?'

The seither hesitated, as if suddenly unsure of her ground.

'Jeh Festrin er, Kalas dottri, Brigs sun, Iels sun, Felins sun, Heniks sun—'

'Henik?'

Now the extraordinary eyes came full open and Festrin One-Eye stepped back, unnerved.

'What? What are you saying?' The Lady Auda pushed herself between the two of them, and pallor accentuated the

normal angularity of her features. 'What bizarre language is it
you were speaking?' She confronted the seither suspiciously.
'It sounded . . . foreign. Certainly not Eyran, or no dialect
of our tongue I ever heard.'

Festrin turned her one eye on the King's mother and
took some satisfaction in the way the old woman quailed
away from her penetrating gaze. 'That, my lady, is the
most ancient tongue in this world. It existed a thousand
years before either Eyra or Istria came into being; before
humankind found its way over the Dragon's Backbone and
trailed out of the emptiness of the Bone Quarter like a colony
of ants; aeons before the Eternal City was founded, or the
earth was cultivated; while dragons patrolled the mountain
fastnesses and great herds of undomesticated yeka roamed the
plains. It has no name: it needed none, for when it first was
spoken, there was no other language on Elda.'

Auda's eyes narrowed. She did not believe a word of it,
but to press the point risked being drawn into madness. 'And
who is she – do you know her?' She stared down her long
nose at her son's wife, then up at the seither.

'I – no,' said Festrin, avoiding the old queen's avid attention. She knelt beside the Rose of the World and made to
touch her, then drew back as if afraid to do so. 'We have never
met. But, my lady—' and she addressed this last to the woman
on the ground, '—I think my great-great-great-grandfather
may have known you.'

'Six generations back?' Auda scoffed. 'The girl can be no
more than two and twenty, and even your father has been
dead these forty years and more. Are you completely out of
your wits?'

Festrin blinked her one eye. 'Even were it a single genera-
tion since this lady was known, I have not heard this language
spoken in these isles since my father died: I had not thought
any were left who knew it.'

'*Sudrinni, alla ieldri segthir,*' the Rosa Eldi said suddenly.

Something in her demeanour had changed in the course of these few minutes: a light seemed to shine out of her, a new confidence, or something yet more crucial.

'*Alla?*'

'*I Istrianni.*'

The seither looked stunned. 'I have not travelled as widely as I should have done. I have been very stupid. Had I only known—'

The King's mother looked from one to the other as if they were both insane. 'I haven't got time for this nonsense in the middle of the night,' she raged. She glared at the seither. 'Quite what I can have been thinking of to summon your help, I cannot imagine. And as for you—' she curled her lip at her son's wife '—you need not think you have deceived me with this charade of bearing an heir for my boy. Anyone with half an eye can see you're not pregnant. Well, your desperate ploy will soon be clear to all, and then we shall be rid of you, and I shall have no need for this freakish creature – no great seer, she; for her one great eye appears to see far less than my two rheumy orbs!'

And with that, she stepped smartly back into her chamber and slammed shut the heavy wooden door.

The Rosa Eldi swayed upright. 'It is true,' she said to the seither in the northern tongue. 'There is no child in me.'

'Ah, my lady.' Festrin bowed her head. 'If you are who I think you are, then there is ample reason for that sad truth.'

The Queen looked stricken. 'If I cannot conceive, then I fear for my life.'

'I could help you leave this place—'

This only had the effect of making the Rose of the World even more despairing. 'No! I cannot leave: do not think to make me.' The thought of being separated from Ravn produced something akin to a physical pain in her chest.

Festrin threw her hands up in conciliation. 'No one can make you do anything you do not wish to do, my lady.'

The Rose of the World regarded her curiously. 'I do not understand what you can mean by that,' she said, thinking of the way Rahe had kept her in the wooden box, removing her only for his pleasure; of how Virelai had sold her the length and breadth of the Istrian coast; how the whim of men had blown her this way and that, like a piece of chaff.

'Perhaps I can help in some other way,' Festrin offered, although she could not think of anything miraculous.

She hefted the knapsack she had left by the door and patted it solicitously, thanking all that was sacred that she had had the intuition to leave it outside the old woman's room. The idea of her most precious crystal and the herb-knots made by her great-grandfather lying in the avaricious claws of such a bitter woman was not a comforting thought.

'It is a ship!' the Rosa Eldi cried.

She seemed, Festrin thought, as excited as any child seeing its first moving image in a crystal; and in many ways she was like a child, partly formed, learning new skills, new information every day. She had decided in the space of the last few minutes, and with a sureness she could not put into words, that to disrupt this delicate process by blasting it with what she believed she knew about the beautiful woman seated opposite her would be both dangerous and damaging. And so she held her tongue, and her thoughts, in check and gave herself up to the scrying instead.

'Let me see.' She placed a hand on either side of the rock – a small quartz orb with which she travelled, since she always left her great master crystal in the safety of her sea-bordered cave on the hidden island of Blackshore – and then recoiled. The rock was alive with weird energies. Tiny lights flickered in and out of the interior facets as if the orb contained a lightning storm. She waited a few moments for the charges to ground themselves, then replaced her hands and gazed into the crystal's depths. The image was indistinct, as if she were seeing it through a fog, but this seemed to be caused by the aftershock of the last user, for when she bent all her concentration upon it, the mist burned away, layer by layer, until she could see not only the vessel, but every thing aboard it with preternatural clarity. The ship looked Eyran, at least in its design; but the crew which manned it appeared a ramshackle bunch indeed. Festrin had never travelled beyond the Northern Isles: to sail too far from her rocky home seemed to her tantamount to relinquishing the seat of her power: for it flowed to her through the very ground of Eyra; but she recognised the origins of many of these folk from descriptions in the knots and scrolls salvaged during her great-great grandfather's flight from the South, and from her own experience of wandering the wharves and docks of Halbo and its surrounding ports, where Empire sailors and merchants brought their trade in years gone by: there was a dark man at the helm with the distinctive clan tattoos of the Farem hilltribes, which was fascinating in itself; and a number of ragtag sailors of indeterminate origin. A small, round man wearing a steel skullcap looked vaguely familiar to her; but the man at the steerboard she knew well. Joz Bearhand! She remembered him as a small child at the steading at Whaleness, fighting his brother with a stick, and clearly getting the best of him, even though the other lad was older by a number of years. Hadn't he gone as a sell-sword? She frowned. Her memory was becoming hazy with the years. She had lost track of her age in any but the most general terms; but many seithers lived beyond a hundred and twenty years, and she knew she had not yet attained that longevity. If it were a mercenary ship, it would certainly explain the ill-assorted crew. But why had the crystal chosen to offer the Rose of the World this particular view? She scanned the other occupants of the vessel more closely, dwelling for a long time on a tall, broad-shouldered woman with her hair bound into a complex arrangement of braids and a mouthful of pointed teeth; then her eyes shifted to the figure with whom this fearsome woman was conversing. The latter was a pretty girl, with long dark hair flying wildly in the wind and soft brown eyes. She was dressed in an ill-fitting tunic and boots that were too big for her; but it was not the incongruity of her presence on this ship full of seasoned hands and motley adventurers that made Festrin catch her breath, but the swell of the woman's belly – to all but the most observant eye camouflaged beneath the oversized folds of the gathered tunic.

'There are indeed mysterious forces at work in the world,' the seither whispered. She took her hands off the crystal and gazed in awe at the Rosa Eldi, a most bizarre stratagem already beginning to take shape in her mind.

'Who are you, and why do you come to my door at such an hour?'

Rui Finco had just emerged from a lingering bath in water scented with rose petals, assisted by two veiled girls who had insisted on spending an hour and more rubbing aromatic oils into his back, which he fervently hoped was a prelude to rather more interesting and energetic pursuits. Jetran ways were not to his usual taste, which tended towards the pragmatic: a bath was for removing the day's grime, and required hot water with no additives other than a loofah and a willing, and preferably naked, companion, and the time thus saved in bathing to be spent rather more productively between the sheets; but the slavegirls in Jetra were more exotically-minded than those in Forent, where they had got used to their lord's rough and ready attitude to bathing as a preliminary to sex; and he was getting a little impatient. He wrapped his silk robe tighter around his muscular frame, which merely served to emphasise his impatience, and surveyed the man who had interrupted his evening with undisguised hostility.

The man – dark-skinned, tousle-haired and broken-nosed

– looked like a hard bastard. Rui judged him to be around eight and thirty years, or possibly a little older: judging by the network of scars on his arms and face, he had seen a fair bit of action, though none of them looked fresh, which meant that he was either a veteran of the last war, or a mercenary so good with a blade that none had got close enough to mark him in recent times. Maybe both were true. Which could make him useful; unless he was here as an assassin, and one with sufficient gall to march up to his chambers and murder him where he stood. Rui's eyes slid to the sword he kept propped by the door-jamb, wondering whether his reflexes would be fast enough to save his skin if this were the case, and knew that if the assassin was good he wouldn't stand a chance. When he looked up again, he caught the man's own gaze returning from the same spot. Rui stared him out, watching for a signal, but the visitor held his hands up. He was weaponless.

'My apologies for disturbing you at this late hour, my lord. My name is Galo Bastido,' he said gruffly, in the heavily-accented Istrian that marked him as a native of the northern coast.

The Lord of Forent waited.

'Until recently I was the captain of the Altean militia.'

That was a surprise, given the accent. Rui thought quickly. Altea: capital of the Vingo lands in the far south of the country; the elder son of the family a cripple; the younger now posted, along with the men his family owned, to Tycho Issian's command. Leaving this Galo Bastido positionless and mostly likely penniless, for he did not look like a man who would swallow his pride and accept a lesser rank under the auspices of some callow youth.

'And you come seeking my favour?'

'I have a proposition for you, my lord.'

The slavegirls were waiting. Their warm mouths and lithe bodies beckoned, demanded his attention. He pushed the

thought aside. Another few minutes' delay after all that
damned massage would signify little. 'Come in,' the Lord
of Forent said after barely a pause, and ushered Bastido into
the anteroom. The girls, well-trained as they were, took one
look at the newcomer, read the situation as one which did
not require their immediate presence, slipped quickly into
the bedchamber and took up their stations there, their veiled
forms still visible through the gauzy drapes which separated
the two rooms.

Rui Finco cast himself down on one of the long couches
and waited.

'Well?' he said.

Galo Bastido dragged his eyes away from the doorway to
the bedchamber. What it was to be a lord in the Eternal City.
Was it just the money, he wondered; or did an inherited title
make such a difference? If it was the latter, then he was cursed;
if the former, perhaps there was still the possibility of him
taking his destiny squarely into his own hands.

'You will need ships, my lord, if you are to storm the
North.'

'Evidently. Our wrights have set to acquiring the necessary
materials to construct a fleet. We are working on the plans.'

'Aye, sir, plans; but no vessels.'

Rui regarded the man askance. 'What are you saying?'

'My father was a sea captain. I learned all he knew at
his side on our own ship, trading with the Northern Isles,
before the war. Then he died in battle and we lost what we
had won. I ended up in Altea Town, peddling my soldiery
skills; stayed there for twenty years, working my way through
the ranks.'

So he was older than he looked.

'Go on.'

'I can sail a ship and navigate as well as any Eyran,
my lord.'

Rui sighed inwardly. 'I am sure your talents will be put

to good use in the time to come, Bastido; be sure to come to me again when we have our fleet.'

The conversation was not following the course Bastido had planned. He said, more quickly than was strictly polite when addressing a member of the nobility, 'I have . . . friends, my lord . . . in your own city. I ran into some of them on the road to Jetra and they told me something which might be of interest to you.'

The Lord of Forent inclined his head and allowed a silence to fall between them which indicated his willingness to hear the man out.

Galo Bastido cleared his throat. 'The Eyran king has a shipmaker,' he said, 'except he hasn't any more.'

Rui's eyes narrowed. 'I know this,' he said, remembering the mercenary woman's glee in relating this news to him.

'I know where he is. My cousin told me. He had it from a mercenary he met in a tavern. Rockfall, he said, the greatest of the Westman Isles. That's where the shipmaker is now.'

'I know this too,' Rui said dangerously. 'You'd better have something to add to this old news or I'll have your feet burned for trespass.'

Galo Bastido looked unperturbed by this unpleasant threat. 'My father's ship is in dry dock in Lanison Bay, my lord; has been these many years since my elder brother died and it passed back to me, but I was earning too well in my post in Altea to be interested in taking to the sea again. Give me some men, my lord, and I will sail them to Rockfall and bring the northern king's shipmaker back to Forent for you.' He paused and lowered his voice. 'And as many barbarian women as you could wish. I hear they are wild, my lord, quite wild.'

Galo Bastido watched Lord of Forent's gaze flare with interest and then turn dreamy. Was it the prospect of an Eyran-designed fleet that so fired his imagination, or the thought of filling his seraglio with northern harlots? he wondered. Either way, his daring request seemed to have met with favour.

The next day, after spending some of the coin he had received as an advance against the success of his venture on a trio of skilful whores and a skinful of the finest wine he had ever tasted, the Bastard left the Eternal City with fifteen armed men and a promissory note entitling him to his pick of Forent's militia. The ship might require a bit of work, he mused, and delay their departure for a while. It had been a ropy old vessel at the best of times, and the best of times had been more than twenty years ago; but there were surely men in Forent who could make it seaworthy enough. Besides, what could be better than having coin in his pouch and a new city to explore while waiting to set out on a quest financed by one of the great lords of the Empire? Feeling twice the man he had been in years, Galo Bastido set his spurs sharply to his horse so that the blood ran down its flanks, and urged his new squad into a gallop.

As the ship sailed into sight of Halbo's great sentinel pillars, the crew took down the alarming carved stempost that gave the *Ice Bear* its name. 'No point in making trouble for ourselves,' Mam had said succinctly. It was, anyway, to be hoped that the King had forgotten the small matter of Dogo and Knobber making such a hash of stealing his own ship the last time they had been in town. Perhaps bringing in the vessel Rui Finco had thought to use as a template for the Istrian's fleet might win him around, if worse came to worst: though she had more of a mind to keep the ship for their own use. Sailing rough seas was not something she would ever get used to; but it was by far the most efficient means of long-distance escape from an awkward situation yet to be devised. Mam and horses did not get along at all.

For his part, Persoa stared and stared at the towering cliffs with their carved stairways and minuscule windows. Nothing had prepared him for such massive architecture: even in rich Istria no one had had the vaunting ambition to so tamper with the natural landscape. He could not imagine being *inside* the living rock: it made the small hairs on his neck and back rise like a dog's.

Selen drew the folds of Mam's huge tunic across her belly and then donned Erno's cloak as well. She wanted to judge for herself what type of place this was and what manner of people the Eyrans were before she disclosed her condition. Not all could be as honourable as Erno Hamson; nor as straightforward as the mercenary crew. Having little memory of her earlier life, she had not expected to be surprised to have such a thought: the Selen Issian she had left behind in the seas off her homeland would have been appalled to have taken ship with a band of rogues and cut-throats; but she had found them unfailingly good company. If a little coarse. And she liked her new name: Leta Gullwing.

Persoa had offered her the first: it was his sister's name he told her, very seriously, for she reminded him of her. But when she had asked him where she lived now, what her life was like, he had gone quiet and changed the subject. 'Gullwing' had come from Mam; and when she had asked a reason, the mercenary leader had shrugged. 'There was one passing overhead as we picked you up,' was all she said.

A new identity was a little more problematic. Dark hair and dark eyes were a rare combination in Eyra: they had settled on the Galian Isles as her place of origin, especially after Erno had privately explained to Mam what he knew of Selen's heritage. 'Her father is a deeply unpleasant man,' Mam had concurred. 'I'd heard of him even before the Gathering. A bigot, a fanatic and a bully. She's well out of his hands and I'd do much to keep it that way.'

Erno had mixed feelings about returning to his homeland. On the one hand, he would be amongst his own kind, and could no doubt find himself a way to eke out a living in

Halbo; but he yearned for Rockfall, if only to walk once more on the ground Katla Aransen had walked upon; to enter the hall where she had been born, to remember her laughing in the meadow and splashing across the strand. But he knew he could never set foot on the island where he had been raised ever again: his life would surely be forfeit to the Rockfall clan for the part he had played in Katla's death. And at the very least, he knew he could not look the fearsome Aran Aranson in the eye.

The password had changed since the last time they had come into Halbo; but Joz struck up a cheerful conversation with the men on watch and they were soon waved through. It would never have been so easy in Ashar Stenson's day, Mam thought darkly, remembering the dour old king. One sight of a bunch of Istrians on an unknown vessel and the whole royal guard would have been aboard the ship before you could say 'Sur's prick'. Even so, they anchored the *Ice Bear* in the outer harbour and waited until the sun went down before going ashore: cover of dark was always the best cloak.

A few curious folk had gathered on the dock, and although impatience carried most of them away by the time Mam gave the order to lower the boats, a knot of twenty or so onlookers remained. In large part they were idlers and touts: hawkers of dodgy goods and women of dubious virtue. Mam pushed past them without a second glance. But as Selen and Erno disembarked from the faering, a very tall, hooded figure detached itself from the crowd and followed them into the quiet backstreets.

'Try harder, damn you! How difficult can it be, for Falla's sake? She's in Halbo – it's not even as if you have to search for her!'

Virelai sighed. There was little point in attempting to explain to the Lord of Cantara that crystals did not work in such a geographical manner: it was all about the power of concentration, guiding the vibrations that were focused in the rock with one's will and clarity of vision. He bent his head over the globe again and thought hard about the Rosa Eldi.

Ever since Rui Finco had put an end to the counterfeiting of the slavegirls to slake Tycho Issian's obsessive desires, the Lord of Cantara had been gradually going out of his mind, it seemed to Virelai. Unable to find surcease from the torments of flesh and imagination, he had taken to pacing the corridors of Jetra's castle at all times of the day and night, and usually ended up in Virelai's chambers demanding some new potion or sight of his love in the great rock. Sometimes he merely sat on the bed and stroked the cat which, tethered as it was to the bedpost, was forced to suffer his attentions with bad grace. Twice, Virelai had glimpsed the Rosa Eldi – but on both occasions she had been locked in a passionate naked embrace with the northern king, and rather than endure one of Tycho's violent, jealous rages, Virelai had desperately sought another distracting image. The first time, he had managed to palm the Lord of Cantara off with the sight of a rabble gathered in the agora of his city around a vast, blazing pyre on which half a dozen nomad women were being immolated while the priests threw safflowers into the flames to consecrate the burning. Tycho had become quite excited by this vision and had insisted that Virelai spend the rest of the night searching the land for other such events. It had not been difficult to find his master many more scenes such as this to salivate over, for a fanatical fever had the Empire in its grip: strangers and heretics were no longer welcome within its borders; men were put to the sword, and those women who would not accept the Way of the Goddess (and thus give themselves freely to every Falla-fearing man in the vicinity) were passed into her mercy through the holy fires.

But on the last of these occasions he had stumbled upon something rather curious. It made the hairs rise on the back of his neck, though he could not have said why, for ostensibly it was far less disturbing a vista than the majority of what he had viewed in past days. It was a city of golden stone, upon which late afternoon sunlight fell in great warm pools and stripes, even though here, in Jetra, it was dead of night, which was hard to understand, for the rock rarely showed him scenes that were not of the here and now. Fascinated, he tilted the crystal this way and that and marvelled at the graceful spires and minarets its facets offered up to him, the wide lakes and fabulous gardens filled with elegant statuary and exotic flowering plants. Jetra was a beautiful city; but it had nothing to compare with this. Squinting till his eyes hurt, Virelai peered and peered, until by sheer force of concentration he wrested the rock to his will and made it scan the city in finer detail. But this closer inspection, instead of repaying his efforts with more bounties and wonders instead revealed disappointments: the architecture was in disrepair; the lakes were green with scum and choked with reeds, and horsetails and briars had run rampant through the gardens. In the air above the ruined skyline, lammergeyers cruised the warm winds on their wide wings, their primary feathers spread like fingers; ravens roosted in the tops of crumbling towers; wild cats as thin as rails patrolled the streets and squares in search of vermin. But of the human inhabitants of the city there was no sign.

Eighteen

Covenants

'Who are you and why have you brought me here?'

Selen Issian gazed into the mesmeric green eyes of the woman before her and felt all her anger and fear begin to ebb away. On the docks, when the shrouded figure had stepped into their path, and with a single touch had made Erno – that brave, protective and *powerful* man – crumple to the stones with a bare murmur of protest, she had been overcome first by terror, and then, as she was marched swiftly through deserted streets towards an unknown destination, by a growing and unaccustomed fury. The tall figure whose grasp on her upper arm felt like the chill grasp of death itself said not a word all the way, which served to make Selen – or Leta, as she determined to call herself now – incandescently enraged. By the time she had been ushered unceremoniously into these elegant chambers, she was ready to fly at the author of this abduction with hooked nails and barbed words; but one look at the quiet, beautiful woman sitting small as a child in the great wooden chair had drained her of all but curiosity.

Behind her, the door closed with a soft thud and someone latched it shut. She could sense the tall figure who had brought her here; could feel its compelling stare on the back of her neck like a cold breath; but she would not turn around, for the presence of the woman in the chair – for all her apparent fragility and harmlessness – was even more commanding.

'My name is the Rosa Eldi, and I am the Rose of the

World,' said the pale woman softly, and the words washed over Selen like words in a dream: she knew them to carry greater import than their surface meaning, but could make no true sense of them.

'She is the Queen of the Northern Isles; wife to King Ravn Asharson,' said the voice from behind her and she realised with sudden shock that the tall, hooded figure was also a woman. She had been quite sure until now – from its height, and the power of its grip – that it was a man.

'And what do you want of me?' she asked again, even more perplexed now that she knew who the pale woman was.

For answer, the Rosa Eldi leaned forward in her chair and parted Selen's veiling robes. Abruptly, Selen felt naked, vulnerable. An overwhelming desire to hide her state rushed over her, but her hands hung limp and volitionless at her sides. The Queen of the North spread her long, pale fingers across the pregnant swell.

'Ah,' she said. And, 'Ah.'

Warmth burgeoned in Selen's belly, infusing every vein and artery, every muscle and inch of skin. She felt the child inside move for the first time – the briefest, the lightest of flutterings, like the flick of a tiny bird's wings in the hollow of her womb, and even she, who knew nothing of babies and the journey they took towards life, knew this movement to be early, bizarre; unnatural.

The woman removed her hand slowly. When she lifted her eyes to Selen's face once more, the Istrian woman was shocked to see that where before they had been the cool green of precious jade, now they were dark and shimmering. No tears fell, but somehow that very absence spoke a greater emotion than mere sorrow.

'I must have your child.'

Selen's heart thudded once, heavily. What could she mean? Into the long silence that followed this statement, and her own failure to respond, there came a rustle of fabric and then the tall figure moved into her view. As it turned towards her, the hood fell away from its head. Selen gasped. It was indeed a woman who towered over her, not an ordinary woman, but one so tall she had to crane her neck to make contact with her appalling single eye. A chill crept over her, for the gaze of that eye was unbearably intent. And then her heart began to hammer at twice its normal rate; her knees gave way and she began to fall.

Lightning-fast, the pale woman came out of her chair. The tall woman swept forward to throw an arm around her waist. Between them, they caught Selen and transferred her to the Queen's vacant chair.

'Do not be afraid,' the single-eyed woman said. 'We wish no harm to you or to your child. Quite the opposite. We have a very special bargain to make with you, one from which you both will prosper.'

And then, with the Queen of the Northern Isles, oddly titled the Rose of the World, seated at her feet like a common slave, Selen Issian listened to all the seither had to say of the bargain they might make.

It was almost dawn before Erno Hamson regained anything approaching his proper wits and managed to stagger into a nearby hostelry, croak out his need for a bed to the surly boy left in charge of the now-quiet bar, and crash into more natural oblivion on a flea-infested straw pallet in the back room. He had no memory of how he had come to be lying face down on the cold cobbles of Halbo Dock with the snow settling on his cloak and the foul water of a muddy puddle soaking into his one and only pair of boots; no memory of where the other crew members of the *Ice Bear* might be; no recollection at all of a girl once called Selen Issian.

But as he slept he saw a face – laughing eyes, hair flying in the ocean winds, hair which at first seemed black, but in some lights might be red – and he hugged himself tight and felt comforted.

*   *   *

Just before dawn, a tall, hooded figure emerged from the Queen's chamber and, armed with information gleaned from the careful scrying she had just carried out, took herself off to the Enemy's Leg — a tavern of dubious reputation down near the docks. There, as she had foreseen, the crew of the vessel on which the pregnant southern woman who called herself Leta Gullwing had arrived, were arrayed in all their drunken glory: snoring like old mutts in a pile on the floor amongst discarded tankards and flagons and boots and sea-bags.

She moved amongst each of them, touching one briefly on a shoulder, another on the head. She tarried for a few seconds with her hand on the cheek of a large woman with rings in her ears and a storm of ferociously braided yellow hair who lay with her head pillowed on the stomach of a small round man blowing air noisily in and out of his mouth, and her face softened for a moment. Could she heal the pain she saw within that outwardly tough and fearsome skull? Should she? She lifted her hand with some reluctance. The pain was what made this woman the fighter she was; it was not her place to change this warrior's character. As a seither, her bond with the world was to do no harm; unless it were forced upon her.

Nor could she effect total loss of memory of the pregnant woman: she could but haze and confuse. Some would recall they had travelled here with another; but be unable, for some time at least, to remember whether that person had been male or female, let alone a woman from the Southern Empire who bore a growing child.

In the nights that followed, she would work her way through the occupants of Halbo Keep, intimating to each man and woman as they lay wrapped in sleep that the Queen was looking remarkably well in her pregnancy, her skin glowing and her body softly swelling these past couple of months — longer than that she dared not suggest, since the royal ravens had but recently made their separate flights carrying the portentous news that the King's wife was with child. Illusion would have to suffice where the appearance of gravity was concerned; and she would need to train her mistress in the channelling of her own powers over her husband's perception of her as they lay together naked in the royal bed. It would not be so hard: it was clear even to one to whom sexual obsession was the most alien of sensations that Ravn Asharson saw his wife through many veils of fantasy and self-deception. And men who wished for something as hard as he wished for this child were yet more susceptible to the easy suggestion of such magics: it would not be so difficult.

What was more difficult was that the Lady Auda – well aware of the nature of the visitor she had called forth – had barred her door so effectively that Festrin could not enter her chamber while she slept; not even a seither's spells could break through good oak and iron, or the tangle of repellent herbs the old woman had in her panic strewn across the threshold. Well: let her rant and rail and declare the Queen a charlatan: no one would listen to an embittered crone who so obviously loathed her son's choice of wife, an ex-queen unceremoniously dethroned by a pale nomad whore.

And as to the matter of the child? What good could come of an enforced coupling, the seed extruded in such terrible circumstances by such an evil man? Yet, it was not the child's fault. It might yet grow straight and true, brought into the world in the northern court, which while rough and unsophisticated, and filled with a disparate company of folk, was not the worst place in the world; even a world which seemed poised on the brink of war.

None but she need know the truth of it: that the child thus apparently engendered could never be the product of the marriage of the Eyran king and his nomad bride; not just because of the true nature of its parentage, but because nothing tangible could ever come of the union between any man and the woman who currently presented herself as the northern queen. For it was not a union of equals, in any sense at all: for as cats and dogs, rats and whales; yeka and dragons could not interbreed, neither could any man get a child upon a creature so rare, exotic and remote as the Rosa Eldi.

She wondered when the Rose of the World would recover her true self, regain her memories, bitter though they must surely be, and come back fully into the world.

And she shivered to think what would happen when she did.

Night lay soft around the Eternal City. The generous stone of Jetra's thick walls absorbed light and warmth and held them fast, cradling its occupants against the chill of the darkness, muffling all sound, gentling breathing, lulling the senses. It seemed to swallow the shuffle of his footsteps as he slipped through the silent corridors, feeling like a fugitive. Turning yet another corner in the labyrinth of passageways, he felt disoriented, misplaced, as if he might at any moment step through a doorway and find himself in another era entirely; which might be a blessing, given his current circumstances. Even time seemed held in abeyance in Jetra: it was perhaps, Virelai thought, another reason for the city's ancient title; that and its endurance, against all the odds, surviving the tides of war that had washed endlessly back and forth across this vast plain.

He took a set of worn stone stairs that wound down towards flickering darkness and suddenly found himself at a thick wooden door girded with ironwork. Through its vast, empty keyhole, he could sense the outside world at night beckoning him. The door opened with barely a creak. There were no guards posted at it, for the call to war had taken every military man who could march or ride north to the muster outside Cera, or fanning outwards to the separate provinces, there to recruit and train others in the skills that would doubtless be required in the days to come. Which largely, Virelai considered sourly, would consist of being able to swim the Northern Ocean, given the rather crucial lack of seaworthy ships available to an invasion force set upon storming Eyra. It was not that Istria's leaders were entirely unaware of this setback, but rather that they appeared to have moved a stage beyond the lack already, reassured as they were by the Lord of Forent's assertion that a fleet would be constructed in no time. So the warlords who would advise the vanguard on their strategy cheerfully gave themselves up to the formation of elaborate plans for the siege of Halbo rather than addressing the problem of how they might actually reach Ravn's capital city, from which they were separated by several hundred miles of turbulent ocean.

Virelai knew what would be coming next: he had witnessed his two masters discussing it when they had thought him otherwise engaged. They had forgotten about the seeing-stone, of course; and there was no reason for them to suspect that little by little he had mastered the art of reading a man's moving lips. Initially, panic had overwhelmed him. What did he, Virelai, escaped mage's apprentice and one-time hawker of fake maps, know about the construction of ships? Absolutely nothing: it was a northern art, not something he had learned at his master's knee; and while he had no idea where in Elda Rahe hailed from, it was most certainly not from the Northern Isles where the art of shipmaking had its home. The tiny sloop in which he had escaped Sanctuary had leaked and wallowed its way across the ocean: he had held it together with much magic and an abundance of sheer good luck; and none of the grimoires he had liberated from the Master's library even mentioned the word 'ship', let alone gave the least clue as to how one might be spirited into being. The shipwright to whom the task should rightly have fallen was dead; his successor mysteriously vanished, and there was no template to work from, either, ever since the blasted sell-swords had stolen the one good Eyran vessel Rui Finco had bought for the purpose at such great expense. Virelai had seen this ship in the stone one night, as he saw so many things, sailing ever farther northwards, manned by a motley crew of mercenaries, deserters and no-hopers. And the girl. The pretty dark one with the radiant eyes and growing curves. Tycho Issian's lost daughter; found once more, but by him alone, for that was also something he'd kept to himself.

But it was not his fear at the likely consequences of failure at the immense task that awaited him which drove him out into the night; but something altogether more pressing and personal.

He was being forced, quite literally, to save his own skin.

As the light from the torch he carried played across the splayed fingers of the hand that pushed open the postern gate, he saw again with barely-contained panic the way the skin there was greying and shedding, sloughing away like sunburn or a snake's seasonal casting. Except that beneath the dead stuff was not vibrant new skin but yet more of the old; and that dull and flaky and crumbling to the touch. He had tried every spell he knew, and several he didn't – workings he had sought in the grimoires he had stolen from the Master, and in all the old parchments and scrolls he had secretly perused in Jetra's great library: to no avail. Even when the cat was being cooperative (which was increasingly seldom: now that it sensed his waning strength it seemed bent on shifting the balance of power between them into its own favour) nothing seemed to stem the decay – if decay it was. What frightened him was not merely the horror of this physical dissolution that threatened to undo him, but that it might herald the leading edge of Rahe's curse and that the screaming demons the Master had promised would attend him would surely descend at any moment.

Only one person he knew could make the sort of scrying that might detect their presence; only one might conceivably be able to treat his sloughing skin; and only one would do it for him out of friendship; for he had no money: Tycho had made sure of that – it was yet another means of binding Virelai all the more tightly to his service.

Alisha.

It had been a shock to see her in the stone again; and this time she had not seen him, occupied as she was with Falo and some cut the lad had sustained on their journey. When he realised that the rose-red walls he could see rising in the background to the scene he viewed were those of Jetra's great keep, his heart had lifted for the first time in months. And so it was that as night wrapped itself securely around the Eternal City he stole furtively into the stables, saddled one of the loathed animals within and urged it out, spurred on by the knowledge that he had barely four hours in which to find Alisha, reveal his distressed and distressing condition to her and return as swiftly and as secretly as he had come.

The nomad camp he had seen in the crystal lay some miles beyond the bounds of Jetra's walls and was well camouflaged against casual scrutiny by a stand of osiers and goat-willows by a curve in the river.

There was no fire burning: nothing at all to mark their position, but he found the curve in the river he had seen with an almost preternatural sense of these things. And without falling off his mount once, a fact in which he took some small pride. A few hundred yards away from the group of quietly cropping yeka and the dark wagons, he tethered the horse to an alder and made his way into the encampment on foot. The caravan with which he had travelled to the Allfair was sadly diminished. Where before there had been twenty and more wagons, now there were but four. The nomads must have divided for their own safety, he supposed, having viewed so many scenes of terrible persecution in the crystal. There seemed to be no safe haven any longer for the Footloose in this world. And by the very action of seeking out this group, he placed them in danger. But he had no choice.

The wagon in which he and the scryer had spent many a lazy afternoon was not among those gathered here; but he recognised the smallclothes set to dry on the line attached at one end to the branch of a goat-willow and at the other to the handle of the door of a more traditional-looking wagon with an elaborate stars-and-moon design painted on the door. He was sure this was the vehicle once occupied by Fezack Starsinger; but the smallclothes — edged in Galian lace and structured to promise sumptuous flesh beneath — were most certainly not those of that ancient, wizened woman . . .

Firming his resolve, he walked up the wooden steps to the stars-and-moon door and rapped softly in the old way they had once devised. At first there was silence: but it was the kind of silence which denoted that the occupant within was holding her breath and listening with absolute and anxious attention. 'It's me,' he whispered loudly. 'Virelai.'

There came a rustle of movement inside the wagon and then the door opened just a crack. Light shone on the eyeball gazing through the aperture. He saw the eye widen; and then, a second later, the door followed suit and Alisha Skylark, clad in a thin shift and a thick shawl stood there, her wild hair disarranged by unquiet sleep and her mouth hanging open in disbelief. She regained her composure quickly, even to the point of raking her hands through her unruly hair. Then she put an urgent finger to her lips, took Virelai by the arm and led him through the camp until they were well out of range of the other wagons.

They came to a halt beneath a stand of willows on the riverbank. Below them, the water rilled swiftly past on its endless journey to the sea.

'I need your help,' Virelai said, at the same time as Alisha asked: 'Where have you been?'

They gazed at each other in some dismay, until at last Virelai repeated his request. 'I am falling apart,' he added.

'Life has been hard on all of us,' she answered automatically, but he shook his head.

'No, no: look—'

The moon was full and its light reflected from the river's surface, lightening the air between them. Virelai rolled up his sleeves, revealing the true horror within. Alisha gasped. 'What disease is this?' she asked, but he just shook his head miserably. For that question he had no answer.

'It has been getting worse for some weeks now,' was all he could think to say. 'I fear there is some curse upon me.' And then, for the first time, though they had been intimate so many times in other ways, he told her of Sanctuary and the Master and the geas that he suspected he had brought down upon himself.

Alisha listened throughout, frowning and nodding. She had always thought the pale woman was his sister; but the story he told was more strange by far. When he came to recount his current terrors, she blanched. 'As if things were not already bad for my people, now you talk of demons?'

Virelai hung his head. 'There is no one else I can turn to.'

'And what about the cat?'

That gave him pause: he had never realised she understood the magical nature of the beast. After a while he said simply, 'It hates me. I have used it too often against its will and now it withholds its magic from me. Indeed, I fear if I were to ask it to cough up a spell for the repair of my flesh, it would reverse it out of spite, and then where would I be?' As a further thought struck him, he added: 'In truth, it frightens me as much as any prospect of demons.'

Alisha raised her eyebrows. 'Frightens you? A little creature like that?'

Virelai shuddered. 'You have not seen it as I have seen it.'

A sudden image of the night-dark beast with the flaming

mouth insinuated itself into a recess in the nomad-woman's mind. It was as demonic an image as any she could conjure . . . But Bëte? It seemed just too unlikely. After all, they had travelled together for months on end: surely she would have discerned during that time if the cat hid within it the monstrous presence Falo had spied in the crystal. And Virelai had always been bad with animals: something about him set them off, made them nervous and skittish, and cats were notoriously neurotic creatures at the best of times. She shook her head minutely as if to dislodge the image. It was a gesture which reminded Virelai of her mother.

'How is Fezack?' he asked belatedly. 'I see you have moved into the old wagon.'

'My mother is dead,' Alisha replied flatly.

'Ah. I am sorry.' Silence lumbered awkwardly about between them like some hulking, blind beast. As much to put an end to it as out of genuine interest, Virelai said, 'And Falo?'

'Well, and asleep,' she answered shortly. 'And I intend that he should stay that way. Wait for me here.' And with that, she caught up the skirt of her shift and ran back towards the wagon, her calves and feet white against the dark grass.

A few moments later, she returned bearing a large and heavy object which she set down on the ground between them. Virelai shivered, recognising the great stone. It was a far more powerful crystal that his own: he knew its history.

'Place your hands upon it,' Alisha ordered. 'Here, between mine.' He did as he was told but minutes later the crystal still remained inert, devoid of reaction. The woman frowned. 'Concentrate,' she chided, but still there came no spark of life. Again she clicked her tongue, and with all his effort Virelai bent his will once more upon the crystal. As if the great stone had been sleeping, suddenly lights shot across its surface and its core became lit with inner fire. Weird lights played across their faces, illuminated the ground around them with purple and red, cyan and gold. When at last the nomad woman took her hands from the stone and sat back upon her heels, her face was stark with repressed emotion.

Virelai scanned her expression anxiously. He had seen nothing but coloured mists, as if the crystal deliberately held back its secrets from him. 'What did you see?' he demanded at last.

'No demons,' she said softly, and her face was full of fear and wonder. And maybe the slightest hint of disgust. 'Poor Virelai. There are no demons. And no sign of any geas, either.'

This confused him greatly. If there were neither curse nor demons whence came this malady? He opened his mouth to ask just this, but she leaned across the great stone and, after a momentary hesitation, touched her fingers to his mouth.

'You must go north,' she said. 'And take the cat with you. Only the Rose of the World can truly heal you.'

'But she—' he started in dismay. The Rosa Eldi was his nemesis; of that he was sure. If he had never spied her in Rahe's chambers he would not have been tempted to drug the Master, nor to steal away from Sanctuary; he would have remained safe in that sorcerous haven, sheltered from this terrible, confusing world in which men schemed to do harm to one another, and in which his very fabric seemed unable to endure.

Then a new thought occurred to him: what if he were to take charge of the Rose of the World once more – steal her away from the northern king when his new masters made their attack upon his capital; and then (somehow) spirit her away her from the obsessive grasp of Lord Tycho Issian? What if he were to take her, and Bëte, and return them to Sanctuary, and there seek Rahe's forgiveness, abjectly throw himself on the mage's mercy? It was at this point that his imagination ceased to function: it was impossible to envisage what might happen then. The Master was not by nature a merciful man;

but would he not be grateful for the safe return of his woman and his cat, if not his errant apprentice? It seemed the best plan he could conceive. The Rose would heal him, and with his renewed strength he would draw sufficient magic from the cat to enable them to slip unnoticed from the grasp of his tormentors. The order he had known all his life would be restored to the world; the damage he had done would be undone. All would be well.

He beamed at Alisha Skylark, who was watching him with intense curiosity. 'Thank you,' he said. 'I know now what I must do. I cannot imagine why I could not see it before.' And then he turned to leave.

Just like that. Alisha stared at his back in disbelief. How like a man: to come to her full of doubts and fears and in need of reassurance, only to leap away again as soon as she had set matters to rights, with all his thoughts bent on a new course of action and no consideration of her at all. 'Wait!' she cried, caught between vexation and concern. 'You will not get far without my aid.'

That made him turn. A deep furrow had appeared in the lily-white forehead. The sight of him so made her anger ebb away abruptly. *At least his face is unmarred*, she thought. Despite his oddness, he had always seemed quite beautiful to her: it was, she realised now, his very strangeness that drew her; he was unknowable, an unfathomable mystery; a man full of contradictions. A man who might do anything, *be* anything. And no wonder, having come from such strange beginnings . . .

With difficulty, she drew her eyes away from his piercing gaze. 'Your skin,' she reminded him, as if he could forget so fundamental a thing. 'You will need some unguent for your skin.'

He smiled, and she remembered suddenly one bright morning when they had lain together as the sun slipped through the wagon's shutters and turned those pale eyes a blazing gold and she had felt her belly flicker with desire and something akin to awe. A terrible sadness swept through her for what might have been, and she turned away, unable to bear the sight of him with all that brightness back in his face, his voice, burning away with new purpose.

'I'm sorry,' he said. 'I did not think.'

He watched Alisha disappear into the shadows of the wagon once more; heard the quiet chink of pots and glasses, the grinding of pestle against mortar, a tender reassurance to the stirring child. Then she came out to him again and with gentle fingers applied the paste she had made to his hands and forearms, where the damage was worst. As it always had, her touch rendered him speechless and languorous, so that his blood seemed to rush to the surface of his skin to meet her. When she stopped, he stood there for a moment, swaying like a man in a trance.

'You are not a bad man, Virelai,' she said softly. 'Please remember that, when the world seems dark around you. What you are is not your fault; no matter how we come into this world, we all have choices as to how we make our lives. I saw no demons in the crystal: no demons, other than men themselves. You will have a great choice to make soon, Virelai, and upon it will rest all there is that is worth saving in the world. Go with love; and do your best.'

And then she pressed a heavy pot of the stuff she had made into his hand and slipped away from him, closing the door of the wagon with a firm click behind her. She stood there for several minutes with her back pressed against the cold wood and her heart hammering away like a wild thing, and listened to his footsteps retreating through the grass.

All the way back to the Eternal City, ducking automatically beneath low-hanging branches and oblivious to the sounds of the night-creatures his passage stirred, Virelai sat the ambling horse in silent speculation as to what on Elda Alisha Skylark might have meant by her curiously hieratic pronouncement. But even by the time the sun came up and he had stabled the animal and made his way without detection to the safety of his chamber, he was still unable to fathom the true significance of her words. But a plan was forming in his head: a plan which involved not only recapturing the Rose Eldi and returning her and the cat to their master; but also the boy called Saro, and the powerful stone he wore about his neck . . .

That very evening the Lord of Cantara came to his chambers. He burst in through the door without announcement, out of breath, and in uncharacteristic disarray for such a deeply fastidious man, let alone one who had just come from making his observances to the Goddess. Virelai could see the safflower stains on his hands, the tracks of orange pollen down the front of his robe, and something else, too; something darker and more obdurate in nature, for where the safflower marks were smeared, as by a hasty brushing of the hand, the other had taken a firm and steady hold of the fabric. It looked, to Virelai's untrained but keen eye to be a significant spattering of blood. *Sacrifice*. Yet another, which surely made it three days in a row. Virelai knew about the cockerel and the lamb: he had had the onerous task of selecting and purchasing both poor creatures, then washing them with all the necessary preparations before they were taken into one of the contemplation gardens and given (usually loudly and against their will) to Falla by one of her grim-faced priests. Today, however, it looked as if the Lord of Cantara had made the killing himself rather than wait for the ministrations of a holy man. The sorcerer found himself wondering what unfortunate beast had had the pleasure of being sent to the Goddess by Tycho Issian's hand, and shuddered. Truly, something must be afoot; and not just as indicated by the number of sacrifices: the Lord of Cantara had a loathing of grime, yet he had clearly not stopped to wash his hands, or to change his clothing. Moreover, his eyes were bulging, and so was the front of his robe.

All this Virelai observed in the few seconds it took his master to cross the chamber. He had learned to read Tycho Issian's moods swiftly: it was a matter of self-preservation. The tented robe was a cause for some concern, though. It was not that Virelai objected to the idea of two men taking pleasure of one another – among the nomads such things were commonplace enough and seemed to do no harm – but the Lord of Cantara terrified him and he could not imagine there being any pleasure to be had from him at all. Reflexively, he stepped between the lord and the ornate desk on which the scrying-stone sat, safely sheathed beneath its dark shroud.

'Show her to me!'

Tycho Issian's voice was hoarse with urgency.

'My lord—'

'Show her to me, now! I must see her.' The Lord of Cantara buried his hands in his hair, clutched his head as if in agony and began to pace the room. 'I have never felt such fire for any woman— It's true that females have always been a curse to me, with their provocative mouths and their lush bodies . . . but usually I worship the Goddess with them and then my desire is slaked, for a time. I've never wished for a woman I could not buy – even at great expense; but *she* – she is different . . . I can't stop thinking about her. She is all I see all through the day; and at night she haunts my dreams. I smell her wherever I go, I hear her voice, even though I've never heard her speak— It's beyond comprehension—' He stopped suddenly and turned to stare at Virelai, his hands falling limply to his sides. 'I think I'm going mad,' he said in anguish.

Virelai did not know what to say. 'Surely not, my lord,' was all he could manage, though he knew in his own mind it was a lie. Mad, yes, and much more . . .

'She makes me *burn*.' Tycho clenched his fists, ground

them both against his groin, forcing down the protuberance
there. Then he approached the table at such speed that Virelai
flinched away; but all the Lord of Cantara did was to grip him
by the shoulders and, lowering his voice, croak out: 'I do not
think . . . I do not think she is entirely human, the Rosa Eldi.
I believe she is touched by the divine. And so, you see, I must
have her. I must save her soul. It is my sacred duty.'

Now, he forced Virelai to sit before him and unveil the
stone. The sorcerer did this nervously; not only because the
lord's erection was pressed uncomfortably against his back,
but also because he was concerned about Tycho making
comment about the state of his hands. Where Alisha had
applied her ointment, the skin was certainly holding together
better than it had; but it was still an odd shade of grey and
even candlelight could not conceal that fact to any with eyes
to see. He had put on some gloves, but in order to scry it was
necessary to make direct contact with the crystal. Reluctantly,
he peeled them off, but the Lord of Cantara did not even
blink, made no comment at all. The grip on his shoulders
remained steady; and almost as if the lord's obsessive need
drove the scrying using Virelai as its conduit, the great stone
rendered up the Rosa Eldi with insulting ease.

There she was, smiling with that strange, bemused smile he
had so often seen on her face since she had fled him, in some
great hall whose walls were adorned with ancient tapestries
and decked with weaponry – barbed spears and crossed
axes, sheaves of swords fanning as if for mere decoration;
halberds and pikes – all fixed within manageable height as
if to provide the occupants with an instant armoury in time
of surprise attack. Amid the ugliness that surrounded her,
the Rosa Eldi was pale and perfect, as graceful as a lily,
as radiant as a safflower. Virelai breathed a sigh of relief:
at least they had come upon her in a public place, fully
clothed and deporting herself in a seemly manner, rather
than cavorting naked with the dark and rampant king, as

had always seemed to be the case whenever he searched the crystal for her before now.

As if the mere sight of the Rose of the World was a balm upon his torment, the Lord of Cantara relaxed his grip upon Virelai's shoulders. Then: 'Ah,' he said, in a great release of breath. '*There* she is. There *she* is!'

A crowd of folk were gathered around her, dozens of them, all pressing close to pay their court. They were all arrayed in rich clothing and fine jewellery: a riot of colour and baubles that flashed in the light of the sconces and the flames roaring high in the hearths. *So much fire*, Virelai thought. To his mind, it was a hellish scene, but the lord behind him whispered in awe: 'See, see— She is Falla rising from the fires of the Holy Mountain.

> '"*Her bare feet soft on smoking coals*
> *Trailing vaporous clouds behind her*
> *And red they were, and white her soles*
> *What man, or god, could bind her?*"

'She is magnificent. Ah . . .'

The crowd knotted, wheeled, flowed like a sea; and then there was the barbarian king, Ravn Asharson, moving with easy grace through his courtiers towards his wife, his long hair shining beneath his silver circlet, the mass of his wolfskin cloak emphasising the muscular set of his shoulders. As if beguiled by him, the crystal followed his every step, revolving so that where before it had offered a view of his back, now it aligned itself with the Rose of the World, so that all that could be seen was the Eyran king as he processed through his people, his proud face, the firelight burnishing his eyes and cheekbones; the fierceness of his smile.

'Damn the thing!' Tycho growled. 'Bring her back: I don't want to see him, that vile whelp! Show me the Rosa Eldi.'

With every atom of his will, Virelai fought the crystal away from its fixation upon the Stallion of the North until at last it veered crazily sideways; unhelpfully refusing him, even then, the Rose of the World, but offering in her stead the view of a quiet chamber, simply furnished, in which a dark-haired girl sat upon a low settle playing a game of knucklebones with a homely-looking woman engaged in picking her teeth with a sharpened stick while waiting for her partner to cast the bones.

The Lord of Cantara hissed; and at that moment the Altean contingent entered the room, headed by Favio Vingo, pushing his eldest son before him in a bizarre wheeled contraption. The older man's face was taut with antipathy for the southern lord, but the boy's eyes burned with fervour.

'My lord,' Tanto began, 'they said we might find you here. I have an idea for a great sphere in which several of the Footloose might be burned together . . .'

Tycho did not even glance away from the crystal to greet his visitors.

Tanto was not to be put off, however. Shrugging his father away and setting his own hands to the wheels, he brought the chair in tight to the table so that he could see what it was that was so absorbing the Lord of Cantara. 'Ah,' he exclaimed delightedly. 'Crystal-gazing: how entertaining. What is it you seek?'

He craned over the table towards the stone and seemed for a moment mazed by its sliding lights and odd perspectives. Then his jaw dropped open.

'Selen,' he breathed.

It was, in truth. Even as he spoke her name, Tycho Issian's daughter raised her head from the game, and a small line appeared between her eyebrows as if she was concentrating hard, or was listening for a distant voice. Tanto almost launched himself over the table to take hold of the seeing-stone; then remembered in the nick of time that he was supposed to be an invalid and subsided into the chair.

'My daughter!' cried the Lord of Cantara. 'So she was stolen by Eyran brigands indeed!'

Now, as if with a mind of its own, and unheedful of Virelai's impotent grasp of hands and will upon it, the crystal veered away again, until with a sickening lurch it offered a set of entirely new perspectives. The first was that of a gloved hand pushing open a stable door in the dark; then they were back in the firelit regions of the Great Hall of Halbo Castle, far up in the vaulted ceiling above the new Queen of Eyra, so that the viewers found themselves staring vertiginously down upon the crown of her head. It was a deceptive angle; but even so, Virelai could tell something was not right, was out of true: for him, the image blurred and flickered. There was magic at work here: powerful magic.

'Falla's tits!' Tanto suddenly exclaimed loudly; but so shocked was he by the view of the Rosa Eldi now offered to him that the pious Lord of Cantara did not even notice the blasphemy. 'He didn't waste his time: she's been well and truly plugged—'

Tycho was blinking rapidly as if he could not believe his eyes. Then: 'She is with child!' he wailed. 'The cur has got my love with child—'

All but Virelai could see clearly that the Rose of the World's belly was distended in a powerful curve away from that spear-straight spine, made all the more prominent by the softly clinging wool of her white gown. Ravn Asharson approached her, kissed her rapturously on both cheeks and then full on the mouth, and his right hand spread itself proprietorially across that lush swell.

By Virelai's ear, there was a great howl of noise. Then the table went over, and the howl was joined by the sound of the crystal striking the floor with massive force and shattering into a million fragments.

The sound of the breaking crystal reverberated through the

castle walls; it echoed through the passages and stairways; fled out into the night. Down in the kennels, the dogs milled about in distress, their tails clamped between their legs; feral cats bolted through the courtyards; geese lifted from the surface of Jetra's Lake, shocked from sleep. In the Star Chamber, Lord Rui Finco – engaged in an absorbing argument about siege tactics with Lord Prionan – lifted his head and winced at the sudden jag of pain that lanced through him; some men cried out sharply, then wondered why they had done so; while others stared wildly around as if disorientated. Hesto Greving dropped the goblet of Golden Spice he had been nursing this past hour as if burned; then stared with dismay at the glistening pool that gathered around his feet, and despite the ache in his bones found himself calculating the waste: thirty-two cantari at least, though he had drunk maybe a half of the cup's volume.

Farther away, a woman crossed a wagon to quiet her son, who had woken, weeping, from a nightmare; and farther yet, an old man cursed in fury as his view of that part of the world darkened and died.

In the gloom of the stables, Saro Vingo clutched his hands to the stone that hung around his neck, while all around him the horses whickered and stamped in alarm, but even the thick fabric of the gloves he had taken to wearing by day and night to keep the world at bay failed to staunch the flow of fiery light which struck out across the beams, the girders and the stalls, limning the occupants in a sunset haze. The moodstone shone through his fingers, so that even through the wool he could glimpse the blur of bone within and he caught his breath in panic, recalling that fateful day at the Allfair, the falling bodies, eyes rolled up to white. If he touched any living thing while the stone blazed, they too would surely perish. It seemed the horses understood this for themselves: they backed edgily away, bumping into one another until they were pressed against the stalls and had nowhere else to go. Then, as suddenly as it had visited, the weird light died, pitching the stables into an even deeper obscurity than there had been before.

Saro stowed the necklace with a beating heart. Then, moving along the stalls more by touch than by sight, he made his way to where Night's Harbinger was tethered. The stallion backed away from him, its feet kicking up the ground-straw, its nostrils expelling air in great plosive bursts.

'Sshh, there: be calm, boy.'

His reaching hand found the horse's sweating neck and he ran his palm down the vibrant flesh, feeling the stallion's pulse ticking quickly beneath his fingers; feeling, too, its nervousness at the unknown force which had disturbed it. He half-expected the beast to rear up at the touch but, ever contrary, Night's Harbinger quieted. Even before the stallion moved, Saro could feel the massy weight of its head in the air above him; then the bay was nuzzling at him, searching for horse-nuts as if nothing at all out of the ordinary had occurred.

Slipping the halter easily over the stallion's head, Saro led him quietly out into the deserted stable-yard, looped the rope around a fence post there and went back in for the bridle and saddle. Finding the bay's saddle amongst the hundred others there in the pitch dark would, for anyone else, have proved impossible without a guiding light; but for once the old nomad's gift proved an advantage. He took off the gloves and ran his hands swiftly over the polished leather, letting the images thus released sweep over him like a warm and fragrant breeze. For fractions of seconds at a time he 'saw' a fat man with close black eyes, a tall lad in blue; a woman, straight-backed with her black hair a flag in the wind – an ancient saddle this, then; for no Istrian woman for a hundred years and more would have been permitted to straddle a horse in such an unseemly fashion. He sensed conflicts, and moved his hands swiftly away. One saddle offered him the image of a spear-struck man gripping desperately to the cantle, before sliding away beneath a ruck of combatants. He saw boys barely large enough to sit astride any creature, let alone a full-grown Tilsen horse, racing like demons across a wind-blown strand; he saw a column of men stretching as far as the eye could see, pennants fluttering from lances held aloft; and then, bizarrely, he was inside himself twice over so that his consciousness seemed to blur and shimmer; and a man came at him on a dappled grey beast. It was such a vivid memory that in this time, here and now, Saro found himself ducking away, just as he had tried to do at the Allfair. He took his hands off the leather before it could remind him of the gutting pain of the Eyran rider's fist under his ribs; then put his gloves back on, picked the saddle up and carried it out into the night.

The empathy was stronger now every day. Even the most mundane household objects awoke and gave up their stories to him at the merest touch. He had no defence against it: all he could do was to order his life as simply as possible, and wear the gloves whenever he was able. He had bided his time with difficulty till this night, for he seemed forever in the company of the Lords of Forent and Cantara, who insisted always on including him in their plans, and that fact combined with the matter of sharing a sleeping-chamber with Tanto had made it impossible to slip away before now. Ever since he had been visited by the harrowing vision of the mayhem that might one day be unleashed by Tycho Issian channelling the power of the moodstone, he had barely been able to eat or sleep. Since the day on which they had arrived, when the tale, pale man with the cold hand and the dead soul had touched him in Jetra's great hall and he had seen wild comprehension flare in the man's almost-colourless eyes at the power of the artefact he wore, he had lived in constant fear that the creature would report that information back to his master. Once the Lord of Cantara discovered the nature of the moodstone, Saro sensed he would stop at nothing to acquire it. The urbane, elegant man he had met at the Allfair had become another order of being entirely in the intervening months: he seemed driven by some inner fervour, some wild, distorting passion which made his eyes burn and his every gesture abrupt and impatient. And Saro had heard him speak about the northerners in terms he could not reconcile with his own few experiences, and with a hatred that went far beyond any root in their two peoples' ancient, conflicted history. And the role he had outlined for Saro to play in this drama – one of treachery, deceit and cold murder – was unimaginable.

The need to escape drove him with a terrible, slow urgency. It made him careful in every movement he made, set all his senses to full alert. He saddled the horse, tightened the girth, then tied the small sack of his provisions and necessities across the bay's shoulder. Then he threw back his head and took a deep breath. Up above, the constellations were as bright as he had ever seen them, the sky as black and vast as all the world. The Northern Cross stood in the zenith, its seven subsidiary stars dancing irregular attendance on the most luminous star of all, the one the Eyrans called the Navigator's Star, and here in the South they called Falla's Eye. How typical, he thought then, for the first time, that the northerners should view their world as so benevolent that it would provide them with guidance and aid, rather than inflict upon them an ever-watchful, ever-judging presence.

I will make my way to Eyra.

Gone were all the manifold reasons with which he had previously caged himself: if the stone were to be kept from Tycho Issian's hands and that terrible revelation of the future averted, to travel as far as he could out of the Lord of Cantara's grasp seemed his only possible course of action. That the stars seemed to have offered him their own encouragement merely added to his determination, so that within moments a sudden notion carried all the force of epiphany, and became a decision as compelling as any made after months of prudent forethought and planning.

Nineteen

The Long Serpent

Katla, working in the forge late into the night on the sword she had promised herself she would make for Tor Leeson's family – to honour the memory of his death, or to sell for whatever price they could get for it – stopped her beating and listened intently. There was, beyond the echo of the hammer on the anvil, a zinging in her head; and in addition to the vibrations her body had absorbed from the iron there was something else – in the air, maybe, or in the ground beneath her feet. She laid down her tools, placed the half-made sword carefully upon the table, and spread her hands on the stone floor in an attempt to locate and identify the sensation; but it was gone, only the faintest resonance of it left echoing in the quartz veins deep below the island. She frowned. Something felt slightly out of true, askew in the world.

Katla glanced back at the sword. It was a fair piece of work; good, but not fine. She had known it all along, ever since the first rough fashioning. Nothing she had attempted since returning to Rockfall after the shipwreck had satisfied her exacting standards, although others exclaimed in wonder over the artistry of the niello tracery with which she had been experimenting, the intricate designs of silver wire winding like serpents around hilt and tang and down into the fuller. But she knew it was mere decoration, fancy patterns to maze the eye and distract from the integrity of the blades. Her heart was no longer in it. The sea-monster had taken something of her with it down into the ocean abyss, along with her brother and her friends.

She wiped her hands on her tunic, doused the fire and left the forge. The long house was in darkness, but she was not tired enough to seek her bed. Instead, she wrapped herself in a thick cloak and chose the track that led to Whale Strand. By the light of a moon which hung large over the island she made her way down towards the cliffs, following the paler sand through the dark furze and brush, and thence took the wider path that issued out onto the beach, her breath steaming in the freezing air. There, she found the Master of Rockfall's great ice-breaking vessel, complete but for its mast, rising from the strand like a ship out of legend. The sight of it made her shiver.

'Beautiful, isn't she?'

Katla almost fell over to hear another voice. She spun around, both hands at her mouth to stifle the cry which threatened to escape her. It was Aran Aranson, seated with his back to a pile of timber, so still he looked himself like a stock of wood.

'By Sur, Da you gave me a shock!'

Her father smiled, but he did not take his eyes off the ship. The expression in them was vague and dream-filled: he seemed like a sleepwalker, Katla thought. 'I'm going to call her the *Long Serpent*,' he said softly.

She sat down beside him so that she could take in the vessel's long hull and elegant curves from the same angle. 'Hmm,' she said appraisingly after a while. 'She's certainly as sinuous as any snake; but is that not an ill-starred name for such a ship?'

A crease appeared in Aran's broad forehead. 'Ill-starred?'

'Is it wise to name your vessel after Sur's greatest enemy?'

'Sur has paid little attention to my prayers over the years,' her father snorted. 'So why not appease the monster that overturned his precious *Raven* and dumped him in the

Northern Ocean? Might leave us alone when we sail into her treacherous waters. It would hardly do to lose another fine ship, would it, now?' His voice was hard and flat. It was the nearest he had come to referring to the loss of the *Snowland Wolf* and his eldest son, in her hearing, at least.

She grimaced. 'It's a good name, Da: mythic and brave, as befits a vessel bound on such a great expedition.' She waited a few seconds before adding, 'When will you set out?' He had, she knew, selected the larger number of his crew: twenty-four men from Rockfall itself and the outlying islands. They had been coming to the steading for weeks now, as tales of the fame and fortune to be won from a mysterious arctic land filled with ancient treasure spread far and wide across the Westman Isles: old and young, experienced seamen and green lads, all eager for adventure and daring deeds. Most of them had wives and children at home; many had land and animals to care for, while others had neither a woman nor a bean to their name and hoped to come quickly by sufficient means to furnish themselves with land and wives and a boat of their own: but the legend of Sanctuary was a tale they had heard at their mothers' knees, and roving the wide sea was in their blood. Even the steadiest man found the idea hard to resist. There were still a few places to be settled, if her father was to take a full crew, and she had yet to broach the subject with him again as to whether she would be one of them.

Aran grinned, a flash of white in the gloom. 'Soon.'

'How soon?'

'A week or two.'

'But the seas will be ice-locked all the way from Whale Holm—'

'Why do you think I had an ice-breaker made for her? I cannot wait till Firstsun to set sail: others will get there first. Some may have set out already, every day she lies unlaunched is a wasted day, to me.'

'What do you mean?'

He turned to her then and his face was set and grim. 'I cannot kick my heels here, Katla: Rockfall holds nothing for me now.'

'Da!'

'My son is lost to me; my wife is going mad with grief, and I can do nothing to set the world aright. Why lie around in front of a choking peat-fire feeding a body that is ageing before my very eyes, waiting for death to claim me a little more each day in hand-measure after hand-measure?'

'So you will go out into the Northern Ocean in the depths of winter and offer yourself wholesale, like a calf to the slaughter? That will hardly make the world aright.'

'If I stay here I, too, will go mad.'

Katla bit her lip to stop herself saying what she truly thought: that the Master of Rockfall might already have turned that corner. But while her head told her his plan was at best folly and at worst wilful idiocy, her heart began to beat faster and the palms of her hands itched as if with incipient sweat, though the night was chill. It was the sensation she often felt before attempting a climb she had been assessing for days. The memory of the voice she had heard, urging her to stay behind, she pushed firmly away, locked it into the small box at the back of her mind where she kept all the doubts and fears and other extraneous matters that tried to assail her as she was making the first move off the ground.

'There is nothing for me here, either, Da. Take me with you. I can row, and free rigging and help the navigation. I am as strong as many a man, and you know I will utter no complaint in even the harshest of conditions. What good am I here, under Ma's feet? She looks at me with reproach, no matter what I do. I cannot cook, or sew or spin or weave or behave in the way she wants me to. I want no husband, and I have lost as much as you; let me come with you.'

Aran Aranson gazed at his daughter and saw how in the fey light her face shone with fervour. She was so like him it hurt. His eyes began to prickle and he looked quickly aside. 'I cannot. Your mother would never forgive me if she were to lose another of her children to the sea.'

'And what about Fent?'

'I have promised him a place.'

Katla was incensed. 'But that's not fair! Why can Fent be risked, and not me? Take me instead of him: you know I am of more use!'

'I have my reasons.' In his mind he saw Festrin One-Eye berating him, telling him to look well to his daughter. He would never admit it to any living soul, but the idea of the seither returning to Rockfall made his stomach turn over; made the hairs on the back of his neck rise like a wary dog's. Besides, Katla had already disobeyed him once in the matter of seagoing expeditions: she would not play that game twice. And Fent was becoming a liability at home with nothing to absorb his increasingly destructive energies. There would be more than one girl bearing red-haired children come the following summer, and they would all have to be provided for. 'My mind is made up in this, Katla, so do not try to wheedle around me, nor think to trick your way aboard. I am not so amenable as Tam Fox: I'd not have hesitated for a moment in putting you over the side.'

The mention of the mummer chief's name filled Katla with a sudden overwhelming despair. If even a man so vital and strong as Tam Fox could be taken by the seas, what chance did any other stand? She found herself staring at the *Long Serpent* with fresh eyes. It was beautiful, but deadly, a slender twig of wood to be tossed at will by waves and storm. Did she really want to cling to its slim gunwales while the wind howled around her ears and pelted her with ice shards and freezing spume?

But in her heart she knew the answer to this question.

No matter what the consequences; yes, yes, yes.

* * *

For the next few days, Katla kept out of her father's way. She could not afford for him to become aware of how his own obsession had gripped her. She had the conviction that if he were to look into her face he would see her thoughts burning there and lock her away in one of the outhouses till the *Long Serpent* had sailed out of the sound. Meanwhile, Aran and his wife had broken their long silence; first with a furious argument, then with tears and softer words, but no matter how brave a face Bera turned to the world, Katla could see the fear in her mother's eyes that having lost her beloved Halli, she would soon lose the man she had borne him to, and most likely Fent as well.

Word of the imminence of the voyage spread across the island. The men who had been chosen as crew expressed some surprise at such an early sailing, into the teeth of the storms and the embrace of the ice; but despite the grumbles, there was a palpable excitement in the air. Like the Master of Rockfall, they were bored with a Westman winter spent engaged in small chores and sleep: adventure called, and they would follow Aran Aranson anywhere he would take them.

The hall was buzzing with chatter and activity. The new sail was woven by day and night, and without the integration of any design, since the Master was in such a hurry. On the morning of its completion, the women took it out into the front enclosure and painted its leeward side with mutton-fat, to catch and hold the wind. The oars were oiled and polished, the better to glide through the water, and the loops of rope which would hold them in place inside the ship were treated with whale oil to keep them waterproofed and supple. The last of the caulking was carried out the next day so that the entire island seemed to reek of pine tar and wet wool. The following morning, the massive mastfish was installed, and the great mast stepped inside it and locked into place so that Morten Danson could be satisfied of the fit. Losing a mast to storm winds and a faulty setting was the simplest way to

lose the vessel and every member of its crew; and while the
shipmaker had no love for the man who had caused him to
be abducted, or for any of the men who would sail with him,
he was damned if he would see his reputation compromised.
The sail was made fast to the yard and hauled up to billow in
the biting onshore breeze. Katla watched, her fingers itching,
as the tumbler, Jad, swarmed easily to the top of the mast to
check the beads and knotting around the rakki and affixed
the shrouds with nimble fingers.

The last of the oak logs which had been towed from the
shipyard were laid all the way from the stempost down the
crunching shingle to the lapping waves. The following day
every able-bodied man on the island took a rope and a hand
in rolling the ship down into the water, and there the *Long
Serpent* was launched, into the sound at Rockfall. All across the
strand men cheered: the launch of such a fine vessel was a sight
to remember. The Master, Morten Danson and his foreman,
Orm Flatnose, checked the lie of the ship, examined the seams
– too loose and the ship would take in too much water; too
tight and when the wood swelled, she would likely spring
planking in a heavy sea – while a half dozen of the chosen
crew hauled up the mast and raised the sail. Satisfied at last,
they brought her to anchor alongside the *Fulmar's Gift*. The
Serpent was a bigger ship by far, and heavier in keel and belly
to compensate for the weight of the ice-breaker; but she was
by far the more elegant of the two vessels. By comparison, the
Fulmar's Gift looked what she was: an elderly ship constructed
of inferior materials and for a less exalted purpose, lumpen
and workaday, her wood blackened by age and scarred from
impact with rock and reef and axe.

For three days, men rowed faerings in and out of the
harbour to the *Long Serpent*, taking with them new buckets of
luting to caulk between the strakes and tar for the seams, while
Morten Danson and Orm, a man with hands like bear's paws,
all palm and muscle and stubby, powerful fingers, checked the

working of the steerboard, fixed the rigging and argued about
exactly how to set the under-yard. When all was done to their
satisfaction, there followed the seachests and firewood, then
the tanned hides, the sealskin bags and spars, to provide what
little shelter could be had on the arctic seas; and lastly the
provisions for the voyage. Chains of women and children
lined the path from the steading to the shore, passing from
hand to hand baskets of rye bread and salt cod, ling and
saithe, blood sausages, pickled mutton and veal, wind-dried
beef, a wheel of cheese, gulls' eggs and chickens' eggs; salted
puffin and whole dried rabbits; an entire seal which had been
soaked in brine. A multitude of heavy kegs containing water
from the stream which ran directly off the mountains behind
the great hall were stowed in the stern in a compartment the
shipmaker had installed there to counterbalance the weight of
the ice-breaker. A small amount of stallion's blood followed,
and a barrel of good beer. It would be good for the crew's
morale, Aran had decided, to be able to have a warming drink
inside them after an exhausting day's rowing.

On the Mistress of Rockfall's orders, two huge sacks of
turnips, kale, onions and wild leeks also made their way
aboard, to make up for the vast, unadulterated quantities
of meat, though she had little expectation that the men
would cook or eat the vegetables without any women
aboard to nag them to do so. Finally, a great fragrant sack
of Bera's famous yellowcakes was passed down the line,
accompanied by much envious comment. It was, perhaps,
the best indication that the wife of the Master of Rockfall
might yet be reconciled to her husband's perilous venture.
What they did not know was that it had been Bera's mother,
Hesta Rolfsen – the woman who had taught her daughter to
bake the delicacies in the first place – who had overseen the
baking of the cakes.

Aran Aranson had taken on another two men: Urse, Tam
Fox's huge deputy with the ruined face, who told the Master

of Rockfall he had no luck with women and needed to earn himself a fortune if he were to buy himself a wife, and Felin Greyship's eldest boy, Gar, a well-muscled lad of nineteen who could hardly string two words together, but could tie a bowline one-handed and with his eyes shut. Against his mother's wishes, Fent, too would indeed accompany his father. That left a bare handful of places to fill, and over a hundred men and boys camped around the steading all vying for the honour. Every time Aran came out of his doors, there were more. It had started with a dozen or so Rockfallers, men he had known for years, and their fathers, too. They were quiet and deferential to the Master, nodding their heads at him, hoping he would remember their family's good name and the hardships they had suffered over the years. Those who arrived from further afield were less restrained. They called out, entreating, or bragging of their prowess, showing off their rowing-muscle, swearing they could navigate in fog or flood.

He spoke to them all, each one alone, quietly and at length. From these last arrivals he eventually chose another man on the day before they were due to sail: Pol Garson, a cousin of Tor Leeson's who had been on a number of expeditions and had done well enough to have his own ship, for a time, until it had foundered off the Cullin Sey three years back during a particularly vicious storm. He could perform dead reckonings and navigate by sun and stars and the natural signs of sea and land; and the callouses on his hands showed that he was not too proud to man an oar. By all accounts, losing the ship had been none of his fault, and when he returned with his share of Sanctuary's treasure, he would provide for Sera Wulfsen and the rest of Tor's family: it seemed a fair and measured choice.

After this, he returned to the long house, shut the door behind him and leaned against it. 'That's it,' he said. 'I can do no more. I'd rather go a man short.'

'Well, tell the rest of them to leave, then,' his wife said brusquely.

Aran looked pained. 'Surely we should give them sustenance first.'

Bera Rolfsen put her hands on her hips. 'There's nothing left. It's all on board your damned ship.'

'Don't let's argue on my last day in Rockfall, wife.'

'My concern is that it truly will be, husband. Will you not wait for the sea-thaw, at least?'

Aran fixed her with a stern eye. 'We have had that discussion, *wife*. Hopli Garson and Fenil Soronson commissioned a ship from Danson before us: they sailed it out of his yard a month or more before Halli stole him away. And there are rumours of other expeditions. They'll already have set sail: every day we linger here, we are farther behind them. It's now or never.'

'Then choose never!' Bera's eyes flashed.

'You know I cannot.'

'Cannot? *Will* not, in truth. For it is your will I see driving this venture, Aran: your bull-headed, obstinate will. I have said it before and I will say it again: the map you took from the Fair is a trick fit to gull fools. Sanctuary is not real, and neither is the gold you dream of, yet you will spend freely of all we have earned over these long hard years and, worse, you will spend that rarest of currencies – the lives of your own family and the lives of the men of Rockfall, whose families depend on them – in order to pursue this mad obsession. For that is what this quest is, Aran Aranson: it is the hunt for a chimera, a fairytale; a wildgoose chase. At the best of times it would be sheer folly; but it is the worst of times, with our eldest boy lost to the cruel sea and cries of war hailing from our capital.

'Oh, do not look at me like that, husband, as if I am some ignorant woman relishing some ridiculous new snip of gossip overheard at the market. I have ears and a tongue and a mind to wield both, and I know what all are saying – that it cannot be long before the Istrians act upon the threats made at the Allfair, and that as soon as the ocean is free of ice, they will bring their ships north to deal flame and sword to us as they did of old. And where will you be then, husband? Here to defend your family, or chasing phantasms in the arctic seas?'

During this tirade, Aran had been clenching his fists together ever more tightly so the skin over his knuckles showed taut and white. Now, as Bera stopped to draw breath, the knife he had been holding snapped in two with a great crack of noise, and splinters of ivory spun out across the room. One struck Bera in the cheek, just beneath the eye and drew blood, though the wound was not deep. She put her hand to her face and the fingers she brought away from the site were wet and red and she shrieked.

'Bones and blood, broken and spilled!' she cried. 'It is an omen, but not one I expect you to heed, for you are deaf and blind to all except your dream.'

'Be silent, wife!' he roared. 'I have no time for such nonsense!' He turned and made to leave, but at that moment, someone bellowed, 'Break a knife, lose a life!'

Aran spun around. Gramma Rolfsen, who had been sitting unwontedly quiet throughout the exchange, hidden behind the loom, now got to her feet, planted herself squarely in front of her son-by-law and took him by the arms with such a fierceness of grip that Aran winced visibly. They made a strange tableau, like two frozen dancers; or a pair of snowbears in mock-fight on their hind legs, except that the old woman came barely as high as the big man's chest. Unfazed by the difference in their relative sizes and powers, Hesta Rolfsen shook him with all her might.

'Will you bring all to ruin, Aran Aranson, with your wild scheme?' she demanded. 'Halli is already lost to us as a result of your madness; and now you would take Fent as well. For myself, I care not a whit that you may perish yourself on this venture, for clearly your wits – such as they were – have already fled to the bottom of the sea in advance of the rest of your sorry hulk; but think of your wife and your daughter: how will they fare without the Master of Rockfall; how will the other women of the islands raise their children and their livestock when you have taken away their husbands and fathers and sons to be swallowed by the ocean tides? You are like your father in all the worst ways, and that man was as obstinate as a blinkered horse and as witless as a hare when the mood struck him. And you'll recall the outcome of his last mad venture.'

The previous Master of Rockfall had almost perished in the hunt for a giant narwhal which was reputed to bear a golden horn. Fully three dozen men had seen the beast and attested to the existence of this wondrous appendage; many of them had been part of his crew when the narwhal had been sighted again; and they had given chase and succeeded in harpooning the monster – which was larger, it was claimed, even than the whale which had been washed ashore on the shingle beach on Rockfall Island in the year of the great storm, from which the strand took its name – only for the beast to ram its 'golden' horn right through the beam of the ship and hole it beyond hope. Water rushed in, the strakes sprang apart and the ship ploughed a straight course for the seabed. Of a crew of thirty-eight, only four men survived, including the Master. The narwhal left a large part of its horn embedded in the ship's timbers. Remnants of these, along with the shard of horn, fetched up among the skerries north of Black Isle: but when men found the wreckage, all agreed that far from being made of gold, the horn was yellow with age and algae only: and was of less worth than a walrus's tusk, for it was so old and friable, it would not even bear carving.

The old Master had almost died of the shame and had lived on at Rockfall, barely speaking, hollow-eyed; a husk of his former self. He had died three years later in the war against the

Istrian Empire. Some said he saw the blow coming and made no effort to defend himself; others said he fought bravely and tenaciously. His son had seen him fall, and knew the truth.

Aran Aranson bowed his head. For a moment it seemed he would waver in his intent. Then, very deliberately, he pried Hesta Rolfsen's fingers from his arms and set her away from him. Without a word, he turned and left the steading.

Katla watched him come out into the home enclosure with his brows knitted into the single black line that marked the onset of his stormy temper; watched the hopeful men gathered there crowd around him like pied birds drawn to a fresh kill, listened as her father yelled at them to pack up their belongings and go home to their families, for he had no need of them. She saw the astonished looks on their faces at the Master's unmannerly words, then Aran was striding off down the track to the strand, his gait all stiff-legged with fury. Fent joined her at the enclosure rail, a whetting stone in one hand and one of her best daggers in the other. She had given it to him to appease him over the knock on the head that had enabled her to take his place on the *Snowland Wolf*, and had then regretted it. It was a pretty piece, one of those she had made before the wreck; but in her twin's hands it had become an extension of him, a weapon that had already drawn blood in two brawls.

'It looks as if we'll be under way sooner than later,' he said cheerfully, holding the blade away from his face to inspect the edge. The dagger gleamed in the cold sun with a deadly glint. 'Ma and Da have had a tremendous fight: I could hear it from the barn!' When Fent looked up, he found his sister's eyes on him, and the expression in them was not kindly. 'What?' he said.

'I know you well remember the seither's words to you.'

Fent flushed an unpleasant red. To cover his confusion, he busied himself with sheathing the dagger.

May all your ventures meet with disaster.

'And you're still intent on accompanying Da?'

'It's his venture, not mine,' Fent said shortly. 'So that doesn't count.'

'But you don't really want to go,' Katla urged. 'You hate ships, you've always said so. You could run the farm while he's gone, be the man of the family . . .'

Fent laughed. 'Why, so that you can go in my stead? Haven't you already done enough? Everyone's telling stories of how my brave sister took on a sea-monster with one of the swords she forged herself, after we pestered Urse for long enough for the true tale. You took my place on the last voyage: this time it's my turn to prove myself.' His head came up and there was a sharp jut to his chin. 'Da's told me as much himself, after the business with Fela's father.'

Fela was a pretty, slight lass of sixteen, the daughter of a bondsman farmer who worked the land two valleys away. In the spring she would be somewhat less slight: she was already beginning to show her three months' child, and after she had missed her courses and come crying to the steading, Fent had turned her away with a hard face, declaring he would not wed her. After which, her father had come to see Aran, and the two men had exchanged harsh words.

Katla nodded once. So that was it: for her brother it was simpler to face the wild seas of the North than it was to deal with an angry man and his heartbroken daughter.

'He won't take you, you know,' Fent said, as if he could read her thoughts. 'You're just a girl.'

Gone were the days when Katla would have reacted with a roundhouse punch to such a remark. Instead, she glared at him steadily. 'At least I'm a girl who knows a bowline from a reef, and a carrick from a clove hitch.'

An unreadable expression passed across her twin's face. 'I have a challenge for you,' he said after a moment's pause and there was a strange glint in his eyes. 'Meet me at dawn tomorrow on top of the Hound's Tooth. And bring a length of rope with you.'

Katla regarded him curiously. What was he up to? Her brother had never shown the slightest interest in climbing before. But Fent met her gaze square on, his grin as wide and guileless as it had been when they were children.

'All right,' she said. 'I will.'

Katla Aransen could never turn away a challenge.

The *Long Serpent* would sail at high tide the next day, Aran Aranson announced, when the seas would run her clear of the circling reefs and out into the ocean swell with the offshore wind. His wife's eyes were red-rimmed and there was an inflamed cut on her left cheek, but she went about her tasks with her head held high as if nothing were out of the ordinary, though men averted their eyes from her and women whispered behind their hands that she must have provoked the Master terribly for him to hit her hard enough to draw blood. Aran turned a deaf ear to them all, and took himself off for a long walk on the steading as the sun started to dip, giving orders to the lads left behind to tend the land and livestock; then he walked into the next valley and settled his debts with Bera's brother Margan, and talked to him until the moon was high.

Katla met him on the way back. She had waited in the crook of the old apple tree for three hours. After the first hour, Ferg had given up whining at her to come down and had fallen asleep among the tangled roots. Every so often, his feet would twitch and his breathing would quicken as he chased phantom rabbits this way and that. Katla envied him the simplicity of his dreams. She knew she would not sleep this night, not until she had spoken to her father one more time about taking her aboard his ice-breaker.

But the Master's face was grim in the moonlight as he strode through the bracken, and when Katla dropped down out of the tree in front of him, waking Ferg, who leapt up barking loudly enough to wake the dead, Aran cursed roundly and foully and walked straight past her so that she had to run to catch him up.

'Da, Da, please stop!'

'I am in the mood for no more words,' Aran said shortly, not slowing his pace.

'You must take me to Sanctuary!' Katla pleaded, all her carefully-worded arguments put to flight by her desperation. 'Please, Da: don't sail without me. I couldn't bear it!' She grabbed his sleeve.

Now Aran Aranson came to a halt. He turned and took his daughter by the arms. His face looked harrowed. 'Do you so want to die?' he asked.

'I will die if I am left here,' Katla declared dramatically.

Her father sighed. 'We are too alike,' he said after a long silence.

Katla held her breath, wondering what would come next.

'You want no marriage; and I have none.'

His daughter frowned. 'What do you mean?' A cold dread suddenly gripped at her stomach.

Aran gave a short, harsh laugh. 'Your mother has cast me off: declared us man and wife no more.'

Katla's mouth fell open. In the Northern Isles a woman could divorce her husband for three reasons: for infidelity, for insanity, or for violence against her. Surely it must be for the second of these, a quarrel over his obsessive expedition? It might seem insanity, in the midst of an argument; but Bera couldn't truly mean it. 'Oh, Da,' she said. Then: 'But you know Mother's temper: she'll have calmed down by now; she always does—'

'Your Uncle Margan is overseeing the settlement.'

He stated it so flatly she knew it must be so. She did not know what to think: her parents, living apart from one another? Maybe even taking other marriage partners? It seemed unthinkable, as if the world had suddenly changed shape. Suddenly, the notion of the voyage seemed a nonsense. 'And you're still going to Sanctuary?' she blurted out.

Aran gave a single, curt nod. 'I have my pride.' His eyes gleamed in the moonlight. When he turned them upon her, they shone so silver it was like looking into the gleaming, empty orbits of an afterwalker. 'If you still want a place on the expedition, it is yours,' he said simply, then walked on, leaving her standing in the dangerous backwash of his anger.

Katla felt the breath rush out of her. An hour ago; ten minutes, even, it was all she had dreamed of; but now? He did it to strike back at her mother, she knew that much instinctively; to demonstrate his power and the rightness of his quest. She felt boneless, dazed by the choice she must make: to go, and by doing so acquiesce in the madness that had already destroyed their family; or to stay at home with an angry, grieving woman and knuckle down as a dutiful daughter?

Katla knew which alternative she should choose; as a daughter, and as a woman. But she also knew that if she remained on Rockfall, her spirit would dwindle and chafe. 'I will go with you!' she shouted after Aran Aranson's retreating back. But if he heard her, he gave no sign of it.

Dawn the following morning found Katla climbing steep ground with a coil of rope draped over her shoulder. Sense had, for once, prevailed over instinct: and so she had eschewed her favourite route to the summit of the Hound's Tooth, via the precipitous seaward face, in favour of the old folks' route, as she thought of it, and was strolling up the well-worn path to the top of the headland at a leisurely pace. Just what her brother had in mind for their challenge when she got there, she did not know, or even much care: it was good to be up and out of the steading, away from all the acrimony and gossip. Perhaps she and Fent could just sit in the early sun and talk about the split between their mother and father, and maybe find some way to mediate between the two of them; persuade Aran to put off the expedition by a few days, or at least until they had made some reconciliation. Even so, she had packed her seachest against the possibility of a noon sailing. And had, of course, not slept a wink.

She was surprised to find her brother already there; and even more surprised to find that he had for some bizarre reason toiled up the path with a heavy wooden chair, which he was now sitting in, like some landless king. She stared at him, dumbfounded. 'What on Elda have you brought that here for?' she demanded.

Fent, lolling in his self-styled throne, barely acknowledged her presence, but gazed out over the wide ocean as if he had not a care in the world. 'Fine view, isn't it?' he said laconically after a while.

Katla frowned. Her twin had never been much interested in scenery. Annoyance made her spiteful. 'How can you sit there, with everything that is going on?'

Fent turned his head lazily in her direction 'There's not much I can do about it, is there? They'll make it up: they always have before. Besides, I've other things to think about.' With a sudden surge of energy he came upright out of the chair. 'I see you were not so caught up in all the drama that you forgot to bring the rope,' he observed. 'So let's get our contest underway.'

She regarded him curiously. 'Well, I am intrigued. What is the nature of the challenge you have for me?'

'Knot-tying,' Fent announced cheerfully. 'You said I didn't know "a bowline from a reef, or a carrick from a clove hitch". So I have devised a game to test our respective skills in that quarter.'

'Actually,' Katla corrected him crossly, 'what I said was that at least I did. I only *implied* you didn't.' She grinned. 'But I know you don't!'

Instead of rising to this bait, Fent sat himself down in the chair again and laid his forearms along its wooden frame. 'I will free myself from any knots you care to bind me with.'

'Ha!'

'And then, you must win free of mine.'

Too easy, Katla thought gleefully. It was a game they had played as children, and Fent always lost. But perhaps he had been practising. She decided to go easy with him: after all, they would be sharing a long, rough passage if the *Long Serpent* did sail at noon, and there was no point in there being bad blood between them if it could be helped. She uncoiled her rope: a fine but sturdy length of twisted sealskin bound with horsehair which gave the cord a certain elasticity as well as considerable strength, and made a beginning by looping an end around the arm of the chair. Leaving a good tail on the rope to make a solid stopper, she bound his arm to the chair in a series of running hitches, then passed the rope twice around his waist and the back of the frame, lifted one of the legs so that she could slip a securing knot to keep the bands in place, then set to work on an elaborate combination of bowlines and sheep-knots. Eventually, she finished the process with a neat fisherman's, using the spare tail of rope, and stood back to admire her handiwork. Not too difficult; but it would surely take him a while to extricate himself.

Fent bared his teeth at her, and his features were as sharp and cunning as a fox's. 'Go sit in the sun, small sister. I'll be with you shortly.'

Katla shrugged and moved away. Her favourite boulder beckoned: it lay in a pool of sunshine which made the rosettes of yellow lichen that bloomed upon it shine like golden coins. There was a depression in the granite into which you could just insert a shoulder and lay your head: it was remarkably comfortable, for a rock.

How long she dozed, she did not know, but when she came awake at last it was because the chill of a shadow had fallen over her. She opened her eyes and found her brother staring down at her. She scrambled upright, surprised. The rope lay on the ground around the chair and showed no sign of unfair tampering.

'I'm impressed,' she said.

'You should be,' he returned. 'It took a good deal of working out. Now it's your turn.'

It was in Katla's mind to call off the challenge and let him win, for there was something in his expression she could not place. Not for the first time, it occurred to her that her twin – who had for most of her life seemed an extension of herself, as she was of him – had lately become a separate being entirely, as alien and unknowable as the strangest stranger. But the stubborn core of her would not allow him the simple satisfaction. She took his place in the chair and watched with a small smile as her brother tied a series of utterly inept knots.

'Call that a carrick-bend—' she started, when suddenly there was something in her mouth, and the smell of earth and sweat assailed her. Powerful hands grabbed her from behind and then another rope went around her – not her own, which confused her mightily – but a thick rope of twisted hemp; and to confound her further, Fent was still in front of her; so who—

The man who had bound her to the chair rather more expertly than her twin stepped now into view. She glared at him over the clout of cloth they had rammed into her mouth, and was only slightly surprised not to recognise him. He was tall and sinewy, with the dark skin of a seasoned mariner and his blond hair worn in a tumble of dirty-looking curls. A large silver earring gleamed in one ear. Fent clapped the man on the shoulder. 'Nice one, Marit. I'd say you've earned your place on the *Serpent*, wouldn't you?'

The other man grinned widely and Katla saw he was missing his two front teeth. 'I'll knock the rest out, you bastard!' she cried, struggling against the rope, but all that emerged was a muffled groan; and the knots gave not a whit.

Her twin placed himself firmly in front of the chair, his blue eyes sparking malice. 'As I said, it's a fine view from here. A perfect vantage point for watching the *Long Serpent* sail out. Thanks to Marit Fennson's expertise, I doubt you'll be able to free yourself, for if you struggle too much, the knots will merely tighten. I dare say someone will think to look for you up here after a while. Or perhaps they won't. Though if you're left for long enough without sustenance you may shed sufficient flesh that you can slip your bonds and crawl back down into Rockfall. It will, at the least, give you plenty of time to remember the occasion when you and my beloved dead brother knocked me over the head and tied me to the pillar in the barn with this same gag in my mouth, so that you could steal my place aboard the *Snowland Wolf*.

'You'll not make a fool of me again for a long time, sister. Fare well.'

Twenty

Flight

In the wake of the destruction of the crystal and the confusion that followed, Virelai took the back stairs down to the yard two at a time, his feet sliding on the age-polished slate, palms pressed against the walls for balance. Only one other person in all of the castle wore gloves like those the seeing-stone had offered up to him in its sudden flash of vision before it had shown the gathered company the Rose of the World flaunting her great belly before the northern court; and while the others were transfixed by that remarkable sight, Virelai had been shocked rigid by that prior, very ordinary glimpse.

Saro Vingo was making his escape from Jetra.

Virelai felt his new-formed plan – so elegant, so perfect – slipping away. It had all seemed to fit into place with the precision of one of the beautifully engineered wooden puzzles they sold for the delectation of rich children in Cera's summer market, and the moodstone the boy carried was its key. Or, as the grimoire he had stolen from Rahe's great library would term it, 'the eldistan'. After his first terrifying encounter with the boy in Jetra's Star Chamber, Virelai had become fascinated by the trinket Saro wore with such apparent ease around his neck, and had searched through every line of the mage's book until he had found this entry:

'In *Natural Alchemia* (Idin Haban c. Swan Year 953) there is mention of moodstones/channel-stones, called in the regions of the far south of the mts, whence such stones most often

derive, "eldistaner". Extremely mutable in their properties,'
he had read in Rahe's swift and spidery hand. 'Only "youngest" are simple moodstones – for amusing diversion only.
Display in outwd fashion passing whims & fancies of one
who holds it in his/her hand. Takes warmth fm holder's
skin. May take on hues which differ greatly fm nat. state.

'Chart shows my own findings:

White = Death

Grey = Emptiness of Mind; failing health

Cyan = Serenity

Green = Wholeness

Yellow = Sickness; tho pale Gold = Wellbeing (further
obs. req.)

Vermilion = Anxiety/Fear/Disruption of Humours

Carmine = Rage

Violet – in its harsh form = Turbulence of Emotion; if
tending towards the blue, denotes Intellectual Activity.'

There followed more in this vein which Virelai had passed
over impatiently. The next entry which caught his eye had
been this:

'"Elder Eldistaner. Ejected fm deep veins of the earth,
typically fm feet or crown of fire-mts, and most esp. from
area surrounding Red Pk, where the Heart of Elda lies."
Larger than usual, darker, and when polished shows compact,
smooth grain. Weighs more heavily in hand and can feel
warm even when untouched for hrs. Idin Haban spks of
telling future w some such; others open mind of holder to
viewer, and one esp. pwrful stone enabled him to make fire
by channelling sorcery. Have w much magecraft channelled
sufficient heat to effect burning of cockroaches, sparrows and
rats, even once a seal to ashes, but V's mind remains closed
to me, if mind he has.'

This made Virelai wince. Had Rahe truly made him the
subject of one of these experiments and if so, when had this
occurred, and why did he have no recollection of it? It was

possible, he mused, that the stone had erased the memory, and there was, as far as he knew, no other being to whom the Master might refer as 'V'. But the idea that the mage had regarded him as so expendable that he would risk his well-being so – or, worse, even wished his destruction – disturbed him greatly. It was as if he were no more to the old man than the cockroaches, sparrows or rats Rahe had so blithely listed. The thought made him seethe and doubt the wisdom of the course of action he was determined on; so he had pushed the doubt away and continued to read.

There then followed a detailed list of every bird, animal and sea-creature which the Master had managed to reduce to cinder, together with the periods of recovery required after each such act. Further down the next page, Virelai had come upon this note:

'More remarkable is Xanon's account in his *History of the Ancient World*, ch. 13 "Among the Nomads" in which he tells how an old woman, by burying one hand deep in the ground, made a stone blaze in a great arc, killing an entire flock of rock-pigeons flying many hundred feet in the air above her. Imagine what a weapon such a stone in other hands wd make.'

Could it be the same stone which Saro bore around his neck, Virelai wondered? Power emanated from the thing in a way that had afforded him the most horrifying and deathly visions. Such a thing in the wrong hands . . . That thought led to another: what if Tycho Issian were to lay hands on such a stone? He shuddered. With the Lord of Cantara in his current unstable state, no living creature on Elda would be safe. It was imperative that the twain be separated, and by as great a distance as possible.

In a fit of morbid dread, he had read on, expecting more and more horrors. Instead, some pages later, he came upon another entry, cryptically worded and strange beyond belief. This he read and then overread, in case he had misapprehended it entirely. But no: its implications were undeniable. A plan began to take shape, the details flowing like the most perfect of weavings. With the stone, if not in his hands, then at least in his company, he could save his own skin. He could return to Sanctuary without fear of reprisal or the Master's wrath. All would be well. A great wave of relief had washed over him. He remembered the momentary bliss of that rare sensation, before anxiety clamped his chest once more.

His plan rested on the slim shoulders of Saro Vingo: lose the boy and he would lose the stone, and thereafter any chance of survival. Redoubling his efforts, he skidded to a halt at the postern gate with his heart thumping and the breath rough in his chest, and looked outside. It was pitch-dark out there and nothing was stirring. Virelai swore quietly. Surely the boy could not have fled so far and so fast? It was true that the seeing-stones could offer deceptions, so the lad might already be far away, the time he had been shown another hour of the night entirely; or safe in his bed, dreaming of his escape on another such occasion. He sniffed the air. The faint scent of horse-dung came back to him, and warm animals. Was the stable door still open?

Virelai stepped out into the night.

Night's Harbinger was in a lively mood. There were mares two paddocks away and he could scent them. When the boy had come to his stall he had thought he was being taken to visit them and had followed the lad eagerly, not even complaining when a bridle was slung over his head. So he was more than a little surprised when he found a saddle on his back and a strap around his belly; but it was only when the boy had grasped his neck and stepped up into the stirrup that he knew something was amiss.

Spinning around, Night's Harbinger tried to bite his rider

on the knee as a mark of protest, all the while snorting fit to wake the dead.

Saro clenched his knees against the stallion's flanks and tried unsuccessfully to quiet him. A moment later, there came the sound of raised voices from the walls above them and his breath caught in his throat. He prepared to press the animal into a desperate gallop; but then the sounds diminished and became more distant as the men passed on without stopping, and no lit torches nor any alarm followed their passage into the castle. Steadying his breathing, Saro urged the horse into a stately walk, heading for the western gate and the grassy plain beyond.

But before they could reach the outer wall, the stallion's ears began to twitch. Then his head came up sharply and he began to dance backwards. Saro fought him to a stiff halt, then stared into the murk to see what had caused him such concern. About twenty feet away, dimly outlined by the moonlight, was a huge dark shape. A pair of fiery golden eyes flared in the darkness, and Saro felt the hairs rise on the back of his neck and gooseflesh prickle down his arms. It was a primal reaction: prey to predator. Cold sweat trickled the length of his spine. He wished, suddenly and fervently and for the first time in his life, that he had a sword.

For the space of several heartbeats horse and rider stood frozen; then the beast opened its maw. It was vast: that much Saro could divine by the glint of moonlight on the wide-apart fangs. Night's Harbinger shifted his weight delicately from hoof to hoof and whisked his tail nervously, but otherwise showed no sign that he had any survival instinct at all. Saro waited for a roar to issue out of the cavernous mouth and for the killing leap that would inevitably follow, but nothing of the sort happened. Instead, the creature closed its mouth again with a faint click of teeth. Saro was filled with the sudden incongruous suspicion that the beast had *yawned*. Was it really so confident it could dispatch him and the stallion? Just as he was thinking this, darkness filled the gap between them, as if something had become between the great beast and its prey. A flicker of something tall and pale . . .

The moodstone began to glow.

'Bëte, desist!'

The voice was deep and commanding. The stallion stilled as if by magic and Saro felt his own will slip into abeyance and his hands, which had been rising to shield the stone, fell limp and useless to his sides. Then the pale thing moved out of his line of sight, and suddenly the beast was there no more. When a cloud passed away from the face of the half-moon overhead, the man called Virelai was standing in front of him. In his arms was a small black cat.

Saro stared past him, but the huge predator was gone, melting into the night as silently as it had appeared.

'Come with me,' the pale man said in the same timbre he had employed before, and although something inside Saro's mind quailed away from the suggestion, his hands tightened on the reins and he heard his own voice replying, 'Yes, I will come.'

It had all been far simpler than Virelai could have imagined. Using the Master's voice of command could be very hit or miss; but here he was with the cat all pliant in his grasp and the boy and his horse following him into the shelter of the orange grove below the city walls. Here they could remain unseen while he hared back into the castle and retrieved his necessaries – the grimoire, at the very least, and as much of the carefully faked silver as he could carry. Up in his chamber, wheezing with the exertion of running twenty-three flights of stairs, he stuffed the cat into its wicker basket, still amazed it had not come out of its trance and tried to bite him with its usual spite, and packed into a sturdy sack the grimoire, some clothes, the ointment, a cloak, a knife, two big bricks of the tin-turned-silver, his herbals, pen and inks, carefully stoppered to avoid spillage, and a set of parchments he had been working on, which could prove most incriminating were they to be found by, for instance, the Lords of Forent and Cantara.

Then he started down again. About halfway to the postern, he realised he should take something for Alisha: it would be bad enough turning up on the step of her wagon without warning, and with the boy, too: two new mouths to feed in the hardest of times, and that without taking into account the danger which would surely follow when the hue and cry was raised, and while a gift was no more than the merest emollient in such circumstances, it at least showed some degree of comprehension of the magnitude of the favour he was about to ask. At the third floor, he took a side door and ran down the twisting corridor as quietly as he could manage with the cat-basket bumping on his back and his bundle of belongings clutched to his chest. He knew exactly what she would most appreciate.

The kitchens were silent except for the snoring of the boys by the bread-oven: even though it was still some hours before the dawn, they would soon have to be up and baking again: the fresh bread and exquisite pastries to be had in Jetra's castle were talked of throughout Istria with nostalgia by those who had experienced them and with longing by those who had not, but they appeared each morning on the nobles' breakfast tables by dint of sheer hard graft rather than as the result of any simple magic. Virelai crept around them and into the cold-pantry where the rarer spices were stored. Hanging from the ceiling in swathes of aromatic green and gold and pink were garlands of safflowers, bunches of hemp and vervain and loosestrife; behind them, in great wide dishes of blue Jetran pottery was this year's harvest of lion crocuses, each triform amber stamen removed with care and gathered to dry for colour and flavouring in a dozen exotic dishes. But Virelai knew another use for the powdered pistils. He picked up one of the heavy pots and poured the contents into a square of fabric, tied it tightly and discarded the vessel. Alisha would love the dish, he knew, but it couldn't be helped. He stowed the parcel inside his bundle and turned to leave. His exit was blocked. In his path was one of the castle dogs – not one of the lords' elegant deerhounds this, but a black-and-tan, brutish-looking mutt with a square jaw and an ugly head. Saliva dripped from its ruckled mouth onto the stone flags.

Virelai smiled.

'Lie down,' he suggested to it. 'Sleep.'

But it was not the Master's powerful command that issued out, but a weak and reedy facsimile. Instead of doing as it had been bidden, the dog growled and took a pace forward into the entrance of the pantry. Virelai took a step back. Inside its basket, the cat stirred.

Dogs were a species of Elda's creatures Virelai had always found problematic. They didn't like him, quite instinctively. In fact, most animals had an antipathy to him, for no reason which was immediately apparent, since he tried to treat them well and was not given to cruelty; but dogs had large teeth and could inflict considerable damage with one jaw-crunching lunge, much like the Lord of Cantara, and the anxiety they caused him seemed to communicate itself. When he could, he avoided them, or tried to make himself as unobtrusive as possible. This beast, however, had made it its business to seek him out and confront him: it would hardly be put off by simple trickery.

Fear made his mind spin. The voice was not working: what else was left in his armoury? The grimoire was well wrapped and in the bottom of the sack: it would take too long to extricate it and find a relevant charm. Even then he would need the cat's cooperation; and the idea of removing the cat in front of such a monster was the sheerest folly. His brain worked feverishly. A tincture of the pistils he had just stolen would cause drowsiness and worse: but he had neither the time nor the means to effect such a treatment. Since all gentler solutions were closed to him, the only course left seemed that of mindless violence. He looked desperately around for anything that might serve as a weapon. Glassware; pottery; dried flowers. It was hopeless. The wished-for rolling pin, ladle or long meat-knife was nowhere to be seen. The dishes were heavy, it was true; but shattered pottery and the chaos that was likely to ensue if he did not kill the dog outright meant certain discovery, capture and the failure of his plan. And with the expensive herb stashed in his pack, a charge of theft to answer.

The dog began to make a bubbling, deep-throated growl. Its ears flattened against its skull. Virelai watched its rump bear down and begin to waggle in a manner that might have been comical, had it not so obviously heralded attack. Without another thought about possible consequences, he picked up the biggest dish he could lay hands on and hurled it with all his might at the beast.

Jetran pottery was famed throughout the civilised world for its elegance and the startling blue of its glaze, which was unique to the potters of the Eternal City. The word for 'blue' in the ancient tongue of the Tilsen Plain was the same as that for 'sky', specifically the deep, unflawed blue of a seven-month sky. What it was not famed for was its sturdiness: the bowl struck the dog square on its massive skull and broke into hundreds of brittle shards. Saffron scattered everywhere, coating the exposed shelves of the pantry, the mutt's vast paws; the floor. But if Virelai had hoped the thing would be distracted by the aromatic pollen, if not by the missile itself, he was to be sadly disappointed.

Enraged by the thump on its head, which had damaged it only in serving to make it bite its tongue, and confused by the yellow dust that invaded its nostrils and caused it to sneeze, the mutt came grimly on, spraying drool and blood as it advanced. Virelai swung the cat-basket around in front of him. It was a cowardly act, and probably a futile one, but it was all he could think of.

Dog and wicker collided with such force that the sorcerer was thrown backwards off his feet, grazing his elbows on the shelving on the way down and bashing his head with a painful thud on the cold stone floor. There, he found himself trapped by the long basket which had wedged itself crosswise between the narrow walls, and by the immense weight of the dog bearing down on top of the basket. Obscure hissings and growlings filled the air, and then the basket burst apart so that he could feel the beast's feet churning into his exposed belly. All the breath rushed out of his lungs; his vision began to speckle and he thought he might vomit. Just as he had decided this was how he would die – ignominiously, on the floor of a pantry, in the act of stealing some herbs in the middle of the night, his throat ripped out by some rabid mongrel – there was a sudden release of pressure. Breath returned, followed by a distant whimpering which might have been his own: he was so disorientated it was hard to tell.

After a few moments' blessed silence, voices sounded out in the kitchens; though whether it was merely the sleepy conversations of the baker-boys, or others wakened by the dog's din, it was impossible to tell.

Virelai sat up gingerly. Of the dog there was no sign, except for the slick pools of blood and slobber it had left on the flagstones. Bits of broken wicker lay strewn around the floor. Bëte was gone.

In her place was the Beast: lion-sized and as black as night. Its fangs were red, its eyes knowing.

Get up, it said into his mind, and his bowels quivered. *Behind you there is a door into the outside world. Open it.*

Virelai moved his head minutely, not daring to take his eyes off the great avatar for fear it would try to rip his throat out, too. Elda knew, he deserved such a fate for thrusting the defenceless cat it had been but moments before into the path of a savage cur. Did the Beast it had become think in such a manner? Did it harbour a grudge? If so, his life was surely forfeit.

Hurry.

By levering himself up on the shelves, Virelai managed to stand. Feeling more confident now that he was on his feet (though there was little logic to this, since the Beast could move a thousand times faster than he could in the event of an attempted escape) he turned and surveyed the back of the pantry. There was indeed – he could just spy out of the corner of his eye – a tiny door there, closed with a simple iron latch. Stupid not to have noticed it before.

The sound of voices in the kitchen got louder and suddenly the Beast was in the pantry with him, its cool fur and hot breath pressed up against him. Shuffling backwards away from the thing, Virelai retrieved his pack and slung it awkwardly over his back. Then, after a moment's thought, he reached up and took down two large bundles of the dried hemp and stowed them in the bundle as well. He had a feeling they might come in useful.

After that he unlatched the door. It opened outwards with barely a creak and suddenly they were out in the night. A cool breeze freighted with the scent of oranges engulfed them.

Good, the Beast said. *Now we go south.*

Virelai blinked.

'No,' he said aloud, 'it is north we must go: north to Sanctuary; back to your master.'

Something tickled the inside of his skull. It felt like having a moth trapped there, a small presence, light and unthreatening. It was, he realised after a short space of incomprehension, a projection of the humour the great cat found in this pronouncement. As if to clarify the matter, it declared:

I have no master. I am the Beast.

Twenty-one

Signs and Portents

By noon the skies were strewn with thin clouds fishtailing high above the horizon. A sharp offshore breeze had sprung up: if it held, the *Long Serpent* would make an auspicious departure from Rockfall, skimming out of the harbour with a full sail, on a straight course north. While the men boarded and loaded the last of their goods and the two sturdy ship's boats, Aran Aranson stood at the prow with his face turned towards the ocean, every line of his expression intent, inturned. One hand rested on some unseen object nestled inside the neck of his tunic; his pale eyes reflected the sky.

Behind him, his crewmen now jostled for position, seeking out the faces of their loved ones who had gathered along the seawall. Some of the wives cried; some stood stony. A gaggle of older women stood off to one side, their arms folded, their expressions resigned. They had seen many departures such as this down the years. Sometimes the sailors came home; sometimes they did not. There seemed little pattern to the luck doled out to such expeditions, and nothing any of them could do to influence the outcome, though in their youth they had, like the younger wives, cut and braided locks from their own hair and bound them with blood and saltwater and tied into them every knot they knew to bring fair weather and safe passage. The folded arms, the resigned faces posed an unspoken question: Why were men such fools, that they were never satisfied with the good lives they had? What drove them to spurn the ground beneath their feet, the daily round of farms and families: what compelled them to throw all aside and chase off across the whale's path on some elusive quest?

They knew the answer, of course: it was precisely those things which drove the men away: the familiar patterns of a life in which the greatest excitement might be damage wreaked by an escaped ram, by visitations of storm, or sickness. The younger women took their men's choice to leave as a personal slight: some marriages never healed from the rift, no matter what riches might be brought home, what tales of glory told around the fire. Bera Rolfsen had been aware of her own husband's restlessness these many years; she had watched him quell his yearnings, put his shoulder to the plough and grimly commit himself to routine and hard graft, the only outlet for his trapped frustrations the annual voyage to the Allfair. She had known it would come to this one day: that his grip on the life they had made together would break apart in some needlessly dramatic fashion. So she watched him now as he stood at the prow of the vessel which had cost their eldest son's life, and though she appeared dry-eyed and impassive, she clutched her mother's hand so tightly that the tips of Gramma Rolfsen's fingers turned purple, then white, then blue. But not once did the Master of Rockfall look back towards the steading; not once did his eyes seek out the face of his wife among those who lined the seawall. Instead, he kept his eyes fixed on the northern horizon, out past the distant cliffs and skerries where ocean and sky melded in a grey haze, and his profile was as hard and proud as carvings of the kings of old, stern men with cold eyes and jutting beards who had died heroic deaths and left nothing behind but their images in wood and stone.

Then his hand fell away from the object hidden inside his shirt and it was as if a spell broke, for he turned suddenly, and seemed to be a man once more. His eyes swept over the scene behind him – the milling folk on the quay, the waving arms, the weeping women – and settled briefly on the figure of Bera Rolfsen, wrapped in her best blue cloak, the hood down so that her fine red hair flew in the breeze. He saw her catch it back with her free hand and their gazes locked for an instant. Something passed between them which might have been acceptance, or at least some form of understanding, then he tore his gaze away once more and, turning his attention to the crew, shouted, 'Yard up!' and strode off down the ship.

Men leapt to their appointed tasks and Aran gave himself over to the practical details of the passage out of the harbour – to the trim of the sail, the setting of the mast, the arrangement of lines and shrouds, the draw of the steerboard. He watched his crew, noting those who moved neatly about the vessel and those who lumbered awkwardly, and hoped the latter would soon find their sea-legs.

As they passed beneath the tall cliffs, black in the shade and patched with guano and lichens, the sail caught the full strength of the wind so that they skimmed past the Hound's Tooth in impressive style and the Master's heart filled with pride. He did not notice the raven which overflew the ship, heading inland on a sure and steady course, its primary feathers spread like fingers. Nor did he realise that his daughter was absent from the ship until well after they had passed beyond sight of the great pinnacle on which she sat, fast-bound, even though her eyes bored down upon him from that rocky promontory and followed the vessel with a burning, tear-glazed intensity until it had sailed far out of mortal sight.

'Did you see her?' Fent nudged the blond man with a sharp elbow.

Marit Fennson bobbed his head. 'Still there, as I told you she would be. My knots would hold a charging bull, let alone a little slip of a thing like your sister. Will you speak with Aran Aranson for me now?'

Fent looked pained. 'Best wait a while. I don't want him turning back for her, or casting you off.'

A shadow fell across them. Katla's brother looked up and found himself staring into the ruined face of Urse One-Ear. The big man grinned. This was a horrible sight at the best of times, and Fent was already feeling nervous. To see a man with barely half a face smiling at you so that his exposed eye-teeth gleamed like tusks made him feel like a seal-pup at the mercy of a snowbear.

'Where's the girlie?' Urse enquired sweetly. 'I have not seen her aboard, though her father said she would be here.'

Marit made himself scarce. Fent watched as he picked his way deftly through the coils of rope, the kegs and chests and cooking implements, to his oar-place and took a seat there, and knew he would have to shoulder this burden alone. Composing his panic, he tried desperately to conjure the plausible excuse he had prepared for his father.

'She felt unwell,' he started, only to stop when he saw the big man's eyes narrow dangerously. He coughed and then started again: 'She thought it best to stay with her mother.'

'There was no sign of her on the quay; though I saw the Lady of Rockfall and her dam standing side by side.'

Fent shrugged. 'Who knows Katla's mind? She is as changeable as the weather.'

There was a long, uncomfortable pause, then: 'In some islands it is believed that newborn twins are joined by a single soul, and that Sur must decide which child shall own it. Where I come from, lots are cast. One babe gets to stay suckling at its mother's titty. The other is given to the sea.' Urse leaned down, placed one of his bearlike hands on the lad's shoulder and squeezed until Fent winced. Ostensibly, the big man was still smiling, but his scar-rimmed eyes were hard as topaz. 'I should like to know how you came ashore again, Fent No-soul. Maybe it is time for the Lord Sur to see his choice made good.'

He held the lad's gaze for two heartbeats longer, then
released him and walked slowly away. Fent felt a chill run
through him. He would have to talk to his father now, before
Urse said anything.

He found Aran Aranson seated on an upturned cask amidships. A square of crumpled parchment, or some other
substance that looked similarly yellow and aged, was spread
upon his knee. The Master traced a fingertip over a series of
lines marked in the upper third of the parchment, every so
often looking out to steerboard and then back down to the
drawing, which he sometimes moved minutely down, or to
the right, as if orientating what he saw in the world to its flat
representation on the map.

Fent breathed a sigh of relief and approached. His father
was obsessed with the map: whenever he handled it, it was
as if it absorbed him so completely that he was unable to
exercise will or temper. It would be the best possible time
to make his lie about Katla.

'Da,' he started, but Aran Aranson waved a hand in the air
as if waving away an irritating sand-fly, so he stopped again.

The Master of Rockfall sighted the position of the sun,
fished in his pouch for one of several lengths of twine
which he selected with some care, then ran his fingers
up and down the knots thereon, his eyes shut tight as if
for fullest concentration. When he opened them again, he
adjusted the position of the map, made a small mark on the
paper with his thumbnail and smiled at his son. 'Kelpie Isle,'
he said, indicating a tiny, jagged outline on the map.

Fent had never seen the map up close before: his father
was possessive of the object, had kept it jealously to himself.
It was, he had to admit, a beautiful, mysterious thing; if you
were interested in pieces of paper – or whatever it was made
of – which purported to show you the world. Fent preferred
to see and experience the external evidences of Elda at first

hand: the abstract held little hold over for him. Even so, he craned his neck dutifully and watched Aran trace his fingers lovingly over the map.

A windrose sat in the top righthand corner, its southern arm pointing diagonally down towards a missing lefthand corner. Around its decorated frame he could make out a number of strange words. Some he could make no sense of at all; which was hardly surprising, given how little time Fent had given to his studies; but the words 'Isenfelt', 'Oceana' and 'Sanctuarii' were clear enough: icefields, ocean; Sanctuary. It made it all sound so simple; especially if it was possible to pinpoint an island as small as Kelpie from these inky squiggles. He blinked, looked up; compared the lines on the map with those etched against the horizon, reached no conclusion. It was an island, and there seemed to be an island marked in approximately that position on the parchment, and that was all he could comprehend. As one of the crewmen – Kalo, the quiet, dark oarsman – threaded his way past them, Fent watched his father's hand curl protectively around the map, rolling it closed against his body and felt a momentary doubt. Could such a pretty, insubstantial object really render up a safe passage to a place of legend? Or had it cast some strange spell over the Master of Rockfall?

Red light was lining the piles of dark clouds gathering on the horizon as the sun went down: the air had taken on an unmistakable chill.

'Da,' he said again. 'About Katla . . .'

The preternaturally good weather that had blessed the Westman Isles these past months had resulted in a succession of unseasonable lambings as ewes mated and birthed quite out of the normal pattern of such things. Even before Aran Aranson had taken most of the good men with him on his expedition to Sanctuary, the flocks were proving more than a handful for the two shepherds charged with their welfare and management. Fili Kolson and his ageing dog, Breda, had finally succeeded in penning all of his sheep in the shieling below the Hound's Tooth; apart from one errant lamb which had taken exception at the sight of a particularly low-flying gull and had bounded away up the rocky pinnacle in complete panic. Breda had snapped at the beast's heels for all of thirty feet, and had then as the ground had steepened unremittingly, had given it up as a lost cause, trotting back to Fili with her tongue hanging as loose as a flag. All Fili could do was to shake his head: when Breda decided she'd had enough neither flood nor fire could intervene. His limbs already woefully tired from a week spent in the uplands, he sighed and pursued the lamb: most likely with the Master gone no one would even notice the loss of a single animal, but he could not help but take pride in the task he had been allotted: even if no one else were to know the difference, the lamb would haunt his dreams.

The creature was maddeningly stupid: every time he came within grabbing distance of its tiny hooves, it danced away in terror, darting ever further up the rocks. By the time dusk approached, it had brought them to within spitting distance of the summit, and Fili was quite ready to fulfil the little beast's worst fears and to strangle and eat it still kicking.

He watched it leap onto a granite outcrop on which the rosettes of lichen glowed gold in the lowering light and vanish from sight. A moment later it was bleating its head off.

'Sur's nuts,' Fili swore fervently.

He gathered his breath and hurled himself up the last few feet of the pinnacle, past the outcrop and into grassy space. The lamb stood there, its sides heaving, its eyes gone round and solemn. Silent bleats issued from its dark little mouth. Fili gave it no quarter, and launched himself at the beast. Grabbing the lamb by the scruff of the neck, he whipped it up and under his arm before it could utter a sound. Oddly compliant at last, it hung there as limp as a dead thing: except that its head swivelled urgently behind his arm, seeking something on the headland. Fili had hobbled its legs and straightened up before he even noticed the focus of its intent gaze. When he did, he almost dropped the beast in shock: for there was a strange shape in the midst of the gloom: it looked like a huge chair, though that made not one whit of sense; and there was rather more to it than that. Some figure appeared to be bound in the seat, its eyes gleaming alarmingly in the half-light.

Fili was a smart lad: he could tie two-dozen knots and counterfeit every ragworm and sand-eel in the islands for bait. And he knew that if you came upon an afterwalker when the light was failing, you'd better be able to run as fast as a sprinting pony, for if it laid its big black hands upon you and got you down on the ground beneath its blood-swollen body, you'd soon be joining it in its nightly depredations and your family would sooner see your head off and buried a field away from your corpse before they'd welcome you in to sit by their hearth any more.

But the figure held his gaze, and as a cloud passed in front of the rising moon, he realised with a sudden start that the thing before him was not an afterwalker at all, but the daughter of the clan-chief, Katla Aransen. He laid the lamb down on the springy turf and dropped to his knees at her side. The first thing he undid was the gag; although when a stream of hoarse and filthy imprecations rent the air, he rather regretted not leaving it till last.

Katla boiled down into the steading, ready for a fight – with anyone, over anything – even though she was tired enough to drop. However, the atmosphere that met her inside the great hall was so bewildering, the fight soon went out of her. No one seemed particularly surprised that she had turned up now after disappearing so suddenly; no one seemed interested enough even to ask where she might have been. In fact, a heavy air of preoccupation hung over the few occupants of the place, deadening conversation, slowing action. Women stood around in huddles, talking quietly, their eyes large and worried. Tasks appeared to have been abandoned, or not started at all: where all would normally have been bustle and application – preparations for the evening meal, the stoking of the fire, folk coming in and out from their chores, the endless mending and making; even down to the tiny details like the refilling of the seal-oil in the soapstone dishes whose moss wicks lit the hall – all seemed to be held in abeyance as if waiting some pronouncement or event. The cook-fire was cold; the spit stood empty, the big iron kettle lay on its side in the dead embers.

Katla stared around her, bemused.

Most strange of all, perhaps, was that her father's high seat was occupied. And not by Aran Aranson – but by his wife.

The Lady of Rockfall sat in the huge, carved chair with her elbows braced on its sturdy oaken arms, chin resting on her hands, gazing vacantly, but with an unsettling intensity, into space. Everyone kept a careful distance from her.

Katla frowned. It was an unspoken understanding, but had always seemed as binding as law, that no one sat in the high seat in the Master's absence. It was a shocking transgression, and one so deliberate it must surely presage ominous tidings; she found herself approaching with uncharacteristic caution.

Her mother's eyes never even flickered.

'Where have you been?' she asked, and her tone was flat and cold.

Katla blinked. 'Tied to a chair,' she said baldly.

If she had expected any reaction, any sign of surprise, she was to be disappointed.

'At the top of the Hound's Tooth,' she went on. 'By my beloved brother.'

Bera's eyebrows shot up, but all she said was, 'A raven came.'

'A raven?'

'From Halbo.' Bera uncurled her right hand, her fingers splaying apart like the fronds of a fern. A twist of twine lay nestled in her palm, where it must have been close-furled for some considerable time. A series of complex knots had been tied into it, punctuated by the red-and-silver hitches clearly denoting the royal court.

Katla took it gingerly, stretched it out and surveyed the arrangement with astonishment. Then she turned the twine upside-down and looked at it from that angle, knowing with a terrible fluttering in her chest even as she did so that she had not been mistaken the first time. When she looked up, she found her mother's eyes fixed on her face.

'We must send a boat after them – there's still time; we might catch them before dawn if the wind remains steady. I'll take the *Fulmar's Gift* and Fili and Perto—' She racked her memory for any of the other Rockfall lads left behind from the expedition who might have been of some use in a boat.

'No.'

Bera's voice was stone-hard.

'What?'

'Even if you reach him and deliver the message, he will never turn back. He is as stubborn as a bull on heat, and has little regard for the King.'

'Then what will we do?'

Her mother made an imperceptible movement that might have been a tiny shrug. 'I shall marshal whichever men I can find in the isles and send them to Halbo. I shall make excuses and beg pardon, though it pains me mightily to do so. And I shall run this household as best I can until my husband returns.'

She firmed her jaw and her chin came up until the tendons stood out on either side of her neck. For the first time, Katla saw how gaunt her mother had become of late, how dark shadows circled her eyes, how hollows had grown beneath the pale rose of her cheeks and lines fanned out from her eyes, gouged her forehead and carved deep grooves which ran down from the corners of her mouth. She was ageing fast; and Aran Aranson's departure ahead of this devastating news had aggravated the process beyond retrieval.

'If he ever does.' Such a bitter tone.

Katla could think of nothing to say, either in her father's defence, or to make her mother feel any better. Her fingers wandered back to the message one more, disbelieving, time.

'We are at war with Istria,' she read there. 'You are commanded to render up to your king all men and ships in the Westman Isles and dispatch them to Halbo forthwith. Any who fail to comply with this decree shall be deemed men of Eyra no more and their goods and lives declared forfeit to the crown. By order of Ravn Asharson, Lord of the Northern Isles.'

The wind held all night, changing strength and direction by only the smallest of increments, which Aran used to his advantage, tacking across the path of the waves and slipping neatly off them, so that the *Long Serpent* skimmed and flowed like the mythical creature after which it had been named. At times it felt just as if the great vessel was airborne: with the night sky so deep and black and the stars mirrored silver in the black water, it was impossible, at a glance and in a drowsy state, to know which element it moved in.

Fent came off his watch two hours after high moon, but he found it impossible to sleep; and not just because of the disturbing motion of the ship or the noisy cracking of the sail overhead. He would begin to drift into an uneasy doze and hear a voice, too close, too loud. Sometimes it seemed to be that of a woman, low, deep and foreign; sometimes it transformed itself into the tones of Urse One-Ear. Once, he felt the big man's breath on his neck, so that he sat bolt upright in panic. There was no one there; no one but Gar Felinson, snoring through his open mouth; and, awake, Fent knew it was unlikely that Tam Fox's lieutenant would carry out his threat, here, on board his father's vessel, in full view of the rest of the crew. *Ah, yes, but at night, in bad weather,* his traitor-mind taunted him. *Who would notice then?*

As it was, Aran had accepted Fent's excuses for his sister's disappearance without a word, had seemed barely even surprised, let alone angry or disappointed. Instead, he had applied himself to the map once more, picking out on its surface the northern coast of Stormness as they passed its tall sandstone cliffs, glowing an uncanny fire-orange in the low spectrum light, the shadows of albatrosses cast in romantic relief against their sheer faces; frowning slightly at the absence of any marking for the series of long reefs there, jutting out through half a mile of surf and turbulence. This failing on the part of his treasure had preoccupied the Master for an hour or more. He glowered; he frowned. His eyebrows joined into the single forbidding line that warned against interruption or comment. He yelled a criticism at Sten Arnason for some apparent misdemeanour with the lines which caused the blond man to glare back, his cheeks flushed. He barked an unnecessary order at Urse, who looked quizzical, but held his tongue. He'd seen enough eccentric captains in his time; unless they were truly mad, these little shows of temper blew over like ocean squalls.

And indeed, a few minutes later, Aran Aranson was beaming. He hit his fist against his thigh. 'Ha!' he exclaimed delightedly. 'Of course! This is no map designed for mere adventures, but for seasoned sailors who know their hazards. Why mark on it every rock and skerry? Let the fools come to grief; let their ships founder; let them fail!'

After that, he had rolled the parchment with infinite care and tucked it away in his tunic, close to his heart. Then he went to sit at the stern, propped up against the skiff, watching the night sky and the ever-steady Navigator's Star as if by his unswerving attention and his will he could hold the ship on its course. Whenever Fent looked aft through the dark hours, there his father sat still and unblinking, the moonlight slicking his eyeballs. And while this night-long vigil might have generated confidence in the crew of another captain, Aran's eerily stonelike watch made the men uneasy. Some of them made warding signs against demonic possession; others turned to their oar-companions and sought solace in shared words.

'Does he never sleep?' Marit enquired of Flint Hakason, a northern islander with a braided beard and scarred hands who purported to have known the Master of Rockfall for twenty years, and to have seen the edge of the world, though none believed him. It was well known Flint saw most things of this nature in the bottom of an empty goblet.

The scarred man laughed. 'Tis my belief he has two sets of eyes like Sada's mother, so he may keep watch by day and night!'

'If you have the virtue of a goddess to set guard over, such may be of great value; but a ship in fair waters and a half-decent crew to place your trust in while you catch a nap?'

'Half-decent, aye. Some of these lubbers haven't sailed beyond Rockfall Sound in their entire lives. Which, in the case of some of these lads, is barely as long as my thumb.' He cast a meaningful glance to the larboard side, where Gar Felinson and the tumbler Jad were engaged in a quiet but intense game of black-pebble-white-pebble. 'We had best pray our luck with the weather holds: Sur help us if we hit a storm.'

But the weather held for several days more, a brisk south-westerly driving them from navigation point to navigation point as if Sur himself had blessed their venture and was easing their passage through the Northern Ocean with all the grace he could muster. The sun shone, the air was sharp and clear: by day, landmarks could be discerned for many sea-miles all around them; by night the stars offered up their configurations in a great celestial map. They passed Whale Holm and there was still no ice. Two days beyond that far landmark, they came upon islands no one on the vessel had ever seen or heard of before: islands which rose up out of the blue waves in great, sheer cliffs, the faces striated with regular bandings of red and black and white. The largest of these it took the best part of an hour to sail past so that the crew exclaimed in wonder and urged Aran to put in in order that they might discern the true nature of the rock – for it looked remarkably like pure sardonyx, and if these were truly islands formed from that prized semi-precious stone, was there any need to seek their fortunes farther north in uncharted waters crammed with ice and who knew what other perils? But the Master of Rockfall turned his face from the islands and continued his northerly course without the slightest appearance of interest, which left the men whispering mutinously until Haki Ulfson pointed out that the islands would be relatively simple to find when they returned from the Master's expedition, and that if they were made up of sardonyx there was clearly more than enough there to make each and every man present – aye, and his wife, sons and dogs and chickens – as rich as King Rahay.

Now the first of the ice began to show itself, floating harmlessly on the surface of the waves in frazil clumps and plates which were opaque and dirty-looking, filled with little bits of detritus and frozen sea-scum. Fascinated, Fent leaned overboard and retrieved a passing disc. Its cold burned his hands so that he yelped and the more seasoned crew laughed at his naiveté, but their laughs soon changed to cries of amazement as he held the disc up to the pale sun to reveal the shapes of tiny shrimps trapped inside the ice. 'You keep fishing those out, lad,' the cook, Mag Snaketongue, told him, 'and we'll have no lack for my broths. But next time, try to find me something a little larger to work with, eh?'

The days continued so mild and fair that they passed seals basking on their backs in the open sea, soaking up the unseasonable winter sun, and so peaceful and contented did they look that no one had the hard-heartedness to disturb their slumbers with harpoon or spear. After all, there was more than enough to eat for many weeks on board, and savouries more tempting to be had from Bera Rolfsen's stores than even the fattest seal-meat. Seabirds circled the ship all day long, so that they got used to the sight of fulmars and kittiwakes, awks and mers: a plenitude of food if ever they were in short supply.

By Aran Aranson's reckoning – by sun and star and the wondrous map – they were within two weeks' sailing of their destination, having negotiated over one third of the voyage with the greatest speed and in the finest conditions any mariner could wish for. Even Fent – never previously happy on board a ship – began to think he could get used to a life on the high seas: there was little work to do when the wind held (for he was not skilled enough to man the lines); the temperatures were extraordinarily pleasant for the depth of winter, when sheltered Rockfall could succumb to the bitterest cold, and Mag Snaketongue had proved to be a better cook than his name or grim aspect suggested, a cook, moreover, who had brought enough herbs and spices away from his own Allfair trip to render even the blandest meats delicious. He became quite expert at knucklebones and the pebble game, and soon most of the crew owed him considerable sums which they promised, with remarkable good humour, to render up to him on their return to the isles. After all, with all that sardonyx to be mined, no one would miss a few cantari, or even their finest livestock. No matter what the outcome of the expedition at their destination, there would be bounty for all one way or another. They were, they told themselves, the luckiest of men.

But their luck was not to hold.

* * *

The wind failed them, first. For days on end it dropped away to nothing, leaving the seas flat and leaden. A thick layer of pale cloud blanketed the sky from horizon to horizon and gave no hint it would ever clear, making navigation by night impossible, for there was not a star to be seen. By day it was not much better, for the sun hid itself from them, indicating its position only by a brief flaring amid the cloud-cover. The hours of light became shorter and shorter, the sun dawning slowly in the south and then disappearing in the same spot, like a whale rolling over in its sleep.

For the next two days a penetrating rain fell without cease, soaking everyone and everything on board. Aran stamped around the ship in a foul temper, hating the waste of time, the lack of progress, feeling the weight of the advantage gained with every lost minute by those other ships which he knew in the very marrow of his bones had set sail for Sanctuary before them.

As a result, he drove the crew hard. They unshipped the oars and rowed till the sun went down, then into the long, long night, with no stop for a cooked meal. When men started to complain at the lack of the good hot food they had become accustomed to, Aran glared so grimly that they quieted and made do with the hard bread and cold sausage Mag Snaketongue passed around, washed down with a mug apiece of smallbeer.

Fent's muscles — unused to such unforgiving punishment — felt as though they were on fire. From time to time he surreptitiously allowed the blade of his oar to skim uselessly through the soft top of a wave to give his arms some surcease; until Tor Bolson, manning the oar in front of him began to laugh at what he perceived as his ineptitude. Then he redoubled his efforts and swore rhythmically and foully to himself for another hour.

By the fifth day, men were complaining of painful blisters on their hands from the constant friction of brine-soaked skin on brine-soaked wood, but Aran would allow no one rest, and even took an oar himself, driving the pace even harder, until his hands were as badly afflicted as his crew's. Blisters bred more blisters, then spread, deepened, got infected, became agonising. Even when they wrapped their hands in strips of cloth dipped in the vile-smelling ointment Hesta Rolfsen had boiled up and bottled for them in a great earthenware pot stoppered with a plug of oily rope, matters failed to improve. By the time seawater boils started to break out on the crew's buttocks, their misery was complete, and when at last Aran relented and allowed the men to row in shifts and sleep between bouts at the oar, those who moved around the ship did so crabbed over like old men, their hands curled in on themselves like dead things.

Still they rowed.

Three hours after sun-up, Urse One-Ear said to his neighbour: 'Cats' paws.'

His oar-partner was a green lad from Fishey with big muscles but no sense of coordination; and despite his claim of great adventures with his cousins out on the high seas in pursuit of belukah whales and once even a narwhal, he looked as if he'd be far happier with oxen and plough.

'What?'

'See: out there.' Urse nodded at the tract of sea they had traversed that day.

Far out beyond the clean white froth of their wake, tiny curls of water were making rough spots on the surface of the dark ocean.

'That's how waves are born, that is.'

The lad – Emer Bretison – laughed. 'Those little things? More like kittens' paws, I'd say.'

'Those little things will catch the wind and grow. They may be no larger than kittens' paws now, but by nightfall we'll be surrounded by lions.'

Emer had no idea what a lion was, but didn't want to show his ignorance. 'The *Long Serpent* will eat them up and spit them out,' he declared.

Urse cast an eye at the darkening horizon and said nothing.

Sure enough, a faint breeze sprang up shortly afterwards – fresh enough to freeze their faces, but not strong enough to warrant raising the sail. It proved fitful in nature, blowing first from the south-west, which, if it strengthened, would suit their course well; then from due west, which would not. Away to the south, tall clouds began to pile themselves up into towers of soft grey which then took on the colours of a bruise, all blue-black and savage purple.

The moon – in its last quarter and providing precious little illumination at the best of times – rose and buried itself behind the banks of cloud, offering only the merest glimmer of light as the wind came out of the south and the clouds began to race across the sky towards the *Long Serpent*.

Wind: at last.

'Ship oars!' Aran Aranson yelled impatiently. Then: 'Yard up!'

The crew obeyed these orders gladly, with the shortsighted relief of men who were fed up with rowing. But Urse One-Ear and Flint Hakason exchanged a glance. They knew the signs of a major storm coming at them, even if others appeared neither to see, nor care. Urse coughed once, and when Aran failed to take any notice of this discreet gesture, coughed again, loudly and horribly. Aran stared at him suspiciously. Urse shook his head. Aran frowned. Urse looked pointedly out to the steerboard side, where the far seas were beginning to stand up tall and advance like some great army. Aran followed his gaze, then turned deliberately and rudely away from Tam's lieutenant and called out: 'Reef the sail to the third point!'

Urse raised his eyebrows, then shrugged and strode over to the yard.

'He's a madman,' he said under his breath to Haki Ulfson as they hauled on the lines. 'If this blow's as big as it looks, we'll lose the sail. And if we lose the sail, we're all doomed.'

'Aran Aranson's a good enough sailor,' Haki replied non-chalantly. 'Storm reef should hold her. I've seen worse: most likely, we'll outrun the blow – she's a fine ship.'

'Fine enough,' Urse conceded. 'But she's untested.'

'Well, now's Aran's time to prove her worth.'

'Even at risk to our lives?'

'Where's your sense of adventure, man?'

Urse said nothing, but his expression spoke his mind eloquently.

The first wave hit the ship broadside and rocked the timbers till they creaked in protest. The next one took her to the steerboard and stern, skewing her path. 'Hold the braces!' Aran yelled at Gar Felinson, and the lad leapt to do his bidding, grasping the writhing ropes until it looked as though he were trying by main force to hold back a runaway stallion.

Those men charged with manning the lines, the steerboard and the beitass took up their appointed positions. Fent, no accomplished sailor, and therefore not assigned any specific task other than bailing, found himself suddenly unemployed. He looked around, deciding where best to put himself. Another wave hit, harder than the last: spray shot over the gunwale and soaked him quite abruptly from head to foot. Cursing furiously, he made a dash for the stern and dived under one of the skiffs. Here, at least, he'd have some cover if there was a storm coming. He'd seen enough storms even from the safety of the land to know he didn't want to be in the path of one at sea. He'd seen storms wrack the shores of Rockfall with horrible regularity in bad winters, rip the turf off houses, down trees, wreck boats anchored even in the most sheltered coves, drive whales and seals up onto beaches far past the usual tideline. Besides, he felt he'd done his duty and more these past days. What was the point of being the captain's only son, if he could not cut himself a little slack? Every fibre of his body ached and burned, his hands felt as if they would never be the same again and his stomach, with the movements caused by this newly active sea, was beginning to feel distinctly queasy.

In addition, under the ship's boat he was out of Urse One-Ear's sight, and therefore, with luck, his mind.

Aran, in contrast, relished a blow. He watched his crew move smartly about the deck, each man focused on his task, and he felt he could indulge himself. With the surefootedness of a mountain goat, he ran the length of the vessel and took up position at the elegantly curved prow, his right hand gripping the gunwale for support, his face turned to the dark northern horizon, the wind strong at his back. Beneath the soles of his boots, he could feel the way the oak accommodated the powerful currents, could sense the keel flexing as lithely as the spine of a leaping cat. The *Long Serpent*! She was his: she was elemental and unconquerable and *he* had had her brought to life out of nothing – out of despair and disaster. And for this: this was what he had been waiting for all his life – this feeling of triumph. He was the master of a superb ship, master of the seas; master of his destiny.

Distant thunder rumbled and a few seconds later a fork of white lightning split the sky.

Now the wind came at them in ferocious gusts. One of these coincided with a broadside wave which took the ship beam to and heeled her over so that water gushed over the side and washed like a river down the deck. Men ran hither and thither, bailing like fury. Like the finely crafted vessel she was, the *Long Serpent* righted herself, directly into the path of the wind, slicing through the tops of the waves and skipping forward like a skittish colt.

Aran Aranson's free hand strayed to the pouch which hung inside his leather tunic, his fingers closing over the shape of the rolled parchment within, and his wolfish face transformed itself from grim concentration to the sheerest exultation.

Thunder sounded again; and almost simultaneously lightning lacerated the clouds, illuminating a nightmarish scene, for the swells were deepening dramatically, rolling closer together; the pitch of the waves growing ever steeper. With a great booming crack, the sail filled with wind so violently that the grease which weatherproofed the wool shot out of the leeward side, peppering the men who stood in range with painful pellets of solidified fat. The lines whipped out of the men's hands and went snaking lethally about the deck. One lashed itself across Haki Ulfson's face, causing him to cry out and stumble. The next minute, he was gone.

'Man overboard!'

The shout brought Aran out of his reverie. Dropping his hand away from the map, he turned to find Urse One-Ear and a blond man whose name he could not recall fishing precariously over the stern with an oar, with other crewmembers holding tight to their waists and legs. For a second through the gloom he saw a white hand reaching out of the dark waves, then the lost man disappeared entirely, only to emerge again in a pool of moonlight twenty feet away in their lee, out of range and retreating fast as the wind carried them forward, his eyes and mouth wide with horror. There was nothing they could do. Engulfed by a huge roller with a heart as black as the night itself, Haki Ulfson was swallowed by the sea.

There was a short lull in which the men stared unbelievingly at the disturbed patch of water where they had last seen their companion; then the storm hit with a vengeance.

'Tie everything down!' Aran yelled, leaping back down the ship. 'Tie yourselves in!'

The crew needed no encouragement. They tied down the provisions as best and as quickly as they could, and then made themselves fast to oarholes and braces, to the mast and the massive mastfish. The experienced men used knots they could

easily undo in the event of the ship rolling; the inexperienced
ones tied themselves in with every single knot they could
remember. Aran and Urse One-Ear found themselves both
at the steerboard. The big man took a step back. A wave hit
hard alongside, drenching them both. Aran shook his head.
'No!' he shouted. 'You take her.' Urse was stronger: if the
Long Serpent had to be wrestled onto the best course, he stood
the better chance against the power of the waves.

Instead, Aran lashed himself to the stern, between the
two skiffs.

Turning, he found himself confronted by a huge wave. It
seemed, he thought inconsequentially in the seconds before
it rolled down at him, nearly as tall as the great oaks from
the Barrow Plantation from which the *Long Serpent* had been
constructed. Which made it as tall as the ship was long. He
remembered how he had stood awestruck in the shade of
those giants seven summers ago when he had travelled with
Margan to survey one of the wonders of Elda. It was a sacred
site; now he wondered whether the destruction of that grove
might not have angered – if not the god himself – at least the
guardian spirits of the place.

That first wave came in under the stern and carried them
far up into the air, so that the Master found himself falling
backwards, held only by his makeshift harness, gazing past
the vertiginous line of sail and mast into the unrelieved night
sky. For a moment the vessel seemed to gain a precarious
equilibrium, balancing on the crest of the wave. Then, she
pitched down so hard that Aran was now staring along the
length of the ship into a deep, dark pit of ocean which seemed
as eager to swallow them as it had Haki Ulfson such a short
time before. They came down with a great crash which made
his head ring and jolted his back painfully into the timbers
so that his breath shot out of him, but the *Long Serpent* held
her own.

Other waves followed the first, now coming hard against

one another and Aran regarded them with his first real taste of fear: if the ship were caught between two of those, he knew she would be snapped in half like a twig. If one were to break directly upon her and her timbers withstood the impact she would still be dragged down, rolled and held beneath the surface by the power of its undertow.

He had never seen such waves, never felt such vicious wind. The force of it was so strong that his hair stood on end, his feet kept lifting off the deck. It smashed the ice it had found floating on the surface of the waves into him like slingshot. He tried to shout an order to his men and heard his own voice stolen away from him like a moth sucked into the night. Powerless to do anything but provide silent witness, he watched casks, oars and tools caught up into the air, saw them spin around one another as if in a maelstrom and vanish into the darkness. Waves came and went. The ship pitched and rolled. Timbers creaked and screamed. Water cascaded down the deck. He watched Urse fighting the steerboard; saw how, even though wracked by the dizzying power of the elements, the big man yet managed to hold the ship into the waves, his head haloed by spinning yellow foam.

Then the sail came free of its lines at last and whipped around the mast like an enraged beast. Now they were entirely at the mercy of the storm.

Aran looked out at the place where he must shortly die. He was surprised to discover that felt no great, all-encompassing emotion at this fact, but rather a vague sense of regret and an even fainter sense of culpability for the lives of the others for whom he was responsible. His fingers flexed, and he found that he had by some odd instinct clutched hold of the map-pouch in the midst of the storm, as if its very touch offered him some obscure, supernatural comfort. There was surely magic in the map, he thought again; and something in him was suddenly sure that whatever charm had been sealed into the parchment would see them through this disaster. It offered Sanctuary in return for his faith. It was his amulet; his talisman.

The sea, however, appeared to be unaware of any such bargain. It was tumultuous, awesome in its sheer destructive power. It might crush them all at any moment. But still the waves held their shape; apart from the spindrift which the wind dragged off their crests, they did not break. Rather, now they began to crash into one another and pile up into a great confusion. For a while it seemed as if the sea was coming from all directions at once. The ship pitched this way and that. The moon buried itself so completely that no light fell on the turbulent waters at all. Time seemed suspended. Aran lost any sense of orientation he had had. A great collision of waves shook free one of the skiffs and the wind got under it and hurled it over the side, nearly taking the Master with it. He held on grimly, thankful he had tied himself to the sturdy gunwale and not the faering; unlike poor Marit Fennson, whose diminishing wail was now lost in the generalised roar of the elements.

The bombardment went on and on, punctuated by vivid bursts of light and ear-numbing thunder. Aran watched helplessly as the blond man who had tried to rescue Haki Ulfson was himself lost to the sea, the cord which had bound him safely to the mastfish sundering under a strain it was never designed to withstand. Another of his crew – he thought it might be Pol Garson – lost his hold on a brace and was picked up by the wind like a straw doll and dashed against the deck. His right arm flopped at an angle which suggested his shoulder had been dislocated and the limb broken below the elbow. Blood ran down his face and was almost instantaneously washed away by another onslaught of the waves, which sucked his inert body perilously close to the edge of the gunwale. There, two men – Erl Fostison and his cousin Fall it looked like, though it was almost impossible to tell through the mixture of lashing rain and seawater –

caught hold of him and saved his life by wrapping the end of the rope that held them in place around his waist. Not that he'd be much good on an oar, Aran found himself thinking uncharitably, even if he survived.

His eyes searched the chaos of the deck for Fent's flying red hair, but his youngest son was nowhere to be seen, which was hardly surprising, since most of the men were desperately hunkered down, trying to keep out of the worst of the wind.

Towards what counted as dawn in this godforsaken region, the storm finally blew itself out, and the wind died away to nothing more than a brisk southerly breeze. It took Aran Aranson several minutes to unstrap himself from the gunwale. His hands were wet and frozen, his fingers red and raw and bruised. He seemed to have no strength at all. Every inch of him ached. The rope had swelled from soaking up the brine, so that even though he had taken care to tie himself in with knots which were designed to be easy to undo in emergency, the influence of the elements had prevailed, turning them stubborn and intransigent.

Then he tottered down the deck on rubbery legs and surveyed the not inconsiderable damage, feeling very little like the hero who had stood at the helm just short hours before.

By some miracle or favour of the god, it appeared that the *Long Serpent* and the greater part of her crew had survived the worst of what the Northern Ocean could throw at her.

Twenty-two

Beasts

Do not try to use the old man's voice on me again. I will bite you.

'I promise I will not, if you will return to your true form.'

I am sure you prefer me as the tiny one whom you can trap and tame, but I do not choose to adopt that guise any longer. This is my true self. What is yours?

'I am what I am. What do you mean?'

You do not smell the way a man should. You have some of the right scent, but more of worms and earth. Indeed, I am not sure I would want to bite you too hard, for fear the taste would linger.

'You have become remarkably talkative since you took on this new form.'

The Beast flicked its tail impatiently but gave no other response.

He started again. 'If you were to kill me, how would you return to your mistress? She is across the ocean and even a cat as great as you cannot swim so far.'

A flicker of amusement. *First a master, now a mistress. Do you truly think of the Rose of the World in that way? How strange you are, worm-man. A worm, in the heart of the rose, in the heart of the world. No, we will go south, to the Red Peak.*

'I do not want to go to the Red Peak: I have read that it is all ash and fire and moving rock. Why would anyone want to go there, except to die? We go north, to Halbo, then to Rahe.'

We go south.

'Nor— Aaah!'

I told you not to use the voice. That was but a mere nibble in comparison with what I might do. We will go where I say, which is not across the ocean. No cat wishes to swim, and I shall not be getting in a boat with you again until the seas run dry.

Saro looked around. His head felt blurry, as if he had woken from a drunken slumber. He blinked and took in his surroundings. He was in a grove outside the walls of the city of Jetra and it was dark. A little distance away from him a horse he recognised as Night's Harbinger was tethered to a tree, rubbing its shoulder against the bark so hard that its branches jiggled. Two or three objects hit the ground in a series of soft thuds and then a powerful scent of overripe orange filled the air. Back home in Altea, where the harvest came later and was less certain, and where every cantari counted, every piece of fruit that could be sold, crushed for juice or boiled up and preserved for the long winter would have been gathered in by now: but here in Jetra they left the fruit to rot on the trees. It was a rich city; rich and foreign and wasteful of its bounty.

The sharp citrus scent served to clear Saro's head. A vague memory of sneaking out of the castle and saddling up the stallion came to him out of nowhere; he recalled looking up at the Navigator's Star. He thought he remembered making a decision to head north; but why that should be, he could not now imagine. North, to Eyra, the land of barbarians, with whom they would imminently be at war: what had possessed him? And yet something nagged at the back of his skull, something that murmured of disaster and ruin if he were not to remove himself as far from this place as possible. He reached for it, failed to grasp it, and was instead assailed by a bizarre collage of images and sounds, uppermost of which was a man's voice telling him to *wait, wait here for my return*. The command had been imperative, ungainsayable; and so he had waited. But now he began to wonder why, and for whom, he was waiting. The necessity of flight, which had impelled him out of the Eternal City in the first place, began to reassert itself with growing urgency. His limbs itched to move, but seemed as rooted as the trees. Concentration even on this simplest of tasks proved hopeless. After a while he became deeply annoyed with himself.

'Falla's tits!' he swore, trying desperately to raise a foot, but his boot remained in obdurate contact with the ground.

As if the curse had woken some kind of demon, a low growl swelled into the darkness behind him; and then Saro began to remember some of what his mind had thought it best to forget. Narrowing his eyes, he stared into the gloom and found that the thing he had believed a figment of nightmare was actually walking in Elda. As if it held the power to materialise at will, it now revealed itself as a huge cat – a vast black beast with glowing golden eyes and massive paws – and if that were not bad enough, at its side was the tall pale man he had inadvertently touched in the Star Chamber, a touch which had disturbed his dreams ever since, as if he had been infected by some illness the man carried.

The stone seemed to respond more positively, though. Like the cat's eyes, it began to glow, emitting a wan greenish-gold light. Illuminated by this eldritch sheen, the sorcerer looked haggard and drawn, though it was hard to ascribe this notion to anything specific: the man's face did not exhibit the usual signs of age, for no frown-lines crossed his smooth forehead, no raven's-feet radiated from his eyes, no gouges marred those colourless cheeks.

Virelai put out his hand in a warding gesture. 'Please,' he said, his eyes fixed on the glowing moodstone. 'Don't.'

At this, the great cat slumped down, lifted a massive leg and began to groom its private parts with a vast, rough tongue and intense self-absorption, so that the rasping sound

was soon joined by a full-throated rumbling which filled the
night air and thrummed in Saro's breastbone. After a while
the combination of the purring and the intense simplicity of
the beast's grooming made something in Saro relax, and as
he did so he found that the pale man's voice no longer had
the same hold over him as it had before. Movement returned
in tiny increments, but rather than lift his feet, Saro's fingers
went instinctively to the moodstone, closing tightly over it so
that the light squeezed out between them, livid and garish.

'No!'

The word seemed imbued with some strange power, for
Saro's hand dropped away from the moodstone as if he had
been burned. Both hand and pendant felt suddenly as cold
and heavy as lead.

Saro frowned. 'You know about the stone,' he said softly.

Through the grey pre-dawn light, the sorcerer held his
gaze and nodded slowly.

'What do you know?'

But Virelai's eyes became uncommunicative, as flat and
dead as those of the giant whiskered fish Saro had once
caught in the stagnant waters of the Crow Marsh. It too had
returned his astonished gaze with this inimical expression –
an expression which spoke of arcane knowledge gradually
accrued by absorbing the experiences of the denizens of those
grim and murky depths – and then whipped its spine back and
forth so hard that it had broken the line and vanished beneath
the surface of the lake. Virelai broke the connection between
them just as effectively, dropping his gaze and moving to
where the stallion was tethered.

Night's Harbinger began to back away, eyes rolling, but the
sorcerer put out his hand. '*Shi-rajen*,' he said to the horse and
it quieted immediately. Then he turned back to regard the
boy. 'Come,' he said, and as if they belonged to the sorcerer
rather than himself, Saro's feet began to shuffle forward.

Behind them, the cat gave a low growl.

You may use it on him, it said into his mind, and on the stupid horse; but remember what I told you.

Dawn announced itself with an extravagant flourish. It came rolling across the Southern Ocean, flushed the wide estuary of the Tilsen River a rich rose red, and cast its rays like Falla's own blessing upon a flotilla of fishing vessels setting out into the placid coastal waters to gather up the lobster-pots and crab-traps they had set the night before. It warmed the terraced hills above Lullea, making the vermilion earth glow so brightly it was as if the colour itself were some rare crop, while down below in the shaded valleys, the groves of olives and pomegranates and orchards of apples, limes and lemons released a freight of rich scents into the air. Further inland, to the south-east of Jetra, in the little town of Lord's Cross with its narrow winding passageways of whitewashed houses and its ornate temple, the tower which dominated the settlement cast a long, long black shadow down the main street like a pointing finger. A mule-borne trader setting out early on his journey from the hill-village of Falcon's Lair to the produce market there that morning with a cartful of persimmons, turned his head at an opportune moment – he never knew what had prompted him to do so – and was gifted with the momentary glimpse of a strange caravan of figures silhouetted on the distant southern horizon.

That evening, in the Hawk's Wing tavern in Lord's Cross, surrounded by a rowdy group of fellow-merchants who had already drunk their way through most of their day's profits, he would not be dissuaded from his assertion that he had spied 'the largest mountain cat ever seen in Istria, walking along as friendly as you like beside a pair of fellows leading a horse with all the lines of a fine racing stallion'. Mountain cats were not unknown this far north; but they tended to be runtish creatures, driven out of their natural habitats by their stronger siblings and rivals; and anyway, whoever heard of anyone other than the Lord of Cera taming one of the beasts?

'Lodu, you should go see Mother Sed tomorrow: get yourself something to improve your eyesight!'

'Is she still practising?' Lodu asked. Most of the nomads had cleared out well before the current round of edicts and executions. 'I didn't see her setting out her stall this morning.' He paused. 'In fact, I didn't see her today at all.'

His friend shrugged. 'I haven't seen her for weeks,' he admitted.

'I heard she burned well,' called an unfamiliar voice from the back of the room.

Lodu turned to survey the speaker, almost as curious to see who it was who had such remarkable hearing to have picked up this fragment of private conversation as to discover the fate of the healer, and found himself looking at a tall, dark man with closely set eyes and a thin mouth currently curved in a cruelly appreciative line, as if the very idea of an ancient crone going up like a torch on one of the Goddess's pyres warmed his immortal soul.

'They burned old Mother Sed?' This seemed unbelievable.

'That's what we do with these cursed Footloose, or have you been living in a cave in the Bone Quarter?'

This last made Lodu indignant. 'She never did anyone any harm.'

Another man spoke up now. 'She practised sorcery, man, and as such was an unnatural creature whose very presence on the face of Elda mortified our Lady Falla. Magic is the Goddess's art: it is sacrilege for any other to draw upon her reserves so. Now she is cleansed away, returned to the Lady.' He made a pious genuflection.

'Sorcery?' Lodu laughed, despite himself. 'She brewed up love potions for gullible girlies and sold the herbs she grew in her own garden: if such is sorcery then my wife had better look out!'

The dark man narrowed his eyes. 'Perhaps she had, my friend. Perhaps she had.'

Virelai swore.

Even though they had managed to leave the Eternal City and pass into the hinterlands without any obvious pursuit, all was not going to plan.

By the time they arrived at the bend in the river where the osiers and goat-willows had masked Alisha's campsite, the place had been abandoned and the nomads long gone, leaving nothing behind but the cold, blackened stones of their bread-oven, an area of bare ground where the yeka had cropped the grass down to its roots, and ruts in the ground from the passage of their wagons.

He kicked one of the stones viciously. It hurt, but not as much as it should have done. He had the deeply unpleasant suspicion that if he were to examine the skin of his foot, he would find the area as grey as a dove's wing.

Saro looked around. It was a cheerless place. 'Why have we come here?' he asked plaintively. The sorcerer had been remarkably unforthcoming on the journey, which had been slow and hard on the legs, especially since with every step southward he sensed that he was travelling in the wrong direction. Even so, and against any shred of will he had left to him, he felt compelled to accompany the man: he could not say why.

'I had hoped to join friends here,' Virelai said gloomily.

This surprised Saro: the sorcerer looked barely human, let alone the type of man to have friends. But after the events of the last night he really shouldn't expect to be surprised by anything ever again. The cat – huge and black, even more terrifying to look at in bright sunshine than it had been when shadowed by the night – had stayed with them every step of their way from Jetra and somehow had proved to be more companionable and less disturbing than the pale man, which set the whole natural order of the world at odds.

Virelai sat down hard on the ground and clutched his head, fingers spread like tentacles across his skull, and as he did so Saro noticed there was a black bruise and a trace of blood around the base of the thumb of his right hand, and what looked suspiciously like toothmarks. 'We are lost,' the sorcerer groaned. 'Now they will surely hunt us down. And if they catch us they will take the stone—' His hands flew up to his mouth, but it was too late: the words were out.

'The stone,' Saro said softly. Something stirred in the recesses of his mind, coalesced; took shape and came into sudden, horrifying focus. The moodstone. In another man's hand – a dark, elegant hand, a killing white light beginning to pulse from between the fingers ... With tremendous concentration, he drew his focus back and allowed the vision which had driven him out of the city in the first place to wash over him with ever more appalling detail. Coruscations of colour assaulted his eyes, followed by a cacophony of groans and growls. And still the images came, dispelling whatever spell it was he had been under since the previous night.

'No!'

With fierce effort, Saro tore himself away from the nightmare, only to find Virelai's strange light eyes with their white-fringed lashes fixed upon him, wide with shock. Beside him, the great cat had risen to its feet as if it might at any moment either leap for his throat or run for its life. Flashes of brilliance, like sunshine on a mirror, danced around them all. When he looked down, he found that he was gripping the moodstone so tightly that his knuckles were white through all its variegations of light.

'Please don't use it!'

Horrified, Saro stuffed the pendant back beneath his shirt; but instead of becoming quiescent, the thing continued to pulse and burn, clearly visible even through the weave of the rough fabric.

'It won't stop!'

Something unspoken passed between Virelai and the cat, and then the great beast took to its heels and in a flurry of displaced dust and water cleared the low willows and the creek with a single muscular bound. Saro watched it breast the low hill on the opposite bank and disappear from view with a certain measure of relief. The lights from the stone flickered and slowly died to a dull glow.

'The thing you wear around your neck is a death-stone,' the sorcerer said at last. 'It is a most rare and treacherous object.'

A death-stone. This was the very same term which the old nomad healer at Pex had used of his pendant as she backed away from him in terror, sharing with him as she did so the horrible image of the men he had slaughtered with it, all unknowing, on the Moonfell Plain. It had killed three on the Moonfell Plain; and was destined to kill thousands in Tycho Issian's hands. Now true fear gripped him: why had Virelai brought him out to this forsaken place if not to kill him and take the stone? His body might lie undiscovered for days: no one would ever know . . . But then why send the cat away? Death at the fangs and claws of a wild animal: it was the perfect alibi for the sorcerer: all he had to do was let the beast have its way with him and then retrieve the stone. Something here made no sense; his mind was still hazed . . . But if he was sure of anything it was that the pendant should not find its way to Tycho Issian.

'Stay back!' he warned the sorcerer. 'You are the Lord of Cantara's servant, and I had rather kill or die myself than allow this stone to fall into the hands of such an evil man.'

'I have no intention of hurting you,' Virelai said. 'The last thing on Elda I would want is for Tycho Issian to have access to a death-stone. He is a madman, a monster.'

That surprised Saro; but who knew the subtle machinations of a sorcerer's mind? 'Give me your hand,' he said suddenly.

An expression of absolute distrust crossed Virelai's face. 'You're going to kill me,' he said fearfully, cringing away.

Impatience made Saro brave. Before the sorcerer could move further out of reach, he caught him by the wrist. The contact was stronger than he'd meant, and fuller far than the passing touch they had shared in the Star Chamber. The torrent of images by which he was usually assaulted on contact with another living being had been bizarrely, hauntingly absent on that occasion, but now Saro was determined. Gritting his teeth, he forced the stone to his will for the first time. At first all he caught from the sorcerer were echoes, like whispers from a distant room, or shattered reflections in a fast-moving stream; that and a marrow-freezing cold. He pressed on, ignoring the chill, concentrating on the fleeting images. With a supreme effort, he separated one from the crowd and examined it. It was pale and vague, a wisp of memory: thin boy's knees pressed hard against an icy floor, small hands polishing, polishing. Another: an old man with an immense, craggy head and a sumptuous beard craned over a table piled high with parchments and diverse objects waving him away with a barrage of unheard abuse; a hand descending again and again; brief flowers of pain. Hunger, distant aches and pains: a sudden pang of loneliness; a cut finger which did not bleed. Snow and ice everywhere; thick mists, a choppy sea. Skin flaking off a grey limb. A black hound, saliva dripping from its maw. A naked woman, half-hidden by her long, long hair. A black cat, big, then small. Tycho Issian, a mad light in his eyes, thrashing out at him with a wicked-looking switch. Then himself, magnified by the sorcerer's terror to the size of a powerful man, brandishing the glowing moodstone—

He broke the contact and sat back, sweating, and tried

to make sense of it all. Fears: many of them, diffuse and scattered. Miseries and discomforts, pain and sadness: but nowhere amongst all these sensations was there any hint of threat or guile.

Retching loudly, Virelai coughed up a thin stream of bile, then knelt and stared at the resultant pool with his arms wrapped protectively around himself. He looked reproachfully at Saro, then wiped his mouth with the back of one limp hand. 'Have you finished scouring me out?' he demanded wearily.

Saro sighed. 'I'm sorry,' he said. 'I had to be sure you were not sent to kill me and take the stone. I know what it can do: I have seen your master laying waste to the world with it.'

Virelai looked shocked. 'Rahe? He would never do that, for all he is old and cantankerous and complains of its evils.'

'Rahe?' The word was vaguely familiar, as if he had heard it somewhere a long time ago. Whatever it was, it eluded him, but it did not matter now, so instead he asked: 'Who is Rahe? I thought the Lord of Cantara was your master?'

'He is now,' Virelai said mournfully. 'But Tycho Issian is worse than the old man: I can well imagine him burning to a cinder anything which prevented him from taking back the Rosa Eldi. That is why I brought you here, to make sure he could not take the death-stone from you and use it for his own devices.'

The Rosa Eldi. The nomad woman whom King Ravn Asharson of Eyra had taken to wife. But what had Tycho Issian to do with such a low-born creature? Unbidden, the obscene image which had presented itself when the Lord of Cantara had embraced him in the Council room returned, luminous amid the carnage: a tall pale woman, her legs wide open to receive . . . Hastily, he banished the sight, the connection between the pair made all too clear. Could basic lust truly propel a man toward such atrocity? He would never have believed it, but then he had always been so naive: after his insights into his own brother's stew of a mind, he could hardly doubt any individual's capacity for evil ever again.

A larger truth presented itself to him then as particularity gave way to generality. It was such a vertiginous fall into comprehension that it left Saro feeling dizzy with shame and horror: shame for his gender and his race; horror for the fate of the world. For it suddenly came clear to him that Tycho Issian had engineered this war, had set the whole of the Southern Empire at the throat of its ancient northern enemy, all for lust. And that he had invoked the Goddess in order to do so demonstrated not only the sham that was their religion, but the stupid, vengeful gullibility of his fellow Istrians, who would swallow the words of any nobleman claiming any so-called just cause – no matter how lame, how fabricated, how hollow – and echo the preacher's hatred a hundredfold and then a hundredfold again until the cries for war swept the entire nation.

Thousands upon thousands would die in the coming conflict; and for what? For the sake of one man's obsession with a woman's privy parts.

His skin turned hot, then cold and clammy. He thought he might faint. The stone he wore about his neck might be the only thing which could stop the madness. He was a peaceable, gentle man by nature; but he knew with the utmost certainty what he had to do. His hand folded over the leather pouch and he felt the death-stone pulse as if in compliance. 'By all that is right and fair in the world, Virelai, I swear that I will stop him, by whatever means I have in my power,' he said, turning his eyes upon the sorcerer. 'And you must help me.'

Twenty-three

Sailings

The Northern Isles had never experienced such a fine winter. Shoal after shoal of herring were landed by the fishing fleets of Sandby and Hrossey; around the shores of Fair Isle, where the ocean usually boiled in and out, leaving sucking maelstroms and treacherous crosscurrents in its wake, the waters were so clear you could see the mackerel lying in the shallows: even the children in their scaled-down faerings and coracles were able to paddle out and catch them in complete safety, landing line after line of them and whooping with delight. Whales cast themselves ashore out of mirror-smooth seas; the seal population flourished. Gigantic walruses were seen in the Sharking Straits, farther south than they had ever been sighted before. Babies grew fat on rich milk; cows calved and lambings continued out of season. Puffins and guillemots lined the ledges of the seacliffs north of Wolf's Ness, an area they usually gave up by the end of ninth moon for warmer regions. The sun seemed to shine for longer than was its usual wont in the short days; but maybe this was an illusion caused by the fact that everyone managed to accomplish far more than they had expected on waking and setting about their tasks, and with better humour, too.

In the gardens around Halbo Castle, roses bloomed in such profusion that their scent pervaded the air as far away as the streets around the docks, masking the usual stench of urine and brine, sweat and tar and semen with a rich and heady perfume. Following a late burst of blossom, the orchards outside the west gate of the city brought forth a second crop of apples. The people of the Northern Isles feasted and rejoiced: their larders and fish-stores were full, their offspring in good health, and the King's foreign wife was robust with his child, which looked as if it were fast coming to term. Who cared that the Southern Empire had declared itself to be at war with them again? Everyone knew the Istrians had neither the good ships nor the expertise to sail them in order to cross the great Northern Ocean and bring battle to them. Let them seethe and simmer and shout up a storm: all was well in Eyra.

For the mercenaries, it was deathly dull. It had been impossible to find enough paying work as a group, so they had split up and taken whatever they could find. They were certainly not the only ones in the same situation: the whole of Halbo seemed awash with bored sell-swords fed up with running errands and fighting petty duels for nobles too useless or frightened to fight their own. Much of the time they fought each other: over dog-matches, card-games, spilled ale, shared billets and shared whores; for a word out of place, the wrong coloured hair or giving another a look askance. Wall-eyed Cnut, whose name came in for plenty of ribaldry as it was, got into so many fights he declared the whole city 'a fucking sinkhole' and rowed off down the coast to Bear's Gut in a faering he'd 'borrowed' from Kettle Jarn, who'd nicked him in the leg the week before.

With Joz Bearhand and Doc acting as guards to Erol Bardson and Dogo last seen dead drunk and borne up by two buxom floozies heading for the seamiest establishment on the docks and not heard of since, Mam and Persoa were left much in each other's company. Erno watched them now across the smoky upper room of the Istrian's Head – a slightly more salubrious establishment than the Enemy's Leg, being some way further up the hill from the wharfside where, supposedly, the head had landed after King Sten's famous retribution – and marvelled for the hundredth time at the mismatch they represented. Where the mercenary leader was powerfully built – for a man, let alone a woman – Persoa had the slight and whippy frame of his native hill country. Where she was blonde, he was dark; where her hair lay in a great profusion of matted braids threaded through with bones and shells, his was shorn close to his head but for a single tail, ringed top and bottom with thin gold bands, reaching halfway down his back. Where her features were broad and blunt, his were fine and sculpted; her eyes were blue, his black; and he was the most politely spoken assassin Erno had ever encountered. Whereas Mam . . .

Their heads were close together, and Persoa had his hand on the mercenary leader's leg as he inclined his ear to listen to what she was saying above the general din. Erno couldn't imagine any other man getting away with his life, let alone his fingers, after making such importunate contact with Mam's thigh: but then, no one else was likely even to consider doing so. Fearsome, foul-mouthed and possessed of a terrifying set of sharpened gnashers, Mam was hardly likely to be any sighted, sober man's first port of call when he was overtaken by lust; but Persoa seemed enraptured by her. The pair had taken to sharing the same room after a couple of weeks back in port and ever since Mam seemed always to be laughing or smiling, happy to share a joke or a pleasantry: which was, as Dogo put it, like watching a shark wink and grin at you before it bit your head off: bleeding disturbing and highly unnatural.

As if she felt the weight of his gaze, Mam looked up suddenly. She grinned and said something to the hillman, who threw his head back and laughed so that Erno felt disconcerted and vaguely annoyed: what had he done that they should laugh at him? Then the mercenary leader stood up, placed a hand on the heavy oak table which stood in her way and vaulted powerfully over the top of it, landing with such a thud that the floorboards creaked and flagons of ale on the surrounding tables trembled and spewed froth onto their owners' hands. No one uttered a word of protest despite the general air of antagonistic boredom, except for one man who had been sitting with his back to Mam, who swore loudly and spun around with his fists balled for a confrontation. Erno watched as the man's face registered his mistake, saw all the fight reflex ebb out of him and how he turned quickly back to apply himself studiously to the scattered knucklebones, as if the fact that his winning throw had been so rudely disrupted had merely served to create a new and fascinating pattern to be considered.

'Can't sit around here all day,' Mam announced cheerfully. 'Things to do.'

She winked at Persoa, tapped her eyebrow and then the side of her cheek. Erno watched the hillman nod once and make a complicated gesture, then head towards the back stairs like a snake weaving its way through grass. When he looked back, the mercenary leader was gone. It never ceased to amaze him that such a big woman could move so swiftly and silently: a great attribute to have during close-quarter assassinations, but rather less so when asking someone to follow you.

By default, he elected the door to the sleeping quarters, moving through the crowd with rather more circumspection than Mam employed. It was not that he was a small man – he was taller than most by half a head – but he was a sell-sword neither by heart nor nature, and he preferred to avoid a fight whenever he could. So it was that by the time he emerged through the far door, Mam was already waiting for him on the other side, wearing an impatient grimace and a lot of weapons. Before he could open his mouth to say a word, she slung his sleeping-roll at him. He stared at it like an idiot.

'Come on,' she said. 'We've got a job to do.'

Down at the docks they found the rest of the band gathered:

Joz Bearhand, Doc, Dogo and Persoa; and about a dozen other mismatched men and one woman. They were loading up a couple of faerings with supplies and weaponry – a lot of weaponry, it seemed to Erno, for a small crew. 'What's going on?' he said to Mam suspiciously.

The mercenary leader grinned at him. 'Well, that would depend on who you were to ask,' she replied cryptically.

'I'm asking you.'

Mam made a face. 'Tell you when we get on board.'

'On board what? And who says I have any intention of leaving the city at all, on foot, horse or blasted ship!'

'Not much going on in Halbo, unless you want to watch a load of overdressed, over-ambitious and overbearing lords and fortune-seekers all trying to pussyfoot around our beloved, besotted King and his knackered old advisers.'

He raised an eyebrow. There was clearly a fine distinction to be made between fortune-seeking and free-booting.

'Besides,' she went on. 'I thought you'd rather go to Rockfall and see Katla Aransen than hang around here.'

Erno stared at Mam so hard his eyes ceased to focus. For several heartbeats her face swam in front of him, became thin and tanned, one wicked grin becoming another, more beguiling by far. Flame-red hair, tousled and boyish, replaced the twisted blonde braids. He felt dizzy, then hopeful; then terrified she was playing some appalling trick on him. Finally, fear became fury. He rounded upon her. 'Katla Aransen died at the Allfair. I loved her, and if I hadn't left her she would still be alive. And yet you taunt me like this! I have always known you to be a hard woman, Mam, but I never thought you were a cruel one!'

The mercenary leader was taken aback by this outburst. Erno had always been both quiet and biddable, a polite young man, who looked as if he might well be handy with a sword if push came to shove, but who was unlikely to answer back, let alone hit you in the face. Now, however, his face was flushed and his eyes were wild with unreadable emotions: it looked as though he might well let fly. Mam took a judicious step back: her watchword was to avoid the avoidable, and it would hardly improve her authority if one of her crew were to smack her in the face in full view of the rest, let alone the new recruits. She'd have to wound him, for sure; but the delicacy required to deliver a non-critical flesh wound had never been something she excelled in: provoked, she was more likely to deprive a man of an arm or leg . . .

'Hold fast!' She stuck out a hand, fingers splayed. 'Who said Katla Aransen was dead? She got a little singed, for sure; but the last time I saw her she was as sparky as a shore-sparrow, sinking Old Bilgewater with the best of us in the Enemy's Leg.'

That stopped him.

'How?' he said, and, 'When?' This last with deep suspicion.

Mam made a brief calculation, then waved her hands. 'Came to Halbo to see relatives is what she said, though I knew that for a story. Strangely enough the King's shipmaker went missing shortly afterwards. A couple of moons ago, does it matter?'

Erno's eyes became as round as a lost child's. He began to tremble. For an instant Mam thought he might even weep. Then: 'She's alive,' he breathed. 'Alive.'

'Put some back into it!'

The whip cracked down once, twice and the man shrieked. When the lash curled back, tiny red droplets spiralled lazily off into the air before coming to rest on the planking, where they became indistinguishable from their surroundings. Captain Galo Bastido's father's galley had been kitted out for war in the finest old traditions, and that included painting the floors a deep red ochre since it was said that if men could not see blood washing down the decks in battle, they were less likely to panic or surrender. The Bastard secretly wished he could have left the wood unfinished: in his experience, maintaining discipline could only be improved by the sight of a little spilled blood.

Even with liberal use of the whip, they had not made as swift a time as he would have wished. The weather had been against them: mild and fair, where strong southerlies would have suited them better, they had been forced to row for days now, and he kept the men working through the nights, too. They had lost only two so far: one who had somehow freed himself of his manacles and leapt overboard as they passed north of Ixa, and the second who had fallen prey to some foul illness which made him retch and spew and shit. Him they had tipped over the rail on the fourth day when it came clear he was getting no better and was likely to infect others. Being two men down was not ideal: Bastido had thought about putting into Cera and pressing a couple of drunks into service; but that would have meant losing the best part of another day and the draw of the adventure and the rest of the Lord of Forent's money was too hard to resist, let alone the acclaim and advancement which would surely be his on the successful completion of his mission. So instead he had wielded the cat himself at one end of the galley and entrusted the region from the stern to the midships to Baranguet, a small, squat man with the hairy, muscular arms of a Gilan ape and a bad temper; a dangerous combination in other circumstances. When he smiled at you, it was to display the curved yellow teeth of a rabid wharf rat. Baranguet made his own whips and had several terms Bastido had never encountered elsewhere for the different strokes one might apply with them. He was a vile man, but a useful one.

The rest of his crew were Forent men for the most part, loaned for the task by Rui Finco himself. They were north-coasters in origin, big, dark men more used to guard-duty and street enforcement than life on board a ship. It was as well the weather had been calm; half of them had been incapacitated for days with sea-sickness – even the slaves had laughed at them, until he had let Baranguet loose. Now a group of them sat louchely around the foredeck, gambling with the red and white stones used in the popular game of mares-and-stallions; the others, he imagined, were taking turns with the two whores they had smuggled aboard. Bastido disapproved – not of the whores, obviously, but of the lapse in discipline this unauthorised initiative represented – and had considered casting the girls overboard to discourage any further backsliding until it became apparent he'd likely have a mutiny on his hands if he did.

He knew all their names now: Pisto, darkest of them all, who rarely spoke and bore a cruel scar down the side of one cheek which raised the corner of his mouth into a sneer; Clermano, who wore his greying hair cropped to his skull and had a notch cut into his forearm for every man he'd killed; Nuno Forin and his brother Milo, who seemed to spend more time belowdecks with the women than anyone else and who chattered away to one another in a dialect no one else could follow; big Casto Agen, a seemingly mild-mannered man who had reputedly won a thousand bare-fist fights before being recruited into the Forent Guard; three sea-wardens, Gaido, Falco and Breseno, who were supposed to know something about ships and sailing, but who had succumbed to the rolling waves quicker than any of the others; a pair of swordsmen from Forent Town, who regarded themselves as the elite among the crew and kept themselves apart; and Gasto Costan, whose wife had left him for his brother. He had taken his case to the priests of the Sisters, and the pair had subsequently been found and burned, a fact that seemed to please Gasto enormously. 'Every year on the same day I roast a pig,' he had boasted cheerfully on the first day aboard. 'It reminds me of the smell.' The others had roared with laughter. Galo Bastido, self-styled bastard, had been surprised to find himself somewhat disgusted by their levity, and even more so by his own gut-reaction, which was to remove Gasto Costan from the ship as swiftly as possible.

But it was hardly nursery maids he needed for the task in hand. Turning his eyes to the far horizon, he scanned for any sight of the Eyran islands, and found none. Eight days was already longer than he had spent on any kind of water before now, let alone this vast expanse of nothing. It was easy to believe in the existence of a god whose element this was, a god of storms and tides and winds; a god who populated his kingdom with souls drawn from wrecks and out of the mouths of sea-creatures. Where was the Goddess when you most needed her? And what good could fire and ash and a horde of elegant, sharp-toothed cats do you in a place like this?

The Bastard shuddered, feeling the limitless depths of the Northern Ocean sucking away beneath his feet, and raised his own whip again.

It was good to feel the sharp air of the Northern Ocean on his face again, good to feel the blood racing through his veins; good to feel his heart beating with anticipation. They could not cast off from Halbo docks fast enough for Erno Hamson: he paced the deck and tutted loudly when some of the crew spilled a sack of grain they were trying to manhandle aboard, struck his forehead with the heel of his hand when a rain of knives clattered out of that sack alongside the golden barley, and almost vaulted over the side of the ship to help retrieve whatever illicit cargo this might be.

'Keep your hair on!'

He looked around, saw no one; looked down. The little round man, Dogo, stood beside him, grinning widely.

'You can't chivvy the wind,' the mercenary told him sagely. It was not a saying Erno had heard before, and he'd thought his grandmother used all the epigrams there were to know, indeed, had probably originated half of them herself. 'She won't go stale, you know.'

Erno fixed the little man with a stern eye. 'What do you know about it?' he asked churlishly.

Dogo tapped the side of his nose. 'If there's something I don't know about women, it's not worth knowing,' he declared modestly. 'Anyhow, who else'd want a girl as thin as a stick, with hair like a bogbrush and the temper of a cornered mole?' And dodged Erno's furious palm with a nimbleness that belied his rotund shape.

'How does everyone know?' he asked Mam plaintively that night after the Istrian coast had disappeared from sight and the Navigator's Star beckoned them north amid the clearest of winter skies.

Mam laughed. 'Joz saw you with her at the Allfair,' she said at last. 'Watched you watching her; saw the pair of you kissing outside the Gathering. He's soft like that, is Joz.'

Erno felt the blush engulf him, starting with a terrible heat in his chest, which then rushed up into his neck and ended by making beacons of his ears. The embarrassment of being spied on like this was one thing; but the shame of Katla discovering him to be in possession of a love-charm which had persuaded her into his arms was another entirely. 'It wasn't like that,' he protested. 'I— She— It meant nothing.'

The mercenary leader put her hand on his arm. 'She's a great girl, but an unforgiving one, Katla Aransen,' she said. 'Best show her your tough side when you see her: she'll not lie down for a soft man.' And then she guffawed loudly, leaving him wondering exactly what definition of the word she had meant by this.

Later that night he lay there in the dark, wrapped in a sheepskin bag against the cold, and listened to the sell-swords talking in low voices, in their carefully contrived codes, which were designed to keep eavesdroppers none the wiser. He knew enough to follow the gist of their discussion, if not the more intricate details. It transpired they had managed to gull the money for the expedition – including the ship, the crew's wages and the cargo – out of two entirely separate sources – the Earl of Stormway and Erol Bardson – for two entirely different reasons. Bardson was under the false impression that they would sail to Fair Isles and Wolf's Ness and there raise a muster among his malcontents, whom they would arm with the weaponry they carried in their grain sacks. These rebels would then return with them, put in down the coast and from there trek overland to enter Halbo from the northern gate when the moon was hidden in nine nights' time. He grinned, despite himself, imagining the unpleasant Bardson waiting in vain in the depths of that black night, planning his incipient kingship. With luck, Erno thought, he'd be caught bloody-handed at the gate and despatched as the traitor he was.

The Earl of Stormway was more likely to see some return on his investment, since his scheme sat rather better with the sell-swords' own plans; or rather with Mam's whim to reunite Erno with Katla Aransen, and gain a sackful of cantari into the bargain. Their task? To deliver up to Stormway the shipmaker, Morten Danson, whom the Rockfallers had abducted from under the King's very nose. If Ravn Asharson – who had seen too little of the world – had no interest in the war Istria had declared, then Stormway – who had seen too much – was determined to take matters into his own hands, it seemed. The old man had already set about bolstering the northern fleet: with Danson overseeing the building of new ships, they could not only defend themselves from attack, but carry fire and fear into the heart of the Istrian Empire.

It was, he considered, ironic that their plans should coincide with Eyra's best weal, for by the standards of those by whom he had been raised, the mercenaries were unprincipled, unpatriotic, untrustworthy ruffians. Yet he felt strangely comfortable in their company: they asked little of him that he could not willingly give and had found in the time he had spent among them more peace and pleasure with them than he could ever have imagined possible. It was true that their tasks in that time had been less nefarious than usual, but he could not help but like them, even so.

He propped himself up on an elbow and withdrew a long piece of red cord from the small pack he had been using to pillow his head. This he held for a few quiet minutes, and then began to knot the following making:

> This for Mam, the gnasher of teeth,
> fiercest of fighters, most fearsome of foes
> happy am I to be her friend
> for her heart is fenced round with thorns.

He paused, then:

> This for Joz Bearhand, wielder of dragons
> bold in battle, bravest of bare-serks
> no man's justice more to be trusted
> most joyous of tales in the telling.

Doc proved more difficult, for Erno had spent less time in his company, and found him alternatively dour and unforthcoming, or ponderously drunk and appallingly garrulous about all manner of inconsequential information. He could not find a pattern he liked, but in the end settled for:

> This for Doc, so tall and so thin
> a mettlesome mine, a mountainous mind
> kindest is he, though swift with a clout,
> skullcapped swordsman and scholar.

> This for Dogo, the halfling, the fool,

dangerous with dagger, a death-dealing dolt
drunk he will dog you, this giver of laughter.

He came to a stop at this point, for he felt someone's eyes
upon him like a tangible touch, and when he looked up it was
to find that the hillman, Persoa, was watching him intently,
his head on one side, like a bird of prey watching a mouse.
Then the hillman dropped one heavy eyelid in a slow and
deliberate wink and lifted the reed-pipe he held to his lips.
Sitting there crosslegged, illuminated by the flickering light
from the tub-fire, he looked exactly like the drawing of the
goat-man in the bound parchment book he had got from a
trader in Hrossey Market, called *The Song of the Flame*, which
recounted many ancient southern tales and legends.

Suddenly his fingers were busy again.

Persoa the assassin, the tattooed man
Eldianna, enigma, Elda-born, elder-born
Sits like Panios playing on his pipes
Protector, predator, predictor and priest.

He looked down at the cord and frowned. He had no idea
why he had tied these last knots – they seemed to have
come from somewhere other than his own fingers. Hastily,
he wrapped the cord around his hand and stowed it in the
sack, then laid his head down on it as if to contain the
knowledge he had stumbled upon.

Sleep came slowly that night. When it did, he dreamed of
Katla Aransen, though he had promised himself he would not.

Twenty-four

Ghosts

They managed to pull Pol Garson's arm back into its socket, but his cries were so loud the albatrosses fled shrieking from the topmast, and when they bound and splinted the broken bone below the elbow, he fainted clean away.

'He'll be no further use to you,' Urse One-Ear said quietly, wiping the sweat from his hands onto his huge, leatherclad thighs.

Aran Aranson nodded abstractedly. They had lost five men to the storm in all – Haki Ulfson, Marit Fennson, a blond man whose name he had never fully committed to memory, and two young brothers from the southern part of the island, Vigli and Jarn Forson. What he would tell their mother when – if – they ever returned to Rockfall, he did not know. Men were lost at sea all the time; but to lose two sons at once was hard. He watched the rest of the crew moving busily around the ship, mending the lines, securing the sail, bailing out the slopping water from the bilges, and made a mental count of those who had survived. Tor Bolson and Fall Ranson at the prow; Emer Bretison, Gar Felinson and Flint Hakason hauling up the sodden sail to let it dry in what little breeze the day granted them; the men from Black Isle running an efficient chain of buckets from midships to stern; Erl Fostison and a couple of the Rockfall lads retying the halyards. He watched Mag Snaketongue and a boy from the east shore making an inventory of the supplies to ascertain

what – if anything – had been washed overboard during the
storm and experienced another bright flash of memory from
the height of the tempest. Haki, arms flailing, disappearing
over the side. His death was a loss to them all, for the
Westman Islander had more knowledge of arctic sailing
than the rest put together; Aran had been counting on his
skill with pack-ice and leads to navigate them safely through
the shifting, treacherous regions they must surely negotiate
between here and Sanctuary. Without Haki, their survival
was likely to depend solely on their captain's judgement and
whatever the map might choose to divulge.

The map.

He touched the weatherproof pouch inside his shirt briefly
for reassurance, though he knew from the constant warmth
it gave out against his skin that the map was still intact inside.
His fingers throbbed and burned as they rested upon it,
generating a current of heat which travelled the length of
his arm and eased the aching muscles in his neck so that
for a moment it was as if the summer sun had made an
unseasonal appearance and blessed him with its caress. Feeling
unwontedly optimistic, the Master scanned the horizon for
any sign of land, suddenly sure the world was about to
yield a secret to him. To the north and east the skies
were as mottled as a broken egg, all bright, yolky yellow
and scarlet-blotched. It was not the good clear sky a sailor
would hope to see after a blow, a sky washed clean by the
storm, suggesting fine weather and good winds to come, but
a sky which promised further difficulties in store. It was like
glancing into the bloodshot eye of a mad bull. Aran looked
away again, disturbed, and wondered suddenly where his son
might be. It occurred to him with a sharp stab of foreboding
that he had not actually seen Fent through the events of the
night before; had no memory of seeing him tied to gunwale,
brace or thwart, or baling with the others in the aftermath.

Turning in circles, he stared around the *Long Serpent*: in

vain. Of his only surviving son there was no sign at all. Gritting his teeth against rising panic, he walked grimly down towards the stern casting glances about him all the way. Men who found his eye upon them looked away again swiftly and busied themselves about their tasks, for there was something fearful about his aspect that brought to mind grandmothers' tales of trolls and tree-sprites.

Amidships, Mag Snaketongue – a man either more courageous or more foolhardy than the rest – stopped the Master of Rockfall by a hand on his arm.

'We lost some of the watercasks, sir.'

Aran stopped dead as if registering this new nightmare.

'Two out of the four.' Mag grimaced. 'Thought they were tied in safe, but the rope got caught on a sharp edge somewhere and frayed through—' He held up the ragged ends for his captain's inspection.

Aran's eyes darted over the evidence. He took a deep breath and the cook winced, quailing from the tirade that was sure to follow. But the Master passed him by, merely looking distracted.

The boy from the east shore slipped out from behind the cook and watched Aran Aranson make his way down the ship. 'Did he hear you?' he asked anxiously. It was his first voyage and he felt at fault, even though no one could have foreseen the way the rope had frayed.

Mag Snaketongue shrugged. 'If he does not order Urse to turn the ship around and head back for the nearest island we'll know he didn't.'

But the Master of Rockfall, instead of stopping to speak to the big lieutenant, stationed as he always was at the steerboard, carried on up to the stern without even turning his head.

'Sur's nuts!' Mag firmed his jaw as if preparing it for a blow, and set out after his captain.

In the depths of the storm he had hit his head hard on one of the upturned thwarts, and as the world became soft and dark around him he thought he had heard a voice calling to him from the heart of the maelstrom, *Death is coming, but not for you. I am coming for you, or you for me. All shall be well, all things shall be well.* And then it had told him more, much more than he wished to hear, until he thought he was losing his wits, or wished he was.

The giant, the madman and the fool, to me, bring them to me.

This last pronouncement tumbled around and around his skull just as he tumbled around beneath the faering in the throes of the gale, disabling and distorting everything he had believed to be true and right, just as his limbs and back, his shoulders and head were bruised and damaged by his rough contact with the wood.

When the light suddenly fell upon him, it was like a physical pain in the centre of his head. He shut his eyes tight and cried out—

'Babbling away about death and madmen and fools,' Mag reported to the knot of men gathered around the cookpot that night. 'Don't ask me why. Hit his head hard, that's all I know: he's got a lump the size of a goose egg above one eye.'

'Serves him right,' Tor Bolson growled. 'Skiving off like that. Fancy hiding himself under the ship's boat when we needed all hands. Captain's son, and all. Fool of a boy.'

'Seems to me we're the fools, for not throwing him overboard when we had the chance,' Erl offered, licking the wound on his arm where Fent had bitten him. 'Before his da noticed we'd found him.'

'Aye, he's a vicious little weasel, that one,' Flint agreed. 'And crazy as a snake now.'

'Keep your voice down,' Emer said anxiously, looking back over his shoulder to where the Master of Rockfall knelt over his son in the stern of the ship. 'They say the Rockfall clan have strange powers.'

Flint Hakason snorted. 'Don't be daft.'

But Erl persisted. 'Katla Aransen got roasted at the Allfair, her arm was all withered and burned as black as the branch of a lightning tree, is what I heard; but then there she is right as rain in no time. You can't tell me that's natural.'

'That was down to the seither who visited, though,' Tor said sagely.

Erl Fostison made the sign of Sur's anchor. 'Safe haven,' he muttered superstitiously. 'Seithers are unlucky at the best of times. It's my belief she washed the keel of the *Long Serpent* in blood, like Ashar Stenson did with the *Troll of Narth*.'

'Aye, well if she did, I'll not complain,' Flint said cheerfully. 'Since the *Troll* came through all its sailings in one piece.'

'Besides,' added one of the Rockfallers matter-of-factly, 'the seither disappeared well before the keel was carved.'

'Ah, yes,' Erl said darkly. 'But you have to ask yourself just where it was exactly she vanished to!'

If they had hoped the Master would turn the ship and head for supplies and safety, they were to be disappointed. Obstinate as a dog with a bone, Aran Aranson cut the water rations to a single cup a day. 'You can drink your own piss if things get bad,' he'd roared at Flint Hakason when the man protested the lack of wisdom in this decision. 'That or jump overboard and catch a passing whale to carry you home.'

Emer, who did not have the sense of a chicken, scoffed at Flint's ill temper and fished plates of ice from over the side, hugging them to himself greedily.

Gar Felinson tried to reason with him, but Flint caught him by the arm. 'Let him find out for himself,' was all he said. 'He'll not learn any other way.'

It was not just the water which was running low. Two sides of beef, a keg of hard bread and all the cheese had been stored in the ship's boat which had been lost over the side during the blow. Mag Snaketongue calculated that if they went easy they might have just enough to get them to their destination if the wind held; but nowhere near sufficient for a return trip, unless the famed isle of Sanctuary yielded more utile treasures than cold, hard gold. This information he decided to keep to himself, given that the ship's captain would hardly welcome the news, and instead thinned the ingredients for the nightly stew until the crew began to complain it tasted of bilgewater.

For three days, the winds blew strong and true as if Sur himself was showing his approval of the Master of Rockfall's folly. Then they fell away entirely till the sea was smooth and still, and the sun speared down through the cloud-layer, keeping the temperature far warmer than was to be expected. The ice was a floating carpet now, fragile and lacy: as they rowed, the *Long Serpent* cut through it as if it were merely duckweed on a pond. They passed a corpse-whale, its mottled skin all grey and white and marbled, its long snout protruding into the air. Men touched their amulets and signed the anchor, for it was well known that such a sighting did not bode well for any expedition. There was much mutinous talk, but no one had the gall to organise an uprising: and so they kept on rowing. On the fourth day, they rowed straight into a sea-fog so thick they could barely tell whether it was day or night.

Without sight of sun or stars, moon or land or any other sign on which they might take a bearing, it was impossible to navigate. 'With any luck,' Fall Ranson confided in his rowing partner, 'we're heading back to Rockfall after all.'

When the fogs had not cleared on the third day, the Master relented and allowed his crew some rest. They bundled themselves in their sheepskins and sealskins and lay like fat chrysalises, scattered about the decks. A few of the younger lads played knucklebones; the older men whittled and made cats'-cradles and prayer-strings for their wives. If they ever saw them again. Urse, alone of them all, kept his station at the steerboard like a figure carved from granite.

It was during this slow time that Fent, who until now had been feverish and raving, made something of a recovery. One moment his pupils were wide and dilated, flooding his eyes with a violet tide; the next, they were their wily blue again, the colour of a winter sky, or the silver-blue of a newly whetted knife. He sat up. He smiled, his dog-teeth white inside the red bloom of his beard.

'They are coming,' he said.

But when his father pressed him as to what he meant by this, he could not say.

A little while later the Master of Rockfall felt something tickle his wrist. Barely registering the touch, he waved his hand and the sensation ceased. A couple of minutes passed, and then there came a faint buzzing sound. Again, he became aware of a vague pressure, an itch of movement. He looked down.

Settled upon the back of his hand, calmly washing its front legs together was a large black fly. He blinked and stared, but it made no attempt to escape. It took him a moment or two to register what its presence signified, then looked up, appalled and yet excited. Land: they must be close to land. The fly bumbled off, its body heavy, its wings slow against the chill of the air.

'What?' said Urse sharply. 'What is it?'

'A blowfly,' Aran said, amazed. 'It was a blowfly.'

'Never.' The big man shook his head in disbelief. 'How could there be flies out here? It's too cold, too remote.'

But now they could all hear the sound: a low hum which reverberated in the eardrum, thrummed through the cords of the neck, echoed in the skull. And then the mists parted.

Men stopped whatever they were doing. Knucklebones dropped with a rattle to the planking and no one looked to see the patterns they made; knives hovered over whalebone and walrus tusk; needles buried themselves in leather and wool. Everyone stared openmouthed as the vessel hove into view.

Silent and eerie, it emerged out of the fog like the ghost of a ship, for its wood was silver with ice and neglect and it wore tatters of white haar around its mast. How it was propelled none could see, for there were no rowers at its idle oars and no sail adorned its yard but for a few ragged threads and shrouds. It came towards them prow-first, its stempost carved into a yawning dragonhead, but no voice hailed them as it approached, only the ever-louder hum which seemed to paralyse them all. When it was only feet away, Aran Aranson leapt to his feet as if breaking through a spell.

'Ware ship!' he cried and grabbed up an oar.

Beside him, Urse One-Ear did the same.

All along the deck men followed suit. Wood grated on wood as the crew of the *Long Serpent* fended off the dead vessel that was bearing down upon them. At last the pale ship rocked to a halt, the ice-laced waves of the Northern Ocean slapping softly against its sides. Like men frozen in time, they waited, oars poised like weapons, though in what form their opponents might show themselves, none wished to conjecture. Too many tales of spectral ships haunted them, tales told by grizzled sailors in dockside taverns, by leery uncles with squints and tattoos and questionable pasts, by bards and entertainers who had travelled the islands collecting and elaborating upon the stories passed down by ten generations of seagoing men too old now to do anything other than frighten the daylights out of green lads set on making their fortune on the ocean wave. Tales of vessels manned by afterwalkers hungry for the flesh and souls of the living, corpses grown vast and black and swollen with gas and evil spirits and ill-will, lumbering about the creaking boards of their foundered craft in search of something to rend and tear. Ships abandoned for no good reason in fair weather and calm seas, their rigging still set for a good blow, their sails full of wind, casks of ale unstoppered for the evening rations. Tales of longships manned by crews of skeletons, their white bones rattling as they rowed into shore . . .

'Hold her steady!'

Aran Aranson was a brave man, men would later agree; brave or maybe rash, but the sort of captain you wanted, who led by example rather than sending others to do what he had neither the heart nor will to do himself. So it was that the Master of Rockfall with a mighty leap found himself on the deck of a vessel called the *White Wyrm*, built – as he was about to ascertain, with rising dread – by the same shipyard he had raided for the men and materials to create the *Long Serpent*, a ship with a fine ice-breaker attached in Morten Danson's own inimitable fashion; a ship built to the same specifications and for the same purpose as his own.

He steadied himself on the rocking deck, fighting down the fear he felt clawing at his chest like a starving wolf. The humming sound engulfed him now. It was hard to think with such a noise in your head, hard to maintain a plan of action or any rational objectivity. It made him want to run for the safety of his own vessel and leave this eerie hulk to float on through the fogs. But he knew he could not allow such a mystery to pass by unexamined. Could not out of sheer personal, morbid curiosity, let alone his duty as a captain – to his own men, who would look to him for reassurance and answers – and to the families and friends of this ship's ill-fated crew, to whom he must surely carry back grim news.

Girding himself for the worst, he raised his head. What met his searching eyes was a bizarre and perplexing sight. A shifting blanket of black covered everything in sight. It took him several seconds to comprehend the nature of this blanket, and when he did he felt the nausea rise in him and ran about the deck, waving his arms around and yelling until his throat was raw. The blowflies rose in a reluctant cloud and hovered gently a few inches in the air above their feast, ready to drop back down again once this nuisance had ceased. But once he had glimpsed the horrors beneath their black iridescent cloak, the Master of Rockfall could not allow them to settle. The remains of the *White Wyrm*'s crew lay in defeated piles around the ship, some with their hands over their heads as if to protect themselves from assailants, others curled tightly into balls like children in the grip of some nightmare. What was left of the legs of another pair stuck out of the ship's single overturned skiff in the hull. Flies rose from barrels and kegs, from casks and the bony frames of fish and seal and sheep. They sat on the prominent brow of an ox-skull and cleaned themselves. Maggots crawled through eye sockets and the holes where strong noses had once jutted; through the gaps between sharp white teeth and the spaces between rib-bones. One delicate skeleton, coiled in on itself like the corpse of a dead wasp, marked the demise of the ship's cat, and as soon as he registered that detail, Aran Aranson knew with chilling certainty exactly whose ship this must be. He had already suspected as much from the set of the vessel herself, but there was only one man he knew who insisted on sailing everywhere with his cat – a massive marmalade moggy with snaggle teeth and an unpleasant disposition towards anyone other than its master.

Once the initial wave of horror had swept over him and he had contained the bile that threatened to burn its way up and out of his gullet, he set about the ship, searching for its captain. Though could one recognise any man from this jumble of gleaming bones and frayed strands of yellow tendon? For there was little distinction to be made between the pathetic bundles on whom death had so ignominiously laid its hand. As he bent to examine each corpse, he was surprised to realise that the smell was less extreme than he would have expected – you had to say that for blowflies: they were efficient in their disposal of carrion; for they had stripped the flesh voraciously and expertly from the dead men, leaving only the toughest sinew and the hair in their wake. Blond braids, therefore, identified Fenil Soronson at the last, propped against the steerboard as if making a last-ditch attempt to sail them out of this disaster; blond braids and the distinctive necklace of sardonyx he had bought at the last Allfair and wore Empire-style around his throat, much to the derision of his fellow Eyrans, who had ribbed him mercilessly for buying back a bit of precious stone he had himself most likely shipped to the Moonfell Plain the year before, and paid a hundred times and more its worth just to have it polished and threaded onto leather thongs – an expensive bit of Istrian tat.

With shaking hands he undid its button-and-loop clasp and slipped it into his belt-pouch.

Hopli Garson he identified with more difficulty, for the little man was nearly bald already, even before the assiduous depredations of the insects; but eventually he found a man whose hand, pared down beyond elegance to a stark arrangement of gristle and bone, grasped the pommel of a weapon fashioned, unmistakably, by his own daughter. Aran remembered him buying it from the stall at Forsey Market three years earlier; it was one of Katla's first sales: she had been thrilled to bargain Hopli to a good price, arguing how long she had taken to fashion the intricate combination of metal and crystal in the hilt. It was a fine piece. His heart contracted to see it, and just for a moment his thoughts fled away from this gruesome place, back to Rockfall, to his difficult daughter and his estranged wife, and he wondered whether he would ever see them again, or whether his fate was to remain here on this silent, freezing ocean, his bones glimmering in the moonlight, his empty eyes staring forever into the mists. With a shiver, he pushed this forlorn image away and reapplied himself to the task at hand. Loosening the dead man's grasp from the pommel of the dagger so that the bones clattered emptily against one another and fell away, he stowed the weapon in his belt. Then he continued his grim inspection of the vessel.

How long he spent in this awful enterprise, he could not tell. At one point someone from the *Long Serpent* called out to him, enquiring whether he required aid, but he ignored the voice and went on his way about the deck, kicking out at the flies, trampling the cascades of pale maggots that tumbled from whatever he disturbed, taking note of the disposition of the bodies and the way the oars were shipped and the lines were tied. He paid particular attention to the alignment of the carcasses he found amidships, turning them over distastefully with his foot, and watching in fascinated repulsion as the maggots swarmed up and over his boot. He scraped them off with the dagger, cleaned it against the gunwale and carried on his grim inspection.

At last he made his way back to the starboard side of the *White Wyrm*. The crew of the *Long Serpent* awaited him there, lining the gunwale of their ship in such numbers that the vessel listed awkwardly. Their eyes were round with foreboding. No one wanted to ask the inevitable question. It fell to Pol Garson to speak up. He stood there, hugging his injured arm to his chest. Sharing the pain of a dislocated limb with your captain made a bond between you, he believed, like fighting back to back in battle in the old days. It gave him the courage required to break the tense silence. 'What did you find, sir?' he asked softly.

'All dead,' Aran said hollowly. 'Each and every one.'

Now the silence was broken, like water bursting through a breach, everyone had a question.

'Are there no survivors?' called one man; and 'Whose ship is it?' asked another.

'What took them?' Urse One-Ear's voice was gruffer than the rest; it boomed out across the space between him and his captain. His eyes took in the absent sail, the shredded rigging, the ominous huddled shapes barely visible through the thick fog.

The flies were starting to settle again. Aran picked up an oar, circled it wildly and drove as many as he could out into the sea.

Urse shuddered. 'It's not natural,' he said, framing the thoughts of every living man present. 'Flies in such abundance, in such a place. By rights they should not be able to survive in such a northerly region.'

'It's been unseasonably warm,' Aran returned flatly, knowing even as he said it it was not the entire truth. He had sensed something beyond nature there, something which had made the hairs on his neck rise in primal reaction. Ancient tales of necromancy, of seithers and blood-magic had made his spine prickle with every step he took on board the accursed vessel. But he would not speak of such to his crew: sailors were already more superstitious than old women. He fixed his eyes on Gar Felinson. 'I'm sorry, lad,' he said, and watched the boy's face pale. 'It's your father's ship, and he is no more.' He raised his voice so that all might hear. 'This is Fenil Soronson and Hopli Garson's ship,' he declared and waited for the shocked reaction to pass away. 'It is the *White Wyrm*, which they commissioned from Morten Danson back in eighth-month—' The men did not like this either; for they stood on the deck of her sister vessel, a ship with similarly elegant lines and an ice-breaker fashioned in the same manner, and if one such craft had come to grief in such a fateful manner, might their own not also betray them?

Ignoring the rising babble of voices, the Master continued: 'They must have put their expedition together with too much haste, for they did not pay as much attention as they should to the quality of their supplies. Someone sold them spoiled meat. The flies you see came inside the carcasses as eggs, swelled into maggots and ate their way through everything – supplies, rigging, the sail – a tempting banquet with its sheep fat still fixed in it: judging by the condition of the ship, I'd say the sail was already eaten away before the storm hit us; or they were in other realms entirely when the blow struck—' And here the men clutched their anchors and whispered prayers.

Aran Aranson indicated the strewn bodies. 'Any of you with the courage to come aboard this place of death will notice that there's not a single boot left on a single foot; and what good Eyran would voluntarily lose his boots? There's no wind I have ever experienced which can suck the footwear off a man: maggots ate them; ate them right off their feet. The whole ship must have been swarming with them.'

Urse was awe-struck. 'But how could that be? What man in his right mind would allow such a thing to occur?'

Aran shrugged. 'The crew were probably already weakened from eating the spoiled meat. Many seem to have died in their sleep; others at their oars, as if they were feebly attempting to row themselves away from the fate that had them in its clutches. But their luck was bad: the eggs kept hatching, the maggots kept coming, and when they had swelled fat and healthy, they took their adult forms and cleaned away what was left.'

He imagined the state the *White Wyrm* must have been in: its decks crawling with maggots, a wriggling yellow-white carpet of them eating everything in their path. Too exhausted by ill-health and ill-luck, the crew had fallen prey to disease and madness, one by one, a sad, volitionless lapse into death; and then their dead flesh had made a new banquet for the greedy worms. Aran Aranson shuddered. He hoped the crew of Fenil Soronson's ship had been dead before the creatures began their new round of feasting.

With Fenil's choker in his pouch and Hopli Garson's dagger tucked into his belt, he leaped from the death-ship back onto the decks of his own.

'You and you!' he called, addressing Fall Ranson and the lad from the east shore. 'Make brands from the spare sailcloth and dip them in whale-oil. Fire the ship. Swiftly now: hurry!'

They ran to do his bidding, and were joined by Tor Bolson and Erl Fostison, all glad of something practical to do to break the awful tension of the waiting and the news.

By now, the flies were gathering on the *Long Serpent*. Men swore and cursed the unclean creatures, swatted them, thrashed at them, stamped upon them, reflexes full of primal revulsion, all the time trying not to think what scraps of their fellow sailors they might last have fed upon. It was, in any case, hard to credit that mere maggots and flies could wreak such chaos, could take a proud, powerful vessel like their own, similarly crewed by strong men like themselves and reduce it to this lifeless hulk, floating directionless in this misty limbo, out of sight and protection of the god.

Aran lit the brands from the brazier. 'Push her off,' he shouted, and the men pressed the *White Wyrm* away with their oars.

When they were clear, the Master of Rockfall hurled two flaming torches through the air, one with each hand. They turned end over end, scattered flaming droplets as they spun, then fell with a thud onto the deck of the other vessel. Immediately, he followed that pair with two more, taking no chances. For several moments nothing happened. Perhaps there was nothing flammable left upon the *White Wyrm* for the fire to feed upon. The crew of the *Long Serpent* held their breath. Then a line of red flowers ran out across the deck and up the mast and a great cheer went up. For half an hour they rowed away, tracking the whereabouts of the stricken vessel by a corona of crimson light which drifted slowly astern of them through the fog; then that too died away to nothing.

Twenty-five

Among the Nomads

They followed the great cat for the better part of three days through rocky brakes, down thorny tracks and dried-up streams. They skirted pine forests and olive groves, abandoned villages with tumbled-down walls covered in sand and creeper. At night the pungent scent of resin swept down out of the hills and enveloped them; during the day it was all dust and heat and the rank sweat of Night's Harbinger as the stallion plodded along behind them, head down and mulish with the baggage he carried. They edged their way fearfully along narrow cliffside paths littered with pebbles which skittered down into the void below with any misplaced step; they clambered gingerly over piles of boulders and slid down scree slopes on the other side; they were bitten by mosquitoes where there was standing water and by dustflies where there was not; they got burned by the sun on their faces and necks, pricked by thorns and brambles, blistered by the sand in their shoes. All the while the big cat loped unconcernedly ahead, its vast paws floppy and relaxed, detouring every so often to examine the smell at the base of a tree or in the hollow of a limestone cave, before trotting off again as if assured of the rightness of its course.

As they went, Saro tried to engage his companion in conversation, but he seemed preoccupied and distracted. It was only when they came upon a songbird lying flapping on the ground, one wing savagely torn – by Bëte, or by some other predator? – that he showed any sign of emotion, bending to examine the small creature with genuine concern.

'We should put it out of its misery,' Saro said quietly.

Virelai turned his face up towards his companion. Such pain was etched upon those white contours, it was as if he felt the bird's agony for himself. Saro handed him a large stone, but the sorcerer winced away from him and would not take it, so in the end Saro firmed his jaw and did the deed himself. They both stood staring down at the tiny corpse, and when they straightened up, the light fell on Virelai's eyes, which Saro realised with a start were glistening with unshed tears. 'It was better that way,' he said softly. 'We could not leave it like that: it would be cruel.'

The sorcerer hung his head. 'I know you are right, but I could not bring myself to do it. I have suffered enough hurt myself to wish to avoid deliberately inflicting it on another, no matter how right the cause.' He paused, as if remembering something. Then he declared, 'Every creature has the right to its own life, no matter how it came into this world.'

Saro was not entirely sure what to make of this. He agreed with the sentiment, of course, but it was disturbing to find himself in sympathy with this strange, pale man.

'How did you come into the world?' he asked at last.

'I have not the least memory of that.'

Saro laughed. 'Neither do I!'

The sorcerer cheered visibly. 'Don't you?'

'I doubt many do.'

Virelai pondered on this for a while. Then he said, 'The Master told me he found me as a baby in the southern mountains, left out on a rocky promontory under the stars to survive or perish as the spirits willed it. By chance it was he who found me and took me to his stronghold to raise me as his own.' It was more of a recitation than a revelation, using almost the exact phrasing the mage had employed for its repeated tellings. It might have been graven in his head, but still it felt hollow and sham, a mere collection of sounds, for he had no pictures in his mind to accompany the words. And he had never discovered why the Master had been wandering those desolate wastes in the first place: Rahe had been most evasive about that. 'I was travelling north,' was the most he would say; but always changed the subject if his apprentice asked where his starting point had been.

'That was a cruel thing to do.'

Virelai nodded. 'I often thought so, especially when he treated me hard. It would have been best he had left me where he stumbled upon me and let the wolves and eagles take me to feed their own.'

Saro was shocked. 'No, no! It was the hill-people's cruelty I meant.' Though having Tycho Issian as his master must surely be the reason the sorcerer was fleeing from Jetra in the middle of the night.

'Ah.' Virelai gave that a moment's consideration. 'I am told that albino babies are considered unlucky.' He stood up, dusting off his grey robes and gazing disconsolately around. 'Certainly, I don't feel I carry much luck with me.'

'Do you believe in luck?'

'The Master always said a man's luck was what he made it; and if that is so, I have surely been a poor craftsman.'

The cat, Bëte, reappeared through the trees in front of them. She seemed impatient with them, as if they were errant cubs who had failed to keep up properly. When she came to a halt beside them, she looked from one to another as if trying to ascertain what had passed between them; then she looked down at the bird, sniffed it to see how long it had been dead. Then with a swift paw she tossed it into the air. Feathers scattered as her jaws closed around it, and then it was gone and she was on the move once more.

Saro and Virelai exchanged glances, then shouldered their packs and fetched the horse.

On the third night, they spied a spiral of campfire smoke

drifting out of the valley below them, at which point Bëte sat down heavily and began to wash her face with intense self-absorption, licking a paw and rubbing it across her cheek and forehead until her fur gleamed with spit and her whiskers bristled. Every line of its body spoke to Saro without any need for the unspoken communication which seemed to pass between Bëte and the sorcerer. It looked both prideful and nonchalant, as if it had done to satisfaction the task it had set for itself and was now leaving the simpler remainder of the job to its two witless human companions.

'Do you think it's them?' Saro asked Virelai as they made their way down the steep hillside as noiselessly as a dark night and an unmarked path would allow.

'If it's not,' Virelai said moodily, 'and the damned creature has led us three days out of our way out of some perversity of humour then I'll skin it myself and sell its pelt at the first market we come to.'

It was, however, a nomad encampment: a ramshackle collection of carts and wagons were huddled together under some scant trees like a bunch of old women sheltering from a rainstorm. In the clearing, a group of yeka – the shaggy plains beasts who drew the vehicles – cropped uncomplainingly at a tiny patch of withered grass while the folk of the caravan sat clustered a little distance away around the remains of a fire whose embers glowed a dull bluish red.

'They have tried to disguise their fire with magic,' Virelai whispered. 'But they could do nothing about the smoke. They must be exhausted, or weakened in some way.'

Even so, he approached warily: no one easily received unannounced visitors at such a late hour, and if they did have any magic defences in place he did not wish to run headlong into them. Before they had gone more than a few yards into the clearing, a figure detached itself from the group and came running towards them. It was a child, Saro noticed with a start; and then with an even greater shock recognised it as the child he had cannoned into at the Allfair when he had taken Tanto's money to Guaya.

'Falo!' Virelai said, himself much surprised. 'How did you—'

The little dark boy laughed. 'I have been watching you for three days now. Nothing is hidden from me,' he boasted. 'Where is the cat?'

Virelai and Saro exchanged a glance, but before either of them could say a word Falo was looking past them and grinning from ear to ear, his eyes as round as plates. A huge black shape hove into view and a vast hum rumbled through the air like thunder.

'Bëte!' the child cried, falling to its knees to embrace the creature. 'Bëte, you have come back!'

As the boy made this apparently mad and sacrificial gesture, a woman arrived, shrieking. 'Falo, Falo, come away! By Elda what are you thinking of?'

She managed somehow to insert herself between her child and the figure of the monstrous black beast, which made no move to eat either of them, but looked from one to the other with an apparently magnanimous golden gaze.

Falo squirmed clear of his mother. 'It is Bëte,' he insisted, as if she were being deliberately obtuse. 'See, Bëte and Virelai are back.'

The woman gave the cat one more suspicious glance, then as if deciding there was no immediate harm to be had from it, turned to examine the newcomers.

'Alisha,' said the sorcerer, spreading his hands in supplication. 'I'm sorry, we had nowhere else to go. The cat led us to you.'

The nomad woman regarded him expressionlessly as if assessing the veracity of this statement, but if she viewed any evasiveness therein, she decided not to pursue it. Instead, staring fearfully at the beast she asked the question Saro had been itching to ask for the past several days. 'How can this great monster be the little black cat I knew as Bëte? What magic is this, Virelai?'

The sorcerer hung his head. 'I do not know how she does it, or why,' he admitted. 'I have no control over her at all.'

The nomad woman said nothing in response to this, and when he looked up again he found she was staring at the beast, her mouth hanging open in astonishment, her eyes all hazed and inturned.

'Alisha—' He made a move towards her, concerned she had suffered some kind of seizure, but she put out her hand, fingers splayed at the end of a straight arm. Even though she uttered not a word, the gesture was clear: *Stay back, do not touch me!*

The air between the three of them was charged with something at once hieratic and at the same time quite ordinary, as if a perfectly normal conversation were going on just out of earshot. A moment later the spell broke. Alisha rubbed a hand across her face as if recovering from a blow, and staggered a pace back into Virelai's arms. Saro noticed how the sorcerer's embrace tightened on her, and that she did not immediately pull away. There was obviously some relationship between the two of them, but what its exact nature was he could not have said. Something more than friendship and less than trust was the best he could manage, but even this seemed insufficient.

Since children are rarely the respecters of intimate moments, it was Falo who interrupted the silence. 'Mama, you see? I was right, wasn't I?' But if she knew what he meant by this, she offered no response, save to wave Virelai and Saro ahead of her and to whistle for the horse which had slipped loose of its tether and come quietly down the hillside after them, as filled with curiosity as Saro himself. Saro watched amazed as the stallion – known for its chariness, its unpredictable temper and sharp teeth – nuzzled the nomad woman's hand and followed them all through the clearing toward the burnt-down campfire and the expectant faces which awaited them there.

The nomads gave them food – a hot stew, flavoured with wild thyme and sage, of maize and root vegetables and something chewy but unidentifiable as anything other than an item of plant origin, served with rounds of the hard, flat bread they baked between stones placed beneath the fire. Saro was surprised to find it delicious, raised as he had been on a diet of rich meat and soft breads. He could not in fact recall the last time he had eaten a meal which did not centre around meat – cuts of lamb and mutton, legs of chicken and geese, pâtés of pressed ducks' livers, slabs of beef hung till it was ripe and tender, gamefowl and deer, rabbits and hares, succulent fish from the Marka River, blood sausages thick with pigmeat and garlic.

When he said as much to Alisha she laughed and said something in the lilting Footloose language which made the rest of the group laugh too. Saro looked from one to another of the nomads, unsure as to whether they were sharing a joke at his expense or merely joining in the general gaiety. They were a diverse band – not quite the wild and exotic caravan of performers and entertainers he'd secretly been wishing for; and Guaya was not amongst them. Indeed, there were no children other than the boy, Falo. There were instead two old men with heads like pickled walnuts and rings in their ears and a gaggle of women so generic in appearance as to surely be sisters, their ages ranging anywhere between fifty and eighty-five – he was not used to looking at women's faces and therefore found it hard to judge. They were all equally dark of skin, wrinkled and sun-marked, and intricately adorned with beads and chains and inked patterns and piercings – in their ears, their noses, their lips, their brows, and the Lady knew where else. They wore tiny scraps of many-coloured fabric, feathers and shells in their white hair, and they all whistled and clacked their teeth when they laughed, which was often. They spoke no word of the Old Tongue. They were utterly alien to Saro; but he liked them immensely, though he could not say why.

Alisha was the youngest woman. When she smiled at him he found himself suddenly and unexpectedly envious of Virelai. She had a generous face — wide-cheeked and wide-lipped — and eyes an extraordinary green-blue, very startling against her dark gold skin, which was several shades lighter than the complexions of the rest of the group.

'We do not eat our fellow creatures,' she replied to him at last. 'We share the world equally as comrades and neighbours, and it would be strange to eat your friends, do you not think?'

She used the word 'strange', rather than 'wrong', Saro noticed, as if not passing judgement on him but rather offering up an observation, inviting his own consideration of the matter. He had never thought about it much, he realised, beyond the brief sympathy he experienced for the rabbit or the deer in its death-throes from the hunt when he was out in the hills with his father and brother and present at the kill: if he did not see where his meat came from, he ate it and enjoyed it and gave its provenance no consideration, and for this now he felt ashamed. He liked animals, and was good with them: the villa's cats came to him and rubbed their cheeks against his legs, reared up to his hand for caresses; the dogs ran around after him, bumping him with their noses; the colts followed him around the enclosure whether he carried horse-nuts with him or not. And because the cooks never served him dishes featuring cat or dog or horse, he thought nothing of what it might be that he *was* eating. The idea of an animal suffering to supply him with a meal was suddenly terribly uncomfortable. Inside his tunic, the moodstone started to glow a deep and purplish red like a second heart, pulsing through the pouch and the thin fabric of his shirt.

As if alerted by a sound, everyone stopped talking. The old men regarded him curiously; the old women bent their heads together and signed to one another.

'*Eldistan,*' someone said into the quiet.

Alisha narrowed her eyes as if remembering something difficult. 'I saw you!' she said at last. 'At the Allfair—' She clutched her hands to her mouth, trying to stop the words coming out.

Saro gazed at her, dismayed. 'What did you see?'

Something about the anguish of his expression must have touched her, for she said more gently: 'I was with my mother – Elda take and restore her soul. We were watching the events of the Fair in our great crystal. It is not always a perfect viewing device and sometimes seems to have a mind of its own, but on that day it was offering us far-sight rather than giving us visions of past or future, and we saw you, in the midst of the melee, walking about like a blind man. You were making your way toward the girl on the pyre, the one so full of lifeforce that the only way the men of the Empire knew to extinguish it was to try to burn her up. Your hand was on the moodstone you wore around your neck and it blazed through your fingers like a fire; but then—' she paused, her brows knit in confusion and the effort of recalling distant details '—there seemed to be a defraction in the crystal: we could not quite see how this came about; but it was as if you came into contact with something, other, something magical, and then the eldistan came into being. White light shone from it, a killing light . . .'

'I did not mean to kill them,' Saro said simply, remembering his nightmares which had shown him the three men he had touched with the stone falling white-eyed at his feet. 'I did not even know what I was doing . . .' He stopped, frowned. 'What do you mean, "the eldistan came into being"?' He looked once at Virelai, from whom he had first heard the term, but the sorcerer shrugged his incomprehension.

'The majority of moodstones have few powers in their natural state,' Alisha said softly. 'But some have far greater properties. Of those, most lie dormant, never to fulfil their potential. And a killing-stone—' she took a breath. 'It is said only the Goddess can make a killing-stone. It becomes the repository for her wild magic.'

Saro stared at her, his mouth dry. 'The Goddess? Falla?'

'Falla, the Lady, One of the Three, the Mother – she has many names.'

'But how could a goddess – the Goddess – be wandering about the Allfair and nobody know it?' Saro cried, suddenly angry. 'It's all just tales for children.'

Beside them, the great cat stretched its vast jaws into a yawn which then turned into a high-pitched yelp, sounding unnaturally close to humour. Alisha reached out and ran her hand over its ears and brow. It leaned its head back into her palm, closed its eyes till they were golden slits and purred. When she looked up again, her eyes were as golden as the cat's.

'We are all such children in this world,' she said softly. 'We understand so little. *I* have understood so little. Until now.' She looked at Virelai, and her gaze was softened by affection and sympathy. 'My dear,' she said huskily, 'you were blessed, did you but know it, for the woman you travelled with is the Rosa Eldi, the Rose of the World indeed: she is the flower at the heart of Elda, the Lady herself.'

Virelai blinked. He opened and closed his mouth like a fish fighting for air, but no words came out.

'And Bëte—'

Saro gasped as a revelation struck him. 'Of course: Bëte – it is the old word for "beast"! I read it in one of the books in my father's library. It derives from "Bast", which was the name of—' His heart thumped, once, hard against his ribcage, as he understood the full import of what Alisha was telling them. 'You mean the cat is also one of the Three? And the woman—' He saw again Tycho Issian's obscene image of her, legs spread . . .

All the nomads began to speak at once then. The old women came forward and began to pet the great cat, which rolled on its back and wriggled its spine in delight. Saro felt disorientated, displaced. How could any of this be true? The entire world felt infinitely mutable and undependable, as if someone had told him his true home was the moon, or that he might sprout wings and horns and begin to speak in tongues. Transformation and magic. These were not concepts which underpinned the world in which he had been raised, a world in which it was more important to bargain a man to a good price for a piece of horse-flesh and carry out due observances to a deity no one ever expected to see or, Lady forfend, actually touch.

It seemed that Virelai was having an equally hard time assimilating the idea. 'She is a goddess?' The term had little currency for him. In the tiny world which was Sanctuary, Rahe had been the sole lord and master, deity of all he surveyed. There was no room in such a world for a goddess.

'Not *a* goddess,' Alisha said kindly. '*The* Goddess. Elda incarnate, as one of the Three; the embodiment of the world's magic.'

'And the cat is another?' He fixed it with a deeply suspicious look, as if it had somehow engineered this situation for its own advantage, merely to gain the dubious attentions of this raggle-taggle troupe.

'So Sirio is the third?' This from Saro.

'Sirio, Sur; the Lord and the Man: yes.'

This was a new shock. 'But Sur is the northerners' god. I do not understand. How can we all believe in the same deities and yet hate one another so much?'

Alisha translated this last for the rest of the group, who all nodded and smiled and touched the tips of their fingers to their foreheads and chests.

'They say you are a very wise young man,' Alisha said, 'for you have gone straight to the heart of the problem.'

'But I cannot answer the question.'

'Maybe there is no answer,' Alisha returned. She thought for a moment. 'Maybe there is not even a question.'

'I do not understand how she can be a goddess,' Virelai interrupted, impatient with the insubstantiality of all this. 'A goddess must have power. The old books say the Three made Elda and have the power to remake the world day by day; but if the Rosa Eldi had such power, then how could Rahe have mastered her, why did she not use it in her own defence? Why did she travel with me all those months, letting men have her wherever we went? Why would she go north with the barbarian king? Why? I do not understand any of this at all.' He looked stricken, appalled, utterly bemused.

'Power,' Alisha mused. 'What is power, I wonder? Is it the ability to defend yourself or others, and wreak damage as you do? To make those around you do your will? To order the world as you would prefer it to be, even if this were not how others wish it? I do not know. All I do know is that my people have for generations thought the Three were lost, which is why our own abilities have dwindled; but something has changed in the world these past months. Magic has returned. Wild magic; the Goddess's bounty.'

At this, one of the older women came forward and placed her hand on Alisha's arm. She smiled at Saro and Virelai in turn and addressed them in the nomad language. Then she subsided with a satisfied nod.

'Elida can follow what you say, but cannot speak the Old Tongue with any facility,' Alisha said. 'But what she says is that in the oldest days, there was no dividing line between men and animals, between the people and the land: our essential nature was the same – we were incomplete without each other. The Three together – Man, Woman and Beast – make one whole and perfect being, and that each of us contains the best and the worst of them, as we do of all things. She also says the power we have is to know ourselves and to love and accept the world, to let it flow through us and around us and give the best of ourselves back to it. It is to be like the Three, the absolute expression of ourselves in all we are and believe and do. We all make the world in this way, by choosing who we are and being a part of all things.

'She has an ancient soul: she has seen much. I like to listen to what she says: it is always worth thinking about.'

Saro digested this for some time. Eventually he said, 'What she says seems to me to be more about happiness than power.'

Alisha smiled. 'Perhaps they are one and the same?'

He frowned. 'I do not understand what this means for me, for any of us.'

The nomad woman made a wide, inclusive gesture. 'We must all find our own way,' she said simply. 'Each alone.'

Saro put his head in his hands. Thoughts whirled about his skull like moths around a candle. Did he know who or what he was? He was not even sure who had fathered him, or if the matter of his parentage made a jot of difference to his essential nature, whatever that might be. Every time he tried to think about it, his entire being seemed diffuse, amorphous, unshaped. He felt detached from the world, rather than a part of it; unrooted, disconnected. In the end, it was hard to regard himself as important enough to have a self which required the need for absolute expression. All he seemed to be any more was the one who wore an eldistan, a death-stone: a man destined to be a pawn in the hands of others. He felt despair set in. 'I think if I let the world flow around me and through me, as you say, and do nothing disaster will follow.' He looked up as if hoping she might reassure him otherwise. 'I have seen a future, you see, in which my stone falls into the hands of an evil man who would use it to destroy everything. He is making a war between the peoples of this world so that he may take the Goddess for himself.' He paused, thought some more.

'But he cannot know who or what she is! No one does.'

'I do not think,' Virelai said slowly then, 'that she even knows herself.'

Alisha considered this. 'That may have been true for a long, long time,' she said after a while, 'but the magic is getting stronger all the time: I sense she is coming back to herself.'

Twenty-six

Wreckage

The fact that he had created these fogs himself and sent them out to haze the boundaries of his world, to veil Sanctuary from the overly-curious, did not improve his temper. But now they were in his way.

He had concocted them in a rage, furious to see ships suddenly bearing down on his hideaway through seas he had always believed to be impassable in the depths of winter, fortified as they usually were with great ramparts and barricades of ice, infinite expanses of fractured, dazzling icefields broken only by treacherous leads and crushing bergs which would loom up like great massifs and move inexorably southwards, ready to crush and sink, to swamp and avalanche the unwary, the unlucky; the trespasser. But somehow, somehow, trespassers were approaching.

He had swung the viewing-crystals in his ice-tower in such a rage that prismatic lights had shot this way and that – violet and gold, turquoise and scarlet – illuminating a chamber left to rot and ruin during his long sleep. Vast white spiders hung in the shady junctures between ceiling and wall, their webs great dusty curtains flecked with chitinous wingcases and discarded legs; the spiders pale ghosts of the monsters he had created in his early days on the island and then lost interest in, as he had so much else in this goddess-forsaken place. And then, suddenly, there, there! Aboard a vessel which had the deep temerity to brave these supposedly uncharted waters, a captain

– a tall, vain man with blond braids and an intricate confection of chalcedony at his throat, consulting, of all things, a *chart*.

The crystals could be remarkably precise when he could be bothered to wield them delicately: in the grip of a curiosity so intense it was like a hand around his throat he had flicked the levers a hair's breadth to left and right, brought the third level of lenses into use for the first time in decades; swore at the dust which clouded them and blasted them clean with a single merciless spell which left them gleaming and painful to the eye. He brought them to bear upon the parchment clutched in the tall man's hand, adjusted the focus a smidgeon; and stared.

It was like a fist to the gut, a winding; a blow. There, inked in the hand he had so painstakingly taught his student – his one, his only, his beloved boy, his Virelai, greatest creation of them all – was a map which charted with intricate and unstinting detail the watercourses of the Northern Ocean, the way to Sanctuary. It was not entirely accurate, of course: how could it be? All his apprentice had ever had to go on was his own poor attempts to chart his strange and eventful journey to this wild place, and those had been filled as much with fancy as with fact. But somehow, somehow, the boy had woven magic into them – he could sense the spell the thing cast by the way the blond man craned over it, hid it from the view even of his navigator, as if he coveted its every curve and recurve, every line of its windrose and indentation of coastline; every letter of its legend. Some sort of compulsion emanated from it; a kind of delusion. What had he offered them? Rahe wondered, but knew even before the answer had formed in his head.

It would be treasure: gold. It was always gold with men. They were fools for it, made mad by the promise of its rare lustre. Even amidst his rage at the boy's treason and guile, he could not help but laugh. It was a bitter laugh, as creaky as an old gate: it echoed around the tower-room like a bat in a cave, a dark thing rarely seen in the light. It took him by surprise, this laugh, made him stop abruptly so that a grey silence wreathed the chamber again, and the spiders, which had ventured into the centre of their webs at the sound, as if sensing some form of life, crawled back up their trembling lines into obscurity once more.

'They will find no gold here,' he said aloud. His voice was hoarse from disuse and dehydration, but it made the words no less true. There was no gold in Sanctuary; no gold but pyrites, great glittering lumps of it excresing in the carved-out tunnels and corridors of the fastness. Fake and worthless, brittle and chill. Fool's gold, the perfect gold for fools. True gold came only from one other source. He, of all beings, knew well where that might be, but his memory did not wish to engage with that knowledge at this time: it shied away like a fretful pony.

There were other ships, too. Some he recognised; others he did not. There were ships, it seemed, wherever he looked! Some were ancient; some the natural storms of the place had dealt with without the need for further interference; others drifted helplessly, lost and rudderless. Some lacked crews; others had ventured too far north and been taken by the ice. He watched in satisfaction as the floes closed in on one stricken vessel and crushed her to splinters while her crew watched hopelessly from their tiny boat. What prospect of survival did they stand in these realms? He smiled and smiled. None, none at all. If the cold did not get them, then storms or hunger or lack of water would carry them off; and madness would come before the end.

Even so, he was taking no chances. Gathering the remnants of his spellcraft, he sent impenetrable fogs out into the Northern Ocean to confuse even the most skilful of navigators and confound the pathetic shreds of magic which Virelai had managed to set into the maps he had made, chilling mists so dense they would swallow any wind that dared to blow near

Sanctuary. And so, becalmed and bedevilled, the trespassers
gave up their ghosts, their spirits coiling like smoke into the
choking fogs, thickening them further, filling them with wails
and cries which the uninitiated might take for the forlorn calls
of lost seabirds.

The effort it took rendered him insensible for three days,
and when he came to, it was in a mire of his own making
and the tower-room was filled with foul odours and the
echoes of his babbling. He crawled to the viewing platform
and searched the myriad vistas in a haze of fury and despair
until something had caught his interest and held it, an echo,
a vibration. It was way out beyond the fogs which obscured
his sight, but it caught at his senses like a cat snagging his
sleeve. Something rare and true: obsession and madness, an
immense and wasted energy: a reservoir to be drawn upon.
He could feel it like a lodestone. He peered and peered, but
the fogs he had made were reluctant to disperse. Angrily, he
swung the prisms again, and again.

Out on the open sea, a sail: plain and red. An elegant
vessel with serpentine lines. Levers creaked and dust flew
as more precise lenses were brought into play. There! A
tall dark man with a determined face standing at the prow
with his hand pressed against his heart. No, not his heart,
but something which lay beneath his clothing, nestling out
of sight, something he valued more than life itself. Beside
him, a giant of a man with a ruined face and a single, tattered
ear. And behind him, a thin boy with red hair and wild eyes.
A dark rancour burned in those eyes, such an untapped well
of it. Suddenly, Rahe felt the old cogs and levers moving not
in his hand, but in his head. It was as if providence itself spoke
to him out of the origins of all things.

A madman; a giant; a fool.

The refrain of an ancient verse played over and over in
his skull, like a mantra or a spell; or the nonsense of a
child's song:

> *Man, Woman, Beast*
> *Madman, Giant, Fool*
> *When Death comes to the Feast*
> *Wild Magic over all shall rule . . .*

The skies darkened, heralding a storm out in the world which mirrored perfectly the pressures moving monstrously inside him. He felt suddenly larger than he was, more than himself, a consciousness which yawned over all of Elda. The pressure built, spilled over, flooded out.

Madness was all he had, so madness he sent forth . . .

It was only when the last glow of the maggot-eaten ship had faded from sight that Aran Aranson turned to order the sail set, and found that two of his crew were missing. He scanned the decks for sight of Tor Bolson – a strapping man who always wore a 'lucky' scarlet jerkin should not be hard to spot – but he was not amongst the knot of men dispersing amidships, nor was he at his appointed rowing place. It was as he was making a mental knot for the rest of the crew that he realised another was absent, too: a short dark boy who had come from the eastern isles, and who, despite southern slave origins, had a sure hand about the rigging.

'Urse!'

The big man was at his side at once.

'Have you seen Tor or,' he searched his memory, 'Bran Mattson?'

Urse looked surprised at the question. Then he, too, turned to scan the deck. 'I saw Bran with Jan and Emer last,' he said slowly.

Aran identified the Fishey lad at once. Emer Bretison was the best part of seven foot tall: he was hard to miss. Beside him, a slight man with his fair hair in a tight tail was working to swing the yard free of the shrouds. He stepped swiftly down the ship towards them. 'I'm looking for Bran,' he said briskly.

Jan stopped what he was doing and regarded his captain blankly. 'He was—' He looked to his left, then to his right and frowned. 'He was standing beside me at the gunwale when we fired the *White Wyrm*,' he said slowly. His eyes became wider. They were very blue, Aran noticed; the blue of speedwell or forget-me-not and when, as now, they were not quite focused, they made him look both vacant and childlike. Then, as if something had struck him, he spun around wildly, his gaze leaping over his fellow crewmember in something approaching panic. 'He was with me,' he started again, 'and then—' He turned back to his captain, horrified. 'He's gone. But how—?'

Aran's eyebrows became a single forbidding black line. He turned to Emer. 'And you?'

Emer shrugged and went back to his task. 'Maybe he took a nap under the skiff,' he said provocatively. That Aran had not punished his son for his cowardice and dereliction of duty had not sat well with the rest of the crew.

The Master of Rockfall stared hard at the back of Emer's head for a few tense seconds. Then, as if deciding not to pursue the remark, he addressed himself to Jan. 'Say nothing,' he warned, and ran back to Urse.

The big man gave him an almost imperceptible shake of the head. 'No one has seen him since before you boarded the *White Wyrm*,' he said when Aran was in range, though he kept his voice down.

Neither man was under the remaining skiff, nor hidden amidst the supplies and sea-chests. No one was up the mast, wrapped in the spare sailcloth, or trailing in the wake. For a wild moment, Aran had a vision of the mismatched pair – one huge and blond, the other dark and wiry – afire aboard the ghost ship, and pushed the image firmly from his mind. He was the only living man to have set foot on that vessel in many weeks, of that he was certain.

By the time the moon came up it was clear neither Tor

nor Bran was any longer aboard the *Long Serpent*. The crew started to speak of evil spirits, things which would suck your soul out of your ears, out through the pores of your skin, gasts which appeared in the form of seductive enchantresses, clothed in weed and shells and sea-haars, which would wrap themselves around you as warm as any land-woman and kiss the life right out of your mouth, every breath and heartbeat. But even gasts and afterwalkers left the emptied-out bodies behind them, and of the two missing sailors there was no trace at all.

Aran sat watch that night, all night, with his back braced against the mast. There was nothing to see outside the ship, star nor moon, nor horizon; for the fogs hung around them, as impenetrable as ever. But it was not spirits that he watched for, nor afterwalkers returned from the dead ship, nor anything which had come out of the sea. Neither coincidence nor supernatural intervention had lost him his crewmen, of that he was sure. And so he sat there, with one hand on the pommel of his dagger and the other balled into a fist, and waited for what the next day would bring.

Sure enough, the morning brought a new freight of horror. In the early hours a second ship sailed through the thinning mists towards them, propelled by neither wind nor oar and haloed by the dawn light like a sundog. Even so, when they had rowed in close enough to grapple the vessel towards them, it was clear that whatever disaster had occurred here was less than supernatural in origin. The stricken ship's timbers were split and silvered by the elements and within seconds of setting foot on its creaking deck, Urse and his captain could see that its crew were dead, every one. This time, the flesh was still upon the corpses, though it was darkened to a vile purplish-black, dried almost to the point of mummification, blotched and livid where boils had swollen, burst and dried to pits. Their faces were the worst, for the eyeballs – yellow white and crazed as ducks' eggs left too long in the nest – appeared shrivelled in their sockets and the lids were shrunken and parched and cracked like an old harness. All that remained of their lips were ragged black lines etched against teeth that jutted long and shockingly white from dark and desiccated gums. Their noses, if such they could be termed since barely a knuckle-length remained, were shrunken and withered to obscene and noxious flaps within which the lining showed as black as spent coal. What remained of the rest of their skin was stretched tight as tanned leather across their fog-dewed bones. They lay in heaps, tangled together or curled into fetal shapes, their staring eye-sockets and open mouths testament to the agony of their passing. There was not a single maggot, not a single blowfly aboard the ship. There was still salt-cod and wind-dried meat packed in two unopened kegs, and a dozen or more hard cakes of unleavened bread wrapped in hessian in a chest beside them; but the water casks were as dry as tinder, and a broken sun-still made from a square of sailcloth contained nothing more than a thick crusting of sea-salt.

Urse shook his head. 'Poor bastards,' he said with feeling.

Pragmatically, they took the bread, fish and meat back with them to the *Long Serpent*, but no one wanted to touch it, let alone eat any of it. It was as if the supplies were as damned as the crew of the unnamed vessel had been, as if the food might contain the curse which had carried them away to Sur's Howe.

Later that night, another of their number vanished.

Urse One-Ear was on last watch, but he neither saw nor heard anything, did not even notice the man was missing until Pol Garson took him by the arm the next morning. 'I cannot see Erl anywhere,' he said quietly. 'And I do not think it is my eyesight which is at fault.'

Urse checked the ship from stem to stern, then woke his captain with the grim news. Aran cursed roundly. 'I should have taken the whole watch,' he said, though his lids were red-rimmed from lack of sleep.

The big man bridled. 'I was alert the whole time.'

'Then you are suggesting he disappeared on my watch?' The Master of Rockfall's eyes flashed dangerously.

Urse shrugged. 'All things are possible until we know the truth of it.'

Aran Aranson's temper was legendary in the Westman Isles, though it was said he never struck an unfair blow. Even so, there were many who would have paid to watch a bout between the Master of Rockfall and Tam Fox's giant, Urse One-Ear; between the temper of the one and the size of the other the betting would have proved close. But as it was, the captain merely shook his head.

'There is something horribly awry here, Urse,' was all he said. 'I do not hold with stories of the undead or demons in spirit form; but men cannot simply vanish into thin air.'

'I have heard of expeditions on which men simply lost their wits and the will to live and have cast themselves silently overboard when the attention of others was distracted,' Urse ventured.

'There is madness here,' Aran replied, 'but I do not believe it was in the lost men.' He paused. 'Although all things are indeed possible until we know the truth of it.'

Twenty-seven

Katla

Life at Rockfall continued in much the same manner as it
always had when its menfolk were away. The women carried
on the chores of the fields and farm, salted fish, baked bread,
spun wool and wove cloth and dug and dried peat for the
long fire. They mended the drystone walls to keep the sheep
in, and the chicken coops to keep the foxes out. They patched
the barn wattle and added new turf to the hall's roof where
the extended summer sun had burned brown patches into the
green. They milked the cows and the goats, separated whey
and curds, bound wheels of cheese in muslin and scraped
barnacles off the hulls of the boats they hauled up out of the
harbour before the worst of the winds came.

But rather than revelling in her new responsibilities, Katla
hated every minute of this enforced domesticity. With hardly
any men present except for the shipmaker and occasionally a
couple of elderly fishermen who'd seen enough of the sea,
the balance seemed wrong: she felt the atmosphere to be
stifling, contained, small-scale. The talk was all of women's
matters: who was pregnant, who was not; which soapwort
worked best for the skin, whether camomile made the hair
lighter; how eating fish livers made eyes shine and nails grow
long; why it was best to add salt to scones and honeyed butter
to carrots; why a bone spindle-whorl worked better than a
wooden one. None of these details held the least interest
for Katla, whose brush with conception had left her chary

of anything to do with sexual matters, whose skin was as brown as the husk of a nut and whose hair had grown out into a shaggy mass as ragged and unkempt as a head of red kelp. Her eyes were bloodshot from the smoke and the wind and her nails, if not bitten down to the quick, were broken and scraped by her escapades on the rockfaces of the island: other women's secrets about how to enhance one's beauty and attract a husband were as dull and as alien to her as the precise knot required to slip a fishnet tight shut or make fast a halyard were to her female companions.

Worst of all, there seemed to be no way of avoiding conflict with her mother. Whatever she did was wrong: when she carded wool it was in a rather more haphazard fashion than the meticulous Mistress of Rockfall demanded; when she peeled vegetables for the nightly stew, Bera told her off for cutting the skins too thickly and losing the best of the flavour. She could not sweep a floor properly, it seemed, nor even mend a torn tunic, let alone weave or sew or spin with the rest of the women, all of whom seemed to have learned these mysterious skills at birth and without a cross word from their mentors. In pique, she took to running the length and breadth of the island again, ostensibly gathering mushrooms and mussels and gulls' eggs, netting coneys and speckled trout, picking reeds for the floor or for new baskets, bulrushes for tapers and torches, but more often simply running for running's sake, not even knowing what it was she ran from.

Today, her job was peeling carrots. An entire barrelful of them. Bera had set the keg down in front of her with a thud and a grim look which brooked no objection. 'By noon, Katla,' she said sharply, 'or I'll give you the turnips too. And if I find the peelings are any thicker than my thumbnail, you'll be peeling mangelwurzels for the rest of the week until you've got the knack of it and won't waste any more of our precious stores.'

Quite why anyone should need to boil a barrel-load of

carrots and three dozen turnips, let alone a sack of inedible mangelwurzels, Katla could not imagine: except as a punishment for some unspoken transgression. She stared at the heap of hateful vegetables then, vengefully, at her mother's retreating form and set her jaw.

Gramma Rolfsen cackled. 'That'll keep you out of mischief for a few hours!'

Instead of rising to the bait, Katla reached into her tunic pouch, took something from it and held it out to her grandmother. On her palm lay a neat-looking metal object somewhere between a stick and a knife. Hesta Rolfsen frowned and picked it up. She held it in front of her face, then selected a turnip and ran the item away from her across its rough surface. The stick/knife skittered and jumped. 'Useless thing,' she said in disgust.

Katla laughed. She took both turnip and implement back from her grandmother and drew the blade across the vegetable towards her instead. As if by magic, a sliver of purple skin spiralled to the ground.

The old woman exclaimed in amazement.

After a moment, 'It peels,' she said, unnecessarily.

Katla gave her a gleeful grin and lowered her voice so that none of the other women present would hear. 'I knew she was going to make me do the carrots today – I saw her collecting them from the barn last night,' she said. 'So I sneaked into the smithy to devise something which might make the job easier than using my poor old belt-knife. I could shave a pig with this, the blade's so keen!'

She had been forbidden access to the smithy by the Mistress of Rockfall as a form of punishment, and when Katla had objected on the grounds that with the men away it was surely the best use of her time to forge as many weapons as she possibly could in case they needed to defend themselves, Bera had simply laughed. 'Can you imagine Marin Edelsen wielding a sword against a raider?' she had asked, quite sensibly. But this made Katla all the more mulish. 'I could teach them the basics,' she'd said; but her mother was having none of it. 'One hoyden is quite enough in my house: I was hoping the presence of the other girls might civilise you; but I can see that given your head the rest of them will be turned into ruffians in no time at all. Household duties only for you, my girl, till I decide otherwise.'

And thus it had been this past week and more.

For the next hour, even with the miraculous new tool, Katla peeled carrot after carrot, and took the top layer of skin off several of her fingers into the bargain. She watched a drop of her blood run the length of one of the vegetables and seep down into the pile. By rights, she should sluice them off with well-water, but just now she could not be bothered. *Since they're sucking my soul out of me, they may as well taste it*, she thought bitterly, and reapplied herself to the job with renewed vigour. For a while she drifted into a sort of pleasant haze and the pile of unpeeled carrots dwindled rapidly.

A particularly loud noise roused her from her reverie. It was Magla Felinsen, talking as only she knew how. It was impossible to attune your senses elsewhere, for the woman had one of those voices which cut through all others, a voice which would be audible even through a howling wind or the heart of a wildfire.

'And so I said to Suna, "Suna Bransen," I said, "if you want to look like the Troll of Blackisle, you're going the right way about it. With hair like that you need to add a little wool-oil into your rinse-water, which will sleek it down a bit." And do you know what she said to me?' Magla put her hands on her hips so that the ladle she'd been using to stir the pot dripped slowly down her apron and onto the floor. Katla watched one of the slyer cats detach itself from the shadow of the benches and slip under Magla's guard to lap at the spilled broth. Having consumed this, it looked up speculatively at the dripping ladle and a tremor of intent ran through the muscles of its haunches as if it would launch itself at the implement; then Magla started gesticulating extravagantly with the spoon and the cat ran for safety. Little globules of fatty gravy flickered into the air and fell sizzling into the fire. '"Magla Felinsen," she said, "you may wish to smell like a rancid old ewe, but I most certainly do not; and when you've finally managed to get Arni Hamson to offer for you perhaps I'll ask for your advice"!'

'How ill-mannered,' said Simi Fallsen. 'Anyone can tell her people came from the east.'

'And what about that awful hair of hers, flying about all wild and bushy and uncontained – it looks like the tail on a manky old mare!' giggled Thin Hildi.

'Poor Suna. Such an uncouth girl,' said Kitten Soronsen, shaking her pretty head in mock sorrow. 'So like our beloved Katla!'

Everyone, except the subject, laughed loudly at this: they had got used to regarding Katla as fair game in the matter of appearance and manners, and she usually accepted their ribaldry in good part. Throughout the merriment, Kitten Soronsen smiled in her disturbingly equivocal fashion, with a sly quirk of those cruel, chiselled lips which made a dozen local lads go weak at the knees and stammer in her presence. It was always hard to know, when she made such observations, whether her teasing was affectionate or unsufferably rude, and no one ever dared challenge her for fear of being made to look even more stupid than she had already rendered them. Katla glared at her, taking in her perfect complexion and elegantly braided locks, bound with blue ribbon and the tiny silk flowers some admirer had bought for her at the Allfair, and was shocked to feel a moment's regret at the contrast between them. That twinge made her temper snap.

'Why do you think everybody wants to be like you, Kitten Soronsen? You think you're so fine with your pretty hair and your perfect face and your smooth pink skin. Just because you've got men paying you court from half a dozen islands, buying you little gifts and making you pretty rhyme-strings, you think you're better than anyone else. But eventually you'll end up the same as any other woman owned by a man – with babies hanging off your tits and your belly as soft and drooping as an old sow's and your arms elbow-deep in smallclothes and nappies, and it will be exactly what you deserve.'

Even before the words were fully out of her mouth she knew she had overstepped her mark. Kitten was catty, it was true, and vain and mean-spirited; but one jibe about her messy hair was hardly just cause for such a tirade. Despite this, it was with some satisfaction that she saw the girl's face darken and her blue eyes flash with rage. Then Kitten Soronsen hurled the wooden spoon she had been using hard at Katla's head. Katla, of course, ducked it neatly. It flew over her shoulder and hit Marin Edelsen square on the bridge of the nose, causing her to squawk with shock and pain. Blood began to spurt out of her nostrils, down onto her best linen apron and well-stuffed tunic, and over Thin Hildi as well, who took one look at the scarlet drops and fell down in a faint.

Morten Danson, who as usual had been snoozing on the bench beside the fire, came awake with a start and stared around him in a disorientated fashion as if he had forgotten yet again where he was.

Seeing her projectile miss its mark, Kitten Soronsen leapt as neatly as her namesake across the long fire, buried her hands knuckle-deep in Katla's hair and began pulling viciously. A physical onslaught on the two-time wrestling champion of the Westman Isles Games was not the most sensible ploy, but Kitten Soronsen was stronger than she looked, and angrier than a nestful of hornets. Katla had not expected such an assault: taken by surprise she lost her balance and went down cursing with the other girl on top of her. The two of them landed with a thud in a slippery pile of vegetable peelings.

The barrel went over too, spilling the rest of the carrots here and there, so that when Kitten tried to get to her feet she could get no purchase and fell back on Katla, knocking the breath out of her.

Gramma Rolfsen began to cackle and wheeze and clap her hands together in delight. 'A catfight! How I love a good catfight. Go on, Katla, show her what for!'

At this point, Magla Felinsen joined in. 'Bitch!' she cried, hitting out at Katla's hands and arms with her ladle. 'Mangy fox-haired bitch! Hit her, Kitten: rip her ugly little face off!' Then she started yelping as Hesta Rolfsen began laying about her with her stick.

Even occupied as she was trying to lever her attacker off her with a forceful knee, Katla was surprised by the intensity of Magla's dislike. What had she ever done to provoke her, she wondered; but only for a moment, because now Kitten was clawing at her eyes, her fingernails as hard and sharp as talons. Perhaps there was something in all that guff about fish-oil making your nails stronger, Katla thought inconsequentially as Kitten gouged at her. She closed her lids tight, feeling the girl's thumb press down hard and tried to wrest her head away, to no avail, because someone else was snarling and kicking at her. Dimly, she could hear her grandmother swearing like a fishwife, the rise and fall of her wicked knobkerry, then a howl of outrage as the old woman went down. Fury flooded through her then.

The floor began to tremble beneath her tensed muscles. Her breath came short and sharp. Heat welled up inside her. And then a voice echoed in her head. 'I need your eyes, Katla Aransen,' it said. 'Take strength from me.'

She had no idea whether the voice came from inside her own head or from without, but she felt a great wave of energy invade her body, through the layers of her clothing, through the peelings scattered on the floor beneath her, through the stone flagstones, and from far far down inside the molten guts of the earth, as if every natural element she was in contact with were joining forces to instil in her their particular vigour: linen and flax and carrot and rushes and granite and crystal and boiling magma.

There was a sudden lightness, a cry; a thud. She opened her eyes, sat up, abruptly unburdened.

Kitten Soronsen was twenty feet away from her in a crumpled heap at the foot of one of the central wooden pillars which supported the hall's roof. She was breathing erratically, for Katla could see the rapid rise and fall of her embroidered tunic, but other than that she was not moving. The room had gone very quiet. She stared around.

'Katla Aransen!'

The voice broke the spell. Everyone started talking at once.

The Mistress of Rockfall advanced upon her daughter. Bera Rolfsen was a diminutive woman, but her temper was well known from Black Isle to the Old Man of Westfall. The onlookers moved nervously out of her path. Two of them – Tian Jensen and Fat Breta Arnasen – ran to Kitten's side and sat her up against the pillar. She had a dark bruise already spreading across one cheek and her right eye was swollen shut, Katla could not help but be satisfied to note.

Then there was nothing in her line of sight except Bera's flushed and raging face. A swift hand descended with a crack and sharp pain flowered across Katla's cheek. Her hand went instinctively up to the site of the blow. It was years since her mother had struck her so, not since she had inadvertently ruined the silk dress Aran had brought back for his wife from the Allfair one summer, which Bera had hung on the washing line to shake out the wrinkles. Katla had at the time been deeply engrossed in devising a new technique for crossing from one sea-stack to another, by looping one end of a rope around the top of the first and making fast the other end to the second, tightening off the slipknots with a bowline to keep the rope tight; then sliding down it with her feet up and her ankles crossed over the cord, hand over hand. It had seemed sensible to practise the concept in the backyard, seven feet off the ground, rather than out at the Old Man, towering a good two hundred. The washing line was robust and new — a fine, strong length of narwhal skin, chewed into softness and stretched between the posts with utmost care. But she hadn't taken into account the fact that the post which supported the far end of the line had been out in the weather these past three winters. The support had cracked apart with an ear-splitting snap, depositing Katla, line and dress in a horrible tangled heap in the mud. She'd borne the black eye her mother had given her on that occasion with a certain resignation: she knew she had deserved punishment, and a quick smack in the eye seemed immeasurably preferable to being confined to the hall for weeks on end, as was her mother's usual practice when chastising her offspring.

Bera stood back, hands on her hips. 'Katla, I am ashamed of you: you are no better than a hoyden, a troll.' Bright scarlet spots in her cheeks attested to the depth of her anger. Her gazed raked the hall, moved from one downcast face to the next, settling for a moment on Marin's blood-covered hands and apron, then on Gramma Rolfsen, but the old woman pretended to be engaged in cleaning something from her shoe and would not meet her eye. Her expression showed her absolute contempt. 'Look at you. You are all no better than a rabble of farmyard cats with no tom to keep you in order, spitting and hissing and tearing out each other's fur.'

Indeed, Katla noted, there appeared to be a handful of blonde hair caught up in the disarray of carrot peelings and rushes, a few inches away from a hank of dark red hair. She didn't remember dragging at Kitten's hair, but there was a certain degree of gratification to be had from the thought that she had inflicted some small damage on those perfect tresses.

Bera returned her furious attention to her daughter. 'And you are the worst of them all. I ask you to spend your morning completing one simple task—' She scanned the mess at her feet, where carrots lay scattered among their shed skins, ripped-out hair, trampled reeds and spilled food, then bent and, quick as a striking snake, retrieved one of the peeled vegetables and held it up in front of Katla. 'See this?'

The carrot was somewhat the worse for wear, but even so it was obvious even to the incurious that the peeling it had suffered had been partial to say the least. Little strips of browner flesh showed dark against the pale orange stem. Katla gazed at it unrepentantly. She shrugged: her blood was up and she was sick and tired of Rockfall, of her mother, and particularly of these grim and stupid chores.

'So what?' she heard herself say, as rudely as the hoyden Bera accused her of being. 'The dirt will come off in the boil; and anyway, whoever heard of anyone dying of eating a little carrot skin?'

It was clearly not a view her mother shared. Bera's skin flushed a darker red; her eyes sparked a dangerous blue.

'You cannot cook, you cannot sew, you cannot spin, or weave or mend or be entrusted with the simplest of tasks. And you look – what was it, Magla, you so graphically suggested?'

The big woman stared fixedly at her feet and said not a word.

'Like "a mangy, fox-haired bitch". Wasn't that the phrase?'

The atmosphere was distinctly uncomfortable. Katla could not help but grin at Magla's embarrassment; was still grinning when her mother turned back to her, her face livid where the older woman had struck her. She watched her mother's gaze rise to take in the welts her fingers had left on her daughter's cheek, but if she regretted the blow she had struck, her remorse was by no means apparent.

'Indeed. Mangy – well, certainly ill-kempt; fox-haired,

well you can blame your mother for your colouring, at least; but that is where all resemblance between the two of us ends, Katla Aransen. You seem inherently incapable of shouldering your fair share of the daily tasks, of taking the least little bit of pride in what you do or how you appear — no, that you won't do, can't be bothered to do, out of sheer pigheadedness and the strange belief that you are in some way different to the rest of us, with our sagging breasts and soft bellies and our families to raise and care for. What makes you so special, Katla, that you expect us all to run around after you, providing you with food and clothing and shelter? You may be able to hammer out a decent sword and beat the lads at their own games, but somewhere along the path from sweet infancy to standing insolently before me now with your lip curled and a gleam in your eye, you went wrong, my girl. The trolls must have taken you, Katla Aransen, for you are no daughter of mine, I swear. I am ashamed of you, ashamed to the core of my heart. And not just for provoking fights or for this—'

The carrot struck Katla's arm and bounced off onto the flagstones.

'If you thought I did not know about you and that . . . that creature Tam Fox, you'd be wrong.'

Bera had hit her full stride now: she was beyond caring what anyone thought, was beyond noticing that every woman in the hall was quivering with the effort to receive and absorb every word she spoke, ready to relay the information to friends and relatives the length and breadth of the Westman Isles just as soon as they had the chance.

'Ma!' Katla was appalled. 'Say no more!' Shock made her thoughts slow and stupid. How on Elda could her mother have known? Tam Fox was dead and drowned and she had told no one— Memory returned, a thorn in the gut. 'Gramma, how could you?' She rounded on her grandmother in fury and watched the old woman grimace.

'I'm so sorry, my dear, she caught me out.' Hesta Rolfsen shrugged apologetically. 'You know how sly your mother can be when she suspects something. And how determined.'

Katla watched a glance pass between them and saw how her mother's expression contained both triumph and shame, and how her grandmother's eyes flashed and her chin lifted in challenge.

'What man would have you now, after you've slept with a man like that?' Bera went on in disgust.

Katla's indignation boiled over in a great volcanic gush. 'A man like what?' she shrieked.

'Bera . . .' Gramma Rolfsen warned.

But mother and daughter were in this too similar: neither would back down now: words would be spoken which could never be forgiven or taken back.

'One of the Old Ones,' Bera hissed, and around the room women murmured and made the sign against evil. 'A very devil.'

Katla frowned. A devil? One of the Old Ones? Tam Fox was no seither: he had had two perfectly good eyes and was as human as any man she'd known. Wasn't he? Something made her shiver, a sudden superstitious chill.

'You shouldn't speak ill of the dead,' Hesta said softly. She touched her fingers to the woven charm of corn and cat fur that hung from the chain around her neck. It invoked Feya, Sur's kind sister, goddess of grain and good fortune.

'Dead? That one? I'll believe it when I see his mouldering bones and festering flesh washed up on Whale Strand!' Bera snorted. 'He may have taken my own firstborn down into the waters as a gift to Sur, but I doubt very much he gave up his own soul to the Storm Lord!'

'You can't blame Tam Fox for what happened to Halli! I was there, not you: I saw what happened. A sea-monster, risen from the deep—'

'So you say.' Her mother's face was vicious with pain.

'Ships and sea-monsters and islands full of gold – you're as bad as any man, seduced away by tales for the simple-minded, abandoning your own for some pathetic adventure far from home and leaving everyone else to get on with doing all the work and making a life for what's left of your family.'

Something about this seemed unfair, but Katla was too angry to step back and view her mother's misery with any cool detachment. Instead, she balled her fists and shouted. 'It's all your fault anyway! Halli wouldn't have died if it hadn't been for you. It was you who drove Father away in the first place, with all your whining and nagging and idiotic, bloody chores. At least he dreamed of something different, something exciting, something . . . amazing. It's so boring here, with your pathetic attempts to shore up your silly little life – mending pigpens and patching aprons and knowing how to peel a fucking carrot properly – as if it mattered, as if any of it matters! And all these simpering ninnies and their sad plans to trap and marry men and start the whole grim round all over again – I can't stand it here! Da would have gone mad if he stayed, just as I'm going mad in his stead. I don't want you, or anyone, making my life – I'm going to make my own life, and it won't be confined to somewhere as small and safe and stupid as Rockfall. Yes, I'd have sailed with Da if Fent hadn't stopped me! And how can you blame him for sailing north? You drove him away, cast him out – he told me! Uncle Margan is helping you divorce him and overseeing the settlement!'

Bera's hands flew to her mouth and her eyes went dark with shock. Betrayed, bewildered, embattled, she stared around the chamber. The crowd of women gazed back at her, sharp-faced with curiosity. This was more entertainment than they had had in years; better by far even than the Winterfest and the mummers.

Gramma Rolfsen regarded her granddaughter miserably. 'Oh, Katla, how could you hurt your mother so?'

But Katla rounded on her. 'And you're no better!' she stormed. 'You probably conspired with her to drive him away.'

Hesta's mouth fell open, but Katla had turned her attention to the other women. They regarded her warily, as avid as a horde of rats, hungry to snatch any more tiny bones of scandal to gnaw upon. If they'd suddenly sprouted whiskers and fur she'd not have been surprised.

'What are you looking at?' she cried. 'You're all the same: a load of small-minded, bigoted, hidebound fools. You'll never do anything for yourselves, never leave the islands, never take a single risk or do anything out of the ordinary. You'll marry some dull man and spawn a dozen dull children and die fat and tired and lumpen in your own stinking beds. Well, I want none of it and none of you!'

They stared at her in silence; then Kitten Sorensen started to laugh. Katla glared at her furiously, but all this served to do was to set the rest of them off as well, and it was with the sound of their derision, as shrill as the braying of a herd of donkeys, ringing in her ears that Katla Aransen left the steading at Rockfall for the last time.

She ran until she could run no more. She did not even know where she was going until she found herself down on the barnacle-covered rocks at the foot of the Hound's Tooth with the sea lapping away on the platform down below. Above her, the great granite spike reared up, hundreds of feet tall, glowing an improbable rosy gold in the afternoon sun. There were still flowers in bloom on the seaward ledges despite the lateness of the year: she could see their pale heads nodding in the breeze – sea-pinks and campions, the lavender-blues of scabious and vetch; and amongst them all the bright yellow rosettes of lichen she had only ever seen here in the Westman Isles. Suddenly, her fingers burned. Her palms itched. It was as if the rock were calling to her. Carefully, she slung the shortbow she had snatched up on her way out of the hall over her back and tucked its lower horn into her belt to stop it slipping. She tightened the knot which held her arrows in place, then slung the quiver across the opposite side and adjusted the leather strap until it was snug beneath her breast. Then, throwing her head back, she surveyed the extent of the cliff and the sunlight fell warm on her upturned cheeks. A gull slid past overhead, its shadow falling cold across her for a brief instant, then she stepped up onto the first ledge, inserted a fist into the cool depths of a ragged crack and laughed out loud as a dozen tiny springtails popped out of the crevice onto her arm and away into the rocks below.

The explosion of energy she received from the granite took her by surprise. She had been used, from her earliest years, to experiencing a certain rapture from the rock as she climbed, a certain connection with its surfaces, with its crystals and minerals, its smooth planes and its rough textures, but she had always considered this phenomenon to be some outward expression of her delight in the freedom her upward movement gave her, as if the life-force inside her was too great to be contained by mere skin and simply spilled out into whatever she came into contact with. Now, however, she knew it to be more than this. Whatever the seither had done to her, or whatever she had done to the seither, in that strange, powerful moment of gift and acceptance, had in some way involved a third force, something which had entered the moment from another place, beyond Rockfall, beyond the isles entirely.

Now she felt it again, this time as a constant presence which flowed into the muscles of her arms and thighs and made the usually steep and taxing climb seem a far less challenging prospect. Every time she reached up for a hold and curled her fingertips over the edge it was as if the rock flowed out to meet her and fused for a crucial second with her skin. Every time she poked a toe into a crack or balanced on a tiny incut, it seemed that the granite swarmed outwards, cupping her foot, ensuring that she didn't slip. It was like dancing – a slow, sensual combination of moves as elegant and formal as a courtly reel, something at which Katla had never excelled because it bored her so much. By the time she reached the summit and wrapped her hand around the final hold there – a huge, frictive lip that curled out and up into the bizarre shape of a rabbit's head – she could feel the blood beating gently but insistently through every inch of her body. Her head sang, her heart swelled. Sitting on soft pillows of sea-pink with the sun on her face, the tang of the salt-breeze in her nostrils and her feet dangling over the edge, she felt more alive than she had ever felt before.

For a few seconds she was in bliss; then the memory of the argument with her mother came flooding back to eclipse everything else like a black cloud across the sun.

Damn her, Katla thought. She unstrapped the bow and quiver, laid them down beside her on the spiky turf and kicked her heels hard against the rockface. Damn them all. The injustice of Bera's revelation made her face flame. It was not that she was ashamed of her liaison with the mummers' leader – far from it, in fact: when she examined the memory of that night and morning, as she did from time to time, taking it out as she might a keepsake cord, knotted with faded flowers and trinkets, all she felt was a terrible sadness at the loss of such a vital man, that she would never again have the opportunity to repeat that thrilling, forbidden coition – but that it was no one else's business and she hated that they would all tattle about her and think themselves better for keeping their legs closed and their minds set on a good marriage. It would be hard to return to the steading. She considered her options. They were few and far between: she could take a faering, hope the weather stayed fair and row the twenty miles of sea between here and Black Isle. But Black Isle was poor and she did not know what work or shelter she might find there:

its folk had enough difficulty fending for themselves at the best of times, and were unlikely to welcome an outcomer, especially the daughter of the Master of Rockfall, who had seduced all their men away on his wild-goose chase. She could row north into the choppier waters past the Old Man and on to Fostrey; but it was a more hazardous crossing and the place was largely deserted. She could stay on Rockfall and throw herself on the mercy of Old Ma Hallasen, for example. She had her bow and her arrow: she could bring in rabbits for the pair of them as part of the bargain. But the idea of kipping down with the mad woman's goats and her brace of odd cats was hardly attractive. The thought of returning to the steading, however, was worse by far.

Pride: she recognised it in herself and knew it as a failing, drove her to say things she did not entirely intend. But it could also be an attribute which drove her harder than those around her, and as such an advantage and a blessing. Even so, it was difficult to swallow; it sat hard and round in the throat and kept her spine rigid and her head up.

And it was then that she spotted the ship.

It came into view from her right, far out on the ocean, where it had just cleared the long, tapering line of jagged black cliffs which guarded Rockfall's eastern shores. It was a tiny silhouette at this distance, but even so, she could make out its clean lines and single dark, square sail. Her heart leapt up into her mouth. He had come back for her – of course he had, when he had realised Fent's cruel trick. Or they had met with ice which was after all too impenetrable at this time of year and had decided to wait till spring to relaunch the expedition . . .

She stood up and shaded her eyes, squinted into the bright sunlight. Should she run down to the harbour to greet them, or wave them in from up here on the Hound's Tooth? Somehow it seemed fitting that she should do the latter, waving madly from the same spot, give or take a few yards, where her beloved twin had left her bound and gagged.

So she sat and waited for the vessel's approach, grinning from ear to ear. She would get the chance to see the legendary Sanctuary after all. It was like a miracle, as if the voice she had heard in the rock, as if its presence and its force were watching over her with absolute beneficence. She could not help but grin from ear to ear.

Moments later, the ship tacked sideways to catch the wind and she saw the second sail, smaller, running out to a boom. Her hands flew up to her face. Not the *Long Serpent*, then; and possibly not an Eyran ship at all. She stared and stared, unable to believe what was coming ever more clearly into view.

At once, she was on her feet and running, yelling at the top of her voice, though there was no one for a mile or more to hear her. Down below, at the steading and around the harbour, women went about their tasks and their gossip without the slightest suspicion that, by the time the sun had set on Rockfall this night, the course of their lives would be changed forever.

Twenty-eight

Seafarers

Mam ran a hand down the length of Persoa's smooth back and sighed. Her mind was a delightful, rare blank: this was the closest she came to contentment and restfulness. That evening, just as the sun's light dipped, they had beached the ship on a wide sandy shore of the island known only as 'Far Sey', made a fire and cooked their first hot meal in several days. After half a keg of stallion's piss, the boiled mutton and wild leeks had been almost palatable: and most of the crew had made their way through a second keg, which had given her and the eldianna sufficient opportunity to erect a makeshift tent out of the spare sail and a framework of branches to keep prying eyes at bay. It had been four days since they had touched one another: shipboard life was hardly conducive to sexual liaisons for any but the most exhibitionist or intoxicated, and Mam had had an urgent need to feel his hands upon her. Now, by the flickering light of three lichen wicks floating in a bowl of seal-oil, she was examining his remarkable tattoo, tracing the lines with surprisingly gentle fingertips for a woman of such massive and ferocious appearance. On his long, lean, dark back, the intricate whorls and curlicues of his tribal markings exploded into an extraordinary riot of colours and shapes. The first time she had seen Persoa naked she had nearly fallen down in amazement: northern sailors sometimes came home from exotic climes with tattoos acquired while they were drunk and disabled in some seedy dockside dive, the generous gift of their so-called friends, and were usually either obscene or misspelt, often both; some made their own simple inked designs when bored at sea; but she had never in all her life seen anything remotely like the hillman's markings. Mythical creatures and places wrapped his entire torso, front and back, like one of the tapestries in the King's great hall. Personally, she had little interest in art or, even less, in artists (a more useless collection of self-involved, egotistical and spineless folk she could not even bear to imagine); and no time for those ridiculous tales of gods and goddesses, fabulous beasts and bizarre magics which so seemed to fascinate the rest of the population, both north and south; but even she had to admit that Persoa's tattoo was one of the wonders of Elda.

She had forgotten its mysteries while they had been apart – or perhaps had pushed them away into the recesses of her memory for the sake of ease of mind – and then had been too enraptured by other functions of his anatomy to spend much time in examining it while they were in Halbo, but now, sated and curious at last, and with the fitful light thrown by the improvised candles across his skin, she found herself fascinated once again. Across the wide planes of his back the Farem Hills gave way to the classic conical mountains of the southern range, with their fans of volcanic ash and smoking fumaroles. Above them, dark clouds floated like an omen, punctuated by flashes of lightning and downpours of rain and golden hail, while down below, stretching across Persoa's left flank and onto his belly, the scene of Falla's flight from some unseen pursuer played itself out in gorgeous detail. She was about to roll the hillman over, when something caught her eye: the Red Peak looked different. She peered closer. The great mountain appeared to have split apart in some way, exhibiting a flaming crimson interior. He must have had the design touched up recently.

'Nice work,' she said softly. 'Forent or Cera?'

For a moment there was no reply, then Persoa said dreamily, 'I don't know what you're talking about.'

'Your tattoo, my wildman; your tattoo. Did you get the new work done in Cera or Forent?'

Persoa rolled onto an elbow and turned to face her, his expression bemused. Mam found herself confronted by the sight of his dark golden chest and a belly licked by flame; and then became thoroughly distracted by the sight of his thick, velvety cock twitching back to life. With a firm hand she pressed him back onto his front and held him down with consummate ease. The hillman turned his face to her over one shoulder, and the candlelight reflected in depths of his black eyes.

'I am, as ever, all yours to do with what you will, my kitten.'

No one sane would ever think of calling Mam 'my kitten'. Uncle Garstan had once tried to call her 'my little cat' while bending her over a haybale in the byre and fumbling with her smallclothes; and as if to bear out this nomenclature, she had twisted in his grip like a feral beast and scratched his face as hard as she could. He'd not had the opportunity to repeat this exercise: she'd kneed him in the groin, stolen his knife and a small pouch of silver and left his farm for good. But when Persoa spoke to her thus, it made her want to purr.

'You've had your tattoo changed,' she said matter-of-factly, trying to focus that fact, rather than the other entrancing thing she had seen. 'The Red Peak is erupting.'

Persoa's face was a picture in itself; and not just for the swirls of dark ink. 'Erupting?'

'There's flames and smoke coming from it, and—' She picked up the candle and held it closer to his buttocks. Two or three small drops of hot oil slipped lazily over the lip of the dish. Persoa yelped and bucked, but Mam was not to be shifted from her purpose. 'And here,' she said, tracing the track of hair that ran down between the two big muscles,

'there's something else.' Leaning in, she spread his cheeks
with the powerful fingers of her other hand and the hillman
wriggled uncomfortably. 'Hold still,' she admonished him,
'I'm not going to do anything unnatural to you.' She paused,
grinning. 'Unless, that is, you wish it.'

Another drop of seal-oil spilled onto him and ran down
into the crack.

'I thank, you: no.'

'Well, see here – ah, you can't: well, let me tell you what
I see. The Red Peak has split apart near the roots of the
mountain and something has half-emerged from it – a figure,
it might be, though it's hard to tell in this light. Or in this
position.'

'A figure?'

'All black and spiky it is – like a goblin or a sprite.'

Now Persoa mustered his not inconsiderable strength and,
throwing off the mercenary leader, leapt away into the corner
of the tent, his face contorted with horror. The soapstone dish
went flying, hot oil flaming out across the dark space between
them, and a line of fire immediately ran up the edge of the
sailcloth. Seconds later, it had taken hold and their shelter
was well and truly alight, but even so, the eldianna remained
where he was, clutching his knees to his chest and moaning
over and over, 'The Warlord, the Madman, the Warlord, the
Madman; Lady help us all . . .'

Mam stood up and with her bare hands ripped the burning
sailcloth from its makeshift frame and hurled it away from
them. It roared through the night air like a comet, attracting
the attention of the rest of the crew.

'Gods blind me,' Joz Bearhand muttered, looking up from
his throw with the sheep's bones to take in this bizarre tableau.
He had never seen his leader unclothed before; and had never
had the least wish to do so, and now he knew why. If truth
be told, he liked his women well-formed, but not on such
a scale. He found himself wondering what in the world she

did with them to keep them out of her way in a fight and then remembered seeing the yards of stiff linen amongst her things he'd taken all this time for bandages. And bandages they were, in their way, though not for your regular sort of wound.

'Take a look at the pair on that,' Doc breathed in awe. 'Have you ever seen such monstrous— Ow!'

'Have some respect,' Joz chided him. 'If Mam knows you've been gawping at her tits, she'll be wearing your bollocks on a string round her neck before you can say "Feya's sweet box".'

After that, they all shut up.

Oddly, no one said a word about the episode for the rest of the night; nor indeed when they set sail again the next morning; and no one dared ask why the eldianna went about his tasks with the staring eyes of a man in shock, or why the tent had gone up in flames in the first place. As one of the younger Halbo sell-swords confided to Erno: 'She's a strong woman, Mam. The last time I saw a man rendered such a gibbering wreck was after he took on Three-handed Ketya and her sisters at the Sailors' Relief. Poor man never walked the same again.'

A knot of girls had gathered on the quay to wave and call out their greetings to the approaching ship: from her vantage point on the landward path down from the Hound's Tooth, Katla could just about make out the forms of Kitten Soronsen, Magla Felinsen and Thin Hildi – who appeared to have made a miraculous recovery from her collapse – out on the mole, along with Forna Stensen, Kit Farsen and Ferra Bransen and some old women who might be part of the Seal Rock clan, or were possibly Old Ma Hallasen and her friend Tian: at this distance it was hard to tell. What she could see, however, was that in the few seconds it had taken for someone to report the sighting of the sail and the general scramble from the hall down to the harbour, Kitten had somehow contrived to change her overdress and was now wearing her best scarlet silk tunic, which set off her hair and eyes so well. She was likely to attract rather more attention than she'd bargained for, wearing that, Katla thought grimly. And not from some good, honest northern sailor, either. She had given up trying to shout to them: all their concentration was towards the sea and no one was looking in her direction at all. Squinting, she could see Fat Breta wheezing her way down the steep path from the steading in the company of Marin Edelsen, and behind them Otter, Magla's mother, in company with the Mistress of Rockfall, Bera Rolfsen herself; and behind her came old Gramma Rolfsen leaning on her sturdy stick.

Gritting her teeth as a blackberry runner snagged hard across her shins, Katla redoubled her efforts. The ship was within striking distance of the sound now: surely anyone with eyes to see could tell that this was no Eyran vessel, let alone her father's elegant new ice-breaker? But the girls knew next to nothing about ships and the old women, who had seen southern vessels before in these waters twenty years and more before, were hazy of vision in these latter days. Katla cursed them all for their stupidity and their age. 'It's not the *Long Serpent*!' she wailed for the hundredth time, even though she knew that rather than carrying to the Rockfallers down below her voice would be wafted away into the rising heat of the air like the cry of a gull. Could she make it down there to warn them in time? It was a long way from the top of the Hound's Tooth down to the harbour; even by the easy path, which was three miles and more from summit to sea level, it would take a good half hour; and the easy path debouched in a more northerly part of the cliff from where the top of her ascent route had brought her out. This descent path was more direct, but it was far steeper, pocked with rabbit-holes which would happily swallow your foot and snap your ankle, and studded with boulders and outcroppings of granite hidden beneath wild flurries of brambles and gorse and bracken. If she did not watch every step she made, she was like to break her neck and die unseen and undiscovered and no use to anyone.

From this stance on the seaward face of the headland, the path now began to curl away from the coast, following a rock-filled gully down into the valley behind the harbour: she would not be able to see either ship or her folk for several minutes; and her cries would be masked by the landscape. Nothing for it now than to run and run and hope she could reach the women before the crew of the ship were able to disembark. *And if these are raiders, then what?* A voice nagged in her head. *None of them bears a weapon, nor knows one end of a sword from the other: what hope for them, if that is the case? Perhaps,* the voice insinuated, *it would be best if you were to cut your losses. After all, what more do they deserve after all they have said to you, the way they have treated you? Run inland and save yourself, slip around to the back of the steading and fetch your sword and belongings: make good your escape while the visitors are fully occupied down at the quayside . . .*

Katla growled softly. She had given up trying to understand whence such voices came, whether they were internal dialogues she held with herself or from some other source entirely. *Shut up!* she told this one sternly. *I cannot listen to you and run as hard as I must.*

Head down, the breath tearing raggedly through her chest, Katla ran.

The *Long Serpent* was indeed far, far away from its home port at Rockfall, and one could say not simply in terms of geography. The mists had cleared from around her mast and the men were rowing again; but they rowed through icy seas in mutinous silence, and their number was much diminished. Since the disappearances of Bran Mattson and Tor Bolson, three more men had gone missing, despite the constant watch set by the ship's captain. Aran Aranson had not slept for four days. His eyes were sore and red-rimmed, the sockets deeply outlined by thin skin as dark as a bruise. He was not always attentive to what was said around him, and when he did listen, he was short-tempered. He ate what Mag Snaketongue put before him, but without relish or comment; he declined to drink hard wine or ale; he consulted his map often. Most of the men avoided him; some gathered in small groups when their shift was done and spoke of losing one other man overboard and then turning the ship for home. None would know the truth of it, they said softly; but though they almost believed it, no one would volunteer to make the first move. Urse watched them and knew their thoughts. He gave Emer Bretison, their ringleader, a hard stare, saw how the big lad held it for several seconds before wavering away into confusion and knew they would not act on their conspiracy. He did all this not out of some misplaced loyalty to Aran Aranson, but because it was his view that they had of their own free wills joined the expedition, and that by setting foot on board the *Long Serpent* they had accepted all consequences of that initial act of greed and risk. The mysterious loss of his shipmates, however, fell somewhere outside this covenant: he did not know what to make of that enigma at all, except that, like his captain, he refused to give credence to tales of afterwalkers and spirits.

Once, in the depths of the night, he had heard a faint cry and a splash, but cloud had lain before the moon and he could see nothing. In the morning Jad the tumbler had been missing, though none save himself had seemed to mark the boy's absence; when they had, Fall Ranson had muttered darkly about the lad being exhausted by the rowing and in despair about reaching any destination other than Sur's Great Howe, until Flint Hakason had quieted him with 'And would you be next?'

Now the ice became thicker and harder to navigate.

Great white sheets of it spread northwards away from them through the near-constant half-light, split by snaking black leads and channels. The *Long Serpent* plunged into the first of these with Urse at the tiller, roaring directions to a crew mesmerised by their sudden new surroundings. The farther they penetrated into this freezing maze, the more bizarre the formations became. At first, there were merely small scatterings of hardened ice bobbing in the dark water like jewels. When these struck the hull it was with a noise quite out of proportion to their size, and the timbers rumbled and creaked as though they might burst apart at any moment. For hours on end, Aran lay half over the prow, fending off the larger lumps with a long gaff, but still a thousand of the smaller balls hammered into them, denting and scraping the hard oak of the strakes.

Under a chill pewter sky, smoky wisps of vapour curled up around the passage of the ship like gasts, hovering in the twilit air as if waiting their moment to coalesce and take their fearsome night-time shapes. They wreathed themselves around the form of the Master of Rockfall, silhouetted as he was out on the prow, as though they might insinuate themselves into his very being and take his body for their own. As the pewter gave way to the rose and violet of the arctic sunset, they entered another territory altogether; one which promised imminent sight of the mythological, for it was more bizarre than anything any of them had ever seen. At first they came upon bergs which towered around them like sentinels or giants or fabulous castles, the smooth planes of their ancient ice tinged with gold and vermilion and purple. As they passed, the ship's wake rolled out down the leads like tidal waves, and when these collided with the bergs it was with a sound like distant thunder.

'My god,' Mag Snaketongue breathed, his dark eyes dimly reflecting the sights before him, 'it looks like the end of the world.'

But things were only to get stranger.

As the light faded, they heard what sounded, freakishly, like a voice in the distance.

'Terns?' Jan asked, looking toward Flint Hakason.

The dark man cocked his head, like a dog listening to something beyond normal hearing range. 'Maybe kittiwakes,' he said after a pause. But he did not look convinced.

'It's too dark.' Aran Aranson declared, his face stern, 'and we're too far from land.'

'Fulmars,' Urse asserted. 'Sounds like fulmars to me.'

The rest of the crew listened. For several moments there was nothing to be discerned except the swirl of air over the surface of the floes, and the eddying of ice crystals which brushed their faces and caught in their beards. Then the noises came again, high and cracked and broken by both distance and wind.

For several moments the men of the *Long Serpent* strained towards the sound, their bodies frozen in stasis. 'By the Lord Sur,' Pol Garson said at last, and his voice was low with dread, 'it's a song.'

Now they could all hear it: the pitch and roll of notes on the wind, too rhythmic for nature, too melodic for chance; and too far from civilisation to be expected; yet still too distant from the ship to be anything but elusive and baffling to the ear.

Mag grasped his captain's arm. 'Let us turn back,' he urged, his fingers digging into the other man's biceps like claws. 'Let us go away from here before it is too late.'

'Aye, Captain, let's take to the oars at once!' cried Gar Felinson, his grizzled head nodding fervently with his request.

Urse One-Ear concurred. 'I do not like the sound of this at all.'

Now all the men were talking and moving at once, panic making their movements fast and jerky. Several ran to their rowing seats, set their oars in position and looked expectantly at their captain; others ran to the gunwales and stared fearfully into the darkness with their hands on the hilts of their daggers. Flint Hakason marched to the mastfish and unlashed one of the harpoons he kept there, his face set in the grimmest of expressions.

The noises got louder, resolved themselves into distinct and horrible particularity. Whatever it was out there in the darkness, it seemed to be experiencing some difficulty in carrying the tune, for the notes wavered reedily, or were swallowed away into the gathering gloom of the night. But despite all this, the lyric soon made itself apparent as belonging to a song all too familiar to every man present, it being *The Seafarer's Lament*:

> 'A maiden fair and free was she
> A maiden fair and free
> She gave herself so joyfully
> She pledged herself to me
>
> But I did travel far away
> Across the oceans blue
> Beyond the islands where she lay
> My own dear love, and true
>
> While over stormy seas I sailed
> A-dreaming of my lover
> Her love for me withered and failed
> She betrayed me with another
>
> Many a friend has gone from me
> As I have sailed the stormy sea
> And now the icy depths do call
> My path leads to the Lord Sur's hall
>
> For nothing keeps me here today
> All I care for has passed away
> My love, my heart, my youth and breath
> I wish for silence, peace and death.'

As the last notes died away, an apparition soughed into view: a battered boat with a tattered sail which flailed like rags in the breeze. It was a small faering; last hope of the storm-wracked and shipwrecked. Its timbers were damaged and weather-bleached, and of its parent ship there was no sign. The men of the *Long Serpent* made the sailor's sign against disaster and clutched their silver anchors as if the pendants had the power to ward off every evil in Elda. They craned their necks for sight of the singer, and for a long while the darkness obscured their view.

A few moments later, they wished it had continued to do so.

A solitary figure sat in the boat. Its face was blackened by the elements and its eyes were staring pits, reflecting the fire of the torch Aran Aranson held aloft. Gappy teeth showed through smeared lips. Its hair and beard were long and matted with some coarse substance which had also leaked down over whatever rags of clothing it had left to it. Its boots were gone, exposing one long white foot and a single grisly stump. In its hands it held what appeared to be a complex arrangement of ivory, whilst heaped all around it, as in one of the long barrows of legend, was a pile of bones and a scatter of skulls.

'By Feya's eyes!' cried Emer Bretison, unmanned by the implications of this appalling sight enough to call on the women's deity.

There was a rattle as Flint Hakason dropped the harpoon. 'God protect us!'

'Vile, murderous bastard!'

'How? What?' asked Fall Ranson slowly, his already-protruding eyes seeming to stand out as on stalks. He continued to stare and stare at the ossuary surrounding the figure in the faering without the least understanding of what he saw. 'The crew – what happened to the rest of the crew?'

'He's eaten them . . .'

Now they could not help but focus on details: how long legbones lay shattered and split open, the marrow gone; how a knife lay buried in what was left of a ribcage; how a skull had been cloven in two, revealing a glossy, empty cavity.

And at last, Urse: suddenly recognising the item the survivor clutched in his clawlike fingers. 'By the Lord Sur,' he uttered in horror. 'He's eaten his own foot . . .'

'He has, he has!' An insane shriek of laughter split the air. 'He's eaten his own foot!' Fent echoed, his wild eyes shining.

A moment later there came a strange whistling noise and a thud; and the cannibal fell backwards into the pile of bones. The pale stump of the survivor's leg twitched convulsively for a few seconds, then the corpse fell still. A harpoon lay embedded in his chest and beyond that ravaged cage, into the timbers of the faering. It was a weapon designed to secure a narwhal or a whale: unleashed on such puny prey, the force with which it struck was disproportionate, savage. Soon, dark wellings of seawater had begun to pool around the skeletal remains; in no time the faering was awash.

Aran Aranson turned his back on the deathly scene. He stalked across the deck of the *Long Serpent*, took his oar-seat and began to scull with a vengeance. Men took their places around him and unshipped their oars rapidly, relieved to have a practical task to set themselves to. Within minutes, the ship had passed the scene which would haunt each man until his dying day.

For some, that would come sooner than for others.

For Bret, the lad from the east shore, it was to be the last sight he laid his sweet blue eyes on; that and the dark wave that came up and engulfed him as Fent Aranson slapped one hand over his mouth and with the other pushed him roughly and swiftly over the side and into the churning wash of the ship.

Twenty-nine

Raiders

Even as Katla emerged from the twisting defile out into the heathland at the foot of the cliff it was already too late. By the time she had cleared the boggy mire around Sheepsfoot Stream and run full-tilt down the steep shingle lane past Ma Hallasen's bothy, where the old woman's ragtag collection of goats and cats watched her pass with similarly inimical golden, black-slitted eyes, the strange ship had entered the inner harbour and the women of Rockfall were in the agonisingly slow process of realising their error.

The vessel which even now was loosing its landing craft into the home waters of their port was not the *Long Serpent*; nor indeed, as Katla had realised precious minutes earlier, a northern ship at all, but a long, lumbering, lashed-together travesty of a boat from another continent entirely which had against all odds braved the hazards of the chancy Northern Ocean and won through intact. It was captained by a man even his friends (of which he had few, and those were now dead, in the main) called 'the Bastard', and crewed by a callous band of cut-throats, criminals and malefactors from every corner of the Southern Empire.

But rather than grasping these facts and at once taking to their heels, the women on the mole were transfixed by curiosity. The newcomers were exotically attired and weirdly cleanshaven. With their dark skin and darker hair, they looked nothing like the big, raw, fair-complexioned, shaggy-bearded men of the Northern Isles. Instead of homespun and leather, they wore bright-coloured silks and linens which shone with beads and metallic stitching. Their belts and chains were of silver and bronze; they had silver rings on their fingers and beaten silver bracelets on their arms, chalcedony necklaces and filigreed earrings encompassing droplets of amber which shone like gold in the falling sun. Instead of battered leather hauberks they wore gleaming mailshirts; instead of notched iron axes they carried slim silver swords which glimmered redly in the failing light.

'Run!' cried Thin Hildi, who was less stupid than she looked. 'Run, run for your lives!'

Ferra Bransen and Kit Farsen stared in disbelief as she lifted her skirts, revealing mismatched and wrinkled woollen stockings and a pair of pigshit-crusted pattens, and hared back up the mole, her wooden shoes clattering on the pitted stonework. There, she overtook Kitten Soronsen in her best crimson shift and Magla Felinsen, who stared openmouthed at her skinny, retreating backside as it jiggled past. 'Ridiculous creature,' Kitten sniffed haughtily, 'scared off by a bunch of traders. I wonder what they've brought with them? They are very finely turned out: perhaps they are showing some of their wares. I'd not say no to a look at some new jewellery and a length of bright emerald Galian silk—'

Beyond them, Thin Hildi encountered a knot of old women who called after her, 'Where are you off to so fast, Hildi Rabbitfoot; is your house burning down, or your dog eating the dinner?'

One of the Seal Rock women nudged her neighbour with a grin. 'She's gone to put on fresh drawers,' she chuckled lewdly, 'in case the smell of the ones she's got on drives all the men away!'

This kept them all cackling contentedly for several moments, by which time the first of the ship's boats had reached the seawall and two men had run up the iron ladders there, knives gripped in their teeth.

Even the sight of these ne'er-do-wells did not alert Magla Felinsen. She turned to her friend to comment on the elegance of their oiled black hair and their aquiline profiles and found Kitten Soronsen gone: her crimson figure a lurching shape at the landward end of the mole. When she turned back, the men were upon her. One of them grabbed her roughly by the wrists and held her there with one hand, his head cocked assessingly. With the other hand, he squeezed her left breast hard.

Magla was enraged. If a northern man had conducted himself so, even in his cups, she could have demanded that her male relatives chastise him with their fists and knives, or have had him driven off, or force him to cough up a hefty fine. He and his entire family would have been shamed by his behaviour. He would never have been able to marry well in the region and would most likely have had to take to the high seas for the rest of his life.

It was a brave or foolhardy man who would take on Magla Felinsen. She was a woman well known in the Westman Isles for her loud and unforgiving mouth, and this she turned upon her attacker now.

'Take your hands off me you filthy heathen! How dare you touch me so without the least word of greeting or any formal introduction! You should be ashamed of yourself, groping a woman in such a way. Do they teach you no manners where you come from? Where do you come from, anyway?'

The man recoiled from this tirade with a look of distaste. Holding Magla away from him at arm's length, he turned to his companion and uttered something complex and unintelligible in the sibilant southern tongue, and the other man laughed and returned a comment of his own. Then, with an expression of the utmost nonchalance, he drew his free hand back and punched her hard in the face.

Magla's eyes went wide with shock. Then she crumpled to the ground.

The sight of Magla Felinsen thus assaulted reduced the other women to complete panic. Forna Stensen, Kit Farsen and Ferra Bransen all shrieked and took to their heels, almost catching up with Kitten Soronsen in their desperate flight. The old women stopped gabbling and gawping, grabbed up their skirts and legged it for the path with an unlikely turn of speed for such ancient crones, looking for all the world like a bunch of hedgehogs surprised by a fox and sprinting for the cover of the bramble-patch. Fat Breta, all red in the face with the effort of running down the hill to the harbour, now took a gulping great breath, turned around and wheezed her way back up, with little Marin Edelsen pulling her by the hand.

Bera Rolfsen, the Mistress of Rockfall, was entirely bemused. She and Otter Garsen had been walking sedately down to the quay, deep in conversation as to the merits of punishment and reward in the raising of difficult daughters and had thus failed to observe the details of the incident involving the latter's wayward child and the Istrian sailor. It was only when Thin Hildi dashed past them crying 'Raiders, raiders!' followed swiftly by Kitten, head down and running so hard she did not even notice the rips and tears the thorn bushes were dealing to her bare shins, that they realised something was surely amiss.

Bera scanned the scene below, saw how even the old women were moving swiftly away from the harbour and instantly appraised the situation.

'My god, Otter,' she said, catching the other woman hard by the arm. 'I suspect these newcomers are not the sort of visitors we wish to welcome to our shores or our hearths. Let us make our way back to the steading, barricade the doors and make such a stand there as would make our husbands proud.' She waved to the women running up the path towards her. 'Quickly, quickly – back to the hall!'

'But—' Otter started, squinting at the scene on the seawall in horrified recognition '—what about my daughter?'

Bera gazed dispassionately down at the mole. 'I do not think there is anything we can do to save her at the moment,' she said firmly, 'and it will hardly ameliorate matters if we allow ourselves to be taken by these raiders, too.' She paused. Then: 'Can you shoot a bow, Otter?'

The older woman stared at her in disbelief and her mouth fell open. She thought for a moment. 'Well enough . . .' she said doubtfully.

'Then,' said Bera Rolfsen, gripping her by the shoulder, 'we shall do what we can to save ourselves, and then her.'

From the gap between the hawthorns where the path took a sharp turn back on itself, Katla was afforded a single tantalising glimpse of the events unfolding down below in Rockfall's harbour. She watched as two of the visitors lifted the form of Magla Felinsen aboard one of their ship's boats and frowned. Was she dead? Unconscious? What had happened here? She couldn't quite imagine why foreign men – or any man, for that matter – would want Magla Felinsen either dead or alive, though she was prepared to admit she might be a little prejudiced on the subject and that you could never account for taste. She was, however, relieved to see that something had occurred to turn the tide of the women's curiosity and that they were all fleeing back up towards the steading. She assessed her choices.

She could slip back up the Hound's Tooth and lie low till the trouble had blown itself out. This seemed attractive for a brief, spiteful moment which passed like a butterfly on the breeze, despite the low urging of that other voice. She could run back to the steading and join the others in whatever defence they could put together there; but this idea she dismissed almost immediately. She was one of very few who could wield a weapon and she'd be wasted at close quarters, jostling for elbow-room amongst a hall full of panicking and useless women. She'd have to swallow her pride and take orders from her mother, too: unthinkable. Better, then, out in the open on her own. Out in the open, she could run and shoot and stab and take the enemy by surprise. And, she thought with terrible pragmatism, if the worst did happen, she would not perish like a trapped rabbit, holed up in the hall with the other women, but outside, with a sword in her hand.

She ran on, looking for a suitable spot for an ambush.

Exhibiting an unlikely turn of speed for a woman who had borne eight children, five of whom had perished in childhood and a sixth in his twenty-fifth year, and been weighed down by her daily tasks for well over twenty years, Bera Rolfsen sprinted up the harbour-track towards Feya's Cross, the intersection with the path which ran down from the steading's enclosure. Here, the hawthorns knit themselves together to form a natural arch over the track which during the fifth moon's cycle became a froth of white blossom exuding a rank and sexual scent of blood and heat – as was only fitting for trees dedicated to the fertility goddess. In earlier times it had been a Rockfall tradition for girls who wished to wed to rise before dawn on the first day of spring and run down to the strand to sit in the dark at the water's edge, thinking about the lad they loved while the sea washed up between their legs, praying to Sur for his favour. Bera Rolfsen remembered the day she had done this herself, dreaming of a tall young man with a chiselled face and intense, deepset eyes, how she had run back up the path and stood beneath the arch of may until the first rays of the sun had filtered down between the branches to freckle her face with rosy light and then stretched up and picked a single sprig of blossom from the centre of the arch without mishap, and with it Feya's blessing. And – superstition or not – her wish had come true: three days later Aran Aranson had ridden his sturdy little pony over the crest of the island to ask for her hand. Over the years, however, the apex of the arch had become higher and more difficult of access as a result of this constant Mayday pruning, until that it was only a very athletic girl who could succeed in the feat of picking a spray without the thorns pricking her or ripping her shift. Either presaged disaster: a single drop of blood spilled meant miscarriage of the first child; torn fabric a rift in the marriage; or worse still, no wedding at all. Soon, no one seemed able to carry out the task without inviting disaster and the ritual was abandoned. Even so, the spot remained a site invested with much sacred dread and excitement by the girls of the island.

The Mistress of Rockfall rounded the corner into Feya's Cross now and almost fell over Kitten Soronsen, who was lying half across the path and half in the hedge, trying feverishly to disentangle her red shift from the hawthorn without tearing the silk. Her pretty beaded slipper – a gift from Haki Ulfson, and a thoroughly impractical item of footwear for running full-tilt up a rough track – lay empty and wedged beneath an exposed root in the middle of the path, bearing mute witness to her fall.

'For Sur's sake, girl!' Bera snapped, taking in this tableau, 'Get up and run!'

Kitten turned a tear-stained face to the Mistress of Rockfall. 'I can't,' she sobbed. 'My dress is caught on the thorns. It's my best one, my – oh!'

Bera stood over her, a length of ripped red silk in her fists. Her knuckles were white.

Kitten looked horrified. 'Now I shall never marry!'

'If you do not make it to the safety of the steading, it'll be more than your pretty little shift that gets ripped,' Bera returned grimly, and watched the girl quail. 'Get into the hall and gather up sticks and staves and anything that may be thrown to do hurt,' she continued, dragging Kitten to her feet. 'Or none of us shall henceforth have the luxury of choosing the man with whom we lie!'

Her face as white as the Mistress's knuckles, Kitten Soronsen leapt to her feet and ran away from Feya's sacred hawthorns as fast as her legs could carry her.

Bera caught her breath, then redoubled her pace. At the top of the hill, she spied Thin Hildi's scrawny figure climbing the wall into the home enclosure.

'Hildi! Hildi!' she cried.

Wobbling on the rockover point of the wall, the girl looked over her shoulder, saw that it was the Mistress of Rockfall who addressed her so peremptorily and promptly fell backwards into the meadow.

Bera crested the rise, sprinted across the rough grass and scaled the stone wall with surprising agility. 'Come with me!' she ordered, grabbing Hildi by the arm to drag her upright.

Having no choice in the matter, Hildi obeyed, though her feet stumbled to catch up with the rest of her. Thus connected, they sped across the meadow towards the smithy. Once inside, Bera let go of Hildi's arm and took down the ring of keys which hung from the wall above the tool bench. The two dozen iron keys clanked unhelpfully together. She stared at them in disbelief, having little idea which key fit which lock in hall, barn, smithy, stable or store, then threw them down onto the stone floor in disgust.

'No time for niceties,' she declared, grabbing up an iron bar from the bench. A moment later she was prying unceremoniously at a massive oak chest which served as the steading's weapons store. Two moments later, the wood around the lock splintered apart. She stared into its dark interior.

'Sur's teeth!' she swore loudly.

Thin Hildi's hands flew to her mouth. She had never heard the Mistress of Rockfall curse: she was such a genteel woman, always punctiliously polite even when furious.

'Sur's giant prick and bollocks!' Bera went on, delivering a vicious kick to the box.

The chest was empty apart from a couple of rusty old knives and a handful of arrows with loose heads. Someone had taken everything they stored there against just such an emergency, but whether all the weaponry had been dealt out to Aran's expeditionary force, or whether someone else had helped themselves to the contents, she could not imagine. Strangest of all was why anyone having rifled the contents so thoroughly would then go to the trouble of relocking the chest. Unless they wished the theft to go unnoticed.

There was no point in further conjecture. She looked around determinedly. On the shelf below the bench was the beautiful sword Katla had promised Tor Leeson's mother, and the two daggers she had been making as show pieces. The latter were awaiting Katla's fine niello work, and were as yet dull and unadorned. As ornamental daggers they would win no prizes; but the points and edges were forged as sharp and true as any warrior's blade.

Three weapons, no matter how well forged, would hardly see off a band of ruthless raiders. Bows and arrows, spears and javelins were what they needed: they must hold the visitors at a distance or they'd be lost entirely, for she'd give long odds against their chances if they had to fight hand to hand with strong, trained men.

At least there were throwing spears, a dozen or more, racked along the eastern wall. Bera grabbed up the knives and sword and thrust them at Hildi. Then she took down spear after spear and pushed them into the girl's arms until she could carry no more. 'Take these and run back to the steading!' she said urgently, and spared no time watching the girl's staggering gait as she trailed awkwardly back towards the hall.

The barn, Bera thought suddenly. Aran and the boys always kept their bows in the barn.

Running swiftly across the courtyard, and praying that they had not been taken on board the *Long Serpent* (for what? her mind questioned ironically: shooting gulls in dull moments between fending off icebergs and stormwaves?) she had a clear view between the trees and noted that several of the women were now in sight at the top of the hill, and that down in the harbour, the raiders had disembarked onto the quay and split into two groups. One group had fanned out to the east and were running into the defile that led up past the Hound's Tooth. They would have little joy in that direction, she thought with a bitter smile. Unless they had a penchant for goats and cats. You did hear odd things about pirates and raiders; anything was possible: Old Ma Hallasen's beasts had better be prepared to defend their virtue. The rest were pursuing the fleeing women, and had almost gained on Ferra Bransen, whose skirts were impeding her progress.

Nothing to be done there. Setting her jaw, Bera ran the hundred yards between the smithy and the barn and found – thank Sur! – Aran Aranson's long hunting bow hanging where he always kept it, and a fine sheaf of arrows wrapped in oilcloth below it. She unwrapped the cloth with a swift flick and counted a couple of dozen ash shafts fletched with swan's feathers. Good, but not good enough. These arrows were made for long flight; she would also need some sturdy yew shafts for use at closer range. A quick scout of the tack room offered further hope: three more shortbows and a bucketful of shafts of varying types and age. Many were black and pitted with age and pocked with rust, and some had barbs which had broken off in some unfortunate prey; but Bera Rolfsen did not give a rat's arse for their condition: what was to come was hardly likely to be a contest with points awarded for skill or precision.

Scooping this trove into her arms, the Mistress of Rockfall hared across the hard-packed ground between the barn and the hall as fleetly as a girl of eighteen. By the time she reached the door, the first of the raiders was clearing the top of the hill. There was no time to waste.

'Bar the doors!' she cried, hurling her harvest of bows and arrows to the floor, where they spilled with a great clatter.

'Ferra is not here yet—' someone started.

'We cannot wait for her!' Bera slammed the wooden door shut and dragged the iron latch and lock across it. 'The benches!' she shouted. 'Barricade the door with benches!'

The women did as they were told without another word of protest. Otter Garsen ran to the pile of weaponry, swiftly selected a whippy long-bow of elm and ran to the far end of the hall where a ladder led up into the loft-space. There, she climbed stiffly up into the eaves and with her belt-knife began to dig away at the turf from the underside. 'Help me!' she called down, and one of the Seal Rock women caught her meaning and came running and together, they began to excavate a hole in the roof.

'Who amongst you can use a bow?' Bera demanded loudly.

Her question seemed to fall on deaf ears. No one made any response. She looked from one woman to another, saw how they looked away shamefaced, perceiving a lack in themselves they would never have perceived as a lack before. At last Tian Jensen said, 'My eyes are not what they were but in my younger days I stuck a few rabbits.'

Bera picked up a long-bow and a dozen swan-flighted arrows and handed them to her. 'You'll find your targets may make up for your eyesight,' she said, 'for these men are somewhat larger than rabbits and may not run so quick, either.' She turned to Morten Danson, sitting so quietly in the shadows at the back of the hall that it was as if he were trying to melt away into them altogether, and fixed him with a sharp look. 'And you, sir shipmaker, which would you rather – a hunting bow to take them out from the roof or a sturdy shortbow for closer range?'

The shipwright held her gaze. 'I have no quarrel with these men,' he said.

Bera laughed bitterly. 'Ah, but do they know that?' she said, almost to herself. She selected a shortbow of yew and horn and threw it to him. He fumbled, then caught the bow before it hit the floor and stared at it as if it were a conger eel and he had no idea which end to hold to stop it biting him. The arrows which followed it clattered around down him. He sat there for a moment, looking bemused, then gathered them up and made his way to one of the windows.

Bera assessed the meagre weaponry they had accumulated. Then she marched around the hall, doling them out: a spear for the young and fit, who might stand some chance of using it; a dagger for all those but the most arthritic, who could not grasp one anyway. Kitten Soronsen she came to last. 'Spear or dagger?' she asked softly. The pretty girl's face was pale, smeared with blood from the thorns and stained with tears. Her eyes were as large and round as an owl's.

With shaking hands, Kitten took up one of the showpiece daggers. 'I never thought I would say such a thing, but I wish now I had trained with Katla when she asked me to,' she said softly.

Gramma Rolfsen took an elm-shafted spear with a cruelly barbed head. 'Any man running onto this,' she announced, 'will not be going far.'

The sword that her daughter had forged for Tor's mother, Bera kept for herself. It felt beautifully weighted in her hand, surprisingly light and powerful. Her palm buzzed from the contact as if with a live thing. She executed a few assessing twists and turns with the blade, remembering the only lesson she had ever had from her husband almost twenty years before when he had sailed out with his father to war against the Southern Empire. 'Eyran weapons are for stabbing and slashing,' Aran had told her. 'Do not be too delicate with the blade: try to take an attacker on at elegant swordplay and you are lost. Put all your weight behind a stroke and you can take a man's leg or arm off, shearing straight through the bone. And once you have done that, you need no longer worry about him.'

She shuddered and sheathed the blade. With luck it would not come to that. Picking up a hunting bow and a quiver of arrows, she ran up the ladder and swarmed up through the ragged new hole in the roof to join Otter and the Seal Rock woman, there to greet the visitors.

The wind was fair from Far Sey. Erno stood at the helm and felt the sting of the salt wind as it whipped his hair across his face. The only way they might sail faster was if the ship were to sprout wings, which seemed unlikely, since in all of Elda only Sur's own ship, the *Raven*, a vessel possessed of rather special powers, had been known to have done so. But with the sun shining down and an unseasonable warmth encouraging the grey seals to bask in the waters around the islands, he had the inalienable sense that all was well with the world and that Katla Aransen – despite the strange history between them – would soon be in his arms. It had, he reminded himself for the thousandth time, been on her command that he had sailed away from the Moonfell Plain; though why she had urged him to do so still remained hazy. It was only in his dreams now that memories of the Istrian woman returned to him, and when he caught the fleeting tails of such dreams, he thought her dark hair and gentle eyes a figment, a concoction of his senses, and felt the guilt roll over him like a stormcloud.

'We'll see Rockfall harbour by dawn tomorrow,' came a voice at his shoulder.

He turned to find Joz Bearhand there. The giant of a man was barely a knuckle's length taller than he was: they stood almost eye to eye. The older man's grey eyes were shrouded and watchful.

'Aye,' nodded Erno. 'At last.'

'I hope we shall be in time to find the shipmaker there.'

'Where else would he be?'

'If he's been stolen to make Aran Aranson a ship, out on the ocean main, I'd think.'

'I'd heard Morten Danson was a landman,' Erno grinned. 'Never set foot on a ship that wasn't firmly anchored in a safe harbour.'

Joz shook his head. 'I do not understand how such a man can build ships which can withstand the strictures of an arctic storm.'

Erno thought about this for a moment. Then he said: 'Katla Aransen has never to my knowledge been to war, yet she forges the finest weapons this side of the Northern Ocean.'

Joz Bearhand patted his sword hilt fondly, then gave a concessionary shrug. 'Ah, she is an exceptional woman, I'll give you that.'

'I'm going to wed her,' Erno said firmly.

A great gale of laughter burst out of the huge mercenary. Erno regarded him fiercely. 'Why do you laugh so?'

The older man wiped a hand across his eyes. 'Lad,' he started, 'you have a great deal to learn about the world if you think your life will progress so simply. Women are odd and contrary creatures,' he paused, to consider this statement, then continued. 'And Katla Aransen is, I have to say, one of the odder of the breed. She is of such a character that it does not lead me to imagine she will come to you like a meek little heifer led on a gilded rope.'

This conjured in his mind a somewhat unlikely image. 'I know it,' Erno said fervently, remembering her feisty nature and odd turns of humour; her pigheaded opinions and her unconventional views about marriage and children. Then he remembered her wild hair and her laughing eyes, and the way she had kissed him outside the King's tent at the Gathering. Suddenly his heart felt high and clear.

What could possibly go wrong?

Katla Aransen was certainly at her wildest now. Having scaled a granite outcrop above the path out of the harbour she had taken up a stance there, shielded by a dense bank of gorse. She had allowed a dozen of the men to pass her without mishap: there was nothing in this direction for them anyway but Ma Hallasen's bothy and the tumbledown ruins of the old fishing community at Seal Point, before the Great Storm had drenched that part of the island and the survivors had moved away. Her concentration was bent on the stragglers. She had one sighted down the shaft of her arrow between the grey fletchings, her eyes following his movements as keenly as a falcon's might the progress of a shrew in the grass. The first of the stragglers was dragging an unwilling Ferra Bransen along the path, while a second man cut her dress from her back in measured sweeps of his elegant sword so that strips of the linen fluttered in ribbons to the ground. They were having a high old time of it, laughing and joking in their pretty southern tongue. Ferra's face was bruised where they had hit her and one eye was swollen shut and crusted with blood. Katla waited until their companions had disappeared around the bend in the path, then drew back her hand until she felt the perfect tension in the string, and released it with a whisper.

The arrow took the first man so cleanly that he did not even have the chance to utter a sound. Nocking another shaft in an instant, Katla sighted on the second man with a gleeful grin. It was the first time she had ever knowingly killed another human being and it felt remarkably satisfying.

The second man stared about him in confusion, unable to fathom what had just happened. His companion had pitched face forward onto the path, with the arrow – a short, sturdy quarrel fashioned by Katla's own hand from yew and iron and designed for rabbit-hunting – buried so deep in his eye that his head was resting at a relatively normal angle for a man asleep, or suddenly unconscious. Meanwhile, Ferra Bransen (who had the brains of a sheep, Katla thought) instead of legging it for safety as any sound-minded person would have done under the circumstances, stood rooted to the ground in open-mouthed horror, her hands batting madly about as if she was swatting flies. With a sigh, Katla shot the second man as realisation of the ambush struck him. The shaft took him neatly in the centre of the chest with a thud, and he fell over backwards into the brambles.

It seemed almost too easy. Easier than shooting rabbits, certainly.

Katla waited to make sure no one was going to double back to find two of their number dead and look for the culprit, then she swarmed down the earthy bank at the back of the outcrop and emerged onto the path a moment later with her bow and quiver swung over her shoulder and a short sword in her hand, just in case.

'Come on, Ferra, let's get you somewhere safe,' she said, gripping the girl by the arm.

But whilst Ferra's body might be standing there on the path to Seal Point, her mind was somewhere else entirely. She stood like an afterwalker with the dying sun reflecting in one unblinking pupil and made no move to save herself at all. Katla rolled her eyes. 'By the lord,' she grumbled, getting a shoulder under Ferra's left armpit, 'you deserve to die, so you do.'

A vast amount of sweaty effort got Ferra Bransen to the relative safety of the fish-drying sheds. Katla stashed her inside with a sigh of relief, bolted the door to stop her from stumbling out, wailing like a gast, and then made for the steading.

Captain Galo Bastido drew his men to a halt at the wall surrounding the steading's home meadow.

'Remember,' he warned them, 'our priority here is to capture the man called Morten Danson and take him back to Lord Rui Finco alive and unharmed so that he may fashion ships for the Istrian war effort. After we have him safe and secure then, and only then, may you have your way with the women.'

He watched the Forin brothers, Milo and Nuno, exchange an amused glance, as if nothing their leader could say was going to stop them having their fun, saw how Pisto Dal stroked his scarred cheek thoughtfully, and how the two swordsmen stood back as if waiting for others to do the dirty work for them. It might well be dirty work, too, he thought, assessing the view in front of them. The steading's main hall was a long, low structure built sturdily from timber, stone and turf. It was designed to withstand high winds and lashing rains, debilitating frosts and freezes. The main door was closed tight and no doubt bolted and barricaded from behind. There were three women up on the roof with weapons in their hands, looking defiant. There was, however, not a single man in sight which was a curiosity in itself, and though he could glimpse a crowd of faces at each of the small, hide-shrouded windows, he could have sworn not a one of them wore a beard. But whether the hall was occupied by men or by women, it made no odds to the Bastard. He had been in similar situations before and he knew how such a building might be taken. And it was not without considerable loss of life.

He climbed the wall and stood carefully out of arrowshot. 'Greetings to you people of Rockfall!' he shouted in the Old Tongue and waited for a response.

None came. The women on the roof stood there, nocking arrows to the strings of their bows as nonchalantly as if they were about to shoot chickens for fun, as he and his brother had as children on their grandfather's farm. One of them looked old enough to be his grandmother.

He drew a deep breath and went on: 'My name is Galo

Bastido and I am the captain of this force. Istria has declared war on your islands and we have come from the Empire city of Forent on behalf of its lord to bring back the shipmaker, Morten Danson. Send him out to us and we will sail away and leave you in peace. If you do not, we shall take him by force and many of you will die unnecessarily!'

Behind him, he heard Baranguet crack his knuckles and make a bawdy comment to his neighbour.

A slightly built woman – one of the three standing on the roof – who wore her hair in two long, deep red braids, took it upon herself to speak for the people of the island. 'Be off with you!' she shouted in the Old Tongue, her Eyran accent rendering the words harsh and guttural. 'We have no intention of opening our doors to you or allowing anyone to be taken onto your vessel without a fight.'

Bastido laughed. 'I can assure you, madam, that you do not wish to pick a fight with us! I have here thirty trained warriors, all raring for a scrap!'

'And I have fifty!' Bera lied.

'Fifty defenceless women, more like!' Baranguet called out. 'And each of them ripe for the picking if you are anything to go by!'

His captain rounded on him furiously, though he kept his voice low. 'It would be far better to take the shipmaker without a battle, Master Whip; wounded women fetch a poor price on a slave block . . .'

Up on the roof, Otter Garsen took the Mistress of Rockfall by the arm. 'Bera,' she urged in a low whisper, designed for no one else, including the Seal Rock women behind them, to hear, 'perhaps we should let the shipmaker go to them. What good is he to us, except to send the lot of us to Feya's weaving room for all eternity?'

'No,' Bera returned fiercely. 'Morten Danson has already undergone the indignity of being abducted by my family, and I have lost one of my sons into the bargain. He may not be a man much to my taste, but I will not hand him over to a rabble of Empire mercenaries like this. The Rockfall clan has some pride left.'

'They look like fearsome men,' Otter continued. 'What chance do we stand against them?'

'That we shall soon discover.'

'Can you not at least lie and say Morten Danson is not here?'

Bera snorted. 'We Rockfallers do not lie. It is a matter of honour.'

'Honour will see us all die.'

'If we do, it will be with honour, nevertheless.'

'Then it shall be with many of our enemies lying dead at our feet,' Otter declared grimly.

Bera Rolfsen said nothing more. Instead, she waved her sword at the Istrians. 'Women we may be: defenceless we are not. If you imagine we represent an easy harvest, you and your men may try your luck, Captain Galo Bastido; but you will find no easy pickings here, and the only crop you will reap shall be one of spears and arrows!'

Bastido shrugged. 'Ah well, madam,' he called back, 'have it your own way. You cannot say we did not give you a fair chance!' He turned to his men. 'Try not to hurt them too much,' he said loudly, 'at least not visibly. Remember each of them alive and hale will fetch over three hundred cantari in Gibeon's market!'

Just as the Istrains began to move forward, one of their number cried out suddenly and fell down. It was one of the north coast men, a wiry, dark-skinned man known as 'the Gutter', who'd worked the fishing fleet off Cera for over twenty years and had a way with a gutting spike. Fittingly, an arrow jutted out of his abdomen. He writhed about like a thrashing snake, clutching the shaft with gore-slimed hands and making the most horrible noises, until Baranguet cut his head off and quieted him. 'Belly wound,' he said matter-of-factly to Bastido, who looked faintly appalled. 'They rarely survive a belly wound, and he was making a terrible racket.'

Pisto Dal laughed. 'I never liked him much anyway.'

It was left to Clermano, the most seasoned of them all, to wonder whence the stray shaft had come. It had taken the Gutter, who had been standing towards the back of the group, in the left side; and it seemed too long a shot to have come from the hall.

Clermano was not the only one wondering this. Otter turned to the Seal Rock woman; but her arrow was still nocked; and Bera had not yet opened her quiver. She called down into the hall below, 'Did one of you do that? Speak now!'

It was left to Kitten Soronsen to reply. 'No one here has loosed an arrow: how that came about is as much a mystery to us as it is to you.'

Oblivious to the snagging thorns, Katla Aransen climbed swiftly down from her stance on top of the hawthorn arch and sped silently west, in the lee of a drystone wall, her bow bumping against her spine. Where the wall turned at a right angle to meet the home field, she stopped and peered over. She was now directly behind the raiders, some of whom were engaged in slinging the headless body of their recently dead companion into a ditch, whilst the rest were opening quivers and nocking their ornate, southern-style bows. *Not much range on those*, Katla noted. *They'll have to get in close to the steading to be effective.* She saw how her mother and the women on the roof of the hall had their arrows trained on the visitors and nodded in appreciation. She had never seen her mother in such a light before. Her chest swelled with unexpected pride.

The raiders fired off a few testing bolts, which flew straight and true, but fell well short of their intended targets. Their leader said something to his men in the hissing Empire speech, and they began to advance. *Go on*, thought Katla, *just another few yards . . .*

Another few yards and Otter Garsen made good on her promise, taking one of the raiders right through the throat with a quarrel fletched with black-tipped goose feathers.

One of mine, Katla thought cheerfully, beginning to enjoy the situation. She extracted a similar arrow and fitted it to the hunting bow. Then she sighted it on a big man wearing his black hair in a tail and his right ear ringed with silver. With a whisper, the shaft whipped through the air between them and took the southerner between the shoulderblades. No question as to where that shot had come from: like a hare she scurried the length of the wall, keeping well down all the way. At the corner, she bobbed up. Three shafts looped over her head. She felt the breeze from them skim her hair. Two of the raiders detached themselves from the group and came after her.

'Nuts!' swore Katla, and ran away down the hill towards the copse, whooping with laughter. Once in the stand of oaks there, she shinned up one of the rough-barked monsters and pressed herself along a branch. It was awkward drawing the bow in such a position, but she and Halli had mock-hunted one another since the age of four, and she always won. The first man came crashing into the wood like a boar on heat. She shot him in the chest. The second man arrived a few seconds later. There was no way she could sight another arrow on him in time. Slipping her arm through the bow to stop it falling, she took her thigh-knife out of its sheath and waited for an opportune moment. This man was more wary than the first. He did not see his fallen companion until he had trodden on his outflung arm; but instead of bending to examine the body, he leapt away backwards and Katla's knife embedded itself in the moss where he had been standing.

He turned his face up to the oak. A puckered scar ran the length of one cheek, gathering the skin on either side into obscenely pink and shiny folds, which stood out harshly against the walnut brown of the rest and the corner of his mouth was pulled up into a ferocious half-grin which exposed two sharp yellow teeth just like a rat's. Fascinated by the disgusting irregularity the scar gave to his features, Katla scanned his face, then watched in horror as his black eyes fixed on her amongst the yellow, thinning leaves and the left side of his mouth curved up to match the right.

'Got you!' he said in the Old Tongue.

It was the last thing Pisto Dal said. Katla's second knife, a finely weighted object with a chunk of sardonyx in the hilt and a damascened blade, inserted itself with a gristly thump in the place where his nose would normally be. She watched his eyes roll down to view this new protuberance, then back into his skull. His legs folded under him and he crumpled to his knees, ending his life in the traditional position of the devout Falla worshipper.

'No,' Katla said softly, letting herself down out of the oak. 'Got *you*.'

By the time she had retrieved and cleaned her precious knives and got back to the top of the hill, matters had taken a turn for the worse. The raiders had got in close to the hall, too close now for arrow-shot from the windows. Only two of their number lay dead in the home meadow, though several dozen goose-fletched shafts pincushioned the ground. Several spears lay scattered like sticks. Another two men were limping, and had bloody fabric tied tightly around their legs, at calf and thigh respectively. Some of them had swarmed up the corner of the hall and made it onto the low turf roof. Of Bera and Otter there was no sign. One of the Seal Rock women, however, lay unmoving up there with two thick shafts protruding from her torso. The men on the roof were digging at the turf.

Inside the hall, Bera Rolfsen had something of a mutiny on her hands.

'Send him out!' demanded Tian Jensen again. 'He's not one of us: we don't care what happens to him.'

For his part, Morten Danson looked like a man in shock. His face was still and white and his hands were shaking. Even so, 'Send me out then, Mistress Bera,' he said. 'They want me to build ships for them: they cannot afford to kill me.'

'That we will not,' Bera returned fiercely. 'Even if it would save the lives of those few of us here, to allow them to take you will result in many more lives being lost in the long run if you help to build them a fleet of vessels with which to storm Eyran shores.'

The shipmaker hung his head. He did not know what to say. He did not want to be taken captive by these rough foreign men, that was for sure; but neither did he wish to be held responsible for the deaths of these mad Rockfall women. Besides, if the raiders took the hall by force, might he not be killed anyway, by accident?

'He could build flawed ships for them,' suggested Forna Stensen guilefully. 'Then they would sink in the Northern Ocean and take their accursed crews down with them and Sur can build up the walls of his howe with their bones.'

Morten Danson nodded vigorously. 'I could, I could!'

Bera laughed bitterly. 'If you think they will leave us be when they have their hands on you, then you are a greater fool than even I took you for, Master Shipwright. Once they have you safely bound, they will come for us: they may well be happy to collect whatever fee this Lord of Forent may pay them for your safe delivery; but these are not men who will be so easily satisfied.' She turned to the gathered women and addressed the room at large. 'Take a look at them. These men are a rabble, a mob of hired hands and ne'er-do-wells who would sell their own mothers, grandmothers, aunts and lovers if it would make them a single cantari of profit or gain them a moment's advantage. You have all heard tales of the Southern Empire and the illicit appetites of their men. They respect women so little that they cover every piece of them except those parts which may accord pleasure. And you saw what they did to poor Magla Felinsen—' At this, Otter Garsen moaned and knit her hands, but Bera went on mercilessly: 'And how they dealt with the man who fell with the arrow in his gut. These are not honourable warriors bound by a code of fair behaviour; they will kill for what they want and take whatever is left for profit. Mark what I say and imagine how they are even now calculating our worth on a southern slave block!'

Some of the women began to cry. Bera turned on them angrily.

'Tears will not keep these raiders at bay!' she cried, fixing Fat Breta and Marin Edelsen with an unforgiving look. 'Dry your eyes and prepare to temper your blades with Istrian blood if you wish to save your lives and your virtue. I cannot promise you that we shall prevail, but we shall not shame our menfolk by giving ourselves up like calves to the slaughter.'

Sniffing, the women regarded their spears and knives dubiously. Then they gripped the handles harder and turned their faces to the windows with new determination.

'Let them come,' said Hesta Rolfsen resolutely, shaking her elm-spear at the raiders. 'And if we die, we die bravely.'

Behind them, one of the roof-climbers pitched foot-first onto the floor. Fat Breta charged him with her spear. The point glanced off his mail coat with a screech and she tripped over the shaft and landed in a tumble at his feet. The raider, a lithe young man with almond-shaped eyes and a winning smile, extended a courteous hand to her and Fat Breta, who had never had any man smile at her, and certainly none as pretty as this one, took it without a murmur. The second man dropped through the roof at this moment and grinned at the first. 'Hens in a coop,' Milo Forin said to his brother in the impenetrable dialect of the north coast, squeezing Fat Breta's hand reassuringly. 'And well fed ones at that!'

Marin Edelsen plunged a dagger into his side and he fell over, looking surprised. She watched him collapse, looking even more surprised than he was and the reddened blade fell from her fingers. With a growl, Nuno Forin sprang at her and caught her by the throat. He looked wildly around at the shocked women, then back at his brother, who had staggered to his feet. The wound had not been deep, though the blood was still seeping.

A spear whirred through the air and took Milo Forin in the chest with such force that he was pinned to one of the roof supports. He expired there without a word. Gramma Rolfsen rubbed her hands down her apron. 'Well,' she said, 'it seems I haven't lost my throwing arm.'

Nuno Forin held Marin in front of him to protect himself from a similar onslaught. What had appeared a relatively simple task had taken a desperate turn. With his free hand he drew his sword. 'Door!' he said in the Old Tongue. It was one of the few words he knew.

No one moved.

'Door!' he said again, and waved the sword around.

'Leave the door alone,' Bera said coolly.

Marin began to wail. The raider tightened his grip on her throat and she stopped. He dragged her towards the barred door, watching the women as he went, his handsome face suddenly ferocious. When he came level with Kitten Soronsen, he paused, his attention captured by the bright crimson of the silk tunic. His black eyes looked her up and down assessingly. Then drove his knife into Marin Edelsen's throat and shoved her body aside, so that it cannoned into one of the old Seal Rock women, providing sufficient distraction for him to take Kitten hostage instead. His free hand travelled up and down the crimson silk, closing for an appreciative moment on her buttock. She stood stock-still, shocked by the sudden death of her friend, her fingers opening and closing around the shaft of the spear she held; then it fell with a clatter from her grasp. Nuno Forin pulled the pretty blue ribbons with their tiny silk flowers from her hair and, twisting viciously, wrapped her long braids around his fist and pressed the point of his sword to her throat. A thin welling of blood spilled down over the blade and dripped onto the shift and the floor. Thin Hildi gasped as Kitten's knees began to buckle.

'Door!' he demanded again, holding the fainting girl upright. He made a mime of sawing off Kitten's head if they did not comply.

Two of the women closest to the door started removing the benches which formed the barricade. 'Don't!' shouted Bera.

'We can't just stand by and see her killed.'

'Then watch from the window as they rape her before your eyes and then kill her anyway!' Bera returned angrily, but the women continued in their endeavour until the door came free and Nuno Forin pushed his way outside. As he passed, Otter Garsen tried to pull Kitten from his grasp, but he swung his sword around in a tight circle and she cried out. Three of her fingers dropped to the ground, twitching, and she fell down in shock.

Outside, the raiders cheered and whooped as Nuno Forin made it back to them, pushing Kitten Soronsen in front of him.

'How many are in there?' Bastido demanded.

'Maybe twenty. All women,' Nuno replied. He grinned around at his companions. 'No one touches this pretty bird but me. You can have the stringy old hens and the overstuffed turkeys.'

'What about the shipmaker?' the Bastard persisted.

Nuno shrugged, 'He stands shaking by the window like a palsied rabbit, his eyes fair popping out with fear.'

'Perhaps he is more frightened of the women of Rockfall than he is of us,' Clermano quipped. 'I have heard they have teeth between their legs instead of hair!'

Now Bastido and his men sent a shower of spears and arrows down on the steading, aiming for the holes the men had made in its roof, but they knew they were doing little damage with them when the women sent them back again, hurling them out of the windows or shooting the arrows from the gables. Night fell and the raiders began to complain of being cold and hungry and bored with their slow progress.

Galo Bastido knew what they meant by this. He had two more stratagems left to him. One might involve significant loss of life; the other was hardly less pleasant. First he had his men gather tinder and light a fire. Then he took Baranguet aside and made his thoughts known. His lieutenant grinned, then approached the giant, Casto Agen. 'Hang onto Nuno Forin,' Baranguet said softly. 'And do not let him free until I tell you.'

The bare-knuckle fighter stayed where he was, frowning, and the firelight played over his wide features as on a wall. It took him a little while to assimilate information; half a minute later he grabbed the north-coaster in a headlock until Nuno's face went bright red and he started to wheeze.

Galo Bastido pulled Kitten Soronsen to her feet, his eyes on the steading, the interior of which was now lit with a reddish glow which silhouetted the heads peering out of the windows. Then he shouted into the gloom, 'We are bored and cold and need some exercise to warm ourselves up. Let the shipmaker out now or we shall treat you to a very special entertainment of our own devising!' He pushed the girl towards his waiting men. 'Strip her!' he commanded.

At once, a group of raiders surrounded Kitten, each of them grinning maniacally. Given such licence, their hands were suddenly everywhere at once. The girl shrieked as they pushed her from one to another, each one tearing away a strip of cloth before passing her on until she stood before them, naked and terrified. Bruises the size and shape of hands stood out on her pale skin; gashes and gouges made by fingernails leaked crimson blood.

'By the lord,' Bera said through gritted teeth, 'they are devils.' She put down the fine sword Katla had made and took up a hunting bow, nocked an arrow and sighted down the shaft. The loosed barb took a short dark man in the upper arm so that he howled like a dog. Three more arrows followed the first. One of the sea-wardens fell to his knees with a shaft in his gut; the other two fell harmlessly short.

The big man holding Nuno Forin let him go. Two of the raiders pushed Kitten Soronsen to the ground and held her down and the north-coaster began to fumble with his clothing.

Otter Garsen shook her bandaged hand out of the window. 'Your pricks will swell up and turn black if you touch her!' she yelled in the Old Tongue. 'This I swear by the Troll of Fairwater! Your balls will shrivel up and fall off and your guts will twist in agony!' She paused to draw breath, then bellowed: 'Your kidneys will boil and your ribcage will burst open and propel your heart out of your chest and you will die in the most excruciating pain!'

Bera raised an eyebrow. It was not so much the content of the curse which surprised her, but the older woman's knowledge of the common language, some of it quite technical.

She watched the men look from one to the other. Then Nuno Forin dropped his breeches and fell to his knees in front of Kitten Soronsen. For a moment, they thought he had done so in order to engage in the rape; then they saw the goose-fletching sticking out of his back. Before anyone out there could react, another man fell dead. A fleet figure scooted past the men like a wraith and disappeared into the darkness.

'Katla!' Bera breathed. 'That was Katla!' She turned to the women. 'We shall not give in!' she announced. 'Take up anything you can throw or shoot. Let us show them what Rockfallers can do!'

Within moments, a hail of missiles engulfed the raiders. First it was sticks and staves and cooking implements; then it was all manner of bizarre objects.

Gramma Rolfsen grinned gleefully down at Fat Breta and Forna Stensen who were propping her up in a precarious fashion through the hole in the roof. 'Hold me steady, girls,' she demanded and took aim with Fent's old catapult once more. A large ball of cow-dung enclosing a damaging collection of sheep's knuckles and pebbles struck the knife-fighter, Clermano, squarely on the jaw, knocking him flat, if more with surprise than force. She followed this up with a bag full of rivets and some fire-blackened stones from the bread-oven.

The raiders abandoned the pale form of Kitten Soronsen and took shelter behind the wall.

'This is ignominious!' cried Baranguet. 'Let us storm the hall at once!'

'No,' replied his captain. 'We must resort to my last stratagem.'

He sent some men down to the wood to collect sticks and twigs and others to the outbuildings to fetch whatever dry straw or hay they might find there. These they fashioned into tied bundles. Two of the Forent men ran with armfuls of the tinder to the right of the steading while the remaining two sea-wardens, Breseno and Falco, piled their faggots on the left side. These they set fire to. The women inside ran about gathering buckets of water and casting them out of the windows to quench the flames, and when the water ran out, they threw out whey and stew, which were somewhat less effective. Before too long, fire had caught hold of the structural pillars. Then the raiders shot flaming arrows into the dry turf of the roof. Soon, the hall was full of smoke.

'My god, Bera, we cannot withstand this,' Otter wheezed. 'Send out the shipmaker, for Feya's sake.'

Through the dense and choking air, Bera Rolfsen stared

at her old friend, taking in the bloodstained bandage around her ruined hand, the misery etched on her face, her streaming eyes. Then she turned to Morten Danson. 'Go,' she said simply.

The shipwright stared back at her. He looked angry, but instead of uttering any word of recrimination he made his way to the door and unbarred it. Opening it just a slit he sucked in a mouthful of clear air and shouted into the night, 'This is Morten Danson, shipmaker to the King of Eyra. I am coming out: stay your hands if you wish to take me to your lord alive!'

Then he stepped outside. After several moments' silence, Bera heard the sounds of celebration in the raiders' camp. She peered around the hall. It was hard to see through the smoke now, for it was as if thick blue curtains hung in the air. She could make out faces only where lanterns had been lit: in the blurry haze she marked how soot ran from Kit Farsen's nose in two long grimy streaks, how Thin Hildi had, with remarkable practicality, bound a damp scarf across her nose and mouth; how the older of the Seal Rock women was clutching her chest as if it hurt. Her mother, Hesta, looked defiant, even though her eyes were red-rimmed and seeping and she had had to prop herself against a pillar; while Forna Stensen, three times and more her junior, looked as if she might expire at any moment. At the back of the hall, someone was wheezing like an afflicted donkey. That would be Fat Breta, Bera thought with a moment's irritation. There really was no choice here. Fire had caught hold of the central pillar now, and flames leapt from the edges of the roof where the turf was driest. If they remained inside, they would die like bugs in a burning tree; if they went outside and gave themselves into the hands of the enemy—

It was unimaginable; but it was life.

'Hark to me!' Bera croaked at last, her voice competing with the crackling flames. 'There is no more to be done to save ourselves, for if we stay here the fire will take us; and if we leave, the raiders will take us. You must each make your choice according to your will.' She coughed and took a while to collect herself. Then she finished with: 'It is a poor choice, and for that I am sorry. I had not thought it would come to this.'

There were tears in the Mistress of Rockfall's eyes now, Otter Garsen noted, and she doubted they were merely a result of the smoke.

Nevertheless, she held herself straight and proud as the women began to shuffle towards the door, slowly at first, then, when the clear air of the outside began to pour in, with swifter, more purposeful steps, until they were able to peer out into the darkness where, in the middle distance, in the lee of the enclosure wall, the southern raiders lounged in the grass, basking in the heat of their own fire and supping noisily from casks of wine. They called encouragement to the women, but since most of them spoke only Istrian, no one really understood what they said, which was probably as well.

'No!'

The voice was disembodied, invisible; hard to locate, for it seemed (impossibly) to come from the sky. The women looked around wildly, half in and half out of the doorway. Tian Jensen looked up onto the roof and gasped.

'There is a gast up there: it is hag-riding the roof timbers!'

And indeed when they all stared upwards it did seem that an afterwalker had taken up residence on the roof-tree, for a dark figure with wild and spiky hair was sitting astride the central beam, its legs dangling on either side of the wood, and with huge hands it flung flaming divots of turf down all around them.

'It must be Magla, come back from death, vengeful because we did not save her!' cried Kit Farsen.

If anything, this possibility seemed even more frightening

than the prospect of the southern raiders, who were at least warm flesh and blood, men with understandable natures and appetites. The Rockfall women – raised on the glorious, overblown superstitions of the Northern Isles in which the unquiet dead who refused to lie peacefully where they had fallen or been buried rose up blackened with rot and fury, swelled to twice their normal size and wrought havoc on the farms, livestock and folk of their home region, all began to shriek and run away from the apparition.

'No!' cried the voice again. 'Come back and help me put out the fire. Save yourselves!'

But Fat Breta, Thin Hildi, Kit Farsen and Forna Stensen were already sprinting across the home field; and the old women from Seal Rock, surprisingly spry for their age, were not far behind them. But Otter Garsen stood rooted to the spot, despite the fiery turf raining down around her, staring fixedly upwards. The figure on the roof did not look much like her daughter; for all that an afterwalker could change their shape and manner of speech beyond recognition, she was suddenly sure it was not Magla.

'Otter!' shouted the thing on the roof. 'Where's my mother?'

It was Katla Aransen. Otter's mouth dropped open. She turned and dashed back into the hall. 'Bera, Bera!'

The smoke was thick and roiling. Some of it churned upwards to escape through the holes Katla Aransen had made in the roof, but the rest hung dense and choking: she could not see the Mistress of Rockfall anywhere. The building seemed deserted. On she went, her good hand pressed to her face. The hall's central pillar was now ablaze from top to root and lines of greedy flame had begun to run along the rafters, illuminating the damaged loft-room and the roof beyond. When she turned around, her route back to the door had gone, veiled by new billows of smoke. Her task suddenly seemed foolhardy and pointless: surely no one could be alive in here? She must have been transfixed by the sight of Katla on the roof and missed Bera Rolfsen as she left the building with the others. She turned, and stumbled over the body of the dead raider, went down with a crash and put out her arms to brace herself. Agony as hot as any flame shot up her arm as the ground impacted with her ruined hand. The pain seemed to clear her head. The smoke was less dense at this level: she peered through it and thought she saw two pairs of feet not far away. Gritting her teeth, she crawled towards them.

One pair of feet indeed belonged to the Mistress of Rockfall. Bera Rolfsen stood coughing and wheezing in front of her aged mother. They appeared to be engaged in a fierce debate but from down below, Otter could not hear what was being said. Slowly, painfully, she got to her feet.

'Mother, I cannot leave you!'

Hesta Rolfsen had seated herself in Aran Aranson's great carved chair, her hands gripping the dragonheads at the ends of the armrests as if she feared her daughter would try to drag her from it. She was too short for it: her feet swung freely like a child's; like a child her face wore an expression of absolute obstinacy.

'Here I sit and here I will stay. Rockfall is my home: I am too old to leave it.'

'Who says you will have to leave? The raiders will not bother to take you and the old folk.'

'Why should I wish to live when my home is burned down and my daughter is taken from me, while I remain a broken, helpless old woman, of no worth even on a southern slave block?'

Bera Rolfsen made a sound of utter, futile frustration. 'Then you will die here in the fire.'

In response, the old woman merely folded her arms and stared at a point a few inches from Bera's head, which is how she came to spy the blurry outline of Otter Garsen.

A toothless grin stretched itself across her face. 'Otter, Otter my dear. Have you come back to die with me?'

'No!' Otter coughed, 'I have come to take you out of here to join your kin. Katla Aransen is on the roof, trying singlehandedly to save the place from burning to the ground!'

'I fear she is too late and too little to do that,' Hesta said sorrowfully. She reached out and took her daughter's hand, patted it softly. 'You save yourself as best you can, my darling girl, and Katla too. Even if it means going with the raiders, at least save your lives. I am too old to see any more of this world; but much still lies before the pair of you, and if you do not survive, then who will be left to avenge my death?'

This last was ungainsayable.

Bera fell to her knees to embrace her mother one last time, then she rose and, taking Otter's arm, made her way blindly through the burning hall.

But their way to the door was blocked: some of the roof timbers had charred through at their centres and fallen down across the room. Smoking wreckage lay in their path, through which great gouts of flame burst up sporadically, and there seemed no way through. When they looked up, they could see stars through the holes in the roof. *Perhaps*, Bera thought, *this will be the last thing I see: the Navigator's Star which is no doubt at this same moment lighting my husband's journey into the icefields of the North.*

It might have been a comforting thought in other circumstances. In her current situation, the sight merely made her angry: angry that she should be forced to experience this unpleasant fate; angry that Aran had left her and taken all the men with him, rendering Rockfall defenceless.

'Damn you, Aran Aranson!' she yelled into the night. 'Damn you and your expedition!'

A head appeared. It was a charred head, all black and

filthy, with wild hair and bright eyes. It looked like a sprite. It was Katla.

'Mother, Otter – here!' A coil of sealskin rope fell down through the hole towards the two women. Loops had been knotted all the way up its length at three-foot intervals.

Bera laughed. 'Up you go, Otter!'

With only one good hand, it was hard for Otter Garsen to make the climb up the rope-ladder, but she had no wish to die in the smoking ruins of Rockfall's hall. Up she went in an ungainly fashion, grabbing for each hold with a fervour born of panic, hanging on with the elbow of her right arm while her left searched for purchase. She disappeared through the hole in the roof and a moment later the sealskin rope came looping down again.

It was a glorious winter's day. The sun shone like scattered gold upon the sea, there was a chill in the air and a stiff breeze filled the sail and drove them at a good clip toward the straits and the Long Man. As they passed beneath the shadow of the great stack, Erno Hamson gazed up at where its sheer pink-white crown glowed in the sun, sending a haze of sparkles of light shimmering off the crystal veins amidst the granite and remembered how it had always been Katla Aransen's avowed intent to climb to the top of that looming three hundred foot tower.

'But once you got up there, how on Elda would you get down?' he had enquired in horror. He had never had a head for heights, had no wish whatsoever to be led to the top of some terrible, exposed lump of rock in the middle of the sea, no matter how much he loved her.

Katla had just thrown her head back and laughed. 'I'll think of something!' she had declared cheerfully. It was her attitude to everything.

He could imagine her now, sitting astride that narrow summit, one leg dangling down the east face, the other down the seaward side, watching the gulls slide past with her eyes half shut in purest delight, like a cat replete with thieved delicacies snoozing off its illicit feast in the sun.

He could not wait to see her.

They sailed into Rockfall harbour in the hour before noon, having made slightly less good time than Mam had expected due to a capricious wind which had seemed to change its direction every time they reset the sail. The harbour was empty. Aran Aranson's longship, the *Fulmar's Gift*, was not at anchor; nor were any of the myriad little boats usually moored there. Erno supposed they might be out at sea, gathering in whatever fish there were for the taking in the mildness of the season. He scanned the landscape that came into focus as they rounded the first harbour. An ominous coil of dark smoke spiralled up into the air over the steading and was carried away over the hillside beyond. He narrowed his eyes. Something was wrong with this scene. They kept the fires burning in the hall most of the time, for cooking as well as for warmth, but the dense blackness of the smoke struck a wrong chord. A chill ran through his heart.

They sailed into the inner harbour. No one came out to greet them, and Erno felt the muscles of his chest constrict.

'This is not right,' he confided to Joz Bearhand. 'The Rockfallers are always hospitable.'

'Perhaps they are being wary,' said Mam, strapping on her swordbelt.

A grinding noise on the steerboard side of the bow made them all jump. Persoa ran lightly up onto the gunwale and looked over the side. 'It's a big piece of wood,' he said. 'I can't quite see what it's from.'

Dogo fetched the gaff and he and Joz caught the object and brought it to the surface for closer inspection. It was the remains of a small craft, deliberately holed below the waterline. They looked at one another. The further they penetrated the inner harbour, the more wrecked vessels they encountered – a skiff, keel-up, its strakes ruined; a faering foundering in the mud, a fishing boat, its hull all smashed.

Erno's face was white. 'Enemies have been here,' he said fearfully.

'Perhaps the Rockfallers did this themselves to prevent others using them,' Mam said softly, though it did not look as if even she believed her own words.

When the ship hit the shingle on the gently shelving shore, Erno was the first out into the surf, mindless of the cold water, the state of his carefully chosen clothes, or anything save knowing what it was that had happened here. The mercenaries followed shortly after, though Mam left Persoa in charge on board and made sure the crew were armed and ready for action if it were required of them.

'Challenge anyone who passes,' she instructed them. 'Ask them the name of the swordsmith who works on this island, and if they do not know it's a woman, or that her name is Katla Aransen, kill them.'

As they ran up the lane from the harbour past the fish sheds, something whimpered and clawed at the silvered wood of the third hut.

'A dog,' said Joz dismissively. 'Just a dog got itself trapped.'

They opened the barred door with some care: even a trapped and weakened dog could give you a nasty bite. Instead, out fell Ferra Bransen in a ragged dress and stained shift. Her face was swollen and she kept babbling at them. There were black bruises on her arms and one of her eyes was crusted with blood. They couldn't get any sense out of her. Doc wrapped her in his cloak and carried her back down to the harbour to Persoa.

In the undergrowth leading up to the steading they found the battered body of a black–and–white dog, and a little farther on the corpse of his companion, the shepherd, Fili Kolson.

Grimly, they continued on their way. Near the top of the hill they came upon the thorny arch known as Feya's Cross.

A strip of red silk lay forlornly upon the ground, trodden into the path by the passage of many feet. Erno picked it up, frowning. It reminded him of the betrothal dress Katla had worn at the Gathering; but the image which intruded itself upon his mind was of a small dark woman wearing that garment instead, which made him frown harder. He pocketed the piece thoughtfully. A little further on and a horrifying vista presented itself.

At the top of the hill, the home meadow stretched away from them, strewn with discarded weaponry. The Great Hall of Rockfall lay beyond, a smouldering ruin. Charred timbers stuck out of it like the ribs of a dead animal. He gave a loud, hoarse cry.

Crows lifted from the field in a clatter of wings, cawing with displeasure. It did not take much imagination to know the manner of the feast they had disturbed. Bodies lay tumbled here and there: men, in wargear and southern dress; women face down, their skirts bundled above their waists so that their private parts were immodestly exposed to the unwinking eye of the bright noon sun.

Erno Hamson fell to his knees. 'My god,' he said, over and over.

Mam marched to the burned hall, her jaw set so hard that the sinews stood out on her neck. Her sword was out, though it did not seem likely there would be any practical use for it other than the digging of graves. Doc and Dogo mooched speculatively around the bodies, removing an item here, an item there. Joz stared about him, his beard jutting fiercely. He sheathed the Dragon of Wen and walked from one corpse to another rearranging the clothing of the women. He did not put anything past Dogo. Each one he turned over was older than he had expected from the mere fact of her rape. It seemed southern raiders cared little for the age and dignity of their victims. It did not surprise him: he had seen sights like this, and worse.

Erno had not. He tailed the older man, grimacing at
the revelation of each face and feeling guilty at the relief
he felt every time it was not Katla. He recognised Tian
Jensen and Otter Garsen and thought a couple of the others
might be from the Seal Rock area. There were no young
women here.

'Taken for the slave markets,' Joz said gruffly as if hearing his thoughts. 'Taken to be sold to brothels in the
southern towns.'

A red wave of fury engulfed Erno. Surely Katla would die
rather than allow such a fate to befall her? But even as he
thought this, the conviction came to him that even were
such to be the case, he had rather a thousand times over see
her alive and ill-used, than dead and untouched. He looked
up, his eyes blurry with unshed tears, and saw Mam coming
back out of the hall, a fine sword in her hand. He recognised
the style of that sword: it was unquestionably one of Katla
Aransen's finer pieces of work. His heart lurched sickeningly.
'What?' he croaked out. 'What have you found?'

'You might ask who,' Mam said and her face was grim.
'But I do not know. You must come and undertake the task
of naming them.'

It was with heavy steps that Erno Hamson made his way
into the hall where he had been fostered since he was a child
of eight, the place he had long considered his home. It was
a ruin. The roof beams had fallen in and so had the ceiling
and much of the turf. Little fires still smouldered where the
pieces of turf sustained them. Light drilled down through the
curling blue smoke in harsh shafts, illuminating the legs of a
dead man, the outstretched hand of a young woman. 'Oh
no,' he breathed, and now the pent tears spilled.

Under the timbers was the body of little Marin Edelsen.
Her eyes were wide blue and her expression was surprised.
A red wound gaped in her neck.

And beyond her, in the high seat of Rockfall, sat Hesta

Rolfsen, Katla's grandmother, matriarch and conniver in schemes, a redoubtable old woman with a scurrilous laugh and a wicked eye. She had boasted to all who would listen that she would outlive them all, that she intended to survive Sur himself and his battle with both wolf and snake. But now she was stone dead with her feet set neatly together on the floor and her hands clasped around the carved dragonhead armrests. Her limbs were burned so that the bones gleamed white ivory amongst all the char, but even as death had eaten at her, she had flinched from her seat not at all.

Thirty

Pursuit

Tanto Vingo had discovered that his brother had escaped from Jetra when he sent two of the cheapest and most disfigured whores he could find to Saro's room dressed so immodestly that their slit tongues and scaly arms were on view to all, knowing that talk of it would be over all the castle by morning. When the women came back bemused and weeping to report him gone, Tanto fell into the most terrifying fury. He hurled himself out of his wheeled chair, he foamed at the mouth; he drummed rigid, and previously inert, limbs in a powerful tattoo upon the floor. The coarsest of swearwords poured from his mouth. He cursed: the Goddess, her adepts, her cat, her fires, her devotees, the Southern Empire, its lords, its women and whores; the Eternal City, Jetra's castle, the guards, Lord Tycho Issian, his sorcerer, his crystal, all nomad magic-makers, his father, his uncle, his ancestors, and of course his brother. It was a tantrum the like of which none of the Jetran women had seen before, never wished to see again; and they had seen far too much of the world as it was. They thought he was possessed by demons, or by the spirits of the long-dead which walked the chilly corridors of the fortress when all warm flesh was safe abed. When he levered himself upright and took out his wrath on the whore named Celina, ramming her against the wall and smashing her head on the plaster till she passed out, Folana fled in terror from the chamber and ran to fetch help.

She knew the passages of the castle well: in her youth she had been comely enough to earn a few cantari from the nobles of the city, before plague and punishment had come to her and left her as she was now. So instead of seeking the guest quarters, she took herself swiftly to the servants' parlour and pleaded with the second steward to intervene.

Frano Filco found Tanto Vingo's father and uncle in the company of Lord Rui Finco and Lord Tycho Issian. Frano had served in Jetra's Castle for fourteen years and only been flogged the once: he was deference itself. 'My lord,' he said, bobbing his head and misaddressing Favio Vingo. 'My lord, your son is . . . unwell.'

Favio looked surprised. His turbaned head bobbed awkwardly. 'Saro? He's just a bit lily-livered, is all: no stomach for war: probably just feeling a bit off-colour before he marches out with the troop.'

Frano shook his head. 'No, lord, no: your other son—' He searched and failed to recall Tanto's name. 'The—' He had been going to say 'cripple', but thought better of it just in time.

'Tanto?' Now Favio was on his feet, looking anxious. 'What's wrong with him?'

But Frano would say nothing: the wrath of nobles was unpredictable and could fall down upon you for a word out of place. Instead, he led the men to Tanto's chamber, where they found the subject on the floor with the naked prostitute, inscribing something redly into her yielding, unconscious flesh with a fruit knife.

Fabel Vingo and Rui Finco looked away, embarrassed, as Favio fell to his knees at his son's side and took the knife away from Tanto's unresisting fingers, all the while crooning, 'Tanto, Tanto, calm yourself: all will be well, my boy, all things shall be well.'

Tycho Issian took in the scene with a raised eyebrow, then

moved a little distance to the left, where he might have a better view of the whore's legs.

'Fetch Cleran,' the Lord of Forent said softly to Frano. 'Quickly. Take the whore back to where she lives and give her this for her silence—' He tipped a stream of silver coins into the man's hands. 'And this for yourself and Cleran—' More money followed.

'The boy is possessed,' Tycho observed curiously.

'No, no,' Favio denied. 'He is merely unwell, unsettled by something.' He cradled his son's head. 'Tanto, my boy, tell me what has happened—'

He glanced down at the whore's arm, where bleeding letters spelled out three letters of a familiar name and knew with sudden horrid instinct that his second son had fled the city. He had been half-expecting it these past days since plans for the coming conflict had escalated to the point of detail and he had watched Saro's face grow paler and more haggard as Lord Tycho Issian had described his plans for storming the northern capital and bringing redemption to its womenfolk. He had his own misgivings about the Lord of Cantara's sanity, especially when the man started raving about the punishments he would inflict upon the Eyran king, and Saro was a delicate boy; too delicate for the task assigned to him, it seemed. Even so, he managed to feign a degree of surprise as Tanto wailed: 'Saro's gone, escaped us all! Little bastard—'

Now it was the Lord of Cantara's turn to be furious. 'Sir!' he said stridently, fixing Favio Vingo with his mad gaze, 'Is this true? Has your second son deserted?'

Favio looked unhappy at the use of this word. Desertion carried a heavy penalty in time of war. Even if Saro had left Jetra, he would prefer to think of his departure as a leavetaking, an absence, a straying. 'I know not, my lord,' he replied.

Fabel stepped forward and took his brother by the arm. 'I will go look in his chambers,' he said reassuringly. 'I am sure there is just some misunderstanding here. Saro would never willingly shirk his duties, however distasteful he might find them.' He shot the Lord of Cantara a pointed look which went entirely unnoticed, and strode off down the corridor, relieved to be away from the unhealthy atmosphere.

But Saro was not in his chambers, nor was he in the solar, nor the kitchens, nor out in the gardens. No one had seen him. And when Fabel took himself off down to the stables and found his prize stallion also missing, it was hard to deny the likelihood that the boy had run away. Moreover, it soon transpired that the Lord of Cantara's strange servant – the albino known as Virelai – had also disappeared.

This last transported Tycho Issian into a towering rage. To lose the boy was one thing, for he could easily be replaced: there were a hundred such younger sons vying for the favour of the foremost lords of the land; but to lose the sorcerer was another disaster altogether. They had amassed a considerable stock of false silver now, it was true – enough to pay for the construction of the ships they needed; but his plan for rescuing the Rose of the World from the grasp of the barbarian king pivoted on the deployment of a sorcery which the apprentice mage had been perfecting these past months. He was indispensable.

Overstepping his authority, he sent out the criers to declare a bounty: for Saro Vingo's head, seven thousand cantari: for the safe return of his servant and the black cat with which he always travelled, twenty thousand. No one dared gainsay him. Hesto and Greving Dystra, nominal heads of the ruling Istrian Council, having worked themselves up into a fluster, finally granted an audience to the deserter's father, then added another ten thousand cantari for the capture of the Vingo boy alive and well, and a further five hundred for the stallion.

Reports of sightings came flooding in. The three had been seen – in company, and journeying alone – as far away as the Blue Woods in the north and the Bone Quarter in the south. Riders sped out from the Eternal City in all directions. A large contingent on fleet horses set out for Altea Town, in case Saro Vingo had foolishly headed for his homeland. Others travelled north-east to the White Downs and thence to Forent. A small group of six riders made for the Golden Mountains and the Dragon's Backbone: it was deemed unlikely anyone would wish to seek shelter in such a wild and inhospitable area. The Southern Wastes were left to a volunteer force of hardened bounty hunters, for no regular troops would venture there: besides, if the heat did not kill the travellers, then the monsters which were reputed now to roam the area surely would. Another contingent took ship down the Tilsen River in order to beat the deserters to the ports at Galia, Tagur or Gila. The troop bound to investigate the sighting in the Blue Woods stopped in Lord's Cross to water their horses, and made a swift visit to the Hawk's Wing tavern to sample the renowned local brew.

Word got around that the soldiers were looking for 'a young nobleman turned traitor by the name of Saro Vingo, an albino servant, a black cat and the stallion which carried the honours at the Allfair'.

One of the regulars tapped the captain on the shoulder. 'Would that be a racing stallion? A black one?'

The captain shrugged his arm away from the man and fixed him with a suspicious stare. He did not like to be approached by strangers in quite such a forward manner, particularly one who did not honour him with a 'sir'. 'Indeed. What do you know?' he asked shortly. 'Have you seen such a horse?'

The man was tall and dark with closely set eyes and a thin mouth, which now twitched up into an unpleasant smile. 'Not me personally, no; but some days back a gentleman by the name of – what was it now?'

He made a good pretence of rummaging through his memory until the captain grew impatient and tossed three coins onto the bar. The dark man picked them up, bit one of

them hard and then examined it closely. As if this very act had
jogged the information out into the light, he grinned broadly.
'Lodu,' he said. 'Lodu saw them – or said he did – two men,
a big cat and a racing stallion.'

No one had mentioned before that the cat was big, but
the captain supposed that was a relative thing. 'This Lodu:
where can I find him?'

The dark man shrugged. 'No idea,' he declared, and
grinned again.

'Falcon's Lair,' said another man indistinctly.

'What?'

'Little hill village south of here. That's where Lodu Balo
lives.'

It took them two hours to reach Falcon's Lair, by which
time the entire troop was on the edge of mutiny. They had
been looking forward to a jar and a game of cards all the hot,
grimy way from the Eternal City to Lord's Cross: trekking
into the steep hill country to the south, in the dark, with no
prospect of an ale at the end of it, was a decidedly unpopular
decision. Having wasted another half hour trying to locate
Lodu Balo's house, which lay not in the tiny village itself, but
a further mile into the hills up a narrow, treacherous path fre-
quented by owls and bats, they were in the mood for a fight.

The woman who opened the door to them was tiny, dark
and bore the clan tattoo of Gola down one cheek and a crystal
around her neck.

'Footloose!' hissed the sergeant.

The woman shrieked and tried to close the door again,
but the captain jammed his foot in it and forced it open.
Five soldiers piled in behind him. Inside, the cot was bare
and simple. On a low table in the centre lay numerous
bunches of mixed herbs – rosemary and thyme, oregano
and marjoram, hensfoot and pyrea – tied with raffia ready
for hanging to dry. The captain picked one up and sniffed
it suspiciously, then recoiled sharply.

'Witchery!' he declared, throwing the bundle down on the floor and stamping on it hard. He turned to the troop. 'Take the rest of this stuff and burn it.' He paused. 'Her, too.'

'What?'

The man who had entered the room from the adjoining chamber was blinking his eyes rapidly, as if he were unaccustomed to the light. His jaw was stubbly; his breath stank of garlic and wine.

'What are you doing in here? And where are you taking my wife?' asked Lodu Balo in a bellicose tone.

The sergeant grabbed him by the tunic and hoisted him up so that his feet were dangling. 'That is a nomad magic-maker, a Footloose whore: what are you doing with her?'

Lodu looked horrified. 'She's my wife, she's been my wife for twenty years. She's not Footloose, she's hillclan.'

'Then why's she messing around with this filthy sorcery?'

'She grows herbs – I sell them at the market, alongside our produce—'

'So, you admit to selling spellcraft, do you?'

'No—'

A fist caught him in the gut so that he doubled up with a bubbling breath. By the time he straightened up, three of the soldiers had dragged his wife outside. He could hear her crying, 'Lodu, Lodu, save me!', cries punctuated by wheezes and yelps, as if someone were kicking her as they might a stray dog.

'I swear!' he wailed. 'I sweaaarrr . . .'

The captain put his face close to Lodu's. 'Two men, a "big" cat and a black stallion. Mean anything to you?'

Lodu's eyes went round as plates.

'I—' he stammered. 'I saw them, yes, on the crest of the hills south of here.'

'When?'

'Market-day, last month,' he blurted out, suddenly full of relief, for it was not something he had done, nor his hill-wife, either, which had brought these soldiers here. 'Very clear, I saw them, heading south, and what struck me as odd – apart from the cat, you know – was that these two men had this fine horse and neither of them was riding it; yet they'd clearly been walking all night – it was just past dawn and I'd set out early for the market at Lord's Cross to make sure the fruit didn't get overripe in the heat and, well, there's nowhere for miles such lordly men could have come from . . .'

'A day's walk from Jetra, maybe; or a night's?'

Lodu nodded.

'And they were headed where?'

'South,' Lodu replied eagerly. 'South and east. The sun was behind them, I remember it well.' There was no sound from outside: they must have let his wife go. Something occurred to him. 'Is there a reward for this information?' he asked, licking his lips.

The captain smiled pityingly at him. 'Reward? Falla's reward maybe.'

Lodu frowned, trying to work this out. He had never been quick off the mark; but even if he had managed to grasp the man's meaning it would have made little difference to his fate. The frown was his last expression. The captain clubbed him over the head with the pommel of his dagger so that he crumpled to the floor.

The captain patted the pouch of coins he carried at his belt. 'Why should a peasant prosper, when it's us who has to do all the hard work?'

The sergeant smiled broadly.

Outside, the night sky was lit by the fire in the sheltered vale below the cot, which illuminated the grove around it, crisping the late olives and lemons, so that these fragrant aromas melded with those of burning herbs. But even these appetising scents could not mask the powerful stench that lay at the heart of the blaze. Together, the captain and his sergeant tossed the unconscious body of Lodu Balo on top of the blackened corpse of his wife, dusted off their hands and went back into the house to find whatever provisions they might stock up with for their long journey south. South and east.

By a bend in the Tilsen River, where the osiers grew high, they found the remains of a fire and the marks of churned-up ground. Evidence of an encampment of some sort: but the ruts left by cartwheels surely had nothing to do with two men, a cat and a horse.

'Now what?' asked the sergeant.

The captain kicked the blackened stones apart. 'Fuck knows,' he said viciously. 'Where would you go if you was deserting?'

The sergeant laughed. 'I'm hardly going to tell you, am I, chief?' He took in the cheerless vista around them. 'Certainly not out into this bloody wilderness, that's for sure.'

There was a cry from the riverbank. One of the soldiers had found pawprints and the rest had gathered around to stare at them.

'Ain't natural,' said one. 'Mountain lion's got no business down here.'

'No mountains for a hundred miles!'

One man placed his hand in the hardened mud. The impression of the cat's paw engulfed it.

The captain whistled through his teeth. 'Wouldn't want that one with its head in your lap, would you?'

The man shuddered and withdrew his hand quickly as if the beast might magically spring up out of its own spoor.

The sergeant regarded the print thoughtfully. '"Big cat", the peasant said. "Big cat." I was wondering how on Elda he'd managed to spot a domestic cat at such a distance. Something weird is going on here: there was a fair bit of talk back at the barracks about the albino, stuff he got up to for the Lord of Cantara—'

'Bastard, that Tycho Issian,' someone said, and there was general agreement.

'Magic and the like . . .'

'Whores, too.'

'So what we got if we add all that together?' the captain asked, scanning their faces. They looked blankly back at him. He clicked his teeth impatiently. 'We got shapechanging and sorcerers and Footloose and treachery.' He dropped his voice and took the sergeant aside. He had known Tilo Gaston since they were lads: they'd trained together, got drunk and beaten the hell out of each other outside a dozen taverns in the Eternal City. Did he trust him? Perhaps not entirely, but money usually sealed a man's mouth. 'We got conspiracy in the highest places here. No wonder there's a high price on their heads: and I reckon we can get it a fair bit higher if we catch 'em, too. Lord of Cantara had some shady ancestors, I'd heard. Someone said something about a nomad father—'

'You'd better not go round saying that in public,' the sergeant muttered, looking back uncomfortably in case any of the others had overheard. 'People disappear around Tycho Issian, and not by magic, neither.'

'Ah, no, I wasn't thinking of saying it in *public*.' The captain winked and rattled the coin-bag. Then he raised his voice. 'I'll bet my arse this was their meeting point,' he said to the troop at large. 'Those dainty little hoofprints back there belong to no yeka I ever saw, so I'd say our quarry have taken up with a band of nomads. Even if they haven't, and they just happened to have crossed paths, the worst we can do if we follow these tracks is to find and roast some Footloose. And the best? Well, the Lady knows: but if you keep imagining what you might do with that reward money, it might take your mind off the heat and the flies.'

Travelling with the nomads was the most enjoyable experience of Saro Vingo's young life. Almost, he forgot the context for their journey: for the tales the old women wove and the knowledge they possessed about everything they passed made him feel the world was a significantly different place to the one he had grown up in: that it was wider and purer and more mysterious and far, far more ancient than he had ever imagined. It made him a little less despairing than he had been since the empathic gift from Hiron had opened his eyes to the horrible true nature of much of humanity; at times he even felt optimistic.

They had been skirting the low foothills of the Golden Mountains for the last two days and were now taking a much-needed rest beside a small stream shaded by overhanging rowans.

'This is lady's smock,' said Alisha, holding up a bunch of tender green stalks topped by delicate pink flowers. 'It's a moon-plant: good for the stomach. Good to eat, too.' She peeled some out of the bunch and handed them to him.

It tasted pleasantly like watercress, if a little more bitter. Already he had learned the names and uses of a dozen fungi, and three dozen plants and herbs – lad's love (for cramps in the muscles); thorn apple (for breathing problems); henbane (for swelling of the testicles); mullein (for bruising and for piles); rampion (for fevers and discoloration of the skin). He had learned that powdered willowherb would stop excessive bleeding, that a decoction of dove's foot in wine could ease aching joints and that one of soapwort might fight those diseases contracted in unhealthy brothels. Such applications made the world seem more benevolent, as if the Three had provided all their folk might ever require, free for the picking.

It was from Virelai that he learned a parcel of rather more disturbing information: that potions made from the root of the salep orchid could harden the male genital organ for a day or more; that the pounded woody stems of the spurge could cause miscarriage and that fresh dog's mercury could kill a mouse, a dog or a man in a most unpleasant manner, depending on how much was administered. He asked Alisha now whether any of this were true, blushing when he got to the bit about the orchid.

'I do not know where he gets all this terrible stuff from,' she said, laughing indulgently. 'Books, he says, the old man's books.'

'Who is the old man?' Saro asked softly. He remembered the vision he had had when he touched the sorcerer. For an elderly man he had not appeared kindly.

Alisha shrugged. 'I believe he raised Virelai from a baby, but given all that, he will not talk much about him. I do not even know his name.'

'I do,' Saro said, surprised. 'Rahe.'

The nomad woman's eyes went wide. 'Ra-hay?' she asked, separating the sounds.

Saro nodded slowly. The way she said it reminded him of something.

'King Rahay?'

'I don't think he was a king. He never mentioned a king,' Saro frowned. 'I touched him once, Virelai, I mean; to see if there was any malice in him and there was a torrent of images – I saw an old, old man, surrounded by parchments and scrolls, and bottles of all sorts, in a fortress made all out of ice. And there was a woman too, with long, long golden hair . . .' He laughed nervously. 'Sounds ridiculous, doesn't it? Like something out of a fairy story.'

Alisha nodded absent-mindedly. She looked towards where the sorcerer sat with the old women, helping them wring out the washing in the stream. Then she turned back to Saro, gazing deep into his eyes. 'I do not know exactly who or what Virelai is,' she said very quietly, 'but I have more than suspicions about the old man. Long ago – hundreds of years maybe – in the time of my distant ancestors in the Far South of Elda, beyond the Dragon's Backbone—'

'But there isn't anything beyond the Dragon's Backbone,' Saro laughed. 'Everyone knows that.'

Alisha looked indignant. 'But there certainly is: it is where my people came from. Yours too.'

'My people come from Altea,' Saro said stubbornly. 'They've been the ruling family of the area for generations.'

'Does having power over people mean so much?' she asked gently.

Now it was Saro's turn to be indignant. 'I didn't mean that. I just meant that because the family is considered important in the region, records of every birth and marriage and death have been noted down: we're proud of our heritage – we know who we are, where we've come from.'

'Apparently not! All the people of Elda came from the Far South, so long ago that stories of that time have passed into legend—'

'Then why do the legends speak of the Far West, then?' Saro asked mulishly, as if he might catch her out.

Alisha laughed. 'That has always amused us. Have you never wondered why both your people and the Eyrans hold dear tales of the Far West?'

Saro looked thoughtful. 'The Eyrans came from here – from Istria – originally. We drove them north, and then out of the southern continent altogether. So I suppose that's why some of the stories are shared. And why Sirio and Sur are similar in sound. But Far West and Far South – well, you couldn't get that wrong – all those Eyran navigators and adventurers planning to find the Ravenway to the Far West – they could hardly sail across the mountains, could they?'

'You wouldn't think so, would you?' Alisha said. 'Since my mother died – you'd have loved her, I think: she was quite a character, wore her hair in a little white topknot, and about a hundred silver chains around her neck, and she was just the kindest of women – I've been trying to remember all she told me; what her mother told her, and her mother before her. And I've talked with Elida and Jana: they know much, too. One thing I do know is that Far West is a corruption of "farvasti", which means "the elder folk" in the Old Tongue. And the elder folk come from beyond the mountains to the south of here.'

Saro closed his eyes. Things were going on in his head, things over which he had no control. Little bits of information were marshalling themselves like the pieces of a puzzle, realigning themselves, coming to the fore of his memory. His eyelids flew open. 'Rahay – he was King of the West – just like in Guaya's puppet-play – but he wasn't, he was King of the South, and his name is Rahe, and he is Virelai's mentor, the Master: he was the one who found the Goddess hundreds of years ago and stole her away!' He stopped and stared at her, aware of what he had just said. 'But no one lives for hundreds of years—' He regarded her, waiting for her to interject or agree, but she just watched him magnanimously and said nothing, so he went on with his thought process, letting it spill from him like a waterfall. 'And your people – the nomads, the Wandering Folk – are the People, just like in the old books: the ones with the earth-magic, the ones who channel the powers of Elda. Except—'

'Except we have little of the Craft left to us – indeed, until the Rosa Eldi came back to the world, we had very nearly lost our magic altogether. Yes,' replied Alisha. 'And you are of the People, too – all of you, both Istrians and Eyrans: but you are of those members of the People who marched away into the world determined to make a different kind of life, who turned their backs on magic and the old ways and went to war with one another instead, and made power and money and land more important than love and truth and the heart of Elda.'

'But if the Goddess is returned to the world, and we have the Beast with us, then if we can find Sirio, all will be restored?'

Alisha smiled at him. 'It seems so simple, doesn't it?'

There came a cry from somewhere on the hillside above them, where the path wove down through the rocks. Saro came upright as if he were on a spring, but he could see nothing. The cry was followed by a deep-throated roar, then by screaming.

'We do indeed have the Beast with us; and it sounds as if she has company,' Alisha said grimly. She ran downstream towards the rest of the caravan. 'Visitors!' she called, waving her arms. 'Let us pack up and away.'

At once the nomads were on their feet, moving quickly. Saro was impressed by how calmly and purposefully they reacted and wondered if this was because they were by nature a phlegmatic folk, or whether such attacks had become common experience to them. Virelai and the men began to herd the yeka together; the women slung the still-wet washing into the backs of the wagons, gathering up their utensils and belongings as they ran. Saro untethered the stallion and stared behind him, up into the hills where the sound of Bëte's roar had thundered. For a moment he could see nothing; then there was a movement amidst the bracken and birches: horsemen, with cloaks of deepest blue. His mind raced. Not a roving band of marauders or brigands, then . . .

'Leave the wagons!' he yelled. 'Leave everything and run!'

Alisha, pushing Falo up into their cart, stared at him.

'Soldiers!' Saro cried, grabbing the boy down again, and watched her face go white. 'It's us they're after,' he added, knowing this suddenly to be the truth. 'Virelai and me.' He could imagine how his brother might have inflamed the Lord of Cantara into taking this swift action. It was as well Tanto could not ride, he thought, or he'd be leading the troop, and then no one would be safe. He looked past the nomad woman to where the sorcerer stood, swaying slightly like a pale aspen in a breeze. 'Virelai!' he called. 'They've come for us – soldiers from Jetra. You and I must face them, hold them at bay for as long we can, let these folk make their escape.'

'We need our wagons,' one of the old men said quietly, leading his pair of yeka forward and harnessing them with slow, sure hands. 'Our lives are in our wagons.'

Saro felt hot frustration scour through him. 'You will have no lives if you do not leave your wagons!' But still the old man persisted with his task until he had the animals yoked.

A moment later, the first of the soldiers came crashing down through the trees, his sword waving wildly. The tip of it was reddened. Then another appeared behind him. His sword was sheathed: he needed both hands on the reins to control his careering horse.

The nomads, seeing the nature of the threat in sudden, vivid colour, were galvanised; but still they would not abandon their carts. Saro, who wore no sword, looked desperately around him for a weapon.

'Here!' It was Falo, wielding a long, stout stick of age-pitted holly-wood. 'It was Amma's,' he said, holding it out for Saro, 'though I don't think she ever hit anyone with it.'

Saro's hands closed over the smooth wood of the staff, and allowed the expected wash of memories and experiences to flood through him – sunlight and dappled ground; a young man; an old man; the pain of a birth; a powerful sense of protectiveness, a deep connection with the world. Against the skin of his chest, the death-stone began to pulse with a pale green light . . .

'Run away,' Saro said to the boy, and his own voice sounded strange to him, deeper and slower and from a long way away, as if it were being drawn out of him by an unseen hand. And Falo must have seen something too, for the boy's eyes went wide and then he turned and sped away down the riverside track.

Fingers gripped his arm and he started, shocked by a sudden

chill. The sorcerer took his hand off Saro as if burned. His gaze was violet, intense.

'The stone . . .' he breathed. 'Saro – do not use the stone—'

Too late. Saro's fingers had already closed over the pendant. As the first soldier charged at them, he drew it out and pointed it at the man. A coruscating light haloed the stone, sending out darting rays and sparks. The soldier's horse shied and whinnied and banked abruptly to the left so that the man lost his stirrups and fell head first into the river. The horse galloped past them with its eyes rolling. Seeing all this, the second soldier hesitated. For a brief, hallucinatory moment, Saro could make out each mark made by the claws Bëte had raked down the horse's flank; then the soldier had wrestled his sword out and was shouting at them. Saro's fingers burned with sudden heat which travelled the length of his arm, through the shoulder joint and into the muscles and bones of his neck and skull. He closed his eyes and wished the man away. There was a cry; a thud. When he opened them again, the soldier lay unmoving, his sword arm flung wide; the weapon spun away across the ground.

He turned, shocked, to say something to the sorcerer, but Virelai was off and running for the cover of the trees in the wake of the nomads. He was on his own. When he turned back, two more soldiers were on the hillside. They must have seen the events which had overtaken their fallen comrades, for their movements were cautious: then, instead of hurling themselves down the slope, they wheeled their mounts about and headed back uphill. For a few seconds their silhouettes were visible against the sky, then they disappeared.

Saro let go of the pendant. His head ached and his stomach felt hollow with dread. The first man he reached was plainly dead, his eyes rolled up into the sockets to reveal yellowed corneas and the barest rim of iris. The second man, however, was floundering around in the shallows of the river in an uncoordinated fashion. 'Help me!' he spluttered at intervals. 'I'm drowning!'

Saro hauled him out onto the bank and he lay there coughing and wheezing and throwing up trickles of water and bile. The contact rendered a number of images – a sensation of exhaustion and angry boredom, heat and dust and thirst; aches from the saddle; a faint disgust as a woman's body burned in a pyre, face down, her heavy peasant shoes jerking convulsively; fear as a huge black cat loomed out of undergrowth causing him to stab down again and again with his sword . . .

Saro took his hands away. 'Why are you here?' he asked.

The soldier blinked. 'Deserter,' he croaked, pointing at Saro. 'Sent to bring you back. And the pale man, as well. Got to be punished, that's what Lord Tycho said. Example to others.' He coughed again, wiped the resultant ejecta away with the back of his hand. 'Supposed to bring the cat back, too.' He paused, laughed. 'Trouble is, no one told us how big the damn thing was!' He hauled the leg of his ripped breeches up to inspect the damage. 'See?' he said.

Flaps of skin hung like ribbons on his thigh. The water had made the blood thin and red again where it had been starting to coagulate. It pulsed out of the wound, staining the dry grass beside him.

'Still, I got the bloody thing, I think,' he said with some satisfaction. 'Right in the side.' He thought about this for a moment, then: 'Got a bandage?' he asked.

Saro stared at him blankly. Was Bëte dead? He had heard no roar since the first shriek on the hillside; no other sound from her at all. Despair came to him again, as dark as a cloud. He got up and walked away, leaving the soldier where he was, looking after him with a confusion bordering on outrage.

The stallion, Night's Harbinger, stood a little way downriver with his head dipped into the water, drinking unconcernedly. But where was Virelai? Saro walked into the bushes where he had last seen the pale man, ducking under branches, stepping over roots and brambles. He found the sorcerer curled up at the foot of a huge rowan, clutching his knees to him and rocking to and fro like a distressed child. When he saw Saro standing over him, he looked terrified. 'Please don't use the stone on me,' he begged.

Saro shook his head. 'I won't,' he promised. 'I'll never use it again.' He removed the pendant from around his neck. 'Here, you take it. I do not want it: I never wanted it – all it has been to me is a curse.'

But Virelai scrabbled away from him till his back was up against the tree and there was nowhere else for him to go, his features set in a feral rictus. 'Oh no,' he protested. 'Not me.'

Saro frowned. 'Then let us bury it here, or cast it into the river: then no one can use it.'

The sorcerer shook his head. 'Others may find it, and that would be worse.'

'Are you sure you will not take it?'

Virelai looked appalled. 'Not I,' he said. 'It is too strong for me.'

Defeated, Saro put the thing on again and tucked it back under his tunic. 'Let us go and find Alisha, then,' he said at last. 'I think the soldiers have gone.'

When they emerged out onto the riverbank again, the wounded soldier was no longer where Saro had left him, and neither was Night's Harbinger. But the ground was churned where he had last seen the stallion: it looked as if the beast had taken to its heels and headed after the nomads.

At a bend in the river, they found the caravan. Or the remnants of it, at least.

Of the four wagons, two were upright and seemed intact; the other two lay on their sides with their wheels spinning. Three yeka lay where they had fallen, necks or legs broken; so did the two old men. Elida, they had pinned to a tree with their lances. She sagged, spiked through the torso and shoulders, and twice through the legs. It looked as if someone had made a poor attempt to cut off her head, then abandoned the task.

Falo lay splayed out on the ground. He was covered in blood. Some distance away, his severed arm still clutched a long club, the end of which was matted with blood and hair. Of his mother there was no sign.

Saro fell to his knees at the boy's side and gently turned him over. His face was untouched, his skin as clear as a spring morning. There was a slight smile upon his lips, as if he were asleep and dreaming of something pleasant. He was quite dead.

Virelai began to cry. Great howls of rage and sorrow welled up inside him and burst out into the air like bats out of a cave. He ran here and there, pushing at the wagons, pulling blankets and clothing and wet washing out of them in case Alisha was somehow hidden by them. Saro watched him, feeling dead inside. It came as no surprise to him when the soldiers reappeared: ten of them, most armed to the teeth, three with arrows trained on him. Their leader walked forward, brandishing his sword in one hand, and pushing Alisha forward with the other. The man with the wounded leg sat astride the stallion. Saro wondered how he had managed to subdue the horse sufficiently to mount him, then saw the cruel way the halter had been knotted around the beast's mouth and neck.

'That's him!' the wounded man – Gesto – cried, indicating Saro. 'He's got a magic stone on a pendant – he killed Foro with it: I saw him!'

The captain looked wary. This was what Isto had reported, too, and he trusted Isto's word beyond Gesto's any day of the week.

'Take off that pendant you're wearing and throw it down in front of me!' he shouted to Saro. 'Carefully, or I'll gut the woman.'

Alisha's hair was in wild disarray and there was blood on the side of her face. Someone had bound her hands roughly: even at this distance he could see with a terrible clarity how the cords cut so tightly into the skin above her wrists that her hands had gone purple.

Something in him made him want to use the stone, to sear them in its awful heat, to scour them from the face of Elda. All of them: Alisha, Virelai, the stallion; even himself. Such destruction, such oblivion seemed for a moment appallingly attractive, a blessed relief, a perfect escape. Then the moment passed. With shaking hands, he removed the pendant, and cast it down on the ground in front of the troop's captain, where it lay on the grass with the cold, white, killing light dying out of it.

They kept their captives well bound and separate on the ride north, for fear they would somehow make spells between them; for if a simple stone could kill a man without leaving a mark on him, who knew what other resources these renegades might draw out of thin air? The pendant lay swaddled inside the captain's saddlebag, wrapped first in silk – the blue kerchief his daughter had solemnly bestowed upon him when he was sent to the Jetra garrison – and then in a woollen mitt, in memory of the old verse his grandmother used to recite when putting away her special things, which had fascinated him as a child:

> *Silk and wool and soft calfskin*
> *If you want to keep the magic in . . .*

If it had been a calf which had donated its hide to make the leather of his saddlebags then it was probably the oldest and ugliest calf in history, Captain Vilon mused; but it was the best he could manage under the circumstances.

No one had ever carried old Festia Vilon off to the pyres;

but she might be less lucky in these times. His mother did not seem to have inherited Festia's wild imagination, if imagination it was; but he suspected that if *he* were to delve into strange practices himself, matters might be different, for beneath his fingers the old woman's artefacts had buzzed and throbbed as if alive. He knew what was inside – his long-dead grandfather's fingerbones, some pieces of crystal and two soft, amorphous lumps of yellow metal reputed to have come from another land and another time – keepsakes, more than charms, which the old woman took out and stroked and muttered over every day, which seemed to keep her happy and did no one any tangible harm. But the memory of that odd sensation was why he had no intention of touching the Vingo lad's pendant himself.

The soldier he had sent to retrieve the thing had refused, until he had held a dagger to the man's jugular; but the stone had done nothing at all, just lain in the trooper's trembling, sweaty palm like the harmless, insensate thing it most probably was in all but a witch's hands.

Sitting astride the dead man's horse, his hands bound and a smothering bag tied over his head in which someone had recently kept an overripe cheese (some nonsense about the searing power of a witch's eyes) Saro wished for death. Clutching Virelai's arm when the soldiers had appeared had undone him entirely, for the chaos of panic which had churned through the pale man had travelled swiftly through the contact between them and swept him screaming away beneath its awful tide, made him limp and lifeless, unable to defend himself, let alone anyone else. Even now he could still 'see' the images which had filled the sorcerer's mind: Virelai himself flayed and tortured over his loss of the cat; thousands of nomads set upon wheels of fire or pressed beneath great stones, as if their magic was some essence within them which could thus be extruded.

And this was not the worst of it.

Back in himself again, Saro knew the true depths of despair. What happened to him, to Virelai; even to the martyred nomads was nothing in comparison with what lay in store for Elda. He had had an intimation of the horrors to come: when old women and beardless boys could be hacked down and tormented without conscience or reprisal, the world was already fatally tainted, poisoned, awry. Power in the wrong hands – no, he corrected himself, recalling the ease with which he had erased the soldier's life – in *any* hands, was an abomination. And now the pendant was travelling north to Jetra where it would be taken to the Lord of Cantara, complete with reports of its lethal abilities, and everything he had seen – the terrible scouring of the world – would surely come to be. And yet it was not that previous nightmare which haunted him now: it was not Tycho's face which he saw gloating over the death-stone, its virid rays making a ghastly mask of his avid, moonlike face; but Tanto Vingo's: his brother's.

'How can I bear to see the future unfold, and know I could have prevented it?' he thought miserably. 'Lady Falla, if you hear me, if you truly are in the world, prove it to me and take my life now. Snuff me out like a candle's flame and let me pass into the darkness, for I wish to exist no longer.'

He waited, silent beneath the suffocating hood; but his prayer remained unremarked and unanswered.

Thirty-one

Sanctuary

'Are you quite mad?'

The voice which hissed in his ear made him leap more violently even than the hand which grasped his shoulder with fingers of iron. Caught in the act of pitching his latest victim over the stern, Fent Aranson whirled around to confront his discoverer.

Aran Aranson's eyes were dull with horror and set in deep black rings born of exhaustion; but a grim light flickered in them, like the embers of a peat-fire. He stared from the pale, narrow face of his son out into the dark, spooling waters of their wake. There was no chance for the fallen man; the waves had closed over Bret Ellison's head and he was well on his way to Sur's feasting table now.

'I knew it was you,' he said quietly. 'I have known for days. Ever since we lost Tor Bolson, though I never seemed to be watching at the right time to see it with my own eyes. I have kept asking myself why I am cursed in this way, but for that I can find no answer. Tell me, Fent, why have you murdered these men?'

Instead being weighed down by fear and guilt, Fent shone as if lit with an inner light at the chance to talk about his crimes. His pale skin glowed like the moon itself and crazed blue starlight shot from his eyes.

'He requires only the three,' he said cryptically. 'The madman, the giant and the fool.' The wide grin he gave his father was proof enough of which of the three Fent himself might be; and after that, he would say no more.

Aran Aranson led his youngest son to the mast and bound him there with soft but strong cords, having first removed the remaining harpoon to another place of safety. Urse was the only other allowed to tend him: they fed him and twice a day untied him so he could make his ablutions. The Master of Rockfall would answer no questions from the crew as to why he had taken these measures; but thereafter no man disappeared in the night, and people drew their own conclusions.

The ice closed in, the black, watery leads between the floes becoming shorter and narrower and less easy to navigate. The light seemed to lie forever just above the far horizon, a beckoning band of violet and blue which promised another life, another world, just out of reach. In the hours of full darkness, the Navigator's Star seemed to hang directly overhead: but did it signify a beacon or a warning? It was so cold, men barely spoke for fear of losing the little warm breath their bodies contained. They wrapped themselves in all they owned. Any exposed skin became reddened within moments; left for longer, it turned white, then numb. Each man asked himself in constant, inward monologues why he had come here, what madness had invaded his soul that he had voluntarily taken up Aran Aranson's invitation. No one had a satisfactory answer for himself: the lure of gold and wealth seemed pointless and nonsensical in this inimical place. Mere survival gradually overtook all other goals; but even survival required some form of forward movement, and there were many days when they made hardly any progress at all. The wind fell away, and rowing became difficult, for lack of open water for the oars to scull or through their own lack of strength. Spurred on only by Aran Aranson's singleminded will toward their mythical destination – a place most of them had long since given up believing in – they used the oars as poles to push the ship through shallow channels, they pressed the ice-breaker into sheets of ice which bowed and then fractured, giving way to the forward momentum of the ship; they slipped into the wake of great bergs which carved their own aimless courses through the ice; and all the time they despaired.

At last, the floes closed in altogether so that the much-vaunted ice-breaker could gain them no further headway. The *Long Serpent* ground to a creaking, protesting halt, its bow rammed hard into a great floe, and the ice crowded all around to engulf the vessel in its inexorable embrace. Nothing they tried could free them: they were stuck fast. The Master of Rockfall waited a day to see whether the movement of the ice would open up a channel; but instead the ice began to crack the ship's timbers. There was no choice. 'Get everything off the ship!' Aran shouted and, together, they evacuated everything of practical use – the remaining ship's boat, the kegs of meat and barrels of water (solid frozen now and bursting the iron-bound seams), the weapons and spars; the shrouds and halyards, even the great dark sail.

With this last, they fashioned a tent, using the mast as its central pole and roped it taut to great boulders of ice. They made ice walls to seal its base, and ice beds and chairs inside. They furnished these with whatever furs and cloaks and sealskins they were not already wearing; they salvaged any wood they could for fires.

This purposeful activity kept them warm and occupied for a day under a sun which gave off such a thin, pale light that the whole world lacked shadows. It was an eerie, luckless, limbo place; and the gradual dying of their ship as the ice took it in its giant, crushing fist filled the air with ominous banshee sounds, so that many of the crew plugged their ears with wool and sang to themselves to mask the noise.

While his men rested, Aran Aranson sat for a long while and watched as the ice devoured the ship which had carried all his dreams. Then he took aside Mag Snaketongue, Pol Garson, Urse One-Ear and Flint Hakason, the most experienced men on his crew. 'We cannot stay here,' he said. 'Here, we will subsist on our few stores, then on whatever we can catch or find; and then we will die, one by one and horribly. There is little chance of rescue so far north: the only others who will venture here will be those like ourselves, bound on an expedition for the Hidden Isle, with little wish to take on board castaways with whom to share their few provisions.'

Urse nodded slowly, having already reached this conclusion for himself. Pol Garson nodded. 'This is a land which devours both ships and men,' he said. 'But if we cannot stay here, where can we go?'

'Onward, to Sanctuary,' Aran replied. 'Overland.'

'Over the ice?' Flint Hakason sounded appalled.

'But we do not know where Sanctuary is, even if it exists,' said Mag Snaketongue, voicing all their thoughts.

'I have a map,' said the Master of Rockfall proudly. He drew the piece of battered parchment out from the interior of all his layers of clothing and unrolled it in front of them, crouching down to flatten it against his thigh.

They gathered around him to peer at this precious item. The Westman Isles and their surrounding seaways were recognisable to each of them, each section of coast beautifully delineated by a delicate and accurate hand; and the farthest islands and corners of the mainland were also thus rendered; but beyond these known landmarks the Northern Ocean gave way to a world of shifting ice; and who could possibly be expected to map such a mutable place so that a man might follow a straight course through it? And indeed, the north-ernmost quarter of the map contained very little useful detail – a wavy line here, an amorphous shape there; the foreign-sounding 'isenfeld' scrawled across one great swathe of white space; and at the heart of a gorgeously drawn windrose in the far righthand corner, a word beginning 'Sanct'.

Urse reached out his hand to smooth out this corner of the map, but Aran jerked it away from him like a child with a jealously guarded toy. Untouched by the magic the artefact contained, the giant stepped back, frowning.

'It's a very pretty thing,' he started hesitantly.

Flint Hakason was less impressed. 'It's completely useless!' he snorted. 'Is that what you've used to bring us to this godforsaken place?'

Aran Aranson leapt to his feet, his eyes ablaze. With one hand, he stowed the map inside his clothing; with the other, he grabbed Flint Hakason by the throat. 'I am the captain of this expedition,' he said through gritted teeth. 'Are you questioning my judgement?'

Flint was a hard man, not easily cowed. He wrestled himself free of the Rockfaller and glared at him. 'I'm not going one step further with you,' he announced bitterly. He lifted a pendant out from under his thick fur cloak. 'See this?' he said, waving the intricately worked silver anchor in Aran's face. 'I will place my trust in Sur now, rather than in you.'

And with that, he turned his back on the other four men and stalked back to the waiting crew. There, he took a piece of string and cut it into a number of uneven pieces which he then balled up into his fist so that only the heads showed. 'I'm leaving this fearsome place, and this cursed expedition,' he announced, 'and I'm taking the ship's boat, some provisions and five of you, if you wish it. I'm going home. Who'll come with me?'

For a moment there was silence. Everyone had seen the confrontation between Flint and the captain and they feared Aran Aranson greatly. But even in their devastated and exhausted state, they feared death more. Suddenly there was a great clamour. A dozen or more of the men, roused from their lethargy, clustered around Flint Hakason and began eagerly to draw out the pieces of string. When each of them had a length, the mutineer declared: 'Longest win a place.'

Emer Bretison roared with delight. 'Ha! I'm with you, Flint. Homeward bound.'

Flint looked less than pleased. 'Don't expect to get any more to eat than the rest, son, despite your great size,' he warned. He looked around the rest of the men with the strings held out on the palms of their hands, then looked relieved. 'Ah, Jan – looks like you'll balance the boat a bit.'

Jan was a slender lad, no bigger than a girl, but with a whippy frame and tough, stringy muscles. When he grinned, he showed sharp canine teeth amidst his straggly blond beard.

In no time, it seemed, Flint Hakason had a boatful. Between them, they hoisted a keg of meat and a sack of hard bread into the skiff, alongside their furs and skin-bags, while Aran looked on, his brows drawn into a single black forbidding line. He made no effort to stop them.

Flint Hakason and his five mutineers shouldered the skiff. It was heavy with provisions, and they were tired and weak from the killing cold, but there was a new purpose in their eyes: they were going home, even if they had to walk for days to find clear water. He turned to the rest of the crew who crouched uncomfortably around the sail-tent, rubbing their hands, avoiding each other's eyes. 'Cheerio, lads,' he said with loud bravado. 'We'll have the fires burning back in Rockfall to greet your return.' He looked to Aran Aranson. 'I hope you find your magic island,' he said, but there was no trace of sarcasm in his voice. 'I hope you come back laden with gold.'

Then he and the five others trudged off southwards across the floe, the loose snow crust squeaking and crunching beneath the soles of their boots. Aran and his crew watched them go. No one said a word.

★　　★　　★

At dawn the next day, Aran Aranson made an announcement.

'I am continuing with my quest,' he said and watched as his men looked from one to another in disbelief. He cleared his throat and went on: 'A captain without a ship is no captain at all: you may make a free choice as to whether you wish to accompany me or not, or whether you wish to remain here with whatever shelter and provisions you need until the weather improves and you can make your own escape, or until I can return for you and take you to safety.' He paused, taking in their hooded expressions, their distrust. Yet these were the men who had travelled from miles around Rockfall – a hundred miles and more in some cases – clamouring to come on this romantic expedition. Now it seemed as soon as disaster struck, they had no backbone at all, were more afraid of the unforeseen death which might await them in the wide, white yonder than the certain death which stalked them here on this grim floe. From their silence he deduced that he would be making the long trek north alone. So be it. He felt disgusted by their cowardice, angry at himself for caring. He took up the harpoon, checked his belt-knives and patted his sack. He had in there a big hunk of flatbread, as hard as seasoned timber, some dried fish which had lost even its rank aroma in this freezing place, a bag full of smoked mutton which would have to be soaked and heated if he were not to break his teeth on it. Three fish-hooks, a length of twine, some seal-fat to smear over the exposed parts of his face. He was ready.

'I'll come with you.' Urse One-Ear stepped forward. 'I have travelled all my life: waiting around is not for me.'

'And I have no wish to sit here and watch my bollocks freeze and fall off,' Fall Ranson declared.

Pol Garson stood up. 'I'll come with you, Captain. My wife always told me I'd never make a name for myself. I'd like to prove her wrong.'

No one else spoke up. Aran scanned face after face and watched as each one looked away. His eyes came to rest on the cook, Mag Snaketongue. He was a tough man, older than most, and Aran trusted him. But the man's expression was guarded.

'Someone has to cook for the lads,' he said simply.

The Master of Rockfall's hand went instinctively to the place where the precious map was swaddled. One small part of his mind knew exactly why Mag had refused to accompany him; but the greater, obsessive part refused to acknowledge this reason. He gave the man a quick nod, then sought out his son.

Fent was sitting on an upturned keg, stabbing repeatedly with a broken stick at a hole in the ice. His face was shrouded by his fur-lined sealskin hood. Aran called his name. The boy made no sign that he had heard his father at all, just kept stabbing and stabbing at the ice. Tiny chips flew up, glinting palely in the low light. Aran raised his voice. 'Fent!'

The lad's head shot up, his eyes flaring blue between the white of his face and the deep red of his fringe and beard. He looked disorientated, disturbed, as though suddenly woken from a deep sleep.

'Get your things together. You're coming with me.'

Fent looked evasive, as if he might bolt at any moment; as if he thought his father might be trying to trick him into following him to a quiet place where he would slaughter him on the spot and leave him for the skuas. 'Where?' he asked suspiciously.

'To Sanctuary.'

If the Master of Rockfall had been expecting mulish obstinacy from his youngest son, he was to be much surprised. Instead of protesting, Fent Aranson leapt to his feet, beaming from ear to ear. His whole demeanour had changed from that of a compulsive child to that of an energetic man with a task to accomplish. 'I'm ready!' he declared.

He carried nothing with him – no pack, no weapon, no spare clothing. Aran ducked into the sail-tent and quickly harvested a few necessary items, which he stuffed into a sheepskin bag which could be slung across the back. When he re-emerged, it was to find Pol Garson in a head-to-head confrontation with Gar Felinson over a haunch of smoked mutton. 'There are more of us than there are of you,' Gar growled.

'Leave it!' shouted Aran, brandishing the harpoon. 'We'll catch what we can on our way.'

Pol Garson shrugged and let go the meat. 'Have it and welcome,' he said to Gar Felinson. 'I have eaten enough sheep in my time to lay their stringy old carcasses from here to Sanctuary and use them as stepping stones!' He turned to the Master of Rockfall. 'Lead on, Aran Aranson, I have a taste for more exotic meats!'

They walked for two days across the sea-ice. It was so cold, it hurt to breathe: they could feel the freezing air deep in their lungs like a wild animal, tearing at the ribs. The hair in their nostrils froze. Their brows and lashes became clumped with ice particles: if they closed their eyes for more than a few seconds, the lids stuck together; icicles formed in their beards and hair. Apart from the light cast by the sun and moon, the landscape was unchanging – grey-white ice, white spindrift, ridges and creases of driven snow, low, ruckled peaks and rifts, rendered romantic and eerie by turns by gradual shifts through red and purple and blue. The world seemed to hover always on the edge of darkness; then at last the sun would sink into the distant sea and night would gather, the moon taking so long to rise that it looked as though it might at any moment lose its battle and drop back into the depths whence it had come.

They walked and walked like mechanical men, one foot in front of the other, over and over and over. This long, monotonous exercise rendered them exhausted and thirsty; they rested only for short intervals, ate and drank and carried on, giving little thought to eking out their supplies. And all the while, the Navigator's Star winked overhead, urging them northwards.

On the third day, a long black lead opened up, splitting the floe apart in front of them. They chose to follow the righthand branch and for what seemed an age trudged along beside the dark water.

On the fourth day, they ran out of the meat they had brought with them from the *Long Serpent*. They had seen no signs of life till now, but Aran Aranson refused to be downhearted. He sat beside the lead for hours, harpoon poised, watching for bubbles which never came. They moved on; again he made himself a fishing stance, where he sat far into the night like a statue made of ice; but no luck came to him and they were reduced to resorting to the remains of their hard bread, which they soaked in meltwater puddles in order to render it chewable.

On the fifth day the lead narrowed and finally closed up again without offering the sight of a single seal or fish and Aran threw the harpoon down in a fit of temper and walked off, leaving it in the snow. A cunning look crept over Fent's face. He darted forward, picked the weapon up and clutched it to his chest; but equally swiftly Urse One-Ear stepped into his path, eased the harpoon away from him with sure, slow hands and slung it over his own back. Later that day they found the frozen corpse of an arctic fox, a tiny thing barely larger than a Westman Isle hare, with a mangy white coat and a round, obdurate skull. Something had gnawed off one of its hind legs and then, disturbed or bored, had abandoned the remainder. Urse drew out of his jacket a pair of flints and a precious bundle of dried moss and they made a small and shabby fire which gave off just enough heat to unfreeze the scraps of meat left adhered to the pathetic bundle of bones, and this little sustained them through another night's walk.

At the end of the sixth day, their water ran out.

Salt had formed uneven crusts around the edges of some puddles amidst the sea-ice, as if it had been leached out of the meltwater. Aran and Pol sipped a little liquid from the pools while the others looked on, licking dry lips. After a time, it seemed that Aran and Pol had suffered no ill effects, so they all refilled their waterskins and trudged on.

On their eighth night beneath the pivot of the stars Fall Ranson, who seemed such a rugged man, dropped in his tracks. Urse turned him over, his face haggard with dread.

'He is stone dead,' he announced.

Pol Garson lifted his anchor-pendant to chapped lips and whispered the words of Sur's blessing. 'Lord of Oceans, take this man, Fall son of Ran, son of Grett the Black, to your deep howe and there let him feast with heroes.' But was this forsaken place land or sea, or some limbo in between? They could only hope that Sur would make a fair decision.

Aran took from the body the dead man's knives and flints, and his pack. Then they mounded snow over him as best they could and carried on.

The next day, just a few hours past sunrise, Pol sat down on the ice. 'I can go no further,' he said indistinctly, for his tongue was swollen and his face was numb with cold.

Without a word, the giant picked him up and slung him over his shoulder, and this was how they continued for the rest of the day.

That night as sun and moon hung uncertainly in the balance they set up camp and made themselves as comfortable as they possibly could without shelter, food or a fire. It was hard to sleep. Even though they were in the midst of a wilderness, they were surrounded by strange sounds which seemed louder with every second of falling darkness. The ice cracked and sighed all around them, and beneath it they could sometimes hear the susurrus of the sea, a constant reminder that the floe on which they lived and walked floated bare inches above thousands of feet of freezing black water. Far off, bergs roared and calved like monsters out of myth; and once they heard a thin cry like the noise a rabbit makes when taken by a fox. Each sound was unnerving in its own right; in concert they set the nerves and teeth on edge, making the men jumpy and anxious.

'This is a daunting place.' Urse spoke softly but it seemed as though his voice boomed out into the emptiness.

'This is not somewhere men should be,' Pol said. 'I sense we are not wanted here.'

Fent laughed hollowly. 'Ah, but we are, we are!' He rubbed his gloved hands together excitedly. 'And we are nearly there.'

His father regarded him curiously. 'How can you know that?'

But Fent's eyes hooded themselves again and he did not reply.

Just before what passed as dawn in this region, Aran sat bolt upright. Beside him, Urse stirred sleepily. 'What?' he whispered. 'What is it?'

The Master of Rockfall put a finger to his lips. In the grey morning light, he looked as though he had died and been recently disinterred. Black shadows carved themselves into his skin, delineating the skull beneath. His beard was dense, his expression stark. He was not a man for wild imaginings: Urse listened with all his might. Some distance away from them, something was moving. He could hear it – a soft rhythmic crunching muffled almost to silence, wisps of sound exaggerated by the stillness of the air.

Aran Aranson pushed himself slowly to his knees, and stared like a hawk into the crepuscular south. A moment later, his right hand reached for the harpoon . . .

It was vast.

It moved with magisterial grace.

It was the king of its domain.

Aran had seen such pelts spread out for sale in the grand market at Halbo. There, they had seemed gorgeously outlandish; their pale straw-streaked white a rare and elegant contrast to the dark, common skins of the woodbears of mainland Eyra. Those had been larger than the usual pelt, the pawpads as large as platters, the pile as shaggy as the fleece on an eight-year-old ram, the heads solid and massy. But they had not prepared him for the sight of his first live snowbear.

Inexorably, it headed for them, showing no urgency in its rangy stride, its small black eyes fixed unmovingly on their little group. Even as it approached them, time seemed to slow, for the Master of Rockfall was able to take in the most minute of details: the way the front legs swung out in fluid, powerful circles; the way the fur rippled along its flanks like the wind through a wheatfield; how the pelt shaded from a pale cream on its back to a soft lemony yellow further down and a gold as deep as ripe corn in the curve of its haunches; how its head described a brutal wedge of bone; how the fur around its black mouth was stained an ominous dark red.

'Run!' cried Pol Garson, hauling himself upright.

'No!' cried Urse, who knew bears. 'Lie down, lie down and cover your head!' And he fell to the ground as though dropped by an unseen spear, covered his head with his gloved hands and lay as still as a rock.

But Pol was too frightened to heed any advice, good or bad. Feet slipping and scrabbling amidst the snow-covered ice, he bolted.

It was all the bear required to trigger every hunting instinct it had been born with. It broke into a trot, which ate the ground away beneath its feet in a most fearsomely efficient manner. The ice trembled; and so did the men.

'Pretend you are dead!' Urse reiterated, and Aran dropped

to the snow and lay there, face down, heart pounding, hands curled pointlessly around his head, feeling as though by doing this he was performing the most foolhardy action of his entire life.

He waited. The bear thundered closer, its footfall reverberating in the bones of Aran's chest and neck, thrumming through the cavern of his skull. He began to mutter the only prayer he knew: the Mariner's Prayer, for sailors in peril on the ocean:

> 'Master of the seas,
> Hear my prayer:
> In storm, tempest and turmoil
> In hazard and in harm
> In flood and fear I call on you
> Heed my words, O high one
> Bring me safe home.'

The snowbear passed right by him and carried on. A moment later, there was a terrible, gurgling cry. Aran raised his head: he could not help it. Fifty yards away – less – the bear was atop Pol Garson, pinning the man to the ice as easily as a cat might pinion a mouse. The man was struggling hard: that much could be seen by the futile flailing of his boots; but the snow around him was turning pinker by the second. Aran doubted a man with both his arms strong and serviceable would be able to fend off such a monster, and Pol's left arm was still recovering from the dislocation, so he stood little chance. Even so, he still felt responsible for him and could hardly stand by and watch him being eaten alive. Knowing that such an action might herald his own death if he failed to make his mark, he shouldered the harpoon and ran as close to the mauling as he dared. It was not a pleasant sight. Pol Garson had no need to concern himself with the recuperation of his arm any more, for the limb had been torn away at the root, tossed aside by the bear like a discarded tidbit. Fighting down nausea, Aran fired the harpoon. It struck the snowbear fair and true in the crook of the shoulder; but the beast merely roared in outrage. Abandoning its victim, it spun menacingly around, head swinging, blood dripping from its teeth.

Then it charged at Aran Aranson with murder in its pebble-black eyes.

The Master of Rockfall prepared to meet his death.

In the few seconds it took for the creature to eat away the ground between them, two things happened: a knife, tossed end over end, struck the bear harmlessly on its rump and spun off into the snow; and a small, quick, dark, nimble figure slipped in under the bear's guard, retrieved the knife and with a peel of shrieking laughter struck the monster again and again and again in its unprotected belly.

All at once, mayhem ensued. The bear howled a great howl of agony and terror and reared up so that its blood and entrails poured out onto the snow. Then it crashed back down, its massive paws striking the floe with such impact that the ice shuddered and cracked apart. For a moment, the snowbear hovered, with one paw on either side of the slow fracture, then the ice parted catastrophically and the beast fell down into the night-dark waters, taking its attacker with it.

Fent's mouth opened to scream, but the shock of the immense cold robbed the sound from him so that all that emerged was a violent hiss of air. The snowbear turned to regard him, its expression one of supreme loathing and malevolence. Then, with every iota of strength it could muster, it launched itself at the boy. Fent's knife-hand rose suddenly out of the water striking down at the great head, the blade a flash of silver in the twilight. The bear roared its contempt and with one swift and merciless bite took the hand off at the wrist, knife and all, then sank into the icy sea beneath the surface of the floe, taking the stolen items with it.

Now Fent began to scream in earnest, his eyes black pits in the wax of his face.

Urse One-Ear flung himself down on the floe, grabbed the boy's hood and hauled. 'I have him!' he called to Aran Aranson, who throughout these few seconds had stood rooted to the ice like a man in a nightmare, unable to move a muscle.

Now, as if released by the big man's cry, Aran scrambled across the ice and caught his son by the arm. Blood pumped from the stump where Fent's right hand had been, congealing thickly in the arctic air; sensibility was already beginning to ebb from the boy's eyes.

By the time they got him out of the freezing water, Fent was unconscious, his breathing slow and shallow. Tremors wracked his body. Aran stared down at him then up at Urse, every line of his face etched with despair. 'By Sur,' he sobbed, 'I cannot bear to lose another son!'

They wrapped him in every warm thing they had; they chafed his skin, they heated what little fresh water they had and poured it drop by precious drop between his blue, unfeeling lips. Even though the bleeding had stopped, Urse burned the end of the stump and bound it, while Aran held his nose and looked away, as appalled by his own squeamishness as by the horror of the situation. Fent did not regain consciousness.

At last Urse said, 'We must move on. If we stay here we will all die.'

The Master of Rockfall turned dull eyes to him and nodded. The giant slung the limp body of Fent Aranson over his shoulder and together they trudged on.

That night there were strange lights in the northern sky. Pale streams of green and pink shimmered across the far horizon like vast banners of silk furling and unfurling with slow, ethereal grace, as though blown by the softest of summer breezes. The two men stood transfixed by this remarkable sight for several minutes then, without a word exchanged, corrected their course minutely so that they were walking directly towards the bizarre phenomenon as if drawn by some unearthly magnetic power. As they walked, the lights played across their faces, softening harsh planes and lines, masking their pain and despair, and all the while the snow at their feet gradually took on the colours of the sky overhead, so it seemed that they walked in a magical world.

Eventually, however, those wonderful lights faded from the sky and full darkness engulfed all again, and that time was the worst; for they were far adrift from the land of men, isolated beyond recall, with no fare and no hope to sustain them, so that every aspect of their venture seemed doomed to failure.

It was in this most miserable and despairing state that they stumbled upon a great hole in the ice revealing the black waters beneath, and close by that, the unmoving body of a gigantic snowbear. Urse laid Fent gently down on the ice and went to examine the beast. It was unquestionably dead, and without any doubt it was the bear which had attacked them, for its belly, washed clean of blood by the arctic waters in which it had swum or been washed to this place, bore the marks of the puncture wounds dealt out to it by Aran Aranson's youngest son.

'By the gods,' Urse breathed, 'we may yet survive.'

So it was that they made a small and pathetic fire by sacrificing to it the spare leather pack and the last of Urse One-Ear's precious moss, and set about butchering the carcass of the beast. As Aran gutted the monster and laid open the odiferous walls of its stomach, out tumbled a collection of fishbones and foxbones; flesh and foods in varying states of digestion; and a most unnerving artefact. The Master of Rockfall extracted this last with dubious care and held it away from him with his brow furrowed and his nose wrinkled in disgust. Then he leant forward and dipped the item into the chilly water. Where before it had been encrusted with globules of matter and viscous fluids, now it emerged bright and shining. It was an object made from the worked metals of the Northern Isles, an item owned by the seafaring men of most families. This particular artefact was rather more distinctive and familiar than most: Aran Aranson had taken especial note of the detail which adorned it: had hardly been able to avoid doing so when its owner had waved it before his face and declared his trust in the god whose symbol it was, rather than in his own. It was Flint Hakason's pendant, the silver-worked Sur's hammer he had always worn about his neck.

Aran recoiled in horror and the thing fell from his fingers and landed noiselessly in the wind-blown snow. It lay there like the reminder of another life, like an accusation. No man would voluntarily be parted from such an auspicious object; and Flint Hakason was no exception. As they excavated the bear's internal cavity they came across further horrible and undeniable evidence of the creature's last meal before it had attacked them.

'I cannot eat this bear,' Aran declared fervently. 'It is surely the worst luck in the world to eat a beast which has eaten one's shipmates.'

'Worse to die for want of a meal, with such a creature lying before you and your shipmates unavenged.'

'Fent avenged them by taking its life.'

'Aye, and it seems the bear has come grievously close to taking his.'

Aran thought about this for a short while. Then he nodded. 'We will eat the bear. But save the heart for my son.'

They charred and ate the best of the meat they could find on the beast and, thus reinvigorated, they then cooked the snowbear's heart and Aran carefully chopped it into tiny pieces and pushed them into his son's mouth. When there was no response, they sat Fent upright and bent his head back until the passage lay clear, and Aran washed the pieces down with water while Urse stroked the boy's throat until he swallowed automatically. But still Fent did not revive, and it was with heavy hearts that they cut up what they could carry of the bear's butchered carcass and walked on into the night.

Fent Aranson lay wrapped in darkness, and a vein beat steadily in his neck. He was aware, yet not aware, floating in a state between wakefulness and sleep. He felt warm, and cold at the same time. He existed in two regions at once – that of living men and that of the dead – yet neither seemed ready to claim him as its own, and it appeared that he was not in a position to decide his own fate. So he lay inert, slung like a sack of turnips over the giant's shoulder while his father walked before him and did not even know the moment when they crossed the lonely, snow-blown boundary which demarcated the end of the world of men and passed into the land of legend.

Epilogue

In the hour before midnight, the Queen's labour pains began. She had been talking with her lady-in-waiting, a pretty dark, rather fat girl from the Galian Isles who sat beside her and who went by the uncommon name of Leta Gullwing. The girl then imparted this knowledge to the forbiddingly tall figure who stood always behind the Queen's throne.

The healer from Blackshore turned her single eye upon the courtiers present. 'The hour of birth has come upon the Queen. Leta and I will take the lady to her chambers,' Festrin said loudly, and her voice reverberated off the stone walls and high beams of Halbo's Great Hall. 'No one else may be permitted to attend the event. The Queen must be entirely relaxed and comfortable if this birth is to go well.'

'Who are you to make such a pronouncement?' demanded Erol Bardson, feeling the seither's magic upon him and resisting it as hard as he could. His chin jutted belligerently. 'This is a matter of state; not one of convenience.' If a child was to be born to his rival he wanted to be there to witness it: like many other malcontents, he had given credence to the rumours which surrounded the Rosa Eldi's true state – that she was not pregnant at all, that she had surrounded herself with illusions which distracted the eye and mazed the mind. And if there was indeed a child inside the pale woman, the chirurgeon he had bribed to assist at the birth was well briefed and knew exactly what to do.

Despite the invisible blanket of calm that Festrin had laid across the company, his was not the only voice to be raised in protest. Auda, the King's mother, ranted and railed; the ladies of the court complained that it was traditional they be present to help the Queen in her time of need; the lords argued that it was crucial they bend a knee to the babe as soon as it emerged; but more than one of them was inspired to make this affirmation not out of loyalty to the Crown, but out of sheer prurient curiosity as to the precise nature of what their lord's enchanting wife had between her elegant legs.

But Ravn Asharson, King of the Northern Isles, fell to the ground at his wife's feet and embraced her so that his head rested upon the great swell of her belly. 'My darling,' he said fervently, 'is it truly your wish to retire with only these two ladies to attend you?'

Mutely, the Rose of the World nodded her head, her beautiful green eyes beseeching.

Ravn sighed. It was a sigh of regret; but also, as he would admit only to himself, one of relief as well. Much as he craved a healthy heir for the northern throne, he adored his wife so greatly that he could not stand to see her suffer a moment's pain; and he had heard that many men – though hardened by years of battle and bloodshed and all the atrocities which war could offer – had fainted clean away at the sight of a child making its forcible passage into the world between the thighs of the woman they had married. Those thighs . . . He shivered at the memory of their silken grasp around him, and pushed the thought away. That would come again, soon enough; but first let her come safely through the birth. He sent up a silent prayer to Feya, the women's deity and hoped Sur would not hold it against him.

And as for leaving his beloved in the hands of the seither – well, the one-eyed woman terrified him; but he did not doubt her skills.

He stood up and addressed the company. 'It shall be as my queen wishes,' he declared.

The babe was born a scant hour later. It was a messy birth, and Leta Gullwing lost a lot of blood, for the child was large for its somewhat shorter than usual gestation period, as well as vigorous and determined, and the girl's channel was narrow. But while the Rosa Eldi, looking somewhat appalled by the entire event, held the bloody, purple-headed child at arm's length and wondered what in the world she would do with it, Festrin had snipped the cord which connected the baby to Selen Issian and with this last piece of evidence removed, applied herself to the Istrian woman's wounds.

Then the seither wrapped the child in the royal blue of Ravn's house and carried it down to the Great Hall.

'Eyra has a new prince!' she announced. 'Long live Ravn Asharson, King of the Northern Isles, and his queen, the Rose of the World; for their union has been blessed by the birth of a fine and healthy boy.'

It was not precisely a lie.

From his tower room window, he watched the first visitors ever to survive the perilous journey – a dark man and his huge companion, carrying the limp form of another – enter his hidden kingdom along the thin isthmus of ice he had opened for them.

'The giant, the madman and the fool,' he murmured with some satisfaction.

He rubbed his hands together. They felt cold and dry and ill-tended. He looked down at himself and found that he was wearing no more than a thin, urine-stained shift, that his beard had grown past his waist and was spotted with food and worse; and that an overgrown yellow toenail was protruding from a hole in his threadbare tapestried slipper. The adventures of the voyagers had been altogether too gripping of late: he had not been taking good care of himself. As the world's most powerful mage, it would hardly do to appear to them thus: an air of majesty and gravitas was surely required.

Summoning the shreds of his magic, the Master of Sanctuary descended the winding ice stairs and prepared to greet his guests.

Iron and water; water and iron. Salt and mineral and ash. This is what the blood tastes like. My blood; spilled on the ground and on my leg. The flavour is strong and invigorating; it fills my senses. Lick and lick again. Hair with the blood; annoying but no more than that. Down it goes. All good nourishment.

The wound is deep: I feel the draw of the healing muscle as I stretch. The fibres have knit quickly, maybe too quickly, as our kind often mend too fast for our own good. I will have to clean it, to worry at it and drain the pus if it goes bad.

Sleep has strengthened me; but sleep has also taken the others away, too far to pursue: too far in the wrong direction. I feel their presence in the world — the pale man, the quiet one and the woman like the flickering of gnats over a distant pond; but they are heading north, north with the cruel men, north with the death-stone, Falla's tear.

There is nothing I can do for them, even had I the strength to follow, to claw, to kill.

No: my course takes me south, south to the Red Peak. My lady may be lost to me; but my lord has awoken: I can sense his presence. If I listen hard enough, I can hear him — in the earth, in the rocks. Mountains shift, lava flows, boulders shatter as he moves.

He calls me, he calls me and I come . . .

POCKET
BOOKS

Sorcery Rising

Book One of Fool's Gold

The Allfair. A place for old enemies to put aside their differences for a time and come together for trade and revelry. The hardy, seafaring Eyrans come from the North; from the South, their old enemies, the Istrians, slave-owners who drove the Eyrans from their lands; and the nomadic peoples – the Footloose – purveyors of charms and harmless potions.

Katla Aransen and her family have sailed to the fair to trade their goods. The Vingo clan have travelled from Istria to purchase a bride for their appalling eldest son. Tycho Issian has come to sell his daughter to the highest bidder. King Ravn Asharson, Stallion of the North, seeks a political alliance; while others seek his downfall.

But there is a disquiet in the air. For centuries, Elda has been bereft of magic; but this year something has changed. A mysterious force is abroad once more, and at its centre a triumvirate of strangers to the Allfair: a mysterious, coldly dispassionate man, his oddly intelligent cat and a woman of such surpassing beauty that all who see her fall under her thrall. Magic is returning to the world, and no one will remain unchanged.

ISBN 0 7434 4040 4
PRICE £6.99

POCKET BOOKS

This book and other **Pocket Books** are available from your bookshop or can be ordered direct from the publisher.

0 7434 4040 4	**Sorcery Rising**	*Jude Fisher*	£6.99
0 7434 3065 4	**Hidden Empire**	*Kevin J. Anderson*	£6.99
0 7434 3066 2	**A Forest of Stars**	*Kevin J. Anderson*	£6.99
0 7434 2897 8	**The Praxis**	*Walter Jon Williams*	£6.99
0 7434 6852 X	**The Jaws of Darkness**	*Harry Turtledove*	£6.99
0 6710 3754 4	**Ares Express**	*Ian McDonald*	£6.99
0 6717 7370 4	**Felaheen**	*Jon Courtenay Grimwood*	£6.99
0 6717 7369 0	**Effendi**	*Jon Courtenay Grimwood*	£6.99

Please send cheque or postal order for the value of the book, free postage and packing within the UK; OVERSEAS including Republic of Ireland £1 per book.

OR: Please debit this amount from my

VISA/ACCESS/MASTERCARD..

CARD NO:..

EXPIRY DATE..

AMOUNT £..

NAME..

ADDRESS..

....

SIGNATURE..

Send orders to: SIMON & SCHUSTER CASH SALES
PO Box 29, Douglas, Isle of Man, IM99 1BQ
Tel: 01624 836000, Fax: 01624 670923
www.bookpost.co.uk
Please allow 14 days for delivery.
Prices and availability subject to change without notice.